Urban Ms

A special limited edition featuring the novels of
Marcia Williams:

Baby Mother
Flex
Waiting for Mr Wright

Published by:
The X Press
PO Box 25694
London, N17 6FP
Tel: 020 8801 2100
Fax: 020 8885 1322
E-mail: vibes@xpress.co.uk

Printed by Omnia Books Ltd, Glasgow, UK

Distributed in UK by Turnaround Distribution
Unit 3, Olympia Trading Estate, Coburg Road, London N22 6TZ
Tel: 020 8829 3000
Fax: 020 8881 5088

ISBN 1-902934-16-4

This collection of novels is dedicated to Martin, the man of my dreams.
Hope you enjoy them.

Marcia Williams

ABOUT THE AUTHOUR

•Marcia Williams is a full-time mum, a full-time local goverment worker and a 'full-time' writer. She has also edited *In Search of Our Sisters' Gardens* (a collection of classic short stories by black women) and *Soul Survivors* (an anthology of female slave narratives). She lives and works in London.

THE BIRTH OF A BESTSELLING AUTHOR

When Marcia Williams sent a manuscript to The X Press in 1996, the company was already established as the foremost purveyors of black interest fiction in Europe, if not in the world. There had been one success after the other - *Yardie*, *O.P.P.*, *Baby Father*, *Cop Killer*, *Wicked In Bed*, *Moss Side Massive*, *The Blacker The Berry*, *The Ragga & The Royal*, *When A Man Loves A Woman*, *Dancehall*, *Single Black Female*, and *Drummond Hill Crew* were some of the titles that kept this publisher at the top of their game, and made authors like Victor Headley, Patrick Augustus, Naomi King and Yvette Richards successful within their various genres. Marcia Williams was to take that success to another level with *Flex*, *Waiting for Mr Wright* and *Baby Mother* (a female answer to the hugely successful *Baby Father* by Patrick Augustus - now a four-part BBC TV drama series). *Baby Mother* was an instant must-read for black women and white women with black partners.

I had the pleasure of working with Marcia as her editor. As well as bringing up two beautiful daughters on her own, Marcia was also holding down a full-time job and writing fiction at night. How did she find time to write 100,000 word novels, you ask. Beats me. I used to travel down to her yard in Kidbrooke, south London, in the evening, and we would work pretty much through the night. I would return home to get my beauty sleep, only too aware that Marcia would have to rise and shine in a couple of hours to get her daughters ready for school, and then to make it to work herself. Still, in her three novels (*Flex* and *Waiting For Mr Wright* followed swiftly on the heels of *Baby Mother*), she managed to capture the voice of the urban black woman.

Dotun Adebayo, The X Press.

FLEX

Pamela, Joan and Marion are three friends who share the good times and the bad moments of 90's women. 'Flex' is the story of their lives told in their words. This unusual novel also features the stories of four men - Colin, James, Shaun and Paul who are the romantic interest for the women.

Written with great wit and insight, 'Flex' is the black woman's story which gives the men the right to reply!

WAITING FOR MR WRIGHT

Television personality Errol Wright has everything going for him: A booming career; a beautiful home; and most important of all, a caring woman and a wonderful son.

But a chance meeting with Anne-Marie is to have unforeseen and devastating consequences on his and his family's lives. Obsessed with his on-screen image, Anne-Marie is convinced that this is the man she has waited so long for. She will do anything to get her Mr Wright, but girlfriend Yvette is just as determined that no one is going to break up her happy home.

BABY MOTHER

High-flying lawyer Jennifer Edwards is always worrying that her wayward teenage sister is going to get pregnant by some absentee baby father. Little could she imagine what fate had in store for her.

Flex

"EASY NUH, MAN. WHA' YOU AH HEGS UP OVER?"

Hegs up? Hegs up?! Bwoy, he was lucky she couldn't run down that phone line and ram her fist down his throat. Man had the damn cheek to call her number and tell her how he's thinking about her and her ripe body. Only last week she'd had to throw his outta-order backside out of her house because he'd taken the damned liberty to raise his hand and slap her. Slapped like she was a child bad-mouthing its mother! Had he honestly expected her to stand for that? Did he have no idea who he was dealing with? This was Joan Ross — a strong black woman. Not some dibi-dibi schoolgirl with stars in her eyes.

First, she had kicked him in the shin. And while he was bent over nursing his leg, she'd balled her fists and brought them down hard on the back of his skull. He'd looked so comical sprawled out on the carpet that, despite her anger, she had laughed hysterically. Embarrassed, his eyes full of shock, he'd scrambled to his feet issuing a stream of obscenities.

"Sticks and stones, Stevie bwoy. Sticks and stones," Joan had taunted.

He'd not touched her again, but had left, slamming the door behind him. And Joan hadn't seen him since.

All that aggro over a gallon of blasted petrol. She was glad it had happened sooner rather than later on in the relationship, when she might have fallen too deep to care. If he had filled up the car as promised, there would have been no argument. If he hadn't been such a prick she would have given him lovin' like he'd never had before. Stephen was tall, dark and athletic — exactly how she liked her men. She would have rocked his world. Oh well, it was his loss. As far as Joan was concerned, he was history. She disconnected him and placed the telephone receiver back in its cradle.

Still angry, she walked across the room to where her cigarettes lay on the armchair. She shook one from the packet and lit up. Men had to be aliens, she concluded, puffing out a cloud of white smoke. Brothers from another planet, an experiment gone wrong. Only an alien could expect a sane woman to take him back after what Stephen had done. Only aliens have brains between their legs. Only an alien would consider a hard-on to be a matter of life or death — damn the consequences as long as they can find somewhere to put it.

Since Joan had split up with her baby father (she hated that term, but she couldn't think of a more appropriate description), Martin Baker, two years previously, she'd had countless men in and out of her life. She wasn't proud of the number, but that was one of the hazards of searching for Mr. Right. How else was she supposed to know if this one or that one was the right one unless she tried them out in every aspect?

Joan sighed to herself. She felt like she was the only woman in the world without a man. Her best mates were both living with their men — well, Pamela was, and Marion had her part-time lover. Even Joan's mother changed her male 'friends' with the seasons. But were any of them happy? Really happy? Donna, her younger sister, was already married. She seemed to have fallen off the face of the earth since her wedding day, and was now rarely seen. Donna had given up her job as a receptionist for Lewisham Housing Services because John didn't want her to work. She had lied, saying that the job wasn't that important anyway. For Joan, that had signalled the complete loss of her independence, and she had let her know what she thought about it. This is what had caused the rift between them. Joan regretted that. Donna had once also been a strong black woman, but nowadays if John didn't like something, neither did she. She even had to ask her husband for pocket money. Joan couldn't see how her sister could possibly be happy.

She lit another cigarette. She felt like a good bitching session. Stephen had wound her up and she needed to let it out. Pamela would love this one. "Kick him, yes," she'd say.

Joan had known Pamela for four years. Just like Joan, she had wasted some of her best years on one no-good, confused black man after another. And she was only seeing James because he was more like a housemaid than anything else. He was always ironing, cooking and — check this — attending to Pamela's every need, and those of her girlfriends when they came round! Marion and Joan called him Jeeves behind his back. He even paid half of Pamela's bills. So far James had lasted ten months, but, knowing Pamela, she would soon get bored. She was, after all, a hot-blooded Scorpio in constant need of passion, which she wasn't exactly getting from her live-in butler.

Joan's other best mate was Marion, the youngest of them all. Joan had known her since she was eight years old and knew how gullible she was. Marion's man, Gerard, was an extremely good-looking bloke, but he was a bastard. A dominating womaniser who couldn't give a damn about Marion and what she wanted. He only visited her when he was at a loose end or when he needed a boost. Yet Marion was ever ready to forgive and forget, and would do virtually anything for him. Joan couldn't stand him. Neither could Pamela. The gossip between them was that Gerard had to have "somet'ing sweet" between his legs. There was no other explanation.

Joan uncurled her shapely legs from the sofa. Her oversized red T-shirt dropped to below her knees. Grabbing her phone index from the coffee table, she left the living room and climbed the stairs, smoke drifting like a fine mist in her wake. At the top of the stairs she stood at the doorway to her daughter's bedroom. Shereen, or Sherry, was now four years old and already talking like a big woman. Joan flicked the light switch and looked over at her daughter's bed. The girl was spread out on her back, her angelic face a picture of peaceful sleep. Her mouth hung open and she breathed lightly. This was Joan's pride and joy. She fought the urge to wake her daughter just for her own comfort.

Joan sighed. She wished she could spend more time with her daughter, but she was an ambitious woman and if she didn't work twelve hours a day she wasn't going to get far in her career. It hadn't been an easy climb to get to be features editor at Icon Press. Especially with her relationship with Shereen's father disintegrating about her.

Martin was a believer in hire purchase, credit cards, cheque-books, and overdrafts. It had put them in debt, which Martin had left her to pay along with the mortgage. Now she had to work all the hours she could manage just to keep her head above water.

Stephen, the latest man in her life, had lasted two months. One thing about Stephen, he was "wicked in bed"! She was going to miss that, if nothing else. Before Stephen she had been seeing Colin, Martin's brother. Joan and Colin had been in and out of each other's lives for a year and a half. Shereen's uncle was another one of those black men who just won't/can't commit. Which isn't the same as a womaniser. Colin could stay faithful as long as he could come and go as he pleased, as long as he wasn't "living" with the woman and marriage wasn't on the cards.

It had been good at first, and Joan had felt such a fool when she'd let her feelings rule her head. She'd fallen in love, he hadn't. She had kept giving him pressure, and he'd kept making excuses. So in the end she had told him to get the hell out of her life. She was twenty-seven, and she had no time to waste on immature men. She'd wanted commitment — she still did. And all she was left with now was her phone book full of ex's.

It was eleven thirty on a weeknight, and she suddenly found herself becoming horny. She, of course, had a new, improved, bigger, better, feel-real, three-speed, pump-action, clitoris-stimulating vibrator at her disposal. But that wasn't what she wanted tonight. No, her bedside buddy wasn't enough. She wanted a man. A hard, hot body.

So there she was, flicking through her phone book with one hand, cigarette in the other, Aaron Hall telling her how much he's missing her, and getting hornier by the second. Page after page she turned, scanning the names one by one. There were so many losers among them — Joan hadn't got that desperate yet.

She had to laugh at some of the memories that surfaced from those names. There was Kinky. He would turn up with handcuffs, blindfolds and wicked leather gear. He liked to have whipped cream licked off his body.

Then there was Ego. He was so selfish that he would bring a bottle 'round to her house and then proceed to drink it on his own, unless she asked for some! They'd been out four times and not once had he said, "I'll pay." They'd halved the bill every time. But he always expected dinner when he turned up at her house empty-handed. He got turned on by getting Joan to remind him of how big his manhood was, how he made her feel, how jealous her girlfriends were when she told them what she was getting. And all this while they were actually doing it!

Then there was Inexperienced. She had tried to teach the boy that she had a whole body and not just a hole between her legs. She'd taught him the gentle art of 'head to head' massage. She'd shown him all her tender spots and asked him, God knows how many times, to slow down. But he was too eager to hit the jackpot.

Oh yeah, then there was Mr. Love. She could laugh about him now, but at the time it had been kind of scary. This man had told her that he loved her on the first date. Joan had laughed, "Yeah, right, you don't know me from Eve." He'd called her every day after that, told her how much he missed being with her and was forever asking if he could come over. Then he'd started to turn up at her house nearly every night, always with a little gift for Shereen. One morning Joan had picked up her mail to find there was a letter addressed to Mr. Love. Curiosity got the better of her and she'd opened it — it had come to her house after all. The letter was from someone interested in Mr. Love's offer to sell her house.

Mr. Loverman, on the other hand, was different. Nice, easygoing, clean-cut, fair-skinned, and packing a lethal weapon. Sexual perfection!

For a moment, Joan considered calling Mr. Loverman up. Just to say hi, see what he was doing and how he was doing, maybe arrange to meet up — like tonight. Her thoughts were interrupted by the buzz of the doorbell. Startled, she looked at her watch. It was nearly midnight. She wasn't expecting anyone, but a sudden premonition told her who it was. She slid off the bed and crossed to the window that overlooked her front garden. A car came 'round the corner and lit her uninvited guest with its headlights. It was Colin.

He was the answer to her prayers. She ran her fingers through her short Halle Berry style hair, to give it that casual windswept look. The cut emphasised her high cheekbones, slanting, exotic eyes and full lips. Joan was not the world's prettiest woman, but she was interesting looking, with mysterious, dark eyes that men found irresistible.

The doorbell rang again.

Joan opened the front door to a confident, boyish grin on Colin's ruggedly handsome face. He stood six foot three before her (firm from head to foot), appraising her with deep brown eyes beneath long lashes.

She looked him up and down. She caught his eyes resting on her chest, where her nipples had risen to bullets in the cold breeze. She pulled her dressing gown closed and crossed her arms over her chest.

"Yes?" she asked nonchalantly.

"All right?"

"Yes, thank you." She stared at him, one eyebrow raised in question. She knew why he was there — for exactly the same reason she wanted him there — but she was going to make him work for it. She didn't want him thinking her house was a pussy takeaway.

"So you're not gonna let me in?"

"For what?" She pushed up her chest.

He rolled his eyes. "I didn't come all this way to stand on the doorstep."

Greenwich to Plumstead. All this way?

"Then what did you drag your arse up here for?"

He ignored her rudeness. "How 'bout I tell you inside?"

Joan wasn't going to stand there and freeze her nipples off just to spite her ex-lover. She let him in and he stood in the hallway waiting for her to lead the way.

"I s'pose you want something to drink now that you've got me out of bed," she said.

"Wouldn't say no."

No you wouldn't, would you, Colin? Wouldn't say no if I dropped my drawers out here in the middle of the street. But if I asked you to stay longer than one night you'd sure run fast enough in the opposite direction.

He dragged out a chair and sat at her dining table like he was at home. Damned cheek! If she weren't so hot for some action, his backside would be walking its way back to Greenwich.

"So how's Shereen?" he asked. "Bet she missed her Uncle Colin."

"Shereen's fine," Joan answered without a hint of warmth in her voice. No thanks to you and your family, she wanted to add. His brother had walked out on her, and when push came to shove so had he. Even their mother had taken Martin's side in the break-up. They were one confused bunch of people. But now that he was here, sitting in her kitchen, she knew that she still wanted him. She also knew that he was here because he still couldn't get her out of his system.

She smiled to herself as she made the coffee. Maybe she would just use and abuse him, she considered. Mek 'im beg. Yeah — that sounded better.

"I missed you, y'know," Colin mumbled. "You and Shereen," he quickly added.

"So?"

He huffed. "You still mad at me?"

She wasn't mad at him. What was there to be angry about? He wanted his freedom; Joan wanted to settle down. She couldn't force the man to want what she wanted. They had to go their separate ways or end up hating the sight of each other.

She handed him his coffee and, pulling out a chair, she sat down beside him and continued playing hard to get.

"Colin, I'm over that." She waved the very idea away. "Don't take it personal. You see, my mates were all settling down and I just wanted to give it another try myself." She crossed her legs and leant one elbow on the table. "You just happened to be around at the time."

His eyes dropped to the pine table, and he studied his fingernails as though he'd never seen them before. Poor Colin — he'd never been very good at verbal expression. Joan sipped her coffee and watched him over the rim of the mug. He was one hunk of a man. She was remembering his body under those loose clothes. All she had to do was reach across the table and she could have him if she wanted. She licked her lips. Colin was hung like a horse, and Joan often thought he made love like one too. Just climb aboard, do your thing, then dismount. Foreplay didn't occur to him! But that didn't bother Joan, because he knew just how to rock her world without it. She was getting goosebumps just thinking about him naked. Just then he reached across the table for her hand. "I…"

"Yeah?" She fixed him with a smouldering, dark gaze.

"I…" He paused, frustration clear in his furrowed brow. "Cho, you won't understand."

"Understand what?"

"I'm trying to tell you…" He breathed a sigh. "I love you."

Joan bit her tongue to stop herself laughing but her shoulders shook anyway. Hurt, Colin snatched back his hand.

"Sorry," she giggled.

"Joan, I'm trying to be serious here." He threw his arms open, then slapped his palms on the table in frustration.

"I'm sorry, Col. But even you've got to admit, you saying 'I love you' sounds ridiculous."

"Yeah, well, I've been thinking — and I think you should give me another chance."

"To do what, Colin?"

"To check out this relationship stuff."

Was he for real? She started giggling again. "Well, if you put it like that, how could I possibly refuse?"

Colin reached up and twisted his baseball cap backwards. "Come on, man. This ain't easy, y'know."

Joan got up and walked 'round to his side of the table, her T-shirt clinging in all the right places. "You're serious, aren't you?"

"Ya know dat."

"Come here," she commanded in her huskiest voice.

Her juices had been flowing all night; now was her chance to satisfy her lust. Grinning like a monkey, he stood up and faced her. She looked up into his eyes. Her arms curled round his neck and she drew him down to meet her waiting lips.

That was all it took to seduce Colin Baker. He pushed himself up against her, nearly lifting her off her feet. Oh God, she loved it when men did that. He wrapped his tongue around hers, and his long, strong fingers did the same to her ample backside. She felt like singing "Hallelujah", but her mouth was too busy.

His hands travelled down to her naked thighs, then back again to her bottom. His mouth seemed to be everywhere at once. Joan's dressing gown dropped to the floor and her T-shirt rose over her head. She was standing in her kitchen stark naked while he was still fully clothed. It was her turn to do the undressing. She yanked his jacket down his back and his track suit bottoms down to his knees. Then she knocked his baseball cap off his head. All he had on now was a baggy string vest. His lips and tongue were working on one nipple and then the other. Feeling his crotch press against hers gave her a rush, his penis hanging like a baseball bat between his legs. That was when she went weak at the knees and her legs gave way. Colin supported her. Lifting her with ease, he laid her on the dining table, panting, gasping and moaning, all ten and a half stone of her.

He mounted her like a stallion and she screamed out for Jesus. All that pent-up frustration was being exorcised like the devil from a woman possessed. He thrust back and forth as she pumped up to meet him. She could have sworn he was getting bigger inside her. Thank goodness I bought solid pine, she thought to herself. She pulled at his shoulders, begging him to make her come, and he obliged as only he could.

Joan shuddered with the after-effects of an orgasm that must have woken the neighbours. It was over in about ten minutes, but it was the best ten minutes she'd had in months.

He was standing above her, his finger tracing a line down her body from her neck to her breasts and down to her belly button.

She raised herself up on her elbows and looked him dead in the eye. "This doesn't mean we're an item again," she breathed, still catching her breath. She was telling him straight, leaving no room for doubt.

"What have I done now?" He bent over to pull up his pants and she uttered a low sigh as she caught a last view of his tight, hairy buttocks before they were tucked out of sight.

She began to feel exposed sitting there on her dining table as naked as a fertility goddess, so she covered her chest with one arm and slid off.

"Don't get me wrong, Col. The sex was wicked — but that's not enough any more. I don't need a man to come and go. Literally."

He had the cheek to kiss his teeth, then made her shiver by tickling her hip with a light, playful stroke. "Who says it's gonna be like that? Ain't we having a good time?"

She couldn't be bothered to answer him or give him the chance to confuse her. She knew what she wanted. She wanted a man who was going to be there for her and Shereen. She wanted a man to be a provider, a lover, a friend, her life-support emotionally and physically.

Grabbing her dressing gown from the floor, she slipped it over her shoulders, tying the belt around her waist. Boy, she needed a cigarette. Joan left the kitchen and headed up the hall to the front room. Colin followed her and stood just inside the doorway, leaning against the frame like he was waiting for something. Joan inhaled deeply, regretting the boredom and frustration that had driven her to start smoking again.

"I know what I want," Colin blurted suddenly. "I want you. I can't even look at you without wanting to touch you." "Here we go again," Joan tutted. "It always comes down to sex with you, doesn't it?"

He shook his head. "Are you paranoid about sex or what? I didn't mean it that way." He came closer. "Me? Paranoid?" A false chuckle gushed from her lips. "What do you have on your mind one hundred per cent of the time?"

"I'm a man, aren't I?" he grinned, lifting his shoulders in a shrug as if to say, "It's not my fault."

She kissed her teeth, flipping her eyes to the ceiling. He took the opportunity to slip his arm around her waist. "I just don't want the whole marriage thing yet," he breathed in her ear.

She turned her head away from him. "Yeah? Well I do. Shereen needs a father. I need a companion. If you don't wanna be tied down, then there's the door." She pointed with the lighted cigarette. God, she wished it was a spliff.

"I can't just leave," he insisted. "I love you."

"Yeah, right. Well you might find it easy to say, but can you show me? An' I'm not talking about sex."

Colin let go of her, stood up and began pacing up and down, arms crossed over his chest. In his string vest, with his bulging muscles, he looked like he had just stepped out of an action movie. She could sense him stirring in his boxer shorts. Sex on legs.

"I think we should go back to just being friends. Like the old days."

"Is that what you want?" He looked deep into her eyes, defying her to say yes. She caught her breath. What she really wanted to tell him, of course, was that it wasn't what she wanted. He was so much like his brother that she couldn't help but have feelings for him. "I think it's for the best." Her cigarette had burnt down to the butt and, she decided, so had this conversation, despite its unsatisfactory outcome. She took his hand off her bottom and stubbed out the cigarette in the ashtray. Still holding his hand, she led him to the door.

"You throwing me out?"

"I've got work tomorrow. It's late." She fetched his jacket and cap from the kitchen and handed them to him.

"You'll never realise how much I care about you, y'know." He kissed her forehead. Kissed her again, on the lips. Give a man an inch…

"I'll call you," he promised.

"I know." Joan opened the front door to the cold once again, and pulled her dressing gown tighter over her chest.

"Colin, if you weren't such a coward, you could have had me twenty-four seven," she called after him on impulse.

He turned. "I know," he said smugly, and walked away into the night.

COLIN

Women can't resist me. I'm not boasting, honestly! They call it charm. All I know is I can weaken any woman's resistance with a touch. Forget love. I'm only interested in sex. Pure sex. Slow and sweet, or wicked and wild — it's a good way to forget your troubles. Good exercise, too.

I told Joan a man and woman can't be "just friends", it don't work. So I kinda replaced Martin, my brother, in her life. It was fun, with regular sex. I wanted her for her body and she wanted me for mine, though I liked to kid myself that it was for my mind. Then one night she turned 'round and asked me if I loved her. I thought it was a joke, so I laughed. Unfortunately she was being serious, and when I said no, she got vexed and locked me 'arf. Since then, it's been the cold shoulder. I thought it would be cool, y'know, plenty more fish in the sea an' all that, but I couldn't get her outta my mind. All that thinking was ruining my sex life! I didn't even feel like checking any other women. To my surprise, I found that I was in love — and I wish I wasn't. Because Joan can be one miserable woman. I blame my brother for that. He took the best five years of her life and threw them back in her face. Left her with the baby and a mortgage. Well, that's Martin for you. I am not my brother's keeper. All I can say is that his loss is my gain.

MARION'S EYES SHOT OPEN. WAS THAT THE FRONT DOOR? SHE slowly eased herself into a sitting position, one ear cocked towards the bedroom door. Only one other person had the keys to her flat. She heard a shuffling of feet in the hallway. Gerard was home. She glanced over at the clock. It was nearly midnight. Some eight o'clock this was!

"Yeah, baby," he'd said this morning, "dinner'll be fine. Eight o'clock? I'll shut the shop on time and come straight over."

Marion pursed her lips. It wasn't the first time he'd stood her up. Maybe if she asked him to stop making promises, then there wouldn't be any to break.

She ran her hands over her naturally wavy hair, tidying her ponytail, then swung her thin legs off the bed and smoothed down her satin and lace camisole and French knickers set. She checked herself in the dresser mirror. She'd wanted to look sexy for him tonight and had doused herself in Champagne, the perfume he'd bought her.

She hadn't meant to fall asleep. She'd wanted to be ready and alert, with dimmed lights, chilled wine, silk lingerie, seductive music — the works.

She heard him go into the bathroom opposite. Was he freshening up for her? She tiptoed to the bedroom door, opened it and peered outside. A trail of clothes ran from the front door to the bathroom — a pair of men's shoes kicked off carelessly, an overcoat thrown over the back of a chair, a tie and suit jacket thrown over the back of the sofa. She wanted to head straight for the bathroom but couldn't fight the urge to put the articles away. As if by instinct, she collected the clothes and folded them neatly. Then she knocked hesitantly on the bathroom door.

"Gerard?"

"Hi, babes," his muffled voice came through from within.

"Can I come in?"

"If you want."

She opened the door and entered the pink bathroom. Gerard stood naked, about to climb into the steaming, cologne-scented water. His shirt and boxer shorts lay in a heap on top of the wash basket, his trousers on the towel rail. The sight of his firm body still made Marion's heart race, even after a year together. She picked up the discarded clothes. The faint musky smell of aftershave wafted off the fabric before she dropped them inside the basket and replaced the lid. "I thought you were asleep," Gerard said, easing himself into the bath with a satisfied sigh.

"I was... I cooked..." she added a subtle reminder. Gerard Thompson was six foot two and a healthy twelve stone. His features looked as though they had been carved from marble, with a rigid, handsome jaw, high cheekbones and almond-shaped light brown eyes. He was stunning to look at. His fair, cool complexion came from a mixture of Bajan and Indian parentage. "I'm sorry, babes. Mum called. She needed some help shifting furniture. I've been promising to do it for ages. You know what Mum's like." He raised a thick eyebrow at Marion. "When she wants something done, she wants it done now. Anyway, she fed me. We'll have your dinner tomorrow, yeah?"

Marion lowered her eyes and nodded in barely noticeable agreement. No, it wasn't okay, but there was nothing she could say. Yes, she did know what Gerard's mum was like, and her son treated her like a queen. Mrs Thompson — Claudia to everyone who knew her personally — would always come before anyone else in Gerard's life. Marion wanted to ask him why he hadn't called. What was the point of having a mobile phone if he never used it? Instead she said, "I missed you."

He grinned patronisingly. A grin that said, "Of course you did". "You too. Come here."

She stepped over to the bathtub and knelt on the mat. Gerard placed a wet hand on the back of her neck and pulled her to him. He kissed her open-mouthed, exploring her mouth with his tongue. She responded passionately.

Gerard released her suddenly and yawned. "Boy, I'm knackered. Any more of that wine left, babes?"

Wine? What did wine have to do with how he was making her feel? Was he truly as insensitive as he acted? She could feel a trickle of water running down her back as she sat back on her heels like a puppy waiting for its master's attention. Her large, naive eyes gazed at the man she loved. Gerard pretended to be oblivious to the effect he had on her. He liked to say he gave her as much as he could give — which left her wondering if that meant he had nothing else to give, or perhaps she had only a share of what was on offer. "A little." She wiped bath water from the back of her neck.

"Get us a glass, will you?" It wasn't a request, it was an order. Gerard knew all about giving orders.

"Sure." She stood to leave the bathroom, turning at the door to look back at him. Gerard blew her a loud, theatrical kiss and she forced a smile. How did he do it? How was it that he could so easily twist her around his little finger? Why was it that she couldn't go right up to him and cuss him out for standing her up? So much for a romantic night in.

And what could she have said? "How dare you help your mum out? I wanted you here, wrapping your arms around me, covering my body with kisses and whispering sweet nothings in my ear"? No. The one time she had tried that, Gerard had dialled his mother's number and handed Marion the phone, saying, "Tell her how you think you're more important than she is." She never did, of course.

Marion returned to the steamy bathroom with a glass of chilled wine. Gerard lay back in the bath, his eyes closed. Aching for him, Marion thought about climbing in. With a clink, she set the glass down on the side of the bath.

Gerard opened his eyes. "So," he said sleepily, "what did you do today?"

Slightly flustered, Marion answered, "I went window shopping."

"Yeah? Anything interesting?" He reached for the bath gel.

"I had a look at some rings."

Gerard sat up and sipped some of the wine, tasting it, then gulped the rest down in one. "You don't have enough rings already?" he asked offhandedly.

Marion took the gel from his hands and fished his flannel out of the bath. "Not them kinda rings. Engagement rings," she said, soaping his back.

"Why? You leaving me?" His head turned round to catch her eye, his expression serious.

Marion swallowed hard. They'd had this conversation before in various forms. There was no subtle way to broach the subject any longer. Gerard had become fed up with indulging her dream of settling down, buying a home together, getting married and having kids.

"Very funny, Gerard," she chuckled nervously. "You know we were talking about getting engaged the other day."

Gerard shrugged her hands off his shoulders. "Excuse me! You mean you were talking about it. I'm not getting married."

"No, not straight away," she compromised. Why was it that getting a man to talk about love and marriage was the hardest thing in the world? She had hoped that after a year of being together Gerard would feel the same way, but it didn't seem like it now.

Gerard stepped out of the bathtub, dripping water on to the cork-tiled floor. He wrapped a towel round his waist while he dried his muscled upper body with another. Marion sat on the edge of the bath watching him, her eyes travelling from his buttocks down to his tapering thighs and bulging calf muscles. God, but he was beautiful.

"I'm going out," he said finally.

Her head snapped back towards him, her eyes widening in surprise. No, I must have heard wrong.

"But you only just got in," she reminded him.

"So? This ain't my home. I've got some business to take care of." He splashed Giorgio Red, his favourite fraicheur, under his arms and across his chest.

"This time of night?"

"Yeah, this time of night," he answered, mimicking her. He swiped mist from the mirrored bathroom cabinet and felt his chin with the back of his fingers. Deciding he didn't need a shave after all, he turned and exited the bathroom without a glance at Marion.

Tears welled up in her eyes as she remained seated on the edge of the bathtub. He wasn't wearing his favourite aftershave to go and visit his mum. She'd suspected for some time now that she wasn't the only one receiving the pleasures of his flesh. Every time they argued he would pick himself up, freshen up and disappear. At times like that it didn't seem to matter to Gerard whether they stayed together or not. She breathed deeply, trying hard to stop the overwhelming emotion that rose from her stomach and gripped her heart. What had she done wrong? She did her best to regain her composure and wiped her eyes with the heel of each hand. Seeing her cry would only make Gerard angry.

Stifling a sob, Marion left the bathroom and headed for the living room to avoid a confrontation. The stereo was already cued up, and all she had to do was press a button on the remote and the room filled with the sound of the Whitehead Brothers singing "187". How appropriate. Gerard's love was about as regular as a damned bus, and just like public transport you spent more on it than it was worth.

She flicked off the light and flung herself on to the soft grey sofa, her slim frame hardly making a dent in the cushions. She sat there in the dark, a thousand thoughts racing around in her mind. Lately, it seemed that all they ever did was have sex (it wasn't making love any more) or argue. She was tempted simply to end it, tell him it was over.

The light suddenly came on.

"Marion, you seen my pager?" Gerard walked over to the sideboard, searching frantically, lifting neatly placed ornaments, books and recently opened mail and dumping them back into disorder. She breathed deeply, willing her voice not to break when she spoke. "I think so... I can't remember where."

He kissed his teeth. "Don't gimme that. Or are you trying to stop me going out by hiding my t'ings?"

"Of course not," she protested.

He came around the sofa and hunched down, facing her. "What's wrong wid you, eh?" He brushed a tear from her cheek with his thumb. "You want to own me? I don't treat you like property and I don't expect to be treated that way either, you know what I mean?"

Marion just looked at him. Another tear trickled down. She sniffed. Gerard opened his arms wide to show that he had nothing to hide. "There ain't no more, babes. You listening to me?"

"Yes, Gerard." Even as she spoke, Marion knew that it didn't matter whose bed Gerard ended up in tonight, she would still take him back. She knew she would let him keep the front door key and allow him to come back whenever he liked. She knew, because this was the man she adored.

"Now, if you feel bad about me missing dinner, then I'm sorry." He took her fingers in one of his smooth hands. "I'll make it up to you, okay?"

"Yes, Gerard." She felt numb.

"That's my girl. Now, where's my pager?"

She wanted him to go. Go now, she thought. Leave me alone.

"Try the bedroom, bedside drawer."

He patted her hand, then let it go. Smiling smugly, he rose from his haunches, leaving her feeling empty and cold.

A few moments later the front door slammed and Marion was alone again. She bawled openly, her body racked with sobs. He hadn't even said goodbye. Her tears soaked into the fabric of the sofa. This was worse than not having anyone at all. She knew now that she wouldn't see Gerard for a week or more. That would be her punishment for bringing up the subject of marriage again. Hadn't he warned her about trying to corner him? Yes he had, that same time when he'd said that, as soon as he was ready, she would be the first to know.

Marion had become Gerard's property a year before, when they were both attending Lewisham College. She was twenty-one and Gerard six years older. They weren't in the same classes, but their breaks had coincided and they would meet up in the canteen. All the girls had fancied Gerard, especially those who denied it. Some of the guys probably fancied him too.

Gerard had oozed confidence, while Marion, a psychology student, had lacked it. But he'd noticed her nevertheless, one day in the lunch queue. Marion had been with her classmate Simone, who was chatting about Valentine's Day a week away. Gerard had stood two places behind with three of his friends, noisily discussing a boxing match and taking bets on who would mash up who for the heavyweight title. Simone had informed Marion loftily that her steady boyfriend, Conrad, who she had been with since she was sixteen, was taking her to Paris for Valentine's. "Four days in gay Paree," she'd swooned, "all expenses paid." She was so excited, she wanted the whole canteen to share her joy, and wouldn't stop talking about it loudly.

Marion had followed her friend to a table and they'd sat down with their lunches. Halfway through the meal Marion had looked up and caught Gerard looking straight at her, smiling. She'd averted her eyes instinctively, but every time she looked back in that direction he'd been looking at her.

For several days after that Gerard would nod or smile whenever their paths crossed. Her friends would nudge her and giggle, but Marion would simply smile back shyly, too afraid to imagine that it would ever come to anything. Gerard was, after all, the resident Adonis. What could he possibly see in her?

Marion had started looking forward to every new college day, looking forward to a smile or a nod of acknowledgement. And she had started dressing better too, and making sure that her hair was knockout before she left home in the mornings.

Then one day it had happened — again in the lunch queue. This time he had been standing right behind her. She'd reached over the counter for a plate, but Gerard's hand had reached for it first and handed it to her. Her heart was thumping hard and fast as she croaked, "Thanks."

"S'all right," he'd said. "I'm Gerard, by the way."

She'd smiled weakly and turned to go.

"Hold on."

She'd turned back to face him. He'd grinned down at her. "And you are…?"

"Marion," she'd replied.

"Nice."

He'd squeezed her free hand, smiling favourably and nodding his head in approval as his eyes undressed her.

Marion had felt embarrassed as her whole body tingled and her nipples hardened. Did the "nice" refer to her name or her body, she'd wondered as she hurried off to her table. He didn't let her off that easily, though. He had sat at her table that day and every day from then on, making her laugh and showering compliments on her. This guy wasn't just good looking, he had charm and a brain, and (to Marion's surprise) they had a lot in common. Gerard seemed to know so much and was very ambitious, just the way she liked her men. Still, she had let him ask her out four times before she accepted. On that first date at the Roof Gardens nightclub, he had been the perfect gentleman. He had done nothing more than kiss her when he dropped her home, and she'd floated through her front door deeply in love.

GERARD

No, I don't think I'm God's gift to women, I know I am. I am every woman's dream. I'm more than good looking. I've got my own business, I've got brains, I treat women well. Buy a lady presents and take her out — sometimes. Not too often, or else they start to take it for granted and then give you hassle when you don't.

I treat 'em all different, because no two women are the same. Take Marion and Debbie for instance. Marion wants me to be her exclusive property, like I'm wearing a sign saying "For Sale". I'm sure she done picked out her wedding dress and the church already. I'm not going to tell her straight out why she isn't my ideal wife because I don't want to hurt her feelings. She's too... fickle. She too easy fe cry. Catch her when it's her time of the month and she'll bawl for any lickle t'ing. And she spends too much time taking care of me. What's wrong with that? I don't need another mother.

Now, Debbie — she's totally different. She loves the fast life. She likes fast music, men, cars, money, food. You name it, it's got to be fast for Debs. There's no talk of babies and marriage with her. She knows what she wants and goes out and gets it.

I like being with Debs. Marion is just someone to relax and chill with. Because I can't relax with Debs, she's always on the go.

PAMELA KING SHUT AND LOCKED THE BATHROOM DOOR. SHE ran the shower until it was pleasantly warm, then stepped in and let the water cascade over her body. She soaped herself vigorously, washing away his scent. Already she began to feel better.

When she'd finished, she climbed out and stood naked in front of the mirror-tiled wall. She untied her shoulder-length hair and let it fall freely. Her body was perfect. Fifty sit-ups a day made sure that her stomach stayed flat. She occasionally went to the gym, more for the social aspect than the keep-fit. Otherwise, she contented herself at home with the aerobic step and video tape, the exercise bike and the stairclimber she had bought herself for Christmas.

She didn't have a mark on her smooth skin. She turned sideways. Her pert backside and firm breasts curved out sensually from her body. She leaned forward to study her face closely. Stunning brown eyes framed by long upturned lashes stared back at her. Her straight nose was almost European, her skin the colour of coffee cream. She was beautiful. So why did she feel so damned depressed?

She knew why — and as she dried off her body with a large lilac towel she thought of the man lying in her bed. Before he had come into her life, living with someone had never entered her mind; it would severely cramp her style, she'd thought. She thought back to the days when she had three or more men virtually queuing up to be with her. She could have had a different man for every night of the week if she'd wanted it. She'd had her boops, her ruffneck, her sweetboy, her buppie — even her toy boy.

She missed those days, when she never knew who was around the corner. The unpredictability of a new lover and all the flirting, the teasing, the chat-ups, the chase and the capture. The life she was living now was just not for her. Living with James had been an experiment. Her first married man. They met at a party. He'd been very open and had told her all about his wife and two kids. A couple of weeks into the affair, he'd suggested that he should come clean and tell his wife about it, then he and Pamela could stop all the ducking and diving and be together properly. Pamela had thought she'd dissuaded him. "After all," she had purred, "why spoil a good thing?" Two months later James had moved in, claiming that his wife had found out and thrown him out of their home. Pamela had her doubts, but he said that he had nowhere else to go, and she felt that she had little choice but to let him move in temporarily. Now she knew what living together meant, she wanted to move on. She'd had enough of sharing her possessions, fitting her life around somebody else's, putting up with habits, not being able to make arrangements without informing your partner. James would be perfect if she ever needed a housemaid. He cooked, cleaned, ironed, massaged her feet, and even did the shopping. But his idea of excitement was having sex on a Sunday morning.

Shaun, Pamela's 'ex' who never was a boyfriend, had called two days earlier and asked if he could see her again. Irresistible Shaun. They'd had a thing going, on and off, for four years — before James had come on the scene. Hearing his voice again down the telephone line had made her tingle with the memories. She felt she couldn't refuse him, didn't want to refuse. Shaun was the ideal tonic to get her back in the swing of things. Boy, they had learnt some positions together. Shaun — Mr Stan' 'Pon It Long! James was no comparison.

Pamela heard the alarm go off in the bedroom. Seconds later James came into the bathroom and stood behind her, rubbing sleep from his eyes. "Morning," he grinned. He was obviously pleased with his performance half an hour earlier.

"Morning," she replied brusquely, beginning her face-cleansing routine. She removed a cotton wool ball from the tube on the low window-sill and caught his eyes in the mirror. He smiled, a smile that she had once thought cute but now irritated her. Five foot eight, he matched her in height, if slightly underfed. Very fair skinned, he was often mistaken for mixed race. His hair was cut in a fashionable short back and sides. He was so thin that, when he had first moved in, Pamela had cooked everything fattening she could think of to put a bit of meat on him. She'd even suggested he visit the gym. Eight months later he was still maaga.

He reached out and stroked her hair. She tensed.

"Coffee?" he asked.

"Please."

She breathed a sigh of relief at his departure. Please don't let him get horny again this morning, she prayed silently. Once a day was quite enough. Shit, once a week was too much. He did nothing for her any more — if ever.

She was smoothing cocoa butter over her full breasts when he came back with the coffees. He placed hers on the window ledge and sipped his.

"Has something changed between us?"

Pamela held his gaze, then bent over to moisturise her legs. His eyes were on her, lustfully following the curves of her lithe body.

"Pam?"

She stood up, shook her dark brown shoulder-length hair, then pushed it off her face and took a sip of her coffee. It was perfect. She reached for her bra from the towel rail. "Everything changes, J, nothing stays the same." She clipped the front clasp of her bra and pushed her arms through the straps.

"But it's not changing for the better, is it?"

No answer, just a deep sigh.

"I mean, do you still love me?" James asked.

Pamela put her hands on her hips and turned her eyes to the ceiling. Why in hell had he chosen this morning to have this conversation?

"Look, James, love is an emotion. It's like being happy or sad. There are different degrees of love, you know what I'm saying?"

He frowned. "You didn't answer my question." He looked like a little boy with stubble, who'd just been told he'd never see his parents again.

"I love you, James," she said softly. "I'm just not sure how much. Maybe it's not enough for you," she added lamely, trying unsuccessfully to convince herself. She pulled black lacy panties on and hoped her answer had satisfied him.

"Is there someone else?" He was looking at her with lie-detector eyes.

Where the hell did he get that from? He had been watching a lot of soaps lately. And did he suspect, or was he just groping in the dark as usual?

She hoped she was looking at him earnestly. "No. No, there's no one else." At the moment she wasn't lying.

James looked at her helplessly, then his shoulders slumped and he hung his head.

"I'm going to get dressed," she said, easing past him and out of the bathroom.

James came into the room and stood in the doorway, a midnight blue towel around his waist. He didn't look too happy.

Personally Pamela liked a good argument, but James wasn't the type. He gave in too easily and always let her win. This inevitably infuriated her, but he refused point-blank to argue back.

"I need some answers before we leave this flat today."

Pamela turned to him, her mouth dropping open. For a minute there he'd sounded angry. She placed one hand on her hip impatiently.

"Pammy, are we breaking up?" He was dead serious.

She reached for her hairbrush on the dresser and turned back to her reflection. "What makes you think that?"

"You want a list?"

"Do you want us to finish?" Pamela brushed her hair vigorously.

"No. But I don't want us to go on like this," he huffed. "You don't respond to me when we make love, you avoid staying in with me. When I suggest we go somewhere you've always got something better to do. You sleep in nightclothes every night with your back to me. I can take a hint."

She sighed and twisted her mouth to one side. "It's true. My feelings have changed." She looked at him for a reaction. His lips were tight and his eyes searched hers. "Maybe if you moved out we could take it from there."

He gasped as if he'd been punched in the stomach. "Move out? But I've got nowhere to go."

"It wouldn't have to be immediately. Just start looking, eh?" She turned her back, dismissing him with a toss of her head. And when she turned back a moment later, James was gone. She heard the bathroom door shut, the lock turn and the shower begin to run.

Remorse began to rise in her chest, but Pamela beat it back down. There was little point in apologising. It was what she wanted. It was for the best, even if it meant that she would have to find his share of the rent somehow.

She pulled her hair back and braided it, tying the end with a red velvet scrunchy. A smile turned up the corners of her mouth. Today could be the start of a new chapter in her life. She punched the air triumphantly. "Yes!"

On Monday she had taken him to the annual Afro Hair & Beauty show. She had picked out what he would wear. He had to look good — after all, she did.

Pamela had tonged her hair into ringlets and expertly applied a touch of bronze colour to the ends. She'd worn a red crĺpe de Chine trouser suit and silver jewellery, and to add the finishing touch she'd put on her most expensive Ray-Bans. For James she had picked out black trousers, a white polo-neck, and a black and white striped blazer. They looked like a couple out of Ebony magazine.

As they had driven to the Alexandra Palace, they'd passed countless groups of women of colour, all making their way to the venue: ladies with ponytails or elaborate beehives, waves, wigs, hairpieces and the most amazing outfits. The Afro Hair & Beauty show was, after all, the unofficial Miss Black UK.

It was still early, two o'clock, when they'd arrived. The air was charged with a buzz that was unmistakably a 'black thang'. Pamela had felt her ego rise in her chest as they'd walked towards the main hall, James two steps behind her. She knew she looked good and she knew that everyone else knew it too.

"Where to first?" James had asked, consulting his programme.

Pamela had kept cool. "Let's just walk," she'd said, taking the lead.

Having walked around the whole hall once, Pamela regretted bringing James along. This wasn't the place to take your boyfriend to. The atmosphere was right for singles who were looking.

They'd both become bored pretty quickly. James was interested only in the "Battle of the Barbers" on the Soft Sheen stand, with four hairdressers snipping their way through the best style they could come up with in twenty minutes.

Meanwhile, Pamela had scanned the hall from behind her shades, checking out the talent. A tall, fair-skinned model had strolled by, and Pamela's eyes had followed him. The man noticed her and grinned handsomely back.

She'd turned to James. "Back in a minute... going to the Ladies'," she'd told him as she fell into step behind the model.

Having got Tevin's phone number, she'd circulated on her own. By the Hawaiian Silky stall she was surprised to bump into Marion's boyfriend, Gerard. His face had spread in an uncomfortable and guilty smile when he noticed Pamela. The two young girls at his side had something to do with his unease.

"Gerard! Fancy seeing you here," Pamela had smiled wryly.

"A'right, Pam." His eyes had darted shiftily around the room. He was dressed in a red blazer with a black T-shirt and trousers. His hair, recently barbered, had shone with S-curl gel, as had his immaculate goatee beard and moustache.

Pamela had shaken her dark curls, enjoying his discomfort. "Enjoying yourself?" she'd asked, turning her attention briefly to the two gum-chewing girls, barely teenagers. They'd been dressed in the typical uniform of their age group: coloured denim, baggy, with extra-extra gel on their heads just in case they ran into a tornado.

"Not really my scene, y'know. I jus' brought these two out for the day," he'd said.

"Yeah, right," Pamela had grinned. "So aren't you going to introduce me, then?"

"Max, get a picture of that guy on stage, that's a wicked suit, man!" the girl closest to Gerard had yelled. Max, her companion, had backed up, pulling a camera out of her pocket and taking a snap.

Pamela had waited for the introductions, and Gerard had had no choice but to oblige. "This is Debbie and Maxine, friends of mine," he'd said, emphasising the "friends". "Satisfied?"

Pamela had lifted an eyebrow. "The question is, aren't you?" she'd said pointedly. Then she had cut her eyes at him and left him fuming inside.

She wouldn't mention it to Marion, she'd decided, unless she found it necessary. It was none of her business. If Marion was naive about men she would have to learn the hard way.

By the time Pamela had got back to the Soft Sheen stand an hour later, she had collected two more phone numbers, one of which had been forced on her by a photographer who wanted her to pose for him. James had been so engrossed with the different heats of the "Battle of the Barbers" that he had barely noticed Pamela had been away.

She'd let that slide. She had managed to enjoy herself without James tagging along. The day hadn't been a total waste of time after all. And she had the phone numbers of men with potential to add to her list.

JAMES

I can't see why some men refuse to learn how to cook. I love to cook and clean. And I can look after kids just as well as any woman can. I've got three kids of my own to prove it. But I need a woman to care about in my life. I love being part of a couple.

We met at Pamela's twenty-fifth. She came over and chatted me up! Even when I told her I was married and had kids from two different women, she didn't so much as bat an eyelid. True, she was a little bit tipsy, but this woman was for real. We got on so well that I went up to see her at her flat the next day and I knew then that I was in love. Maybe I fall in love too easily. I just feel good when I'm with her. Even when we're just relaxing with a bottle of wine and playing Monopoly.

We are so different. But as the saying goes, opposites attract. Pamela likes to rave. I understand. She needs her time to herself. Why should she stay cooped up with me all weekend when she has a lot of friends to see? I don't mind. Any problems we're going through I'm determined to sort out. I can't just let it end, I love her. When something's worth saving you work at it. We won't let a few ups and downs split us up.

PAMELA SAT AT HOME IN HER SATIN PYJAMA SUIT WITH A GLASS of brandy and Coke in her hand and sweet soul music oozing out of her stereo system. James was out visiting his children. She wasn't expecting him back until late, and she intended to get completely sozzled before then.

The phone rang, interrupting a fantasy of sex on the beach with Shaun. She answered on the fifth ring.

"Pam, it's me."

"Maz. A'right love?" She settled down in the cream armchair, throwing her legs over the arm.

"Not really." Marion's voice sounded low, depressed.

"Man trouble?" Pamela guessed.

"Yep."

Whenever Marion needed to tell someone her troubles she called Pamela. Joan, being the eldest, would only lecture her. "So what did the bastard do this time?"

Marion explained. Gerard had come and gone the night before without a word of when he'd be back. Pamela listened, ice tinkling in her glass as she twirled the brown liquid around before raising it to her lips and sipping. The brandy warmed her throat and continued its heated trail to her stomach.

Pamela had heard this story before, several times in the last few months, in fact. Gerard needed someone to cut him down to size, she concluded, and Marion definitely wasn't that someone. He took advantage of her too easily.

"I've told you before, Maz, you're too good for him. He doesn't appreciate you."

"That doesn't help, Pam. I still love him."

"Don't mek love turn you fool, y'know."

Marion sighed. "Maybe it's my fault."

"You should never blame yourself with someone like Gerard." Pamela wanted to say more. She wanted to tell Marion about the Afro Hair & Beauty show, or the times she'd had to fight off Gerard's advances. About six months previously, he had found her phone number in Marion's phone index and started calling her. At first she had mildly flirted with him. He may have been her friend's man, but he was a wicked-looking specimen and she couldn't resist playing with him. She saw no harm in a little fun, but she had absolutely no intention of letting it get any further. After a few calls, though, he had started to come on strong, dissing Marion to her, and saying how he thought he and Pamela would make the perfect couple. Pamela had told him in clear, expressive terms what he could do to himself. He hadn't called again. Since that day, there had always been a frosty atmosphere between them that Marion noticed but couldn't quite place. Gerard treated Marion badly enough; Pamela wasn't about to hurt her friend further by telling her the truth. So she changed the subject. "I haven't told you, I've got good news: I got a promotion."

"Congratulations, Pam."

"It's only temporary, but, you know, extra money for three months isn't bad." That morning, Pamela had gone into the Loampit Vale nursery where she had worked since leaving college, and had been called into the office by the senior nursery nurse. Margaret, her first-line manager, had been ill for some time. The doctors had suspected cancer but Margaret, being the kind of person she was, had laughed it off. It had unfortunately turned out to be worse than first diagnosed.

The job would now go to Pamela while Margaret was on sick leave. It wasn't the way she would have liked to gain a promotion, but a hundred pounds extra a month was not something to be sniffed at.

"More good news," Pamela whispered conspiratorially. "Shaun's back."

Marion's voice was full of surprise. "Are you sure you want him back? That was over a year ago."

"You know it could never be over, not with Shaun," Pamela giggled.

"But what about James?" Marion asked.

Pamela tutted. "James bores me silly. I've asked him to move out, but he reckons he can't find anywhere else to go."

"How can you do that to him? He'd die for you."

"That's an idea," Pamela laughed.

"Pam!"

"I was only joking. I've been drinking — it's gone to my head. I need

24

some excitement."

"If that's the way you feel, go for it," Marion said unconvincingly.

"I will. We've got a problem, though."

"Yeah?"

"Well, we're supposed to go out tomorrow night. We can't use his place, his parents are staying for the week, and I can't exactly bring him here," Pamela frowned. She couldn't even do as she pleased in her own flat. James was becoming a liability.

"Sorry, Pam, can't help you," Marion interjected. "I'm babysitting for Joan. She's staying over at Colin's tomorrow night, apparently."

Pamela smirked. "You're kidding! She told me they were done."

"Yeah, well, he doesn't think so."

"That means her house is free tomorrow night?"

"I suppose so."

"What d'you think?" Marion wasn't committing herself to a promise that had nothing to do with her. "Ask her yourself. So long as you don't use her beds, there shouldn't be a problem."

"I wasn't thinking about the bed, Maz."

"The bathroom?" Marion laughed, catching the hint of what Pamela had in mind. Joan had a large en suite bathroom. Tiled floor, circular bathtub and a shower stall. The girls had often shared jokes and fantasies about using her bathroom for adventurous sex.

"Yes, girl. I'm getting goosebumps just thinking about it."

"You'd better call her, then. Let me know what she says — and, Pam, I want details afterwards." "You know that. I'll call you later, yeah? Bye." Pamela rang off. She sat there, easy and relaxed, with a mischievous grin on her face. She savoured the thought of Shaun and herself in Joan's bathroom. Shaun knew how to please a woman, any time, any place. She could hardly contain her excitement as she picked up the phone to call Joan.

"All right, Mum. We'll come down this Sunday for dinner."

Joan's mother kissed her teeth. "Fe dinner! I tell you I want to see more ah yuh, an' so yuh want me to feed yuh."

Joan rolled her eyes. "Look, I'll tell you what. How about if we come down on Saturday and stay till Sunday evening? I'll cook the whole weekend."

"Dat soun' bettah. I'll see you Sat'day, then."

"Yeah. Bye, Mum."

Joan hung up and reached into her handbag for a cigarette. Talking to her mum always gave her a smoker's appetite. She complained about not seeing enough of her and Shereen, but refused to come and visit, claiming she couldn't leave the house empty "fe teef to come tek weh me t'ings dem."

Joan lit a cigarette, sucked in deeply and exhaled. The phone rang again. "Yeah, hello?" she answered abruptly.

"Hi, J."

"Pam! How you doing, girl?"

"Safe. How're you?"

"Alive."

"Oh, don't. You sound like Marion. I just spoke to her and she's depressed over Gerard."

"Yeah, I know."

Pamela kissed her teeth. "She better sort him out soon. He was at the Afro Hair Show the other day, with a couple of schoolgirls."

"Yeah! Does Marion know?"

"I couldn't tell her that. Besides, I've got no proof he was with them."

"You can bet he wasn't there just to hold their hands, though."

"Speaking of holding hands, I heard a rumour you're seeing Colin tomorrow night."

There was the tiniest pause. "Marion, right?"

"She mentioned she was babysitting for you, that's all."

"He came round last night and we talked," Joan said wistfully.

"Yeah, and the rest. You and Colin never just talk." Pamela chuckled. "You can't hide that stuff from me. I know you too well."

"All right, nosy. I had him on the kitchen table." Joan smiled. She got warm just thinking about it.

"You lie!" Pamela screamed.

"Why would I lie? It was gooood. He's still got it."

"Well, I've got news for you, too. Shaun is back in my life."

"No! What did I tell you about you two? You kept telling me it's really over this time."

"Yeah I know, but the boy is just too tempting… J, I need a favour."

SHAUN

You see me, I'm a sucker for pretty women with long, tight legs, clear skin, a fit body and kissable lips. But did you ever hear of someone being instantly turned on to someone else without any contact? No? Then let me tell you, it can happen. It happened to me when I was just seventeen years old, and it hasn't worn off yet.

When I first met Pamela she was the same age as me and had her own place.

For a seventeen-year-old to have her own flat was wicked. A group of us would hang out there regularly.

At seventeen, girls are only for one thing. I'd had my share of them and more. But Pamela always stood out in a crowd. She had this kind of aura about her. Anyway we got close, just hanging out together. She was studying for her BTEC in nursery teaching. I had no time for school, but used to meet her outside college every afternoon. When I finally got 'round to asking her out, I kinda like acted like I was playing, y'know. I said, "You ever thought about us going out, y'know, as boyfriend and girlfriend?" She looked at me with those sexy eyes and said, "Ain't we going out already?"

I tell you, my heart must have risen up outta my chest into my throat and did a little soca dance. I was so choked I couldn't speak. That night we went back to her place and made it official. I thought I was good, but she was a lot more experienced than me, and taught me about a woman's body and what she wanted. I loved every moment of it.

Even at that age I knew I didn't have anything to offer a girl like Pamela except my looks and body and what I had learned about satisfying her in bed. I had her hooked on sex with me, you know what I'm saying? We always seemed to be at it. We couldn't go to a party together without having to slip out into some back alley to get some.

The relationship was intense and we broke up and got back together whenever it got outta control. Then she moved that guy in. I had gone to visit my parents in St Lucia, and when I got back I found Pamela shacked up with some man. At the time I just said fine, it's your life, even though it hurt me. But now I've got one more chance and I'm going to make sure I get her back.

MUSIC PUMPED OUT OF THE FIFTH-FLOOR FLAT WHERE PAMELA lived. Marion rubbed her cold hands together and knocked again, louder this time. She hated waiting around in this neighbourhood. There was never anyone around — at least no one she would want to meet. Deptford wasn't exactly Hampstead, and the Pepys estate, with its reputation of old, was one of the least desirable addresses in the area.

Pamela finally answered the door, her face covered in a green face-pack. "Hello, love." She wore a cut-off top and a pair of shorts, emphasising her hard, flat stomach and long legs.

"Are you deaf? I've been knocking for about five minutes. It's cold out here, y'know." Marion dropped her bag containing her toiletries and outfit in the hallway and shrugged off her coat.

"Sorry, Maz. Joan's got the music up loud." Marion followed Pamela into the flat. The three girlfriends had decided to meet at Pamela's flat to get ready to go out. In stark contrast to the block Marion lived in, Pamela's flat was very stylishly decorated in cream and red. Cream-coloured leather settee and armchair, red carpet and red aluminium shelves. A glass-topped marble coffee table centred the room, and a large black-framed mirror dominated one wall.

Joan, her lips slightly puckered in concentration, sat on the settee building a spliff as Marion entered. She glanced up briefly. "Hi, Maz."

"Getting in the mood I see," Marion said disapprovingly. Joan ignored her and carried on rolling her joint.

"I'll get us some drinks," Pamela said, and motioned with her head for Marion to follow her. They stepped into the adjoining kitchen and the door swung shut behind them.

"What's happening there, then?" Marion asked. "I thought Joan had given that stuff up."

"Who knows? Colin. Her mum. She just needs to chill out every once in a while."

"Okay, it's her life." Marion let it go. "So how did it go with Shaun?"

Pamela remained cool, not giving anything away. "I'll get the drinks and then I'll fill you both in. Joan's begging me for the details too." She opened a cupboard stocked with alcoholic beverages. Bacardi, whisky, brandy, Southern Comfort and Malibu were definitely in effect.

"You planning to open an off-licence?" Marion joked.

"You know I like my tipple, Maz. Besides, I often need a stiff drink when James is around." She crossed to the fridge and swung the door open. Still more alcohol. Several four-packs of lager and half a dozen bottles of sparkling wine. She pulled out a bottle of Asti Spumante and poured a glass for herself.

"Where is he, anyway?" Marion asked.

"I chucked him out," Pamela said seriously.

"You didn't!"

"He's only gone to his cousin's." Pamela threw her head back, laughing. She loved winding Marion up, it was so easy. "Look, make yourself useful." She handed her friend the ice bucket. "Take this through. I'll bring the drinks in shortly."

Joan stood by the window, gazing out over the estate. The living room was full of the pungent aroma of ganja.

Marion deposited the ice bucket on the coffee table and sat down on the settee, her short, slim legs crossed.

"Joan!" Marion raised her voice over the music.

Joan turned with a faraway look on her face. "Sorry, Maz — miles away."

"You all right?"

Joan rocked her hand back and forth. "So-so." She went over to the stereo and turned down the volume.

Pamela came in with the tray of drinks and placed it carefully on the table. "Get stuck in. We're gonna get well plastered tonight."

"You mean you've still got the energy, after Shaun?" Joan winked.

Pamela flung herself on to the sofa with a graceful air. "Shaun's good, but not that good. Anyway, you can talk. You've had Colin two nights in a row."

Joan and Marion exchanged looks. They both knew the truth: Joan and Colin hadn't spent the night together. They had argued, and Joan had walked out on him. She hadn't gone back to her own home because Pamela and Shaun had been there, so she'd ended up crashing on the sofa at Marion's. She hadn't been in the mood to talk about it then, and she still wasn't now.

Marion and Joan had grown up together on the Meridian housing estate in Greenwich, by the Cutty Sark. They had lost touch when Marion's family had moved to Abbeywood. After five years they'd met again at the funeral of Marion's younger sister, Jacqueline. For two years now the friends had been very close again, just as if they had never parted. A mutual acquaintance had introduced them both to Pamela shortly afterwards, and the two friends had become three.

"So?" Joan persisted.

"You eager, eenh?" Pamela teased.

"Don't keep us in suspense, Pam," Marion pleaded. She knew Pamela was dying to tell them about her night of lust anyway, so why the delay?

"Awright, awright." Pamela paused. "It was wicked! Five hours of non-stop bed work." The girls let out whoops of excited laughter.

"I'm telling you, he made my toes curl," Pamela continued, gesturing with her hands. "I stopped counting the orgasms after number eight. You know when you feel like you're gonna explode…" Pamela went into graphic detail of how Shaun had given her the good stuff and she had lapped it up, all of it. "I swear he's got bigger. I was like, okay, so I haven't had a decent man in months, but when I held it in my hands it was t'ick an' heavy." Pamela held one hand out as if she was weighing something in her palm. "I was feeling it all up in my chest… And you know what really turns him on?" A wicked grin spread across her face. "When I bite his bottom. I swear, my teeth just have to go near his backside and he goes wild."

Joan screamed with laughter and Marion wiped away tears from the corners of her eyes. "No, I'm serious. You should try it, then tell me if I'm lying. They love it. Bite his bottom, man." By the time Pamela had finished, Joan was on the floor holding her sides and Marion was swaying, laughing hysterically.

Pamela took a swig of her brandy and Coke. "I've got to wash this stuff off my face, I probably look like the Wicked Witch of the West. Back in a minute." With that, she disappeared out of the door.

The girls slowly recovered from Pamela's tale. Joan slid back on to her seat and reached for her cigarettes. "Pamela kills me, man." She shook her head. Marion got up and went over to the stereo to select another CD, still chuckling to herself. She flipped through the stack, occasionally pulling one out and reading the list of tracks. She turned to look at Joan as she heard the flick of the lighter. She had been smoking a lot more than usual, and Marion knew from experience that this was a sign she was feeling low. "You sure you're all right, Jo?" she asked.

"Safe. Why?" Joan dragged hard on the cigarette and leaned back in the chair.

"You're chain-smoking again," Marion noted.

"Am I? Didn't notice, y'know." She shrugged. "I only light up when I feel the need."

"So how's Colin?"

Joan shot her friend a look of frustration. "We've gone back to being mates — yet again. He's just a big kid, Maz. I need a man." She played with her lighter, nervously flicking it on and off.

Colin had wanted them to go back to sex on casual terms. She was adamant that it wasn't what she wanted. After hours of arguing back and forth on the subject, she had given up trying to make him see her point of view.

"So you dropped him again?"

"Yeah, no big deal. We ain't got nuttin' anyway." Joan half-smiled unconvincingly.

Marion decided to let it drop. She slotted an R. Kelly CD into the machine and grabbed a handful of peanuts as she sat down again. "How's Shereen?"

"Fine." Joan smiled. "Better than her mummy."

"I think we all need a break, a holiday."

Joan took a puff of her cigarette, rested her head on the back of the sofa and let her thoughts drift away.

Marion continued. "Like that weekend in Paris. We just packed up and went. Forgot about men, work, London..."

"Yeah, Maz, but who can afford it now?"

"Mmm..."

The conversation fell dead again.

Pamela walked back in, fresh-faced, her hair held back with a red hairband. "So, does James suspect anything?" Marion asked her.

"He might. He's been asking a lot of questions recently. I told him I was at Chantelle's house Thursday night. I don't care if he does think something's going on, I'm enjoying myself." She snuggled back into the leather armchair, curling her legs underneath her bottom.

"You're too wicked, Pam," Joan jokingly scolded.

"Innit, though? The man left his wife for you and, eight months later, you're cheating on him," Marion chided. She had a soft spot for James, and thought Pamela fortunate in having him. "What's good for the goose is good for the gander," Pamela said smugly.

"Damn right," Joan agreed. She was starting to feel light-headed. "Men think they're the only ones who can play around."

Pamela grinned. "Shaun told me he loves me." "And you believed him?" Joan sniffed.

"He was telling the truth. I know him."

"Yeah, whatever." Joan kissed her teeth and downed the last of her Malibu and pineapple.

Marion frowned. "Never mind her. What you gonna do? James loves you too."

"But he's so boring. I used to miss him like crazy, before he moved in. Now all we seem to do is watch telly then go to bed — to sleep! A woman cannot live by TV alone." Pamela raised her glass of wine to her lips and gulped down a mouthful.

"Which one of them gives it to you how you want it?" Joan asked.

"Shaun does — but woman cannot live by cock alone either."

Joan stubbed out her cigarette in the ashtray. "You two need to swap men. Gerard could put Pamela under manners, then James and Marion could live happily ever after," she giggled. "After all, you do fancy James, don't you, Marion?"

"I just think he's a nice guy, that's all," Marion murmured.

"You want him, you can have him," Pamela offered.

Marion pulled on the tops of her knee-high boots, loosening them a little. She gave an exasperated sigh. "A good man is hard to find."

Joan reached for another cigarette. "You don't really know what a man's like until you live with him," she said.

R.Kelly's "Bump n' Grind" pumped out of the speakers. Pamela threw her arms in the air. "This is my tune, man." Then she sang: "I don't see nothing wrong, with a little bump an' grind." The girls joined in. Joan dragged Marion to her feet and started gyrating to the beat. Pamela, giggling, joined in, bumping and grinding around the marble coffee table.

"Oh God, you do it long enough, you can actually feel it," Pamela laughed.

"Feel what?" Marion asked, bumping hips with Joan.

"The man's t'ing, you dope."

The track ended and the girls collapsed on the settee. Joan picked up a magazine and fanned herself with it, beads of perspiration trickling down her nose. Pamela refilled her glass with brandy and Coke and slid back into her seat.

It was nearly time to go.

The red Maestro cruised slowly past the crowd queuing outside the South London club. Granaries was going to be packed as usual. Girls shivered in short, expensive dresses, sacrificing warmth for style on this cold spring evening, while the guys posed, looking cool in their finest clothes.

Heads turned at the sound of the heavy garage track booming from Joan's car speakers.

"You sure we're getting in there tonight? Look at the queue!" Marion shouted above the music.

"Never mind 'bout the queue, did you see the men?" Pamela craned her neck to check out two guys who were eyeing the girls as the car passed. She smiled back teasingly. Joan turned the volume down on the car stereo. "Don't you think you've got enough men already? Girl, save some for the rest of us." "Nothing wrong with looking." Pamela pouted into her Fashion Fair powder compact mirror and dusted her nose lightly.

Joan steered the car into a parking space round the corner. They climbed out and began to make their way back. Joan was dressed in an all-in-one flared trouser suit. Pamela wore a silver baby-doll dress that just about covered her butt by five inches — her usual style. Marion was wearing sexy black batty rider shorts with lacy footless tights and a studded bra top. It suited her petite figure like it was made for her.

It was only a quarter to one when they entered the hot and sticky club, but it was already packed. Pamela's eyes scanned the dancefloor for men with potential. A mellow soul tune pumped from the speakers as a crowd of bodies rocked gently in time.

The girlfriends made their way down the mirrored corridor and past the mini waterfall which ran down the centre of the stairwell, to the Ladies', just to make sure nothing had slipped and that they looked as good as they had before leaving home. Even the rest rooms were crowded, with women queuing for the lavatories. In front of the mirrors, a line of women touched up, made up, adjusted bra straps, straightened hemlines, pulled tummies in, pushed breasts up, and patted hair into place, before asking their homegirls for a last opinion:

"Do my boobs look all right?"

"There's nothing wrong with your boobs. You wait till you've had kids — going without a bra will be a thing of the past."

"I should have worn my strapless, push 'em up a bit."

"Leave those tits alone. Bwoy, anyone would think you loved groping yourself."

"I do!"

Pamela pouted into the mirror and giggled. She shook her breasts and concluded that they looked fine. Then the girls strode confidently back into the club.

"Ready for a drink?" Pamela offered as the girls squeezed their way to the bar. Traditionally, she always bought the first round. Drinks in hand, they made their way back through the crowd to their favourite spot at the back of the dancefloor, by a row of small tables. From this vantage point they could observe all the talent available.

The swing beat changed to hip hop. "Drum an' bass crew, hol' tight, your time soon come," the MC announced. The roar went up from the ravers.

Half an hour later the music slowed way down to lovers'. Men mopped their heads with limp handkerchiefs or flannels, and women fanned themselves with invitation fliers. On the dancefloor one of the ravers twisted seductively, her knee firmly in her dancing partner's crotch. His hands groped her backside. Joan recognised the girl. "Look, it's Christine!"

Pam laughed loudly. "We know who's getting some tonight then," she howled.

Christine was a well-known man-eater. She was a mini-mampy with an insatiable sexual appetite and, judging by the way she was dancing, she had found another victim. Her sequined bottom rose slowly, then dipped again as she wined away blissfully. Marion was hot. She had been dancing throughout the drum n' bass set and, as a result, her clothes were now sticking uncomfortably to her body. As she watched the couples dancing close, she wondered what Gerard was doing. She couldn't remember the last time she had danced with him. They didn't rave together any more — they didn't do anything together. She looked over at her friends. Pam was giving the eye to an extremely good-looking fair-skinned man who was grinning back, hand on his chin contemplatively. Marion watched as he said something to his friend, who then turned to get a good look at Pamela. He nodded and smiled as if giving his friend the go ahead. The man began to make his way over. Suddenly, from behind, a pair of arms encircled Marion's waist and a firm male body thrust up against her. She spun 'round, ready to slap somebody. Instead she came face to face with a pair of familiar eyes on a dark, attractive male face. A look of pleased surprise filled her face.

"Paul, baby!" She embraced him, kissing him on both cheeks.

"See how you stay," Paul joked, holding her at arm's length. "Me nuh like the way you just dash me weh. I ain't heard from you in months."

"I didn't forget you. Busy, y'know," Marion said.

"Yeah?" Paul raised an eyebrow wryly.

Paul was a memory Marion thought she had forgotten. The last time she had seen him he had a full head of hair. Now he was fashionably clean-shaven and wore an earring.

Paul looked to her left. "Is that Pam?"

"Yeah. As usual she's rubbing up man," Marion laughed. She tugged Joan's arm to get her attention. "You remember Joan."

Always the charmer, Paul took Joan's hand and kissed the back of it with a bow of his head. Then he turned back to Marion, and taking her hand in his, he flashed his sweetest smile and put an arm around her waist, drawing her to him. "I want to talk to you," he whispered in her ear.

"Talk, then."

"Just a chat, man. Come on, I don't want to shout. Come to the bar with me. Your friends aren't going anywhere. Come nuh." His eyes smiled at her warmly.

Marion tapped Joan on her shoulder and mouthed, "Back in a minute."

Joan nodded as Paul took Marion by the hand and led her to a quiet table.

"Want a drink?" he asked.

"Yeah, a Canei, please."

Paul nodded and left her at the table. Marion watched him weave his way through the crowd to the bar. He looked so fine. He was not a tall man, five foot eight, but women never failed to notice his ebony black physique. Marion remembered how he used to be able to turn her on simply by looking at her in that certain way of his. Just the thought of his dark, hard body set her skin tingling, especially his tight buttocks. Her mind drifted back to one particularly passionate night in her living room. Paul taught karate to kids, and he was good, but that wasn't all he was good at, she recalled.

Paul returned with the drinks a few minutes later and sat down beside her, the scent of Aramis oozing from his body. Marion smiled to herself as memories came flooding back.

Paul caught the faintest smile in her eyes and, full of confidence, he held the stare. Then his smiling eyes travelled down her body, from her face, to her breasts, to her legs — all the way down — and back up again. "I could eat food off your body, you know that."

Marion smiled modestly. Paul loved complimenting women. It seemed to give him a buzz. "You're looking fine yourself. Still training?" she asked.

"Yeah, man, it's my life. So where's your man?"

Marion knew he was going to ask that sooner or later. It was pretty standard as chat-up lines go and, being a man, Paul was looking for that green light to give him the 'go ahead'. She was glad she wouldn't have to lie.

"I hope he's in bed, dreaming about me," she replied coyly.

"I dream about you." Paul ran his forefinger gently down her bare arm, looking enticingly into her eyes.

"Yeah?"

"Yeah, man, all the time." His eyes dropped to her smooth, slim legs. "Those shorts... I looked over and said to myself, no one else looks that good in shorts, it has to be Marion."

"Don't bullshit, Paul," she chuckled.

"Who's bullshitting?" he said with mock astonishment. "You make my nature rise, girl."

Marion fought the urge to lower her eyes to his crotch. "Stop it, Paul. I told you, I've got a man."

He leaned on the table with one elbow and rested his chin on his knuckles. "You happy?"

"Yes." She lowered her eyes.

"Like we were?" He knew she was still attracted to him.

Marion hesitated. "It's different. I don't want to talk about us, we're in the past. It's over."

The music changed to a down-tempo groove. Paul got up and offered Marion his hand. He wanted a dance — up close and personal. Marion didn't know if she could trust herself hip to hip with him, but she stood up anyway and let him pull her close. She could feel that he was already slightly aroused. He placed a hand on her lower back.

Their bodies moved together, hips rolling to the up and down beats of the track, and Marion let herself go with the flow. It didn't take long for the combined effect of alcohol, music and breathlessly good winin' to wash away Marion's memory of her man at home, in bed and dreaming about her.

Paul's hands caressed her gently, following her spine as they danced. His warm breath, close to her ear, made her tremble. Then he nibbled her neck.

A dance with Gerard had never been this good. Not even close.

The record came to an end, but Paul wasn't finished. The next track was equally arousing and he guided her arms back around his neck.

This guy knew how to move, and he was moving her.

She clung to him, and any thought of Gerard disappeared like a bubble bursting. It was Paul she was dancing with and that was all that mattered.

Hadn't she loved him once? It was not so surprising that feelings began to resurface. Not just sexual feelings either, but how Paul had loved her, really loved her. Yes he had, and now she wanted — no, needed — some of that sweetness back.

Gerard forced his way back into her mind. Marion suddenly pulled herself away from her dancing partner and made to leave.

"Where you going?"

"I've got to find my friends," she insisted.

"When we gonna meet up again?" he asked, dabbing his brow with a handkerchief from his back pocket.

She shrugged. "I'll call you."

He laughed. "I've heard that before."

"No, really. I will call."

"A'right then. An' tell that man of yours, he better treat you right, or he'll have me to deal with. Seen?"

Marion smiled, she leaned towards him and kissed his cheek, stepping back quickly before he got the wrong idea.

Flustered and hot, she returned to where she'd left her friends. Both of them had their arms wrapped around good-looking men. She fanned herself with a beer mat, thinking about Paul and Gerard. It had only been a dance, but the rush of emotions it evoked worried her. Paul was irresistible.

But what of Gerard? She was sure she loved him. Who wouldn't? A six-foot-two tower of ambition. Paul, though, had stirred up emotions Gerard knew nothing about.

Oh, cruel world that would make Paul her past and Gerard her future. Was that all there was to it? If only she could be like Pamela and share her love, with no feelings of guilt. What was she thinking? Marion suddenly realised that she had had too much to drink.

The girls swapped notes on the car journey home. Joan had got the number of a guy named Charles. He was thirty-five years old and the manager of a busy cinema in Islington.

"Dollar signs all over him, I'm telling you. He didn't look bad either," she said.

"The guy I was dancing with last — now he was nice," Pamela interrupted.

"Another pretty bwoy." Joan tutted. "Don't you ever learn?"

"They have their uses," Pam smirked.

"I'm so glad I'm off the market," Marion piped up.

"I'm not exactly 'on the market', but it don't stop me browsing," Pamela laughed. "And anyway, didn't I see you disappear with Paul?"

"Paul's a friend," Marion said defensively.

"A 'friend' you had a passionate affair with." Joan looked over her shoulder at Marion as they pulled up at traffic lights.

"Yeah, well, I've got morals."

"Listen to her, Miss Goody Two Shoes," Pamela teased.

A black Saab pulled up beside them. The driver rolled his window down and grinned at Pamela. Pamela nudged Joan and the three of them burst out laughing.

The man was no Denzel Washington. In fact, Shabba Ranks would have been stiff competition.

As the lights changed Pamela wound down her window and shouted out, "If I had your face I wouldn't need a backside, mate."

Marion's mouth fell open with embarrassment as their car sped through the lights, leaving the other car behind.

"Nice car, shame about the face," Joan giggled.

Marion curled up in the back seat and pretended to sleep, her mind too tormented to join in the fun.

PAUL

When I was fourteen my parents split up. Dad went back to Nigeria, leaving us in England with our Jamaican mother. She struggled to bring the three of us up. No way would I let my woman or my kids struggle like that. No way.

At the moment I'm single — by choice. I haven't met anyone I want to be with. It's like everyone out there is on the lookout for a partner. I've been there, been hurt, and now I just wanna chill.

Women are like assault courses. They have their ups and downs. Some of them are easy, some difficult. The ones that look easy have their little surprises. They'll pump you up, then bring you down hard. But, hey, if the right woman came along... who knows? As the saying goes, can't live wiv 'em, can't live wivout 'em.

There's one woman I'm interested in. She's my ex but, hey, if t'ings never work out the firs' time...

She was going t'rough some emotional stuff back then. I couldn't handle it. That was two years ago. I've matured since then. And, hey, if she came along today... I'd gladly take the stress.

Marion attracts me like a magnet. She's so innocent... I jus' wanna take care of her. When I saw her at Granaries it was like sump'n jus' open up again. I'm not one of these brothers who can't express how they feel, so when we started dancing I let her know exactly how I felt with every move and every caress. Now the ball's in her court.

PAMELA STIRRED BEFORE OPENING ONE SLEEPY EYE. THE SPACE beside her was empty — James had already left for work. He worked one Sunday a month, and would be gone until four in the afternoon. So it was her turn to cook. As James had cooked all week, she couldn't complain.

She opened the other eye. The bedroom was a mess, clothes and underwear scattered everywhere. Even last night's raving clothes lay in a pile on the floor — surprisingly, James hadn't cleared up after her. Squinting, she looked at the clock. It was two in the afternoon. Luckily, she never got hangovers.

With a prolonged yawn, Pamela lifted herself up into the lotus position. She sat like that for several minutes, breathing in deeply and out slowly. Then she got up and, pulling an oversized T-shirt over her naked bottom, skipped across the peach bedroom carpet into the bathroom. She ran a hot bath, and added plenty of scented bath oil.

Pamela sank into the perfumed water and closed her eyes. This was like a slice of heaven. She stroked warm bubbles over her thighs and thought of Shaun. As the image became clearer, her hands became his. Her fingers moved over her body, tracing a moist path up her stomach and over her breasts. Her fingers stroked and teased her nipples into hardness. The water lapped around her as she sank lower into the bubbles. Her right hand ran down her body to her flat stomach and below to her pubic hair. She placed her painted toes on the rim of the bath and parted the fur with her fingertips, lingering on her clitoris before entering herself. She moaned with the increasing ecstasy of her own foreplay. She dragged her fingertips slowly back up the path to her clitoris, while her left hand continued to massage her nipples. All she could feel was Shaun kissing her, caressing her, pumping away deep inside her. She massaged her clitoris to a tempo that was getting faster with each beat. Heat was rising from deep inside, spreading over her neck, chest and face. Eventually she gasped aloud as her most sensitive nerve throbbed.

Pamela had brought herself to a delicious climax, and beads of perspiration now stood out on her forehead and upper lip.

It was James who had turned her into an expert in the art of fantasising and masturbation. He hadn't been performing to satisfaction. For weeks, the only sex they'd had was made up of quickies, amounting to little more than a kiss and a quick fumble, then off with the clothes, followed by hurried strokes as though he were running for a train — and that was it; he'd roll over and leave her to conjure up a dream lover. Pamela had known from the start that sex wasn't as important to James as it was to her. And at first she'd thought she could cope with that. However she now knew that, far from being ready to slow down, she was hungrier than ever. Shaun, she knew, was ready and willing to satisfy her — and the more she thought of him, the more it seemed like James was history. She just didn't know how to tell him.

Perhaps her mates were right. Maybe she was a bitch. Her parents had certainly thought so. It was as though they'd blamed their only child for the three miscarriages her mother had previously suffered — all boys.

She remembered being dolled up, bows in her hair, wearing a pretty dress and her best coat, to go to church every Sunday with her parents. She recalled the boring sermons, the smoke drifting from melting candles, and all the old people. Often she would drift off, only to be rudely awoken by a nudge in the ribs from her mother's Bible or umbrella: "Wake up, child. You don't sleep in the Lord's house. Pray for your brothers."

But she hadn't known any brothers. She was the last born and the sole survivor, yet her mother would remind her daily of how she'd nearly died bringing Pamela into the world. So much pain and suffering over a girl child. Pamela was made to feel that the only way she could make it up to her mother was to do all the chores in the house.

At around the age of twelve, Pamela had begun to rebel. She knew there was more to life than the strict Catholic school she attended. Reggae music became her high, and she saved her meagre pocket money to buy herself a cheap Walkman from the market. As she got older and realised her parents would no longer lift a hand to her, she got braver. Every way she could think of, Pamela turned their rules around. They were old — what could they possibly do to stop an unruly teenager? Her parents had turned on each other instead. When she left home there was no love lost between any of them.

The telephone began to ring in the living room.

The caller was persistent, and the phone continued to ring as Pamela tried to ignore this intrusion into her private thoughts. Eventually, tutting her frustration at being interrupted, she grabbed a large towel from the bathroom rail and stepped dripping from the bath. She padded her way out of the bathroom leaving a trail of water behind her, and picked up the phone in the hallway. "Hello?"

"Hi, babes," Shaun's crisp tone came down the line.

"Hi." Her voice mellowed instantly.

"Is the coast clear?"

Pamela leant against the red and grey striped wall, holding up the towel with one hand. "Yeah, he's out at work."

"What took you so long to answer the phone, then?"

"I was in the bath."

"So you're standing there naked?" His voice was trickling down the phone line like warm syrup.

She could almost see the look on his face. "Yeah. Nothing but a towel to hide my modesty." She was playing into his hands.

"What modesty?" Shaun laughed, sending shivers down her body. She raised one foot and rested it high on the wall, stretching her lean muscles. Her wet hair was clinging to the back of her neck and shoulders. She ran her tongue over her lips. "I can be modest, y'know," she beamed.

"Yeah, sure," he chuckled. "Are you doing anything this evening?"

Pamela sighed. "If you can call having dinner with James doing something, yes. Why?"

"My parents left this morning," he declared. "I want to see you."

"I want to do more than see you. I want you butt naked and sprawled out on a bed," she smiled, her eyes lighting up.

He chuckled again, and lowered his voice to a sexy growl. "And then what would you do with me?"

"Wouldn't you rather I showed you?" Pamela purred.

"Boy! You've got to come round now, cause something just came up." Pamela laughed. Men were so predictable. "What time?"

"Eight?"

"Make it seven. James might wonder if I go out that late." There it was again — having to consider James before making her own plans.

"Okay. Want me to pick you up?" His voice was eager now.

"No, I'll make my own way. Just give me a lift back."

"I'll be waiting."

"Ready and waiting?" she teased. This was so easy; he was putty in her hands.

"Damn right."

She giggled, licking her lips. "See you later." She hung up, smiling confidently to herself. She was ready for him now. It was just after three. James would be home in about an hour. Pamela sauntered back to the bathroom and immersed herself back in the warm water.

Tonight wouldn't be quite as boring as she had thought.

"You decide to leave that wimp yet?" Shaun nudged Pamela's naked bottom with his bare foot.

She was lying on the threadbare carpet, flipping through Hype Hair magazine.

It was the first time either of them had spoken in ten minutes. They had made love within half an hour of her arriving, and were now chilling out in the living room. Getting out of dinner with James had not been a problem. He hadn't stood in her way. All he wanted to know was when she was coming home. She had no idea — and that was exactly what she had told him.

Shaun, wearing nothing but baggy shorts, sat on his black foldaway sofa bed, remote control in hand, busily flicking through the cable channels. A half-eaten pizza lay in its box on the second-hand wooden coffee table. Pamela had decided that she wasn't that hungry after all, and had eaten only the mixed salad. She was dressed in a large T-shirt she'd found in Shaun's wardrobe. Shaun nudged her again. The T-shirt rucked up, baring her buttocks.

"He's not a wimp," she replied irritably. She hated talking about James when she was with Shaun; it spoiled the mood. "Any man who can't please his woman is a wimp," he sneered.

Pamela sat up in front of him and crossed her legs. Her long, dark hair fell about her face. She had about her an after-sex glow that brought her natural beauty out to its fullest. "It's not that. It's just that you've spoilt me. After having champagne, who wants to go back to Babycham?" She flashed a cheeky grin.

Shaun ran a hand over his barely-there hair. He grinned back. "So, I'm champagne now, am I?" His dimples deepened.

"Yeah. Bubbly, sweet, strong, and very addictive." Pamela drew out the words sexily and let the T-shirt slip back just a bit, giving him a glimpse of her pubic hair.

But Shaun knew her too well. He knew she was avoiding the issue by trying to take his mind off it. "You didn't answer my question," he said paternally.

Pamela switched to the defensive. "Which one?" She twirled a finger in her hair, distractedly turning to gaze at the television.

"Don't play games with me, Pam. Are you gonna chuck him out?" He was starting to sound like her father and she wasn't so sure she liked him telling her what to do. "I told you I asked him to go. What more do you want from me?" She bared her teeth and her eyes flashed fire.

Shaun, taken aback, moved to touch her.

"Just don't, Shaun." She shrugged his hand away.

"What did I say?" He lifted his shoulders.

She sighed. "It's like you're hassling me. I shouldn't have to take that from you."

"I know, but I want you to myself."

"And I don't want to make any mistakes. You know what it was like with us. There were so many ups and downs. James is stable, helpful, supportive..." She was counting the points off on her fingers.

"Boring," Shaun interrupted.

"Okay, so I can't have everything." She half-laughed.

Shaun glowered. "I can be all those things too, y'know. I've grown up since I was going out with you. Don't tell me you can't see that?" Shaun's fair skin had one drawback: when he was upset, the tips of his ears went pinky red. Pamela saw this happening now and her spirits rose again. She was glad she was having this effect on him. It meant she still had the power. She raised a cynical eyebrow. Shaun remained serious. His usually playful eyes were staring into her face. He leaned forward, resting his elbows on his knees. "Being away from you made me realise how much I want you. You're meant for me, man."

She cast down her eyes. She wasn't sure if she felt the same, but it wouldn't hurt to keep him sweet. "I dunno."

"You want to stay with him?"

"No, not any more."

"Then get rid of this geezer. I don't like sharing you."

"It's not that easy."

"Why not?" He raised his voice now. "It's your flat. Just pack his bags and throw them out. Or do you need some help?"

He was giving her orders again. "You see what I mean? A minute ago I told you not to talk to me like that. You don't listen to me." Pamela uncrossed her legs and stood up, the T-shirt dropping down to hide her nakedness. She wandered over to the glass-fronted drinks bar. This was a relic from when Shaun's parents still lived in England. Its front was the shape of a yacht and had a gold railing round the top. Pamela picked up a bottle of Southern Comfort and poured some of the orange-brown liquid slowly into a glass tumbler, her back still turned to Shaun.

As he watched her, he wondered what was going through her mind. Did she really like this guy or was she just using him? His possessiveness was compounded as he admired her small, tight buttocks moving under the T-shirt. He felt the beginnings of arousal and pushed the thought to the back of his mind. "What's wrong with you? You turning soft in your old age?"

Pamela spun round, breasts jiggling enticingly, her nipples pointing at him through the thin fabric. He licked his lips.

"Don't test me, Shaun." "Or you'll do what?" he challenged, almost smiling. To him, her anger made her more beautiful.

"Just don't put pressure on me. I've come here to enjoy myself. Do you have to ruin it?"

Shaun couldn't resist her any longer. Fighting Pamela was like punching a brick wall — you only hurt yourself. "Come here," he said, opening his arms.

Pamela stepped lightly towards him, stopping in front of him, glass in hand.

He took the glass and placed it on the floor. "Why did I ever let you go?"

"Because you're a fool?" Her eyes were drawn to his erection.

He smiled, dimples deepening. "I was. I know what I want now, though."

"Yeah? What?"

"This," he said, squeezing her bottom.

"Give me time — an' you can have it all."

"Don't take too long, y'know. I got women queuing up to take your place."

Pamela thumped his arm playfully. "But you're turning them all down, aren't you?"

It was his turn to tease. "For now. So long as you keep me happy." She grinned. "In that case…" She mounted his lap, wrapping her legs around his back. "I want to make you happy now." She pressed against his groin, feeling his penis jump.

"Yeah, well, I'm not in the mood," he joked, his eyes shining. He pushed her hands away. Pamela kissed his lips, tickling them with her tongue, playfully nipping them with her teeth. She let her breasts brush against his chest. Then she slid herself down his body and nudged his semi-erection with her lips. She could see it grow instantly. She took him into her mouth and he moaned softly.

Releasing him suddenly, she grinned up at his face. "Changing your mind yet?"

"Okay, you've persuaded me." He pulled her up to him and kissed her passionately.

Shaun never let her down.

If only he didn't want to own her like all the others, she would enjoy this so much more. But right now he was pleasing her, the best way he knew how.

AT WOOLWICH, MARION STEPPED HURRIEDLY FROM THE BUS clutching the bulky pushchair. She waited while the young girl with the screaming infant followed.

"Thanks a lot," the girl said, taking back the buggy and struggling to get it open. She couldn't have been more than sixteen, Marion thought, and her own mother suddenly sprang to mind. She had been younger than that when Marion was born.

She breathed in deeply and made her way across the market. Today was going to be hot. June was only a few days away, and already the temperature was seventy-five degrees.

There was only one class of people in Woolwich: working class. To Marion, they seemed to have no direction in life. Working in a library, she encountered many disillusioned faces daily.

At college, she'd had dreams of becoming a journalist. Her tutors had told her she had talent; she had the certificates to prove it. But the opportunities were few and far between. Six months down the line, she was still not in full-time employment. She had a dead-end part-time job that just about paid for her shopping every week.

But still she had a dream. Though her sights had narrowed and it was no longer top priority, it was there somewhere.

Heading towards the library, she allowed her mind to wander. It was a habit she hadn't managed to break since childhood. At school she had been one of those children who, when asked a question about the subject of the lesson, couldn't answer because she had been gazing out of the window. After Jacqueline died she had daydreamed constantly, usually in the form of "what if"s. What if Jacqueline hadn't been working so hard? What if she had gone into hospital a day earlier? What if she could have been cured? What if the consultant had been on duty when they arrived at the hospital? Could he have saved her?

What if their mother had still been around? If anything, Marion blamed Gwendolyn, her mother — there had been no real father to speak of. Jacqueline's father was a married man, who had no intention of leaving his wife or acknowledging the baby as his own. Marion's father had been nothing more than a sixteen-year-old boy who, after being verbally abused by Marion's grandfather, was thrown out of the house and told never to come near his daughter again.

The closest they had come to a father was Derek. He had moved in when Marion was five years old, and stayed for ten years. During this time Marion's mother lost two babies by him before getting herself sterilised. Derek was allowed by their mother to take over the girls' upbringing completely. Gwendolyn was totally under his control, so it followed that her children would be too. They were told to call him Daddy, and to follow the new rules he set out in their home: "Tidy your bedroom, you have fifteen minutes."; "Do your homework by six o'clock."; "Hoover up the place."; "Do the washing up."; "Go and get my newspaper." Fetch this, that, come, go, do, don't... His rules were hard and fast, and any rebellion was met with a beating from his belt. He would make them stand in front of him, holding out their small hands to receive their punishment. The girls would invariably be bawling before the strap had actually touched them, pleading with their mother, who would simply say that they should have done as they were told.

The girls hated Derek with a vengeance, and would often sit and plan how they could get rid of him. Their plans ranged from calling the police after a beating, to drugging him and throwing him into the Thames. As they were both kids at the time, there was no way they had the guts or the know-how to do it.

What their mother saw in the man, they never knew. He certainly wasn't good looking. Maybe he had charisma. He was intellectual; he'd been a law student when they'd first met. His skin was as dark as plain chocolate, and his affected Queen's English always made him sound like a foreign student. He was forever being mistaken for African. He always spoke to outsiders as though he knew what he was talking about. This superiority had fooled Marion's mother — but not the children.

The man was evil. When the bills had got out of hand from his gambling and strangers kept turning up on the doorstep demanding money, Gwendolyn had finally started to fight back. This, of course, made the situation worse. Derek would threaten to kill her and the children, or throw them out on the street. These turned out to be empty threats, but the beatings were real enough.

He stole from her to pay his debts, forging her signature in the social security books and drawing on her money. Many times Marion found her mother in tears, for no other reason except that he was in her life.

Eventually Derek moved on. Another woman, another life to ruin. A profound peace fell over their home after his departure. At last, they had their mother back.

Then Gwendolyn married, and practically left them to fend for themselves. Jacqueline was forced to find work instead of continuing with her studies.

Jacqueline had refused to go to their mother's wedding. From the beginning she had been adamant that she wasn't going to celebrate a marriage between her mother and this white man from Birmingham. Marion had attended simply to keep the peace, although in her heart she did wish her mother the best.

By now, Marion was a year into her BTEC in journalism at South Thames College, and was also studying psychology at Lewisham. Jacqueline had managed to get a job at Hennes in Oxford Street as a salesgirl. She never complained, but woke at six every morning to get ready, and came home in the evening shattered. Marion promised her that as soon as she finished college they would swap over, so Jacqueline could go to college and complete her education. She wanted to be an Environmental Health Officer. Sadly, she managed only four weeks' work experience with the local council before her illness prevented her from continuing work. As the disease progressed she would sleep more during the day, and she started taking a lot more of her pills even when she wasn't in pain — or at least she said she wasn't.

When Jacqueline died, Marion felt alone until Joan and Pamela started to call her regularly after the funeral. Eventually they made going out together a regular thing. In time, her friends became closer than family. There was nothing she couldn't share with them.

Marion was the only black woman on the staff. A part-timer, she found she would often be called into work on days when promotions were happening. The week before, some bright spark had suggested they have an Afro-Caribbean make-up demonstration. They had booked a beautician to come in today to make up volunteers' faces while the onlooking public learnt what colours suited them and how to apply them correctly.

Marion was all for encouraging the black community into the libraries — but like this? Using make-up as bait was not her idea of encouragement. Why couldn't they have asked the community for ideas on what they would have liked to see? They might have had a book-signing by an X-Press author, or a speaker on black history, or a successful black businessperson to come in and say how they had achieved what they did.

Role models — that's what Marion felt were needed. Not someone telling you how to look pretty by dabbing on make-up. What about black men? Was this supposed to interest them?

About an hour before the beautician was due to arrive, Marion and Parminder, an Asian colleague, were instructed to pace the streets of Woolwich handing out flyers advertising the demonstration. They walked down Powis Street, the busiest shopping area in Woolwich, then stood outside Woolwich Arsenal station for fifteen minutes.

"You know why they picked us, don't you?" Parminder asked. She was the same height as Marion, with shoulder-length black hair, a chubby figure and a thick Asian accent.

"Course. We're their token blacks. When it suits them, we can appear to be very important to the organisation."

Parminder tutted and handed out another leaflet to a woman with a scarf round her head who was dragging three toddlers along beside her.

"You know, I've tried three times to get a promotion in this place," Marion said. "I had the experience required, and they still wouldn't give me a permanent job."

"I know. I'm a qualified librarian in my country. When I come here they tell me I must take exam again."

"So you have to start at the bottom because they think your country is too backward."

"It seems that way," Parminder said, clearly disgruntled.

Thrusting leaflets into the hands of people in a hurry was one of the most humiliating things Marion had ever had to do. Nobody was interested. After an hour or so there were flyers floating off in all directions. To top that humiliation, when the beautician finally turned up at the library she was white, had never done coloured skin before, and hadn't brought the right shades.

Five black women turned up for the session. They sat watching the chief librarian get made up in colours made for her skin colour. Every now and then they would glance at their watches. Half-way through, two of them stood and made hastily mumbled excuses before exiting. Marion didn't blame them, if she could have left she would have. She was glad she was working only until four o'clock, because her jaw ached from putting on a forced smile for each new customer during the day. Standing once again at the bus stop, she thought about how much easier life would be if she could get a full-time job, and therefore be able to afford a car. She had passed her test at eighteen, and she hadn't been able to afford a car then either.

One good thing about working part time was that she could keep her hand in with her writing. She wrote articles for women's magazines. She knew the competition was fierce and, although she kept having articles returned, they would usually come back with a note of encouragement. Some would say that, although the article was not right for their publication, they had enjoyed it and would like her to keep trying.

As soon as she got home Marion ran a quick bath to freshen up. Lying in the water, she felt as though she'd lived in this flat forever.

It had been four long years, she thought, letting the warm water soothe her aching legs. Two without Jacqueline. When their mother married and left, they had been moved out of their three-bedroom council house in Abbeywood, into this dingy flat in Charlton. The flat had two bedrooms: Jacqueline's room (as Marion still called it) was a narrow six by fifteen foot room with a built in wardrobe; Marion slept in the fairer-sized twelve by twelve foot room. The living room was large, with doors leading out on to a self-contained balcony. The kitchen was a neat L shape, badly in need of decorating since there had been a flood upstairs.

Marion stepped from the bathroom in her bra and knickers.The scent of her Body Shop deodorant and body oil followed her into her bedroom. The room was decorated in pastel pinks and blues. She found baby colours relaxing. This was her thinking room. A small desk and bookshelf were to the left as one entered and on the other side of the bedroom stood

Marion's all-in-one dressing table and double wardrobe. One side of the wardrobe had become Gerard's. It had happened gradually, starting with the odd jacket left over a weekend, then clean shirts had appeared, toiletries, a second pair of trousers, underwear... To Marion it felt right, even if it meant that she had to fold her clothes and use the airing cupboard shelves.

She had never understood the stories of women fighting or killing themselves over men — until she had fallen for Gerard. He knew a lot of women. On the few occasions they went out together, they would always end up bumping into someone he knew. The heat of jealousy rose up and boiled within Marion each time. It wouldn't be so bad if he didn't act as though she wasn't standing right there by his side. He would chat intimately to the females, making promises to visit them and swapping phone numbers, and not once would he introduce her.

It hurt. Once she had actually tried to introduce herself, fed up with being treated as though she didn't exist. Gerard had shot her a look that had burnt right through her, before shutting her out of the conversation again. He had a life that she had nothing to do with. It was something else she had come to accept.

She removed a simple black catsuit from the wardrobe, along with a short, crocheted cream top. Slipping them on in front of her mirror she imagined being single again. Being without Gerard. It wasn't as though she had to put up with him. She could get other men. It was the thought of being out there again that put her off. Meeting a man, getting to know his pros and cons, getting to know another body, judging his feelings, with him judging yours... Relationships were too unpredictable, yet she would rather stay in this unpredictable one than start all over again. Besides, she loved Gerard. Faults and all.

GERARD

Hot. This kind of weather makes a man restless. My mum would cuss if she saw the way I was sitting in her chair: "Tek yuh naked skin out de chair, Gerry. Yuh no have no manners?" She'd probably grab the towel from my body and whip me with it.

But she ain't here, she won't know. I've just been for a five-mile jog. I like to keep myself trim.

I need a woman bad — right now. It would be a crying shame to let this fine body go to waste on a day like this. Debbie should be home now. She don't go nowhere on Sundays. She's at college doing sociology and psychology. She have ambition as well as beauty. We met at a dance in Dalston. She lives in Brixton.

She's young, twenty one, but she have a vibrancy I cyan't resist. She's feisty too, but I like that. She can stand up for herself. There ain't no comparison between her and Marion.

Marion can cook and care for me, and she's willing to listen to my troubles and pamper me when I need it.

Debbie is wild, man. I doubt she even knows how to use a cooker. But she makes up for it in other ways. Thinking about her just mek the restlessness rise, y'know what I mean? I'm gonna call her. She'll do nicely.

IT WAS A BEAUTIFUL, SUNNY DAY. THE SKY WAS BLUE AND cloudless, and a light breeze prevented it from becoming too hot. Perfect weather for a barbecue. Joan stood in her bedroom, dreamily looking out of the window at the street below. Her Asian neighbour across the road was stripped down to his shorts, washing his dark blue Peugeot 405 by hand. Two boys raced their skateboards down opposite sides of the road, their friends cheering them on.

The little girl stepped daintily across the lavender carpet, not making a sound. A cheeky grin dimpled one cheek as she crept up behind her mother and encircled her legs in her little arms, giving them a gentle squeeze. Joan turned to look down at her daughter. "Shereen, how can you frighten Mummy like that?" "You left me on my own." The little girl pouted. She was dressed in a pink corduroy skirt with a matching jacket and a white T-shirt, like a miniature cowgirl.

"I was only up here. You miss me?"

Shereen put on her pretending-to-be-shy look and nodded.

"All right." Joan picked up her daughter and hugged her small body to her chest, careful not to crumple the flimsy material of her own clothes. She wore a short, flowing, navy dress that moved when she did, bought specially for the occasion. "I'm coming back down now. You got your bag all ready to take to Grandma's?"

"Yes. An' I put in my Barbie and Ken."

"Did ya?"

"Yeah. 'Cause Grandma only got soft toys, not real dollies," she said with an air of authority on the subject. Joan smiled. Her mother made rag dolls and teddy bears. Over the years, they had accumulated quite a collection. Shereen would stay at her grandmother's house on occasional weekends. For a fifty-two-year-old woman, Grace was still very lively, and Joan had no worries about her becoming reclusive. Joan's father had gone back to Jamaica ten years previously, taking her brother Patrick with him and leaving the two sisters, Joan and Donna, with their mother. At first her mother had carried on like she couldn't care less, even though she had cussed all sorts of bad words about her husband's "fancy piece dem". Then all of a sudden she hadn't mentioned him any longer. When Joan or Donna asked her whether he wrote, or if she had heard from him, their mother would pretend she didn't hear or change the subject. Soon they stopped mentioning him altogether, as though he had never existed.

Joan drove towards Wandsworth to drop Shereen off at her grandmother's before going to the barbecue.

Charles, the man she had met at Granaries, had kept in touch. He seemed mature, interesting — and interested. But Joan had been at this stage in a relationship before, when you had met the man in question only once, in a club or at a party, but always in the dark. You'd talked a couple of times on the phone, and he'd sounded like so much fun, you couldn't wait to meet up again. And then you find when you do meet up that he's nothing like you remember and you have nothing in common.

Since she had stopped seeing Colin, and after the episode with Stephen, Joan had decided to look for someone who was more than simply a 'good man' — he would have to be a good father too. But the men she met didn't seem to know what they wanted. It was as though the older they got the more they struggled against being tied down. As soon as she mentioned children, you could see the interest drain from their eyes. Joan pulled into her mother's driveway. The house was pre-war, three storeys high. Her mother had the first floor and basement, and she let the upper floor out to a young black couple. It was lunchtime. The smell of cooking wafted towards them. When Shereen rang the bell, they were greeted by a new face at the front door. Joan eyed the old man suspiciously, wondering what the hell this guy was doing answering her Mum's front door. He looked very dapper in a smart suit. His hair was completely white, and he was clean shaven. He must have been at least sixty-five. She looked past him for any sign of her mother.

"Er, hello."

"You must be Joan. Come in, darling." The little man stepped aside to let them into the house and closed the door behind them. Shereen clung to her mother's coat as they followed the stranger through the hallway and into the kitchen. "Grace, is yuh dawta," he called. Grace was fifty-two last birthday, and looked no older than thirty-eight. Joan's friends were always complimenting her, saying they looked more like sisters. They even wore the same sized clothes. Grace was in the hairdresser's at least once a week, prettying herself up for one of her many admirers. If

Joan got there early enough in the morning she could catch her mother bouncing up and down in front of the television to a keep-fit video. Joan had to admire her mother, but she hated the fact that she still went on dates. Mothers of adult children shouldn't be doing them kind of things, she'd constantly tell her. And she refused to think about whether her mother still had sex. That was just too gross.

Grace stood at the cooker, stirring a pot of spicy chicken. Joan's stomach contracted hungrily. She hadn't eaten all day, saving herself for the barbecue food.

"Joan, you early," Grace stated, turning to them. Joan kissed her on the cheek. "You did say two o'clock. I didn't think two hours would make that much difference. I've got some things I want to do before I go out. Besides..." She cast a sideways look at the man seated comfortably at the kitchen table. "I didn't think I'd be interrupting anything."

"Oh I feget, you never meet Clyde. Clyde, This me eldest, Joan. Joan, a Clyde dis. 'Im is a fren'."

"A friend?" Joan raised an eyebrow. She thought she knew all her mother's friends.

"Doan question me, Joan," her Mother warned, and turned her attention to the little girl still clinging to her mother's leg. "So, Sherry, you have a kiss fe yuh Grandma?" Shereen let go of her mum's leg and, without taking her eyes off Clyde, she ran up to her Grandma and kissed her firmly on the lips.

"Ehhh! T'ank yuh, love."

"I'm gonna go now, Mum. I'll pick Shereen up at dinner-time tomorrow."

"Yes, good. I'll see you then."

"Clyde, maybe I'll see you again. Shereen, be good for Grandma." Shereen waved and Clyde nodded and smiled.

Boy, her mother had more boyfriends than she did. What was this world coming to?

Following the directions Charles had given her, Joan swung the car into a narrow street off the Old Kent Road. Already she could hear the music blasting from the speakers, even though she was still one block away. As she turned the car into Drovers Place, she could see people congregating outside the house, some sitting in cars, some sitting on cars. Suddenly she felt very uncomfortable about coming to the barbecue on her own. But that had been the whole idea, she reminded herself — change of scenery, different mix of people.

She parked the car around the corner from the house and checked her hair and make-up in the rear-view mirror. Charles had seemed very eager to see her again when he called. He'd made her laugh with his sarcastic humour and he'd showered her with compliments. She didn't fall for it, but it was nice getting them.

The barbecue was in aid of his thirty-sixth birthday, as if Joan needed reminding that there was a nine-year age gap between them. Charles's tastes were different to hers, and he talked about things that she'd never experienced and wasn't interested in. However, they both loved to party and Charles could really dance. He was an okay guy.

The barbecue was in full swing. The front door stood open and Joan stepped into the house. She glanced around for any familiar faces, but saw none. Most of the people seemed to be outside in the back garden. MC Hammer's "Pumps in the Bumps" was blasting out of the speakers so loudly that Joan could feel the house vibrating. Her earrings tinkled with the buzz. She edged past people she didn't know, through the living room and into the sun-filled garden.

It was an elegant affair, with 'nuff chat, food and drink. Everybody seemed to be mingling, standing in twos and threes or huddled into picnic parties on the grass. The huge speakers under the willow tree oozed music to the residents of the neighbouring streets. Joan scanned the garden, her eyes coming to rest on the plume of smoke that rose lazily into the blue sky. The barbecue. Heading in that direction, she quickly spotted Charles, surrounded by a bevy of women, laughing as usual, looking cool in black cotton shorts and a long white shirt that billowed in the gentle breeze. His hairy legs ended in sandalled feet.

Joan eased up behind him and wrapped her arms round his waist and squeezed. His body tensed, just for a second, then he craned his neck to see who his seducer was. "Jo! Hello, sweetheart." His eyes creased as he smiled at her. Charles was tall, dark and charismatically handsome, the kind of good looks formed by personality. His forehead was lightly ridged with fine lines and tiny crows' feet adorned the corners of his eyes. Whether he liked it or not, time was catching up with him.

"Hi, Charles. I hope you've got my plate ready."

He slid a hand 'round her waist and answered in his natural Jamaican accent, "Everyt'ing ready. You want a drink?"

"Yes, please."

"Saaf or hard?" he teased with a glint in his eye.

Joan laughed, catching the innuendo straight away. "I'm driving. I'll just have a pineapple juice."

"Right, I'll be back. Don't go away." He squeezed her hand gently and walked back towards the house. Alone again, Joan surveyed her surroundings. She had never been to Charles's home before. From what she had seen of the inside, he had expensive tastes. The garden was landscaped, the path from the patio doors running straight down the middle before branching off in different directions. One branch ended in a flower display, another in a rockery. The main path ended at a pond bordered by love-seats.

Charles returned with the drink. "You looking good," he said, handing Joan the glass.

"Thank you, Charles," she answered modestly.

"I did t'ink you change yuh mind."

"About what?"

"Seeing me."

"Well, I had nothing better to do." She lit her cigarette, hiding her smile.

"You t'ink yuh smart, but one of dese days, Joan, some guy gwine tame yuh."

"No one tames me until I want to be tamed."

"Awright, we'll see." He gave her a look as if to say, "I take that as a challenge". "You hungry?"

"Starved."

"Then come nuh. Mek we fine sump'n fe yuh." He took her hand in his and led her to the front of the queue for hot food.

Time was flying, and Joan was having fun. Three hours later, although she didn't know it, Joan was pissed. Well out of it. The spiked pineapple juice had gone straight to her head.

Charles made her laugh. He'd introduced her to some of his male friends, who had taken it upon themselves to be her bodyguards for the rest of the day. Any man who came near her was politely but firmly shown the runnings.

It was now evening. She and Charles sat alone on a love-seat by the pond. Coloured bulbs strung out in the trees above their heads cast dancing shadows over the garden.

Charles slid his arm around her waist and pulled her close. "How's my sexy lady?" he whispered softly into her ear. A light breeze had blown up, and Joan clutched his jacket around her shoulders.

"Me? I'm fine," she giggled.

"Did you drive?"

"Yeah, the car's round the corner. Why?"

" 'Cause yuh not driving home." He kissed her forehead. "I'm fine, Chas." She didn't sound convinced. "I've only had pineapple juice — I think." Her voice didn't sound like hers anymore. It reminded her of when she was on a sensi buzz.

"You get drunk on pineapple juice?"

Joan giggled again and looked at him. She shook her head foggily and tried to focus her eyes but wasn't having much luck. "I'm drunk?" she slurred.

"Nuh worry 'bout it. Me will drive you home."

She hugged him with arms that had no strength in them. "My hero," she teased.

Charles helped her to her feet and walked her back through the house. Inside was empty, except for a few stragglers and two older women tidying up in the kitchen. Charles stopped to introduce Joan to them. "Aunty Gen, dis is my wife," he told a tall, grey-haired woman, who turned and smiled at them. Joan tried to smile back, but not being able to feel her lips she wasn't sure she'd managed it.

"From when you married? Chile, tek no notice of de bwoy's nonsense." The woman had a beautiful smile.

"I don't," Joan replied.

Charles looked into her bleary eyes. "How you mean? You don't think I'm gonna mek an honest woman of you?"

"It'd be more like me making an honest man of you," Joan said. "Now take me home before you have to carry me," she said, slipping her arm through his.

"Bye, love." Aunty Gen waved and resumed her washing up.

Joan must have fallen asleep on the way home — or passed out. Charles kept glancing over at her as he drove. She was his kind of woman. His friends had even asked him if she was available. He'd made sure they got the message: this one was his. And the only way he could be sure that he would be driving her home, was to spike her pineapple juice with Bacardi.

He wanted to spend some time with her alone, get to know her better. As far as he was concerned, she was already his. He just had to make her realise.

Charles parked the car in a space opposite Joan's house. She woke as the car's engine shut off.

"You all right?" he enquired, leaning towards her.

"Mmm," she answered, peering out of the windscreen. "You coming in?"

"If you want me to."

Joan didn't notice the seductive tone in his voice. "You might as well, unless you're gonna walk home, it's late," she yawned.

Charles wasn't going to argue.

He accompanied her inside. She kicked off her shoes in the hallway and hung his jacket, which she'd been wearing in the car, on the banister. She told him to go through to the living room while she made some coffee.

"Nice place you 'ave 'ere," Charles commented, when Joan returned with the coffees.

She walked over to the stereo and slotted a Keith Sweat cassette into the machine. "Thanks. It was hard work." She stepped back to the sofa and sat down at Charles's sandalled feet. All thoughts of sleep slowly vanished as she sipped the coffee and looked up at his handsome, mature face. A coy smile played on her lips. Soon she had something else on her mind.

"I t'ink I've met my match," he told her.

"Why do you say that?" "Yuh mek me nervous," he said, smiling. "Look, how me hands dem ah shake." He raised a trembling arm.

Joan laughed.

"Cyan I kiss you?" he asked, leaning forward.

She regarded him quizzically. Was this guy for real? "Do you always ask first?"

"Naw, man. I tell yuh, it's you doing this to me. Yuh too mysterious."

She eased closer. "Some men like mystery."

"I do. 'Nuff time pass since I met anyone like you."

"Has it?" she purred, resting her hands on his bare knees.

"Yeah." He touched her nose with a finger, and a little smile played on her lips. "You're beautiful, you know that?"

She suddenly wished he would stop talking and kiss her. A sexual tingle was rising in anticipation from her vagina. "No I'm not. An' you don't need to compliment me to get a kiss."

His smile broadened. "What me haffe do?"

"Come closer."

Charles leant forward a bit more. At first he merely tasted her lips with his own. Then, as she kissed back, he became bolder, his tongue pushing past her lips to meet hers. He can kiss too, this is promising, Joan mused. She closed her eyes and enjoyed. The kiss lasted for what seemed like minutes, without him attempting to touch her elsewhere. Joan decided to make a move instead. She crawled up on to the sofa and climbed on top of him, still kissing, forcing him to lie back. His hand moved up inside her top, and she gave a sigh of exhilaration. Too soon. His hand stopped. There was no fumbling for the bra strap to unclip the clasp. There were no fingers on her thighs, rising higher to search for gold. Not even an erection pressing into her stomach. She resigned herself to the fact that maybe she was just too fast. This guy obviously wanted to take it slow. She kissed his cheeks, his neck, and slid down his body so that her head rested on his chest. His torso was soft, but she could tell that at one time it had been hard with muscle. She listened to his heartbeat.

"This feels good," he murmured, eyes closed.

Joan frowned. What felt good? They hadn't done anything except kiss. Could this be what older men are about? Maybe nine years was too big a gap. He only wanted a woman to be comfortable with.

His hand stroked her hair. "You know how to make a man feel good."

"I do?" She looked up at him, resting her chin on his chest.

"Yeah. I feel close to yuh, you know? Like I know yuh fe years. I jus' want to hol' yuh, not get sexual or anyt'ing. It jus' feel right, y'know?"

"Don't take this the wrong way, Charles, but I don't want to get heavy with anyone right now."

"Why not? You have someone else waiting on yuh?"

She hesitated. "I don't want to go into it. But this is our first date. I like to get to know a man a little, before planning a future together. I mean, you hardly know me."

He raised her face from his chest, his big hands gripping her arms. "I know you, Joan. I told you, dis feels right."

"For you." She could have slapped herself. What was she thinking? She might never meet another man like this, and here she was giving him the cold shoulder.

He sat up straight, forcing her off him. She sat beside him feeling awful. He held one fist in the palm of his other hand and stared at the coffee mugs, standing untouched on the table.

"I'm sorry, Charles, but I can't lie to you," she blurted. "I'm in love with someone else. He just doesn't feel the same way as I do. At the moment I feel it would be unfair to lead you on."

He cut his eye after her. "More fool you," he said tightly.

"Don't get offensive with me. I thought we were good mates. We've been getting on fine until now."

His head bobbed in comprehension. He understood what she was saying. He placed a hand on her knee. "Awright. We'll tek it slow. Is not like yuh saying yuh don't want to know..." He watched her face for an answer.

"No, of course not. I like you," she assured him, making her expression as sincere as possible. It was the truth, after all. It just wasn't the kind of "like" that he wanted it to be.

"Good." He stood up. "I better go, you get some sleep." Now he was back on his feet, he appeared to perk up slightly.

Joan stood up too. "Are you sure? If you wait till morning I'll drop you."

"Is awright. I'll catch a cab." He kissed her quickly on the lips. She went to kiss him again, but he gently pushed her away. "Slow, remember?"

Damn! Just now she wished it wasn't slow. She followed him to the front door, lifting his jacket from the stair banister. "You'll probably need this now," she said.

"T'anks. Later, then."

"Okay," she said.

"Bye, beautiful." He kissed her cheek and left.

For a while she just stood with her back against the door. What had happened here? Was she losing her touch, or just a little touched in the head? This man would have been good for her. Single, own house, car, no live-in dependants. In the back of her mind she knew it was her love for Colin that was blocking her emotions for anyone else. She cursed him, before stamping her way up the stairs to bed.

CHARLES
There comes a time in every man's life when all him want is a good home life. I work 'ard all my life since I was fifteen. Get up early in the morning, come home late. For eight years I had a woman in my life and I took her for granted. Now, after five years on my own, I want a woman to give me de chance to treat her right.

All it takes is someone like Joan to turn my life around, I'll show her what a real man is all about.

THE GROUP OF MEN AND WOMEN FILED OUT OF THE CONFERENCE room, chatting, discussing work or plans to meet for lunch. Although they were smiling now, the meeting that had just concluded, between the editors and writers, had become heated. The editors had complained that there didn't seem to be any enthusiasm any more. The same old stuff was being published. They needed something for the nineties. Everyone, the boss had told them, had to pull their socks up or else outsiders would be brought in, and that would mean job losses for the existing staff. Being commissioning editor of features, Joan had no worries about her job. She remained seated as the room emptied, scribbling mindlessly on the lined pad in front of her. Two days had passed since the barbecue, and all she could think about was Colin. The fact that she hadn't heard from him for three weeks was beginning to bother her.

Charles had called yesterday and suggested they go out somewhere. No ties. Joan had told him she would let him know. She'd made up an excuse about having a lot of work on at the moment. She had no intention of calling him again. Colin was different. With him she wanted to be more than "just friends".

"Penny for them." A voice close by brought Joan out of her reverie.

Sarah, blonde, slim and sexy, bedroom fantasy of many of their male colleagues, perched herself on the edge of the desk. She wore a low-cut see-through blouse over a lacy slip, and a smart scarlet skirt. Her blonde hair — never tidy, she seemed to like the wild-child look — was piled high up on her head and secured with a butterfly clip. Long tendrils that had worked their way loose were falling around her face and down her shoulders like a blonde waterfall.

"My thoughts are worth more than that, Sarah." Joan swivelled her chair around to face her. "Just trying to plan my life out in my head." Joan could always talk to Sarah. Being the only other female of her age group in editorial, they tended to find comfort in each other's company. There wasn't much they didn't know about each other's lives.

"It's not just work, is it?" Sarah asked, crossing her waxed legs.

Joan half-smiled. Was she that easy to read?

"How's the love life?"

Joan raised an eyebrow. "What love life?"

"Like that, is it?"

Sarah was in the process of buying a home with her boyfriend of three years. White girls always seemed to be getting engaged, married or moving in with their boyfriends. It seemed as though white men knew what they were doing when it came to love and women. Black men didn't have a clue — except for sex.

"I've had men throwing themselves at me, Sar, but I just keep throwing them back. I haven't found the man who's good enough for me yet. Instead I lie in bed and dream up my perfect lover."

"Colin, right?"

It must have been written all over Joan's face

"So, you heard from Colin?"

"No. Don't know if I want to, either. You know when something's just not going anywhere; I need to move on."

"Yeah, I had that problem with Graham. Plus he was cheating on me." She removed the butterfly clip and shook her hair free, letting it cascade over her shoulders before grabbing a bunch in the centre and tying it up exactly as it had been.

Joan sighed. "Anyway, I've got more important things on my mind than men."

"Like what? What do we spend most of our time talking about?"

"Men," Joan had to agree.

"We make them important. No wonder they feel they can treat us as they do."

"You've got nothing to worry about, anyway. You're moving in with Daniel in two weeks."

"I was lucky this time. Look, if you're having trouble sleeping at night, just call Colin. Use him. They do it to us. Why go without, 'cause you don't want the rest of him?" Sarah could be so cocky sometimes, but she was right. Why not? It couldn't hurt, could it? "I might just do that."

"Good." She punched Joan playfully on the arm. "Fancy a coffee break?"

"Yeah, why not? Let's go round the corner to that neat little deli and order cappuccinos and a slice of that double chocolate gateau. And no more talk of sex and men, okay?"

"What does that leave us with?"

"Money and kids?"

"Oh no, how depressing. Can't we just have a little sex?"

"I didn't know you were that way inclined," Joan laughed.

They arrived back at the office just after eleven thirty. Joan went straight to her desk. Sarah took time to freshen her make-up, a routine she performed five times a day.

Joan shared an open-plan office with four others including Sarah. The editor's office was partitioned off at the end of the room.

"Anything been happening? Anyone called for me?" she asked a male colleague.

Geoffrey looked up from his PC. "Actually, yes. I wish you'd tell me when you're leaving the office," he spat indignantly. "I spent five minutes trying to find you." "Well excuuuse me," Joan exaggerated. "Just give me the messages and spare me the heartache." The nerve of some people! Anyone would think she'd taken the whole afternoon off.

Geoffrey tutted, running a hand over his spiky hairdo while shuffling through the papers on his desk with the other. "Francis Dixon wants to know when her article will be published, claims we've been fobbing her off for three months."

"Damn! I'll call her later. Forgot all about that." She'd get Sarah, or her secretary, Jayne, to deal with Mrs Dixon. The woman had written an article on collecting African artefacts, and had expected it to be snapped up straight away. It was a good article, but it needed a hook. And Joan hadn't found it. She scribbled a note and handed it to Jayne.

Easing back in her swivel chair, Joan stared at the phone, fingering the cover of her phone index thoughtfully. Three weeks. Was she really missing Colin bad? She certainly couldn't stop thinking about him. All she had to do was swallow her pride and call him. Surely he'd be glad to hear from her. After all, the last time he had come round they'd had a laugh and terrific sex too.

The thought of Colin's body made up her mind. She flicked through her address book until she found the number to the adventure playground where he worked.

"Hello?" Colin's deep voice came on the line, and Joan's heartbeat quickened just for a second.

"Col, it's me. Joan."

"J! How you doing?" His voice sounded smooth.

"Good," she answered. "And you?" She rested her elbow on the desk, a little smile dancing on her lips.

"Fine." There was a pause. She wondered if he could hear the thundering beat of her heart.

"I miss you," she blurted out.

"Yeah?" He sounded surprised.

"What d'you mean, 'yeah'?"

"What do you want me to say?" He sounded peeved.

"You could say you missed me too."

"Joan, I've been busy."

Her heart sank. This had been a bad idea. "So what does that mean? You couldn't pick up the phone?"

"Did you want me to?"

"Of course I did! We're still friends, ain't we?"

"Friends, yeah."

"So... are you seeing anyone?" she asked in as casual a way as possible. She doodled on the desk blotter, squares, triangles, then hearts trapped inside them.

"Sort of." He coughed nervously.

Bloody hell, Joan thought, it was like getting blood out of a stone. "What's 'sort of'?"

"I am," he owned up.

"Oh. I see."

Silence again.

She changed the subject abruptly. "Listen, I've got to go now, but could you come round later?" She was chasing him. It was the first time she had chased a man and it didn't feel good.

He exhaled loudly, as though it were a big decision. "Err, yeah. I could sort something out. About nine, all right?"

"Okay. I'll look forward to it."

"Bye." He hung up.

Joan replaced the receiver slowly, feeling worse than she had before she made the call. She needed a cigarette break. She had already decided that she would have to seduce Colin tonight. She had no intention of giving him up to another woman without a struggle.

JOAN PREENED IN FRONT OF THE BATHROOM MIRROR FOR THE third time in half an hour. Her hair was slicked back and it gleamed in the light from the bulb overhead. She applied some more lipstick, blotted it, then dropped the tissue into the bin already full of bathroom disposables.

It was ten o'clock. Colin was an hour late. She walked over to the window and looked up and down the street. Nothing, no sign of him. She lit an incense stick, Afrodisia, to take her mind off things. Then she picked up the latest copy of Black Beauty & Hair magazine and sat on the edge of the sofa, not wanting to crease her white chiffon blouse. The smoke from the incense flowed like a cloud across the ceiling and was already filling the room with its pungent aroma.

The knock at the front door startled her. He was finally here. She jumped up in excited anticipation, before checking herself. Take your time, girl. He kept you waiting. She straightened her clothes, did a slow twirl in front of the mirror on the wall, dimmed the light, and went to let him in.

He was dressed reasonably smartly, in black jeans with a black denim shirt hanging over them. A new pair of black boots adorned his feet. His height gave him a menacing look that wasn't him at all.

He sat on the sofa beside her and Joan got him a drink. She wanted to jump on him and have her wicked way, but she also wanted him to make love to her. Sweet and slow. Which wasn't his style at all. Oh well, she thought, it's never too late to learn. He was being very quiet. A wildlife programme was on the television, and instead of meeting her eyes he pretended to watch it.

"Have you gone off me?" she asked after a while.

He turned to her with a grin. "I could never go off you."

"Then why haven't you called?"

"I thought you wanted it that way."

Just like him to transfer the blame. She slid a hand on to his leg and smiled seductively. "Can you stay tonight?" Knowing that he lived alone, she knew he couldn't have an excuse not to.

"Maybe," he replied coolly.

Joan was becoming impatient. "Maybe what?"

"If you give me good reason to." She studied his face, looking for any hint to what he was thinking. "I know what you're doing, you know."

"What?" "You're playing hard to get."

He mocked her with his eyes. "Me?" He raised his glass to his lips and sipped, watching her over the rim.

"Yes, you."

"I don't know what gave you that idea. I'm just playing things the way you wanted them."

She decided to try again with the seductive tactics. Her hand travelled up his thigh. "Suppose I want to change the way things are."

Colin remained immobile. "I suppose you expect me to just go along with it."

Joan snatched her hand back. "You haven't gone off me, so what's the problem?"

"The problem is you're using me."

"How can I be using you? Or have you gone off sex?"

"Now who's got sex on the brain?" Humour shone from his eyes, but Joan was getting seriously irritated.

She pouted. "I thought we had a deal."

"Our deal, as you call it, was to be friends. Remember?" His eyes were laughing at her. He was actually enjoying this.

"Yeah, but…"

He interrupted. " 'But' nothing. I don't need this any more." His foot tapped the carpet soundlessly.

"You're saying you don't need me any more? So it was just sex. Now that you've got a replacement, you don't love me any more."

"Maybe I don't."

Joan glared at him. His face remained cool, but a little muscle in his jaw jumped, giving away his true emotion. She pulled away from him, moving up the sofa. Her lips were pushed up into an angry pout. Her eyes narrowed under a bunched brow.

Colin brushed invisible lint from his jeans. "Sorry, J."

She didn't move. "Don't even talk to me," she hissed.

"I didn't mean it." He moved closer and put his hands on her shoulders. She felt herself melting and tried her best not to think about it. "Then why say it?"

"I've got other things on my mind. Forgive me?"

She turned to face him, tucking one leg up under the other, as she always did. It gave Colin a sense of déjà vu.

"You don't have to stay if you don't want to," she said, knowing full well she wouldn't want him to leave.

"I do. I still care about you," he added, "even though we are just friends." He stressed the overused phrase with a grin.

Her mouth curved ironically. She looked into his deep brown eyes and asked, "Do you still love me?"

He grabbed her, and before she realised what was happening they were on the floor, covering each other with kisses. Their hands explored each other, seeking the flesh beneath the clothes. The questions remained unanswered, but Joan didn't care. For the moment, she had what she wanted.

She threw her arms around his neck and kissed him hard. Colin sent his tongue deep into her mouth. She let one hand slide down into the front of his shirt and ran restless, searching fingers across his hairy chest.

"Do you want me, Colin?" she whispered into his ear.

His hand on her breast, he groaned, "Yesss."

She slid down his body and used both hands to unbuckle and unzip his trousers, while he worked on the buttons of her blouse. Their eyes remained fixed on each other's. Joan squeezed the strong swell of his muscled thighs as she drew his trousers down his legs. His cock was like a raging bull ready to charge, its head straining against the flimsy material of his boxer shorts.

She stood up, and with her blouse hanging open from her shoulders she turned her back to him. She let her blouse drop to the floor. Then she half-turned and glanced at him for a reaction. He had his hand on his huge erection and was working it slowly up and down. She grinned wickedly and drew down the bottom half of her clothing, bending to give him a full view of her buttocks.

Colin stood and came up behind her. He grabbed the offered flesh with his big hands and squeezed. She gasped as he rubbed his cock against the crevice offered up to him.

He was big, hard and hot. His hands travelled upwards to cup her breasts and he gave her nipples a tweak, groaning hungrily. It sounded like a grizzly bear — mean, but exciting and vigorous.

"Come on, baby, fuck me," she whispered huskily.

"I'll fuck you," he promised, "until you see stars."

She raised her entrance to him, moist in anticipation of his cock filling her. Her hands crawled around to his hips and she gripped him as he plunged deep into her vagina.

Perfect rhythm. She felt as though she could come straight away. He seemed to get deeper with each thrust, as though she was sucking him inside her, like a kid with a lollipop.

A little harder, a little faster. They began breathing more heavily as they neared climax. She could feel his balls slapping against her, exciting her further. He felt so close, so hot, she was melting and breaking up into a million pieces all at the same time. Every nerve in her body was jumping, alive. She felt his orgasmic swell inside her, the first pulsing of his penis coinciding with her own explosion, moving ever closer, and it seemed as though her whole body shook with the final tumult of their release.

Afterwards, she lay on the floor in his arms. He had gone quiet again. She leaned up on one elbow. "Something wrong?"

"No. Just thinking."

"'Bout what?" Finally, she thought, he's going to talk to me. She knew there had been something bugging him all night.

"Us… life, y'know."

"No, I don't know. Explain." Joan sat up fully now. Her small breasts, nipples erect, hung above him. Colin knew Joan well enough to know that she wasn't going to let this go. He also knew with a knot in his stomach that he would have to tell her. His face was illuminated by the mute television. "I told you I was seeing someone…"

"Yeah, but that's nothing serious." She paused. "Is it?" A trace of worry had entered her voice.

He breathed deeply. Joan's heart lurched into her throat. She thought she knew what he was going to say. She set herself up to hear that Colin was falling in love with someone else. There was no way of preparing for what she was about to hear.

He looked serious. "I've been living with her for about three months." He hesitated, swallowing hard before he continued. "The thing is, she's pregnant."

Joan's voice was low with disbelief. "What? Is this some kind of joke?"

"I haven't finished."

"What? You mean there's more?" she gasped.

"I told her I'd marry her for the baby's sake," he blurted out.

Joan shot up off the floor. Realising she was naked she grabbed her blouse from the sofa and held it clasped against her chest. She felt as though she was in the middle of a very bad soap opera. "I can't believe you're doing this to me." Rage and humiliation swept through her, making her every nerve taut. "What we just did... what was that?" She motioned at the floor with her hand as though the actions were still going on.

He sat up now, feeling vulnerable (angry women can be dangerous creatures). He knew he'd hurt her. Trying to find a way of telling her had been on his mind all night. She had to know. And yet he hadn't wanted her to.

"Answer me," she screamed.

He stood up and stepped past her. "Look, I didn't mean for that to happen. I can't resist you. I love you, remember."

"Oh, you love me so damned much that you're gonna marry someone else." She began to shake hysterically, torn between tears and terrible laughter.

"It's not like that. I'm doing it for my kid."

"You're telling me the only way you'd have married me is if I got pregnant?" she spluttered.

He pulled his shirt on and retrieved his trousers from the floor, dragging them on as quickly as he could. He zipped and buttoned them, leaving the belt dangling.

He bent to retrieve his boots and Joan dived for them first, and dashed them at him. "You bloody user! You're a bastard, Colin! Just like your brother! Why couldn't I see that before?"

He silently took the boots, pulled them on and tied the laces. His cheek smarted from where the heel of one of them had hit him.

She watched him with narrowed eyes, her breathing heavy. At that moment she hated him. She hated him with a vengeance that she had no idea how to act out. She'd thought she hated Martin when he had walked out, but that feeling had nothing to do with the fire inside her now.

Finally, Colin looked up. Anger like the venom of a horde of scorpions stung him from her eyes. He didn't want to face her. He stood, fully dressed now, and picked up his jacket from the chair by the door. He turned and looked at her again. She stood there, completely naked, the chiffon shirt lying discarded at her feet, her whole body shaking with the pent-up fury inside her. All of a sudden her clenched fists flew open and she dived for him. Her hands reached for his face, open palms flailing as though she wanted to beat him to death. Colin stood there and let her hit him, feeling her blows rain down on his chest and across his head. There were tears coming from her eyes, but Joan wasn't crying. She was screaming, yelling, venting her outrage. He grabbed her wrists as he felt her sudden strength ebbing away. "I'm sorry, J. Believe me." He let her go and she stepped away from him.

Heaving, she swiped away the betraying tears with the back of her hand. "Get the fuck out of my life, Baker." Her voice sounded both harsh and winded.

"So much for friendship," he said, then ducked as Joan bent and picked up a glass from the coffee table and hurled it at him. It missed by inches. He exited hurriedly, closing the door behind him. He paused momentarily outside the door to listen to her continuing tirade.

She would get over it. They always did.

COLIN
Got in from work and Lois had cooked dinner. While I was eating she ran me a bath. This is the kind of life I dream about having when I'm sixty, not twenty-nine!

Lois was all right before all this baby stuff. There are some girls you shouldn't make a habit of, and Lois is one of them. I made a big mistake with this one. I thought we were both out for the same thing, y'know — exciting sex, a laugh, few drinks... Boy, I must have been tripping when I got mixed up with this one. I know she got herself pregnant deliberately. She's that type. I give it too good, that's my problem.

Why do we black men always trust you women when you say, "It's all right, I'm on the pill"? The pill ain't gonna stop me from catching sump'n deadly.

I've only known her a few months. She goes for kinky sex. Likes being tied up and covered in food, and then to have the food licked off her. That's what kept me going back, jus' to see what she would come up with next.

Her getting pregnant wasn't part of the deal. When she told me, it was like someone dropped a heavy metal safe from a great height on to my head. She took away my power and freedom to finish with her.

I have always said that the woman who has my first child will be special to me. So I had my hands tied. Lois had to become special.

There's something weird about her, though. Apart from the kinky stuff. She gets into all my business and flies into a rage for no reason. Not my ideal woman. I think she just needs a strong man to calm her down. Me?

I don't know, but I'll give it a try.

I feel real bad about Joan. All that stuff I said to get her back. I do love her. She should have been my baby mother.

Lois knew all about Joan, and I know she was as jealous as hell. Boy, I should have dropped that when she started acting them ways. But as usual I was following my dick.

I don't wanna blame Joan, but in a way it's her fault too. She's the one who wanted us to be just friends. She expect me to go without, so that she can have her independence? Things don't go like that.

They say things always happen for a reason. What the reason for this is, I don't know.

THE INDIAN RESTAURANT WAS ONLY HALF FULL, BUT THE atmosphere was bordering on rowdy. A group of young white guys were celebrating something, and the beers were being consumed as fast as the waiters could serve them.

James looked up from his meal. "The food all right?" he asked.

"Yeah, fine," Pamela mumbled unconvincingly. The rose-scented candle in the centre of the table was giving her a headache — or maybe it was making a headache that was already there worse.

James pushed his plate aside. "What's wrong? You've been quiet all evening." Pamela looked up at him. She had invited him out because she had hoped that on neutral territory she would be able to talk to him about them going their separate ways. Now she didn't know how to start.

"Pam?" he pushed, breaking her thoughts.

"I'm tired, that's all. Don't waste your food on my account." She'd meant it to sound courteous, but instead it came out somewhat agitated.

To think that two months ago, she and James had been planning to buy a house and have children together. She shuddered involuntarily at the thought.

She regarded him with a perplexed stare. He wasn't a bad-looking guy, a bit paler than she liked her men, but he couldn't help that. He was in love with her. She saw it in his eyes, felt it in his touch. He never raised his voice to her in anger. He was living in her home, and he respected that. He did his share around the house: cooking, cleaning, paying his share of the bills. She knew she was the envy of many women, including Marion. What on earth was she doing? James had given up so much for her, even his wife and baby.

Pamela reached over and touched his hand, feeling his knuckles beneath her soft palm. She smiled. "I'm sorry. I spoilt the evening. I promise I'll make it up to you later." There was a gleam of mischief in her voice.

James's expression changed swiftly from a frown to a smile of excited expectation. "I've got some making up to do myself. Why don't we get out of here?"

All the way home, James was caressing her. Although to her it felt more like harassing.

Pamela tried to get more enthusiastic about this, but the more she tried the more she thought about Shaun.

This would definitely be the last time, she affirmed. She couldn't possibly go on like this.

As soon as they got into the flat, his hands were everywhere. James was practically floating on heat. Pamela went into the bedroom and undressed slowly. She slipped on a full-length satin négligé before going to the bathroom. She was so tense, she felt like a body builder after a workout. She shook her shoulders and arms to try to relax. James stood in the bathroom doorway. He was bare chested, his belt hanging loose around his small waist. He watched her pull the brush through her long black hair, and then tie it back with an elastic band. He loved her hair. Indeed, he couldn't think of anything he didn't love about this woman. He watched her slim body move sensuously underneath the satin nightgown, feeling his manhood begin to stir. He took a stride towards her, encircling her waist and pulling her body close. Then he buried his face into her neck and took her flesh between his teeth. He was as horny as hell. Pamela tensed as he sucked at her flesh, but she let him lift her nightie and caress her smooth buttocks. She felt him fumbling to undo his trousers, to release himself, and heard his belt buckle hit the floor.

He was nothing compared to Shaun. Shaun would at least make sure she was enjoying it as much as he was before even attempting to enter her. James simply spread her legs with his hand and pressed himself into her. There wasn't much of him; he slid in easily.

Pamela grimaced. She wasn't ready, not in the least bit turned on. She shut her eyes and thought of Shaun as James, oblivious, continued to pump in and out of her with uninspired strokes. Each motion of his hips was accompanied by a low grunt. Pamela clenched the muscles of her vagina and moaned loudly. "That feels so good," she cooed expertly. "Do it faster." This, of course, would bring him to a quicker climax. He thrust into her with one final, shuddering lunge, and she felt his hot seed filling her. It was over before it had begun. James wilted, gripping her hunched shoulders, and his thrusts slowed and stopped. He withdrew. Kissing her on her shoulder and pulling up his trousers, he whispered, "I'll see you in the bedroom," before leaving the room.

Pamela froze. Was he expecting more? Hands still braced against the sink, she stood up straight and caught her reflection in the mirror. She didn't even want to face herself. Her cheeks hadn't flushed, her pulse-rate hadn't risen a beat. She was as cool as if she'd just taken a shower. In fact the shower stood more chance of stimulating her.

She turned on the taps to fill the bath. She had to wash him off her. His fluid was already oozing out, tracing a sticky path down her leg.

"Not for much longer," she hissed quietly.

JAMES

Something's going on. Maybe it's just me, but Pamela always seems distracted these days. I try to please her and all it does is upset her. It's like she's got non-stop PMT. I agreed to go out with her the other night. I thought she was going to come out of this mood she was in. Have a nice meal, go home, have a few drinks, and then a bit of you-know-what. It sounded perfect.

I get the feeling she's hiding something from me, but I don't know what yet. She asked me to move out of her flat about a month back. When I asked why, she said something about needing her space back. But I never get in her way or stop her from doing what she wants to do. Couldn't, even if I tried.

She keeps going on at me to get out more. What's the problem? I'm happy staying in, being with her. The way I treat her she should be ecstatic. Maybe it's just a phase she's going through.

We need a holiday, some time away together, away from distractions like her girlfriends, her work, the mystery telephone caller she keeps telling she'll call back later. I'm not a suspicious person. Everyone has their secrets, I don't think she's cheating on me...

No, the problem is definitely that we need to spend more time together.

I'm going 'round to the travel agents first thing Saturday morning to find a holiday to surprise her with.

If there's one thing I know how to do, it's treat a lady well.

WALKING HOME, MARION STRUGGLED WITH HER UMBRELLA TO shelter from the downpour that had seemed to come from nowhere. Gerard had called her at work to tell her he was taking her out tonight, and to be ready for seven. Marion had tried protesting — she didn't get home until seven most days when she worked late — but Gerard had insisted. So she'd taken the last hour off work and stepped out into the pouring rain.

Arriving home at quarter past six, lower half soaked despite the umbrella, she was miserable and not in the mood for going out. She had been feeling nauseous, depressed and lethargic the last few days, and today was no exception. All she wanted to do was get into bed with a cup of hot chocolate for company. She ran a bath. As she lay in the water she wondered what the occasion was. Gerard hadn't said why he'd suddenly decided to take her out. They never went anywhere together any more, unless it was shopping. He'd told her to wear something dressy, sophisticated. She had grinned, despite her suspicion at his enthusiasm to show her off.

The bath had revived her sufficiently for Marion to start looking forward to the evening. She poured herself a glass of wine before searching her wardrobe for something suitable to wear and deciding on a lilac velvet dress she had worn only once. Gerard liked it; when she'd worn it he'd said he couldn't keep his hands off her.

Seated in front of the mirror, dressed only in her underwear, she applied her make-up while the curling tongs heated up. She sang along with Usher's "Can You Get With It?" The wine was already giving her a buzz.

She didn't like to wear very much make-up: eyeliner, lipstick and a fine layer of powder was all she felt she needed. She wrapped her hair into a french twist and a small beehive, then with the aid of the curling tongs she created tiny ringlets to fall around her face.

She slipped into the dress, feeling the smoothness of the silk lining against her skin. She stood in front of the full-length mirror on the wardrobe door and admired the way the shaped cups pushed up her breasts, giving her extra cleavage.

Gerard arrived at quarter to seven, looking stush in a bottle-green suit with a white polo-neck sweater. He wore two gold chains, one a belcher that Marion had bought him for his last birthday. He gave her a look of proud admiration as he entered the bedroom, coming up behind her and kissing her cheek.

"Nice, very nice. New dress?" he asked.

"No. I wore this the last time you took me out, remember? You liked it then too."

"Oh yeah," he said vaguely. He stood behind her, checking his hair in the mirror while she put dangling gold earrings in her lobes.

"So, what's the occasion then?" she asked.

"Sorry?" "Why are we going out tonight?"

"Oh, a business contact invited us to dinner. They're married, so I thought I'd better bring my other half." He ran a hand over his S-curled hair, smoothing down a single stray hair, then smoothed his moustache on either side of his top lip before wiping his hands on a towel which hung on the back of the chair.

"Are we supposed to be married, then?" She applied powder to her nose and chin, spreading it gently with dabs from a cotton wool ball.

"Well, I didn't tell them we weren't," he answered.

"I suppose he'll guess anyway, when he sees there's no ring on my finger." "Just say we're engaged then," he said, then quickly added, "but only if he asks. Wear one of your other rings on that finger. Just for tonight." He reached over her shoulder for his aftershave and sprayed it lightly under the collar of his polo neck.

Marion beamed. She turned around and kissed him on the cheek.

"Watch it, I don't wear lipstick," he smiled, swiping at his face and checking his handsome reflection in the mirror.

She watched him, feeling an admiration that was fuelled by hunger, as he dusted his spotless lapels. She didn't care that this man loved himself more than anything else in the world. He was her man, and she loved him.

The drive to West London took them nearly an hour. Gerard was full of talk about their host, and Marion paid attention as he briefed her on his background. "His name's Brian Mack. He owns a chain of electrical retail shops, and he's looking to get into mobile phones — which is where I come in." He tapped a finger to his chest. "He wants a partner to run that side of the business, right? So tonight, we'll..." he searched for the right word, "negotiate — see whether he buys me out and hires me or whether he buys into my company as a silent partner. You follow me?"

"Yeah. If you want my opinion, Ger, I don't think you should sell out. If he decides he doesn't like you, you could be out of a job, left with nothing." "I didn't ask for your opinion," he answered bluntly. "I've thought of that already. I've got a contract to cover it — I'm no fool, y'know." A muscle bunched in his jaw and he gripped the steering wheel more tightly.

Marion knew she had struck a nerve. She wasn't sure what her purpose was to be tonight, but she hoped he wouldn't bring her into the business side of the conversation. He never listened to her ideas anyway; on the rare occasions when he did, he'd pretend he had come up with them.

A cyclist swung out in front of the car. Gerard braked sharply and slammed on the horn. He stuck his head out of the window and shouted, "Blasted idiot, shoulda killed your raas."

Marion didn't realise she'd been holding her breath until she started feeling light-headed. She let it out slowly. She reached forward and turned the car stereo on to avoid any further conversation. Gerard was obviously uptight, and this wasn't good considering they were going to a business meeting.

The car turned into a quiet residential street. Beautifully landscaped gardens lined the road. Some houses had elaborate gates surrounding them, like film stars' homes in the movies. Perfectly trimmed hedges, mowed lawns, patios... these houses had to be worth at least two hundred grand, Marion thought, in awe of what she was seeing.

Gerard pulled into a wide driveway outside a pretty mock-Tudor house. He parked the car outside the garage door and turned to Marion. "What d'you think?" He was smiling again, his eyes lighting up as though they had never known anger.

"This is where they live?" she asked dazedly.

Gerard just kept smiling knowingly. Marion was overwhelmed, and had every right to be — this was a world so very different from her own. Brian Mack was raking the money in, and Gerard wanted to be part of it. Electrical goods, whether they be mobile phones or start-of-the-art studio equipment, would always be in demand.

"These are white people, right?" Marion asked, opening her door.

"Nope." Gerard checked his face in the mirror before exiting the car. "One day I'll have a house just like this." He looked into her eyes for a second over the car roof.

Marion, who never missed intonations in speech, had caught the fact that he had said "I will" and not "we will". But she let it go as usual. She slipped her arm through his as they walked up the red-brick path to the house. Gerard rang the bell and the porch light came on instantly. Marion half-expected alarms to start ringing too.

The door was answered promptly by a tall, slender, dark-skinned woman. She was dressed in a short, deep red, crushed velvet dress with a plunging neckline. Around her neck she wore a diamante choker that caught the light and completely mesmerised Marion with its brilliance. The woman's smile spread as she grabbed Gerard by the shoulders and loudly kissed the air by each of his cheeks. Marion noticed her green contact lenses and instantly disliked the woman.

"Gerry! On time, I like that." She must have been at least six feet tall in her high heels. Marion came level with her chest as she stepped inside.

"And you must be Marilyn," she giggled, brushing her hand through her long brown woven hair. Was there anything about this woman that was real?

Marion momentarily held her gaze, just as the woman's bosom held Gerard's eyes. "Marion," she corrected pointedly. Gerard dragged his eyes away from the woman's cleavage, but not before Marion caught him running his tongue over his upper lip.

They followed the woman into the hallway. It was as Marion had expected: expensive, everything dressed up as much as their hostess. The hallway and the doors were all of the same dark wood. Lamps lit the hallway, three on either side.

"Marion, this is Patrice Mack," Gerard introduced.

Patrice offered her hand. Those had to be false nails! Marion shook the outstretched claw lightly, ignoring the way Patrice had held it as though she was expecting Marion to kiss it. "Something smells good," Gerard said, nose in the air.

Patrice took his jacket. "I do hope you like lamb. The cook didn't receive very much notice, but she has excelled herself tonight."

After relieving her guests of their outdoor clothes Patrice, to Marion's horror, took Gerard's arm and swanned off down the hall to their right, leaving Marion to follow, fuming. Gerard hadn't taken the least bit of notice of her. They entered a semi-lit study. Brian Mack appeared from behind a large wooden desk. Marion was surprised at just how small he was compared to his tall, voluptuous wife.

"Brian, I told you to stop work for now. We have guests," Patrice scolded. Brian Mack was a man in his early forties. His round face was bearded and the beard was speckled with grey, while his hair was dyed jet black and gently waved giving him a distinguished look. He was dressed casually in a short-sleeved, blue and white striped shirt and navy trousers.

"Gerard and Marion!" His deep voice filled the room, reminding Marion of her deputy head teacher at school, whose voice had boomed across the assembly hall. Brian stepped from behind his huge desk with his arm extended, shaking their hands in turn. "Nice to meet you at last, Gerard. Patrice hasn't stopped talking about you."

Marion's eyes whipped from Gerard to Patrice, and she caught the look that passed briefly between them. Patrice's expression was one of self-satisfaction, and Gerard's lips turned up just slightly, his eyes sparkling as if a happy memory had just come to mind.

"Nice to meet you too, Brian. Let's hope we can do business," he said in his best posh voice.

"And Marion, the good woman behind the successful man! You are the very angel I'd imagined." He held her hand a little longer than necessary and looked too deeply into her eyes.

"Thank you," she answered, pulling her hand free.

Brian turned to his wife, who was busy patting her perfect hairstyle into place. "Patrice, will you do the honours? I've just got to finish up here." He waved a hand over his desk.

"Not too long, Brian," Patrice said, once again taking Gerard's arm as though he were a blind man needing guidance.

As they left the room, Patrice continued to talk as though Gerard was the only one there. "It's such a pain, Brian working as much as he does. He really does need a partner, y'know. Then I wouldn't get so lonely." She pouted, flashing her green eyes to Marion. "Marion really is a lucky girl." They entered another room down the hall. "Sometimes," she giggled, "I fantasise about burning his study down, but that would only mean he'd be out of the house more often, in one of his shops — so I just can't win."

The room they had walked into was huge, as big as a small school hall. Marion gazed about in awe as Gerard strolled in and made himself comfortable on the sofa. At one end on a raised floor stood the dining area, six chairs surrounding a long black wooden table. Light danced off the crystal glasses placed at each setting. The entire area was seductively lit by candles. The other end of the room had probably been decorated by Patrice. There were four large framed photographs of her around the walls, each in a different pose, all very artistically composed. The largest dominated one wall. In the picture, Patrice lay back on a chaise long, wrapped only in a length of African cotton, her nipples pointing at the ceiling, her hair hanging to the floor. Those cat's eyes seemed to stare at Marion wherever she stood.

Patrice caught her looking at it. "Brian is into photography when he has the time. He likes shooting me, especially naked," she giggled.

Maybe he should use a gun next time, Marion thought wickedly. "Nice," was what she said aloud.

"Please, sit down. What can I get you to drink?" Before Marion could open her mouth Gerard had answered for her. "You know what I drink — and Marion will have a Bacardi and Coke."

Marion shot him a look, which he ignored. What was going on here? Whatever it was she didn't like it. If she had any way of getting home on her own she would have left there and then.

It wasn't just the fact that he had ordered her drink. She wanted to know how on earth he was so familiar with this woman, and why he hadn't mentioned her before. For the time being, she knew her curiosity must remain stifled, the questions unasked. Maybe she was just being paranoid — or was that look in Gerard's eyes lust?

Gerard watched Patrice approvingly. Now here, he considered, was a black woman with class. No wonder her husband couldn't handle her, he was twice her age. Gerard had had a hard time controlling her four nights ago. Patrice was insatiable, but he'd soon tame her. He had absolutely no objections to helping her out in that department. The merger had been Patrice's idea. She knew everything about her husband's business, and often put other firms in touch with him. She found Gerard irresistible. He not only had a face and body she wanted to eat, but a good business brain too. She was sure this was a unity made in heaven. She mixed their drinks and brought them over on a sparkling glass tray. She took a seat in the unusually shaped cream leather swivel chair opposite, and crossed her legs suggestively. "Brian and I have big plans for your business," she purred, looking directly into Gerard's eyes.

"So do I," he answered proudly, with the same suggestive look in his eyes.

"I know. Which is why I want to get the two of you together." Her voice oozed in a sickly way that turned Marion's stomach.

Marion couldn't help but feel invisible. The only way she was going to get in on this conversation was by barging in. "So, Patrice. How long have you known Gerard?" she asked shrewdly.

Patrice answered promptly without missing a beat. "It must be two months now..." She looked to Gerard for confirmation.

"Yeah, 'bout that," he said, giving Marion a look of uncertainty.

Marion continued regardless. "It's just that he's never mentioned you. I'd assumed it was your husband he was dealing with." She took another sip of Bacardi.

Patrice, visibly flustered by Marion's intonation, uncrossed her long legs. "That reminds me — I'll just go and chase Brian," she said, rising from her designer chair and making her way to the door.

As soon as the door was closed, Gerard turned on Marion. "What the hell do you think you're playing at?" he exploded.

"I only said what I thought, Gerard. Maybe she's got a guilty conscience."

"About what?" he challenged her, trying to keep his voice from getting too loud.

"I don't know — you tell me." Marion knew she was pushing it. Now wasn't the right time to have this out.

Gerard pointed his finger at her threateningly. "Don't delve into my business, okay? I didn't have to bring you here, y'know. Just enjoy it — an' don't mess up." The last words were delivered through clenched teeth.

Marion's wide eyes lowered and her lips quivered. She felt her heart sink into the pit of her stomach. He had just confirmed that something was going on. She raised her eyes and stared at him disbelievingly as he downed the rest of his sherry in one gulp. Her friends were probably right — she deserved better. Marion knew that, if only she could stand up to him without being afraid of losing him, maybe then he'd show her some respect. She felt tears sting the backs of her eyelids. She had so many questions buzzing in her head that a headache was emerging from the back of her skull and forcing its way round to her temples. She suddenly had the scariest feeling that this had been planned, just so that Gerard could show his mistress off in front of her. To show her what her competition was. Well, if he wanted a wannabe-white black woman, he wasn't the man she had thought he was. They both started as the door opened and Brian entered, followed by Patrice. Marion and Gerard sat rigidly at each end of the three-seater sofa. You could have cut the air with a knife.

"Sorry to keep you waiting," Brian apologised. "Dinner is now served." He gestured with his hands that they should take their places at the table.

Patrice directed them to their seats. Marion found herself placed opposite Brian and next to Gerard. Patrice sat opposite Gerard. "Cecile will serve dinner. We don't always have a cook, by the way," she said to Marion. "She's borrowed from neighbours of ours. I can cook just well enough to get by," and she issued that irritating giggle again. A shudder passed through Marion.

Brian took Patrice's hand. "Not that you need to cook to win your man's heart," he said. Marion felt a twinge of pity for this man, who obviously thought his wife was faithful to him.

"Isn't he sweet?" Patrice giggled.

"Mmm," Marion smiled back weakly.

A door opened in the panelling behind Brian and Patrice and an olive-skinned woman entered, pushing a food trolley. She placed warm bowls in front of them and served them with soup. Once she had withdrawn Brian started up the conversation.

"I see you're engaged," he said to Marion. "Have you set a date?"

"We..." she began.

Gerard placed his hand over hers, silencing her with a squeeze. "Not yet. We're saving first. Start things right, y'know." "Of course," Brian agreed, impressed.

"I told you he was sensible," Patrice added.

"That you did," Brian said, nodding appreciatively.

Marion sat, quietly fuming. After the soup, Brian opened a bottle of vintage wine and poured for all of them. Marion drank hers in big gulps and prayed that no one would notice just how much she was consuming, despite her promise to herself to give it up. It was the only way she was going to be able to get through the evening.

All they seemed to talk about over the main course was business. Thus Marion was kept out of it, and the drink was dulling her senses enough for her not to care. The food was perfection, right down to the Tiramisu. While they drank their coffee, Brian never stopped complimenting Marion, while his wife giggled and made eyes at Gerard.

After dinner they retired to what Brian called his studio. It was at the top of the house, and took up the entire attic conversion. Plush cream carpet covered the floor and even two of the walls. There wasn't much furniture, except for a few low easy chairs at one end, a coffee table and a well-stocked drinks cabinet. They were told to take off their shoes at the door and to make themselves comfortable. Gerard had no trouble making himself at home, acting as though he already knew the place. By now Marion was unsober, what with the drink before dinner and the wine with dinner, and now Brian offering her brandy. Before long Marion had allowed the warmth of the alcohol and the comfort of her surroundings to obscure her earlier feelings of jealousy, and she relaxed in an oversized easy chair.

Gerard sat across the room from her, Patrice snuggling up next to him. It meant nothing to Marion.

After all, they were socialising. Brian put on a CD and the room was filled with the voice of Diana Ross. He sat beside Marion and placed an arm across the back of the chair behind her head. "You're a very attractive woman, Marion," he told her. She shifted away from him, feeling uncomfortable under his gaze. He turned to Gerard. "Don't you ever worry about men trying to steal her from you, Gerry?"

Gerard seemed amused by the question. "They can try, but she belongs to me." He smiled at Marion then, and she shivered involuntarily. Suddenly she felt like the doomed victim in a vampire movie.

Brian turned back to her and took her hand in his. She was still looking at Gerard, but he was already in deep conversation with Patrice. Their eyes held each others and their voices were too low for her to hear.

"Your fiancé is a very open-minded man," Brian was saying.

"He is?" Marion could barely hear herself, as if she were speaking through cotton wool.

Brian's face loomed closer. "You know, I find it very hard to relax. Patrice is always trying to find new ways of taking my mind off my work. I think this is her best idea yet." His arm fell on to her shoulder.

Marion flinched. What idea? Her brain was doing somersaults trying to figure out what was going on. Across the room Gerard and Patrice were joined together in a passionate embrace. Her leg was thrown across him, and her fingers ran through his wavy hair. Marion giggled as she imagined Gerard doing that to Patrice and the hair coming off in his hand. She was really out of it.

Brian's hot breath was on Marion's face and she tried to push him away, but her arms felt heavy and she didn't think she could stand up if she wanted to. Brian's beard brushed against her cheek and then he was on top of her, tongue probing her lips. She was unable to stop him; his weight was crushing her into the chair. She tried to call Gerard but her voice stuck in her throat. As she struggled Brian groaned in her ear. "Enjoy, Marion, enjoy."

Again she looked for Gerard but he had disappeared, along with Patrice. She was alone with this old man. The image of him having a heart attack on top of her made her giggle again, and she became sure she was drugged. She began to feel herself passing out, and fought it, knowing what would happen if she did. She had no idea where the strength came from, but somehow she gathered it, and with the palms of her hands on Brian's chest she shoved, twisting her body under him. They both tumbled to the floor. Marion moved quickly despite her intoxicated state. As she struggled to her stockinged feet the room swam around her. The door up ahead was dancing in time to the beat of "Why Do Fools Fall In Love" and moving farther away. She managed to lunge for the handle, gripping it tight and dragging it open. Brian moaned from the floor behind her — she must have hurt him, but that wasn't her concern. She just wanted to find Gerard and get out of this madhouse.

There was a key on the outside of the door and she turned it, locking Brian inside. Steadying herself against the banisters, she stepped as quickly as possible down the carpeted stairs to the first floor. She could hear the sounds of a bed creaking and muffled noises coming from the hallway to her left, so she hurried towards them, needing to locate Gerard, knowing and yet still dreading what she would find.

This door wasn't locked. She shoved it and it swung open to reveal a large four-poster bed in a semi-dark room. The two bodies on top of it were unmistakably Gerard and Patrice. Gerard, naked, was on his back, being ridden by a writhing, bouncing Patrice. His hands fondled her breasts and she was groaning with ecstasy. Marion heaved and felt a rush of vomit race up from her stomach. She bent double as it came spewing out. She passed out, but before she lost consciousness she distinctly heard a hammering, like fists on wood, and Gerard exclaiming, "Shit!"

Marion came to in the car. Her throat was dry and she had a cramp in her stomach. Gerard was driving like a madman and she bounced from side to side as he took the corners. "Ger?" she whispered. "Shut up, just shut up." His face was a mask of stone.

Marion squeezed herself into the corner of the seat by the door. She was shaking uncontrollably. She was sure that Gerard had planned the events at Brian's house, and she had spoiled his plan.

Knowing Gerard like she did, she was afraid she'd get more than verbal abuse if she pushed him to talk to her, so she shut her eyes to fake sleep — or further unconsciousness.

Gerard took her home, made her take a bath and then took her to bed, intending to complete his unfinished business. He made love to her body only, and she felt as though he was with someone else. Tears filled her eyes as he rode her silently in the dark. He had used her in the worst way tonight. She wanted him to talk to her about what had happened. Why Brian Mack had expected her to have sex with him. Why he had gone off with that woman, leaving her for that old man to maul.

Marion lay still as Gerard finished. As her thoughts began to rearrange themselves, she slowly began to convince herself that the whole night must have been an awful mistake, that Gerard had been drugged and seduced also. Gerard grunted and turned his back to her. She was sure that, when morning came, he would be able to explain the whole sordid affair. She fell asleep curled into his back. He snored lightly, completely sated. She breathed in his scent and squeezed herself tighter into his back. Somehow that night she managed to dream only sweet dreams as her subconscious struggled to replace the nightmare.

GERARD
The best laid plans... Y'know, I thought about taking Debs. But she wouldn't have fit in. Marion can look good, knows when to keep her mouth shut, and usually goes with the flow. Not this time, though.

I couldn't believe it when she burst in on me and Patrice. I was having a good time, y'know what I mean? I did t'ink Marion was too, getting herself drunk and flirting with Brian.

The way Patrice was throwing herself at me in full view of her husband! Only a fool wouldn't catch the drift. I wanted Marion to try sump'n new, different, y'know? Everyone's got this kinky streak in them, I reckon — all it takes is the right person to bring it out. Patrice attracts me 'cause we're two of a kind. The only difference is she married money and I'm making my own by hard work, y'know what I mean? She made the first move. She walked into my shop and asked to make an appointment with the manager. She had good timing — I was running the shop that day. When she came in I was, y'know, kinda worried. A black woman in a suit usually means government business, trouble. Y'know, like solicitors, fraud squad, sump'n like that. She introduced herself and told me exactly what she wanted: a piece of my action. I tell ya, I couldn't wait to get a piece of hers, jus' looking at her, y'know what I mean? What is the big deal with women and relationships anyway? Y'know, nearly all the women I know are in their twenties and they all want me to be their exclusive property. The teenagers and the older women are the ones I have the most good times with. The babies are ripe and ready to be filled with the joys of sex; the mummies are just ready to have a sweet young boy give them the business. No strings, no hang ups.

Soon as I find a replacement — y'know, a nice lickle regular, with her own place an' dat — then Marion's gone. One t'ing, though. I'm gonna miss her cooking.

MARION HAD MANAGED TO GET THROUGH A WEEK WITHOUT Gerard. It wasn't by choice — the morning after the Macks' dinner party she had woken up disorientated and alone, and Gerard had been unobtainable ever since. Every time she called his work place she was told he had "just left". His mobile number was constantly giving her the mechanical voice: "We are unable to connect your call. Please try again later." She'd left copious messages with his mother, until Claudia had had to tell her to stop calling, to let Gerard call her when he was ready. Needing to share her worries with somebody, she had told Pamela about the planned orgy. Pamela had gone absolutely mad. "I hope you told him where to go, Marion," she'd said in a stern voice.

"Well, I…"

"Don't tell me you didn't finish with him."

"All right, I won't," she'd huffed childishly.

"Marion, you are sick. Are you so addicted to this man's dick that you can't give him up? Even after this?"

"I will. There's just a couple of things we have to sort out first."

"Yeah, right. You mean he'll be doing the sorting out and you'll just sit back and take it all."

Marion hadn't been able to think of anything to say. Pamela's words had sounded too much like the truth.

"Listen to me," her friend had continued, "I don't want to hear from you again until you've sent his arse to hell, d'you hear me?"

"Pam!" Marion had gasped, affronted.

"No, I mean it. I love you like a sister, but this has gone too far."

After that, Marion didn't have the guts to tell Joan. She knew her friends only wanted the best for her, but some decisions she had to make on her own. It was her life.

Now Joan had called and invited her out tonight. A night out with Joan would be just what she needed to help her escape from her own prison of misery. Joan had said she had some good news for her. It was about time Marion got some good news. Her life seemed to be one long bad news story.

Neither of her friends knew she was pregnant.

The test had confirmed it this morning, but she'd already known what the result would be. If splitting up with Gerard had been difficult before, it now felt like an impossibility.

When Joan arrived Marion could immediately smell the ganja on her. She didn't say a word — Joan already knew how she felt about her smoking that stuff. Joan didn't need it. She was a much better person without it, in fact.

To match her mood, Marion had dressed completely in black — a short flared skirt and a long blouse, worn with her knee-high black boots and black stockings laced with silver. In contrast, Joan was dressed in white, a crocheted dress that echoed the style of the twenties.

"You ready, then?" Joan asked, eyeing the garments her friend wore. Her eyes may have been faraway, but the rest of her was alive and kicking. She seemed to be bubbling over with some kind of adrenalin rush; her body was one giant fidget.

"Maybe I should change…" Marion turned to go back to the bedroom.

Joan grabbed her arm. "Don't bother. We're only going to King's. You look fine."

"Joan, I can't afford a wine bar." Marion thought of the five pounds in her purse that was to last her the rest of the week.

"Hey, this is my treat. I needed a night out just as much as you," Joan said, and ushered Marion through the front door.

It was still early evening when they got to the wine bar, and the after-work crowd was still loitering. It was mostly men, some of whom turned to look the girls up and down as they walked towards the bar. A few couples sat at the bar, and people were scattered around the room at various tables, chatting loudly over the music.

Joan bought the drinks and the girls sat at a corner table by the PA system, where a young male DJ selected music for the evening. Changing Faces' "Stroke You Up" was playing.

"Remember I said I had some good news for you?" Joan beamed, her eyes staring too intensely.

"Yes," Marion said tentatively.

"You'll love this." Joan touched Marion's arm. "I'm planning a six-month series on black men in one of our magazines." Joan glanced around and lowered her voice, as though anyone might be listening in to their conversation. "I've already got a writer in mind for the job. Someone who's talented, qualified, and ready to start straight away…"

Marion, her mind still churning with other matters, waited for the punchline.

"Well? What d'you say?" Joan asked.

"What?"

Joan threw her hands up in exasperation. "I was talking about you, silly!"

Marion's mouth fell open. "Me? But I couldn't… I mean, I could, but… what about experience?"

"You've got the qualifications, it's your field of work… Marion, this is just what you've been looking for! I mean, what you don't know about black men isn't worth knowing."

Marion shook her head. "It'll be hard work. I don't know... Is there a deadline?"

"You'd have to have a draft plan of each topic ready in October." Joan reached down for her miniature handbag by her feet. "Here, I've brought a plan with me." She removed a square of paper from her purse and carefully unfolded it into an A3 sheet. Marion moved the glasses aside and they spread the plan out between them. Drawn out in different colours was a large seven-legged spider. At the end of each of its legs was a heading. On the body was written: "Project Target: Black Men", and the topics highlighted on the legs were Sex, Money, Love, Ambition, Family, and Future.

"The first one will go out in the December issue," Joan explained. "We'd want this one to catch people's attention, you know, leave them hungry for part two."

"I like it." Marion's eyes lit up as she perused the page.

"These headings aren't fixed," Joan pointed out, "we can always change one or two if a better idea comes up."

Marion's brain was already working with the topics in front of her. This was perfect. She could see her name in a by-line on the front page. This was a once-in-a-lifetime opportunity. All these months she had been scouting for work, trying to sell her articles, and now this job was being handed to her.

"Do you feel you can handle it?" Joan asked.

"This is exactly what I've been looking for."

Marion reached over and hugged her friend. "Thanks, Joan."

"Hey, we're sistas, ain't we?"

"I want to do this, Joan. This is my career, my ambition. I want to do this more than anything else at the moment." She suddenly thought about Gerard — and the baby. How would they fit in? Her eyes misted over.

"You sure?" Joan regarded her quizzically. "You look a little worried."

Marion shook off the descending black veil surrounding her. "No, I'm fine. It's not the work."

"What then? Your man?"

Marion sighed theatrically. "I think Gerard's avoiding me."

"What, again? I thought it was something serious," Joan said flippantly, and sucked on her cigarette.

"He is my boyfriend, Joan." Marion found herself defending him despite what had happened, probably fuelled by her friend's insensitivity rather than any sense of loyalty.

"Yeah, I know" Joan said, "but how long's it been since you had anything good to say about him?"

Marion knew now she couldn't fool herself any longer. There was nothing good about what she had with Gerard. She knew he was cheating on her — he'd done it right in front of her on the last occasion. Even when he made love to her it was like he was fantasising about other women. He cared more about his clothes than he did about her. She blinked smoke from her eyes, raising a hand and wafting it past her face. Joan swapped her cigarette to her other hand. "I'm sorry, Maz, but you know the man's no good. For all you know he's got loads of other women…"

"He hasn't," Marion said a little too quickly.

Joan raised that quizzical eyebrow again. "All right." Marion swallowed. "I think he might be seeing someone else." She studied a spotlight on the opposite wall until her eyes ached.

"What makes you think that?" Joan asked, brushing ash from her white dress.

Marion searched for the right words. "Well, he… he hardly comes round any more, unless it's to eat or to crash out. He never phones. When I call him he fobs me off with excuses, but still he just turns up when he feels like it…"

"Because you let him, Maz."

"What else can I do? I love him," Marion protested.

Joan wanted to slap some sense into her. Sometimes women could be so pathetic. What on earth could possess Marion to love this egotistical bastard? There was nothing in the relationship for her any more, and yet she still clung to him. Her own pride, dignity and self-esteem were going down the drain. It was no wonder he treated her the way he did; he did it simply because he could.

Joan remembered one occasion when she had gone around to Marion's flat to pick her up for a night out. Gerard had walked into the bedroom as Marion was putting on her jewellery.

"What's that you have 'round your neck," he'd demanded.

Joan had raised her head from the magazine she was reading at the tone of his voice.

"What, my necklace?" Marion had raised her hand to touch the silver and gold costume jewellery she wore.

"Is that what it is?" he'd snarled. "Didn't I buy you gold? What you wearing that shit for?"

Joan had had to bite her tongue to stop herself interfering.

"It goes with my dress, Ger," Marion had reasoned pitifully.

He'd looked at her with disgust. "Well you're not leaving here with that thing on."

Marion had reached up to undo the chain and take it off, and Joan found she couldn't control herself any longer. "There is no way a man could come tell me what I can and can't wear on my body!" she'd blasted. "Much less tell me I can't walk out of my own house."

Gerard had glared at her, then decided to ignore her and turned back to Marion, who held the chain in her hands, looking from her friend's face to his. "This is nothing to do with your friend," he'd said, "but if you wanna go out looking cheap then that's up to you," and he'd stormed back to the living room, slamming the door behind him.

His sudden anger had frightened Joan a little, but she was also angry at Marion. If that was the way he carried on all the time, then it was clear that Marion was living her life in fear of his dominance.

"You were never a doormat before you met him," Joan said now. "I can remember when we were kids you would even stand up to your mum's boyfriend when he tried to boss you around. You stood up for yourself."

"I don't want to have to fight, Joan. Not like my mum did. He walked out on her because of her interfering children."

"That just proves that he was no good, and only out for himself — like Gerard." Joan leaned toward her. "He's playing with you. Using you for his own satisfaction and not giving a damn about your feelings. He's a sweetboy, a buppie, a cock on legs."

Marion looked into her friend's eyes. Just who were they talking about here? "How's Colin these days?" she asked with a sneer.

Joan suddenly jumped back, shocked. "We're talking about your love life here, not mine."

"Hit a nerve, did I?" Marion was getting into this. She watched as Joan lit another cigarette with shaking hands.

"I don't want to talk about Colin." She shook her head. "I've made some mistakes in my life, and the Baker brothers were two of the biggest."

"Tell me about it."

Joan suddenly stood up, smoothing her dress down. "I'll get us a refill. Same again?" She didn't wait for an answer but sloped off towards the bar, leaving Marion wondering.

The wine bar had filled up since they'd entered. Most of the crowd hadn't bothered to dress up. There were all walks of life in here tonight,

Marion considered, becoming conscious of eyes watching her. She turned around to the table to her left and saw a young black man smiling at her. She looked past him, then turned to look for Joan.

The fellow was not to be deterred. He nudged his mate, and the two of them strolled over and made themselves comfortable in the vacant chairs at Marion's table.

The last thing Marion needed was to be chatted up. She turned her back on them, having to swivel around in her chair to do so.

"Hi," the first man said.

Marion glanced at the speaker, then cut her eyes at him and turned to look for Joan. She caught her friend's eye briefly and saw the flicker of a frown as Joan clocked the men at their table. Get back here, Joan. I can't handle this.

"So wha'? You cyaan seh hello?" the friend said. He was tall, dark and skinny.

"Do I know you?" she replied without looking at them.

The first guy dragged his chair closer and looked into her face. "No. But you will." He wasn't too bad looking. The first thing she noticed about him was his smooth skin.

"I don't want to know you, okay?" She managed to muster some sternness into her voice.

"Aah, come on. You two looked a little lonely, sitting here all alone. We just want to keep you company."

Marion thought quickly. She wasn't good at this sort of thing. "We're not alone. We're waiting for our boyfriends."

"Yeah? So where are they?" Tall and Skinny asked, smirking.

Joan reappeared by Marion's side like an angel. "Can we help you with something?"

"I can think of something," Smooth Face said.

"Yeah, so can I. But I take it you know how to walk."

"Come on, girls," Tall and Skinny chimed in, "we only want to chat."

"Can't you take a hint? When a woman tells you she doesn't want to know, she means she doesn't want to know," Joan enunciated.

"So you t'ink you're too stush to talk to us?" Smooth Face asked.

"In a word — yes." Joan touched Marion's shoulder. "Come on," she said. "Let's sit somewhere else," and she turned and made off across the room. Marion got up and tagged after her.

"Yaow, sexy! You don't know what you're missing," Tall and Skinny called after them.

The girls totally ignored him, taking a seat at the other end of the bar.

It was the noisier side of the room, but at least the men hadn't followed them.

"What is wrong with some men?" Joan blasted. "D'you think if a man turned me down flat I would keep pestering him? Where is their pride?" She gulped at her brandy and Coke.

"Some of them can't tell the difference between a woman turning them down and one who's playing hard to get," Marion said.

"Whatever," Joan kissed her teeth and shook another cigarette free from the packet. "They should stick to women who at least look interested." She lit the cigarette and tapped the lighter on the wooden table in time to the music.

"Obviously you're not on the lookout for another man then," Marion said, swinging the conversation back to their previous topic.

Joan gave her an incredulous look. "You must be joking. I've had too much trouble with them recently."

"So, tell me about it."

Joan blew smoke upwards through pursed lips. "I'm still not talking about it, Marion." She seemed adamant. Her eyes flicked restlessly around the wine bar.

"Are you sure you don't need to get this out of your system, whatever it is?"

Joan's eyes became too active, darting here and there, anywhere except Marion. She tapped the lighter a little harder at double the tempo of the track. "Bastards," she finally spat. "The lot of them." She crossed one leg over the other. "Y'know, if he'd have asked me to, I would have had his baby. Not without a ring on my finger first, mind you, but I would have done it. But no, what does he do? He goes and gets some whore pregnant instead!" Marion's big eyes opened wider at the mention of a pregnancy, then she remembered Joan knew nothing about hers. She narrowed her eyes. "Are we still talking about Colin?"

"Who else?" Her voice was rising to an unnatural pitch. She rested her elbows on the table in front of her. "I feel so damned stupid. Why couldn't I see it?" She looked to Marion as though she held the answers.

Around them people chatted, laughed and carried on as if they didn't exist. Marion wondered fleetingly what their lives were like. Was there even one couple here who could say they were in a solid relationship? Finally she said anxiously, "I can't believe it, Joan. Why didn't you say something?" "I don't want pity, Marion. And don't you dare tell Pam! I can do without the whole world knowing how I let myself be used. I mean, here I am giving you advice and I can't even see what's wrong with my own life."

Marion stifled a smile. She wasn't the only one who'd fallen for the wrong man. She'd caught her friend in a rare moment of weakness, most unlike her, and Joan had told her more perhaps than she'd intended. Would she still be handing out advice now that Marion knew she had her weaknesses too?

"It was probably a one-off with this girl." Marion allowed the smile to grow. "These things happen. He loves you, doesn't he?"

Joan cut her down. "Love? Get real, Maz! He was probably seeing her all along. He fancied a change and came running back to me, and like a sucker I let him." A vein throbbed at her temple.

Marion wished she could turn back the clock to when they had first entered. This was supposed to be an evening of good news, an attempt to take her mind off her man and her worries. The bad news had all of a sudden eradicated the good. They now sat in silence, Joan puffing away at her cigarette. If only society didn't make having a man so important to the fulfilment of a woman's life, Marion mused, she and her friends would be a lot happier.

Claudette Thompson opened the door and greeted Marion with a hug. Gerard's mother was surprisingly bubbly for a woman in her early fifties. Her jet black hair, which fell below her shoulders when she wore it down, was tied back in a loose bun. She was a few inches taller than Marion and just a little overweight, but the full figure suited her. It was a natural mother figure. She had the same mouth as Gerard, with sensual, cupid's-bow lips. She was altogether a very attractive woman, and Marion sometimes felt jealous of her vibrant personality.

Marion had called Gerard's house two hours earlier, for what seemed like the hundredth time. Claudette had answered and told her that Gerard had gone training. When she realised it was Marion, Claudette had promptly invited her round to the house for dinner. It was just the excuse Marion needed to corner Gerard.

Marion loved being in Claudette's company. She found that they could talk freely about anything, and often forgot that this woman was more than twice her age. Claudette served up a generous helping of steak, stew peas, rice, boiled cabbage and carrots, then sat opposite Marion, smiling, occasionally asking if the food was all right, telling her that she was still a growing girl. Marion laughed, assuring her that the food was fine — she just wasn't used to eating so much at one sitting. Afterwards, Claudette offered her home-made strawberry and kiwi cheesecake. Even though Marion was full, she could not refuse. By ten o'clock in the evening Gerard had still not arrived home, and Marion was beginning to feel drowsy. She explained to Claudette that it was her time of the month and she had to go up to the bathroom. Claudette smiled — those days were now gone for her, she told Marion, and good riddance to them. Anyway, she went on, she was feeling pretty tired and would be heading for bed any minute. Used to Marion waiting for Gerard in his room, she wished her good-night and left her to her own devices.

Gerard's room was just like him. Immaculate. Yet another ego trip. It was decorated completely in black and white, with a mirrored wardrobe covering an entire wall. As if that wasn't enough, there was a mirror above the black ash dresser and another smaller one on his bedside table. His expensive aftershaves and hair-care products adorned the dresser.

Unable to help herself, Marion began to snoop, not really knowing what she was looking for. She opened the top drawer of the dresser, his sock drawer. She knew because she had organised it that way three months previously. Her fingers ran over the paired bunches. She knew several of them were silk, his favourite fabric. Tucked underneath was a small box of condoms, which she picked up, opened, counted and then replaced. The next drawer, his underwear drawer, held no surprises. The bottom drawer however was heaped with junk. She gently pulled it on to the carpet and sat cross-legged in front of it. She didn't feel guilty about going through his things. If they were to reveal any secrets to her, she had a right to know.

Neither did she know what she expected to find. Left-over underwear perhaps, love letters, photographs...

Marion removed postcards, which she quickly read before putting them aside. Nothing. There were some old copies of a body-building magazine called Work It, pencils, batteries, receipts, guarantees, birthday cards, an address book (which she placed on her lap to browse through later), stubs of concert tickets — these interested her. They were for Aaron Hall's and R. Kelly's concerts, to both of which she had wanted to go. Gerard had known this — she had pleaded with him to take her — and yet he had never mentioned going. Marion screwed up her lips to stop herself from making a noise and attracting the attention of Claudette, and dropped the tickets by her side. Disgruntled, she continued her rummage with greater determination. There were passport-size photographs of Gerard on his own. He was smiling in only one of them, and one of the four was missing. Marion was tempted to take one of them, but she forced herself to put them back. Her eyes scanned the remains of the drawer. Screws, envelopes, bits of broken jewellery, cassettes that looked as though they would never play again, half-melted candles — and a Colorama photograph envelope. Her hand reached for it. Dismissing any doubts about invading his privacy she opened it up and slid the prints into the palm of her hand.

Girls, girls, girls. Here was one in her underwear sprawled out on his bed. And another in a bikini sitting by the side of a jacuzzi. Here was Gerard with his arm around another.

Marion flicked through the photos one after the other, her mouth opening wider with each one. Who were all these women? Okay, so the pictures didn't look all that recent, and they had been at the bottom of his drawer covered in all his other rubbish, but if this sort of behaviour was Gerard's thing there was bound to be someone else keeping his bed warm nowadays. She threw everything back into the drawer and slid it back into its slot. She stood up, the address book still in her hand, and glanced back at his dresser. There was another photo envelope, propped up against a bottle of aftershave.

A more recent Gerard, with two young girls at some kind of event. There were several of these, all innocent enough, until Marion came across one of a smiling Pamela, at the same event, and the back view of Gerard's head. Her heart sank. She walked back to the bed and slumped down, the offending photo still in her hand. She felt like running, screaming, yelling, ranting, throwing something, breaking something. She wanted to confront someone. Gerard would be home soon. Then she would have someone to confront. Then she would get an explanation.

Marion's full belly and the heat of the night were making her drowsy. She switched on Gerard's stereo and put a tape in, then kicked off her shoes and stretched out on his black and white duvet. Her mind was turning somersaults, but the mellow soul tune soon had her drifting into a light sleep.

The girl clung to his arm. Dizzy with alcohol, she leaned her weight on his strong shoulders. "You sure this is all right?"

"Debs, I told you, mum sleeps like a log." Gerard eased the front door open and stepped aside to let her into the house. "It is after midnight, y'know," she informed him.

"Since when you start worrying about how late it is?" Holding the latch, Gerard closed the door silently. The hallway was dark and he made no attempt to put the light on. He took Debbie's hand and strode stealthily towards the stairs. With a finger to his lips, he nodded in the direction of his mother's room. Debbie squeezed his hand to show that she understood. They crept up the stairs towards his bedroom at the end of the landing. He flicked the light, bathing the area outside the room in a warm glow, stepped in, and froze as he noticed the figure asleep on his bed. "What the…?" His arm flew up to hold Debbie back.

"What's wrong with you?" she hissed. "You almost had my eye out!" She tried to crane her neck to see what had stopped their progress. She was in no mood for games, she was feeling good — and when she felt this good there was only one thing she wanted to do.

"Hold on a minute." Gerard tried to pull the door back, but Marion had already started to wake up and Debbie had seen her.

Marion heard the voices and slowly came out of her sleep. At first she couldn't remember where she was. Then, seeing Gerard standing in his doorway, it all came back. She saw the girl over his shoulder and recognised her from the pictures. Her brain began to function again.

"Marion, what you doing here?" Gerard asked, trying in vain to keep Debbie out of sight, but she struggled past him. "Who's she?" she squealed.

"Just keep quiet!" He grabbed hold of her arm to keep her from going further into the room. Marion blinked the sleep out of her eyes and swung herself off the bed. "I could ask you the same thing," she said to Gerard. "Who's she?"

Gerard looked at the ceiling. "A friend."

"Who you calling a friend?" Debbie exploded. "You screw all your friends, do ya?"

"What?" Marion's eyes flared. She wasn't sure she had heard right. Was this child telling her she was screwing her fiancé? Who the hell did she think she was? Debbie wasn't waiting for Gerard to make any excuses. "I wanna know who she is, Gerard. Is she another one of your girlfriends?" She faced him with her hands on hips, her large earrings jangling.

Marion stood her ground. "His fiancé," she answered for him. Despite the increasing noise level Gerard seemed not to know how to deal with this situation. He had been standing stock still, like he was trying to blend into the wall. Now his eyebrows shot up and his mouth dropped open, but still he seemed to have been struck dumb.

"Gerard ain't marrying no one." Debbie laughed in Marion's face. She had an earring in her nose which Marion desperately wanted to rip out.

"Well, he would tell you that, wouldn't he? He's got good taste."

"What did you have to do, get pregnant?" Debbie smirked.

Marion flinched, catching her breath. "I don't have to stoop that low to get a man," she spat back, glancing uneasily at Gerard, who still seemed too shocked to intervene.

"Only to keep him, eh?" Debbie cut her eye after Marion.

"Bitch!"

"Don't call me no bitch, right? 'Cause if anyone's a dog in here it's you." She pointed a gold fingernail at Marion.

Marion dived towards her, her hands stretching like claws ready to scratch her eyes out. Gerard suddenly came back to life and stepped between them, so surprised that Marion was actually initiating a fight that he snapped out of his stupor.

"Do something, Gerard," Debbie whined, fending off Marion's grasping hands. "Tell this mad woman where to go."

"Stop the noise, you'll wake my mum," he hissed under his breath.

Marion stopped her attempts to get at the girl. "Is that all you care about?" She crossed her arms in front of her heaving chest. "Just get rid of her. I want to talk to you alone."

"If anyone's leaving, it's you," Debbie said confidently, still ready to fight.

Gerard had heard enough. "Debs! Jus' stop, all right? I'll give you cab fare home," he said.

"You're throwing me out?" She turned to face him, a look of disbelief in her eyes.

"I'll call you in the morning." His voice mellowed as he tried to appease her.

Debbie's shock was replaced by anger. "Don't bother. I don't want to hear from your sorry arse again. I'm not that desperate." She threw Marion a look full of scorn, but underneath it Marion thought she saw a hint of pity in her eyes. Debbie ran down the stairs. The front door slammed as she exited, no longer caring whom she disturbed. Gerard closed the bedroom door. He looked at Marion, who sat back on the edge of the bed. Her eyes were downcast, and she was close to tears.

She looked up at him. "How could you, Gerard? And with someone like that," she sniffed.

"I needed a break." Gerard shrugged. He was thinking about how to get this over with once and for all. He didn't need this kind of business going down in his mother's house.

"Couldn't you have talked to me about it?"

He looked at her as if she'd asked a ridiculous question. "Of course not. I knew how you'd react." He crossed to the bed and sat on the crumpled sheets beside her, his elbows rested on his knees, fingers clasped.

"How long have you been seeing her?" Marion asked, looking across at his solemn face.

"Not long. A few weeks, on and off."

Marion sniffed, fighting back the tears. "Do you want us to finish?" It was the last thing she wanted to say, but it was the question she had come to ask.

"Honestly. I think it's for the best. I don't want to hurt you." He forced an earnest tone into his voice. "We're just not right for each other, you know what I mean?"

"It feels right to me." As the words left her mouth she realised she was lying too. It had never felt as wrong as it did right now. Her head felt heavy again, and her eyes began to swim a little, she couldn't focus.

"But not to me. This is just too one-sided. I tried, but you're choking me. You hang around me all the time. I want to be my own man again." His words stung. The threatening tears finally arrived and she sobbed, her body shaking with emotion. "I... I'll change," she promised, her dignity taking a leave of absence.

"You see what I mean? You just caught me sneaking another woman into my bedroom at night, an' you still want me. Is that normal? Aren't you angry?"

Marion felt a mix of emotions, but wasn't sure whether anger was among them. "I can't be angry with you. I love you." She touched his arm, an unconscious attempt to seek comfort. Gerard backed away from her fingers, as though she was conducting electricity. Suddenly he couldn't believe this was the confident woman he had met just over a year ago. "It's over. I'm sorry, but that's life. Come on, put your shoes on and get your things. I'll give you a lift home."

Marion burst into fresh sobs. Gerard looked at her in disgust. "You're only making this worse for yourself. Stop it, Marion." He grabbed hold of her arm, and she was dragged reluctantly to her feet. She couldn't control her actions. She threw her arms around his neck, clinging to him in desperation. A voice inside her screamed out that she was losing all her dignity, making herself look a complete fool, but she couldn't help herself. She could feel herself doing these things, but it was as if it wasn't her. It was as though she were fighting for her life, trying to hold on to the only person that meant something to her. She was begging him to love her, and though she wanted to stop, she couldn't. He'd finished with her and she hadn't yet told him she was pregnant. "Don't do this, Gerard. I want us to get married and have our baby." He pushed her away roughly. "What baby? I don't want those things yet, and when I do it won't be with you. You're bloody obsessed."

GERARD

Women! I can't even come home to my own bedroom without finding one waiting for me now. I was looking forward to a piece ah Debbie that night, man. The girl couldn't wait to get my clothes off. Instead I find that stupid bitch Marion — on my bed!

What did she expect? That I would welcome her with open arms? Can't she take a hint, man? I ain't called the girl in weeks an' she still run me down.

She don't own me. An' I don't like women telling people they're my fiancé when they know damn well they ain't. I don't want my reputation soiled. The girl's got a screw loose. She had to go, man. This is what happens when you stay too long with one woman. They start getting ideas.

IT WAS SEVEN O'CLOCK BY THE TIME JOAN PULLED UP OUTSIDE her house. She lifted Shereen out of the car and carried her towards the house. She didn't want to wake her just yet; she knew she would only be miserable until she was settled again.

She was fumbling in her handbag for her door keys, Shereen asleep and balanced on one arm, when she heard heavy footsteps coming up the path behind her. She spun around. The figure she saw caused her to freeze on the spot. Martin Baker, Shereen's father, stopped less than three feet away from her. He was as tall as his brother, and they had the same boyishly handsome face, but Martin's was two shades lighter. He had sleepy eyes; Joan had always called them "come to bed eyes". Now she thought they looked as though he'd had too much to drink. His hands were shoved deep into the pockets of the grey trousers he wore. The navy blue blazer and white shirt did nothing to hide the fact that he had lost a lot of weight. He stood there, a tentative smile on his face, like he was waiting for her to greet him.

Shereen was getting weighty. Joan came out of her shock and found her keys. She turned to the front door without saying a word, opened it and stepped in. Martin took this as an invitation and followed. Joan turned around as he reached the door and glared at him.

"What do you want?" she asked acidly, dark eyes flashing from oval slits.

Martin looked at her earnestly. "I…" He paused. "Can I come in?"

"What for?"

"I came to see you... and Shereen." His eyes flicked over the child still sleeping on Joan's shoulder.

"I don't think we need to see you, Martin." She started to close the door, but he put a hand up and stopped it with his palm. "I'm here for my child, I'm not here to interfere. I just want to see my daughter."

"Couldn't you have called first?"

"I did try," he said. "You changed your number, innit? I called your mum an' all I got was verbal abuse."

"You called my mum?"

"Yeah, an' I wish I hadn't. She's still got a whiplash tongue on her."

Joan smiled inwardly as she imagined her mum cussing Martin. But she didn't want to stand on the doorstep discussing her business for everyone to hear. "I suppose you'd better come in," she said with a sigh. She walked in and Martin followed, closing the door behind him. "Go through to the living room," she instructed. "I'll be down in a minute." She dropped her handbag at the bottom of the stairs and ascended. She placed Shereen on her bed in her pretty pink bedroom. As she removed the child's sandals, she wondered why Martin had suddenly appeared. He knew that she and Colin had been getting it on. It had never bothered him, according to Colin. Perhaps he now also knew that Colin was getting married to the pregnant cow.

She went back downstairs. She picked up her handbag and removed her cigarettes, shaking one free as she entered the living room. For some reason she was feeling nervous. She couldn't believe it. She had known this man for seven years — minus the two that she hadn't seen him — what on earth was there to be nervous about? Her palms were slick with perspiration as she bent down for the table-lighter. It was shaped like a baseball cap and looked tacky and out of place compared to her other ornaments, but Colin had bought it for her in Blackpool and it reminded her of the good times.

"You look like you're doing all right," Martin said, looking around the room. "Not as well as I could be. We just about get by."

She leant back in the armchair and crossed her legs. She was sure Martin hadn't turned up just for a chat. After not communicating for two years, he had a lot of bottle to turn up on her doorstep at all.

"So?" she said impatiently. "How's Sherry?"

"Our daughter is fine. She started school a few months ago." "Yeah!" He grinned proudly. "Does she like it?"

Joan blew a stream of smoke into the air. "Yeah, she does. They told me she's one of the brightest kids there."

"That's my girl."

Joan gave him a look of contempt. "So — you've come to see her?"

Martin nodded. "And to make arrangements to start giving you both some money."

Joan pulled the ashtray towards her and tipped ash into it. "And what do you want in return?"

"Just to see my daughter when I can. I've never set out to hurt either of you," he said frankly. "I'm trying to make amends."

"Why now, all of a sudden?"

He shrugged. "I have to face up to my responsibility some time," he said, toying with a large gold and onyx ring on his finger. "I've been out of work for a year and I didn't want to make promises I couldn't keep." He chuckled nervously. "I kept expecting a letter from the CSA any day." He smiled at Joan, but she didn't return it and the smile dropped like a stone. "I started a new job with British Telecom last month. I can afford to be a father to Shereen now." He said it as though he expected Joan to be proud of him.

"You don't buy love, Martin," she told him, unimpressed by his feeble show of responsibility. "I'm sure your daughter would have been happy to see you even if you'd turned up in rags. You're still her father, with or without money." He met her eyes briefly before guilt gripped his insides and he dropped his gaze to the carpet. "I've got my pride, Joan. I couldn't come back empty-handed." He stood up suddenly and pulled his wallet from his jacket pocket. Removing three notes he walked over to her and handed her the money.

Joan took the notes from his outstretched hand. Sixty pounds. She felt like throwing it back in his face. But why should she? Money is money after all.

"I'm sorry it's not more, but I owe more than I earn. I'll give you what I can. Tell Shereen I called, yeah? I'll be in touch."

He dragged his feet into the hallway. Joan stood up and followed him out, fighting an uncontrollable urge to slap him for the last two years absence. She wondered if this small donation was the real reason he had come.

"Aren't you going to ask for my new number? I wouldn't want you just turning up again, I might be... engaged." She made sure he got the meaning by the tone of her voice.

"I s'pose I better." He turned back towards her.

Joan went back into the living room and scribbled her number on a

Post-It note. She took it back out to Martin. He glanced at it before folding it and slipping it into his inside pocket.

"I'll be in touch, then," he said again. He didn't seem inclined to say any more. He leant down and kissed her awkwardly on the cheek. Joan visibly tensed and he hurriedly retreated. She closed the door behind him and strolled back towards the kitchen.

Many times she had imagined what it would be like if he reappeared, but she hadn't expected anything like this. It was curiously disappointing. He hadn't asked her about her love life. He hadn't tried to seduce her, so that she could reject him. He hadn't applied for custody of his daughter. All he seemed to want to do was see Shereen occasionally.

After getting herself that cold drink, she decided to call Marion. She had to tell someone. She lit another cigarette as she dialled. The phone rang and rang. Marion wasn't in. So she called Pamela instead. Pamela would cheer her up. For some reason she suddenly felt like the most undesirable woman alive. Pamela's answerphone clicked on and Joan listened to her friend's husky voice telling her she wasn't in. Joan knew how much Pamela hated people not leaving a message, so she waited for the bleep. "Hi Pam, it's Joan…"

There was a whirring click and the line opened up. "J! How you doing, girl?" "Who you trying to avoid now?" Joan asked.

"I was just being lazy," honestly. "So, what's going on?"

"If I told you that Martin was just here, would that give you a clue?"

"You lie!" Pamela said.

"No. He reckons he came to see Shereen."

"And?"

"He gave me money."

"How much?"

"Sixty pounds."

"Is that all, after… how long is it?"

"Two years," Joan informed her. "It's not what we deserve, but it's a start. He says he's going to give us money regular."

"So, what did Shereen do?"

"She was sleeping, didn't even see him."

"What a shame. You gonna tell her?" "I don't know. I don't wanna get her hopes up in case he doesn't come again."

"You know your daughter better than anyone else, so it's up to you. How do you feel about seeing him?"

"I'm still in shock, Pam. I didn't know what to say or do. He told me he'd called my mum to try and get my new number. She cussed him out

— you know what my mum's like, innit?" Joan laughed.

Pamela joined her. "Good, the bastard. Some of 'em need a good cussing. Like Shaun the other day, getting on my case about when am I gonna throw James out."

"Are you?"

"Eventually, in my own time. I can't go on like this for much longer, though. I can't take the hassle. I'm losing sleep. I'm sure I saw a grey hair this morning."

"Men!"

"Who needs 'em?" Pamela kissed her teeth.

"We do," Joan joked.

"You got that right." They both cracked up. "Listen, girl, I was thinking. Why don't we have a drink up? We haven't had one since last year. We could invite Paul and his mates. Christina and Melanie. It would be a laugh."

"You know, that's just what we need. When?" Joan asked keenly.

"About three weeks, nearer pay day."

"Okay. Let's do it. I'll start making a few phone calls this week. We all pitching in with the food?"

"Yeah. I'll do the curry goat and white rice. Let Maz do the chicken and rice and peas, that leaves you to do simple salads."

"Thank you, Pam. You know I hate cooking, innit?"

"Yes, girl."

"So — you inviting Shaun?"

"D'you think I should?"

"Why not?"

"No, I couldn't. Not if we're having it here. James and Shaun in the same house... can you imagine?"

"We'll have it at my house, then. That way you won't have to tell James. Just say you're going out."

"How'd you get to be so devious?" Pamela gave a little laugh.

"You're my teacher." Joan grinned into the phone.

"Hey, I'm not that bad," Pam said with mock innocence.

"Look who you're talking to. This is me. I know about both the men, remember?" Joan laughed. "I also know about you using my house to carry on your sordid affair. So don't come tell me you're 'not that bad'." She mimicked Pamela's voice.

Pamela laughed. "Hold on a minute, J." Joan could hear a male voice in the background. Then Pamela came back on. "Listen, J. I've gotta go. James just got in and I wanna talk to him before he goes out again. I'll call you during the week, yeah?"

"Yeah, okay. Bye."

Joan decided she still had time to go ahead with her plans for the rest of the night. Martin hadn't totally ruined her evening. Now, where had she put that bag of weed?

MARTIN

I know what you're thinking — just another absent father. But I have my reasons. A lot of black men couldn't tell you why they left their wife and kids. I know why.

She drove me away. While she was just a clerical assistant everything was fine, then within three years she got two promotions with Icon Press. We never saw each other.

She was always working. She'd leave before I got out of bed, leaving me to take care of Shereen, make her lunch, get her bathed and dressed and then drop her at the minder's before I went to work. Then she would bring work home with her, as if it wasn't bad enough that she was at work nearly twelve hours a day. There was no room in her life for me any more. I wasn't important. She became this New Woman. Strong, ambitious, cold. And always too tired for sex.

I know this is gonna seem like a cliché, but I had to find someone to fill the empty space she had left in my life. There was this girl at work. I didn't mean to have an affair. I took her out to lunch to start with. Then we would meet after work for a drink. Then she would invite me 'round for dinner. We understood each other. It felt good to enjoy myself with a woman again. A woman who was interested in me. She wanted me, made me feel good about myself. After six months of seeing her we decided it was time I made a decision. Things were getting pretty serious, and I'm sure Joan knew all about us, but either she was waiting for me to tell her or she didn't care.

The way I left her was cowardly, I admit it. I couldn't tell her face to face, so I just waited until she'd gone to work as usual, took Shereen to the minder's, then went back home, packed and left her a note. I had taken voluntary redundancy from work without telling her, so she couldn't reach me there. I just disappeared from their lives.

It's hard to go back. But I want my daughter to know her father cares. I know angry women can use their children against their absent fathers, and I never want that to happen to us.

A HEAVY RAIN TAPPED CEASELESSLY AGAINST THE WINDOWPANE heavy rain tapped ceaselessly against the windowpane like hundreds of tiny fingers, bringing Marion back to the land of the living. She had slept only fitfully, the kind of sleep brought on by an exhausted mind. Gerard had driven her home from his house the night before. They'd sat in silence for the entire journey. The only sounds were the traffic and her sniffing and sobbing. He'd opened the front door with his key, then pressed it into her hand, saying he wouldn't be needing it any more. He'd helped her undress, as though he were undressing a child. He'd tucked her in, kissed her forehead, then switched off the lights and left. She'd felt physically and emotionally paralysed. She'd eventually cried herself to sleep. Now her head felt heavy and her eyes ached. It hurt to open them. The last time she had felt this way was after Jacqueline died. Her sister was only nineteen when sickle cell had claimed her life. Marion had cried for three days before drying up into a state of numbness. Then it had started all over again at the funeral. Marion now felt the same empty, worthless feeling. What was the point of life? What did she have left to live for?

She ran her hand across her flat tummy. She did have something to live for. Gerard's baby was growing inside her. Only five weeks old now, and its father didn't even know. He wouldn't want it even if he did. This thought brought fresh tears, but it hurt to cry and she forced herself to stop. She turned over on to her stomach and pulled the cover over her head. What had she done? She would now have to face the world as another single black mother, just like her own mother had done. Once, she had promised herself she wouldn't let her children go through that — struggle, stress, stepfathers...

The phone rang and startled her. She snatched up the receiver. "Hello?" she answered breathily, expectantly, the vague notion that it might be Gerard filling her with anticipation.

It was Joan.

"Maz? Did I wake you? Sorry, I just had to talk to someone. I tried to call you last night... Maz? What's wrong, babe?" Joan could hear nothing but anguished cries on the other end of the line. Her voice became concerned as she immediately forgot her own problems. "It's Gerard, ain't it?"

"J, I don't know what to do." Marion hitched and coughed.

"I'm coming over, all right? Right now."

"But Shereen...?"

"She's at a neighbour's. School holidays she's round there most of the time. See you shortly."

The connection went dead as Joan hung up. Marion felt like such a fool.

Forty-five minutes later the doorbell rang and Marion dragged her feet to the front door. Joan dropped her handbag and shook raindrops from her jacket. She hugged Marion's tiny frame to her as they stood in the hallway. "You don't even have to tell me what happened," she said. "That bastard wasn't good enough for you anyway."

Marion made a dry clicking sound in her throat, as though she were trying to swallow something that didn't want to go down.

"I bet you haven't even had a hot drink yet," Joan said, walking her back to the living room. "Come and sit down and I'll get us both a cup." She made sure Marion was comfortable on the sofa before she went into the kitchen. She took off her damp jacket and put the kettle on. "What was it, then? Another woman? He just couldn't keep himself still. What did I tell you about them sweetboys?" she yelled back to Marion.

Marion slumped back into the sofa, not seeing, hardly hearing. Her head throbbed and she wanted to curl up into a ball.

Joan's voice continued in the background: "I knew you'd get hurt, but you can't say anything to a woman in love. I know. My mum warned me when I told her I was moving in with Martin, but I was in love. He promised me marriage, and I went ahead and had his baby. Now where is he?" She came back into the living room with two steaming cups of coffee and put Marion's mug on the coffee table. "That'll wake you up a bit." Then she sat next to her friend on the sofa. "So — talk to me."

Marion, dressed only in an oversized T-shirt and panties, looked at Joan with red, swollen eyes. Joan shook her head in pity. She thought that her friend looked like a mirror image of herself after Martin had walked out on her. She put her arm around Marion's shoulders.

"It's over. He told me," Marion said. "I went round to see him. To find out where I stood. I was going to tell him about the baby, I nearly did too…"

"What baby?" Joan interrupted.

"That's exactly what he said. Then he said he wouldn't want me to have his kids anyway. Joan, he had a girl with him…" Tears threatened again with the memory. "She laughed at me when I said I was his fiancée. She didn't even know about me."

Joan's face registered incredulity. "Hold on a minute." She raised a hand. "Rewind. You're pregnant?"

Marion moistened her lips and reached for the chain she wore around her neck. Her sister's. She toyed with the small gold key on the end of it. "Yeah. Five weeks. And he still doesn't know."

"Boy, Marion, when you keep a secret you keep it good. I don't believe that guy! The bastard was dipping elsewhere and you were pinning your hopes on marriage." Joan shook her head again and handed Marion her coffee.

"There's something else," Marion said quietly.

Joan studied her face curiously.

"I think he might be seeing Pamela too." Joan smiled. "Get outta here! Our Pamela?"

"I saw photographs of them together." Marion looked up at Joan with a dead pain in her eyes.

"What do you mean 'together'? Kissing? Naked? Holding hands? What?"

"They looked as though they were just talking. It was at that hair and beauty thing. Pamela told me she went with James. She never mentioned seeing Gerard there…" Joan shook her head, stifling a laugh. "Pam did go with James. She told me all about it," she explained. "She bumped into Gerard with two girls there. Come on, Marion. You know how Pamela hates Gerard. What, did you think she was making it up? She wouldn't do that to you."

"But she was always trying to get me to leave him. And why didn't she tell me she saw him there?"

"Marion… Maz," Joan comforted, "she didn't tell you because she didn't want to upset you. She wanted you to break up with him for your own good, not so that she could have him."

Marion realised that what Joan was saying was true. "I'm sorry," she said, "I haven't been thinking straight. Tell me how stupid I am."

"No, it wasn't your fault." Joan squeezed her shoulders. "Pam will probably die laughing when I tell her." Her tone became more serious. "But why did you let yourself get pregnant?"

Marion's eyes told her what she had already guessed, and she answered her own question. "You hoped it would save your relationship." "Now tell me how stupid I am." Marion gulped the warm coffee; it felt good going down.

"So you're gonna have an abortion?"

"No!" Marion's answer was sharp, direct. She was hurt that Joan would automatically expect her to get rid of her baby.

Joan's mouth dropped open and she stared at her friend in disbelief. "What?"

"I'm keeping it. It's my baby too. I got pregnant deliberately, how could I just kill it?" "You know I'll be here for you." Joan squeezed

Marion's hand. She didn't agree with most things Marion did, but when you can't change a friend's mind you support them the best you can. "Does your mum know?"

"No. She'll probably kill me. I'll tell her over the phone, it'll be safer. Besides, I'm in no mood to go trekking up to Birmingham." "Maybe you should go an' visit for a while. You could get away from things. You wouldn't accidentally bump into Gerard." Joan raised her eyebrows meaningfully on the word "accidentally".

"I wouldn't do that, Joan. But you're right — I should go away for a while. I couldn't face work now anyway."

"You're too naive for your own good, you know that? Right now I feel like hugging you and slapping you at the same time." Marion laughed, surprising herself.

"That's better." Joan smiled. "I suppose you'd better call your mum."

"No, not yet. I've got some things I want to clear up first, bills to pay, y'know. Thanks, Joan. I don't know what I'd have done if you hadn't come round. I haven't cried so much since Jackie... y'know."

"Yeah." Joan gave her hand another squeeze. "But believe me, men aren't worth it. D'you think he's losing sleep over this? I doubt it. Especially as he's got this other woman."

"Girl," Marion corrected. "And she blew him out anyway. I swear she was about nineteen. I could've killed her."

"Remember, she didn't know about you either. It's him you should have killed."

Marion had called the library on Monday morning and taken the rest of the week off. She'd told them she had a family crisis, too personal to go into. It was true, in a sense, so she hadn't really lied. It was now Wednesday evening. She lay in bed, the sheets twisted around her body, staring at the Artex ceiling, but not seeing. Jodeci played on the cassette player on her bedside table. An empty packet of headache pills lay next to the machine, along with three mugs with varying amounts of coffee in them. Discarded clothes, newspapers and magazines lay scattered on the floor or half hanging off the bed.

She'd tried to begin working on the assignment from Joan, but writing about men wasn't easy when you were trying to recover from a break-up. She'd tried to write to Gerard. She knew the message she wanted to send him should have been angry, remonstrative, but all she had managed to produce was a series of pleading letters. Then it was poetry, reminding him of how it had been in the beginning. None of her attempts had got further than the waste bin.

She took a couple more pills and vomited them back up a few minutes later. She knew it was morning sickness, but nobody had prepared her for feeling so wretched. The phone rang. She let it ring several times before reaching over and picking it up.

"I'm still waiting for that call," a distinctive male voice told her.

"Paul?" Her voice was hoarse, sleepy.

"Yeah — Paul. You were supposed to call me, remember?"

She remembered. She had meant to call Paul ever since their last meeting, but other things had crowded her brain. "Yes, but..."

"No buts, Marion. What's happening? This man got you under manners?" he joked.

What man? she thought glumly. "No, Paul. In fact, we..." she coughed, "err... broke up." She had to force out the words.

"Sorry, babes." She heard the smile in his voice, and imagined him gloating. "I haven't called anyone in a while."

"You sound terrible. Want some company?" "I don't know, Paul. I wouldn't be very good company." She didn't know if she could face another man right now, there was too much to think about. But then again she needed a break from thinking, especially about Gerard...

"But I would. I could be there in half an hour."

Marion sunk back into her pillow and made up her mind. "Okay. But make it an hour."

"Yeah? I can come up?" he asked, somewhat surprised.

"Yes," she gave in.

"Want me to bring anything?"

"A bottle of wine would be nice."

"You got it. I'll see you later then." Paul spoke jubilantly.

"Bye." She hung up and looked around the room. The whole flat was a mess. She couldn't let Paul see the place like this.

As she set to work tidying hurriedly, she caught sight of herself in the dresser mirror and couldn't believe what a wreck she looked. Puffy bags under her shrunken eyes, dry skin and chapped lips. She went into the bathroom and turned on the cold tap, splashing her face with icy water. Then she ran a bath, took off her bra and panties and stepped into the water. She scrubbed her body, feeling it tingle with life as she rubbed the soap over her still flat tummy. When she'd got out she covered her body in Body Shop musk oil. Going back into the bedroom she found a purple satin french knicker set that Gerard had bought her on one of their shopping trips and put it on. She massaged Luster's Pink Oil into her hair and tied it back into a ponytail. She sat on the white stool in front of her white dressing table, and selected her favourite lipstick. Gerard hated the scarlet red. He said it made her look like a whore. Marion, though, thought it was sexy, and put it on. She smiled at her new defiant spirit, and applied eyeliner. She put on her dressing gown and went to the living room, where she brought the large mirror out from behind the sofa where it had been hiding for a week and hung it back on the wall. She was practising seducing pouts in front of the glass when the intercom rang.

Here he was. Paul. She took the offered bottle from him and placed it gently on the floor. He took her into his arms as she closed the door behind him, and she buried her head in his neck and squeezed him back. He kissed her tentatively on the lips. She returned his kiss, surprising herself. So he kissed her just a little harder, plunging his tongue between her lips. His hands held her in the centre of her back, drawing her into his embrace. Marion felt her body responding, her panties getting wet, as his sense of urgency rubbed off on her. Backing up against the passage wall, she let him open her dressing gown and grind his hips against hers. Then he began to travel down her body, kissing her breasts, sucking her nipples, taking her flesh between his teeth, exciting her further. He gripped her bottom, pulling her so close that there was no air between them.

Marion felt only the slightest pang of guilt as she led him into her bedroom, teasing him with her body, her lips, her eyes. She ran her fingers over his shaved head. He didn't need any encouragement, he was already hers. Neither of them said a word as he removed the skimpy lingerie she wore and showered her body with kisses and love bites. She totally succumbed to Paul's lovemaking. His jacket had fallen on the floor by the front door. His T-shirt was at the bedroom door, his shoes at the bottom of the bed, and now his trousers were being worked slowly down his hips. His breathing was coming hard and fast as he moved her hand to his strong erection. He was as hard as the head of a hammer, hot and thrusting. She guided him, wanting him inside her body, needing him to come inside her, then gasped as she took the full length of him. Her brown legs wrapped themselves around his buttocks. He kissed her cheeks and neck more excitedly and drove his hips faster against her as they approached their climax. They came together, his muscular body tensing as it shook with the sexual explosion. She clung to his broad shoulders, her nails leaving indentations in his back.

"Girl, what did you do to me?" He rolled off her, breathlessly, on to his back.

Marion turned over and leant on one elbow, her other hand resting on his chest. She studied his features. His jaw reminded her of Gerard's, strong and chiselled, but there the similarity ended. His skin was dark, like chocolate, and shiny with perspiration. She ran her fingers through the curly hairs on his chest. Gerard's chest was smooth, hardly a hair on it. They were so different. Light and dark, tall and short, headstrong and easygoing. They would make very different babies... Marion pushed that thought to the back of her mind. She had loved Paul once, and she could again — for her baby's sake.

PAUL

You know, I've known Marion two years now — and if anybody did tell me dat one day she would seduce me, I would have put money on it never happening. Marion's not that type. But sometimes it's good for a man to be in the right place at the right time. When a woman jus' break up with her man, the next man moves in and dries up all the tears.

From her performance tonight I feel sure Marion wants me back.

Like that night at the club. I'm no mind-reader, but I know she was feeling the feeling.

If we're gonna try this thing again, I would have liked to go slower. Give her time to get over her man. Give me time to get to know her all over again. But I guess it's all out of my hands now.

CARNIVAL BANK HOLIDAY WAS HERE AGAIN, AND THIS YEAR IT promised to be one of the best. Thirty years old, the carnival was now the biggest street event in Europe, and literally millions of people were flocking to a few streets in West London for the biggest alldayer of the year.

As usual the forecast had been for rain, but so far the clouds were staying scattered and, despite the cold breeze, the sun looked like it was here to stay.

Joan, Pamela, and her old schoolfriend Rebecca (Marion had decided that, in her condition, carnival wasn't for her this year) sat in the Ford Fiesta in a typical carnival traffic jam. Carloads of ravers were on their way to the festivities. On the pavements, posses of people were following each other in an expectant procession. The sound of revellers could already be heard from the Harrow Road. Soca music, whistles and foghorns blasted their welcome.

Half a million men in one place! Pure manhunt ah gwaning.

Rebecca drove. With her Brownstone cropped hair, dyed cinnamon for effect, and her tight, slim body enclosed in a simple grey track suit bottom and a clinging white bodysuit, she cut a striking figure. Pamela wore a baggy white T-shirt over track suit bottoms, and Joan had opted for a tight-fitting lycra shorts catsuit.

"Hey, ladies! Any room in your car for me?" The young man spoke with an American accent, and his flashing white teeth immediately drew the girls' attention. They looked with amazement at the vision by their car. He was beautiful from head to toe, dressed in navy and white Fila shorts and jacket. His hair was waved high at the front and gelled back into waves at the back and sides. His fair skin was smooth and spotless. A wicked looking specimen.

"Oh yes, baby," Rebecca replied, winding her window all the way down. "Just park yourself right here on my lap."

The man grinned. "See you there, ladies. I love you all," and he blew them an exaggerated film-star kiss before jogging back to his friends on the pavement.

The girls erupted into screams as they caught a glimpse of the other guys, craning their necks to get a look. "Oh God, they're gorgeous," Joan gasped, leaning over Rebecca to ogle them.

"Follow them, Bec." Pamela shoved the back of the driver's seat as if it would make the traffic disappear. "Did you see his eyes? Oooh." She bounced up and down in the back seat.

Rebecca laughed. "How can I follow them when I can't even move forward?"

Joan watched the men cruise out of their lives. "We are definitely going to enjoy this carnival."

Pamela caught the eye of a tall, dark-skinned brother who nearly walked into a lamppost with distraction. "Men — men everywhere," she sang to the tune of "Trailer Load Ah Girls". "From London, Canada and the USA. Men, men everywhere. I wanna give you one, so bring your body right here."

"Bwoy! I jus' caught a glimpse of that guy's chest," Joan said, half-hanging out of the window, a bottle of Cisco in one hand. "Yaow, big chest!" she yelled across the street.

Several heads turned, including his, and he flung his jacket open, revealing that he had nothing but his jeans on under it.

The girls burst into catcalls as the traffic started moving again. "I woulda loved to rub my hands all over that body," Joan cooed.

"Yeah, well, you'd have had to race me for it," Pamela teased.

It took them ten minutes driving around the back streets of Kensal Rise to find a parking space. They finally slotted the car into a gap just vacated, and walked the three quarters of a mile back to the centre of activity. Whistles at the ready, bottles of Cisco grasped in their hands, mini rucksacks strapped to their chests, the three girls merged into the throbbing crowd that was milling around Ladbroke Grove.

With eyes like a radar, Pamela was homing in on every good-looking male they came across, which began to be so many that eventually she gave up looking in four directions at once and concentrated on looking ahead.

As soon as they hit Ladbroke Grove station the movement came to a congested stop. A float carrying gaily dressed dancers was trying to drive down the road while crowds of people were trying to get around, backwards and forwards. The impatience of the younger, fitter party-goers forcing their way through by whatever means necessary was causing children and the elderly to be squashed in between. Tempers were fraying. Dragging their belongings with them, the girls emerged on the other side of the commotion and forged ahead, regaining their composure.

They followed the rhythm of a garage track and headed east. This is what they had come for — to rave. They blended into the crowd, jumping to the beat. Whereas there had been a slight chill in the air before, the girls were now feeling the heat of all the bodies around them: twisting bodies, dipping bodies, pumping bodies, gyrating bodies, jumping, dancing, pushing, groping. There was so much going on that if you stopped to think about it, it would make you dizzy. The heady smells of Caribbean chicken, patties, sugar cane, coconut, and the smoke from charcoal barbecues filled the spirited air.

Having finished the drinks they had brought with them, Pamela queued up to purchase some more. Handing over the bottles of Thunderbird wine from behind his wooden blockade, the Asian storekeeper grinned. "All for you?"

"Naw, man. It's for me and my sisters," Pamela replied with an air of street tough.

"You very pretty. Come back later. You teach me dance, yes?" he leered, baring yellow teeth.

Pamela shook her head, laughing. "Naw, mate. You stay there." She giggled to her mates, making fun of the man who hadn't quite got the joke.

Joan placed a hand on her shoulder. "Pulling crusty Indian geezers now, Pam?" she jibed.

"That ain't funny. Don't go spoiling my rep," Pamela mock-scolded.

Father MC's "Hit You With a Sixty-Nine" came blasting from the speakers some way up the road. The three girls linked arms in a bid not to lose each other as they rushed towards the heavy bass, whistles to their pouting lips.

By nine o'clock, all the sound systems had packed up and the remaining revellers followed the carnival floats or chilled out by the mobile food stalls. Food and drink was not cheap, but as they say, "when you belly bawling for hungry, if you have the money you pay". The girls bought chicken, a drumstick each, which didn't even touch their hunger. It seemed that people just did not want to go home. The floats were now travelling down the main road on their way out of the route, and yet people were still dancing in the streets, caught in the hypnotism of carnival.

After having countless male members shoved up against their backs all day, the aches and pains began at eleven thirty, and the girls decided to make their way back to the car with the phone numbers they had collected. Pamela had the most numbers, never failing to catch the males' attention and hold it. Rebecca had bumped into old friends, and Joan had bumped into old boyfriends. Taking their numbers had been nothing but a courtesy.

"Bwoy, my legs are gonna be killing me tomorrow," Joan moaned, slowing down her pace now they had left the crowds behind. She was glad Rebecca was driving.

"Naw, it's my back, that's where I can feel it." Pamela placed a hand on her lower back and rubbed with her fingers.

Rebecca groaned. "Can't you feel any pain in your pelvis, all that 'wuk up yuh waist'? Mine feels like it's gonna drop off."

Joan laughed, leaning on Rebecca's shoulder. "God, we mus' be getting old."

"Oh, don't!" Pamela gasped. Only twenty-five, old was the last thing she wanted to feel.

They turned on to a long residential street — and realised they were lost.

"We didn't come this far up." Pamela looked up and down the street. She was positive they had walked too far.

Joan on the other hand felt they were still on the right track. "Yes we did. Don't you remember? I was complaining we'd walked miles," she corrected.

Rebecca cut in. "No, I think she's right, Joan. We've come too far up. Let's walk back a bit."

They turned on their heels and went back the way they had come. Three guys stood on the corner they'd turned. Rebecca recognised them as guys they'd met during the festivities. She made a comment about how they hadn't got their numbers.

As soon as the words were out of her mouth, one of them turned and addressed Pamela, who was lagging behind.

"So, you can't even stop and say hello?"

Pamela stopped, squinted her eyes at him blankly. "Do I know you?"

He raised his eyebrows in surprise. "You don't remember me?"

Pamela looked him up and down. He was quite presentable. Intelligently good-looking, and had a friendly smile. No, she didn't remember him, and she told him so.

Rebecca jogged her friend's memory. "You remember, Pam, when we were dancing at that soul sound system — the one that got shut down 'cause of the fight."

"Yeah." The guy nodded, pleased one of them recognised him. He turned back to Pamela — obviously that was where his interest lay.

Realisation dawned on her heart-shaped face. "Oh yeah. I remember now," she smiled.

He put on an offended look. "Huh! Diss me like that after I told you how good you can dance…"

"Sorry." Pamela touched his arm, already going into a natural flirt.

"My name's Gary, by the way," he said.

"Pam." They shook hands.

"So, where you going?" Gary asked, his friends still hanging back. The shorter of the two was wrapping his arms around himself in a bid to keep warm; the other, a tall fellow in red corduroy, was eyeing Rebecca. "We're trying to find our car," Joan said, wrapping her cardigan tighter around herself. "Yeah? So are we. It's around here somewhere."

Rebecca, ever so quick, suggested they look for the vehicles together, then whoever found theirs first could give the others a lift to look for theirs.

"Come on, then. It's cold out here, y'know," said the short guy.

"So, what's your names, then?" the guy in the red corduroy asked.

The girls introduced themselves, and the other two men gave their names as Desmond and Marcellis. Joan fell in love with the name Marcellis. It was so different. She decided to take him under her wing, and as they walked down the road automatically pairing off into couples, she wrapped her arm around his shoulder.

The girls found their car first. The six of them piled into the Fiesta and followed the guys' vague directions. When finally they came to the car nobody moved. They had got into the flow of easy conversation, and nobody seemed to want to end it just yet. And so they chatted for hours in the confines of the Fiesta. The men appeared to have their heads screwed on. They were all employed in good, professional jobs, and seemed interested in what the women had to say. Joan told them about Marion's writing, and the fact that they were looking for men to interview. The guys jumped at the chance of having their views published. So Joan steered the conversation to sex and relationships. Desmond came over as being very bitter about women, claiming that he had to ask a woman what she wanted all the time. Women, according to him, didn't communicate. Gary, on the other hand, said that women didn't know what they wanted. They said they wanted one thing, and when they got it they still weren't satisfied. Marcellis, the youngest and quietest of the group, said that he enjoyed being single. There were times when being part of a couple was something that he wanted, but he wasn't ready for long-term commitment.

The conversation continued long into the night, the six of them so relaxed — perhaps as a reaction to the day's frantic activity — that they were soon talking as though they were friends of old. It was five o'clock in the morning before everyone decided they would have to go home and get some sleep — they all had work the next day.

They swapped phone numbers, and Pamela suggested that the boys should come to their party.

By the time Rebecca had pulled out into the empty West London streets, Joan's mind was buzzing with ideas for the articles. She had taken Marcellis's number only because he seemed like promising material — plus he had promised to pose nude for her — a picture for her bedroom wall. If that wasn't worth a phone call, what was?

"MUMMY, I'M THIRSTY." SHEREEN LOOKED UP AT HER MOTHER with her father's sleepy eyes.

Joan was in no mood to be hassled. "In a minute, Shereen," she said. It was hot, she was tired, and this was the third time the child had asked for a drink in five minutes. They had been shopping for Shereen's school clothes for the new term in September.

"Mummy! Look, Mummy! It's Uncle Colin."

"Where?" Joan asked distractedly.

It was him. Wearing a black track suit and baseball cap. His muscular arms bulged beneath the vest he wore. The girl beside him, with her arm around him, kissed him. Colin smiled sweetly at her.

"Why don't we go and say hello, Mummy?" Shereen whined.

Joan had to think fast for an answer. "We haven't got time love," she said. "Come on." It sounded weak, but Shereen was tuned in enough to her mother's moods not to press the point.

It was very crowded in Lewisham today, as it was most days. They walked down the alleyway commonly known as the Black Market. Here there were shops and market stalls that sold clothes, Jamaican patties and West Indian bread, a black greeting card shop, and a hairdressers.

Joan was seething. She had finally seen Colin's pregnant girlfriend. They were shopping together. Probably choosing paint for the baby's room. Her heart jolted at the thought. That girl was going to have Colin's baby. Joan suddenly felt a deep sense of loss. She had thought she was over Colin Baker, that nothing he did mattered any more. But that wasn't true. Joan unlocked the car door, still in a daze. Shereen clambered into the back while Joan unlocked the boot and slung the bags of shopping in. She couldn't get Colin out of her mind. She swung the car around and headed towards Wandsworth. Shereen would be spending the rest of the weekend with her grandmother.

"Hi, Mum." Joan kissed her mother on one of her soft cheeks.

"You awright? You look a bit peaked."

"Yeah, I'm fine." Joan lied.

They entered the house. Joan took Shereen's bags into the back bedroom. As she came out she bumped into her daughter running back up the passageway, a handful of jelly beans in each of her little fists. Grace sat in her favourite armchair, a green velvet recliner with its own built-in cushions. Its position gave her a view of the street and anybody approaching her house, which was why she had reached the front door before they were out of the car. She had picked up her knitting. A beautiful soft beige speckled mohair wool hung from the needles.

"What you making this time, Mum?"

"Somet'ing nice and warm fe de winter. You like it?" Grace held up the side she had nearly completed.

Joan picked up the pattern from the table beside her. "Oh yes, that's nice. Can I borrow it when it's done?"

Grace laughed. "Me len' you anyt'ing, me naw get it back."

Joan regarded her mother with a hurt look. "That's not true, Mum. What about that long black dress?"

"De ongle reason yuh did bring dat back is 'cause yuh hav' nuttin' to fill it wid." Grace laughed heartily, pushing her glasses back up on her nose.

Joan lifted the shopping bag she was holding. "All right, so I didn't inherit your chest." "You going out tonight?"

"Yeah. Night club."

"I hope seh you meet a nice young man."

Joan thought of Colin. "I'm not looking, Mum."

"Dat is when yuh fine dem."

"Don't start, Mum. I've had it with men."

Her mother gave her a knowing look. "So you seh."

Joan quickly changed the subject. "You heard from Donna lately?"

Her mother huffed. "De laas me hear from your sister, is a pos'cyard she sen' from…" She frowned, trying to remember where her younger daughter had gone on holiday.

"Canary Islands," Joan filled in.

"Yes. She nuh call me. She doan even visit her own madda. You hear from her?"

Joan shook her head. "Same as you, Mum — a postcard."

"She t'ink seh she big now she get married, she doan need family no more."

Joan wasn't worried about her sister. As far as she knew, her husband John took care of her as he should. But she was upset that Donna wasn't keeping in touch. Last Christmas she had gone to John's family instead of visiting Grace, and on New Year's Eve she'd turned up on her own.

"Mum, I'm gonna go. Got lots to do."

"Okay, bye then," Grace said without looking up from her work.

"Bye, Shereen. Be good."

"All right, Mum. Bye." Shereen's eyes were fixed on the television. Joan left thinking how lucky she was to have her family. So why did she still feel so unfulfilled?

COLIN

I want respect from my woman. You know, I want her to look up at me and feel proud. I want respect for what I do, what I achieve, what I am. Money is only one way of gaining respect. You have to prove that you deserve it. A man who doesn't respect himself can't expect it from others.

Bwoy, did that come from me? I must be getting deep. You know who should hear me talk like this? Joan.

THE COOING OF THE PIGEONS STRUTTING OUTSIDE HIS BEDROOM window brought Shaun out of his sleep. He stirred. With his eyes still shut, he became aware of the warm body by his side. He turned over, leaning on one elbow, and gazed down at her. Pamela looked as innocent as a baby. He had never known another woman to look this good after what they had done the night before. Her black shoulder-length hair half covered her face, and he swept it clear with a single stroke. A quick glance at the alarm clock told him it was time to wake her up. He leaned over and ran his tongue over his lips, wetting them before placing a tender kiss on her neck. Then he ran his tongue down her neck to her shoulder. Pamela moaned and turned on to her back. Shaun's eyes travelled down to her full breasts. "Pam," he said softly. She didn't move. He called her name again, this time shaking her gently. Pamela groaned and threw her arm over her eyes. "No more, Shaun. I'm tired."

Shaun threw his head back and laughed heartily. "I'm not offering you anything. Get up." He gently shoved her again.

"What?" she cried irritably.

"Didn't you tell James you'd be home this afternoon?" he asked with a smirk on his face.

"Shit! What time is it?" She sprang up, her hair falling about her head like a badly fitting wig.

"Three thirty," Shaun informed her, slightly amused.

Pamela flung the covers off. "God, Shaun! Why didn't you wake me?" She jumped naked from the bed.

Shaun leaned back on the headboard, arms folded behind his head. He watched her with a grin as she stalked about the room, grabbing her clothes from the floor. "I'm sure I've told you this before, Pam — your body is a gift."

"Shaun, don't go getting horny on me now. James is probably already suspicious." She turned to him, not completely unaware of the effect she had on him, and yawned. "Make us a cup of coffee, will you?"

"Is that an order?"

"Damn right." She reached for the door handle and Shaun made as if to get up and go after her. She dashed out of the room, laughing.

Slowly Shaun got out of bed. He could hear the bath water running. She was going back to her man. Or was that her other man? The irony of it hit him: Pamela belonged to no one; she did exactly as she pleased, when she pleased. The thought of sharing her angered him, but he had no choice. She had already told him it was share or get nothing, for the time being anyway.

She was too good for James. The wimp. She'd told Shaun she had stopped having sex with James since she had started seeing him again. And he believed her. After all, James couldn't be much of a temptation compared to him.

He ran his hand over his short, neatly cut hair, and wondered if Pamela wanted his company in the bath. He smiled to himself, showing perfect teeth. Pamela's call from the bathroom brought him back to the present. "Shaun, where's my coffee?"

"Coming," he called back. Forget the coffee — he would give her something to think about on her way back to James. Soon she would be back with the wimp, but one day she would be Shaun's for ever.

Pamela bounced into the flat. She was in a good mood. The only damper was coming back home to James. She could hear the sound of the television coming from the bedroom, and assumed that was where he was. She dropped her bags gently in the hallway. It wasn't until she reached the living room door that she heard music coming from inside. Puzzled, she opened the door and stopped in her tracks. James sat on the floor, his legs underneath the coffee table, his back resting against the leather two-seater. He had a drink in his hand, and she could smell the pungent aroma of ganja. It hung in the air like a cloud; he could only just have finished smoking.

His slightly red eyes rose to meet hers. "So, you decide to come home?" he slurred.

"I told you I was coming back this afternoon." She crossed the room to the window and pushed it open.

His half-shut eyes followed her. "I thought you meant lunchtime. I cooked for us." His voice was unusually rough.

"Oh, good. I'm starving." She tried to remain cheery, but James's behaviour worried her.

She made her way quickly to the kitchen, avoiding his eyes. "You mean Rebecca didn't feed you?"

"Sorry?" she called back.

"You were at Rebecca's, weren't you?" he asked accusingly. He had got up and followed her to the kitchen, moving with a sluggish, apathetic tread. Now he stood in the doorway, barely filling the frame. She turned to face him. He looked paler than usual. A faint shadow covered his chin and cheeks, as though he hadn't shaved in a couple of days. She'd only been gone for the weekend. "Yes. Look, what's all the aggro about? I'm hungry and tired," she said, forcing toughness into her voice.

"Up all night, were you?" He raised his eyebrows questioningly.

"We were, as a matter of fact." she turned to the pots on the hob, switching the gas on low, "watching videos."

"Why are you lying to me?" he yelled suddenly, startling her. "About what?" she said, her pretty brown eyes taking him in.

His hand turned into a fist. "Rebecca called last night, asking for you." Pamela's heart stopped and then started again, beating twice as fast. She pushed past him and stepped into the living room. He grabbed her arm. "How do you explain that?"

Her heart was in her throat, but she said calmly, "What time did she call?"

"What difference does that make?" he sneered.

"Because I stopped at Marion's first, then got to Rebecca's a bit late. I probably hadn't got there yet."

"You're still lying to me!" His grip on her arm tightened. She was more surprised than frightened. Was this really James?

"What do you want to hear?" Her voice rose again, letting loose her anger. "That I spent the weekend with another man?" She dragged her arm away forcefully and marched into the hallway. She lifted her bags and carried them into the bedroom, where the TV still blared. He was right on her heels. "Well? Did you?"

"Just stop this, okay?" She crossed to the television and switched off Patricia Routledge in mid-sentence.

"No! I want the truth. Are you seeing someone else?" he asked directly.

Pamela no longer saw any reason to deny it. She figured she had nothing to lose. She pulled herself up to her full height. "Alright. Okay. You want the truth? I am seeing someone else." She said it almost with pride. "I've been seeing Shaun again."

His eyes widened, and then narrowed to tiny slits. "I knew it! He hasn't been back two minutes and you're jumping back into his bed. Fine. If that's what you want, I won't stand in your way." He sidestepped past her, went over to the wardrobe and, bending over, removed his suitcase from the bottom shelf.

Pamela was suddenly cautious. "James, you don't have to leave."

He continued opening drawers and loading his stuff into the case.

"Do you honestly think I want to spend another night with you, when you've been with him? I can't believe I wrecked my marriage for you."

Pamela sat on the edge of the bed. "I didn't tell you to leave your wife. I was happy the way we were."

"So why didn't you say so?" He stopped packing to glare at her.

"You were the one who kept saying you wanted to tell her about us. I thought I was ready to settle down again. At first it was nice having you around."

He rounded on her. "Nice! You mean like having a dog, a friendly companion?" "No. A companion, yes — but not a dog, James."

James sat on the end of the bed, his back to her. "How could you do this to us? I thought we had something good." He glanced at her briefly before facing the dressing table again.

She could see his reflection in the mirror. His face started to crumble and for one awful moment she thought he was going to cry.

"We did once," she said.

"Then why? And with Shaun — when you know how I feel about you and him."

"I wouldn't have done it with just anyone. You know I still have feelings for Shaun. I can't help that. I had to find out if there was still a chance for us," she said calmly.

"What you really mean is you couldn't control yourself, right? Is that how it was with me? You just lost control and I got sucked in?" His anger was rising again, his moment of weakness gone.

"Listen to me, for God's sake," Pamela said earnestly, almost fiercely. "This isn't all my fault. I gave you a chance to save this relationship." James stood up. "What — by throwing me out?"

"I asked you to move out," she corrected, "to give us some space. I wanted to see if I could miss you again. I used to enjoy waiting for you to come round; it was something to look forward to."

He waved her explanation away. "That's your excuse. You just wanted me out of the way so you could move him in."

"You think I'd move you out to move another man in?" she asked seriously.

"Why not, if you can jump from one man's bed to another?" he shouted at her, a look of disgust in his eyes.

There was a tense silence for a few seconds. James started to pack again. Pamela felt her blood begin to boil. He had no right to make her feel this way. This was her life, and she intended to live it the way she wanted to.

"If that's what you think," she said, "then you might as well go."

"Well, what do you expect? I feel used. All I can think of is you and him... together."

"I felt exactly the same way about your wife."

"Don't change the subject," he snapped. "We're talking about you and Shaun here. I've never even met the guy and I hate him. Does he know about me?"

"Of course."

"Then maybe you two deserve each other." He jabbed the air with a thin finger. "You both couldn't care less about the people involved when you take someone's partner."

Pamela raised her hands in the air to halt his tirade of verbal abuse. "Hold on a minute. Take someone's partner?" she said, incredulous. "You gave yourself to me. I saw you more than she did because you were using the brain between your legs and not the one in your head."

James's hand swung up and he took a stride towards her. Pamela flinched, expecting some kind of violence, but his arm dropped by his side.

"You don't know how close I came to hitting you."

"So why didn't you?" she dared, knowing she would have grabbed the nearest lethal object and killed him with it if he had.

"Don't tempt me," he muttered, walking past her into the hall. He removed his training shoes from the hall cupboard and proceeded to put them on.

Pamela looked at his pitiful figure and mellowed a little. He didn't have anywhere to go. He'd probably end up on a mate's settee. "I know you're feeling hurt, but I never wanted us to finish like this." Her voice was calmer now, though still a little shaky. "I wanted you to realise it wasn't working out."

"Maybe you should have thought of that before..." He paused, sucking air between his teeth, his face a picture of restraint.

"Before what, James? You might as well say it — you can't hurt me any more than you already have done."

"Before freeing up yourself for another man." He ignored the look of horror on her face and grabbed his jacket from the cupboard, slinging it over his arm. Without looking back, he opened the front door. "I'll be back tomorrow to pick up the rest of my stuff. Then you can have your key back."

He left, slamming the door as hard as he could.

Pamela jumped. She was so angry she felt like breaking something.

After all she had done for this guy, he had turned 'round and insulted her. As far as she was concerned, it was good riddance to a dull ride. She had already made up her mind that she was never going to put herself in that position again. From now on it would be me, myself and I.

JAMES
I can't believe she did that to me — to us. I know I'm not the most passionate of lovers, but I make up for it in other ways.

I feel used and betrayed. Pamela took my heart and ground it into the dirt with stiletto heels. I don't think she even realises how much it hurts. As far as she is concerned she can do as she likes, by whatever means necessary. And yet, even after the way she treated me, I still can't bring myself to hate her.

Maybe I was too hasty in leaving. When I left Pamela's I jumped on a bus and headed straight for Brixton, to my brother Phil's place. I told him I had had enough of living with someone. I needed to play the field for a while. I told him I had given Pamela the push. Phil slapped me on the back and said he was glad I had come to my senses, he was beginning to think I was a Boops. If only he knew the truth.

I wonder if Darlene will take me back? After all, it was only my first affair. There was bound to be a few hiccups in the first years of marriage. Besides, I still own the house. I'll make a trip up to Stockwell to see her.

I miss Pamela so badly. I've already phoned her three times today, but she hung up on me.

THE CONFERENCE HAD BEEN ARRANGED FOR MARION'S presentation to the members of the features team and six magazine editors. Marion had been working for a month on the outline for the articles. Joan hadn't seen the finished draft yet, and she was just as nervous as her friend, who was being extremely secretive. Apparently there was a new man in her life, but as yet she was keeping him under wraps.

There was a tentative knock on the conference door, and Joan's secretary Jayne entered, followed by Marion. Joan crossed the room to greet Marion as Jayne left them alone. "How d'you feel?" she asked.

Marion forced a nervous smile. "How do I look?"

Joan looked her up and down. "Skinny, but you'll do," she laughed. "No, seriously, you'll be fine. Just think confidence. You certainly look the part."

Marion did indeed look businesslike. She wore a dark red and white vertically striped blouse under a red skirt suit. The brooch on her lapel was eye-catching without being dazzling, and her hair was tied back neatly with a maroon scrunchy.

Jayne appeared again with two steaming cups of coffee. The two friends sat opposite each other at the conference table. Marion had brought an A3 portfolio with her, which she opened between them. "Did you get the photos of the guys developed?" she asked. For the past two weeks they had been scouting for volunteers. It seemed that men were only too glad to have their views heard. It had been easy to get them to pose for pictures too.

"Of course," she replied. "The slides are all set up and ready to go."

They continued to look over Marion's plan until the executives started to arrive. They all looked so formal and efficient that Marion's earlier nervousness rose again. But there was no going back now. Adrenalin was pumping fast around her body as Joan got up to introduce her. The room hushed. "Ladies and Gentlemen, Marion Stewart on black men." Joan met Marion's eyes and gave her a smile of confidence as she rose on shaky legs. They shook hands before changing places. Marion cleared her throat. "Thank you, and good morning." She nervously smoothed her skirt down over her narrow hips. Removing the film of moisture from her palms, she took a deep breath and stood up straight. "As you know, I have been commissioned to write a series of articles on black men." She turned to the flipchart behind her. On the board were the topics' titles in the order they were to be published. "The mysterious black man," she said in eerie voice. "What makes them tick? I see we have a few sisters in the room and only one black brother." She looked directly at the man sitting at the back of the room. He was a well-dressed fortysomething, and he shuffled irritably in his seat. "Don't worry, I won't embarrass you." She gave him a friendly smile before turning back to the rest of her audience. "Wouldn't we all like to know what was going on inside the heads of our partners? When they say one thing, do they really mean another? How many of us read between the lines, or even insert lines ourselves to fill in for the unspoken words? And how many of us get it wrong?" She smiled again. There were enthusiastic nods and a few coughs from the men in the room. "Well, hopefully, after reading my articles you'll never have to ask these questions again. You'll know."

Her audience were now all leaning forward with interest. Including Joan, who seemed entranced by Marion's transformation. Joan glanced around and took in the same look on the faces around her.

Marion continued: "We have selected twelve men from our

community to tell it like it is. Jayne, the slide, please…"

Jayne, who was sitting at the back of the room, turned off the lights before switching the projector on. One by one images of the twelve black men were flashed on the screen, accompanied by a short verbal commentary on each one.

"Every one of these men has volunteered to give us his honest, unbiased views on sex, money, love, ambition, his family, and the future." Marion noticed everyone was busy scribbling on their notepads. She swallowed. "The age groups range from eighteen to thirty-five years. The majority are in the twenty-one- to thirty-five-year bracket. This was intentional: most of the black magazines target this group also, for advertising purposes."

The last slide was now showing, containing all twelve men. "These are the representatives of the black male community in London. You have in front of you an outline of all the topics. Now I'll take you through each one, detailing exactly what we are looking for from the men."

Marion was very thorough in her breakdown of each article. Basically, each man was to be given a set of questions and a tape each month on which to record their thoughts and opinions. The tapes would be sent back to the office and Marion would use the best selection in her articles.

When Marion finally finished, Joan led the applause. "Brilliant, Maz! You were great," she congratulated.

Marion beamed. She felt good.

"Ready for some questions?"

"Yeah," Marion said confidently.

The questions focused mainly on the method of collecting data, how honest it would be, and how much would actually be expected to go into print. Marion answered them all without hesitation. She had thought it all through thoroughly.

The assembled executives were each given a draft of the first article so they could see the points of interest for themselves. As they filed out of the conference room they all shook Marion's hands. Then Marion and Joan left to celebrate over a cappuccino and chocolate gateau at the local deli.

The phone was ringing as Joan hurriedly turned the key in the front door. Leaving it open, she dashed to pick it up. Shereen came in behind her and shoved the door closed.

"Hello?" Joan answered breathlessly.

"Jo? It's me." Her sister's voice was almost unrecognisable. She sounded like she had a mouthful of marbles.

"Donna? You sound terrible?" She hadn't heard from her sister in three months?

"Jo, I'm in the hospital..." came the reply.

Joan's head suddenly became light and she sat down hard on the edge of the sofa. "What? What's wrong? What happened?" she asked in quick succession.

Donna's breathing was laboured. "I want you to come, Jo. I'll tell you when you get here. They're taking me up to X-ray soon, but I'll leave a message at reception for you. Please come soon." She sniffed, and then breathed deeply into the phone.

X-ray! That meant she had broken bones! Oh my God. "Where are you, Don?"

"King's College."

"Okay. I'll be about half an hour, Sis. Hold tight." She hung up.

The pictures that raced through Joan's mind were not pleasant — all she could think of was that Donna must have been in some kind of accident. She hesitated by the phone, wondering if she should call their mother, then decided that Grace couldn't do anything from where she was. She didn't want to take Shereen to the hospital. She grabbed her handbag and called Shereen back from upstairs. "Shereen? You're going to stay with Natalie for a while, okay?" Joan dropped her daughter off at their neighbours' house and drove to the hospital.

The man behind the reception desk stood up slowly as Joan approached. Jowly and red-faced, he held her with dull, yellow, glassy eyes, peering out from a field of flesh. "Can I help you, miss?"

"I'm looking for Donna Marcus, my sister. She told me she was in here."

The man tapped out a few keys on his keyboard and squinted at the screen. "Down the corridor, to your right, and through the double doors, love. Cubicle six." He pointed with a fat finger.

Joan absolutely hated being called "love", but she ignored it and followed the man's directions. She stepped through the plastic swing doors and looked along the curtained cubicles. Number six was on her left. She wandered over and gingerly pushed the curtain aside. Donna lay on her back on a cot. Her eyes were closed. She held a bandaged arm across her chest and her breathing was deep and rasping. Her cheeks were bruised black and purple, and there was a nasty gash on her forehead.

Joan brushed her cheek lightly with her fingertips. Her eyes flickered open. They were still vague as she focused on her sister. "Jo?"

"Hi, babes. What happened to you?" she enquired softly.

"John…" Donna's throat clicked as she tried to swallow. She lifted her eyes to the glass of water on the bedside trolley.

Joan brought the glass to Donna's lips and let her sip until she raised her good arm to stop her. "He's not here?" Joan asked.

Donna tried to shake her head and winced. "He came in drunk this evening," she said through swollen lips. "He jus' started hitting me…" She sucked back saliva that was trickling from the corner of her mouth. Joan's eyes opened wide in horror. "John beat you up?" she uttered hesitantly, hoping she had heard wrong. A flare of anger ignited in her head.

"I swear, Jo. I didn't do anything to upset him," Donna sobbed.

Joan leant over and put an arm around her shoulder, mindful of her bandaged arm. "Men don't think they need an excuse," she said between clenched teeth. "Where is he now?"

"I dunno. He ran out when I blacked out. I tried to fight back but it only made him worse."

Joan felt tears come to her eyes. She tried to hold them back. "Have you told the police, Don?" Her face became authoritative.

Donna closed her eyes and took a sharp intake of breath. "No," she whispered.

"Why the hell not? Don't tell me you're letting him get away with this." Joan's voice had risen to a yell before she remembered where she was and brought herself under control.

Donna sniffed pitifully. "I can't, he's my husband. For better or worse, remember?"

Joan glared at her sister as if she'd gone completely mad. "You've got to be joking! Well if you won't, then I will." She made as if to get up and leave. Donna's good arm shot up and grabbed her jacket. "Please, Jo. I can't leave him. He's not always like this," she cried. She was pitiful. Joan kissed her teeth and gave her sister a look of contempt. She had read about women who stayed with abusive husbands, but she'd never thought her sister would be one of them. She had never thought of the women in her family as weak, now here was her sister telling her she can't leave a man who would beat his wife up. How could she still think of that bastard as her husband? She sat back on the edge of the bed. "You're going back to him, then?" Donna continued to sob.

"Why on earth did you call me? You knew how I'd react. You'd have been better off calling Mum."

"Mum would have made me…" she sniffed, "come home."

"Wouldn't you be better off?"

"I married him, Jo."

"That doesn't mean you have to live a life of misery. I mean, look at you." Joan's eyes scanned Donna's injuries. They had cleaned her up pretty good, no doubt; she must have looked as though she'd been in a car accident. "How did you get the gash on the head?"

"I fell over the coffee table."

"God, Donna!" Joan sprang up as if pricked by a needle. "I can't take this. You're not going back there. You're going to come home with me, and then we're going to the police and we're getting him slung out."

"Don't, please, Jo."

"I don't want your waterworks. I'm doing what's best for you," Joan told her. Her patience was wearing thin. "Mum and I'll take care of you. You can work, y'know. Just 'cause he didn't want you to, it doesn't mean you can't."

"Jo?"

"Yes, babes?" Her voice softened.

"I'm scared."

Joan climbed on to the bed and stretched out alongside her sister. She took her in her arms. No words were needed. Donna knew her sister would take care of her.

On Monday afternoon Joan left work early and went round to Donna's flat. She knew John wouldn't be around. He'd probably be running scared. The flat was dead quiet. It didn't look as though anyone had been there since the incident. In the kitchen, a pot he had thrown across the room lay on its side on the floor. Congealed gravy spotted the walls.

Joan left it all and went into the bedroom. She found a holdall and packed Donna's belongings. She threw things from the bathroom into a carrier bag, along with some of Donna's cosmetics from the dressing table.

Joan left the flat in a hurry. She didn't want to hang around to face that madman if he returned. She had already planned to move the sofa-bed into Shereen's bedroom. Donna could stay with her in there. Their mother would have to be told, of course. She would suspect something anyway, as soon as she knew Donna was staying with Joan. Grace was the least of their problems, however.

John would come looking for her eventually. Hopefully, before that happened, Joan could persuade Donna to have him arrested.

Joan arrived later that afternoon at the hospital to find Donna a lot more cheerful. She was sitting up in bed chatting to a young black nurse.

"Hi, Sis," Donna smiled through her bruised lips.

Joan looked at her. "You've cheered up. What's happened?"

The nurse turned to Joan. She was pretty, with soft, wavy hair and the kind of eyebrows Joan had always envied, naturally arched. "Your sister is a very brave woman. You should be proud of her." She turned to smile at Donna, and patted her on the hand before leaving the two of them together.

"Well? You gonna tell me what happened?"

Donna grinned shyly. "He turned up here, Jo."

Joan was ready to explode. "He what?"

"It's alright," Donna calmed her. "I told the staff what happened and that I wanted to report it to the police. They called the police for me."

"You mean he's been arrested?"

"Yes. I gave the police a statement."

"Oh, Don. I'm so proud of you." Joan got up and hugged her sister. Relief flooded through her and she squeezed Donna a little too hard.

"Joan! Mind, nuh? I'm still bruised all over."

Joan eased off. "Sorry, hon. So when can you come home?"

"I can go as soon as I want. No broken bones. I'd dislocated my shoulder, and it's still killing me, but I'll be all right."

"Good. You're coming home now. Shereen will love having you there."

The two women grinned at each other, and love flowed between them.

"SOMEONE TURN THAT MUSIC UP," CHANTELLED YELLED FROM the kitchen, her curly extensions bobbing with her head to the beat of Tag Team's "Whoomp There It Is". Chantelle was a friend of Pamela's. Her favourite place at a party was always the kitchen, she was proud of telling people, because that's where the food and drink are. As no one else wanted the job of serving people tonight, Joan was only too glad to let her do it. Chantelle was sixteen stone and five foot seven — a woman not to be trifled with. Dressed in a red lace and satin ragamuffin outfit, she gave a massive first impression that always got a second look. Her bubbly personality and perpetually smiling face kept everyone in good spirits.

Behind her, Joan had just finished blending the vegetables for the coleslaw. She tipped them into a bowl and poured on an entire jar of mayonnaise. As she stirred the ingredients together, she rocked and bumped to the music, laughing at Chantelle's antics as she bounced around the kitchen.

Their "drink-up" had turned into a full-blown party. Pamela had gone mad with the invitations. It was only ten o'clock, and so far they had about thirty guests here, only six of them women. They were expecting about a hundred, and Joan hoped more women would turn up. They only seemed to know men, but they knew from experience that men wouldn't hang around for long if women didn't turn up. Marion hadn't arrived yet. She had spent the whole day with her new mystery man, so only God knew when they would drag themselves out of the flat. Pamela and Donna were upstairs getting changed. Joan hadn't changed yet, as she had been busy preparing the food. She finished the coleslaw, covered the container, and put it on the only shelf

in the fridge that wasn't fully occupied with drinks. Then she checked on the curry goat Pamela had prepared, which was bubbling away on the hob.

"Chantelle," she shouted over the music, "turn that off in half an hour, alright?"

"Yes, sista." Chantelle raised her hand. Joan laughed and, moving the table that blocked the doorway, she passed through into the hallway. She nodded or raised a hand to people she knew as she made her way upstairs, taking the stairs two at a time.

She knocked on her bedroom door. "You decent, Pam?" she called.

"Yeah, come in."

Pam stood in front of the full-length mirror on the wardrobe door. The dress she wore was red leather, the sides held together by laces. It just about covered her bottom. Her hair, which had taken an hour and a half to do, was a mass of small tonged ringlets with gold spray on their ends. Joan raised an eyebrow at her. "Who you planning to give a heart attack tonight?"

"Do you like it?" Pamela grinned, doing a spin.

"It doesn't matter what I think, I'm not a man. But if I was, I'd have no choice. Ain't you cold?"

Pamela laughed, turning to get a back view of her dress in the mirror. "Where's Donna?"

"In the bathroom."

Joan looked at her own short black dress hanging on the wardrobe door as she undressed. The dress had a bra-shaped top, and was covered in beads and sequins. She had thought it quite revealing before she saw Pamela's dress, now she would feel overdressed. "What's Marion wearing tonight?" Pamela asked. She bent over to get her shoes out of the carrier bag she'd wrapped them in.

"Sequined shorts and a bra top. She reckons it'll be the last time she'll be able to fit into them. She's still as skinny as a stick, but she says she feels bigger already." Joan, now undressed to her bra and knickers, walked over to the dressing table. "Has she told you who this man is yet?"

"No. But we'll find out tonight. I wonder if he knows she's pregnant." Pamela buckled her shoes and stood up straight, testing the feel of them. "I don't want children. I haven't got time for a kid." She crossed to the dressing table and, removing a Kleenex from its cube box, blotted her lipstick. "And what's she gonna do about her writing when the kid drops?"

"She'll manage. She's come a long way since dropping Gerard." Joan placed her hands on her hips and watched Pamela pouting in the mirror. "Will you stop admiring yourself and go down to greet our guests, dear? Chantelle can't run this thing on her own — and besides, they're mostly your friends."

"All right." Pam ran her tongue over her teeth to remove a smear of lipstick before striking a pose in front of Joan. "How do I look?"

"Like shit, but you'll do," Joan said in a matter-of-fact voice.

"Shut up. Jealousy is a sin, you know that."

Joan grabbed a hairbrush off the bed. "Go, or I'll mash up your hair with this."

"I'm gone, I'm gone," Pamela screamed, ducking out of the door. The music got louder as the door opened, then muted again as it swung shut. Joan stood back from the mirror and studied her body. Not bad, she thought. Never be a size twelve again, though. Having a baby had made her a permanent fourteen. Chantelle had styled her hair for her. It was tonged then brushed into a page-boy style. All she had to do now was shower and make up, then slip her dress on. Donna emerged from the bathroom, freshly scented with a towel wrapped around her slim body.

"About time, too. How long have you been in there?" Joan joked.

"I was relaxing," Donna said defensively. "Boy, can't have a moment's peace in this house." She stomped over to the dressing table.

Joan frowned. She had noticed a distinct change in Donna's attitude. All day she had been distracted, and her mood was getting progressively lower. She moved to her sister's side. "What's up, Don?"

"Nothing," Donna replied, a trifle sharply.

"Don't give me that." Joan caught her eyes in the mirror. "Has John been in touch?"

Donna looked back, surprised. "How did you know?"

"It's the only thing that gets you down."

Donna turned and shuffled over to the bed. She sat down on its edge. "He finally got bail," she said fretfully. "He called here. He knows where I am."

"Mek him come," Joan retorted. "He can't take on both of us, and if he tries, he's gonna be banged up for so long he'll have plenty of time to regret it." She sat next to Donna on the bed, sensing there was still something else her sister wanted to say. "Why didn't you say something before?"

"I didn't wanna spoil your party." Donna sighed. The bass beat of the music coming from downstairs could be felt through the floor. "He wants me home."

"No!" Joan shook her head vehemently. "It's not your home any more." Donna said nothing, but avoided her sister's gaze.

"What the hell are you thinking, girl?"

Donna looked Joan in the eye defiantly. "I married him. I should give it a try, shouldn't I?" She spoke with a faltering passion, doubting her own words.

Joan stood up and pulled Donna up to face her. "Don't talk no stupidness in front of me! You don't need him, all right? When I think of how you looked a week ago, in that hospital… It makes me sick that I didn't kill him myself." Tears of frustration began to well up in Donna's eyes.

"Look, don't cry." Joan's voice softened. What was she going to do with this kid? She realised her sister needed support, but she also needed some good solid professional advice. Joan didn't feel equipped to give her that.

"We are going to party tonight, right? Forget John. I'll go and see a solicitor with you next week, and we'll get a restraining order or something. I won't let him touch you."

Donna wiped away her tears. "Sorry, Jo."

"Come on, wipe your face. I'm gonna shower and then we'll go downstairs and rave."

Donna forced a smile on her face and let her sister lead her to the bathroom.

Joan sometimes wished she could lock Donna away for her own good. But it wouldn't solve anything. She would always be the way she was. No, Joan's job was to bring her daughter up right, to instil a pride in her that would allow her to live her life to the full, not to be dependent on her mother or a man to give her what she deserved.

There were a few good-looking men downstairs. If Joan had been in the swing of things she would be making her move right now, but she wasn't in the mood — for men or a party.

Marion would have her new man. Pamela would have Shaun, or whoever else was handy... This was a bad idea, Joan suddenly thought. It was going to be one long night. She decided she'd get totally out of it, on alcohol and the good weed.

Marion's hand rested on Paul's leg as he drove towards Plumstead and Joan's house. She was feeling so good. Happiness flowed in her veins like wine. Before they had left her flat Paul had made love to her in a way that Gerard never had. His sweet kisses had landed all over her body. He'd even kissed her fingernails, which had made her laugh. His excuse was that he wanted to taste every part of her. He had kissed her feet, sucked her toes, and eaten his way up her body. He hadn't entered her once, and yet she felt as though she had gone to heaven and back. He made her feel confident, beautiful and loved. God, was she loved! It didn't stop.

She couldn't help comparing him to Gerard. She compared everything, from the way they dressed to the way they made love. Gerard could do with tips from Paul on how a real man treats his woman.

Marion looked across at him now, and feeling her gaze on him he turned and smiled at her. His hand touched hers and he squeezed her fingers gently. She felt her heart rise in her chest.

The only thing that bothered her was that, when they were apart, she didn't miss him. She still missed Gerard. Though she wanted to forget him, he was always in the back of her mind. The fact that she was carrying his child meant that he would forever be a part of her life, whether she liked it or not.

She breathed in deeply, inhaling the smell of Paul's aftershave. Calvin Klein. The sweetness of the cologne mixed with his fresh-from-the-shower scent made her want to snuggle up close to him.

She thought back to last night, when he had carried her to the bedroom. She had felt so happy and cherished in his company, it was like the rest of the world didn't exist. They'd talked, and he'd listened to her. He supported her in all she wanted to do. In a couple of weeks, she thought, she would be able to tell him her secret and she would know just how much he cared.

The car pulled up four doors away from Joan's house. Paul switched off the engine and got out, taking the keys out of the ignition. Marion got out and stood by his side, watching him with admiration as he opened the boot and leant inside for the case of lagers he had bought earlier. He was dressed casually in a red sweater and jeans. His hard body was like a mould underneath the material.

"Don't go straining yourself now," she joked.

"As if!" His eyes smiled back at her. Inside, the party was hotting up. As Marion and Paul were let in, Joan spotted them and came rushing over to hug Marion.

"Girl! I thought you weren't coming." There was a glint in her eyes as she looked over at Paul. She asked Marion with her eyes if this was him.

Marion nodded, grinning back.

"Paul — how you doing, man?" Joan slapped his arm playfully.

"Fine thanks. You?"

"Yeah, good." She turned back to Marion. "This man keeping you too busy. Don't let him take you away from us, y'know."

"It's her fault we're late," Paul defended himself. "The girl tried on everything she had and then went back to the same thing she had on to start with."

Joan laughed and waved Pamela over. Pam was in the arms of yet another tall, handsome man. She tiptoed to shout something in his ear, he released his grip around her waist, and she sauntered over, her tight dress not hindering her lithe movement in the least. She grabbed Marion's small waist in both hands. "You're still so skinny!" she exclaimed loudly.

Marion stiffened. Taking hold of Pamela's hands, she pushed them away somewhat roughly. "Not as skinny as you. Where's my drink?"

Pamela hadn't got the hint. "I suppose you'll be off the booze now."

Marion nearly stopped breathing. Paul, still standing by her side, seemed none the wiser. She slipped her arm through Pamela's and headed off towards the bar. Pamela, bemused, was forced to strut alongside.

As soon as they were out of earshot, Marion hissed at Pamela: "Paul doesn't know about the baby."

Pamela looked at her as if she were crazy. "So when are you planning on telling him?"

They reached the bar and Chantelle leaned over to give Marion a hug. "How you doing, Marion?"

Pamela was staring at Marion, one hand on her hip.

"Fine, Chan. You look well," Marion replied, aware of Pamela's piercing gaze.

"Meaning I look fat." Chantelle made a face as if to say "Don't try to fool me".

"Naw, Chan. Just well fed." Marion laughed and ducked as Chantelle's huge hand came flying towards her. "I think you should sack your bar staff, Pamela. Too violent."

Chantelle laughed. "What you having?" "Babycham, please, Chan," Marion replied.

"Yeah, me too," Pamela said, then changed her mind. "No — give me a brandy an' Coke instead." She turned back to Marion. "Well?"

"I'm not telling him until it's possible it could be his," she whispered.

Paul had come up behind them and they stepped apart to allow him to pass the crate of lagers to Chantelle.

Marion smiled at him and he touched her arm lightly before leaving them again. Pamela watched him go, waiting until he was far enough away and distracted by Joan.

"You're gonna con him?" Pamela said with horror.

"Don't start, Pam. I feel bad enough as it is," Marion said despondently.

"How could you do that to him?"

"Please, Pam, just support me on this. I can't lose Paul too," she pleaded, her eyes searching her friend's.

Pamela held up her hands in a submissive gesture. "Leave me out of this one. If he finds out — which he will when the baby is born looking like Gerard — he's going to hate you."

By two o'clock the party was in full swing. There was a queue at the bar and a queue for the toilet. The three guys who were running the sounds had put a tape in and were busy checking girls around the room. No one seemed to mind: the drinks were flowing and everybody was dancing to whatever music came on. Pamela was drunk. Out in the middle of the living room she and her mate Christine were wining around each other to a soca track, their audience cheering them on. A couple of equally drunk men joined in, whining in time to their movements and the music.

Joan was amazed at how Pamela managed to dance in that dress. She sat on the living room window-sill, smoking her fourth spliff. She had got fed up of seeing Marion and Paul smooching. They seemed to be joined together at the hip.

"Hiya, Joan!" A woman's voice brought her out of her thoughts. She looked up and squinted through the haze of smoke at the familiar face.

"It's me — Sharna," the girl obliged.

"Oh God, Sharna!" Joan exclaimed with an air of pleasant surprise. She stood up and embraced her friend.

She had met Sharna at a pre-carnival party the year before, they had met again at the carnival, and had stayed in touch with the occasional phone call ever since. She had posted her an invitation to the party, but hadn't expected her to come.

"Good to see you," Sharna said, hugging her back. "I thought you'd forgotten me." Sharna had a husky voice which made her sound a lot older than her twenty-three years.

"You looking good." Joan eyed the red catsuit Sharna was sheathed in. It fit her slim figure like a second skin. Sharna took in Joan's sequined outfit with a glance. "Thank you. Love the dress." "Just a little something I chucked on," Joan laughed. In truth the dress had cost her ninety pounds — it was a treat she felt she deserved. "Who did you come with?"

"Those girls over by the door." Sharna pointed. "So — you all right, though?"

"Getting by, y'know how it is." Joan shrugged and screwed up her face in a fed-up way.

Sharna nodded distractedly. "Some nice looking guys here." She surveyed the room. "Looks like the girls can have their pick tonight."

"Most of them are Pamela's ex's." Joan pointed out Pamela, who was laughing hysterically with a group in the opposite corner.

Sharna twisted round to look. "She looks like fun. Where's the rest of her dress?" she asked sarcastically.

"Leave her. She always dresses like that. Likes to flaunt what she's got."

"Yeah? Well I better find myself a man before they start queuing up for some a' dat." She pushed a loose strand of hair out of her eyes.

"You go, girl. See you later." Joan smiled encouragingly.

Sharna danced back into the partying crowd and rejoined her friends. Joan remembered at the carnival Sharna had gone wild, wining up with nearly every good-looking man available. Every time Joan had turned around she'd been with someone else. She knew how to have a good time. If Joan was in the mood now she would have joined her. Even Donna was out there enjoying herself.

She walked back through the house, pushing and squeezing past hot bodies to the makeshift bar at the entrance to the kitchen. On the way she was stopped several times by friends and acquaintances who wanted to say hello.

Chantelle stood with her back to the door, resting her ample bottom against the table cum bar. She had company. Rebecca, wearing a long, black, tight-fitting dress, waved to her as she got closer.

Chantelle rose heftily to her feet and turned with a plate piled high with curry goat, rice and coleslaw. "Hi, Joan. What's up, babe?" She swiped at her lips with the back of her hand and placed her meal on the table.

"I'm bored, Chan," Joan sighed, and took a puff of her roach before dropping it to the floor.

"How can you be bored when there's a party going on? 'Nuff man out deh, y'know." Chantelle planted her fists on her large hips.

Joan leaned wearily against the door frame. "Yeah, well, I'm not interested."

Rebecca stepped forward. "I love your house, Joan. Nice and big," she smiled. She had a wide, friendly smile, the kind that made her look as though she was getting ready to laugh.

"Thanks. Chan, d'you want a break? I'll take over."

"Yes, please. Just put my food in the oven for me." Chantelle was already moving the table from the kitchen doorway and giving Joan access. "Come, Bec, let's go shake a leg."

"See you later," Joan called to Chantelle's retreating back. Rebecca turned and smiled at her.

Chantelle had been a perfect barmaid. The kitchen was reasonably tidy, the sink was piled with plastic cups in case they ran out and had to wash some.

Joan lit a cigarette and poured herself a half cup of brandy. She was feeling very light-headed, but it hadn't succeeded in stopping her from thinking. People spend most of their lives looking for someone to love, she pondered. She thought she had found it with Colin, but was now feeling worse than before. Why did love have to hurt so much? All she wanted to do was to get on with her life, but to do that she had to forget Colin Baker.

Sharna, who had been doing a pretty good job of circulating, took an opportunity to get some background information on a guy she had just danced with. She weaved her way through the ravers, searching for Joan, eventually tracking her down in the kitchen. "Joan. You have got to tell me some more about this guy — he says he knows you," she said, leaning her palms on the table.

"What guy?" Joan asked moodily, not in the least interested.

"Come out here and I'll show ya. He says his name is Marcellis."

Joan remembered the name. He was one of the guys from the carnival.

She also remembered that he had been a good looker with a brain. "No, Shar. I don't feel like it," she protested, holding her cigarettes to her chest like a comforter.

Sharna shoved the table out of the way and reached round for Joan's arm. "What is this — a party or what? You are going to enjoy yourself if it kills me."

"I can't just leave the bar." "Like hell you can't," Sharna said, and pulled Joan from the kitchen, forcing her to rejoin the party.

Joan could hardly see anything, it was so dark. The drink and ganja didn't help. She scanned the hallway through squinted eyes and noticed a tall, big-built, light-skinned guy entering the living room. Her attention perked up — he looked all right. The tall man stepped aside and she saw who he had come with. Colin.

Joan's heart stopped and then quickened. She caught her breath and looked around for Pamela. Sharna still had a hold of her hand and was pulling her forward. Towards Colin.

Joan stopped abruptly and managed to drag her hand away from Sharna's. Sharna turned round and questioned her with her eyes.

"Catch you up. Jus' saw someone I know," Joan yelled over the music and whirled back the way she had come. Marion was coming down the stairs with Paul close behind, and Joan managed to hail her. "I've got to talk to you," she shouted when Marion reached her. Paul hung back, waiting patiently.

"What's up?" Marion asked.

"Colin's here." Joan laced and unlaced nervous fingers.

Marion looked around. "Where?"

"I've just seen him go into the living room. Pam must have invited him."

"Didn't you tell her about...?"

"I couldn't."

"How could he turn up here? I'll tell him to leave." Marion started to walk towards the living room.

Joan grabbed her arm. "You can't do that."

"Joan, this is your house."

"I know. Look, I'll just keep out of his way."

"You sure? I could get Paul to do it," Marion offered.

"Just leave it. You go back to Paul before he starts to miss you." Marion questioned Joan with her eyes before squeezing her arm reassuringly and returning to Paul.

She lit another cigarette and decided to go upstairs for awhile. She passed Marion and Paul and made her way to the staircase, looking towards the living room door in case Colin came out and saw her. She was so busy looking the wrong way that she walked right into him.

She looked up, straight into his eyes, immediately became flustered and tried to push past him to get to the stairs, but he gently grabbed her arm, not budging from her path.

"Joan…" Colin began.

"Leave me alone, Colin," she hissed.

He kept hold of her arm. "I've got something to say to you." His jaw was determined and his eyes sincere.

"What? That you need a bit on the side?" she replied viciously.

"Come outside with me?" he asked.

"Hell, no!" She stared down at his hand. "Let go of my fucking arm." Her voice was rasping with barely controlled emotion.

Colin let go of her, and she immediately turned to walk back the way she had come. He stepped in front of her.

"Get out of my way before I dig this cigarette in your eye," she threatened, raising the cigarette to head height.

"Joan, come on, man." He spread his arms amiably. "Five minutes. I won't touch you. After that you can just walk away." He dared to look at her with those damned gorgeous eyes.

Joan turned and stomped towards the front door. It was open and she stepped out into the cold early-morning air. The chill hit her to the bone but she marched on anyway. She could hear Colin's footsteps right behind her and she speeded up, trying to put as much distance between them as possible.

She risked looking back at him. He beamed at her confidently, with more bottle than Wray & Nephew.

Colin took his jacket off and draped it over her shoulders. Joan shot him a look of scorn, but pulled the jacket around her cold body none the less. Colin, feeling even more confident, walked by her side with his hands thrust into his trouser pockets. Joan continued to ignore him.

"Can I talk to you?" Colin asked affably.

She didn't reply.

"I take that as a yes," he said sarcastically. He breathed out deeply, trying to figure out where to begin. "Joan, I'm trying to apologise here. I was totally in the wrong. The way I told you…" He seemed to be trying hard to find the right words. "Lois was no good, she tried to trap me," he explained, his voice tight in his throat.

Lois! What kind of a name is that, Joan thought, images of Lois Lane in Superman's arms springing to mind. She wanted to laugh in his face. So his woman had kicked him out, had she? Colin continued to speak. "She told me she wasn't pregnant when we were having an argument. She tried to fool me. I tell you, you women are the best bloody liars alive."

Joan stung him with another one of her looks.

"We're finished," he pointed out, just in case she hadn't caught his gist. There was still no reaction.

"I'm single again, Joan. Remember what you were saying that night, about changing the way things were?"

She glanced up at his brown eyes. He smiled at her and she turned away fast enough to give herself whiplash. Colin licked his dry lips and got out some more words. "We can do that now. I still love you, y'know."

Joan broke her silence. "What about Lois? Did you love her too?" she spat.

"I thought I could, but you were always on my mind."

Joan stopped and sat on a garden wall. They had reached the bottom of the road. She hated to admit it, but she had missed him. And now here he stood facing her, head bowed, wanting her forgiveness. Many nights she had lain awake dreaming of this moment: Colin crawling back on his hands and knees. Just as she had done two months ago. Making a fool of herself.

She took a step towards him. "What's wrong with us, Colin?"

He looked down at her, meeting her slanted eyes. "What d'you mean?"

Joan lifted her arms and his jacket fell to the ground as she placed them on his shoulders. Colin was caught unawares by the way her anger and hostility had suddenly vanished.

"I love you, Colin. We love each other, don't we?" She waited for his acknowledgement.

"Course." His lips turned up in a sexy grin. Joan pressed closer and felt his rising erection hard against her stomach. "Then why do we keep pushing each other away? All I want is you." She seductively stroked the back of his neck.

He licked his lips and leaned down to kiss her. She felt his breath against her mouth and could almost taste the kiss. "Take me, Colin. I wanna be yours again."

He wrapped his arms around her waist. Heart racing, a strange excitement churned within her. As she gripped Colin's shoulders she swiftly brought her knee up hard into his groin, feeling it connect with his erect penis and testicles. As he hollered in pain, crumpling as though someone had just removed his spine, she jumped back out of reach.

His eyes popped wide with pain and disbelief. Both hands gripped his crotch.

"Don't take me for a half-wit, Colin Baker! Joan Ross ain't no fool. Stay the hell away from me and Shereen. I only wish I'd had something sharper to hand, then your worries about becoming an accidental father would be over." She glared down at him as his watery eyes came to rest on her. His teeth were clenched and he seemed to be having trouble breathing.

She smiled a wicked grin. "Dog!" she yelled, then she turned on her heel and marched back up the road towards her house.

MARION WENT INTO THE KITCHEN, WHERE PAMELA WAS HELPING herself to a plateful of curry goat and rice. Pam's curls had dropped, and where her make-up had worn off she had a sheen to her skin. Chantelle was asleep on a kitchen stool, her head resting on the kitchen counter.

Marion realised she hadn't seen Shaun all night. Pamela must have invited him; in fact she remembered Pamela going on about how no one would see her all night 'cause she would be busy. "What happened to Shaun? I thought he was coming." Marion poured herself a glass of orange juice.

"You asking me? I don't care what happened to him, I'm not his keeper."

Chantelle started to snore. Both girls looked at each other and burst out laughing.

"Boy, she's like a baby, sleep anywhere," Pamela said, glancing at her friend.

Marion smiled. She left Pamela in the kitchen and walked up the hallway. The house was now completely empty. All the remaining guests were outside, chatting on the deserted streets. The moon was dropping and the sun was beginning to lighten the sky. She could see Paul outside the open front door, deep in conversation with a guy she didn't know. She smiled as he looked her way, and he raised a hand and carried on talking. She left him to it and went into the living room to start clearing up.

Plastic cups, cans and bottles littered the floor and every surface. The air was still grey with cigarette smoke. Marion sighed and went back to the kitchen to arm herself with a dustpan and brush and a black rubbish bag. She was on her way back when Joan walked in through the front door. She was grinning from ear to ear.

The girls sat around the kitchen table, a glass of fruit juice in front of each of them. Marion had cleared the kitchen of debris while Joan had relayed what had happened between herself and Colin. They were all physically exhausted, but found that they had so much to talk about they weren't ready for bed. Paul had taken Chantelle home and hadn't arrived back yet. The door was left on the latch for his return.

Pamela leaned back on her chair carelessly. "You know what I fancy right now?" Without waiting for an answer she told them. "A man eating my body from head to toe." She closed her eyes, conjuring up the image.

"So where is your man?" Joan asked.

"Shaun? He's not my man. He's my part-time lover. I've finished with relationships. Did you see that guy I was chatting to?"

"Which one?"

"The dark guy with the moustache. His body was hard. You know, if this was my house I'd have been upstairs with that one."

"You old tart," Marion joked.

"Whatever," Pamela waved her hands matter-of-factly. "I just tell it like it is. Why lie?" She looked pointedly at Marion. "At least my men know what I want them for."

Marion winced. She knew what Pamela was referring to. But she didn't retaliate. Although she didn't feel good about what she was doing, she also knew she didn't have to explain herself to anyone.

Joan diverted the conversation. "I've got some strawberry cheesecake in the fridge. Anyone fancy some?"

"Yes, please!" Marion answered without hesitation. She hadn't eaten throughout the entire party, and dinner the previous evening had been beans on toast.

"Well, I shouldn't really — I'm watching my figure," Pamela joked. "But go on then."

"Girl, you've got plenty of men who'll do that for you," Joan said. She took the cheesecake from the fridge and placed it on the counter. Marion stood up and got some dishes out of the cupboard. "So, Pamela, looks as though you're the only one who's got to sort out your love life," she said.

"Does it?" Pamela looked up curiously, still tilting on her chair, her hands clinging to the edge of the table.

"Well, Paul and I are having a baby, and Joan's finally got rid of Colin. But you, you don't get rid of one before you start with another."

"And I'm staying that way. I can find more exciting things to do than changing nappies or cleaning up after a man," she returned, making a face.

Joan carefully laid a slice of cake on to a plate. "It's not as bad as you make out, Pam."

"Isn't it? I've been there. I mean, you start out all lovey-dovey, and as soon as the guy knows he's got you where he wants you he's playing the field again. I love men, but I couldn't limit myself to one for the rest of my life — and I wouldn't trust a man to do that for me." Marion slid Pamela's plate across the table to her. "Thanks, Maz." Pam picked up a dessert spoon.

Joan had been letting what Pamela had said sink in. "Yeah, but, I've had all that, Pam. I'm twenty-seven now, and I know I'm ready to settle down again. I want to meet a man I can love and trust, a man who makes me feel good about myself. I want to be important to somebody." She looked to Marion to support her.

"You're right, Joan. Love is hard to find. The way I see it, when you find it, hold on to it."

"I'm not saying you shouldn't. I'm just saying I don't think I could," Pamela said through a mouthful of strawberry cheesecake. "The man would have to satisfy my every need. I've not found a man who could do that yet." She took another mouthful and closed her eyes in ecstasy.

"Besides, I've got Shereen to think of," Joan said. "I can't keep parading all these different men in front of her. What kind of example is that to set for my daughter?"

For a full minute the only sounds were the scraping of cutlery on plates. Joan was digesting the fact that she had finally finished with Colin. It felt good but, still, there had been a second of panic there, when she had nearly apologised for hurting him. But she was bigger than that. One thing she knew how to do was rise above her emotions. Marion was wondering if Paul would ever propose. Or whether, when he found out about the baby, he would run a mile. She felt she was prepared for all eventualities. Pamela was enjoying her cheesecake and wondering if both her friends had gone off their heads, talking about settling down at their age. They were all still young. Why on earth would they want to end their freedom? But they were her friends, and if that's what they wanted she would be happy for them, when and if it ever happened. She pushed her empty plate away from her and reached for her fruit juice. "By the way, Joan, whatever happened to Charles?"

"Yeah, what did happen to him?" Marion asked.

"I think I frightened him off."

Marion was intrigued. "How?"

"Well, first I tried to seduce him on our first date. Then I told him I was in love with Colin."

"You never!"

"I thought it would be better to have everything out in the open," Joan said.

Marion looked puzzled. "But you and Colin weren't seeing each other then," she said.

"I know, but I still wanted him. I didn't want to hurt Charles." Joan placed her elbows on the table and laced her fingers, making a bridge.

"That's sweet, Joan, but the guy had money!" Trust Pamela to bring it down to material things.

"Money isn't everything. I didn't feel anything for him." Joan shrugged.

Pam giggled. "You mean he didn't make your toes curl?"

"My mum's got this saying: 'New broom sweep good but old broom know de corner dem'. That's me and Colin," Joan said haughtily.

Pamela chuckled. "Yeah, well, my parents had a saying too: 'When old stick bruck, you mus' push new one in deh'."

"You lie. You jus' made that up," Marion accused.

"God's truth," Pamela said with a serious face. Then, as she thought of her parents ever using a sexual innuendo, she burst into laughter, slapping the table with her palm. She shook her head, sending her dropped curls swinging round.

Marion wasn't sure she found it so funny. To her it sounded as though Charles was a romantic. The man was probably falling in love with Joan. Her friends were much too hung up on good sex. Although she didn't see anything wrong with it, she knew all relationships can't be based on it.

They heard the front door open and close. Paul must have just returned.

"And the man had such a safe body. He used to work out three times a week," Joan continued.

"What a waste," Pamela sympathised, shaking her head. "You know what I'd have done?"

"No, what?" Joan asked expectantly.

"Just flung him down and ripped his clothes off. Or ripped my own clothes off, spread my legs and said 'Take me'." Pamela threw open her arms in a submissive pose. Joan and Marion both screamed with laughter. Even Marion couldn't resist Pamela's humour.

"I couldn't," Joan said. "He would have run a mile. He seemed to have the idea that I was a decent, good woman. He was looking for a wife type. Maybe I should introduce him to you, Marion…"

"I've got a man," Marion said proudly.

"Yeah, but does your man have money?" Pamela made them all laugh again. Marion shook her head. Pamela's idea of a good catch was a rich man with a big dick.

Pamela squirted dairy cream on to her plate and stuck her finger into it. "What does this remind you of?" She held her hand in the air, letting the cream run down her finger.

"A premature ejaculator." Joan cracked up. Pamela screamed, "James!" She held her aching sides in mirth.

"Martin!" Joan yelled.

"You two are disgusting," Marion said, turning her nose up.

"All this talk about sex is getting me horny," Pamela said shamelessly. "I'll have to go home and call my remote-control cock." Standing up, she stretched her arms in the air.

"And who is that this month?" Joan asked, beginning to clear the dishes from the table.

"Shaun, of course!"

"After he stood you up tonight?" Marion asked.

Pamela rolled her eyes. "He didn't stand me up. And besides, I only want him for one thing. Whatever else he does is his business," she said brazenly.

"I'd better go as well," Marion said. "I want to do more writing again later. You wanna catch a lift with us, Pam?" she offered.

"Might as well." Pamela pushed her feet back into her shoes. Marion went to tell Paul she was ready. She came back carrying her and Pam's jackets.

"I'll call you during the week." Joan hugged her back. "It was a good party though, wasn't it?" She was beginning to feel lonely already. "Yeah, our best," Pam answered.

"Course, we should have a Christmas one, or New Year's," Marion suggested.

"You'll be sitting down by then," Joan said, reminding her of her condition.

"Naw. Baby's gonna dance too." Marion lowered her voice as Paul came out of the living room into the hallway.

Joan walked them out to the door, where Paul waited.

He kissed Joan's cheek. "See you soon, yeah?"

"Definitely," Joan told him. She watched them walk down the quiet street to the car before going back inside. In the living room she switched off the stereo. There was nothing left to do down here, so she climbed the stairs. She went into the bathroom and ran a shallow bath. She was washed and out in ten minutes, drying herself wearily, her arms suddenly feeling heavy.

She walked out of the bathroom completely naked, put her head around Shereen's bedroom door to check on Donna, then entered her own room. As she turned to get into bed she noticed the shape of someone under the covers, and recognised the back of Colin's head.

"Colin?"

"Mmmm." He rolled over on to his back and opened his eyes. "Thought you were never coming to bed," he said, throwing back the covers to reveal his long, hard body. Joan almost fainted with the rush of blood to her head. Was this guy so thick-skinned that he still didn't get the message?

"W... wha..." she stuttered. Then she took a deep breath. "Where are all your clothes?"

He sat up. "Over the back of the chair." He nodded towards the window.

Joan stormed across the room. She grabbed his clothes with one hand and pushed the already open window wide with the other. She swung her arm back and the clothes went flying through the air to land in her front garden.

Colin sat there, mouth open. "What d'you do that for?"

"What will it take to get through to you, Colin? Get out of my damn bed, my house and my life!" she yelled, her arms flailing wildly with each order. She grabbed her robe from the bottom of the bed and pulled it on. Colin swung his long limbs off the bed and crossed the room to the window. He peered out, looking for his garments.

Joan stood behind him, hands on hips. "You better go after them before some tramp claims them," she said icily.

Her coldness had absolutely no effect on him. He knew her too well. "I ain't going nowhere until I make you see sense." He stepped towards her and she stepped back.

"What do you know about sense? It's clear you haven't got any or else you wouldn't be here."

Colin continued to advance on her, his flaccid penis bouncing with every step. Her foot touched the edge of the bed and she lost her balance and fell backwards.

Before she could get back on her feet, Colin was on top of her.

"Oh, so you're gonna rape me now!" she scowled.

His eyes penetrated hers. He was serious, but not threatening. "I won't have to." He pinned her arms to the bed, knowing it was the only way to keep her still. "You know you want me, Joan. Why don't you just give in to your brain? You're always fighting what you feel."

She could feel him stiffening against her thigh. "What makes you think that?"

"I know you. I know you like you're a part of me. I know you're scared of being hurt again. But you can't keep pushing me away."

She kissed her teeth and twisted her head away from him to face the wall, her lips screwed into a tight pout. What did he know?

"You know I'm not lying. Look at me and tell me I'm lying," he said.

Joan was suddenly beginning to feel tired. Tired of running, tired of fighting. Tired because it was seven in the morning and she hadn't slept yet. Her body relaxed underneath him. "You gonna trap me like this all day?" she asked, still avoiding his eyes.

"Just promise me one thing."

"I'm not promising you anything."

"Then we stay like this." He grinned, pressing himself closer.

Joan could feel her body betraying her, becoming as aroused as he was. Damn him! "Okay. What?" she said. Anything to get him off her.

"Let me stay. And no more attacks on my physical being," he added.

She turned to face him. "That's two."

"Well?"

She sighed and whispered, "All right."

"Sorry?" He turned his ear to her.

"All right," she said louder.

Colin let go of her arms and rolled off her.

"The things men do to get their own way," she said, rubbing her wrists.

"Sorry, but you're dangerous let loose."

She had to smile at that. Her mother had always taught her to fight back, and she wasn't going to stop now that she had grown up. She pointed in the direction of his groin. "How d'you feel... you know, down there?"

"Can't you tell he's ready and rearing to go again?" He lifted it twice like a lever.

"You're sick, you know that."

"Makes two of us," Colin joked back.

"Nothing wrong with me."

"Oh no?" He raised his eyebrows. "You're the one who's in love with me."

"Yeah… that qualifies me all right." They laughed together. Joan stood up and made for the door.

"Now where are you going?" Colin asked, already making himself comfortable at the head of the bed.

"To get you sheets and a pillow. You'll need those for your bed."

Colin opened his eyes wide. "What?"

"You said you wanted to stay here — you didn't say where." She laughed wickedly. "You're sleeping on the floor, Mr Baker. I want to make one thing clear: we share the same bed only when I want to. It's not up to you when you have my body."

He shook his head. She was sharper than he expected this time of the morning. He was just grateful he had got her to calm down. She wasn't screaming at him any more.

Colin made the most of his makeshift bed on the floor. He placed it right by her bed and held her hand as he poured out his heart to her. He would have promised her anything that night. By the time Donna burst into her sister's room later that morning, Colin was sharing her bed.

COLIN

Oh boy! What have I done?

I think I must have drunk too many last night. I woke up in Joan's bed. She turned over and smiled down at me and said, "I will be Mrs Baker after all." Yeah, I said, then it all came flooding back.

Caught up in the moment I had proposed to her. Or did I? As I remember the conversation went something like this:

She said, "So where do we go from here?"

I said, "Marriage, I s'pose." I was mucking around, didn't think she'd take me seriously. But she jumped on it like a drowning man to a life raft.

"You serious?"

I couldn't take it back. "Well, why not?"

"Okay, then," she said. "Let's do it."

That was it. I was committed. No way back. At the time it felt right. We were saying all the right things an' that. I wasn't thinking past getting in bed with her.

The thing is not to let Lois know I'm seeing Joan again, and not to let Joan find out I'm staying in Lois's flat. Nothing's going on between us. I wouldn't sleep with her again if she paid me — and believe me, she's tried. It's just that I needed somewhere to stay and Lois offered her place. Now that I've got Joan back I've got to sort out the rest of my life.

I may be allowed back in her bed, but that's as far as it goes for the time being.

Sex is out until I prove myself worthy.
Shouldn't be too long now though.

THE NURSERY WAS JUST OPENING UP. PARENTS AND CHILDREN buzzed around, falling in line for the routine of hanging up coats and booking lunches with the secretary. Pamela was chatting to a parent who was concerned that her little boy kept wetting himself at school whereas he never did it at home. Was he being mistreated? she wanted to know. Pamela, who was used to parents' concerns like this, told her that this kind of thing was quite common when children were still settling in, and that if she wanted to she could make an appointment to see the child psychologists who were available for consultation. Immediately the woman's view changed. All of a sudden there was nothing wrong with her child.

Pamela finally turned her attention to the little brown-skinned boy tugging at her shirt hem. His gorgeous hazel eyes blinked adoringly up at her, his cheeks pushed up in a toothy grin. He wore his favourite baseball cap with the peak at the back.

"Hi, Mikey!" She hunched down and gave the little boy a warm hug. He was one of her favourites. So cute, and he was well behaved. "Where's mummy today?" she asked, looking towards the door. Cheryl, his mother, had become a good friend. She would often stop for a cup of coffee and a chat after dropping Mikey off. Cheryl was a gossip. Little happened in her own life, according to her, but she knew everything that was going on in her friends' and neighbours' lives.

"Daddy brung me today," the four-year-old told her, and pointed towards the door. Pamela followed his tiny pointing finger and caught her breath, as in walked God.

She froze, unable to take her eyes off him. This man was Mikey in twenty-five years' time — the same hazel eyes, the handsome, self-assured grin — except that he didn't have the baby cheeks, he had a strong jawline and cool milk-chocolate-brown skin. He must have been at least six foot four. He strode towards them confidently, his hand raised in greeting as he approached. "You must be Miss Pamela," he said, in a voice that seemed to originate in the pit of his stomach and reached across the air to grab her attention. It was deep and mellow, and flowed like a caramel river. Pamela stared at his mouth, his beautiful lips, full and kissable. She stood there like a fool, looking at him like a hungry man looks at a plate of his favourite food.

He was dressed in a navy business suit, with a navy tie over a white shirt. He carried it so well it could have been made for him.

"Shake his hand, then," Mikey ordered, his baby voice bringing Pamela back to reality. Pamela's face broke out of its trance. "Sorry." She smiled, showing pretty white teeth, and offered her hand. "Yes, I'm Pamela." He introduced himself. "Michael." His handshake was firm.

Pamela's hand stayed in his until he let it go, embarrassed. She still couldn't help but stare uncontrollably. This guy even had sexy eyebrows. They were smooth, thick and silky. Pamela had the urge to run her fingers along them; it took a great effort to control the urge. "Is Cheryl all right?" she managed.

Michael nodded. "Yeah, she's fine. She's got a job interview, so I said I'd bring Mikey in for her." He looked down at her and smiled provocatively. "I'm glad I did."

Oh yes, she thought to herself. Yes, yes, yes.

Michael looked around for his son. "Mikey? Come give me hug, I'm going now," he called. He looked round and caught Pamela staring at him again, a stupid grin on her face. He smiled back — encouraging her, she thought. Mikey dropped the bricks he was busy carrying from one end of the room to the other and ran into his father's arms. Michael hugged his child to him with genuine affection, and kissed his cheek. Mikey immediately wiped the spot with the back of his hand, and Pamela laughed with his father. "Cheek!" Michael said, as his son ran off again to his bricks. "He's a lovely little boy. I want my first to be just like him," Pamela said.

"First? You mean you haven't started yet?" Michael asked.

"Haven't met a man worthy enough to have my child," she said smugly.

Michael looked into her eyes as if trying to read between her words. He must have liked what he saw, because he nodded approvingly and threw her a little smile. "Maybe I'll see you again sometime," he said in that deep well of a voice.

"Sure." Pamela couldn't think of anything else to say. She felt awkward. Michael was already walking towards the door as she came up with a brainstorm. "Michael?" she called, quick-stepping towards his waiting figure — and what a figure. "We've got a parents' evening on Thursday night. Why don't you come along? Cheryl said she won't be able to make it, and I bet you don't get much of a chance to see Mikey's work."

He hesitated, striking a pose with one hand stroking his chin thoughtfully. "You're right — I don't. What time?"

Pamela stepped back just a little as she realised she was close enough to smell the mints on his breath, and might not be able to control what her hands might do. "Between four and six thirty."

"I'll be here." The corners of his eyes crinkled engagingly. He moistened his lips with his tongue, then pulled his bottom lip in with his teeth, slowly letting it go, leaving white bloodless tracks for a fraction of a second. "Later then." He brushed her arm fleetingly. Pamela was hypnotised. "Later," she replied, feeling her knees buckle as she tried to walk away. She felt as though she were floating a few inches above the ground.

She had been hit by the thunderbolt.

Oh my God, a voice inside her declared. I'm in love.

Pamela arrived home at nine that evening, exhausted as usual. Keeping control of twenty children under five was tiring work. After work, she had gone straight to the Wavelengths leisure centre for an hour of aerobics followed immediately by another hour of gym. As she had begun her work-out the adrenalin rush had taken over and she'd recovered enough to complete her exercise routine. Now she was completely shattered. Since James had left, home had become very quiet. The men in her life still called, but she wasn't interested. Sex, she was beginning to realise, wasn't everything. She wanted someone to be there for her. She actually found herself missing James. Not for himself, but for the massages and cuddles, the breakfast in bed at the weekends, the morning cups of coffee. Dinner when she came home from work…

Her friends were right — James had been too good for her.

She stripped off her clothes as she walked around the flat, feeling filthy and grimy with perspiration. She ran the bath and went to fetch a robe from the bedroom.

The phone rang on her way, and she picked it up in the living room. "Pam?"

She recognised Shaun's voice and sighed internally. "Yeah. Shaun." She ran a hand through her greasy hair.

"What's up? You sound down."

"I'm tired," she replied. "Shaun, my bath's running. Can I call you later?"

"Yeah, all right. Talk to you later, then."

"Bye." She hung up. Even Shaun was getting boring. The last time he had come round she had fallen asleep next to him. She just hadn't fancied the same old routine.

After she emerged from the bath feeling drained but clean, she still wasn't in the mood to call Shaun back. Let him cuss, she said to herself, switching on the answerphone. She was tired of him; she was tired of them all. They swanned through her life, leaving her unfulfilled and still searching. She knew deep down she was a good person: she didn't bitch; she didn't want to tie a man down with kids; she was fit, attractive, good in bed... her problem was that the wrong men were always falling for her.

The men she wanted, the men who attracted her sexually, were the ones whom so many other women wanted as well. Which was why they felt they had to spread it around, not to leave anyone out. They were unreliable, couldn't make promises (let alone keep them), and only turned up when they wanted something. She understood these men. Hell, she had acted like them enough times.

On the other hand, the ones that promised love, fidelity and total devotion bored her, and they were always the ones that fell for her. They could only ever be taken in short bursts before it became too heavy and she had to escape.

She thought about Michael. Which category would he fall into? She had a pretty good idea that he would be the spread-himself-thin type. But what the hell, she thought. She desired him too much to care and she couldn't see him putting up much resistance if the opportunity arose. Somehow she had to find out if he still shared a bed with Cheryl.

Pamela lay on her bed above the sheets, wearing nothing but a crumpled pink T-shirt and panties. Her hands were clasped behind her head, her knees drawn up making twin bridges. She allowed her thoughts to drift in and out of her mind, unable to sleep and yet not having the inclination to do anything else.

Thursday arrived. The day couldn't go fast enough. For Pamela it had been a long week so far — three days of undeniable anticipation and excitement. One person had stayed on her mind night and day. She felt like a teenager again. Even choosing something to wear to work had been an ordeal.

When Cheryl had brought Mikey in on Tuesday, Pamela had fished around for information about the boy's father. But Cheryl didn't want to talk about Michael — she'd told Pamela he was interested only in his son, and that was fine because she wanted nothing more to do with him. Pamela had smiled to herself. Michael was as good as hers.

Tea breaks and lunchtime came and went. After the afternoon session the children went home, and preparations for the parents' evening began.

"Should be an easy evening," Annette said to Pamela. Annette was a nursery assistant and had been with them for a year. She was nineteen, and all the kids were fond of her. She had the ambition of going into primary teaching; this, she said, was just a stepping-stone for her.

Pamela looked up from her reports. "Oh?"

Annette was chewing gum vigorously, and moved it with her tongue to the inside

her cheek as she spoke. "Yeah. We've only had ten definites."

Pamela put on her voice of authority. "It doesn't mean others won't turn up, Annette. I've been receiving verbal confirmations all week." She was wound up tighter than an elastic band around a pencil.

"Yeah, well, we don't wanna hang around longer than we have to, do we?"

"We'll hang around for as long as it takes," Pamela snapped. "You are being paid."

Annette swallowed her gum, her eyes widening in astonishment at Pamela's unprovoked outburst. She scuttled away to her chores, muttering under her breath.

Two hours into the parents' evening, Pamela was getting to breaking point. Keeping her eyes open for Michael, it was hard to concentrate properly on her job, and she was rushing the other parents through their interviews and not giving them the chance for questions. She was vaguely aware she was doing it, but couldn't help herself. She was as nervous as a cat walking past a dog pound, and her jaw was aching from forcing a smile at so many people for so long. By six fifteen, with fifteen minutes to go, she was convinced he wasn't going to show up. She had seen her share of the parents and the rest of staff were leaving. She began to put away her notes, disappointedly. Lifting the files from the desk, she turned to walk back to the office and nearly bumped into Michael.

"Not too late, am I?" His voice was breathless, as if he had been jogging.

"Michael! No, of course not."

Her eyes travelled down from his face to his smart attire. He was wearing a cream sweater and a pair of smart black trousers. He looked gorgeous. Pamela's pulse quickened. The smile that spread itself across her face now didn't have to be forced, it had a will of its own. She fought to regain her composure, confidence and professionalism taking the place of girlish excitement. "As you can see, everyone else has left. You just caught me."

"I'm sorry. I had to get here from Finchley. You have no idea how many speed limits I broke to do it."

His voice was just as she remembered it, deep and sexy. It wasn't a fantasy after all. She wondered what he did for a living. Did he have a huge wage packet to match the rest of his assets?

"Glad you could make it." She extended her hand to shake his, and dropped the pile of files. "Shit!" she exclaimed, and then immediately covered her mouth with her hand. "Sorry."

Michael laughed, his hazel eyes filled with amusement. "Don't worry about it. I'll give you a hand."

They both bent down, and together they shoved papers back into folders and piled them back on the desk. As they reached for the last file together, their hands touched. It was like a bolt of electricity. Pamela pulled her hand back, and Michael's eyes met hers. Right then she nearly kissed him, their heads were so close. Instead she caught herself, stood up on weak legs, and took the files from his arms.

"Thanks. I'll be with you in a minute," she said, turning her back on him as he rose slowly from the floor, eyes burning into her retreating figure.

Pamela had needed a chance to get her breath back. She had wanted to impress him and show him how classy she was, how in control she was, and boy, had she messed up. She was the one who was supposed to be in charge of developments. That was the way it had always been. But now she felt disturbingly uncertain.

She walked back into the nursery hall with long, smooth strides, aware of him watching her. Walking straight was not easy; right now she would rather be lying down — preferably with him. What was he like naked? She planned to find out. He didn't leave much to the imagination anyway. Sex-appeal oozed from his every pore.

She took him over to a desk in a corner and opened up Mikey's file. As she spoke she was aware that he was probably not listening to a word she was saying — but that was okay, because as far as she could make out she was mumbling a load of rubbish anyway.

His hands were clasped on the table in front of him. "Do you want to go somewhere afterwards?" he suddenly interrupted.

Pamela was taken by surprise. She swallowed hard and nervously shuffled a couple of pages back into the folder. "I... I..." she stammered. What on earth was wrong with her? She never stammered. He covered her shaking hands with his. "I'm moving too fast, aren't I?"

"No!" she gushed. What must he be thinking of her? She wanted a chance to show him the real Pamela. "Why don't you come back to my place? We could get a takeaway, some wine…"

He leant closer across the table, his eyes swallowing her whole. "Sounds good to me. You finished here?" He nodded at the papers in front of them.

"I've just got to lock up." She closed the file in front of her and smiled at him. "Five minutes."

They hardly spoke as he led her towards his car. He drove a late registration Laguna. You've landed one this time, girl, she thought as she admired its sleek lines. He opened the door for her and she slid into the comfortable passenger seat. Michael slid a CD into the player and the sounds of Jodeci issued forth. "Where to?" he asked.

The Caribbean. That was what she wanted to say. "Pepys Estate," she replied. She gazed out at the passing scene as they drove off towards Deptford, occasionally turning to glance at his profile without being too obvious.

His lips were parted as he sang quietly along with the music.

They drove through New Cross, and within ten minutes Pamela had directed him to where she lived. He pulled up outside the tower block. On the way up, they chatted about the state of the area. Pamela told him that if she could afford to move out she would.

"You sure you can trust me to come in?" Michael asked once they had reached her front door.

She gave him a cynical look. "Why? Are you some kind of serial killer?"

"I'm hardly going to admit that now, am I?" His rich voice was heavy with sarcasm. He reached over and touched the back of her neck with soft fingers, smiling slyly.

She shivered. "Well, if you are, then I'd better warn you — I've got a black belt in Tae Kwan Do."

"Yeah, and my name's Michelle," Michael smirked.

"Hello, Michelle." She chuckled and let him into her humble abode.

"I've found my future husband."

Joan laughed sarcastically, pressing the remote control she held in her hand to lower the television's volume. "Yeah, right, Pam. How many times have I heard that? Has he got nice eyes, a firm arse, or just a big cock?"

"All ah dat. But that's not it. I haven't even had him yet. I know this sounds corny, but I think I'm in love."

Joan laughed again. In love! Pamela had to be winding her up. The word "love" wasn't in her vocabulary, much less her heart.

"So…" She controlled the giggle. "Tell me, then. What has this great man done to make you feel this way?"

Pamela hadn't been able to wait to tell her friends all about Michael. He had literally swept her off her feet. Last night had been the best night she'd ever spent with a man without having sex. She didn't know whether it was just the fact that he was so good looking, or the fact that he was a gentleman, or his voice, or just the way he'd treated her. One evening — and she felt as though she could spend the rest of her life with him. "I'm telling you, Joan, this is nothing like Shaun or even how it started with James. Michael took me home last night. We were supposed to get a takeaway, and I swear the thought of food went clean out of our heads. I'm gonna be honest, right? I thought the man was after sex like they all are. I know I was… We were in my living room, I got us some wine and put a soul tape on — the one you made up for me, with 'Slap n' Tickle' on it. We sat there chatting, and then he asks me to dance…"

"What — in your front room?"

"Yes," Pamela chirruped. "So I says, 'All right,' and he took me in his arms in the middle of the front room. I can't even explain how it felt. We just moved together like it was… I dunno. It just felt right, y'know? Then 'Nice and Slow' came on — you know what that record does to me…" She didn't wait for Joan to answer. "And he kissed me. He can kiss! I wanted him badly, and he must've felt it. I was trembling all over, but he just held me, stroked me — and boy did he move me." Pamela screamed. She was so excited she was rambling. "So… what stopped you?"

"I don't know. This is what I'm saying about this guy. We danced, talked, drank a bit too much. He told me all about his job in computers and what his plans for the future are. He even stayed the night — and all he did was hold me. He told me he wanted to enjoy every minute of our time together." Pamela sighed. "I called in sick this morning and we spent the whole day together. He went out and bought us Chinese for lunch." She giggled like a schoolgirl.

Joan was amazed at what she was hearing. Prime steak laid out in Pamela's bed, and she didn't eat it! "There must be something wrong with you," she said, "or there's something wrong with him."

Pamela's voice was all dreamy. "This is different, J. I know I'm falling in love. I understand what you and Marion were going on about now — an' that's saying something."

"Love…" Joan sighed and went into big-sister mode. "You know, love comes with responsibility. You don't know this guy from Adam; how do you know he's not some sort of con artist? Sweet you up one minute and tek all your belongings the next."

"I hear you, Joan. I'm not stupid. I'll take it easy," Pamela assured her. "He's coming back tonight. I'll ask him where this is going."

"You know I only want the best for you. But I know you, you've never been committed to one man in your life. And what about Shaun? Doesn't he think he's your man?" Pamela held the phone away from her ear and grimaced. Joan had to go and burst her bubble. But she was right. To make a go of it with any man she would have to make a lot of changes to herself and her priorities. Shaun believed he was her man. She would have to come clean with him. Anyway, the relationship had gone as far as it was going to go, she thought. There was no point in it any more. She wanted to move on. "You listening to me?" Joan pressed.

"Shaun's no problem. I'll give him the elbow, an' I'll be free to do as I please," Pamela simply replied.

"Boy, you're certainly working your way through the population."

Pamela laughed. "I'm slowing down now."

Although she wanted it to be true, Joan doubted it. Lord knows, she'd been where Pamela was now. A new man who promised the world — until things started to get too heavy. But if that was what Pamela wanted, then Joan resolved to be there for her. She asked if he had any kids.

"Didn't I tell you? His little boy goes to my nursery."

"He's a single parent?" Joan seemed impressed at the thought of a black man raising his child alone.

"No. The kid lives with his mum. I must have mentioned Cheryl."

The penny dropped. "Oh, her! Mikey's mum. So Mikey is Michael junior…" Joan was getting a warning feeling in her stomach. Pamela had mentioned Cheryl, and Joan had the impression that the woman was the kind you didn't mess with. "It is finished between them?"

"Yeah. I even asked her just to make sure. She doesn't want him."

"Did you find out why not?" Joan enquired.

Pamela tutted and rolled her eyes. "It's over, that's all. Do you have to be so suspicious?"

"Let me meet him. I'll look him over for you. I've got women's intuition."

"You'll meet him. Not that you're any authority on Mr Right."

Joan laughed. Even women with women's intuition didn't get it right all the time. "Okay. I'll back off. But jus' you take care. Test the waters before you jump in, and keep me informed."

"I will. I'll see you soon anyway." They said their goodbyes and hung up. Pamela shook her head at the way Joan was carrying on. Not all men were bad. You just had to know how to handle them.

Michael had left Pamela's flat at three o'clock that afternoon. At seven he'd phoned her, just minutes after she'd spoken to Joan. During the four hours in between, Pamela had become completely useless to herself. She'd tried to do housework, but had managed only to move things from one area to another before sinking again into thoughts of Michael. He crowded into every compartment of her brain, invading her mind in a way that confused her. She almost resented it. It was a new feeling for her, and she didn't know whether to fight it or go with it.

When the phone rang she'd been redoing her hair for the fourth time that day. She'd hurriedly grabbed the receiver and issued a breathless hello.

"Hi, babes. It's Michael," he'd said. There was no mistaking his voice anyway.

She'd forced a controlled calm into her voice. "Hi, Mike."

"You all right?"

"Yeah, fine. Jus' doing some housework. How're you?"

"Still at work. Should finish soon, though. You know I was supposed to start at two o'clock? I missed a meeting in Kensington. The boss wasn't too happy." She'd heard a smile rising in his voice. "But it was worth it."

Pamela had remembered the morning and her heartbeat had quickened. She had never believed Marion when she told her how Paul made love without actually "putting it in her", but that was exactly what Michael had done — and he had managed to satisfy her. She'd recalled the whiteness of his teeth and the light in his hazel eyes, his strong jaw, and the dampness between her legs that was a direct result of her contact with this man.

"What're we gonna do, eh?" She'd spoken her thoughts out loud.

"What do you want to do?" His voice had been thick with innuendo.

"I'm not sure, but whatever it is it includes you."

He'd laughed then, loud and richly musical. The sound had travelled down the phone line to grip her stomach in a nervous reflex action. She'd wondered if she'd been too presumptuous. They had only had one night together — one sexless night. Maybe to him it was no big deal.

"So, is it all right for me to come round tonight?"

"Of course."

"Good. Do you have candles at home?"

Pamela had frowned, puzzled. "A couple, I think. Why?"

"A surprise. Don't eat until I get there. By the way, what's your favourite food?"

She'd shrugged, searching her brain. "I'm not fussy. So long as it's not too fatty, I'll eat it."

"I'll be there in about half an hour."

"Okay. I'll see you later."

And now he was here on her doorstep, dressed completely in black, carrying several foil containers of Indian takeaway. Pamela was fascinated by this man's cool confidence.

They spread a tablecloth on the floor and took cushions off the sofa for seats. He lit the candles and placed them in the centre of the spread. He served the food, poured the wine, and generally took over.

Michael's conversation was intelligent, and he seemed interested even in the mindless gossip that she contributed. He had a habit of watching her mouth as she spoke. She found it intriguing, if a little disquieting. Later on, she promised herself, she would stand in front of the mirror to see what was so interesting about her lips.

"So, tell me something." He swallowed and placed his fork on the side of his plate. "This guy Shaun you were seeing… is he definitely out of the picture?"

Pamela nodded enthusiastically. "Yes. It was nothing." She waved a hand in the air.

"When you say nothing, you telling me you were just friends?" Michael quizzed.

Pamela thought about her answer. If there was one thing she'd discovered about Michael in the short time she'd known him, it was that he never asked a question unless he wanted an honest answer. It was his way of getting to know someone, being very direct. "No. More than just friends. We go way back, to when we were teenagers. But over the past few months it's been just a sexual thing, y'know."

Michael raised his glass to his lips, his hazel eyes watching her over the rim. "I can't believe a man would use you just for sex."

Pamela nearly choked on her biryani. "Use me! Naw, luv — it was the other way round."

Michael scrutinised her across the makeshift table, taking in her body language. "Did he know?"

"What?"

"That you were just using him for sex?"

"Well, I didn't tell him any different."

"That doesn't mean he saw it the same way as you. He could've been under the impression that you were his woman."

"Get real!" Though it had a ring of truth about it, she snubbed his suggestion.

"I just don't want to step on anyone's toes. If you're seeing me, I don't want to imagine you with someone else. Unless I'm not good enough for you — then I'd rather you told me and I could back out."

Pamela was completely taken aback. Was he trying to tell her she was going to become his possession? She beat down the urge to tell him where to go with that attitude. But he had a point. If he liked her as much as she liked him, then he had every right to lay down a couple of ground rules. "Does that mean that you'd do the same?" she asked.

"Sure. But I'm telling you now, unless you don't want me, you've got me to yourself."

"Fair enough," she said, and swallowed a mouthful of white wine.

Michael spread out on to his side on the carpet, draping one long leg over the other. He rested on one forearm. "You know, there's something about the way you treat men that makes me think you're a little bitter," he said.

"Bitter?"

"Yeah, like the last two men in your life. You seem to have something against men falling for you."

What was he now? A Psychiatrist? "What're you getting at?" Pamela placed a palm on her chest dramatically.

"I want to get to know you, Pamela. I want to know every detail, but also I need to know if I'm just gonna be another plaything, someone to pass the time with until the next stud comes along. You get me?"

"Michael," she said, placing her glass gently on the floor, "I'm not into mind games. If this was just gonna be a fling I'd have flung by now." She smiled honestly. "I want to get to know you too."

He smiled his bright, white smile and his hazel eyes flashed their satisfaction. "You know, I've been asking all the questions. I probably know more about you than you do about me. Do you want to ask me anything?"

"I don't do that," Pamela replied. "I get to know a man by his actions, not by how he answers my questions. I'd be a fool to take every word you said as the truth, now wouldn't I?"

Michael laughed, the sound ranging from a deep and throaty rumble to a light chuckle. "You always have a knack of saying the right things. I'll have to watch you." He leant over and kissed her lips.

He held her hand as they continued to eat, taking her breath away with the promises in his beautiful eyes. He made her think before she spoke — which was definitely a new one on Pamela. And this was only the start of a perfect evening...

Later, they lay together on the soft leather sofa, illuminated by the flickering light of the muted television. The gentle soul music of Aaron Hall was playing low in the background. Michael's hand stroked her back and he placed light kisses on her forehead. Pamela felt secure. No man had ever made her feel like this. It was alien to her, and to be honest a little frightening. She felt as though she were in a dream and had to keep kissing him to make sure he was real.

"Michael?" she whispered softly.

"Yes?"

She hesitated, choosing her words carefully. "Are you sexually attracted to me?"

"What do you think?" His eyes sparkled at her.

She could feel that he was aroused. She raised her head and giggled, her long hair falling around her face. "I know you're ready, but..."

He stroked her hair back off her face with his huge hand. "You want to know why we're not having sex yet?"

"Well," she replied hesitantly, "yes."

Michael sat her up, took her chin in his hand and made her eyes meet his. "Is that all you want?"

Pamela felt the first ripple of anticipation spreading from between her legs. "What?" she asked, for a second forgetting the thread of the conversation.

"Sex."

She looked directly into his beautiful eyes. It wasn't as though she didn't know how to seduce a man. But for some reason she didn't want to do it with Michael. She wanted him to take her. Wanted to know that he felt the same thing she was feeling. Seducing him would be too easy.

"It's just... what I'm used to."

Michael shook his head. "I want this to be different." He took her cheek in his hand and stroked it with his thumb. "I want you, but I want it to be special." His eyes passed over her like a slow caress, and a shiver ran along her nerves. This was the same feeling she got when he kissed her, of every bone in her body being turned to water. "I'm gonna feel really stupid after I say this, but I have to. I..." She swallowed. "I've never wanted one man this badly." She continued quickly before he had a chance to laugh at her: "I know I don't know you. I just feel like this is gonna be more than just sex." She watched him, looking for a hint of understanding.

"Why do you think I want this to be different?" His voice was soft and deep, like the caress of a warm breeze, warm water, warm sleep. She looked into his eyes, and the expression there took her completely by surprise. She saw open longing there, and desire she couldn't have imagined. He kissed her and she fell into his arms, melting into his body. He covered her face and neck in kisses until she was gasping. Suddenly he stopped and Pamela groaned. "Let's take this to the bedroom," he said. "I'll show you what I mean."

Pamela was already aching for him, and she led the way to the bedroom without letting go of his hand. She moved lithely to the bed in the dark, and subsided on to the red satin sheets, fully dressed.

Michael stood at the doorway. "No," he said. "Come here." He switched on the light. Pamela walked towards him, watching him with puzzled eyes. Her legs felt weak. His hazel eyes were smouldering with desire, taking her in from head to foot as they had done earlier. She stood so close her nipples brushed his chest. As she looked up at him, he smiled knowingly, teasingly. He ran one finger from her nose to her lips, where he let her kiss them before continuing the journey down her body. He gently cupped one firm breast in his hand, rolling the nipple under his thumb. She shivered. His other hand followed the curve of her waist, her hips, and then her buttocks. His eyes never left hers.

Pamela helped him remove her T-shirt and it dropped to the floor. The clasp on her bra was released and it too was discarded. Her breasts were rising and falling with her breathing. He continued to caress her nipples with his thumbs as he ran his tongue over his lips, wetting them before bending to take a nipple in his mouth. Pamela's arms rose to his broad shoulders and ran down his muscular arms, marvelling at how hard his body was. Michael's breathing became heavier as he took her in his arms. He kissed her slowly but passionately, handling her like a delicate antique doll.

She was crying out for him now, mentally and physically. She murmured, "I need you now, Michael."

"I know, baby. I know," he replied, his voice even deeper than usual. He slid her leggings down, leaving her standing in her black lacy panties. She gripped his shoulders as he took her buttocks into both hands, lifting her off her feet. She wrapped her toned brown legs around his torso, lacing her ankles behind his back, grinding herself against his taut body — still fully clothed in contrast to her own semi-nakedness — as if her life depended on it. He let her body slip down his until she was standing on her feet again, her breath coming in short pants, a film of perspiration covering her entire body. Never before had she come so close to an orgasm without penetration.

She stepped backwards and eased herself down on to the satin sheets of the bed. Michael stood in the middle of the room. She watched eagerly and somewhat impatiently as he undressed for her. His chest was as she expected: big, broad, a weightlifter's torso. His arms bulged with the strength she had felt when he'd carried her. His abdomen was hard, the muscles standing out under his skin. He unbuckled his belt and unzipped his trousers slowly. He was watching her watching him, showing discernable pride in his manhood, which stood to attention as he let his boxers drop to the floor. Pamela sighed with anticipation, sure she had died and gone to heaven. She had never seen one that big — and she had seen many…

She stifled a scream as he crept towards her. Starting at her feet, he kissed, nibbled, sucked and stroked his way up her body. Then he rolled her over to give her the same treatment on the back. Every nerve in her was sparking like a live wire. She was moaning his name as he explored erogenous zones she had forgotten existed. The sensation was incredible, unbearable.

His tongue probed her wet vagina. He played with her clitoris, teasing her to orgasm by sucking and licking her just right. He could certainly teach a few men the art of going downtown. It was a skill most men only thought they possessed. As he came face to face with her and she could feel his hardness pressing for entry, she drew her legs up to allow him access, gripping his smooth buttocks in her slim hands. Still he took his time, opening her up with an expertise she admired, finding her magic button. He was treating her like a precious flower he didn't want to damage.

A wave was building up inside her, threatening to break the dams and flood them both. She felt she could drown in her own wetness, and still his finger moved faster in and out, gauging the rhythm. She finally spilt over and shuddered with a huge orgasm, her vagina clenching his knuckles.

Then he entered her, moving his penis inside with a slow, shallow pumping motion at first, then speeding up and deepening until she thought she would explode, then withdrawing again, leaving her gasping, before changing position to start all over again.

She was totally out of control. They rolled around on the bed, pleasing each other equally, until finally Michael joined her in a climax, his eyes screwed tightly shut in the agony of sex. She bit into his shoulder as they collapsed back on to the bed, moulded firmly together.

Hours later, she still lay in his arms. They were both covered in perspiration and had no need for sheets. She fell asleep feeling like the most fulfilled woman in the world.

Pamela awoke to an empty bed and the sounds and smells of cooking coming from her kitchen. For one horrifying moment she thought of James, that last night must have been a cruel joke played on her by her mind. But as she yawned and stretched she smiled to herself, remembering Michael's body. No, it had been too good to be a dream.

She slipped out of bed and ran a hand through her tangled hair. Her mouth still tasted of last night's lovemaking. Wrapping herself in her short dressing gown, she went towards the sounds.

Michael stood at the cooker, his back to her. He was dressed only in his boxer shorts. She crept up behind him and circled his waist with her arms.

"Good morning." He turned round and smiled down at her. She stood on tiptoe to kiss him on the lips. "I hope you're not a vegetarian. I couldn't find anything except cereal, fruit and vegetables, so I went out and did some shopping. We got bacon, sausages and eggs."

Pamela grinned and her eyes sparkled. She must have been sleeping deeply — she hadn't heard him leave or return. "What you trying to do, fatten me up?"

"All the better to eat you," he said. Opening his mouth wide and baring his teeth, he brought his lips down to her neck.

Pamela laughed. "You're too much."

"You didn't complain last night," he said with a grin.

"There wasn't — and still isn't — anything to complain about." She kissed him again and he gave her a quick squeeze before turning back to his bacon. "It'll be ready in about ten minutes," he informed her. "I was going to slip back into bed with your breakfast on a tray, but you beat me to it."

Pamela silently cursed her luck. "Well, I'll go and freshen up then." She turned to leave the kitchen.

"Don't have a bath yet," he called, his back to her. Pamela stopped in her tracks and raised an eyebrow at him. He turned and grinned engagingly before turning back to the frying pan. He used a spatula to flip the bacon over. "We're bathing together, after breakfast. Any objection?"

"No, sir!" She saluted. Michael laughed. Even his laugh was sexy.

They sat cross-legged on the floor of the living room, the October sunlight giving the room an eerie glow. Michael fed her breakfast from his plate. He liked the floor for eating. He said chairs were too formal.

He noticed the book on the coffee table. "You're reading Terry MacMillan?" he observed.

"Yeah," she said through a mouthful of toast. "Only just started that one."

"I haven't read it. Any good?"

"You read novels?"

"What? You thought I couldn't read?" he said with mock indignation.

"It's not that," she said, dusting crumbs from her bare legs. "I just don't know many black men our age who read. Out of about five men I know, I bet not one of them has read a book since they left school."

"I'll read to you in the bath," he promised, as if to prove the point. "Unless you don't fancy it…"

"Well…" She paused, running her tongue over her lips. "I can think of better things to do." She grinned wickedly.

"I know what's on your mind, babe." He spoke directly to her eyes. "But you can get that anytime. I told you I want this to be special. I guarantee you'll enjoy it," he said sincerely.

Michael was right. They lay in the bubble bath, her head resting on his sculpted chest, and he read to her. One hand held the book while the other caressed her body with warm water and bubbles as he spoke in a rough American accent.

Pamela never wanted this to end. Michael was hers, and she had no reason to think that this wouldn't last.

MICHAEL

I've got no intention of trying to get back with Cheryl. She's a bitch. She bitches about money, about me not spending enough time with my son, turning up when I feel like it, and sometimes she just bitches about nothing in particular to get my back up.

Now before you get the wrong idea about me, I'm gonna set you straight. I can't fall in love. No — that's not right — I can, but I refuse to. It's like this fear comes over me. And then I run. I don't like doing it. I don't want to hurt anyone

— especially someone as fine as Pamela.

I thought I could make it work with Cheryl. We were together five years. I'm telling you, I tried. Now I want to try again. I want to fall in love with Pamela. If it doesn't work out, it won't be for the lack of trying.

THE DAY OF RECKONING HAD ARRIVED. MARION FELT LIKE THE world's wickedest bitch. Today was the day she planned to tell Paul about "his" baby. She had convinced herself that the child was his — it would make the lying so much easier. Having gone over the details many times — just as she had when Gerard was going to be the recipient of the news — it was hard separating the truth from the lies. Paul was coming to pick her up from work in the afternoon, ostensibly to give her a batch of interview tapes he had collected from Joan. She knew she would be a bundle of nerves. After all, this would make or break their relationship. She had hardly mentioned kids with Paul since they'd got back together. He liked kids, she knew that, but he'd always said he wanted to be set up financially before he had his own. The fact that he loved her gave Marion strength. After all — love conquers all, doesn't it?

Her writing had pushed her problems to the back of her mind. Joan had bought her a book called Interviewing Techniques for Writers and Researchers, which she had used to compile her questionnaires. One of the interviewees, Marcellis, seemed to know exactly what he wanted in relationships, and was anxious to show a woman he cared for that he was willing to please her. There would be no messing about in his relationships, Marion thought. He would make some woman a considerate husband.

There were other men who reminded Marion of Gerard with their attitudes. Some were bitter because they had been hurt before, and vowed never to let a woman get that close again.

She had read an article about black women travelling to America to find partners. Apparently, England was running short of eligible professional black men, and women were getting desperate. There was an upcoming television programme on Channel 4 called Shopping for Mr Right. Marion would make a point of watching it.

She was definitely enjoying writing again, especially using this enlightening method. Paul had even volunteered to be one of her subjects.

The day ticked by slowly. Five minutes before the library finally closed, Paul turned up. He smiled at her over the counter, his eyes sparkling. "Can I get some service over here?" he said. Marion leaned on the counter with her forearms and kissed him on the lips. He looked so handsome, dressed in a navy blue sweater that laced up from his chest to his neck, and black jeans. He had just had his hair shaved again, and was looking dashingly masculine.

"You ought to leave that till you get home," Sandra, a colleague of hers, called over from the enquiry desk. "You're making me jealous." Paul chuckled. Marion turned back to him. "Never mind Sandra," she said, loud enough for Sandra to hear, "she's got a list of men waiting to kiss her."

Sandra laughed and tossed her long brown hair back from her face. Paul took one of Marion's hands and kissed it. "I'll see you outside."

She put her smile back on again. "Yeah. Won't be long."

Paul left and Marion sighed. She didn't know if she could go through with this. Sandra brought her mind back to earth. "Cor! He's good looking, ain't he? Good bod too."

"Thanks, Sandra. And he's all mine."

"Well, you know where to send him when you've finished with him." Marion smiled.

Paul's attempts at conversation fell on deaf ears as they drove home. Marion's mind was elsewhere. Eventually he gave up and they sat in silence.

Autumn leaves blew around their feet and fell like snowflakes from the trees as they walked hand in hand towards the flats. Paul had asked her if she was all right as they'd left the car. He was concerned. Marion had told him she was fine — just tired, that's all. He had given her a warm hug before taking her hand. She wished he wasn't being so loving. Not now, when she was doing this to him. Paul opened the door with his own set of keys. Marion followed behind, unease churning in her stomach. Paul took her jacket while she went into the living room.

"Fancy a cuppa?" he called after her.

"Not now, P. I'll have one later." She slumped into the armchair. With her head rested on its back, she closed her eyes. She had deliberately chosen the armchair so that he couldn't sit next to her while she told him. She heard him come into the living room and stop by the side of the chair. "What's wrong, Marion? I know when something's bothering you." He was always so sensitive to her needs.

She couldn't put it off any longer. She wished she had thought of writing a note, going away for a couple of days and waiting for his reaction on her return. But it had to be now. They were alone. She had no excuses left. This was it. She cleared her throat. Paul sat on the arm of the sofa opposite. She didn't look at him. Instead, she played with her sister's chain that she wore around her neck. "I've got something to tell you," she said quietly, frowning, her head bowed as she spoke.

Paul leaned forward, hands on knees. "Is this bad news?"

"How would you feel..." she began, and then stopped to clear her throat again. "What would you say if I told you I was pregnant?" Her heart thudded loudly in her chest as she waited for his answer.

Paul's face, which had been wearing a worried frown, now held a look of puzzled surprise. For a second she thought he hadn't got it. There was a silence during which Marion felt as though she was going to pass out. She could hear children playing on the balcony outside — carefree, young and innocent. She wanted to be that young again, never growing up, never having to go through the stress of being an adult...

"Are we having a baby?" Paul came over and hunched down in front of her. He took her shaking hands in his and observed her.

She held his gaze, wishing it were possible to read his mind. She nodded.

He searched her eyes, her face. "How?"

What did he mean, how? Why was he making this harder than it already was? A sudden thought occurred to her: suppose he was sterile or something. She raised an eyebrow at him, and a smile slowly spread across his lips and lit up his eyes as he laughed.

"I mean, I thought you were on the pill or sump'n. I seen you take 'em."

Marion had pretended to take the pill. She kept a packet on the bedside table and pressed one out every morning, disposing of it. She pondered for a minute before beginning her rehearsed speech. "The week I broke up with Gerard I stopped taking them. I didn't think I'd be with anyone so soon..." The lies started tripping off her tongue with ease. "The night you came round, I wanted you... I wasn't thinking straight. I'd been off the pill for a week. I missed my last period and put it down to stress. I did a test a week ago."

Paul stood up and walked slowly to the window. He rubbed his hands across his eyes, then shoved them into his trouser pockets. His back to her, his strong shoulders rose and then came down slowly. "A baby," he said. Marion stared at her hands clasped in her lap. "I can understand if you don't want..." she began, but he rushed over to her. "Don't say what I think you're going to say. Our baby!" He pulled her up to him and folded her into his arms.

A great tide of relief surged in her heart. "You don't mind?"

"We're together, aren't we? How can I mind?" He held her away from him and looked into her moist eyes. "It is mine, isn't it?"

Her voice remained low, her eyelids shading her usually jovial eyes in a modest downward look. "I can't be one hundred per cent sure, but I never missed the pill with Gerard. He made sure of that."

Paul grinned. "So when's it due?"

"May." The baby was actually due in April. She would carry on as though it was premature when the time came.

"Another Taurean like me!" He manoeuvred her over to the sofa and they sat down.

"Can we afford it though, Paul?"

"I'm working. We've got this place. We'll manage." He kissed her forehead.

Marion's eyes flitted to the ceiling. She said a silent prayer: Thank you, God. I'll never ask you for anything else again.

Later, Marion woke uneasily in the dark. Disorientated, she looked over at the luminous clock on the bedside table. Three twenty-three. She tried to remember what had woken her. A nightmare? If it was, it was already fading fast.

Rolling on to her stomach, she hugged her pillows to her. They were soft and comfortable, but tonight they weren't comforting. She was aware of something in the dream, something only partially discernable, as if it lay behind a veil, there for her to see but still out of reach. It was as though her subconscious was putting something precious somewhere safe, never to be found again.

She turned over on to her back and listened. She could hear the rumble of traffic coming from down below, the distant sounds of her neighbours doing whatever people do at this time in the morning. She felt for Paul. Her hand slid along his hot back. He was always hot. She prodded him gently, wanting him to wake up. Paul shifted slightly in his sleep, but didn't wake.

Marion lay with her eyes open for a while, listening to his shallow breathing. As sleep slowly descended upon her once more she closed her eyes — and all of a sudden the dream came rushing back. Her eyes flew open again, warding it off. It was about the baby. Her baby was going to be deformed; something was going to be terribly wrong with it. She had lied, and for her sins her baby was going to be cursed. Paul was a decent guy, who through no fault of his own was being misled, and this deceit would lead to his ultimate unhappiness. Marion sat up in the dark, feeling claustrophobic. She reached for the lamp and switched it on. The whole room came to life, and the shadows which had crowded her consciousness shrank back into the corners.

She looked round at Paul, who was flinging back the sheets and struggling to wake up. "Marion, what's wrong?" he whispered hoarsely.

She took his hand in hers. "I had a bad dream."

"Come here," he said, pulling her back to him. He smoothed her hair away from her face and kissed her forehead.

As he drifted back to sleep, blissfully unaware of her inner torment, Marion lay in his arms, still feeling uneasy. Over and over in her mind she struggled to relieve herself of the terrible guilt and fear that had gripped her. She had had a bad dream, that was all. The baby would be fine, she and Paul would be fine... They were happy. That was all that mattered.

PAUL

Honestly, I couldn't think of anything that would make me happier than I feel now. I love kids. I've always wanted to have my own — with the right woman. I'm twenty-four years old, and I'm ready for some responsibility. I want to be able to to take care of my own family, show people that it's not every black man who runs from the responsibility of bringing up children.

Me and Marion are good together. We jus' cool, yuh know. A kid of ours couldn't turn out wrong. This is our baby, and we both want it. Yeah, maybe I would have wanted to wait a bit longer, if we had the choice, but these things happen.

PAMELA'S REFLECTION STARED BACK AT HER FROM THE SHOP window on Peckham's Rye Lane. She had been admiring the snazzy red sequined dress on the emaciated mannequin, and had been staring so hard that she began to see herself in it.

In the fantasy that slowly began to form in her mind, she was on a stage with Satisfaction, the male strippers. They were wearing dinner suits, and it was her role to undress them, one item at a time, moving from one pumped-up body to the next. She would remove a garment slowly and seductively, toss it aside, and then proceed to caress and squeeze their biceps. This would go on until they were down to their pouches. The oil would come out next, and she would smother their rippling muscles from head to foot. Then it would be their turn to help her off with the sequined dress...

In her mind's eye she turned to them for the finale, and found they were all wearing Michael's face.

She snapped out of the daydream as suddenly as she had fallen into it. Jesus! She was becoming some kind of nymphomaniac. All she ever dreamed of was naked men, and nowadays they always seemed to end up being Michael.

She strolled up the road to the meat market. It was early morning, the best time to shop. Hardly anyone was on the streets. Any later, and getting from one end of Peckham to the other became an assault course, especially at Christmas.

Peckham had always felt like home to Pamela. Her parents had lived here until she was twelve years old. She remembered standing by her mother's side and listening to the conversations she had with her acquaintances as they travelled this very street. Her mother had always bumped into people she knew, from church, from back home, and people who had moved away but still came back to Peckham to shop.

"How you do, Miss P?"

"Bwoy! Not too good, yuh know."

"Wha'appen?"

"Me art'ritis ah kill me, Ma."

"Ah so? So wha' de doctor seh?"

"Dacta! All him a gi'me ah drugs fe mess up me head."

Or, "Ah Pamela dis? Look 'pon how she a tu'n big ooman now."

"Not too big to know her place," her mother would huff, pushing up her chest with crossed arms.

"Is true! Too much ah dem pickney nowadays ha' no respec'."

"Is de parent dem! Spoil de pickney, tu'n dem fool."

"Yuh nuh hear seh Miss Bea son lack up inna jailhouse again?"

"No! Fe wha'?"

"Ah no, me jus' tell yuh so, but de bwoy mash up some white gal face, near kill her."

"Ah true?"

"Then whey me jus' seh? Dem tell me de gal did sleep wid one nudda man."

"Well, she did get whey she ah look fa."

Gossip. Then her mother would go home and relay it all back to her father, word for word. Pamela felt her stomach tighten at the thought of her parents. She hadn't seen them in five years. She had no one except herself to care about. That was good, wasn't it?

The only family she had now were her friends. Her mother and father didn't want to know. Every year she sent them a card. Not once had she received one back.

To them, they didn't have a daughter. She sometimes regretted the way she had parted with her parents, helping herself to the cash savings they kept in a box under their bed. But at the time she'd felt she was entitled to take something on her departure.

Only once had she attempted a reconciliation. Her sour-faced mother had slammed the front door in her face. Her father had come to the living room window of their semi-detached house and peered out at her, stone-faced. When the tears had threatened she'd turned and run away from the hurt and humiliation.

Now, Pamela always spent Christmases with Joan and Shereen. This year, Joan and Colin had invited her and Michael for Christmas dinner. Joan still hadn't met Michael, and was dying to see the man that had managed to conquer Miss Pamela King.

Pamela had bought presents for both Joan and Shereen (Marion was away with Paul and wouldn't be around to share Christmas with them), but Michael's present was harder to choose. It would have to be something unique, and it would have to mean something to both of them.

Back in Deptford and her lonely flat, Pamela picked up her mail at the front door and switched on the answerphone while she unpacked the shopping.

"Pam, it's Joan. Call me back. See ya."

"Hi, babes. Michael. I'll be round eight o'clock. Later." Pamela smiled at the sound of his voice.

"It's Shaun. If you're there, pick up..." Pause. "I want to see you. Call me."

Pamela thought it was probably time to change her number, as Joan had done. Like a spring-clean thing.

The shopping unpacked, she picked up her mail and flipped through it as she crossed back into the living room. Phone bill, junk mail, Christmas card, and a letter from an organisation called NORCAP — probably some charity. She started with the Christmas card — good news first. It was from an old schoolfriend, Yvette. They never saw each other, or even exchanged words on the telephone, but every year without fail Pamela would send her a Christmas card and would receive one back. This year Pamela had forgotten, but it wasn't too late. She put the card aside, a mental picture of what Yvette must look like now entering her head. She had two kids now, and had been engaged for two years. Good for her.

Next she opened the phone bill. Eighty-four quid! She slapped a hand to her forehead. Shocked, she unfolded the itemised statement and perused the list of numbers. She counted fifteen calls to Michael on his mobile number. She would have to stick to using his land line from now on.

The last envelope was the one from NORCAP. She opened it and read the letterhead: National Organisation for the Counselling of Adoptees and Parents. Her brow furrowed as she read further.

> Dear Ms King
>
> We are writing to you on behalf of Mrs Eileen Cummins. Your parents, Mr and Mrs King of Howden Street, London SE15, have given us permission to inform you of your adoptive status. Mrs Cummins, your natural mother, wishes to make contact with you. We realise that a considerable amount of stress is brought about by these circumstances, and want to help both parties through this.
>
> Of course, the decision is yours, and no further contact will be made unless you inform our office, quoting the above reference number, to let us know that you want more information. Mrs Cummins does not have your details, and knows only that we have successfully traced you.
>
> Please do not hesitate to contact us if we can be of any further assistance.
>
> Yours sincerely, Karen Tomkin

The pages fell to the floor. Pamela closed her eyes, but the words still swam behind her eyelids: Adoptive status... Natural mother... ADOPTIVE STATUS.

Marion got up from her desk and closed the window. A football match was going on in the square outside her flats, which made concentration very difficult.

Another batch of tapes had arrived yesterday. She had spent all morning on just three of them. These were for the Valentine's Day issue: Black Men on Love.

There was a definite pattern emerging from listening to these guys talk about their feelings. The interesting thing was that they didn't really discuss their emotions. Anger and frustration, perhaps, but when it came to love and intimacy they either skipped it altogether or watered it down. Men, Marion concluded, clearly have their own language, which women have no chance of understanding. Some men talked of how they could get out of arguments with their women with simple white lies. They would say things like "I'll call you", which simply meant goodbye. They would give potential girlfriends work or mobile numbers, so that their woman wouldn't know they were fooling around. When some said they needed their own space it meant they were seeing someone else. Instead of telling their women how they felt about them, some said they would buy gifts, take them out, or offer to decorate.

The male ego was something that manifested itself strongly in the recordings. Men with no money would come out with, "I believe in equality," when what they really wanted to say was, "You can pay your share; I'm skint."

Marion was concerned by the discovery that a man finds it hard to admit to his woman when something is wrong. If he has problems, he'd rather not share them with his partner, because he would see it as a doubling of the burden, a weakness. How could she possibly help?

One subject explained in detail why he didn't phone his partner if he was going to be late meeting her. It was because he would usually be with friends or colleagues, and a phone call to his partner would make him look henpecked, like he had to ask her permission.

Men hated to ask for anything. "Why should we have to ask when it's our right to receive?" said one. If his woman ever turned him down for sex, he would demand to know who else she was getting it from.

Communication was a big problem. Marion's questions included what men talked to their partners about. The responses ranged from work to what they were going to eat tonight.

One topic they always seemed to avoid in long-term relationships was their feelings. Most subjects said they felt they knew when their partners were happy or sad, so they didn't need to ask them. They said women needed to communicate more as well; even if it meant a disagreement, at least the man would know how they felt.

There were also a few very considerate men, men who talked and listened to their partners, men who expressed their true emotions rather than what they felt their partner wanted to hear, men who put their families before their friends and careers.

One such example was a twenty-five-year-old who said he was raising his two-year-old daughter on his own because when his girlfriend found out she was pregnant she didn't want it. He'd persuaded her to have the baby and had promised to take the child off her hands and raise it himself. Which he did, and never regretted it.

Joan flipped the catalogue shut. She had ploughed through pages of children's toys looking for a present for Shereen. She knew what her daughter wanted: another Barbie doll. Martin had promised to buy her the latest one, which could say twenty different phrases. But Joan was hell-bent on buying her something educational. A computer would be ideal, and it didn't have to be expensive for a four-year-old child.

It was at times like these when Joan thought of how lonely Shereen must be, lacking any brothers or sisters to play with at home. And yet she didn't seem to mind. It was the norm for her. When Joan had the time she would read or draw with her, do quizzes, watch her play. These times were very precious to them both: mother and daughter in perfect harmony.

Joan would sometimes find herself envying Barbie and Ken. The plastic couple shared their baby duties, spent evenings in on the sofa, sunbathed on their roof garden, went raving together, and slept side by side in the same bed under the roof of the Barbie dreamhouse.

At least Martin was back on the scene now — even if it was as a part-time father. Despite Joan's doubts about his intentions, it still halved the burden. She didn't have to be alone any more. And Colin was just as much a father as an uncle to Shereen. She had asked her daughter what she thought of him coming to live with them. In reply, Shereen had asked why Daddy couldn't come and live with them again, and Joan had patiently explained once again that Mummy and Daddy didn't love each other any more, and that now Mummy loved Uncle Colin and wanted to be with him.

It was hard for a four-year-old to grasp, Joan knew, but Shereen had shrugged and said she didn't mind, so long as Daddy could still come and see her.

More than anything else right now, Joan wanted a stable family life for her daughter. She knew Colin was trying, but he had a lot to learn about commitment and about sharing someone else's life. In time, Joan hoped, and with her help, he would learn.

It was also nice having her younger sister living with her, albeit temporarily. They could do stuff together like shopping for clothes, pigging out on a Friday night with a video and a bottle of wine; they had a laugh. Plus, Donna was a permanent babysitter and someone to help with the housework and cooking. The only problem was the lack of privacy. Upstairs was banned for sex unless Donna was out; Joan's creaky bed would give her away every time. There was a new "Do Not Disturb" sign for the living room door, designed by Shereen, for when Colin came round.

For the first time in years, despite all the recent changes in her circumstances, Joan felt as though her life was coming together.

THE VICTORIA COACH TERMINAL WAS VERY BUSY. IT WAS Christmas week, and everyone seemed to be heading somewhere to visit friends or family.

Marion pulled her coat tighter around her as Paul took her arm and they dashed across the road to where the coach was filling up with people. They were on their way to spend a week with Marion's mother in Birmingham. Paul had finally persuaded her to tell her mother about the baby. Sooner would be better than later, he had reasoned, and at least they would be telling her together. They were also bringing the good news of Marion's first published article. She had a copy of the magazine in her luggage.

Marion had let Paul take charge of the arrangements. He'd decided he didn't want to drive all the way to Birmingham, saying he wouldn't have much use for his car there. His real reason for taking the coach was that he wanted to be able to relax with her.

Marion was now six months pregnant — five, if you asked Paul — and the bump was just beginning to show. She was feeling a lot better these days. Ever since she had told Paul about the baby the morning sickness had virtually stopped. The dizziness and lethargy she'd suffered now came about only when she was tired. And Paul was taking good care of her. They were living together now, albeit unofficially. Paul only went home a couple of days a week. He would pick her up from work and make sure she was comfortable at home, sometimes helping out in the kitchen. She'd been teaching him how to cook. He'd said he had to learn, so that he could take over once the baby was born.

She began to nod off half an hour into the journey. They had left home at eight o'clock that morning, having been up at six to check the packing and get organised. Paul cradled her head on his shoulder and wrapped an arm around her shoulder. If there was one thing that Marion could be certain of in her life, it was that Paul loved her.

The coach jolted to a halt and Marion awoke. She straightened up in her seat, blinking the sleep out of her eyes.

"Hi." Paul gave her a squeeze.

She kissed him lightly on the lips. "Hi yourself." She gazed out of the window. "Where are we?"

"Just a coach stop. You all right?"

"Thirsty," she said, licking her dry lips.

Paul reached into their holdall and produced a bottle of orange juice. He twisted the cap, breaking the seal, and poured some juice into a plastic cup for her.

She accepted it and drank it down in one go. Handing the cup back to him, she smiled. "Thanks, hon."

"Anything for my girl." He smiled back. "You still nervous?" He stroked the soft skin of her forearm.

Marion tilted her head back against the headrest. "Aren't you? You've never met my mum and stepdad. It isn't going to be easy. I don't know how you talked me into this." She regarded him with serious, dark eyes.

"You can't tell me that you'd prefer to turn up one day on your mother's doorstep with a child. You have to tell her now."

Marion sulked. "S'pose so."

"I am right," he told her.

"I know." She put her head on his shoulder, her lips pouting a little.

He kissed her forehead. "Get some sleep — you'll need it."

"Mmm," she yawned. She closed her eyes and let him hold her, rocking her back to sleep.

The minicab deposited them outside the row of cottages at the top of a steep hill. Marion had only been here once before, eighteen months earlier. Paul held her gloved hand, carrying their suitcase in the other. Marion had deliberately chosen loose clothing to cover the evidence of her pregnancy. She wore a big baggy jumper over leggings. They stood outside her parents' front door, shivering with the cold and nervousness, daring each other to ring the doorbell.

"Please, Paul. You do it," she asked.

"What's wrong with you?" he laughed. "It's your mum."

"I'm not ready for this. Can't we go somewhere for a drink first to calm my nerves?" She tugged at his hand.

"Later. Let's get this part over with first." He dropped the suitcase to the ground at his side and rang the bell in the centre of a seasonal holly wreath.

The door was opened almost immediately, as if the woman had been standing behind it all along. They looked at each other, and Marion smiled despite herself.

Paul felt relieved. He'd had no idea what to expect at this reunion. The last time he had seen Mrs Wilkins was at the funeral of Marion's sister. She looked a lot healthier now. Gwendolyn Wilkins could have been

Marion, only twenty years older. Their facial features were identical. They were about the same height, but Paul hoped Marion's figure wouldn't spread quite that much with age.

Gwendolyn held out her arms to her daughter. "Marion," she uttered. "Hello, Mum." Marion stepped into her mother's arms and they hugged.

As they stepped apart, Marion's mother let her eyes flit over Marion's body. "You do look well. Rosy cheeks." Paul cleared his throat, and both women turned as if surprised that he was there.

"Oh, Mum — you remember Paul, my boyfriend?"

Gwendolyn held out her hand to him and he stepped forward. Instead of his usual greeting of a peck on the cheek, he shook her hand formally. "Nice to see you again," he said, switching on his smiling eyes — and Marion watched Gwendolyn try to restrain her smile.

"Likewise, I'm sure." She stepped back to let them into the house. "Come in, bring your things. Thomas isn't home yet, but you'll see him later." She ushered them through the pastel-coloured hallway, her bottom rolling from side to side under the black pinafore dress she wore. There was a smell of baking in the air. Marion recognised the aroma of her mother's cinnamon scones, and memories came flooding back. Her mother had always been in the kitchen when they were little, cooking, baking, washing, cleaning. The house always had to be just so, with breakfast, lunch and dinner served at the same time every day.

The low afternoon sun shone on the walls, and sunbeams danced in the air above their heads from a window at the top of the first flight of stairs. Gwendolyn showed them into the living room, where they sat on a cosy rose-coloured sofa that looked brand new. Marion was sure it only looked that way because this was the room they used only for visitors. Her mother went off to make hot drinks for them all, leaving them alone for a few minutes.

"I can't see what all the fuss was about." Paul shrugged.

"Mum's all right on her own. Wait till he gets home," Marion warned, removing her gloves.

Paul couldn't believe it would be as bad as Marion was making out. Her mother seemed to like him, and there didn't seem to be any animosity between the two women. He looked around the modest room. It looked very cosy, but rich. Not exactly the kind of place you would let a child roam free in. A large decorated fir tree stood in the corner by the fireplace. The white lights blinked on and off as if following some inaudible tune. Brightly wrapped gifts already sat beneath it. Gwendolyn came back in with the tea and sat opposite them in the matching rose-coloured armchair. She told Paul he could call her Gwen. Mrs Wilkins was much too formal.

Gwendolyn and Paul were getting on like old friends. He complimented her and made her laugh with tasteful jokes and anecdotes of his experiences. Marion was amazed at the way he manipulated her mother. She couldn't quite believe that this was the same woman who had left her two years ago. Paul held Marion's hand the entire time. Every now and then he would give it a little squeeze or turn to smile at her, his eyes sparkling with charm. Her mother was gently grilling him. She had a way of gaining information that made it seem like simple curiosity. She seemed to want to know every detail of his past, and his plans for the future. Paul coped with it with admirable ease.

As she sat beside him, Marion began to realise just how much she loved this man. Over the past four months she had still feared she might be in love with Gerard. But the truth of the matter was, she had never been in love with Gerard. The realisation flooded her mind as she sat in her mother's living room. She had been in love with what other women thought she had. The actual man was nothing but a fake.

Paul looked over at her and she smiled, realising she had been staring at him. She leant her head on his shoulder and he moved his arm, wrapping it around her waist. Gwendolyn noticed this, and with a silent smile she stood up. "I'll just clear these things away. Paul, I'll show you where the two of you will be sleeping — you can bring your things."

"Yeah, okay," he said, standing up to follow her. He turned to Marion as her mother left the room. "You all right?"

"Yeah, sure." She nodded. In fact she had never felt better. She added, "I love you, Panther." It was the first time she had told him, and she knew it had been worth it to see the look on his face. His eyes smiled at her and he leant over and kissed her on the lips. "Love you too." He was grinning as he left the room to catch up with her mother.

Thomas Wilkins was a big man — six foot five — and he looked as though he had done weightlifting in the past and then let himself go. The fact was that he had spent his youth loading ships and lorries in Liverpool, and his muscles were natural. His features were naturally stern, and he didn't say much.

He arrived home just before dinner. During the meal the talk was light. Thomas said very little.

After dinner they went back into the living room to catch up on all the news from both sides. Thomas put the television on — a Des O'Connor Christmas special.

"So, how is Joany?" Gwendolyn asked, pouring a glass of sherry for them all. She had been calling Marion's friend Joany ever since she was about eight years old.

"She's fine, Mum. She's just got engaged, actually."

Gwendolyn looked up, astonished. She turned to her husband. "Joany getting married! Isn't that nice, Tom?"

Thomas nodded. "Nice," he growled, his eyes not leaving the television screen.

Marion frowned. She doubted he even remembered who 'Joany' was, having only met her once, at the funeral.

"Mum, we… er, have some news for you as well," she said, reaching for Paul's hand.

"Yes?" Her mother's eyes travelled from Marion to Paul expectantly. Marion swallowed hard, trying to find the words she needed to explain her situation to her mother. The lights on the Christmas tree carried on their merry dance as if mocking her. What made it harder was her stepfather had suddenly become interested in the conversation.

Paul carried on for her. "I want you to know that I love this woman." He glanced at Marion. "She's brought purpose to my life, and I'm not planning on letting her go again."

Gwendolyn looked over at Thomas, who was now leaning forward in his chair, elbows on his knees. His grey eyes scrutinised the pair, waiting for the news. He had suspected there was more to their visit than a family get-together; now it seemed he was going to be proved right.

"We're going to have a baby," Marion blurted out, unable to take the pressure of the situation any longer. She waited, watching her mother's face for a reaction. Her heart tried to escape by beating its way through her chest. Gwendolyn's face had frozen, except for the corners of her mouth which had dropped to form an unhappy arch. "Oh," she issued.

"Hmm-mm," Thomas mumbled, and leant back in his chair, a smug look on his face.

Marion ignored him. "We want the baby, Mum. Although it wasn't planned, we really love each other, and we'll do our best to bring him — or her — up."

"Marion, you have no idea," Gwendolyn snapped, cutting her short. "How could you let this happen? After all I've been through with you and your sister, trying to bring you up properly…" Her lips trembled and her voice began to quaver.

Thomas broke his silence. "You have disappointed your mother, young lady. When she heard that you were coming to visit with your young man, she had hopes of hearing a wedding announcement — not this."

"Tom!" Gwendolyn held up her hand, halting his speech. She held her head high, her eyes hard, and turned on Marion. "Don't get me wrong, Marion. I'm happy that I will soon be a grandmother. But you don't know how much bringing a child into the world takes from you."

Paul stepped in to share the abuse. "We have thought about this, y'know, Gwen. We know what we're doing," he said positively. Gwendolyn cut her eyes after him and continued talking to Marion. "How long have the two of you been back together? Six months?" Thomas got up and walked over to the large bay windows, his back to them, feigning interest in something happening outside.

"I'm sure you feel as though you'll never part now — but you wait until that baby is born," Gwendolyn continued, her hands and arms emphasising her words with wide gestures. "When it's screaming in the middle of the night, when you're buried in housework, bills, too tired to make love — then we'll see if you still feel the same. An' how do you even know that this boy will stick around when the going gets tough, huh?"

Marion wanted to scream. It was right there at the back of her throat. She wanted to yell at her mother, tell her that she wasn't a lonely teenager — as her mother had been the first time she fell pregnant. She had Paul, and she had her friends. She stood and walked out defiantly under her mother's angry gaze. She was so upset she couldn't even retaliate, knowing it would mean the end of any kind of decent relationship between them.

Paul stood as well, wanting to go after Marion but feeling he hadn't said what he knew these people needed to hear. He heard Marion's footsteps on the stairs, and then a door slamming above them. He remained standing, and addressed the two people in the room as if from a pulpit. "How could you say somet'ing like that to your only daughter? You don't know what she's been through since you left her. You don't even find out firs' if yuh daughter and I are capable of bringing up our child! Cho', people like you need to sit down and t'ink about what is important in your lives before putting judgement on others." Thomas bristled — Paul could almost see the hair on his head rising — and moved to his wife's side.

Paul started to walk out to find Marion and comfort her, but turned back again. "Y'know, when she told me she didn't want to tell you about the baby, I couldn't understand why she was so worried. I mean, you're her mother. How could you not be happy about a new addition to your family?" He clenched his teeth. "We shouldn't have come. I can tek care of her on my own!" He whirled out of the room, leaving the husband and wife staring at the empty space he had just vacated, their mouths hanging open.

The next morning the four of them sat down to a full breakfast of fried dumplings, ackee, fried fish, plantain and hard dough bread. Marion and Paul had talked through most of the night. Paul had said that he didn't want her to fall out with her mother again, especially not over their child. Marion had persuaded him that they should retreat, go home — that they had been doing fine without family involvement, and could go on doing fine. Paul had given in because he could see her getting more and more upset. They would go to his mother's home instead, he'd suggested. His brother and sister were also going there for Christmas. They would be welcomed with open arms.

It seemed that Mr and Mrs Wilkins had also had a talk of their own.

Breaking the dough bread, Paul informed them that they were leaving on the next available coach. His announcement was met with silence, and furtive glances between Gwendolyn and Thomas across the table. Thomas eventually broke the silence. His stern face showed no emotion as his grey, glassy eyes turned to Marion and Paul. "Gwendolyn has something she would like to say to you both." He nodded at Gwendolyn.

A smile found the corners of her small mouth. "Marion," she breathed, reaching across the table for her hand. Marion let her mother's hand rest on her own, but made no move to reciprocate. "You know how much I care about your welfare," Gwendolyn continued.

Marion still held some bleak anger within her, and couldn't bring herself to speak to her mother, much less look at her. She kept her eyes downcast.

Gwendolyn went on: "When you told me about the baby, all I could think about was myself at sixteen. I was pregnant with you; your father was too young to care, and my parents turned their back on me. I was alone and scared. I know that you're older than I was — and you have Paul, who has proved to be a very caring young man." Her eyes travelled fleetingly to Paul's face, a shadow of regret and apology being conveyed to him. "I want to say I'm sorry, and beg your forgiveness."

Marion looked up at her mother. Tears came to both their eyes. Marion stood, and walked around the dining table to her mother's side. She leant towards her mother and let herself be hugged.

Paul smiled and turned to Thomas. He offered the older man his hand across the table. And black and white met in a friendly handshake.

The decision was made. They were staying for Christmas.

During the week, Marion and her mother went shopping for presents and baby things. They also visited Gwendolyn's friends and neighbours, sometimes with Paul in tow. Gwendolyn's closest friends came round and shared the news which she was no longer ashamed of.

Christmas day was the first traditional celebration Marion had had since her mother had left London. She missed her friends, but a phone call took care of that. The fact that Marion had Paul with her made everything perfect.

By the end of the week, they had so much extra luggage that Thomas offered to drive them back home. They accepted gratefully. The goodbyes were tearful on the women's side. Both promised to keep in touch regularly. The men stood by, hands in pockets, not knowing whether to chat, hug or what.

Back in their own flat, Marion sank into the armchair and kicked her boots off. "I'm exhausted," she sighed.

Having switched the heating back on, Paul entered the living room and hunched down in front of her. "Now that we've got that out of the way, don't I get a thank you?" He took her small stockinged feet in his hands and rubbed them gently.

She smiled indulgently. "Of course you do. Thanks, honey. I couldn't have done it without you."

"You wouldn't have to." He reached up and kissed her, pressing his thumbs on her instep before moving up to her toes. "I've been thinking. Wouldn't it be a good idea if I jus' moved in? What do you think? It won't be long before the baby's born, an' I want to be there with you."

Marion relaxed and issued a moan of pleasure. She was so glad he had brought the subject up; she hadn't wanted to put any more pressure on him. This time it was his decision. "How soon could you move in?"

Paul grinned and, letting her foot go, he hugged her. "Tomorrow soon enough?"

"No. How about right now?" Her wide, childlike eyes danced.

"You got it."

Families. The house was buzzing with the noise of a family get-together. Joan, Donna and Grace were in the kitchen preparing the Christmas

180

dinner.

Choice FM kept them entertained as they chatted and worked. It was the first time they had prepared Christmas dinner together since Donna had left home three years before.

Colin was playing Connect Four with Shereen in the living room — and losing badly, to Shereen's glee. Her babyish laughter could be heard throughout the house. A repeat of The Snowman was showing on the television. Donna had started divorce proceedings against John, on her sister's advice. Joan had changed her number again to stop him harassing her. He wouldn't have a chance to see her unless he was brave enough to risk jail by breaking the injunction.

Although Colin and Joan had decided to get engaged, they had resolved not to tell their families and friends until they were sure it was going to work out. There was nothing worse, in Joan's opinion, than being premature with an announcement.

There would be seven for dinner this year, with Michael and Pamela coming too. This was going to be an occasion to be remembered. They would miss seeing Marion this year, but she was doing the right thing by going to see her mum.

Peeling potatoes for roasting, Grace sat at the kitchen table. Donna sat opposite, mixing batter for the Yorkshire puddings.

"So — Colin. You and him is more dan fren' now?" Grace asked for the second time that day.

The first time Joan had informed her that Colin was coming to have dinner with them her mother had wondered why. Joan had simply told her that he was family and had every right to.

Joan now bent down to the oven to check the turkey. "I've told you, Mum, we've started seeing each other recently."

"How yuh mean, seeing each udder? Yuh sharing a bed?"

"Mum!" Donna giggled.

Joan shook her head. Her mother always spoke her mind. She had taught them to do the same. "Yeah, we sleep together sometimes," she admitted, feeling a heat in her cheeks that wasn't from the oven. "But we're not living together yet," she added.

"Yuh don't t'ink is about time Shereen get a brudda or sista?" Grace dropped the last peeled potato into the bowl and handed it up to Joan.

Taking the bowl, she crossed to the sink to wash them. "I know, Mum, but you don't rush these things. When I'm ready I'll decide with the baby's father."

Grace now turned to her younger daughter. "Dis one married,

181

divorce, and don't even produce one gran' pickney. Nuttin' to bless de union wid."

Donna glared at her mother. There was no way she had wanted to have a child with John. What kind of father would he have been?

Joan jumped in to save her sister. "Don't start on her, Mum. She's young, plenty of time..." She was thanked by a look of appreciation in Donna's eyes.

Grace huffed and stood up to wrap the potato peel in newspaper and throw it in the bin. "You two always stick together. Patrick was de ongle chile I did have pan my side, and yuh faada tek him wey."

Joan tutted. "That's not true, mum. You spoiled Patrick — that's why he was closer to you than us. While Don and I did our chores — and his, sometimes — he was out with his mates. You always let him off."

"We always got the washing up and cooking and cleaning," Donna agreed. "All he ever did was carry the rubbish out every Thursday and hoover the carpets."

Grace screwed up her face. "Cho, a man don't have to learn to wash pot. Dat's what they have ooman fa."

Joan and Donna exchanged looks. Even though their mother was now independent, and had proved to herself and her daughters that she didn't need a man, she always made it clear that it was men who needed women. In Grace's eyes, men left their mothers to live with women, and thenceforth expected the same treatment — their clothes to be washed and ironed, cooked food ready when they got home — plus the added bonus of sex.

Joan deftly moved the conversation on. "So, Don, I forgot to ask you how you got on at that employment agency." "Oh, they took my details, but I haven't done anything in administration for a while. They want me to take some computer course to get up to date with the systems."

"That's no problem. Community college has loads of courses."

Grace joined in. "Yes. Me will bring you de brochure from home."

"I think that's too far out for Donna, Mum. She's better off picking one up at the local library."

"She should be living back at home now, anyway. You have your man and yuh dawta to tek care of. I have plenty room, and I could do with de comp'ny."

"Maybe you're right, Mum." Joan dried her hands on a tea towel and took a seat at the table. "I could do with my privacy again. And Donna could have much more of her own privacy with you. Sharing a room with her baby niece isn't right for a woman her age."

Donna listened to them discussing her life as though she wasn't there. It made her wonder what they said when she wasn't around. Families!

Pamela and Michael arrived, dressed immaculately, just as the table was being laid.

Joan looked at the tall, dark, handsome man in the pure wool jacket, and wondered why she couldn't have met him first. "So, this is Michael?"

Pamela introduced him to everyone. Michael nodded at the smiling female faces, and then Joan took him through to the living room to meet Colin.

Michael immediately homed in on the computer game Colin was playing. "Is that Mortal Kombat?" he asked, settling down on the sofa.

"Mortal Kombat II. You wanna game?" Colin asked, glad for the male company.

"Set me up."

The girls rolled their eyes and left them to it.

"What d'you think of Michael, then?" Pamela asked eagerly.

"If I didn't have Colin I'd be in there making my move right now," Joan told her. "He is gorgeous. What possessed Cheryl to let him go?"

Pamela chuckled. "I don't think she could handle him."

"Well, you can tell him from me that when he gets bored of you, I'll handle him any time."

Pamela slapped Joan's arm playfully. "Hands off," she warned. "And none of that footsie under the table."

Michael and Colin had become instant mates. The talk over the lunch table was football and boxing — boxing being Colin's first love. The women stuck to gossip and their plans for the new year. Grace had already decided Donna was moving back in. Donna told her she had decided to put her name down with the council. It shouldn't be too long, she said, before she moved out. Pamela shot that remark down as optimistic. She told tales of friends who were stuck sleeping on mates' sofas for years because they were single with no dependants. "You'd have to get pregnant to get a flat off those people."

That started Grace on her gran pickney yearning again.

Joan told them that she was planning on changing her car. The Maestro was getting outdated. She wanted a car that matched her status. So, for the new year she wanted something sporty and flash... and yet feminine. The guys joined in at the mention of cars, and there was a heated discussion about what a woman could and couldn't handle.

After a long and indulgent late-afternoon lunch, the women let the men clear the table while they retired to the living room. Shereen was shortly thereafter put to bed, followed closely by Grace an hour later.

The youngsters (as Grace called them) spent the evening chatting, laughing, playing music, drinking — and finally settled down to watch a video.

The two couples paired off.

Donna decided to slip away and retire upstairs to cuddle up to her niece.

SPRING. A NEW YEAR, A NEW SEASON. A TIME FOR NEW beginnings; a time for the problems of the past to be resolved and put behind you. But whatever problems people manage to solve, others always seem to emerge...

That evening it was Martin who put Shereen to bed. Joan had used the time to catch up on some work she had brought home a week ago, and was now clearing the kitchen.

Martin entered the neat room and leant against the counter by the sink. Joan looked up at him and smiled. "Did she settle down all right?" she asked.

"Yeah. She was tired." He rested his palms behind him on the counter. Joan looked so relaxed and at ease with life and everything, that he felt an urge to encircle her waist and pull her close. But he knew it wasn't worth risking what he already had for the satisfaction of a basic human instinct. He had been there for three hours. Usually, after Shereen went to bed, he would leave. Now he was arousing Joan's suspicion by hanging around.

"I saw Colin yesterday," he said.

Joan turned to look at him as she replied. "Yeah? How is he?" She tried to sound genuinely naive. They still hadn't told anyone about the engagement.

"He looked good. His woman must be taking care of him," Martin said, grinning.

Joan smiled to herself; she knew Colin was getting it good. But what was Martin getting at? "So, he's got a woman has he?" "Didn't you know? He's been living with this girl in Deptford now for eight months. He's still there, so it mus' be good."

Joan stared at him with disbelieving eyes. The plate she was rinsing slipped from her hands and splashed back into the sink. "Y... you're joking," she stuttered.

"Naw, straight up! I was shocked too, believe me. Colin never stayed with no one for that long. I was telling him just the other day how he ought to settle down..." Martin carried on talking, but Joan had phased out. There was a rush of blood pumping quickly to her head, her temples were pulsating; she fought to control her breathing but was fighting a losing battle. Something was using a tiny hammer and playing drums in her ears. Colin was deceiving her again. How could he do this to her? They were practically engaged, for God's sake! Tears of anger and frustration pricked her eyes and she pretended to sneeze to cover it up.

"...So when he told me he was serious about someone I just had to meet her, you know what I mean?"

"You met her?" Joan whispered. She turned a plate over in the rack and reached into the suds for another.

"Yeah! They didn't seem real close or nothing, but maybe it's just 'cause I was there, you know?" He nudged her playfully with his elbow.

Bastard, bastard, bastard, she screamed in her head, and slammed another dripping plate into the rack. A grimace attached itself to her face.

Martin turned to her. "You want some help? You look kinda tired."

She shook her head. "I'm all right," she said, then she gazed back at him as a new thought entered her mind. Martin was still an attractive guy. She had loved him once; and now she loved his deceiving brother. What sweet revenge, to sleep with Colin's brother again... She was sure that she could play Martin straight into her hands.

She dried her hands on a dish towel. "Want a drink?" she offered.

Martin looked surprised. "Yeah," he said, unsure. "Why not?" She had never encouraged him to hang around when Shereen was absent. She had always made it clear that the only reason he was here was because Shereen needed her father. Now she was practically giving him a come-on. Women were the strangest creatures alive.

She crossed to the fridge and produced a bottle of Canei. Martin watched her, trying to figure her out.

"Let's go and sit down," she said, grabbing two glasses from the cupboard. She handed him the bottle and led him through to the living room, where she sat on the three-seater settee and patted the space beside her, giving him the full works with her eyes. "I get so lonely sometimes in the evenings," she said. "Not having a man to talk to..."

Martin sat by her side and twisted the cap off the wine bottle. "Yeah, I know the feeling." He filled the wine glasses. Their eyes locked as they took the first sip together.

Joan pulled one leg up under her so that she was half facing him.

"You've really been taking care of yourself." His eyes flitted over her casual jogging attire. "Do you remember when we first met at that party?"

Joan nodded, smirking. "In New Cross. Yeah, I went with Marcia."

"All my friends were after you that night." He licked his lips. "But I got there first." Joan leaned towards him. "I remember, you told me."

He put his glass on the floor by the settee, and his hand found itself on her knee and then rose to rest on her thigh. "You haven't changed a bit."

"Oh, so I've still got an eighteen-year-old body, have I?" she giggled.

His voice became husky. "Your body will always be the same to me." His mouth was now so close she could feel his breath on her lips. "So tell me," she said matter-of-factly. "What's she look like?"

The spell was broken. Martin drew back, a puzzled frown on his face. "Who?"

"Colin's girlfriend."

He pulled his hand away and rested his head on the back of the sofa. "When were you going to tell me?"

Now it was Joan's turn to frown. "Tell you what?"

His eyes drifted to a framed portrait of Joan and Shereen on top of the TV cabinet. "Shereen reckons her Uncle Colin is coming to live with you."

Joan gasped, flustered. Kids! Never know how to keep something to themselves. "It isn't what you think…"

"How do you know what I think? You've been seeing my brother for months, from what Shereen's been telling me, an' you couldn't even mention it."

Joan stood up and turned her back to him. "Colin and I have been seeing each other, but it's only just got serious. We didn't want to tell anyone because we weren't sure how it would work out."

"I'm his brother, for goodness' sake! Family!"

Joan remembered that she was trying to get information out of him, not argue about her personal life. She returned to the sofa and looked him in the eye. "Martin… this other woman, that was just to wind me up, right?" she questioned hopefully.

Martin smirked. "No. He really is living with a girl in Deptford."

Joan felt her heart stop for at least three seconds. She dry-swallowed. "But didn't he ever mention me?"

"No. Jus' like you didn't mention him."

Her anger rose again, and she jumped up and paced the room.

Martin watched with a critical grin on his face. He found the whole situation hilarious. "So, you want to tell me about you and Colin?" he asked. Joan didn't know where to begin. She decided that the the beginning would be best.

"When you left, we started seeing each other." She paused. Martin already knew that his brother had caught Joan on the rebound, although perhaps he didn't know the extent of their involvement. Either way, it hadn't seemed to affect him that much. His eyes were serious, expressionless, waiting. "We were just friends at first; nothing happened until I was sure I was over you..." She told him everything, right up until the last time she had seen Colin. She even told him about how Lois had pretended to be pregnant to keep him, to trick him into marrying her. "Yeah?" he chuckled. "Jus' like Colin to fall for that one. She mus' know him well."

Joan took offence at that remark. The only reason Colin had "fallen for it" was because he cared what happened to his child. She wanted to blast Martin with that one, but there was still information to get from him, and she didn't want to rock the boat.

Martin had raised his eyebrows at the fact that they'd got engaged.

"I wanted him to tell you," she said earnestly. "It was so childish not to tell the family. It was the best way, though. You know Colin — heaven only knows how long it was going to last before he got itchy feet again."

Martin nodded vaguely. He looked up at her as she paused in mid stroll. "You going to dump him?"

She looked shocked at the suggestion, as if it hadn't occurred to her. "I can't. Well, not until I talk to him about it."

Martin raised his hands in a "keep me out of it" gesture. "Don't say it came from me. Colin and I are on shaky ground as it is. You know we weren't talking for a while."

Joan knew all about the year the two of them hadn't talked to each other. Colin had taken her side in the break-up, and was putting pressure on his brother. His mother had taken Martin's side, and the family had become split. Their mother had finally brought them back together the Christmas before last.

"I need his address, Marty. I'll tell him someone else saw him going in and told me about it. No names, I promise."

Martin almost laughed. "Shit, Joan. I can't." He placed his palms on his knees as though he was getting ready to stand.

"I promise, he'll never know," she begged. She got down and kneeled comically at his feet.

"He'll guess." Martin avoided her eyes.

She changed tactics. "I thought you cared about me," she said.

Martin sighed deeply. Women! They always come out with that line when a man tries to assert himself. "I do, but—"

"How else am I gonna find out the truth?" she interrupted. "He'll deny it unless I catch him in the act."

Martin leaned back and thought about it. "He's living in Dolphin Towers. Eighty-nine."

Joan memorised the address and squeezed Martin's hand. "Ta. And don't look so worried. You're doing this for me." She smiled appeasingly, her Egyptian eyes enchanting him.

She poured some more wine and the two of them sat and chatted until the early hours of the morning. Joan had wanted to go straight to Dolphin Towers that night.

She was going to get her man. Tomorrow would do just fine.

IT WAS TEN O'CLOCK AT NIGHT WHEN JOAN PULLED UP OUTSIDE the block of flats. As she stood outside the flat, she could hear the sound of a radio and imagined them together in there. She had had to psych herself up on the way over; now she had to again before knocking on the door. Her heart was beating way too fast. Her palms were sweaty, and a fine sheen of perspiration glazed her top lip.

She breathed deeply and knocked loudly. She heard the sound of a door opening and the radio momentarily getting louder, then slippered feet coming towards the front door. She drew her chest up, hands by her side military style, ready for the confrontation. The door swung open and the same young woman she had seen that day in Lewisham stood before her, dressed in jeans and a jumper.

She looked Joan up and down. "Yes?" Hostility was harsh in her voice.

Joan didn't let it deter her. She cleared her throat. "Is Colin in?"

"Who're you?" the girl asked, standing her ground.

"Just get Colin. He knows who I am."

"He's sleeping," the girl lied.

"Well, wake him up." Joan was getting ready to barge in if she had to.

The girl looked her up and down again, a malignant scowl on her face, before stepping back into the flat. She wasn't much to look at: plain and flat-chested, with short, unstyled hair and a huge backside. Whatever it was that had attracted him, it wasn't her looks.

A moment later Colin came out. The look on his face was nothing short of comical. Joan would have laughed if she wasn't so angry.

He shut the inner door behind him. Dressed in black track suit bottoms and a white T-shirt, he looked as though he hadn't slept for a couple of days.

They faced each other, Colin leaning against the wall in that easygoing way of his.

Joan stood with her hands thrust into her jacket pocket. "Was that Lois?" she asked.

Colin looked down at his feet. "Yeah. How did you find out where I lived?"

"Why didn't you tell me?"

He shrugged. "This looks bad, doesn't it?" He peered at her from beneath his long eyelashes.

"Damn right it looks bad. What the hell d'you think you're playing at?"

"She's renting me a room."

Joan rolled her eyes to the ceiling. "And just what else is she renting?" she jested sarcastically.

He shrugged again, his muscular shoulders hunched in disgrace. He was like a little boy caught stealing. "This isn't what you think. I wouldn't two-time you." He sighed deeply. "I was evicted from my flat. It was before we got back together. I moved in here because there was nowhere else to go," he explained. "Not good enough." Joan put one hand on her hip. "After what she did... Why didn't you tell me you needed somewhere to live?"

"Because I've got somewhere to live! I wasn't out on the streets."

Joan screwed up her face in disgust. "With her?" Colin raised his hands and glanced towards the inner door. "Keep your voice down — she's a funny person."

"I don't give a fuck what kind of person she is. You're my man, or so I thought. If what you said is true, then she's got no hold over you. You could leave with me right now."

Colin kissed his teeth. "What're you talking about?"

"I'm talking about you moving in with me. Get your things. The car's downstairs."

Colin was shocked; he couldn't move. He studied her eyes. "Are you sure?"

Joan stood up straight, asserting her seriousness. "I wouldn't say it otherwise. It seems the only way I can keep an eye on you is if you're coming home to me every night. So — are you coming or not?"

He grinned out of the side of his mouth. "You giving me orders now?"

"If that's the way you want to see it, yes I am."

"You don't believe me, do you?" He searched her still angry eyes.

"I'll believe you if you go in there and come out with your things packed," she told him.

"Okay, you got me." He was still grinning as he stepped towards her. "I do love you, y'know. Even though you're a mad, impulsive fool."

She remained dead serious; she would deal with him properly at home. "Need any help packing?"

His hands dropped to his sides. "I don't think that's a good idea. Why don't you wait in the car?"

Joan huffed and ran a hand through her short, bobbed hair. "Why?"

"Well, Lois ain't gonna be too happy about losing her lodger."

"I think I'll wait right here I wouldn't wanna miss the big farewell," she said defiantly. She was well aware of what she could learn from the next two minutes. If this was an affair, it would be more than a simple goodbye and a handshake. Colin went back into the flat, closing the front door. There was a lot of talk going on inside. Joan strained to hear what was going on, resorting eventually to pressing her ear against the front door.

"Who is she?" she heard Lois say with some spite.

"None of your business."

"Where d'you think you're going?"

"Home."

"Don't talk to me like that!"

"Where's my blue jacket?"

"You can't just leave in the middle of the night."

"Try stopping me."

"You don't care about me."

"You got that right."

Joan heard a loud thump, as if something had hit the wall, and she sprang back as the front door opened.

Lois's voice followed Colin out of the flat. "Get out! Jus' get out! Mek sure you tek everything, else it ain't gonna be here when you come back!"

Colin struggled out with two huge holdalls bulging with clothes and a rucksack on his back. "Grab these for me. I'm going back for my stereo," he said, handing her the bags. Joan dragged them over to the lift and pressed the down button.

The lift arrived as Colin was coming back out of the flat. Joan heaved the bags in and turned to him. He carried his stereo in both arms. He smiled. She smiled back. This was finally going to be it. Colin was hers.

Neither of them was prepared for what happened next. There was an unearthly scream from behind Colin, and over his shoulder Joan caught a glimpse of a raised arm that ended in a kitchen knife. The arm swiped downwards towards Colin's back. Acting on sheer instinct, Joan had grabbed his jacket and pulled him towards her, but the knife caught him in the arm.

The stereo dropped with a load crack as it hit the concrete floor, half in, half out of the lift. Colin uttered a strangled cry and tried to clutch at his injured arm; the knife had pierced the sleeve of his jacket. There was a stunned look on his face as he stumbled and fell, and the lift tried to close on his legs, automatically opening again.

He wasn't too badly hurt, and he pulled himself into a sitting position. There was already blood seeping through his thin jacket. Joan glared across at the woman holding the knife and fury welled up within her.

As Lois came at them again, Joan, free of any baggage, climbed over Colin's legs and ran head-first into the girl's stomach. The wind knocked out of her, Lois retreated and stumbled back against the wall, the knife flying out of her hand. Joan went for her again, dragging her up by her short hair and digging her nails into her scalp. She balled her hand into a fist and slammed it hard into the girl's face, feeling it connect with the bridge of her nose. Then she open-handedly slapped her across her cheek. Lois struggled, yelping and screaming, to grab Joan. She parried a clumsy blow and struck out with her left foot. But Joan was bigger and stronger. She threw the girl hard against the wall by her hair and blood splattered from the girl's nose which, Joan suspected, she'd broken. Splashes of blood landed on Joan's cream blouse and jacket.

Lois went limp, and Joan let her fall to a heap on the concrete floor by her front door. A door opened cautiously down the hall. Joan ignored the African man who came out to stare.

Colin was leaning against the lift door, blood dripping from his arm.

"You okay?" she asked him breathlessly, kneeling by his side.

"Me? I'm fine. Let's just get out of here." He eased himself against one wall of the lift, Joan dragged his stuff in behind them, and they descended.

Back home that night they took a bath together. Colin's stab wound wasn't as bad as it had at first appeared. Joan had bandaged it tight to stop the bleeding. Now she sat opposite him at the tap end of the bath.

He lay back with a flannel covering his boyish face.

"Colin?"

"Mmm?"

"There must be things you don't like about me."

He removed the flannel from his face and lowered it into the warm water.

Joan placed a hand on his knee. "You know I can't be perfect. What would you see as my faults?" she asked.

"Well..." he thought, "you always see the bad side of things..."

"Uh-uh," Joan interrupted, shaking her head. "I'm a realist. I don't sugar-coat things. I tell it like it really is."

"Yeah, whatever. It comes over as pessimism, though. You have bad mood swings too." He paused for thought. "Like when you're angry at me. All of a sudden you come over all passionate or sweet, and then you're angry and bitter again. I hate that. I never know where I am with you."

Joan frowned. Maybe this wasn't such a good idea after all.

Colin continued none the less: "And I don't like the way you lump all men together and judge us as one. We're not all the same. You say 'the Baker brothers' as if there's no difference between us. Nobody is perfect, but we're all individuals. Let a man prove himself before judging him."

"I'd have to have a man prove me wrong before I made a decision to treat him any differently," Joan said, grumpily squeezing out her flannel and then soaking it again. "Anything else?"

He opened his eyes and blinked a drip of water from his long lashes. "Not for now, but you can tell me what you don't like about me." He watched her as her eyes travelled to the ceiling in thought.

"Okay — where do I start?"

Colin twisted his mouth to one side. He looked worried.

"I got one. I don't like the fact that you take advantage of the way I feel about you."

"How?"

"Because you know how I feel, you think you can always come back no matter what — and you've been right so far."

He grinned.

"But did you ever think about how I really feel? It hurts to see myself weaken. I hate weakness in emotions."

Colin said nothing, letting her continue.

"Another thing is, all the years I've known you, you've never changed."

Colin sat up now, drawing his knees up to his chest. Water dripped down his hairy chest and back into the bath.

Joan regarded him across the water. "You look the same, dress the same, you're in the same job... People think you've got no ambition. They look at me and wonder what I see in someone like you. I know you've got ambition, but you're just not doing anything to make it happen. I want other people to be able to see what you're all about."

"I don't care what other people think. I'm me..."

"I know you don't. But it's not about what they want, it's about doing what you need to do to improve yourself."

Colin nodded his head in silence.

"Another thing — you're insensitive," she told him. She fished the soap out of the water and lathered her flannel. "You don't know how to make love. We have sex. Sometimes I just wish you'd kiss my body with little tender kisses from my head down to my toes. I'd love a gentle massage occasionally. Even just to have you lie down with me and hold me without it leading to sex... When I say no to you, you just think I'm playing hard to get. You don't listen to my needs."

"Well, you've never complained before," he remonstrated.

"You don't notice. As I said, you're insensitive. As soon as you get turned on you're only out to satisfy number one."

"That's not true. I go down on you — not many black men do that."

"No, and not many black men know what to do when they get there," she replied pointedly.

This was turning into a massacre. Colin glared at her. "Is that it?"

Joan laughed. "No. One more. You know how to say 'I love you' now. Just try showing it a little more often. And I'm not talking about sex now."

He frowned. "You talking about presents and taking you out and stuff?"

"Not necessarily. Asking me how I am, cooking for me, taking Shereen off my hands when I need a break, giving me a massage when I've had a hard day. Sharing time with me..." She looked into his attentive brown eyes to see if he understood.

"Bwoy!" He scratched his head. "This relationship t'ing nuh easy."

Joan laughed again. "We'll work on it together."

"Mmm, I don't know about that now." He grinned cheekily, the gap in his teeth giving him the look of an urchin.

"Yeah, well, you're in my house now — and I ain't asking you, I'm telling you."

"Yes, miss."

Joan threw the wet flannel at him and it splatted his face with suds.

COLIN

I knew that Lois was a nutter. There was something unhinged about her from the start. I can't believe that the girl would've killed me, though.

But my woman come to my rescue. That's what I call love. Yeah, I like that. My future wife is not only tough where it counts, but she's got muscle power too. Warrior! From the way I see her throwing those punches I better watch myself. I might end up on the end of one of them any time I upset her.

Looks like that's it, then. I'm living in my fiancée's house, with my brother's daughter. I've got myself a family.

Time to grow up, I suppose. Yikes!

MARION'S EYES FLEW OPEN IN THE DARKNESS AS A CONTRACTION jolted her out of her sleep. She turned over and faced the clock, watching the time before the next one. It was fifteen minutes before she felt the tightness again. They were mild contractions, but she knew they could still signal the birth of her baby. But before she woke Paul she had to be sure. He wasn't expecting anything for another month. She had to make it a convincing "premature" labour. She slipped out of bed and went to make herself a cup of tea. The contractions eased off for about an hour, then started again more intensely, the time between each one shortening. She told herself she would wait until they were coming about five minutes apart, but the pain was becoming unbearable. It felt as though her middle was trapped in a vice that was tightening with every new contraction. Beads of sweat stood out on her forehead. She sat on the sofa, her feet placed wide apart, and breathed through them as she had been told to do, until finally she could stand the agonising wait no more. She waddled back to the bedroom intending to wake Paul, but as she crawled in next to him he turned to her, already awake. "Is everything all right?" he asked.

Marion tensed as another contraction immobilised her. "The baby's coming," she panted.

Paul shot upright as though on a spring. "It can't be — we've got weeks yet." He placed his hand on her tummy.

"Don't panic. The baby's fine. I think we should get to the hospital, though."

Paul threw the covers from his legs and reached for the phone on the bedside table. "Where's the hospital number? I'm sure you left it by the phone."

"By the phone in the front room, Paul."

"Oh, yeah." He smiled before hurrying from the room.

Marion lay back on the pillows and felt a kick from the baby. "Not long now, soldier," she whispered. "I can't wait to see you either."

Paul drove like a madman to the hospital. He accompanied her to the labour ward as planned. Marion was already ten centimetres dilated by the time she was wheeled into the delivery room.

Propped up on huge pillows, her knees drawn up to her chest, Marion panted and sweated while Paul held her hand and rubbed her back. It was too late for pethidine. Instead she gulped gas until she was seeing the staff and Paul through a fuzzy haze.

"Do you feel like you need to bear down yet?" the midwife asked. She was a chubby woman with rosy cheeks and a permanent smile, and the trace of an accent that Marion couldn't place.

Marion strained to see through the cloud. The woman's face came into focus for a couple of seconds before fading out again. "The baby's coming on its own," she gasped.

The midwife moved to the end of the bed and examined Marion. "You're right! I can see lots of thick black hair. Let's get this baby born, then."

Marion forced a smile as Paul kissed her cheek and whispered, "I love you."

"Now. On the next contraction, Marion — push."

The wave of another contraction began to build and Marion gasped, catching her breath. Oh God. The pain! "No, no, honey. Breathe with it, you'll find it a lot easier. Breathe out slowly. Breath in... then out. Push, Marion."

Marion screwed up her face and bore down with all her might.

"Okay, now pant... good girl. Another contraction, big push this time, and we'll have baby's head out."

Marion pushed. The pain was unbearable. She felt as though she were trying to give birth to a water melon, and it was ripping her in half. "Never again, Paul. Never again," she hissed.

Paul chuckled nervously.

The midwife was busy turning the baby's head and checking the neck for any sign of the cord. "Listen to me, Marion — your baby's head has been delivered. Now I want you to give one more push and it'll be over, honey. Here we go..."

Marion sobbed. "I can't! Please. I can't do it. Paul, I want to go home," she whimpered.

"You can do it, babes. Just imagine, our baby will be coming home with us…" He gave her a squeeze as the next contraction rolled in.

Marion gave it her all. There was a rush of fluid, and their baby slid into the world. Marion collapsed back on to the pillows. It was over… and she was still alive.

"You have a baby boy, Marion. A beautiful baby boy." The midwife held him up for inspection. "I'll just do his checks, and then he's all yours."

A few seconds later the baby howled, and a shiver ran up Marion's spine. Her baby's first sound. Tears sprung to her eyes.

After efficiently inspecting the infant, the midwife handed the tiny bundle over to Marion. She lifted back the blanket to see her baby's body. He had skin the colour of a Chinaman. Marion looked at the tiny features; he had her small mouth, his father's arched eyebrows, and… she studied his face… she was sure his nose would be Gerard's as well. This child was definitely Gerard's. It would be obvious to anyone who knew him.

Tears rolled down her cheeks.

Paul and the nurses took them to be tears of joy, and Paul hugged her as she held her son. "He's perfect. Thank you," he whispered.

"I know." The baby gripped Marion's thumb in a tiny fist and made sucking motions with his mouth.

"Hungry already?" Paul asked the baby.

A nurse came in and took over from the midwife. "Baby boy? We'll have to weigh him and do his checks, and then you can have a go at feeding him. How are you going to feed him?"

"Breastfeeding. For a while, anyway."

The nurse smiled and held out her arms for the baby. Marion reluctantly handed him over and watched as the nurse walked away with her son, gibbering baby-talk to him.

Paul left her a few minutes later to call Marion's family and his own, and their friends.

After the baby had been returned to her, Marion stood by the plastic crib and looked down at him. He slept peacefully. He was so delicate and tiny. He had silky black hair which was still stuck to his head like a skull cap. Marion placed a hand on his back, reassuring herself that he was still breathing. She could feel the rapid up-and-down rhythm of his tiny lungs.

His father didn't even know he existed. His loss.

She had decided to call him Diallo. She hoped the name would make her son as great a man as she had been told his namesake was.

Paul left them an hour later. He was bushed, and had to work later that day. Kissing Marion hard on the lips, he promised to come back that evening with a couple of members of his family.

Marion slept until she was awoken by familiar voices.

"There she is!" That was Joan.

"Let me see him." And Pamela. Marion sat up sleepily as the girls rushed over.

"Hiya." They hugged her in turn before surrounding the crib.

"Oh, Maz, he's beautiful," Pamela cooed.

Joan pulled the blanket back off him. "Dead stamp of Gerard."

"Don't say that around Paul," Marion warned.

"He's so tiny. Can I hold him?" Pamela asked.

The girls sat around, chatting and passing the baby back and forth. Joan and Marion compared labours, Marion breastfeeding as they talked.

"I remember my breasts the day after the birth," Joan said. "Rock hard, they were. You wait till your milk comes in."

"I know. My mum told me she was leaking through a whole packet of cotton wool a day," Marion said.

"I could do with rock-hard tits," Pamela said, pushing her chest up.

Joan gave her a critical look. "I don't think you could take the pain," she said.

"Ask Michael if I can't take pain," Pam answered with a smile. Her friends looked at her. Everything had to come down to sex with Pamela.

"And how is Michael?" Marion asked. "You seen him recently?"

"Nearly every day," Pamela replied haughtily.

"It happened too fast with you two, don't you think?" Joan put in. "It's like James all over again."

"This is nothing like me and James. That was a mistake." Pamela changed the subject. "How does Paul feel about his son?" she asked, emphasising the "his".

"He thinks he's perfect. He didn't even say anything about the dates."

"I think you're good to go on so long without telling him," Joan said. "Although, you know one day he is going to find out."

"I know. And when that time comes, I'll be ready," Marion declared, her warm gaze coming to rest on her sleeping infant.

East Street, one of the busiest markets in London, was packed with shoppers, the usual Saturday crowd. It was the start of the spring sales, and people were already buying clothes for the summer. Paul had parked the car in Elephant and Castle, and they had walked up to the market through the shopping centre hand in hand, window shopping as they went. Marion carried Diallo in a pouch on her chest, her arm serving as a protective barrier for his delicate head. At six weeks old he was already starting to feel too heavy for her to carry. "We'll have to look at christening outfits soon," she said as they passed a children's clothes shop.

"Yeah. But let's leave that till he's about six months,"Paul advised.

"Why?" "It just seems the right time to do it," Paul said, and Marion shut up.

They stopped and looked at the pushchairs in the shop's window. They hadn't bought one yet. Their cot had come courtesy of her mother, and Joan had given them a baby chair. A pushchair hadn't seemed an essential, but from the speed by which Diallo was growing it soon would be. They decided to go and have a look inside, but as they reached the door a hand grabbed Marion's arm and, startled, she turned to face her accoster.

"I thought it was you!" Claudia Thompson's voice sing-songed. It had been a year since Marion had heard it, and her heart nearly stopped. Gerard's mother stood in front of them, grinning for all she was worth.

Paul was half-way into the shop and stopped in the doorway, standing behind Marion as she turned to face Claudia.

"Claudia! How are you?" Marion asked with exaggerated calm.

Claudia's eyes were on the tiny bundle hanging from her shoulders. She ignored Marion's greeting. "No one never tell me you have baby," she said.

"Six weeks now," Marion said, and immediately regretted it. Claudia hadn't asked how old he was, and it was a clue to his father's identity. Unconsciously, she shielded the baby with her jacket.

But that wasn't putting Claudia off. "Let me have a look, then. Girl or boy?"

Marion reluctantly lifted Diallo into view. "Boy." She watched Claudia's face, knowing the woman would see the resemblance straight away. Claudia looked from the baby to Paul and back again. "That's a handsome baby boy you have there," she said.

"I know. Thank you," Paul answered, and placed a reassuring hand on Marion's tense shoulder.

"Yes, he is a handsome boy. Who does he take after?" she murmured, so that only Marion would hear.

Marion was so tense, every muscle of her body began to ache. "I really do have to get on, Claudia. It was nice seeing you," she said hastily. Claudia gave her a look that said everything. She knew. "Buying baby things?" she carried on. "Expensive, 'int it?" She had a wry smile on her chubby face. "Well, I better go meself, dear. I'll be in touch. You tek care now, y'hear?" She smiled at Paul.

Marion was sure Claudia was going to say something incriminating. But her expression changed and she touched Paul's arm briefly. "You tek care as well. Bye, Marion."

"Bye, Claudia," Marion said. Her throat clicked with dryness and she tried to swallow. Claudia walked away and Marion turned to walk into the shop.

"You okay?" Paul asked.

"Why shouldn't I be?" she snapped, and walked past him. Paul stood behind her, bewildered. He knew Marion well enough to realise she was upset. And it had something to do with that woman.

Marion remained quiet and disinterested throughout the rest of their shopping trip. The appearance of Claudia Thompson had ruined her day. All she wanted to do was go home and shut herself in. She felt her life crumbling around her.

Gerard was Claudia's only son. Which meant — if he didn't already have children elsewhere — that Diallo was her only grandchild. There was no doubt in Marion's mind that Claudia would tell her son about the baby. What he'd do after that was anyone's guess.

GERARD

Now I know my mum is getting on a bit, and sometimes she get mix up — but this time she's gone too far. As soon as I came in this evening she start on me: "How can you let some other man be taking care of your child? Marion is such a lovely girl. How can you have a son and never tell me 'bout it?" I thought the old lady had finally lost it. After I sat her down and made her some tea, she told me how she's seen Marion in the market with her boyfriend and a baby. So? I says. She told me how old the baby was and how he look jus' like me. She had already worked out the dates of when the baby would have been conceived and born.

It got me thinking… Marion was always going on about wanting a baby…

Mum was on at me to go and see her. The last thing I wanted to do was go and see my ex-girlfriend and accuse her of having my child.

I don't know if I wanna get involved in dem kinda business. If the kid is mine — an' I'm still not convinced it is — then it's mine in blood only.

Mum isn't gonna let it rest. She's got this big t'ing about having a grandchild to spoil. I'm gonna put her off as long as possible. I don't wanna have to meet up with Marion again. I'll give mum some story about Marion not wanting me to see the kid.

Women!

SUNDAY MORNING, AND THE AIR WAS CRISP AND FRESH. AFTER breakfast in bed, Pamela and Michael showered together before getting dressed and going for a walk to get the papers.

On Saturday they had spent the whole day in bed. Breakfast and lunch had been served on trays by Michael, and Pamela had got up to prepare and serve dinner. It seemed she just couldn't get enough of him. The past few months had gone by so quickly, yet the feelings she had for him had grown to such proportions that she was beginning to miss him as soon as he'd walk out of the door. She couldn't imagine life without him — and that feeling was definitely a new one on Pamela. Life with Michael was full of new experiences. Only last week he'd taken her for her first taste of Thai food. They'd feasted on squid and oysters — exotic food to enliven her tastebuds — and afterwards they'd taken a romantic walk by the Cutty Sark in Greenwich, watching the ships drift by on the Thames.

Now her arm was around his waist and his around her shoulders as they walked up towards Evelyn Street. Elderly ladies smiled at them approvingly as they passed. Younger people smirked uncomfortably as the couple stole quick kisses. Neither of them had yet used the L word.

They walked through the sixty square feet of greenery that constituted a park on the estate. The sounds of the Sunday morning traffic and the chirping of the birds were the only thing that invaded the space around them. Several times they had discussed her dilemma with her parents. It wasn't easy deciding what to do. Michael had said that if he was in her position he would much rather put it all behind him. Pamela had tried that, and it didn't work. She was too curious about her natural mother. What did she look like? What was she like as a person? Was she anything like Pamela? What had made her give her daughter up? And the big question: who was Pamela's father? All these questions, and more, needed to be answered. Joan had been with her when she'd called the agency. They had been very understanding and offered to send someone round to advise her and give counselling. But Pamela had changed her mind at the last minute; she just wasn't ready to accept her new status as an adopted child.

She felt like a nobody. She had no history — except her false one, which she was only too happy to forget.

A March wind blew up as they turned the corner onto Evelyn Street. Michael pulled her closer, closing the collar round the neck of her jacket with his arm. He had the ability to take her mind off her problems. If she ever needed to talk, he was there. They took the Sunday papers back to her flat. Michael made coffee and they lay on the living room floor, on the lambswool rug he'd bought for her, the papers spread out between them and his Sounds of Blackness album playing in the background.

Pamela opened a colour supplement and flicked straight to the fashion pages. "Mike, what'd you think of that on me?" she asked, pointing to a picture of a long, slinky, backless dress.

"I'd love you in that, but for my eyes only." He turned a page of the newspaper.

"What's the point of that?" She rested her chin on her palm. "Wouldn't you rather take me out and show me off? You could say to the other guys, 'This is my woman. Look, but don't touch'." She giggled.

His hazel eyes came to rest on her lips. "I do that anyway. Whatever you wear you look good in."

"Thanks, baby." She leant forward and kissed him. "You do too," she said — and meant it.

"I do what?"

"Look good in whatever you wear," she told him. "Especially your birthday suit."

Michael flashed that incredible, sparkling smile, and his eyes opened in amusement. "You're too rude, y'know that?" He touched her nose playfully.

"Mmm-mm, so I've been told. Would you like me to show you how rude I can get?" She edged closer, already feeling the heat radiating from his body.

"You did. This morning, last night..."

"See what you do to me?" she interrupted. "Turn me into a raging nymphomaniac."

Michael turned on to his side so that he was facing her. "I think it's the other way around. When I leave here I'm no good to anybody. You drain my energy like a vampire."

"Tell me you don't like it and I'll stop."

"Would you?"

"No. I just said that to test you."

Michael shook his head in mirth and moved closer. He had this way of pulling his bottom lip in and drawing his top teeth across it when he was thinking about something sexual. It was a tell-tale sign to Pamela.

She closed her eyes before they kissed. There was no resistance in her body or mind. She gripped his firm, round arse and pulled him to her, kissing, stroking, the feel of him and the smell of his favourite aftershave filling the space around her until nothing else mattered. Newspapers crinkled and tore as he climbed on top of her and plunged his tongue between her small lips. He pushed his groin against her, knowing she could feel every inch of his growing erection. His tongue traced a path from her ear lobe to her neck.

"Michael?"

"Mmm?" "Do you love me?" she breathed.

Michael groaned. "Mmm? What?"

"I just asked you if you love me."

He released her suddenly, rolling over on to his back. "What for?"

She frowned. "I thought it was a fair question."

He stared at the ceiling. "Depends why you want to know."

"I only asked." In reality, Pamela had no idea why she had asked. But as he protested it became more important to know the truth.

"You asked for a reason." He sat up now, the mood lost, his huge shoulders hunched over his knees.

"So — you can't answer yes or no. I'm not asking you to say you'll marry me."

"I don't know," he faltered. His hazel eyes came to rest on her lips. "I know I care about you. A lot," he added.

"Yeah. And?"

"Jesus, Pam. What is this about?" Irritated and suddenly restless, he stood up. Pamela followed suit and moved to sit on the sofa. "It's about us, and where this relationship is going."

"Don't do this, Pam. It doesn't suit you. Has one of your friends been putting ideas into your head?"

He bent down to pick up the newspapers from the floor.

"I don't need my friends to tell me how to lead my life, Michael. Why are we arguing over this?"

"I don't know. Why did you ask?" The conversation was going round in circles. Having placed the folded newspapers on the coffee table, Michael crossed to the window and pushed it open mechanically. Cold air entered the room, turning the already chilly atmosphere icy. "All right! Just forget it, okay?" Pamela raised her hands in submission. "It doesn't matter."

A silence fell between them. Michael tucked his sweatshirt back into his trousers and looked at his watch. "I've gotta go. I promised to drop in on Mikey this weekend."

"You're running away," she accused.

"Oh come on, Pam. This isn't us. We were doing fine, weren't we?"

"Just go, Michael," she dismissed him. "I'll call you later," he said, picking up his keys.

Pamela stood up and breathed deeply. She was surprised by this elusive side to Michael, but even more amazed at how upset she was. They walked to the door together. "You all right?" he asked, stroking her back.

"Course." She looked up at him. "I'll talk to you later, then."

He kissed her on her nose, and was gone.

Disturbed and frustrated, Pamela went back into the living room. She switched on the television, not caring what was on. Tired now, and unable to get him out of her head, she turned over on the sofa, her back to the television. Everything smelt of Michael. Her confused brain fighting with the niggling intuition that it was over, she fell into a dreamless sleep.

Pamela replaced the receiver and sat staring at it for a moment. She decided she would dial again in a few minutes.

Outside, the wind had dropped slightly but the rain had intensified. It slapped against her living room window, the constant patter sounding like a thousand birds pecking at the glass. The cheap double glazing rattled in its frame.

She reached for the phone again. No, she thought. Leave it. Instead, she hauled herself off the sofa and padded into the kitchen, opening cupboards and the fridge. But she wasn't hungry. Not for food, anyway. She poured herself a brandy, dropped two ice cubes into it, and left the kitchen.

Michael hadn't called for four days now. On Monday she'd paged him and left a message to call her back. She'd left a message on his answerphone too, and still hadn't got a reply. The agony of waiting had made her lose her appetite, and she was having trouble sleeping. Her zest for all things fun in life had walked out of the door with him. She couldn't believe she was falling apart over a man, and so she began to convince herself that it was the stress of her recent discovery of her adoptive status that was getting her down.

Now exercise was the only thing that kept her sane. She worked her frustrations out on her stairclimber and jogged four miles a day. Then she would go to work like a zombie, come home and chat to her mates on the phone — making sure the call-waiting function was in operation — until it was time to go to bed.

She'd been sure Michael felt the same way she did. So she had opened up to him, and now he had thrown it back in her face.

She stomped into her bedroom and sat at the head of the bed. On the table was a photo of Michael she had taken outside the flats. She picked up the frame and touched the image of his face as if to feel the smoothness of his skin.

She reached for the phone again, jabbing out the digits of his mobile number.

Just let me hear your voice...

The phone went on ringing, no answering service this time. That meant he had picked up his messages and left the phone switched on. Still, he didn't answer her call. Where the hell was he? Pamela took a sip of brandy, still holding the phone to her ear.

Pick up...

The ringing continued until she slammed the phone down and unplugged it from the socket. Fuck him! she thought. If he wants to hide, let him. Forget him. Men were like children, she decided. Never said what they meant. It wasn't as though she was soft. Pamela knew she could take it if he called and said it was over. It was the not knowing that got to her. The fact that he knew she must be trying to get hold of him hurt even more. He was deliberately avoiding her.

She downed the rest of the brandy in one and went to the kitchen to get a refill. Deciding it would be easier simply to take the bottle back with her, she did just that. She slammed his framed photograph face-down on the table. "Fuck you!" she told it, and threw herself backwards on the bed.

MICHAEL

So what? It's not all my fault it ended up like this.

I thought Pamela and I were on the same level. Why can't a woman just put two and two together and make four? They've always got to look for the hidden agenda.

I've been with her now for — what? — about eight months or so. We ain't had no problems — an' you know why? Because we didn't mention love and commitment. We just went with it.

I care about her. She knows I want to be with her, because I'm always there.

A man don't need words when he can show how he feels. Putting how you feel in words is like giving a woman ammunition to get back at you with. The only way to keep a woman interested is to treat her right, but to keep an element of mystery there. Something of a challenge, something to keep her digging.

When Pamela came out with that "Do you love me?" line it struck me like a kick in the crotch. I guess I'm still not ready.

I need time to think.

I listen to her message on the answerphone. I want to call her, but I know what she's going to come out with and I'm not ready for that yet. I've got my career and my son to think about. Pamela is important, but that will sort itself out one way or the other.

I'm not even thinking about ending what we have.

ENOUGH TIME HAD GONE BY SINCE THE ACCIDENTAL MEETING with Claudia Thompson in the market place for Marion to feel she could start to relax. For the past two weeks, every time the telephone had rung she'd felt her heart-rate accelerate, every time the intercom buzzed her breathing had nearly stopped. But now the summer was finally here, and June had brought with it long, hot days. Bright, warm sunshine streamed through the curtains this morning, and Marion took this as her cue to stop hibernating.

Paul had noticed her changes in mood. He knew her too well. He had made it his duty to read her needs. In the two and a half months since Diallo's birth he had amazed her by showing a side of him she had never suspected. She would never have guessed he could be so gentle with a new-born baby.

Diallo was filling out nicely. He was a cuddly bundle of joy. The only times he seemed to be miserable was at night, when he was put in the cot on his own, and more often than not he would end up sleeping in the bed with them. He was spoiled by his surrogate father. Paul changed, fed, bathed and played with him. It made Marion feel as though nothing could destroy their bond. The three of them were meant to be together. Even if Claudia had told Gerard about the baby, there was nothing he could do to break them up — and she doubted he would even try. Gerard was only interested in himself. What would he want with a baby?

Paul's help had given Marion time to continue her writing in the evenings and at weekends. She had received several offers of work since her articles were published, and Essence magazine in the States had commissioned her to do a series on nineties black British women in comparison to their mothers in the fifties and sixties. All the extra cash she earned was being spent on Diallo, and the list of things he needed seemed to grow every month. Marion pulled on a pair of shorts and a baggy T-shirt. Her figure had sprung back since giving birth. Paul had treated her to an exercise bike, and she rode ten miles a day.

She put the sun canopy on Diallo's brand new pushchair, dressed him coolly in light blue shorts and top, with boots and hat to match, and left the flat, w

heeling the new buggy out into the heat of the day, feeling the sun's rays lift her spirit.

Joan and Pamela would both be at work now, and Marion decided to pop into Pamela's nursery for a visit. Pamela hadn't seen Diallo in nearly a month, and would be grateful for the company. Marion caught a bus on the Woolwich Road and headed for Lewisham. This part of town was the usual hive of activity. The Lewisham 2000 project was causing chaos for pedestrians and confusion for drivers. Roads had been dug up and diverted, and there were temporary crossings and signs everywhere. Marion found herself manoeuvring the pushchair through the crowds with some difficulty. She bumped into a couple of people she knew. One was a friend of her mother's, and the other was Carmen, an old schoolfriend from her days at St Theresa's. Carmen cooed over the baby, and told Marion how she hadn't changed, saying she still looked sixteen. Carmen didn't have any children yet. She was still looking for the right man. Marion told her she had already found hers and was very happy.

Making her way towards Loampit Vale Nursery, Marion thought about how good she felt. Her life was in order. She had a baby, a man who loved her, friends who supported her, and a caring family. One thing she did miss was her sister's company. Jacqueline would have loved to be an auntie. As Marion entered the coolness of the nursery she spotted Pamela talking to a small child. "Excuse me, any chance of enrolling my son?" Marion said loudly to catch her attention.

Pamela turned to the voice and her face instantly lit up. "Marion, hi! Why didn't you tell me you were coming?" She approached her friend, dismissing the little girl at the same time.

"I thought you liked surprises."

Pamela's attention was already drawn to the baby in the pushchair. "Aaah, look at his little shoes." She worked at the straps of the pushchair and lifted him free. Diallo was fast asleep. Pamela held him in the crook of her arm. "He is so gorgeous, if only he was twenty-five years older…"

"You leave my son alone, you. You'll be corrupting him before he can talk," Marion laughed.

They went over to the book corner. It was the only carpeted area of the room, with cushions and bean bags on the floor. Once they were both comfortable, Pamela asked, "So how are you, girl? I hardl
y hear from you these days."

"Not too bad. What about you?"

"You know…" Pamela shrugged and mopped the corner of Diallo's mouth with his bib.

"Michael?"

"Nothing's wrong exactly." She paused. "It's just… well, I haven't seen or heard from him in a while. I thought we were getting on fine, and then he just went cold on me."

Marion nodded.

"I've called, left messages. He doesn't answer."

"Yeah?" Marion was having flashbacks to her days with Gerard. She remembered exactly how that felt.

"I know I probably rushed into it, but all he has to do is to tell me to back off, you know. He led me on, Maz. I told you about how he used to treat me, didn't I?"

"Yeah." Marion nodded and crossed her legs. Diallo gurgled in his sleep and his eyelids fluttered.

"If I wasn't so caught up in this love thing, I'd forget him. You know me — plenty more fish in the sea an' all that. The only problem is the way I feel about him. All I want to know is where I went wrong — not that I'm blaming myself," she added hastily, "it's just that I want to know one way or the other what's going on."

"Sometimes men need their own space. I've been there, remember?"

Pamela tutted. "This isn't the same. Gerard…" She paused and turned her eyes to the ceiling, trying to find the right words without offending. "Gerard didn't care about you. I know how that sounds, but you know what I mean."

Suddenly Marion needed the comfort of her baby in her arms. She reached for him and Pamela handed him to her.

"Has he been in touch?" Pamela asked. Marion had told her about meeting Claudia.

"No. And I pray to God every night that he doesn't. I have nightmares about it." She shifted Diallo around so that he lay on her thighs, feet touching her stomach.

"I bet you do. And how's Paul?"

"Paul's still as loving as ever." She looked down at her baby. "To both of us."

"You should see Michael with his son. They're so much alike, except Mikey…" She trailed off. "Can't stop thinking about him."

"Not easy, is it?" Marion sympathised.

Pamela shook her head, her ponytail swinging. "Anyway, when're you gonna start raving again? You must miss it."

"I'm not ready to leave him yet." She nodded towards Diallo.

"Don't you trust Paul alone with him?" Pamela asked, incredulous.

"I trust him. It's just that… I think I'd still be worried no matter who had him. I haven't left him with anyone since he was born."

"Love, eh?" Pamela smirked, her pretty eyes sparkling.

Marion smiled back at her.

"I'll make us a cuppa." Pamela put on her cockney accent. "Then we can catch up on some news."

Marion stayed at the nursery for an hour and a half. As the afternoon drew on a breeze blew up, dropping the temperature by a few degrees, and when it was time to go Marion wrapped Diallo in his shawl so that only his head showed above the fluffy white wool. As Marion left, she told Pamela she was glad she wasn't on the market any more. The days of having to be out there, getting mucked about by men, were over. There was no doubt in her mind.

She got home at around four o'clock. The atmosphere inside the flat was still warm, so she left a window open to circulate the air. Diallo sat in his chair in the living room, entranced by the dancing net curtains. Marion left him there while she went to put the dinner on.

While she was in the kitchen the intercom buzzed. Marion didn't even stop to wonder who it might be, but wiped her hands on a kitchen towel and went out to the passage to answer it.

"Hello," she called cheerfully.

"Marion, it's Gerard," the voice came back at her. Marion was sure she'd stopped breathing. She leant her weight against the passage wall, stomach churning, pulse hammering, the intercom receiver clutched to her chest.

Diallo began the first hiccoughs of a cry. Marion pressed the door release button and hurried to her son. A minute later, Gerard entered the flat. Marion stood in the middle of the living room and faced the doorway waiting.

Pamela locked up the nursery door as usual, and waited while the alarm checked and switched itself on. Then she slung her handbag strap over her shoulder and strolled up towards Lewisham High Street.

Recent events had taken their toll on her state of mind. Another man had brought her down again. How many times had she said never again? Well, she thought, Michael could keep his love, and his charm, and his good looks and his hard body — she sighed at the thought of his body. But he had been all she wanted in a man. Pamela had got the idea that if she talked to Cheryl she could get some insight into what was happening. She couldn't think where else to turn. Cheryl had gone out with Michael, lived with him, for five years. If anyone else could shed some light on the subject, it would be her. So Pamela had called her just before leaving work. Cheryl had invited her round and sounded as though she'd been expecting the call.

Cheryl was very thin and tall. She had the Somalian look of high cheekbones and meek brown eyes. She let Pamela into her council flat. The smell of cooking wafted out of the kitchen and seemed to grab Pamela's insides, pulling her in. As she entered the flat, Mikey ran up to her and reached up for a hug. Even though they had only seen each other an hour before, he always carried on as though he had missed her.

"Leave the woman alone, Mikey. You finish yuh dinner yet?" Cheryl nagged.

Mikey skulked away, pouting at being scolded in front of his teacher. "Sorry to barge in on you, Cheryl..." Pamela began.

"Don't be stupid, it's good to have some company." Cheryl waved away Pamela's apologies and motioned towards Mikey with her head. "As soon as he finishes his food he'll fall asleep in front of the TV." Pamela followed her into the kitchen where Cheryl was preparing her own dinner. She took off her jacket and hung it over the top edge of the door.

"Wanna drink?" Cheryl asked.

"Yes, please. Something cold." Pamela perched on the bar stool by the kitchen counter.

Cheryl went to the fridge and brought back a blackcurrant cordial. "We haven't had a chance to chat for ages. How're you doing?"

"Not too bad, y'know..."

Cheryl poked a finger at her. "I know you — you're a raver. What you been up to?"

Pamela shook her long hair off her face. "Too busy to even rave these days," she lamented.

Cheryl cocked her head to one side. "Oh yeah? Doing what?" she asked slyly. She poured cold water into the glasses and handed one to

Pamela.

"You know — work, socialising, dating…"

"Still up to your old tricks?" Cheryl winked at her as she began chopping onions on a wooden board.

"Naw, man. I'm thinking of settling down now."

Cheryl flashed a quick glance of amusement. "What — you?"

"That's exactly what my other mates say. D'you think I'm that bad?"

"Bad ain't the word for you," Cheryl chuckled, looking attentively downwards.

Pamela had to blurt it out before she lost her bottle. "I'm seeing your ex. Michael." Cheryl paused for just a second, but her face showed no hint of surprise. "I thought so."

Pamela looked at her, one eyebrow raised. "What would make you think that?" Mikey came to mind as the source, but she was wrong.

"Him asking about you. You asking about him. I'm not stupid."

Now Pamela felt guilty for not telling her, for making it seem like a conspiracy. "I was gonna tell you, Chel, I just didn't know how you'd take it."

"It's nothing to do with me." Cheryl poured the onions into the steaming casserole on the hob. "Michael and me had it good once." She glanced out of the window. "Yeah, it was good — but these things happen." She wiped her hands on a tea towel and turned her back to Pamela.

"What did happen between you two?" Pamela enquired. "He never said."

Cheryl reached for a pot from the wooden shelf above her head. "He split us up. I don't think Michael can take pressure."

"What d'you mean? He was with you for five years."

Cheryl put the pot on the hob, added oil and turned the flame up. "Michael can be a good man, but he tries too hard." She paused again, reminiscing, then turned to Pamela and rested her back on the counter. "He pleases others before himself, and then when he realises what he's missing he goes looking for it. Then he can turn into the most selfish bastard alive."

Pamela shook her head, wondering if they could be talking about the same person. She'd thought Michael didn't have a selfish bone in his body. Up until a month ago he had always put her first.

Cheryl watched Pamela through knowing eyes and saw the disbelief on her face. "Believe me, Pam, I know what I'm talking about. I know him better than he knows himself."

"I think he's in love with me," Pamela told her, hoping it would change the negativity that Cheryl was giving off.

Cheryl smirked. "Has he said that?"

"No, but men don't," Pamela gushed. "The way he treats me—"

"Means nothing," Cheryl interrupted.

"Maybe it meant nothing with you, but whatever he sees in me must be something you didn't have."

Cheryl bristled. Her eyes turned to daggers, but she breathed deeply and turned back to her cooking. "I don't want us to fall out over a man, Pam. If you want us to stay friends, don't bring Michael up again."

"Fine." Pam stood and reached for her coat. "Thanks for the chat."

"Where you going? I thought you were staying for dinner."

"Sorry, I don't think I've got the time. I'll see you next week, Cheryl."

Cheryl walked Pamela to the front door. "Take care, yeah? I didn't mean anything by what I said, you know. I don't want you to take it the wrong way."

Pamela touched Cheryl's arm, briefly squeezing it, and gave her a look of pity. "Thanks," she said, and left.

The sky had become overcast, threatening rain. Pamela pulled her collar up and put her head down against the driving wind. A car turned into the road as she took the corner, a car she recognised, and its driver recognised her. The car slowed, pulled over, and Michael stepped out. Pamela had stopped on the kerb. She waited as he approached her. He wore an uncertain smile, but his eyes sparkled with charm all the same. Pamela stood with her hands in her jacket pockets. He stopped a foot away, unsure of her mood. They stared into each other's eyes.

They stared into each other's eyes. Marion felt brave. She had her son to defend, and like a lioness she intended to do just that. This was her home, and Gerard had no right ever to set foot in it again. She held Diallo close to her, resting his head on her shoulder.

Gerard stood in the doorway nonchalantly, one hand resting on the frame. He looked even more handsome than she remembered him. His eyes strayed to the baby in her arms, then met hers again. "Why didn't you tell me?" His voice was unnaturally low, as though he too felt he shouldn't be here.

"Tell you what?" Marion wrinkled her brow as if she didn't know what he was talking about.

He looked down at his shoes and shifted his position in the doorway. This seemed to be hard for him too. Marion could sense the turmoil

211

within him. It was very rare for anyone to see Gerard unsure of himself. The only times she had seen him this humble was when he spoke of his father.

He spoke now to the floor, eyes and head cast down. "Mum told me she saw you the other day." He coughed. "Is he mine?"

Marion remained silent. She gazed at him with round-eyed perplexity. Diallo shifted his head, trying to turn to the strange voice in the room. Marion placed a protective hand on the back of his head and kissed him.

"Well?" Gerard's eyes came to rest on her once again.

"Your sperm may have created him, but he's not your child."

"What kinda rubbish is that?" He took a step towards her. Marion backed up, feeling threatened. "What d'you want, Gerard?" She spoke firmly, asserting the fact that she didn't want anything from him.

"Jus' tell me if he's my son." He put one hand to his forehead, rubbing at his temples before letting it drop back to his side. "I've told you..." she began.

"You've told me nothin'," he erupted. The baby started to cry. Gerard saw the fear in Marion's eyes and breathed deeply. "Look, sorry. I didn't come here to upset nothin'." His voice mellowed. "Can I see him?" Marion brought the baby down from her shoulder and held him in the crook of her arm, so that Gerard could see him. Gerard held his arms out, but Marion only gripped him more tightly. "You can look at him, but I can't let you take him."

Gerard laughed at her. "What d'you think I'm gonna do? Run off with him?"

"I don't know what you're here for." She took a step towards him and they met in the centre of the room. She watched his expression as he took his first glance at his son. She was surprised to see a genuine smile, his eyes actually lighting up. It was beautiful. Gerard looked at the baby with the same expression she had seen on Paul's face many times. His eyes met Marion's and she tried to suppress her own smile.

"He is my son," Gerard said with a hint of wonder. He stepped away from her and sat down hard in the armchair, taking a deep breath.

Marion frowned. This wasn't what she'd expected. She didn't want him to care. "Gerard, he's registered as Paul's baby. You can't claim him as yours..." She stopped as Gerard gave her a look that was half disbelief and half anger.

"Why?" he asked.

"What did you expect me to do? You didn't want me. You wouldn't have wanted our baby. Paul wanted both of us..."

"So he knows it's not his?"

Marion lifted Diallo to her shoulder and sat down on the sofa opposite Gerard. She avoided answering the question. "He loves Diallo," she said.

"You named him after my dad?" Gerard's voice broke on the last word, his pitch lowering a little.

"I'm sorry…"

"No." Gerard held up his hand. "Dad would've liked that."

There was a silence between them, as if they were paying a tribute to the dead man. Diallo was hungry and began sucking at his fist and turning his little head to nudge Marion's full breasts. Marion, being by now used to breastfeeding in company, didn't think twice about lifting her T-shirt to feed her baby. Diallo sucked hungrily on the offered nipple.

Gerard stood up and crossed the room to sit next to her. Marion watched his approach and let him sit close to her without budging. He took one of Diallo's hands in his. The tiny fingers gripped his thumb and a smile broke out on his face once more.

"Does he know Diallo isn't his?" Gerard asked again.

"No."

He searched her eyes. "Are you going tell him?"

"Not if I don't have to." There was a hint of pleading in her voice. Gerard noticed it. Clearly she didn't want her new life disrupted. But didn't he have rights too? Some other man was playing happy families with his kid, and he wanted a taste of this life. "I want to see my son," he said.

Taken aback, Marion stared him in the eye. "No," she said adamantly. "You can't do that."

Gerard jumped up. "What do you mean I can't?" The tranquillity of the past few minutes was shattered in a second.

"Paul would be hurt if he found out."

Like a firecracker, Gerard was off again. "I don't give a damn about Paul. He's my kid. I wanna see him grow up." The sound of a key turning in the front door startled them both. Marion's frightened eyes flew to the clock on the wall. It was six thirty. She had forgotten that Paul was coming back home for his kit. She shoved her breast back into her bra, disturbing the semi-sleeping baby, who began to wail.

Gerard had spun around, also surprised by the intrusion. They stood side by side, looking guiltily towards the door, as Paul appeared.

"Hi," he said.

"Hi yuhself," Pamela replied, looking up at him.

"I tried to call you," Michael said, shifting from one foot to the other.

"Oh yeah?" She remained cool. "When?"

"Just now. I've been trying for an hour."

She chuckled sarcastically. "Funny. I've been trying to call you for two weeks."

His gaze never faltered. "I've had some things to sort out. I was kinda busy."

"Too busy to pick up the phone? Or did you lose my number?" He reached out for her arm but she snatched it back.

"Don't be like that, Pam."

"Don't be like what? I'm not some young gal you can just mess around with for a lark, Mike. I'm a woman who deserves respect."

"Course I respect you, babes," he said in his rich, sonorous voice.

"Don't 'babes' me, Michael. You did get my messages, didn't you?"

"Yeah, but…"

She waved away his excuses. "Do you think I would treat you that way? You know how I feel about you, and yet you treat me like that. I don't have to wait around for you, you know."

A middle-aged woman dragging a shopping trolley slowed as she approached, the argument between these two lovebirds seeming more important than getting the tea on the table.

Pamela shot her a look. "Can we help you?" she asked rudely.

Flustered, the woman tightened her scarf around her neck and bustled on her way.

Michael rubbed his hands together and then folded them across his chest. "I apologise. I didn't mean to upset you."

"Upset me!" she yelled. "Who said I was upset?" Michael laughed. "If you're not upset, you're doing a pretty good impression of someone who is."

"Don't laugh at me, Michael." She turned her back to him, hiding her expression. "You have no idea what's been going through my mind. I was thinking you could've been in an accident."

"You serious?" He grinned.

She turned again to face him. "D'you think I'd make that up? I don't like men using me, Michael."

"But it's all right if you use them."

"What? I never used you."

"No. But you used the last two men in your life."

"Oh, so this was to teach me a lesson, was it?"

"This has nothing to do with your past. This is me. Things were just getting too deep, y'know?"

"No, I don't know."

He shuffled his feet awkwardly. "I wanna do the right thing by you. I wasn't sure what I was feeling, you know…"

"Did you sort it out?" Pamela asked.

"I think so." "That's not good enough, Mike. The way I feel about you, you've got to be sure or that's it."

"How can anyone be sure? People are getting divorced every day. I jus' know I want to be with you. Let's go somewhere on neutral ground. I need to talk." "You're not getting out of it that easily. And weren't you going to see Mikey?"

"I was, but they weren't expecting me. I'm not trying to get out of what I have to say. I just want to do it properly." He moved in on her then, and Pamela let herself weaken. She wanted him with an undeniable ache. He kissed her forehead, her nose, and finally her lips, with a gentleness that made her want to cry out with pleasure. She knew her heart was his again. She had needed to let off steam, and now she felt she had — some of it, anyway. Tonight, though, they were going to talk seriously. He wasn't going to get away with puny excuses. Everything he told her from now on would have to hold water, or else she was getting out, love or not.

The smile Paul had been wearing dropped from his face as he studied the stranger in his living room suspiciously. Marion felt sick to her stomach. Faint. There was a hammering in her chest as her heart speeded up. Her legs felt weak. Diallo was stirring fretfully in her arms and she wanted to put him down in his cot, but couldn't.

Gerard stood with his feet wide apart in a challenging stance. Marion was sure he was planning something. The old mocking glint had reappeared in his eyes.

Paul looked from Marion to Gerard, and back again. Marion was about to speak when she saw Gerard's hand come up. She watched helplessly, riveted to the spot, as he stepped towards Paul. The silence was deafening. "I'm Gerard, Marion's ex," he said amiably.

Paul looked over at her again. She could only offer a weak smile that didn't touch her eyes. He shook Gerard's outstretched hand and introduced himself.

Gerard turned slightly and smiled at Marion. It was a crooked smile, that said 'I've let you off this time'. "Anyway," he breathed, "must be getting on. I'll catch you later, Marion. Paul, more time, yeah?" He raised his fist for a touch and Paul returned the gesture. Their fists met in the air.

"Yeah, safe," Paul replied with a feeling of unease. He escorted Gerard to the front door. Marion waited until she'd heard it shut before she moved. She left the living room as Paul was coming back down the passageway, and they met at the bedroom door. He stood behind her as she put Diallo down. "What was he doing here?" His voice held only plain curiosity.

"Just passing by, you know." She shrugged.

Paul walked around to the bottom of the cot and looked down at the baby. "How's Diallo been today?"

"Good. We went for a walk, popped in to see Pam at work." She turned to leave the room.

"Marion?"

She stopped and turned to him.

"What was he really doing here?"

"What d'you mean?"

"Come here." He held one hand out to her, and she approached hesitantly. "I know when you're lying to me. Is something bothering you?" He regarded her with burning intensity.

"Why?"

"Jus' answer me, Marion."

"No," she said, looking past him at the cot mobile.

"Look at me and tell me there's nothing wrong."

She couldn't. She wanted to pull away from him. She was crumbling, her whole world falling apart. She had always known the day would come when he would have to learn the truth, but she would have been happy to postpone it for ever. Now it seemed the moment had arrived.

"Don't make me tell you, Paul," she said. "I can sort it out." She tried to make her voice sound cheerful as Paul continued to gaze at her enquiringly.

"Sort what out? We're in this together. Talk to me, man."

"I can't, honey." She tried the sentimental distraction; it had worked before. She put her head on his chest and pushed her arms around his waist.

His arms remained by his side. "You're shutting me out," he said. "I'm not."

"Is it me?"

Marion shut her eyes and prayed this was all a nightmare. She could hear his heartbeat. It seemed to speed up like a drum roll.

"Marion, I can't go on like this, man."

She opened her eyes. "We're doing all right, ain't we? Does it matter what's on my mind?"

"It matters when I walk in and find your ex-boyfriend in our home, and you're acting as jumpy as a rabbit. I don't like being kept in the dark. What's going on?"

"Don't, Paul," she whimpered. She didn't want to cry, but couldn't help it.

"Is it that bad?" he asked, concerned now.

She sniffed. "You... you... don't realise h-how bad," she stuttered, tears streaming down her face.

He led her out of the bedroom and into the living room, to avoid waking Diallo. They sat side by side on the sofa. He let her cry for a while before trying to talk to her again. "Marion, I've got a class at seven thirty. I've gotta go. When I get back later, we're going to talk, you hear me?" He spoke as if addressing a small child.

She nodded, sniffing, and wiped her face with the back of her hand.

"Good." He got up and left the room to get his martial arts kit. "I'm gone. I'll see you later," he called from the hallway.

"Bye, Paul." The front door shut, and Marion had a sudden, mad impulse. She would take the baby and leave right now. Paul would never know; she would never have to tell him he had been living a lie for nearly a year.

She picked up the phone and dialled Joan's number, convincing herself that this would save everyone a lot of grief. No one could make her tell Paul — not now, or ever.

Paul arrived home two hours later to find an empty flat. A handwritten note left on the coffee table read:

> Dear Paul
> I've gone away for a while. Please don't try to find me. I'll contact
> you when I'm ready. Don't worry, we'll both be fine.
> Marion

He ignored her request and immediately picked up the phone, pressing the automatic dial button for Joan's house. The phone rang continuously. He tried Pamela's number and got her answerphone. Slamming the receiver down, he ran out of the flat, got into the car and drove. He would find her, the silly woman. Just what was she running from?

It took a week before Joan broke down and told Paul everything from the beginning. He had worked on her relentlessly. When he wasn't at her home, he would call Joan hourly to ask if she had heard anything. Then he would talk about how much he was missing Marion and the baby, how quiet the flat was without them. What really got to Joan was when he burst out crying, saying he didn't think he could go on without them. She couldn't take it any more. She had to put him out of his misery. He had a right to know. So she broke her promise to Marion.

Even as she told him, Joan knew he would head straight for Birmingham.

PAUL

I had everything, and I find out I got nuttin'.

Of course I'm going to Birmingham.

I never figured Marion for the devious type. Perhaps deviousness is in all women.

I'm driving, an' all I can see is Marion, Diallo and that fancy ex-boyfriend of hers. I'm so tense. And I'm angry.

Damn! I need to stop thinking for a while to clear my head. I'm on my way to bring her back and I don't even know if she wants to come back. Shit, I don't even know if I want her back. Someone else's baby. What a come-down. How can I tell anyone? I hate her for putting me through this. Yet I still love her. Shit! I'm so fucking mixed up.

MARION'S MUM'S HOUSE HELD THE SUMMER'S HEAT LIKE A furnace. She couldn't stay indoors, but couldn't find the energy to go out anywhere. She took a book from the bookshelf. It was Jilly Cooper's Riders. Not exactly her type of reading material but, unable to find anything better, she poured herself a glass of home-made lemonade and took it outside to the spacious, well-kept garden. This was the kind of home she wanted to bring her son up in.

She lay on the sun lounger, shaded by the umbrella that was attached to the head of the seat. This was more like it. It was the first time Marion had relaxed all week. Her mother and Thomas had taken Diallo out shopping, to show him off. Marion still hadn't called Paul. She felt guilty about leaving him the way she had. She'd convinced herself she was doing it for his own good; it made her feel better to see it that way. She didn't want to see him hurt. But if it were possible to turn the clock back, she would have done everything differently. The sun burnt her legs as she lay in its heat. One chapter into the book, she began to doze off. She dreamt. She was back home with Paul and Diallo, and Gerard had never existed. They were happy, until one day when the doorbell started ringing… A doorbell really was ringing, somewhere outside her dream. Marion drifted back to reality. The doorbell rang again. She sat up too quickly and a wave of dizziness made her stop to regain her balance. She stood slowly, making sure the disorientation had passed before getting to her feet. She opened the front door, a smile readily prepared on her face. And at the sight of her boyfriend — here, at her mother's front door in Birmingham — she began to back up. The banister stopped her progress. She gripped the post with one hand, the look of a cornered animal on her face. What was he doing here? Did he know?

Paul entered the thick, motionless heat of the hallway and closed the door behind him. Although he had shaved before leaving home and his hair was neatly cut, he had the hard look of a vagrant on his face. His jawline stuck out meanly. His dark eyes shone unnaturally, emotionlessly. Dressed completely in black, he looked like a possessed priest out for vengeance. "Are we alone?" he asked, his voice hoarse. He looked around, listening, taking in the stillness of the house. Marion nodded and backed further up the stairs as it became apparent that he did know. "I can explain," she blurted. He approached her stealthily. She cursed the house's shadows — they were making him look like a psycho from a horror movie. The thought sent goosepimples shooting up all over her body.

She took another step upwards. He was only two feet away now. Suddenly frightened by his silence, she turned and darted up the remaining stairs. The bathroom door had a lock on it; she could shut herself in there and pray for someone to come in time. But Paul was fit and flexible. He bounded up the stairs and she screamed as he grabbed her arm, turning her to face him as they reached the first landing. Tears filled her eyes as she began to blubber, "Oh God, Paul. I'm so sorry. I didn't mean to hurt you. I love you, Paul. I wish he was yours, honestly." She reached up to him and saw a flicker in his eyes — sentimentality. It was there for only a couple of seconds before clouding over again. He took her head forcefully in his hands and pulled her to him. He kissed her hard, thrusting his tongue deep into her mouth. She responded hungrily, her mind racing.

Paul was forcing her down on to the stairs, fumbling under the flimsy dress for her panties. "Not here, Paul," she protested, trying to stop him, but he was past listening and ignored her feeble protests. He was already freeing himself from his own clothes. She felt his hardness probing for entry and, although this wasn't Paul's style at all, she opened up for him. She kissed him, wanting to make it up to him. The stairs were hard against her back and buttocks. He thrust into her, deep and high. He grabbed her hair, pulling her head back, giving himself leverage. For a few seconds after he'd satisfied himself they both lay still, breathing heavily. One of Marion's hands clung to the banister. Suddenly Paul stood up and began pulling his clothes together, fastening his trousers. He looked down at her with those hard eyes she'd seen before. She slowly sat up, waiting, thinking it was time to tell all and get it over with. "I'm going home to pack," he said.

Marion's eyes flew wide and she felt cold. "You see how it feels to get used?" he continued. "Yeah, I remember that day. You must have seen me coming. I walked right into that trap. Well, don't expect me to do it again," he sneered. The tears that had only threatened before now came full force. "Don't do this, Paul. I said I was sorry," she cried. He laughed derisively. "You're sorry? For ruining my life? You used me as a meal ticket, for you and your kid. I bet you don't even know if Gerard's the father either." He spat the words at her. Marion cringed, bringing her knees up to her chest and hugging them. Paul turned as he walked down the stairs. "I'm only taking what's mine from the flat." He shook his head. "You should take up acting, y'know that? You had me fooled." With that he left, walking out of her life. Marion sat at the top of the stairs like a tiny orphaned child. She held her knees in her arms and rocked backwards and forwards. She felt as though she could never cry again, she was all dried up. It had happened again. She had lost a man she loved. Whose fault was it but her own?

PAUL

I'm not proud of what I did. Shit! If I could apologise, or even face her again, I would. What's stopping me? Pride. I'm a man. Men don't go crawling back, begging forgiveness. You cut your losses and move on. The woman made a fool out of me. Marion and Diallo became so important to me that all I wanted in life was to make them happy. Nothing else mattered. No wonder she found it so easy to use me. What I did to her must have cut her up bad. But, bwoy, everyone must take responsibility for their actions. You can't use somebody for your own gains and not expect to pay a price. Let me tell you something... men get hurt too.

JULY. THE FLAT HAD A PARTY ATMOSPHERE. IT WAS A DOUBLE celebration: Marion's birthday — plus yet another job offer. This time Marion was going on the box. Channel Four had been in touch. They were running a new six-week series called Mantalk, and they wanted

Marion to be the guest 'expert' in each programme. She hadn't been able to sleep for a whole week after she had received the letter. Windows were open in every room to let what little breeze there was flow through the flat. Marion tipped a packet of peanuts into a dish and put glas

ses and a bottle of sparkling wine on to a tray. She headed for the living room, where Joan and Pamela were rocking to the ragga track on the stereo. Donna was in the bedroom with Diallo — she would be babysitting tonight. The girls were raving for the first time since Marion had had the baby. She had stayed at her mother's for a month, and had arrived back this week feeling revived and ready to face the world again. Pamela had dyed her hair brown two days previously, and she'd had it cut into an ear-length bob. The final part of her make-over was for her to go out and enjoy herself. Paul had been truthful about only taking what was his from the flat. He had left everything that had anything to do with her. He had taken Diallo's framed baby portrait, though, despite what he now knew. Marion had coped well, considering. She now felt at peace. She had direction in her life now — a career, and her son to concentrate her energies on. She tried not to think of Paul, it only ever resulted in sadness. "Marion, did Joan show you the ring?" Pamela asked as she entered with the tray. "What ring?" Marion looked to Joan. Joan held her left hand out. "He thought it would make it official," she explained. "It's no big deal. We've been engaged for months anyway." Though a big kid in some ways, Colin was trying hard to be a responsible father and future husband. Joan loved being part of a couple again. It was good for her.

"The ring is a big deal, believe," Pamela told her. She grabbed a handful of peanuts from the bowl and dropped them daintily one by one into her mouth. "He's showing everyone that he's made a commitment." "It's perfect," Marion said dreamily. "It's all right, I s'pose." Joan looked at it, grinning from ear to ear. Marion sat next to her and took a sip of wine. "So, where's Michael tonight?" she asked Pamela. Pamela and Michael had become a regular item. Every time one of her friends called her, Michael was there or he'd just left or was on his way. They'd joked about him moving in. Pamela had immediately put them straight: no way; no matter how good he was for her, she wasn't giving up her independence again. "He's at Tony's," Pamela replied. "They're coming to Sharna's party later." Joan raised her eyes to the ceiling before turning to Pamela. "You know what that means. You're going with us, but you'll spend the night with him," she said. Pamela waved her away, her scarlet nails catching the light. "He's going with his mates an' I'll be with you lot. We're not joined together, you know, not like you and Colin." "Don't tell me it hasn't crossed your mind, though," Joan pressed. Pamela smiled, modestly brushing salt from her black jeans. "All right, I've thought about it." The truth was that Pamela and Michael had an agreement, and that was that they wouldn't put any pressure on each other. They already knew how they felt about each other. It wasn't necessary to try to force words and action from the other to prove it. "Shaun stopped calling?" Marion asked. "I ain't heard from him for about four weeks. I think he finally got the message." "Boy, that was one stubborn black man," Joan affirmed. "You're not wrong. I thought of all the men I've been with he would understand the difference between lust and love."

Joan nearly choked on her drink. "You what!" She gave Pamela an incredulous stare. "Maz, back me up on this. Wasn't this the same girl who just a few months ago was saying how no one man could satisfy her. An' how all she wanted was sex?" Marion nodded and Pamela laughed. "Oh come on, guys, you know what I was going on about." "No. What?" Marion asked. "Put it this way. I hadn't met him then — and now I have." "Hmm-mmm," Joan teased. "Shut up, you!" Pamela picked up a cushion and threw it across the room at J

oan, who screamed and ducked. The girls cracked up with laughter. "On a more serious note," Joan said, "aren't you going to tell Marion about your meeting?" Pamela had totally forgotten. She had called the agency and spoken to a very nice woman, who'd passed on the details of her natural mother. "I'm going to meet my real mum next week." Marion's mouth fell open. "I don't believe it! You're actually going o go through with it?" "I have to. They say curiosity killed the cat — well, I'm not dead yet. I ha

ve to know." "Well, good luck to you." Marion turned to Joan. "You got a date for your wedding yet?" she asked. She had a lot of news to catch up on. "Mmm — about this time next year." Joan sipped some wine. "I'll have to talk to Mum first. Finances, y'know." Marion suddenly looked at the clock and then back to her friends. "Guess what?" "What?" they said together. "You lot have been here three hours and Joan hasn't lit up once." Pamela now turned to Joan. "Shit, she's right." "Didn't I tell you? I haven't smoked in a month," Joan said proudly. "You're kidding me!" Pamela said, shocked. Joan shook her head. "Honestly, I don't need it any more." She had also lost a stone in weight, but she wasn't bragging. "You see what good love does for people?" Marion grinned as if she had given the love to her friend. She got up to put a new tape on. "So, what has love done for you, Pam?" Joan asked. "Who, me?" Pamela asked, feigning surprise. She thought about it for a while, then answered slowly,

"I'm gonna get real deep here. Love has given me a sense of worth. A respect for men I never had before. Black pride." She raised her hand in a fist and the girls copied her, punching the air. Pamela continued: "I am now more self-confident, proud, and filled with absolute joy. I have a man who I love, and who loves me back." She paused, letting the momentum of her statement build. "Get on with it," Joan said, reaching for the cushion on the floor. "All right... And I'm having the best fucking sex I've had in my life!" She cracked up. The other two laughed with her, enjoying the feeling of unity. Pamela put on her best cockney accent. "Ain't luv grand?" Marion sat down on the floor crossed-legged, her features becoming melancholy. She drained her glass of wine and poured some more. Her friends exchanged looks, their smiles fading as they realised they were probably being insensitive. "You know, Michael's friend Tony is single," Pamela hinted. Marion ran her finger around the rim of the glass. "I'm not interested. I'm tired of all that. I've got Diallo to think of now."

Joan tried to console her. "Maybe Paul will have a change of heart. You know he really loved you — the two of you." Marion smiled weakly. Did Joan know something she didn't? The telephone rang, and Marion was glad — she really didn't want to talk about Paul. "Hello?" she answered. A muffled but vaguely familiar male voice came down the line: "Hello?" "Yes?" Marion said, then the line went dead. Her friends turned to look at her as she held the phone aloft and shrugged her shoulder. She replaced the receiver and they soon forgot about the call as they got chatting again, gossiping about life, love, sex, their future plans, and upcoming raves. They were all a little tipsy when, half an hour later, the door opened and Donna entered the room holding Diallo on her hip. The baby, three and a half months old now, gazed around at the drunken women sprawled over the living room. He spotted his mother and grinned toothlessly. "Marion, there's a man at the door," Donna informed her. "Says he knows you." None of them had heard the bell. "Oooh, a man! Is he gift-wrapped?" Pamela giggled from her place on the floor. "Room service! Bring him in, Maz. We'll share him," Joan laughed, sliding off the chair to slap palms with Pamela. Marion struggled to her feet and left the room, closing the door behind her. It was late for visitors, and she wasn't expecting anyone. Joan already knew who it was, but she'd been keeping it to herself. This visitor was to be a birthday surprise. Joan had been keeping him up to date on how things were for the past month, and so he knew all about the TV offer. If there was one thing Joan was good at, she silently congratulated herself, it was being a friend and counsellor. This was one case she was not going to lose. Donna shook her head in dismay. Sometimes, she thought, her sister and her friends acted like teenagers. She hoped she wouldn't be like that in five years' time. Paul stood in the hallway, hands clasped in front of him. The front door stood open behind him. To Marion, he looked like a lost little boy. A feeling of total euphoria came over her. She was feeling extremely light-headed, and wondered if she was hallucinating. Paul looked uncomfortable, shifting from one foot to the other. "Happy birthday," he said, smiling shyly.

"Thank you," she replied, not knowing quite what else to say. He made an attempt at humour. "You can throw me out if you want."

Marion didn't know how to react. She remembered how she had felt the last time she'd seen him. How hurt they had both been. She wasn't sure what his motives were this time, and wasn't going to let herself be trapped. "I have visitors," she slurred, her wide eyes trying to stay open. "Yeah, I heard," he smiled. They were silent for nearly a minute, neither of them knowing what the other's next move might be. "I need some air. Why don't we go outside?" she suggested finally and he followed her out. They took the lift in silence, Marion watching the numbers descend above the door. All sorts of things were going through her head. Paul pointed as they exited the flats. "My car's just up there." Marion followed him. They reached the car and Paul opened the passenger side for her. Before she got in, she turned to him. "That was you on the phone before, wasn't it?" Paul nodded, embarrassed. Marion frowned and got into the car, and Paul walked around to the driver's side. On the dashboard there was a single red rose with a card attached. Marion glanced at it and then at him. He nodded at the rose. "It's for you." Marion hesitantly picked up the flower and removed the tiny card from its envelope. She read the handwritten words.

Darling Marion, Please forgive me. I want you. I need you. Without you I am worthless. I love you always, for ever, for eternity. I can't breathe without you. Panther

The words wrapped themselves around her heart, and she read them again as her nostrils filled with the flower's scent. She gazed through the windscreen, her face holding none of the mixed emotions she was feeling inside. "Are you sure, Paul?" He leaned towards her and reached for her hand. "I thought about this for over a month. Why d'ya think I'm here? I really care about you…" He reached to embrace her but she pulled back. "What about Diallo? Could you accept him too?" she asked, looking deep into his eyes. He pondered the question for a moment, but he already knew how he felt. "For a year I thought he was my kid. I love him, Marion. I missed both of you." His eyes glistened with the unshed tears of remembered pain. She looked down at his hand holding hers, and knew she felt the same as he did. "Paul, I'm so sorry…" She leaned towards him, and this time he pulled back. "Hold on. There's something else." He swallowed nervously. "I have to know that you want me, and not just a replacement for Gerard." "That's over, Paul. Whatever I felt for him is gone. I love you." Satisfied, Paul reached over her and opened the glove compartment. He handed her a small velvet box. "Happy birthday," he said again. She accepted the box with tear-filled eyes — tears of joy this time. It clicked open to reveal a gold multi-stoned ring. "It's an eternity ring," he told her. As if she didn't know. She had certainly gazed at enough of them in jewellery shop windows. "Why don't you put it on for me?" She handed him the box and held her left hand out. He slipped the ring on to her ring finger. Their eyes met, and as they drew closer their lips did too. They were together again, and that was all that mattered. Paul thought of a saying his mother loved to recite: "Learn from the past and look to the future."

He thought they had both learnt their lesson. The future was for them to make a go of it — honestly, as a family.

COLIN

I've been tamed — under manners, as they say. It ain't that bad. Joan is still Joan. I still love her, an' I want to marry her. I have this feeling… our first will be a boy. Yeah, love's so fine.

GERARD

Nothin's really changed for me, you know. The mobile phone business is going good. I've I'm shacked up with a girl named Beverley now. She's a good cook, takes care of my needs. It's nothin' serious, but she don't know that. Marion and her man decided it was bes' if I stay out of my son's life until he's old enough to understand. Mum has visiting rights, though. Marion an' her got on. Paul — he's all right, y'know. Respect to him still — 'cause he's raising my boy. I'm not ready for Miss Right. Maybe one day… you know how it goes.

MICHAEL

When I think back on what I could have lost, I have to kick myself. Pamela and I have an easygoing relationship. She does her thing, I do mine, but we're doing it together. There's no more playing around. We both know what we want now, but we're not pushing it down each other's throats. I just hope I don't have a relapse.

Fingers crossed, yeah?

PAUL
I've got no complaints. My chile, my wife, my home — perfect. I have it all again. Marion's career has taken off. Diallo's getting bigger every day. How do I feel about him not being mine? At firs', it was hard. I kept trying to distance myself. It's still hard, I suppose. But I can't see myself without him now. Blood or not, I love him.

Marion keeps hinting at marriage. It's a good idea, but right now we can't afford to do it properly. I'm working hard though.

End

Waiting
for
Mr Wright

Yo, dude, wake up and get outta bed! Yo, dude, wake up and get outta bed ..."

Errol Wright pulled the duvet over his head and attempted to sink himself back into his dream, where Janet Jackson was trying to persuade him to give everything up and live with her in America.

"... Yo, dude, wake up and get outta bed!"

Groaning, Errol threw one arm out from under the cover. "That's it man," he grunted. "Cho', me an' yuh nuh spar no more."

The alarm clock fell to the floor with a thud, but Bart Simpson had not yet got the message.

"Yo, dude..."

"Damn!" Errol fumbled blindly for the clock once more, grabbing the damn thing by its plastic head and hitting the shut-off button. A Christmas present from his son, Bart Simpson was the only childish thing in Errol's bedroom. He sat up in bed and waited for the walls to stop spinning. Last night was the final time he would ever listen to his bone-headed mate, Colin. "I've only got a few more hours of being a single man," Colin had said. "You can't turn down a bachelor's last request. Let's invite some ah the lads round..." Well, a few of the lads had brought a few ladies, the drink-up had turned into a wild party, and Errol now felt like a fifty-year-old. The brandy and champagne had poured until five o'clock in the morning, and mixed with the fried chicken, rice and peas and hard dough bread that Colin's mum had brought round, Errol's stomach was now planning a walk-out.

This was not good. He had to have Colin in church in four hours' time, and Errol knew that cameras don't look too favourably on hung-over TV presenters, whether they are the best man or not. Media success had made him more 'friends' than he could handle. They all expected him to have ready money and to be willing to party at the drop of a hat. None of them seemed to realise what hard work it was, how his life didn't belong to him any more.

Errol flopped on to his back and became aware of a warm body in bed

1

beside him. He shot upright again and regretted it instantly: his brain spun and his stomach churned. He fell back on to the pillows and held his aching head, shaved smooth only yesterday.

The body beside him turned over and moved closer. "Col?" she murmured, throwing an arm over his chest.

Errol held his breath. "What's up?"

It was Melanie, one of Colin's ex-girlfriends. How in hell had she got in here? Before she could come to completely, Errol swung his usually strong legs off the bed and gave a sigh of relief when he realised he was still wearing his boxer shorts. He moved as fast as he could in his condition, and grabbed a shirt from the heap of clothes on the floor. Leaving the shirt open he gingerly tiptoed from the room. The door to the spare bedroom was open as he passed on his way to the stairs. Errol's temporary lodger was sprawled across his bed, fully dressed. No wonder his ex had found her way into the wrong room last night. Lucky for Mr Baker... but it could have been very unlucky for Errol if Yvette had decided to pay a surprise visit.

The house was almost deadly quiet. Almost. Somewhere downstairs a radio had been left on. The small modern house in Mitcham was Errol's pride and joy, his treat to himself for getting where he was today. He'd bought it six months ago, paying the deposit from his first wage packet and advance from the job that had since made him a TV personality. Now he had money, an instantly recognizable face, his own home and a brand new car – a far cry from the bedsits he had stayed in during his student days.

He relieved himself in the bathroom, avoiding his reflection in the mirror until he'd woken properly. Coffee – that's what he needed. Hot, black and strong, like himself...

Damn! It hurt to smile. He reached the top of the stairs and very nearly fell headlong down them as he was blinded by the sun's rays pouring in through the skylight. Raising a heavy arm, he blocked the glare from his eyes, gripped the banister, and slowly descended on legs shaky from lack of sleep.

The hall still held mementos of the night before. Although smoking was banned from his home – the guests had had to smoke in the garden – bottles, cans and dirty plates littered the furniture, and the faint scent of expensive aftershave hung in the air. He'd have to call his housekeeper in to deal with it. The party had been Colin's idea and, now Errol came to think of it, the guests had been mostly Colin's friends. Errol pushed open the swing door to his kitchen and stopped in his tracks. A woman stood at the sink, in front of the window overlooking the garden. She was singing along to Smooth's "Undercover Lover" playing on the portable radio, while rinsing mugs under the tap. The black woman's hair was natural and pulled back into a ponytail. Her skin was fair, and smooth as caramel. Very slim, and with a neck that begged to be kissed, she was dressed in a long-sleeved black satin dress, the sleeves made of chiffon. She made an unforgettable first impression.

Errol stood in the doorway, one hand still on the door, his head tilted to one side, and one eyebrow raised. Women were turning up in the most unexpected places this morning!

Her singing voice was rich and confident, and for some reason Errol didn't want to disturb her. For a few seconds it seemed as though his headache had disappeared completely. He let go of the door and it swung back behind him, making a whooshing sound. He saw her jump as she spun to face him. "Errol!" she said with mild surprise. "Good morning."

So, she had the advantage – she knew who he was. Which wasn't really surprising when he thought about it: he was on television every week, and she was in his house, where he'd just thrown a party. But for the life of him he couldn't place her.

"Morning…" He hurriedly began to button his shirt to cover his naked torso and boxer shorts. Her eyes sparkled with amusement as she watched him. Ambling over to the dining table, he scratched his head and asked, "Have we met?"

She turned off the running tap. "Sort of." She was giggling as she reached for a hand towel. "I fell into your lap last night – well, actually it was the early hours of this morning. I lost my ride home and camped on your sofa."

A vague memory crept back into his consciousness like a traveller in the fog. "Your name begin with A?"

"Yeah." She smiled, an enticing smile that was so friendly he had to grin back. Her voice was sophisticated, cultured, the enunciation exquisite. "Anne-Marie Simms." She held out her right hand.

Errol shook it. Her skin was soft – as if she hadn't done a day's manual work in her life – and moist from washing up. His head still ached, but now he remembered her: Anne-Marie had spilt white wine on his silk shirt and he'd had to go upstairs and change. "Coffee?"

"Yes, please." She lowered her eyes shyly. "Sorry, I was going to help myself…"

"Don't worry about it." Errol watched her move back to the sink and retrieve two mugs that she had rinsed and dried. She placed them on the table as Errol flicked on the kettle. He found himself wishing she had found her way into his bed last night instead of Melanie, but he quickly abandoned the idea. After all, he was almost spoken for. Errol had been ready to make instant coffee, but because he had a guest he filled the percolator with water and produced fresh coffee and filters from the cupboard.

"What a night, eh?"

He shook his bald head. "Yeah, what a night!" He tried to laugh but received a bolt of lightning to his temples for his trouble.

Anne-Marie must have noticed his wince. "Feeling a bit fragile?"

He touched a temple gingerly. "Just a bit." His voice was hoarse and deeper than usual. Hopefully that would clear before he had to make the speeches later on. Crossing the kitchen floor, he pulled a drawer open and searched for some pills to cure his headache. "Care for a pain-killer?" he offered.

Anne-Marie laughed, and there it was again: that very open, welcoming smile. "No thanks. Coffee will be fine."

Errol spooned fresh coffee into the filter.

"So, where's the groom?" Anne-Marie asked.

Errol slapped his forehead and felt himself sway. "Shit! I knew there was something I was supposed to do before I came down."

Anne-Marie shook her head, laughing. "I think you'd better go and see to him. I'll make the coffee." Groggily, Errol passed a hand over his head, a gesture he often made when he was thinking. He left the kitchen feeling Anne-Marie's eyes on his back.

Colin was in the same position he'd been in when Errol had gone down to the kitchen. Errol crossed the threshold and yelled, "Colin, man, get up!"

There was no movement from his friend, so he went over and shoved him. "Yo, homie! It's your wedding day!"

That got some reaction. Colin rolled over on to his back. "Wha… ?"

"You're expected in church in less than four hours. Now get your arse up and into the shower!"

"What time you call this to wake me up? You're supposed to be my best man!"

"Stop complainin'. Four hours is plenty of time to get ready."

"It might be plenty of time to dress, but what about my comtemplation time, man?"

"You had that last night." Errol crossed to the airing cupboard in the hall and slung a towel on to Colin's prone body. "I'm cooking breakfast.

4

Be down in fifteen."

Colin groaned and struggled to sit up straight.

Back downstairs, Anne-Marie was sitting at the pine dining table, resting her chin on her hands. "Is he okay?"

Errol found himself feeling glad she was still here. They had only just met, but it felt good to have someone about to ease his best man's nerves. He reached for the coffee pot and brought it to the table. "Fine. I just hope he stays awake."

"You've got a beautiful house, Errol. Do you live here alone?"

"Thank you. Yes, I do."

Anne-Marie turned in the chair, rested one arm across the back of it, and crossed her legs. She took a closer look at Errol Wright and couldn't help feeling that, under the two pieces of clothing he had on, there was a lethal weapon. "I'm a big fan of yours, you know. I wouldn't watch *Do the Wright Thing* if it wasn't for you."

"Thank you again." Errol was used to people sucking up to him, but Anne-Marie seemed genuine. Still studying him as though he were a rare artefact, she asked, "Do you know Marion Stewart?"

"Yes. In fact she's interviewing me on Monday for *Mantalk*."

"Really?" Anne-Marie's brown eyes glittered. "I went to school with her. We're having lunch together on Monday."

Errol raised an eyebrow. "Small world!" Marion was also a close friend of his – she and her boyfriend Paul. He was an honorary godfather to her son.

"Isn't it, though? I'm an author – *Internal Bleeding*..." She said it as though he should know it.

He didn't. "So what's the book about?"

She lowered her eyes modestly. "I hate telling men what I write about. They get very... sceptical."

Errol smiled reassuringly, automaticatically slipping into talk-show-host mode. "Trust me," he said.

She smiled and shrugged. "It's about the pain we go through when our loved one walks out on the relationship."

"Oh?" he said. "From experience?"

"Mine – and others'."

"I see... Well, good on ya. I might read it myself."

The smile lit up every feature of Anne-Marie's face. Like every writer Errol had ever met, for her, praise was as necessary as food or sex.

She watched him through the haze of steam rising from the large mug she held to her lips, her eyes travelling down the smooth outline of his chest. He was gorgeous. Last night she had tried to talk to him and it had been virtually impossible; he'd been most certainly in demand. Now, here, she had him all to herself.

"You know, no one's gonna believe me when I tell them I was with Errol Wright for breakfast."

He ran a hand over his chin, hearing the unusual rasp of bristles on his usually clean shaven face. "Is that your way of asking for my autograph?"

She ran a finger round the rim of the mug. "Does that seem childish?"

Was she flirting with him? It was hard to tell. He'd had women practically throw themselves at him since becoming a celebrity. If Anne-Marie was flirting she was doing it with subtlety. "Course not." He gulped down some warm coffee. "I'll sign a photo for you if I can get a discount on your book."

She giggled, her eyes shining. "It's a done deal."

They shook on it.

"So, did you enjoy your party?"

"It was Colin's party really – a second stag night. Colin must be the only groom I know that isn't satisfied with one going-out party. But what I can remember of it – yes." He met her eyes across the table, suddenly curious who invited her. "Are you one of Colin's friends?"

"Kind of." She went shy again. "Actually, Colin and I were lovers a while back. We still keep in touch."

Errol's spirits dropped as soon as the word "lovers" came from her lips. He avoided her eyes by staring into his coffee. That was it, then. He made it a rule never to go out with anyone within his circle of friends – he'd found that his personal life stopped being personal whenever he let that happen. Anne-Marie was one of Colin's ex-girlfriends, she knew Marion as well... and that made her a no-go zone.

She must have noticed the change in his demeanor, because she quickly changed the subject. "You should eat, y'know. You're going to be much too busy later."

He realised he was a little hungry, and he certainly needed something to soak up last night's alcohol. The coffee had settled his stomach, but now it felt empty. "Toast!" He scraped back the chair on the stone-tiled floor and headed for the wooden bread bin.

Anne-Marie stood up too. "Why don't I make it for you? Then you can check on Colin and start getting ready."

"I couldn't let you do—"

"I'm offering." She held up a hand. He paused for a few seconds. Here he was, standing half-naked in his kitchen with an extremely pretty woman, the first intelligent woman in his life since God knows when, and he couldn't touch her. He'd be making a big mistake. Where was the justice in this world?

She was right, though. He did need a shave, and the traffic heading into town wasn't going to be easy. "Thanks, Anne…"

"Anne-Marie, please."

"Sorry…"

"Don't apologise. My mum just never liked it shortened; I guess it rubbed off."

They stood there, neither of them moving, a slight smile playing across Anne-Marie's eyes and lips. Then the door was thrown open aggressively, and Colin entered as only Colin could: newly cut hairdo so neat he'd have to do nothing to it, bleary red eyes trying to stay open, string vest and baggy trousers crushed and musty. "I smelt coffee. Make us a cup nuh, man – you know dat's your job today." He slumped down on a pine dining chair.

"Cho, what d'you think this is, a café?" Errol scolded, apologising with his eyes to Anne-Marie.

Colin forced his eyes open and they came to rest on Anne-Marie, who was leaning against the counter. His expression was a dreary parody of surprise. "You still here?" he asked, looking suspiciously from her to Errol and back again. Then he smiled. "Oh, yeah…"

Errol knew exactly what was going through what passed for Colin's mind. "It's not what you think. Anne-Marie slept on the sofa."

Colin got up, smacking his lips thirstily. "It's not my business." He pulled a carton of orange juice from the fridge and raised it to his lips, gulping noisily. Nodding towards the bread in Anne-Marie's hand he asked, "You mekking breakfast? I'll 'ave some a dat too." Then he was gone, the door swinging behind him.

"I suppose I don't need to apologise for my friend. You know him already."

Anne-Marie laughed and brushed breadcrumbs from her fingers. "Yeah, I suppose I do."

Their eyes met again, and Errol felt as if he couldn't bring himself to leave her. He could walk out of the kitchen and never set eyes on her again. A self-confessed bachelor, he was already involved in a sexual relationship that had satisfied him for the past year or so. Now he was confused about why a woman he'd just met was making him consider cheating on his girlfriend.

"Hadn't you better get ready?" she reminded him.

"Sure... yeah. You all right down here?"

"Fine," she assured him with that knee-trembling smile. She wasn't Colin's type at all – she had brains and beauty. Just what had she seen in him? A bit of rough? "Right then... I'll catch you later." Errol edged towards the door.

Anne-Marie was fully aware of the effect she was having on him, and it warmed her inside. "Yeah."

Pushing the door, he couldn't stop himself taking one last look at her backside... And the rest of her was exactly the same. Damn!

On the upstairs landing, Errol passed Melanie coming out of the spare room. The girl was cool to hang out with – a little brainless, but that was what Colin had gone for before Joan. Melanie had a bad case of 'bedhead' and redeye. She ran an embarrassed hand through her hair, not that it made much difference. "Hi, Errol! Sorry about last night... I was well gone, man."

He stroked her arm playfully. "It's all right, Mel. Trying to give Colin a send-off were you?"

She giggled. "Sump'n like that." Yeah – she had probably walked into the wrong room on purpose, and instead of the seduction she'd planned had most probably passed out.

Errol's bath took him approximately thirty minutes, during which time he soaped himself with Lynx shower gel, scrubbed his fingernails, and shampooed his head. Washed, shaved and back in his bedroom, he began to feel a little like his old self again.

He liked the pattern of days he had to himself, enjoyed the routinelessness of it all, hated to be jarred or hurried into the day. But this morning was an exception. Today, he was to be a best man for the second time.

Thirty-four and still single, though he had a son. He knew he looked good, though... Didn't he? As if to prove it to himself, he turned to his full-length mirror and studied his body, face and naked torso, turning this way and that, flexing and stretching. What he saw was an inviting, humorous smile, long-lashed brown eyes, silky, arched eyebrows, not one wrinkle... juicy lips, and a male model's jawline. His dark skin was still supple, smooth and free of scars. He stood a solid six foot two, with broad shoulders, hard pecs and pumped biceps. No way did he look thirty-four... Twenty-seven at the most...

"Now here's a dedication that's going out to the bridegroom, Mr Colin Baker. He's gettin' married at St Mark's in Peckham this afternoon.

Your bride, Joan Ross, soon to be Baker, wants us to play 'Tonight I Celebrate my Love for You'. She loves you, man – mek sure you treat her right..." Daddy Ernie spun the track, and as the first bars rang out the groom stepped out of the shower.

Dressed in a towel, Errol smiled to himself and crossed the room to rummage around in his underwear drawer for the g-string he wanted to wear today: Yvette's favourite. He half-turned and directed his voice towards the en suite bathroom. "Colin, you hear dat? Your bride just sent you a dedication over the airwaves."

Colin was mopping himself down with a towel. "Yeah, I heard," he replied proudly. "A my girl, dat!"

Errol laughed and padded barefoot across the bedroom to dust down their hired suits with a clothes brush. Always the best man, never the groom... He hoped Colin knew what he was letting himself in for.

Errol was a very confident man, sure of himself and his future, although he'd never seen himself as the marrying type. His parents were strong, independent, professional people, who'd instilled in their only child a firm sense of confidence and self-worth. "Believe in yourself and you can do anything," his father had told him. "Never be frightened in life," his mother had said. "Face whatever comes your way with dignity and strength."

It was all right for them – they had each other. But Errol had often felt like an intruder in their presence... especially when sex was something they didn't wait until he was asleep to perform.

So when they'd decided to move to the States he had known that this was his chance to practise what they preached. He was eighteen at the time – an adult, with nothing but the thousand pounds they had left him. But he had found himself filled with the energy and enthusiasm of an independent youth with something to prove.

While he studied he'd moved from one friend's couch to the next, struggling to survive on a measly student's grant. After college he'd held down several jobs to repay his overdraft – shelf-stacker, hired hand, mechanic – before finally landing a job with a local paper as a journalist. From there he had made contacts in television, gone back to college to get the right qualifications, signed on with an agent – and his life had changed dramatically.

"You got two more hours of freedom before she slap dat chastity belt 'pon you an t'row away de key."

"There ain't no chastity in my relationship, believe."

"Marriage changes people. You wait – give it six months and you're gonna be making appointments to have sex with your wife," Errol joked. "Leave it out! If that was gonna happen it would have happened already. At least I know where my next lay is coming from, unlike some people I could mention." "Leave my sex life out of this." "But when are you gonna settle down, Errol?" Colin quizzed. "You gonna be left on the shelf if you don't find someone soon."

What was this man on? How could anyone answer that question? Errol stepped to the bathroom door and watched while Colin lathered up his face for a shave. "I chose to have one specific woman because she pleases me sexually; I go out with other women because I also need mental stimulation. Why not share what I've got to offer?" Colin turned to him, razor in hand. "You see! Did you just hear yourself? You got more ego than sense."

"Don't you worry about it, Col. In my own time I'll decide which woman I end up with. You should know how hard a decision that is anyway. Look how long it took you an' Joan to decide you were meant for each other."

"Mmm." Colin twisted his face to one side to get a clean shave. "Joan wasn't easy though, man. I had to fight to hold on to that one." He rinsed his razor in the sink. "You know there's always women on the look-out for eligible bachelors at weddings. Being the best man, you'd best watch your back."

"Easy, star! I'm picking Yvette up for the reception. She should finish work by about seven."

"Oh, she's the one you're sporting tonight?"

"She's not a suit, man. An' jus' watch what you say in front of her."

"Hey, rude bwoy. Dis is me you a talk to." Colin wiped his face with a flannel and threw it across the room. It hit Errol in the chest. "I ain't gonna drop you in it. Stress getting to you?"

"I'm not the one getting married." Errol threw the flannel back and Colin caught it in his fist. He now looked fresh and alert, belying the fact that they had been up until five. "You jealous?"

Errol raised an eyebrow. "Yeah, right! Listen, you got another hour to make yourself look like a bridegroom." Errol could have been in Colin's present situation many times over. Instead he was the ultimate batchelor: eligible, with charm and charisma and good looks. But that wasn't all he had going for him. One thing many women look for in a mate is a man who can communicate with them on their level, and Errol Wright was definitely that man. All it usually took was for him to go into talk-show-host mode and say, "Talk to me." A few sympathetic words, and he'd get them to confide in him. It worked with his guests too. The only problem with his talent was that it had no limits. Once he was on a roll, once he'd got the woman on his side, it snowballed until all of a sudden he realised he was in a relationship.

It also drew a certain type of woman. They would be sophisticated, intersesting, independent, intelligent and attractive – but unfortunately they would be searching for Mr Right. They were usually hard to spot, because everything they said and did seemed so confident and self-sufficient, and it was this I-don't-need-a-man attitude that was deceiving. Errol had learnt one tell-tale sign: they always made the first move. They would be so intent on getting their man that they would soon start to worm their way into his life. Often carrying the scars of being treated unfairly by the opposite sex, these women were on the look-out for a healer, a man who wasn't going to hurt them, one who actually liked women, and not just for the obvious. In other words, someone like Errol Wright. After four of these close calls, he'd simply given up. He'd met Yvette, and they had hit it off straight away. She'd made it clear that she wasn't into changing herself for any man, that a prospective partner would have to take her as she was. So they had gone out for a drink and ended up in bed – and that's the way it remained between them. They were both happy with the situation, and more than anything they were friends. She was his homie lover friend.

Errol slid open the door of his walk-in closet and paused in front of the long row of suits. There was thousands of pounds' worth of clothing here: royal blue, midnight blue, bottle green, khaki green, greys and black... these were his serious suits. Then there were the checks and flamboyant materials for the occasional "special appearances". On the other side of the closet were several rows of shoes, sorted into categories of dress, casual, sport and evening. He selected a highly polished Italian leather pair, to match his suit, then, feeling like Errol Wright, Voice of the People, he left Colin to dress and skipped down the stairs.

He entered the kitchen with a flourish. His eyes fell on the note propped up on the marmalade jar. It was from Anne-Marie: "We'll swap autographs at your earliest convenience." Underneath was her phone number. Errol smiled and slipped the paper into his jacket pocket. Then, grabbing two pieces of cold toast, he switched on the kettle to make some fresh coffee. It was going to be a long day.

The Saab pulled up across the road from the small church, and two young men – dapper, handsome, and groomed to perfection – stepped into the brilliant sunshine of the day.

Martin, Colin's brother, accompanied the groom shoulder to shoulder up the steps of the church, while the best man locked the vehicle and checked out the scene.

Inside, the church was lit from high windows in the roof and along the tops of the walls. A bulky man dressed in black with a white waistcoat was bustling up the aisle towards them, a camera bouncing on his chest. "Where've you been? We need to get some pictures of you and your escorts before the bride's party arrives."

Errol whispered to Colin, "I guess that's the photographer."

"Don't look at me, I didn't find him," Colin hissed back.

Behind the three of them another four men in identical suits entered.

"Oh good, you're all here!" The photographer bustled the group back towards the entrance of the church. "Okay. Outside now, gentlemen. If we could get a move on here…" "Yo, D!" Colin called out to the youngest of the ushers. "You look criss in that suit. A your turn next!" Duane, fifteen years old, waved him away with a shy grin.

Like an army sargeant the photographer lined them all up and started to order them around, telling them to stand up, kneel down, smile, hug, shake hands, even lift the groom up for the bumps.

The groom's mother arrived fifteen minutes later and fussed over him until she had to be pulled away: "Colin, you have you 'kerchief? Put it in de pockit." "Colin, straighten you tie! You don't see you 'ave de pin upside down!" "Colin! Who iron you trousers? De crease nuh straight…"

When she was finally seated behind them, Errol kept Colin's mind occupied with jokes about the bride not turning up, and started a mental countdown to the ceremony that would end Colin's single life. The church was filling up quickly, and they turned and waved to family and friends as they were ushered in behind them.

After a few minutes, the whisper reached them like a wave from the back of the church that the bride had arrived. Colin grabbed Errol's arm and swallowed hard.

His best man grinned. "You feeling it now?"

They stood up together, moving to the altar as the organist struck up the wedding march. The congregation stood as Joan, her daughter and her father, followed by six bridesmaids, stepped in time down the aisle. There was an audible sigh from the females admiring Joan's dress and that of her five-year-old daughter. The little girl dropped rose petals up the aisle as she stepped ahead of her mother and grandfather. Errol did his duty as ring bearer and then bowed out, grateful to be able to take a seat.

"Mm-hmm. Michael, your buns get tighter every time I see 'em." Yvette slapped the fit black man's buttocks, giving him a flirtatious smile before moving on to the next piece of fitness equipment. Michael watched her sheepishly, his eyes flitting to her Lycra-covered bottom, before he stepped up his pace on the treadmill. At thirty-seven years old, he was one of her regulars at the gym. He was also one of the few gentlemen.

The men who frequented The Body Beautiful knew what Yvette was like, which in most cases was why they came. The ones who found her too familiar never returned. This was *her* gym, and she loved it more than her own home. The Body Beautiful was a beauty parlour, offering the services of masseurs and toning tables, as well as a fully equipped gym. And Yvette occasionally took aerobics classes. One day she planned to expand to include saunas. She was still a youthful-looking thirty two – she knew she could eventually achieve everything she wanted. She had an eleven-year-old son – My Man, she called him. Tyrone had used to have this thing about vetting her appearance before she went out for a date. He would tell her if her dress was too short or cut too low, if her hair looked good, or if she had on too much make-up. Tyrone had used to be her protector, the man of the house. Any man who tried to muscle in on his territory was soon put in his place – and if he didn't like it, then he was out. Tyrone was definitely his mother's son.

That is, before she'd started seeing Errol, who had had the boy eating out of his hand from day one.

Errol had walked into their home one evening and shaken Tyrone's hand, then had taken an immediate interest in what the boy was doing. Tyrone hadn't recognised him from the TV; they had talked and played with the computer until the early hours of the morning before Errol told him he was a celebrity.

"Never mind me," Yvette had said as she'd pouted in front of the television. This male bonding shit stinks, she'd thought. Tyrone didn't see Errol as a threat because Errol had shown him respect, that he was friend, not foe, before the boy had even had a chance to consider it.

That had been almost a year ago, and already Tyrone had asked if he could call Errol "Daddy". Needless to say, Yvette had refused, feeling the jealousy boiling up inside her. "He's *not* your daddy," she'd said angrily. But she had been secretly glad that her son had accepted Errol, that he

13

obviously felt the same way she did for the man. Later, when she'd asked Errol how he would have felt if she'd said yes, he'd replied, "I would've been honoured, but I'm not in the position to be a father to him at the moment."

The only thing stopping them being a family, Yvette felt, was both of their need for indepenence.

"Yvette, man, what's wrong wid dis machine?"

"You having a problem there, Kyle?" Another black hunk – God, she loved this job.

"Nothing's happening." The man tapped the side of the console twice.

"Don't you go hitting my equipment wid dem hammer-fists a yours!" Yvette strode lithely to the rowing machine, where the featherweight boxer was getting frustrated. She adjusted her cut-off top so she wouldn't reveal anything as she bent over.

"It ain't lightin' up."

"You tried turning it on?" Yvette flipped a switch on the side of the console and it beeped into life.

Kyle shrugged. "New technology – I still ain't got the hang of it."

"You just a big baby, ain't ya?" She squeezed his cheeks playfully. Observers chuckled as Yvette teased the big man. "Don't worry, babe – when you're ready for lessons you know where to find me..." The inuendo was not lost on her audience. Yvette always caught nuff jokes in the fitness room. She would stride around in her work-out gear, catching up with her patrons' lives and praising them on their efforts to keep fit. She made friends easily – that was how she had met Errol. Speaking of which, it was time to get showered and get out of here. He was due to pick her up in half an hour for a wedding reception.

"Fellas, I'm gone. I'll catch you later."

She was answered by grunts, growls and wolf-whistles. Yvette was making her way through the mirrored corridor of her domain when Babs, the receptionist, met her. She was tugging at the cord of her track-suit bottoms, tightening the twenty-four-inch waist. "I was just coming to get you..."

Yvette was already walking away. "Yeah, well whatever it is can wait until tommorrow. I'm on my way out."

"But you can't—"

"Sorry?" Yvette placed a hand on her hip and cocked her head to one side.

Babs quickly started to apologise. "I'm sorry... It's just that Elaine called. She's twisted her ankle and there's no way she can take the class tonight…"

"What! You're kidding."

"I know you were planning to get off, but the women are already arriving…"

"Shit, shit, *shit*! Why now? I just don't believe this…" It was too late to get anyone else to cover – the class started in ten minutes. Cussing and stamping her feet, Yvette turned and headed towards her personal changing room to get ready. She wouldn't cancel a class; cancelled classes meant lost money and a damaged reputation.

Errol knew he must have looked like a fish out of water as he strolled up Woolwich High Street in his three-piece suit. He had taken his time sauntering up the road from the car park, because he knew that there was no way Yvette would be ready on time. She would still be doing her hair or make-up. He had learnt that the woman didn't know the meaning of time. You had to give her an hour in advance to be anywhere. Although if you kept her waiting you'd soon know about it. He wasn't obsessive about punctuality; it was just that he endeavored to turn up for people on time, even if it meant getting to places early and having to wait around. That's just the way he was.

The electronic buzzer on the door alerted Babs to Errol's presence. She looked up and smiled welcomingly. "Hi, Errol! You're looking good. No gym bag today?"

"Not today, Babs. I'm escorting my lady to a wedding reception." He had a twinkle in his eyes, and his smile brought out his charming, boyish dimples.

Babs was always glowing. She was half-caste, with lots of wild ringlets that always did the opposite to what she wanted. Today she had attempted a ponytail, but her hair wasn't having it and only half of it had stayed in the band. She smirked, giving him a wink. "But you still getting a work-out though, innit?"

Errol winced. The way women just came out with things these days… they didn't leave anything to the imagination. It wasn't as if he didn't occasionally make quips like that himself, but there was a time and a place for everything. "Is it all right to go through?" he asked, eager to be away from Babs's appraising eyes.

"Yeah, but she's still working. She had to take an extra class."

Errol nodded and raised a hand in thanks as he went through the entrance to the staff quarters. Along one side of the corridor was a mirrored wall; flick off the lights and it became a two-way mirror through which the staff could watch the goings-on in both the gym and the aerobics hall, where Yvette was presently taking her class. On the other side were doors that led to the staff room, Yvette's office, and the private changing rooms. At the end of the corridor was another door that led to the patrons' changing rooms, the showers and the treatment rooms. From the outside, no one would ever guess that there were so many rooms in here, and yet Yvette wanted more.

Errol stood alone in the corridor, contemplating whether to wait in her office or take a seat in the staff room, watch a bit of telly. Absently he flipped the light switch, and was suddenly given a view of rows of women doing their step aerobics. Dressed in leotards or leggings and T-shirts, they moved in unison to the beat of "This Is How We Do It" by Montell Jordan. Yvette was at the front of the class, her back to the mirror, shouting instructions and encouragement. Her extensions were tied high on her head with a band, and a layer of perspiration gave her skin a sheen.

She was good – in more ways than one – and Errol felt a surge of pride just watching her. People loved her. She was sometimes too loud, too flirtatious, too outspoken, too tactless and pushy, but underneath all of that was a good woman, an ambitious woman, with pride and much love for her son. She could be just as affectionate as she was brash; it just took the right person to bring it out. It suited them both to be permanent lovers. She knew how to be discreet, and didn't demand to be taken out to the expensive places Errol frequented in business.

And from his vantage point she had a great body. What was it his American cousin always said about black women? "Baby got back," he mouthed to himself, cocking his head to one side and runninng his tongue across his lips. Mm-hmm, Miss Barker definitely had back, as well as front. Tina Turner in her youth – that was Yvette. She even had those lips… snogging lips, legs that went on for ever, and muscles screaming out to be touched, caressed, massaged…

All it took was watching her. He could go to see her at her home thinking, Tonight I'm not going to touch her; tonight we're just going to sit down and talk, have a drink and cuddle up and talk. But what actually happened to him after a few minutes in her company was completely different. His hormones would take over, his dick would start bobbing and throbbing, and before his very eyes she would be a naked Goddess – ripe, juicy, hips pumping…

At first, that was all they had done. They had tried doing the dating thing once – their first date – but by the end of the evening they'd damned near torn the clothes from each other's bodies on her doorstep. They had it going on, uncontrollably, and it just kept getting better.

The class was winding up. The women were now lying flat on their backs doing cool-down exercises. They lifted their pelvises off the floor, holding, then down, then up again…

Errol turned away. Enough was enough. Just watching her do dem t'ings made him not only horny but thirsty too. He headed for the drinks machine and bought himself a lemon Tango. By the time he'd strolled back up towards the hall the ladies were emerging, hot, perspiring, giggling and chatting, some were mopping perspiration from their face and shoulders with towels, others were taking swigs from bottles of mineral water. Errol waited for them to exit before making his presence known. He cleared his throat, as Yvette's back was to him.

"Hi, baby." She sat on a bench and bent to untie her trainers. "Boy, what a day I've had! My brother this morning, going over the books and giving me headache, a self-defence class at the Waterfront this afternoon, then I get back here and have to supervise the inductions for the fitness room – I swear, some of the people we get in here should stick to a skipping rope… Oh, and then Elaine couldn't make it in to do this evening's class so I'm stuck here for another hour… So, obviously, I'm not ready…" She stopped and looked at him. Standing up, she put her hands on her hips. "You listening to me?"

He was leaning against the door's jamb, arms folded over his chest, one leg overlapping the other, the toe of one shoe on its tip. He had that you-know-what-I-want-to-do-to-you look in his eyes and was pulling his top teeth over his bottom lip seductively. "Of course I'm listening to you," he answered.

Yvette kissed her teeth. Shaking her head, she turned her back to him, but he could see in the mirror that she'd allowed a sneaky little smile to play on her lips. Yes, she loved it when he watched her like that. He knew he turned her on in the worst way. And she did have a body worth watching – she wasn't a fitness instructor for nothing. Yvette liked the fact that Errol went in for style in an understated way. Stylish hair, sharp suits… and he had a thing for hand-painted silk ties. He had been known to pay out a hundred pounds for one. She had often told him that he must have come out of charm school with a diploma. But of course she wasn't falling for any of that sweet-boy crap. She was one woman you either gave it to straight or not at all. When they'd first met she'd taken time to impress, which made a difference to Errol. She'd known who he was, and yet she hadn't fallen into his arms or gone all gooey. Still, four months later she'd been hooked. Although she hadn't said anything – Errol had simply exercised his male intuition.

"Well, as I was saying…" she started again.

"I know what you were saying." He approached her slowly, puposefully, his hands in his pockets. "And I'm here to make it all better." Placing his hands on her waist, he drew her to him, the bulge of his erection pressing against her bottom. He was just a couple of inches taller than her. Perfect.

She grinned. "You want some play, bad bwoy?"

"You offering?" He turned her to face him and slid his hands down her back to cup her taut buttocks, the smooth fabric of the leotard she wore arousing him more.

"Looks like you don't wait to be offered."

He took a step backwards, his arms still around her, and looked her in the eyes. He played into her little game. "Is that a complaint?"

Yvette looked around exaggeratedly. "I don't see anyone else in here. Did you hear a complaint? 'Cause it sure didn't come from me." She snaked one arm between their bodies, reaching for his hard-on. Her fingertips ran over the head and her palm cupped the shaft. Errol groaned.

"Aren't you supposed to be at a wedding?" she whispered.

"A reception." He nibbled her ear. "Not the same. We have time."

"Come," she said, taking his hand. "Lets go somewhere a little more private." Following her out of the gym, Errol smiled to himselfself. And there he had been, thinking she loved to do it in public. But he had no objections. Secure in his manhood, he had no problem with women who liked to lead in the bedroom – and Yvette certainly knew what she wanted.

If there were a female version of himself, he knew he'd found it in Yvette. Impulsive and unashamedly highly sexed, she knew he was always ready for her.

The corridor was still empty as they crossed it and entered her private changing room. As soon as the door was closed he spun her round and captured her lips with his own. The kiss was full of heat, passion and longing. Its urgency didn't surprise Yvette, and she grabbed the back of his head in both hands, making their embrace as deep as it could possibly get. Errol inhaled the scent of her flesh – a mixture of perspiration and cocoa butter body lotion. He sucked the skin on her neck, revelling in the way he made her feel – so totally on remote control. His hands were under the straps of her leotard now, pulling them away from her shoulders and down her arms. Her breasts sprung over the top of the material, the nipples erect and pointing at him. His mouth travelled down her neck, kissing, sucking and biting. Just as eagerly, Yvette was fumbling with the buckle of his belt, her fingers working to undo the zipper and release his erection. Then her hands found their way under his jacket. The jacket fell to the floor and she began to step backwards, towards her desk in the centre of the office. Her hands never stopped moving as she worked his trousers over his hips, simultaneously releasing herself from her leggings. He helped her drag his waistcoat and shirt over his head; they spun in the air before being fired across the room to land over the back of her swivel chair.

Errol knew how much g-strings turned Yvette on. They left his buttocks bare and his balls encased in thin fabric, leaving little to the imagination. She eased herself on to the corner of her desk, pulling him against her, cupping his buttocks in her hands and wrapping one leg around his thigh.

There were no words spoken, just heavy breathing and whispers of encouragement, each of them completely immersed in giving pleasure. First he teased her with his erection, giving her a taste of what was to come, rubbing his length against her groin, making her arch her back towards him, almost begging. Then he used his fingers, finding her clitoris and massaging the tiny, erect bud until she bit into his shoulder with pleasure. Then both of them simultaneously gasped as he entered her, tentatively at first, then letting himself go and taking as well as giving what they both wanted.

Suddenly Yvette was pushing him away and she stood, grabbing his hand. They were travelling again. She made him wrap his arms around her as they crossed the room, joined belly to back, heading for her private bathroom. She unlatched the door and they tumbled against it as it swung inwards. Yvette pressed her palms against the cold, tiled wall to brace herself, and Errol kept the pace going and entered her from behind. Again the position was changed after a minute by Yvette. She whirled round, leant her back against the wall, and placing her hands on Errol's shoulders she pulled herself up on to his hips, wrapping both legs round his waist. He entered her with lubricated ease, and she cried out as she took the full length of him. He let her take control, riding his cock as he carried her towards the shower. She cried out, as if the water hitting her were as sharp as a knife's blade. Errol felt the cool stream wash the perspiration from their hot bodies. Yvette's legs began to slip on his wet skin, so she lowered her feet to the floor. Again, he concentrated on her body. She gripped the towel rail to keep her balance as he went to work with his mouth. First he circled her nipples with his tongue, then he took each one in turn into his mouth, flicking their already hard tips.

Then Errol went downtown, giving her pleasure she had never thought possible before he had initiated her to it. Nipping his way back up to her neck he turned her around, all the while massaging her clitoris with his middle finger. He entered her from behind. Taking it slowly at first, then speeding up his thrusts, matching her own movements.

The sex was as good as always, maybe even marginally better. The explosive climax at the end of it left Yvette breathless and weak, but Errol's manhood still stood to attention, glistening and dripping wet, so she made sure it wasn't going to waste.

Marion had spotted Anne-Marie standing alone, and stepped carefully over to her in her bridesmaid's dress. Her friend appeared to be looking for someone and, seeing as she knew only the groom and herself, Marion assumed it must be her.

"Anne-Marie!" She kissed her cheek and gave her a brief hug. "You look great! I heard you were partying last night…"

"The bachelor party, yeah. I went home and had a few hours' sleep." Anne-Maries's eyes were still scouting the room.

Marion followed her gaze. "Are you looking for someone?"

"Errol, the best man. I met him yesterday. Thought I'd say hi."

"Oh, Errol's gone to pick up a friend. He'll be back later. Listen, are you okay on your own? I've just seen someone…"

"Yes, fine, you go on."

The tables and chairs had been pushed back against the walls by now, and the sound system was playing warm-up music. A few people were still dressed as they had been at the service, but others had gone home and changed or brought outfits to change into. A group of kids were chasing each other in and out of the milling adults' legs. One child went skidding past Anne-Marie on his backside, probably ruining a perfectly good pair of dress trousers. She helped him to his feet and, without saying thank you, he dashed off again after the others.

Anne-Marie browsed, walking round the hall and pretending to smile or nod at acquaintances, and all the while her eyes kept drifting back to the door. There had been a sense of fate about her encounter with Errol that morning, a sense of inevitability. A sense of unadulterable, unchangeable purpose. She was sure he had felt it too – and that was why she had changed her mind and decided to come to her ex-boyfriend's wedding reception.

Errol arrived an hour later, dressed in a blue suit. His back view alone was the most beautiful thing Anne-Marie had ever seen. Starting with his shaved head, her eyes worked their way down his long, strong neck and over his shoulders, wide and confidently squared. The length of his spine was impressive, making her fingers itch to trace his vertebrae. The narrowness of his waist was evident even under the made-to-measure blue jacket, and his long legs ended in elegant blue leather shoes. Anne-Marie's heart started to thump as he turned almost fully round, but his arm was grabbed possessively by a striking woman with long, braided hair plaited into a rope that hung down her back. She had a perfect figure, if a little muscular. She was dressed in a sapphire and black dress that passed her calves, and silver adorned her ears, neck and wrists. They crossed the room arm in arm; she walked as though she had a right to be where she was. There was no coy dropping of the hands as some couples do; he was proud of her. She said something to him, and he whispered a reply which brought about a tinkling laugh that hurt Anne-Marie like a slap in the face. She froze on the spot, immediately trying to think of a way she could get out of here without drawing attention to herself. She looked around for Marion, but she was standing at the head table, chatting and laughing with the bride, who was actually sitting on the table-top and smoking. Very unbridelike.

Anne-Marie shuffled towards the door, trying to make herself as invisible as possible. She was almost there when someone grabbed her arm and whirled her round.

"Hey, no dance for me?" Colin was grinning like a gremlin and had obviously had a skinful to top up what he had consumed last night.

"I was just about to leave, Col."

"What? You cyan't do that. The party just start, and all my exes have to dance with me before they leave." He drew her into his arms, breathing beery fumes in her face.

"Are you drunk, Colin?"

He pulled her away for a second and frowned at her. "What you take me for? I wouldn't get drunk at my own wedding. Naw, man – I'm just mellow…" And he drew her to him again, cheek to cheek. As he danced her slowly round she caught sight of Errol watching them, and desperately wanted to let go of this immature, drunk, married man and run into his arms.

He lifted his hand in acknowledgement and she smiled back. But his attention was soon taken away by another woman.

"Colin, who's the woman Errol came with?'

"Woman? What woman?"

"Errol brought a woman to the reception with him…"

"Oh, her." He shrugged. "I don't know. Errol has the agency set him up with models and other celebs for functions – you know, keep his private life private," Colin lied.

Anne-Marie nodded, but her heart rose again. So, there was no competition. As soon as the record was over, she rushed to the ladies' to freshen up.

Errol had seen Anne-Marie dancing with Colin, and was mildly surprised that Joan hadn't got up and slapped him silly for behaving like a fool on her (and his) wedding day. It seemed that they were both out to enjoy the day thoroughly, however, when Joan accepted a dance from another man.

Errol saw Anne-Marie dashing out of the room after her dance with Colin, and decided to follow her. It was a totally impulsive thing – he didn't even know what he intended to say to her. He waited outside the ladies' room, occasionally signing a napkin for a fan or chatting to an old friend.

When Anne-Marie emerged she looked a little stunned to see him leaning against the wall, obviously waiting.

"Hi," he said.

Up close, Errol looked almost regal in his suit. His aftershave tempted her to reach out and touch him. She looked down at her shoes before saying, "Hi yourself."

"I didn't know you'd be here. I would have brought that signed photo."

Anne-Marie smiled charmingly. "I only decided to come this afternoon. I wasn't sure how the bride would take an ex-girlfriend turning up, and then I decided she wouldn't know who I was anyway. And how often do I get invited to a wedding?"

Errol smiled too, glad that she had decided to come. "Enjoying yourself so far?"

"As a matter of fact, no," she said, almost apologetically. "I was getting ready to leave." "Not on my account, I hope. I mean, I just got here and you're leaving."

"I wish I'd brought a date. I see you did."

"Yeah, well it stops all the bridesmaids coming on to me."

She looked up at him, a brand new interest in her eyes. Errol Wright was a man who didn't have an interest in being caught, a man who covered all possibilities. He looked at her carefully; he could tell what she was thinking. She was cool, though, with skin that looked as though she used only the best cosmetics. She had smiling eyes that always seemed to be thinking, digging deeper than she could actually express. Her hair was quite long but she wore it naturally, probably pressed or blow-dried for the occassion and wrapped into a bun. She wore no make up except for the functional lipstick. She stood straight, like one who has been taught the value of standing up for oneself, and she wore a long cream dress and a matching bolero jacket with a pink stone and diamante brooch on one lapel.

"So, are you a little jealous of the bride?" Errol asked.

"Me? No – not for marrying Colin."

"You didn't want him then?"

"No. If I'd wanted him I'd still have him."

"A woman who gets what she wants."

"Always."

"Not a person who gives up?"

"Never."

"Do you always get *who* you want too?"

"I've never really wanted anyone." She caught his eyes and they held their gaze, each trying to read the other's expression.

Errol held up his glass. "A toast," he said, "to the day you get who you want."

Anne-Marie smiled coyly as he handed her his glass to sip from.

"I'd better get back. They'll be sending out a search party for the best man. I'll catch you later..." He ran a hand down her arm, like a caress. He knew women went weak for it, but he'd done it anyway. Errol knew she was watching him as he walked away from her.

Errol opened the glass doors that led on to his roof balcony from the bedroom. It was six in the morning. The sun was not quite in the sky, making little impact on the chilly morning, but he could tell it was going to be a lovely day.

He shivered in his thick white towelling robe, stretched his arms above his head and breathed in, looking down at the tidy gardens beneath him. He remembered the doubts he'd had about buying this place. There weren't too many black people in the area, and although he hadn't been worried about being accepted he'd wanted to feel comfortable with his neighbours, had wanted them to come round for barbecues, at which he could play his own music and the music his friends wanted to hear.

He had a regular housekeeper – a luxury, his friends thought, but when you worked the hours he did it was most certainly a necessity. His suits were always dry-cleaned and hanging ready in his walk in closet; his bed sheets, pressed and sweet smelling, were changed every other day; he had cooked meals to order, and there was not a speck of dust anywhere. Errol was still living in the style his parents had accustomed him to, and he'd done it without their help.

It seemed to him that all his spare time was spent networking. He partied with interesting people – established celebrities and the up-and-coming – with ease. The only problem was that sometimes he did not know what was pleasure and what was business. He still occasionally found his situation unbelievable, incredible. He'd be watching television, and would flick channels to see himself on the screen. Or he'd be walking the streets and spot someone reading a magazine with his face on the cover. So he didn't mind being alone. Loneliness was a welcome rarity in an otherwise crowded life.

Errol began to dress. He couldn't afford to look anything but totally presentable at all times. He put his clothes on slowly, noticing every detail. The light beige Donna Karan wool jacket looked as though it had never been worn; the trousers, clasped at the waist by a Hugo Boss belt, were creased just so, and hung to show off his finely toned figure. Under the jacket he wore a chocolate-coloured short-sleeved V-neck sweater that co-ordinated perfectly with the suit. Mr GQ he most certainly was.

He glanced at his watch. It was about that time again, so he reached for his mobile to make his wake-up call.

"Good morning, my queen."

The greeting made Yvette grin with pleasure. "Good morning, Errol."

Every morning Errol would call her at around seven thirty. He'd wish her a good morning, would let her know that he was thinking about her, giving her a positive vibe for the day. Yvette slid into the armchair by the telephone and curled up her legs. Errol's voice sounded real good, she could almost see him in front of her, wrapped in nothing but a bath towel.

"How are you this morning?"

"I'm fine." She would have gone on to say, "and all the better for hearing your voice," but she didn't want to sound too eager.

"So, my black butterfly, you miss me?" he asked.

"Get real!" She grinned. "You know there's only one thing I miss about you."

He laughed. "My smile, right?"

"What – you have one down there too?"

Errol laughed again. That's what he liked about Yvette. The bullshit didn't work, but he had a laugh trying. Yvette pulled her long, braided hair back with one hand. "What you up to today?"

"The only thing I got on my schedule is an interview with that new paper, *New Nations*."

"So, you're basically free today…"

"Yeah. Why?"

"Well I thought you could cook us dinner. You know how Ty loves your roast potatoes, and the way you cooked that chicken… Boy, it didn't even taste like chicken by the time you'd done with it."

Errol took the compliment in his stride. Yvette couldn't prepare anything more than whatever she could simply heat up in the oven, chop up and boil, or eat raw. "How is Ty?"

"Keeps asking me when you're going to take him to Planet Hollywood."

"Damn. I didn't forget, honestly. It's just time. Why don't we eat there tonight?"

"You serious?"

"Sure. Tell him I'll pick you both up around five."

"You know, Errol…" She stopped as though she had been interrupted.

"What?"

"It's okay. I'll see you later."

"Looking forward to it."

"Me too." Yvette replaced the reciever and pinched her arm. God, was she getting soft? She'd almost told him she loved him. Would that have been a mistake or what?

M onday came sooner than expected. Another timetabled day. Errol ran a finger round the inside of his collar. He was cool, but he didn't feel it. It was swelteringly hot even off the set – or was it just him? The air conditioning was definitely on. He stood in the wings, breathing deeply. Why was he always so nervous before going in front of the cameras? Once they were rolling he was fine; he was Errol Wright, TV personality.

Marion Stewart was coming to the end of her introduction. This was his cue. "… so please welcome presenter of *Do the Wright Thing*, Errol Wright!"

The studio was filled with the sound of his signature tune and rapturous applause. He could see his image on a monitor as he took the stairs down the centre aisle of the auditorium: a tall, dark man, casually smart in a blue suit and white T-shirt, the beam of a follow-spot bouncing off his shaved head, his grin wide, confident, natural.

His hostess stood before him, joining the mainly black audience in their applause. Marion and Errol had jumped on the Channel 5 bandwagon at the same time. Errol Wright and Marion Stewart: young, black, active in their communities, with views and attitudes they wanted to share with the world. As newcomers together they had formed an instant bond. Now they were good friends, comrades against the critics. "Thank you, thank you..." Errol turned to the audience and bowed deeply, dramatically. "Boy, you guys flatter me. I get more applause doing guest appearances than I do on my own show!"

The audience rewarded him with a burst of laughter.

Laughing with them, Marion invited him with a gesture of her hand to take a seat on the comfortable pink sofa opposite her.

Errol shook her hand as though they'd just met, belying the fact that they had spent the last two hours rehearsing the interview and chatting over coffee. He smiled, sat down and crossed one leg over the other. The applause and laughter subsided, and he turned to the audience and delivered a passable impersonation of Eddie Murphy: "Couldn't you just eat this woman up? She's like one a dem Barbie dolls – y'know, good to look at, but you play a little rough and the legs fall off!"

Laughter burst out again. Marion crossed her legs demurely and leaned towards him, her eyes flashing a warning. She knew Errol very well; he was always ribbing her about her size. She waited for the audience to settle. "So, Errol, how does it feel to be on your rival show?"

"Rival?" He raised an eyebrow, a trademark he had made his own. "I wouldn't say we were rivals, Marion. We're like brother and sister shows – you're my female equivalent." He uncrossed his legs and placed both feet on the floor, clasping his hands and resting his elbows on his knees.

"So, you don't see us as being in competition for the ratings?"

Errol turned to the cameras and a mischievous look came into his eyes. Let's be spontaneous here, he thought. "Okay. All you fellows out there – which programme do you watch regularly? *Mantalk* or *Do the Wright Thing*?"

The men in the audience were unanimous. "*Mantalk*!" came the chant.

"Now the ladies..." He stood up. "Which do *you* prefer?"

No less fervently the female cry came up: "Errol, Errol, Errol," followed by screams, just to confirm his point.

26

Marion smiled. It was a good thing she knew this man; she hated people deviating from the script. "That doesn't surprise me, Errol. My show's studio audience is largely made up of men who come to hear what women are all about. And how often do we get to see a young, good-looking black presenter on our screens?"

The audience agreed with applause and wolf-whistles.

Marion chose her next question from the tele-prompter. "Errol, I always thought your over-confidence was put on for the television. Tell me, are you always like this?"

"Like what?" He shrugged, keeping that cheeky grin. "No, of course not. Believe me, Marion, really I'm kinda shy." He fluttered his eyelashes at the camera and the audience laughed again. They were most definitely on his side today. Women were practically sliding off their seats at being in the same room as him. It gave him a buzz better than an aphrodisiac. "No, seriously..." He held up his hands. "I do have two personas, if you like. What you are seeing is the showman; at home I try to lead a quiet life. I read, work out in my purpose-built gym..." He secretly crossed his fingers. "... have quiet drinks at home with just a few close friends. If I was like this all the time I probably wouldn't *have* any close friends."

Marion smiled knowingly. "What is it like to be the first black British male talk-show host?"

Errol leaned back on the sofa and spread his arms along the back. "I'd like to say it's been great, but it is a really challenging job – and I don't mean that in the aspiring way."

"What exactly *do* you mean?" Marion clasped one knee with her fingers.

"Well..." Errol paused, appearing to be considering his answer. "People like yourself, Oprah, Esther, Ricky, Vanessa... you all have the advantage of being female. People respond to you females so much better. With me they feel I'm being pushy, nosy, sometimes even aggressive." He shrugged, and the audience chuckled. Errol did occasionally get tough with his guests, usually when he had to get them to admit to something.

Marion laughed modestly. "For all those aspiring TV personalities out there, what advice would you give them?"

He glanced upwards, then, as a camera zoomed in, looked straight into it. "Opportunity knocks when you least expect it. I started out as a journalist. When I realised what I really wanted to do I got myself a good agent, made them work for me and, after much hard graft and with a firm belief in myself, here I am today. So I suppose my advice is, if you've got talent, find yourself a reputable agent, show them how enthusiastic you are, sell yourself, dedicate yourself to a sole purpose – or two – and go for it. You can't sit around expecting your dreams to land in your lap; you gotta go out and search for them."

"We've seen several of your shows aired now. What else does *Do the Wright Thing* have in store for us?"

"Now, that would be telling…" Errol threw another heap of charm at the audience and grinned. "No, seriously, next week I believe we're showing the programme on teenage parents and single-parent families." His tone became more grave. "And we'll have a special programme for national AIDS week, giving a chance for the victims of this terrible disease to express their feelings about the prejudice shown to them… But on the up side, we do like to break the seriousness of the show with a little occasional fun, so we'll be doing a programme on what the nineties ladies are looking for in a man. We'll have twenty bachelors in the studio for you to put to the test."

This statement was met with more wolf-whistles, howls and screams from the ladies.

Marion asked what all the women in the audience wanted to know. "Will you be one of them?" Errol smiled sweetly and shook his head. "It's a shame, but no."

A communal sigh rose from the studio.

"Errol, why did you choose to accept a position in a form of TV that is so densely populated at the moment by women?"

Without hesitation he answered, "I love the idea of being unique as well as popular. Of course, it's only a matter of time before it catches on. Men were talk-show hosts as far back as black and white TV, black males only more recently – but I hope to be the first of many in England. We have several ideas lined up for a future series. Who knows – you might get a chance to be my guest sometime, Marion."

"Well, thank you… Although I'll know you're only inviting me to boost your ratings!"

Now the audience laughed with Marion. Errol wagged a finger and shook his head in jest. Marion introduced a clip from one of Errol's shows, where he was soothing a weeping teenaged adoptee whose natural mother, after being tracked down, still wanted nothing to do with her. His arms were around her trembling body, her head rested on his shoulder. He spoke with the docile, trained tone of a professional counselor, instilling a pride and strength in the youngster, encouraging her to think beyond this one person to the family she already had.

As the clip ended Errol replaced his glass of water on the table. The audience was full of unrehearsed admiration, and the applause took a little longer to subside this time. "Ladies and Gentleman, Errol Wright!" Marion clapped along with the upstanding audience.

Marion concluded the interview preofessionally, made her thank yous, and the recording stopped. A stills photographer rushed on to the set for shots of Marion and guests, then, once the tape had been checked and the audience departed, they were allowed to relax. "How'd I do?" Errol asked Marion as they left the set.

She stretched her arms in the air, relieving her shoulders of tension. "You're so vain you have to ask?"

"No, I just want your opinion. As a colleague and friend, your view is important to me."

Marion blushed. "Okay. You were good as ever. But do you always have to try and steal the show?"

Errol put an arm across her shoulders. "I guess I'm just not used to being in the firing line of the interview." They walked behind the wings, where the studio hands were going about their duties. "Paul wants to know why you missed training again this week," Marion said coyly.

"Yeah?" Paul had taken Errol to a couple of judo sessions a few weeks previously. Errol had found that it wasn't his sport, but he didn't want to hurt Paul's feelings – after all, judo was Paul's life.

"Yeah."

"Yvette, you know – she's been putting me through my paces. I'll give him a ring later. Will he be in?"

"Yeah, he's baby-sitting. I'm going out for a change. So, you and Yvette getting serious?"

"Who – me? Naw. We see a lot of each other, but I wouldn't be hearing any wedding bells."

"One day someone's going to get you to settle down." She smiled, but there was a seriousness in her voice.

"Been there, done that."

She laughed.

From the shy little woman Errol had met a year ago, Marion was turning into a very shrewd, confident businesswoman. She exuded cunning know-how, and could soak up information like a sponge. Marion half turned as a tall, gangly woman came running up to them, long, curly brown hair flapping about her head. "Marion, thank goodness I caught you," the set manager said, out of breath. "Hi, Errol…"

He nodded a reply.

"What is it, Jayne?"

"Derek wants to see you in his office – now, please."

Marion sighed deeply. Derek was always keeping an eye on her. She felt as though he still considered her his special project. He always introduced her as "my presenter". But, being the producer, it was important to keep him sweet. "Errol, I'm sorry. Look, why don't you meet us later for lunch? I'll be bringing someone with me. Our usual restaurant?"

"Yeah, sure. Two o'clock?"

"Fine." She kissed him lightly on the cheek. "See you later."

He watched her hurry away, chatting to Jayne about the show, before heading to the changing room to remove the special matt foundation used solely for TV and film work. (After recording his first show he had been glad to rush out into the fresh air. He'd been so full of nervous tension that he'd felt he was going to explode. It wasn't until he'd got back to the studio and taken a look at his face in the mirrored lift that he'd realised his face was still covered in the heavy make-up they used to stop the glare of the lights bouncing off your skin.)

With an hour to kill, Errol went window shopping. In Marks & Spencer he bought himself a cold drink, then walked the streets, stopping occassionally in a clothes shop or furniture shop He was always looking at ways to improve his already perfect home; now he could afford to change whatever he liked he did it just for the shopping buzz.

He was gazing into an antique shop window when someone tapped him on his shoulder. Thinking he had been recognised by a fan, he was already reaching inside his jacket for a pen as he turned round. "Are you sure you can afford anything in there, sir?" Anne-Marie was grinning at him in her that open, friendly way of hers.

"Anne-Marie! How are you?" Errol shook her hand. She was in a long, navy-blue suit. The blouse underneath was a pale green, and she wore another of those brooches which always caught Errol's eye. Her wavy hair was pulled back from her face and fastened at the nape of her neck with a clip.

"Fine. I heard you might be walking the streets on your own."

"You saw Marion?"

"I did. Remember? I told you I was having lunch with her today."

He nodded.

"She's still working, so I thought I'd come and find you."

They fell into step, and walked together to the restaurant. The place where they were to meet Marion was very modern and bright, its open-plan dining area tastefully decorated with contemporary paintings on the wall and a mosaic floor. They sat at a table surrounded by windows, but were not worried about gawking passers-by because the building was surrounded by shrubs. Errol was pleased for Anne-Marie's company, and she was just as pleased to be with him again. She'd done nothing all weekend except sit at home alone, and hope that the phone would ring and it would be him.

"Where are your family from?" she asked him.

Errol sipped at his sherry and placed the glass back on the table before answering. "My mother's Jamaican and my father's from Chicago. They met in England."

"Really! So you're mixed race." She smiled.

"I hadn't really thought about it like that. Although I do consider myself to be of mixed culture, like most black people are."

"*Touché.*"

Errol leant forward, his elbows on the table, and turned on his talk-show-host voice. "What about you? Where are your folks from?"

"My parents were both Jamaican. Mother died just three months ago, and Dad... well, Dad went back to Jamaica."

Errol felt gutted that he'd asked. His eyes filled with remorse. "I'm sorry to hear about your mother."

She waved his sympathy away. "It's fine. *I'm* fine. It's more of a relief really: she was suffering for two years before she went... and she did leave me quite well off."

Errol let a reasonable silence follow before he picked up the conversation again. The lunchtime crowd was evaporating as it neared two o'clock. "My parents abandoned me too."

"Oh?"

"Well, I was eighteen at the time. They decided to go back to the USA. I try to visit once a year, but you know... work..."

"Yes, it must be difficult." Anne-Marie nodded. "But at least you have them."

"You don't keep in touch with your father?"

Anne-Marie fiddled with a ring on her finger. "No. He left under a cloud, so to speak. Maybe I'll pay him a visit one day, who knows?"

Errol felt that there was some element to the story she wasn't telling. Something dark, that skeleton in the cupboard. He changed the subject. "I'll bet there are stories you could tell about Marion."

"Well, some... but at school we didn't actually go around together. We knew each other, but just to say hello to. I sometimes sat with her at lunch or when her other friends weren't around. I think we're better friends now than we were then."

"I see." Perhaps Anne-Marie was a bit of a loner, he thought. She had come to his party alone, had turned up at the wedding reception alone, and was now hanging around with an old school acquaintance to whom she was never really that close. But he couldn't see why. She was attractive, intelligent, and a good conversationalist; she should have no trouble making friends.

"Any brothers or sisters?" he asked.

"No. I guess my parents tried it once and didn't like it."

Errol laughed. "I'm an only child too. I believe my parents thought of me as a status symbol. They're both very professional people; they actually had to make time to have a child. I was brought up by a nanny who taught me at nursery age before I went to school."

"A sheltered childhood."

"Quite. I was lucky, I guess, that I didn't end up rebelling. It happens that way sometimes."

"So you had to look after yourself from an early age. I mean, when your parents left."

"Yes – cook, clean, wash, iron for myself…"

"And what do you eat – beans on toast?" Her eyes danced with humour.

"No." He laughed modestly. "I can cook. I taught myself from books. Italian, Chinese, gourmet… I can turn my hand to anything."

"Can I put you to the test?"

Errol raised an eyebrow curiously.

"How would you like to cook dinner for me sometime this week?"

Was she asking him out? Errol rememebered his motto: never date mates or your friends exes. He also knew about women who made the first move. But… "Well, I'd have to check my schedule…"

"Okay. I'll call you tommorrow and we can arrange a date. Give me a chance to see if you're just boasting."

Just then Marion rushed in, flustered but still smiling. "I'm so sorry I'm late. Got held up about half a dozen times. You two getting on okay?"

Errol and Anne-Marie looked at each other and said in unison, "Fine." After lunch they chatted over coffee. They had the whole afternoon, and no one wanted to hurry away.

"I like being in control of my life again," Anne-Marie was saying. "Any man who wants to share it with me now will have to learn to compromise, if he doesn't know how to already." She'd had a fair amount to drink while they had waited, more over lunch, and her voice had risen a little above normal coversational level.

Errol leant back in his chair, studying her oval face. "So how do you stay in control? I mean, you can't change people…"

"I don't rely on others. I make my own plans, have good back-up systems. In a relationship I call the shots; if the man can't handle it then he's not the man for me."

"Hmm." Errol was a little worried. This attitude wasn't gelling with what he already knew about Anne-Marie. She hadn't come across as one of these hard, career-minded women of the nineties before.

"And I don't let others pressure me to conform. Some of my acquaintances seem all geared to becoming like everyone else thinks they should be at thirty. You know – find a man, settle down and have babies. There are more important things in my life."

She was certainly trying to sound convincing. Errol leaned forward. "Such as… ?"

"Well, my career as a counsellor. My writing. I studied hard to get where I am today, came out of a rough relationship to live a fresh new life. No man could give me greater satisfaction than I get seeing my creations on bookshelves all over the country, knowing that others are reading my thoughts and views and living by them."

Marion had listened to Anne-Marie's speech quietly. She didn't understand it. Both these young, attractive professionals giving up on love for their careers? It didn't make sense. What could possibly be more important than love and family? Who did they come home to at nights? Who was around to listen, give encouragement, motivation? Errol voiced the question for her. "I can see your point, Anne-Marie. But, although I'm… a bachelor," he lowered his voice and flicked his eyes around the room, "I'm not planning to be that way for ever. My career is only going to take me so far, and then I'm going to want someone to share my success with me."

Anne-Marie couldn't hide her smile. "You see, it's different for men. A single man can have casual sex to satisfy his needs. He can date as many women as he wants without commitment, and that is considered normal in our age-group. But a woman could only carry on like that in secret. "Did you see that documentary on the single mother who goes to clubs specifically to pick up men? You should have seen the papers. The outcry! 'It should have been banned.' 'This woman has no self esteem – what kind of role model is she for her child?' I actually sat through that programme feeling sympathy for her, even though I knew I wouldn't do something like that myself."

"Sympathy!" Marion turned down her mouth in disgust. "Sympathy for a woman with a baby who sleeps around?"

Anne-Marie tried to defend her position. "She said she does it because there are no emotional ties. The last thing she wants is a man telling her he loves her. She doesn't see why, as a single mother, she should have to give up her independence to be happy. And she *is* happy…"

Marion still couldn't believe what she was hearing. "How can you say that? As a counsellor you meet plenty of women like that – how can you seriously believe she's really happy?"

"In her conscious mind she is. She's a good mother throughout the week, she loves her daughter, and she goes to bed most nights on her own. One night a week, or once a fortnight, she goes out to find a sexual partner…"

Errol rejoined the conversation. "But wouldn't she get known around town as a slut? An easy lay? I know that, if I saw a woman coming into a club on a regular basis and leaving with a different man each time, I wouldn't touch her or have any respect for her. How can she respect herself – after all those men that have had her? These guys might even pass the word around that they can get a no-strings-attached lay if they go with her."

Anne-Marie shrugged. "That's their problem, not hers."

Marion was outraged. "I don't believe it *is* just their problem! She's giving it away for free. She puts up with all the dangers of disease, violence, rape, and she isn't even getting the satisfaction of payment that prostitutes get."

"That's the point! She doesn't do it for the *men*. You mentioned giving it away – well, she isn't just giving, she's taking too. She's enjoying herself; prostitutes are forced to do it. She *uses* the men. She even goes back to their place so she can leave when she feels like it without ever seeing them again."

"That girl needs a man to love her. To show her that sex is more than just sensation. It's emotional too, something to share with someone you love. It's an experience you have to build on. How much love is she gonna get once a fortnight?"

"And what man is going to want her, when he finds out she's had more guys inside her than the Dog and Duck?" Errol added, and Marion nodded.

"You see…" Anne-Marie gestured at both of them with an open palm. "Even in the nineties, attitutudes haven't changed. A man can sleep around and his woman just calls him 'experienced'. But society sees the women who do it as reckless and irresponsible. She's not going to get a pat on the back for bedding twenty men in a year."

"But do women want to be like men?" Errol asked.

"Maybe some of us just want the freedom of choice that men have. Research shows that, although we women are going out there now and acting more like our male counterparts, we're not any happier. And society still frowns on women who don't want children."

"Good point," Errol said. "It's not about acting like men, or treating them like they've been treating women for centuries. It's about fulfilling your potential as a human being, an individual with needs, ambitions and a life to live for yourself – not your peers or your family... nor your man."

"I've managed to have it all, and I'm happy," Marion interjected. "I don't believe that anyone can live contentedly without love."

"Because you could only reach fulfilment through having it all, Marion," Anne-Marie said. "You *wanted* kids, you *wanted* to be a journalist – and as a bonus you're a TV celebrity too. And you wanted love from a good man. In fact you're one big success story!" she added with a grin and a pat on Marion's hand.

"Thank you." Marion smiled, unsure whether Anne-Marie's congratulations were genuine or not.

Errol knew that what Anne-Marie was saying was true. He didn't condone men sleeping around, playing with people's feelings. And he knew that any woman who'd deliberately pick up a new man every time she wanted sex was heading for trouble. Why not just find a steady, reliable sexual partner, as he had? You agree on the boundaries, and if one or the other wants to break it up, it's up for discussion.

"So, what made you decide to stay a bachelor?" Anne-Marie asked.

Errol dipped his eyes and appeared to study something in his drink. "Circumstance. I'm an ambitious, career-minded person. I haven't got time to fall in love and give a relationship what it deserves."

"Is that all?"

"Yeah. And in case you're wondering, it's not a physical problem."

A wry grin appeared on Anne-Marie's face. "But of course not! You are a black man."

Marion laughed as Errol's mouth dropped open. She knew that it was the AIDS-related death of one of his friends that had made him more careful with his sex life. And she was the only one who knew. Errol trusted her.

He quickly changed the subject. "Now Marion's nabbed you for her show I suppose I'll have to wait until the second book comes out before I can get you on mine."

"Maybe the public will have to wait, Errol. But you can have me anytime…" She still had that smirk on her face. Errol was sure she was scheming something.

Embarrassed for him, Marion cleared her throat. "Anyone for dessert?"

"Not for me, I'm dieting again."

Marion gave Anne-Marie a look, but didn't say anything. Errol ordered his favourite hot chocolate fudge cake with cream, and then excused himself to go to the gents.

Anne-Marie couldn't even wait for him to disappear from sight before she quizzed Marion. "What do you think of Errol?" Marion raised her eyebrows. "Errol?"

"Yes." Anne-Marie crossed one leg over the other and leaned back on her chair, her eyes turning to the ceiling dreamily. "Do you think he's interested in me?"

It wasn't the first time Anne-Marie had brought up the subject with Marion, but now it was beginning to get annoying. Marion's brow creased. "I know you're interested in him…"

"That obvious, eh?"

"Anne-Marie, you can't stop talking about him!"

Anne-Marie sat forward on her chair, her elbows on her knees. "But does he talk about me?"

Marion tutted and rolled her eyes. "Errol is a very private person. He wouldn't tell me who he's seeing or who he likes. As far as I know he's single and will stay that way until he meets a woman he can trust to fall in love with."

"So he's not gay then? Maybe he could do with a counsellor, a personal therapist. You know, to help him come to terms with opening up."

Again Marion frowned. This girl was *not* the one for Errol. "Errol is a close friend of mine, Anne-Marie. Leave him alone."

Anne-Marie smiled indulgently. "*Moi*? I wouldn't hurt a hair on his pretty head. I just want to know a little more about Mister Cool; it's my profession. He intrigues me."

"Just don't do anything underhand. If you're going to use him for one of your studies, then make sure he knows about it."

Anne-Marie laughed sarcastically as she lifted her cappuccino to her lips. Marion decided to let it go. "This psychologist you told me about – for the eating disorder programme…" Errol's a big boy, she was thinking – he can take care of himself. Anne-Marie wasn't the first admirer, and most certainly she would not be the last.

When Errol returned to the table, Marion filled him in on what he had missed. "I was telling Anne-Marie about Black Networkers With Attitude. She's interested in joining." "Yeah? Good. We can always do with more opinionated women."

"Well, I do speak my mind…"

"So I discovered." Errol caught her eyes again and felt the same bolt that had hit him that first morning. He wasn't sure what it was about Anne-Marie… something intriguing, something in her eyes. It wasn't a physical attraction, as he had first thought, but it was an attraction.

Marion noticed the two of them and felt a pang of jealousy. Errol had never looked at her like that. He'd always treated her like a little sister. Anne-Marie wasn't even that pretty… She stopped the train of thought. What was her problem? She was engaged to Paul. She sighed. She and Errol were just good friends.

So where are we going again?" Karen flicked her cigarette butt out of the car and turned to the driver.

Yvette sighed exasperatedly. "We're gonna go back to look at that house in Catford."

"What, the mansion?"

Yvette giggled and wound down the window, letting out the cigarette fumes that had accumulated inside her Cabriolet. "All right, so it's bigger than I was going for… but don't you think it suits me?"

"You mean like a leotard or a Lycra dress suits you?"

"Shut up, Kaz! I just have to see the inside of dat place, man. Read out what it says on that property sheet again."

Karen screwed up her mouth and gave her friend a crazy look, but she did as she was told, and reached behind her to retrieve the pages from the back seat. "Right, here we are…" She held the page in both hands, trying to steady it as Yvette took a corner at thirty miles an hour. "Built 1898… probably haunted," she mumbled.

"Just read the damned thing!"

"Semi-detached, halls adjoining, four storeys with mezzanine… Boy, it's one a dem house wid stairs you don't need, innit?" She sucked her teeth and continued: "Four storeys, cellar… A cellar! In a house that old it's probably got bodies buried down dere…"

"Will you stop criticising it until we actually see it!"

"Awright, awright. Chill…" Karen almost laughed: her friend was so eager to get her own place and it had to be just right. Boy, this was worse than shopping for clothes with her! "Where was I? Yeah – cellar, lounge fifteen by fourteen, dining room, kitchen stroke breakfast room, four bedrooms, double-glazed and centrally heated… Like I said, a mansion. What you gonna do with four bedrooms?"

"You don't think I deserve a mansion?"

Karen raised her eyebrows and stared at her friend. "It's not that, baby. You can't afford it."

"No harm in browsing." Yvette pulled a Tina Turner pout. "Even if it is to see what I'm missing."

The September wind whipped at their coats as they stepped out of the car. Yvette's dream house stood opposite, and for a few seconds they stood side by side and just stared at it.

"Well?"

Karen raised her hand to her hair, holding it back from her face. "Not bad, if you like that kind of thing."

Yvette hiked up her sleeve and checked her watch. "They're not going to be expecting us now, you know. But who cares? They wanna sell their house, don't they?"

They linked arms and crossed the road. The door was answered by a woman in her forties with grey hair that dropped to her shoulders in a stylish bob. She looked down her nose at them. "Can I help you?"

Yvette put on her very best negotiating accent. "The estate agent sent us. Sorry we're late, we had a few to see today."

The woman was obviously taken in by it. "Oh, of course…" A smile cracked her face. "I'm afraid my husband isn't here, but I suppose I can show you around." She stepped back to admit them into the gloomy hallway.

Brown wallpaper! Green doors! Who *were* these people – naturalists?

Karen turned to whisper to Yvette. "I suppose you could always brighten it up by painting a mural on it."

"Ha ha."

"We'll start upstairs, shall we? There's a lot to see." They followed her up a flight of stairs to the first floor and the woman showed them a bedroom and a bathroom. "We had three children," she explained. "The last one left a year ago. The place is just too big for us now." She opened the door to another, darker room. The walls were grey and the faded purple carpet was stained and worn. There was no furniture, just bags and boxes, packed and ready for removal. Yvette was thinking ahead. This could be a store room – too small for a bedroom, and not enough light for a study.

Karen gingerly lifted the grey net curtain that covered the small window, and got a view of the most beautiful garden she'd seen in a while. An apple tree stood in one corner, opposite a pond with love seats on either side. Despite a recent change in the weather, the lawn was still green. Because of the slope of the hill behind the house, you could see for miles over the tops of the other houses. "You have a view.'

Yvette rushed over and looked down at what Karen was excited about. "Wow!"

The bathroom was small, a tub and wash basin only, but the next floor up was more promising. Two rooms – one presumably a sitting room, the other a bedroom. *My* bedroom, and study, Yvette thought. God, this is just so perfect! The sitting room cum bedroom looked out on to the street from all four windows. It was at least fifteen foot by eighteen.

The woman went ahead of them, opening doors. On the top floor were the other bedrooms and another bathroom, fully equipped with a shower.

Back on the ground floor was a very quaint "country" kitchen, recently furnished with new cupboards and units and a fitted cooker and oven. Yvette nearly wet herself with excitement when she saw the basement. It spanned the length of the house. The floors were stripped and polished wood, as were the walls and ceiling. A gym – in her own home! With a bit of renovation she could even build a sauna!

Karen could see the euphoria on her friend's face as they drove back home. "You know it's going to cost a fortune to do up properly."

"Look at the outlay as a long-term investment," said Yvette. "I might never get another chance like this."

"And just where are you gonna get the extra ten grand?"

"I'll find it. My brother—"

"Your brother told you you were up to your limit in loans, and the business can only handle the forty thousand for the shared ownership…" Karen suddenly grabbed Yvette's arm. "What are we thinking of? Why don't you just get lover-boy to move in?"

"Errol?"

"Mr Errol Wright himself. He's got money. You've been seeing him for… what, a year? Haven't you thought of living together?"

"Not really. It's not that kind of relationship."

"And why not? Do his feet smell? Don't he take care of you? He hates kids? What?"

"He's got his own house, and I've got my independence. It just never came up."

"Well bring it up, girl. You want that house, don't you? Tyrone would love it! You'd be a family again, in your dream home."

God damn it, Karen was right! Why hadn't she thought of going into this with Errol before? It would be the perfect arrangement. Errol Wright, you are in for the treat of your life.

The Channel 5 building was modest by Canary Wharf standards, standing only ten storeys high, but every floor was taken up with the station's industries. Hundreds of offices, thousands of people, all sheltered under the Channel 5 umbrella.

The lights were on to dispel the November gloom, and for a second Anne-Marie felt a shiver of doubt as she stood outside, a sudden unnerving loss of confidence. Coming to this building before she had merely been a guest; never before had she entered as an employee. A real, honest-to-goodness television researcher.

Squaring her shoulders, she walked through the familiar foyer. She was greeted by the security guard and the pretty-faced, expensively dressed woman who looked up from the reception desk and chimed, "Good morning." She smiled back. She belonged here.

Sitting at her new desk, relaxing in a huge leather swivel chair, she was thinking, This is it. Finally she had got into the world of television. Maybe it was behind the scenes, but there was always the chance – if she made the right contacts, and with her qualifications – of getting on to the other side of the camera.

Her desk was heaped high with forms, files, reports, books, pens and notepaper. Such was the life of a researcher. Still, it hadn't been hard – with her forged references, her published book and her brilliant CV. She had won a place on the programme's research team, a unit which was always trying to improve itself. She shared an office with two others – but that wasn't a problem. After all, she didn't plan to be stuck behind a desk the whole time she was here. Errol's dressing room was one floor beneath her.

She smiled to herself. Hers was a smile that made people want to smile back at her, but underneath it was a scheme – a scheme to get a man who was convinced he couldn't be got.

She had asked around about Errol Wright. No one knew who he was seeing, unless it was someone they had set him up with for publicity. A very private man, he didn't socialise with anyone at work unless he had to. He did, in fact, live alone... even if he was seeing that bimbo from the wedding. But she was no match for Anne-Marie, a woman who knew how to get what she wanted. Without Errol, this job meant nothing. The men she had been with in the past meant nothing. But this one would. She could feel it was right in her heart and soul.

Errol's Secretary Helen arrived promptly at half past nine every other weekday. She worked in Errol's self-made study, a small, light room upstairs, where she opened fan letters and other requests by mail, made phone calls and wrote letters that Errol didn't have time to do personally, and took messages off the answerphone, filtering any through to Errol that she thought he needed to hear. She was extremely efficient. In her late forties, she had two grown-up children and an ex-husband. She had worked in the media field before, and so was perfectly experienced to deal with things on her own. Errol got on with her very well. They even compared notes on the quick, easy recipes that their lifestyles required. She fitted into his life with ease. He was always interested in her stories about herself. She seemed to have led such a full life. She was a school governor, took regular keep-fit classes, held afternoon teas at her house, and was also a hospital volunteer and carer for housebound patrients. Wednesday's work was sorting the post into piles of fan mail, fan mail that needed a reply, requests for appearances, and refusals. Errol always liked to go through the correspondence with her once it was sorted. That Wednesday was also the cleaner's morning in. Mrs Stewart came only twice a week, on request. She was a strong-looking, slim woman in her mid sixties, with salt-and-pepper hair that she kept tied back in a bunny-rabbit ponytail and skin that could have been borrowed from a baby, it was so smooth. That morning she didn't appear in a good mood. "What a mawnin!" she moaned. "Me couldn't put me feet dem outta bed dis mawnin'. Cold! Times like dis me wawn go 'ome."

Errol smiled warmly, used as he was to Mrs Stewart's moans and groans. He was dressed in a cool linen shirt, worn loose outside his beige Armani trousers; his feet were slipped into beach sandals: his relaxing attire. "I was going to say 'Good morning', but I suppose it isn't for you."

She followed him down the hall to the kitchen, shrugging off the oversized coat she wore. Mrs Stewart had been offered the job on the strength of the fact that she knew his family. She had cleaned for his mother, and had been given first refusal for whenever he needed a cleaner. So here he was, stuck with Mrs Chatterbox Gossip UK. "Boy, de floor need a good scrub, eh? Wha'appen? Yuh 'ave anudder party?"

"No, just Aaron."

"Ah, dat boy! Him mussie big now. My pickney, dem big but dem nah leave 'ome. Big man, but dey love dem 'ome comfort. Boy, I was so tired dis mawnin' I coulda just stay in me warm bed. But you know I don't like let nobody down if me healt' don' prevent it. You 'ave yuh breakfast yet? 'Cause if you want I can do the living room first an come back in 'ere later..."

"As you wish. I'll be upstairs." Errol hurriedly exited and joined Helen reading through the mail.

"Looks as though someone's in love," she said as he walked into the room.

Errol raised an eyebrow. He couldn't imagine who she meant.

She held up a letter. "You have a new admirer." Taking it from her hand, Errol sat at his desk. It was a laser-printed A4 sheet of pink paper, signed simply, "Yours".

> I don't quite know how to start, Errol. All I know for certain at the moment is that I love you. I know how that sounds, you're probably thinking who is this woman and what have you done to provoke the emotions I feel for you. It's simple. I am your number one fan, and you are my Mr Wright.
>
> The only problem is that it is much too early for me to introduce myself to you. But soon, I promise, we will be together.

Errol ran a hand over his bald head. "You're right. Any more like that?"

Helen stretched a hand out, palm down, and rocked it. "Some, but none proclaiming love."

"Bin job?"

"You might have thought that, but no. I have a file for the weird ones. You know, just in case it gets a little heavy... Some of them are totally harmless, but—"

"You mean I could be a celebrity with a stalker?" Now Errol laughed.

"Who knows? Trevor Macdonald has one."

He laughed louder. "Okay. File it, just in case."

A few minutes later, Errol was suddenly in need of a cup of coffee. He was about to send Helen, but when he looked up he saw she was far too busy. He would have to go downstairs himself and endure Mrs Stewart's company.

She had finished the dishes and was scrubbing the floor on her hands and knees. As soon as she saw Errol in the doorway she began talking again as though she had just been switched on.

"You know what you need? One a dem Vax, sump'n. Clean, polish, hoover, suck up water – everyt'ing. Me poor knee dem, every time me haffe get up again it tek a few minute before me feel right in de leg dem. An' de danger… I could slip an' cause serious damage to me ol' body."

"I'm sorry, Mrs Stewart. I just assumed you'd turn up with your own equipment."

"Wid my likkle pension? I cyan' afford dem t'ings."

"Then I'll look into it, okay?"

"You're a lovely man," she said, straightening herself with a palm in the centre of her back. "Not like de las' man I clean fa. Ungrateful? Bwoy! 'Im couldn' even manage a fifty-pence bonus at Chris'mus time. An 'im pickney did rude! De crying an carry on…" She shook her head. "His wife did work at a college, I figet which one. I don't t'ink she did right in de head. Never see 'er widout a glass in 'er 'and and she wasn't drinking water—"

Errol poured hot water on to his coffee. "Really…" "They had tenants, treat the house like Deptford Market. De stink! Oh Lawd, if me did 'ave anudder job me woulda stop work fa dem."

Errol removed himself silently.

John Everett, Errol's show's producer, was sitting at his desk, a cup of coffee and the *Daily Mail* in front of him, as Errol entered the office for his early-morning meeting.

"Ah, Errol…" John, a young forty-something, looked up from his paper. "I have good news."

Errol took a seat opposite. He no longer had to wait for an invitation. To John, he was like the son he'd never had.

"The show will be going on again in the spring."

"Well!" Errol grinned, unable to conceal his joy. "Shouldn't we be celebrating? Where's the rest of the team?"

"At the moment this is just between me and you. There are going to be a few changes…" John shifted uncomfortably.

Errol raised an eyebrow and crossed one leg over the other. "Changes?" "New director, new team, new style, and new slot. Must think of the future, eh?"

Errol was perplexed, but it was still good news. "It's your show, John. You must know what's best. But you know what I think. So long as my job's safe I've got no problem with a few changes."

"Certainly. You're our star. We'll have a team meeting later on in the week, after I've briefed the individuals concerned. But I thought you should be the first to know. Now, down to interviews for next week ..."

Errol settled back and listened to his producer. The man had brought him this far and had plans to take him further. He couldn't knock it.

Later that day Errol was hurrying along, late for a recording session and trying to avoid the rain that was about to pour from the gathering storm clouds, when a female voice hailed him just as he reached the entrance to the studio building. Reluctantly he slowed and turned round. Anne-Marie was hurrying up to him, high-heeled boots clacking on the concrete paving. His brow furrowed briefly before he eased his face into a relaxed smile. "Hi! Fancy seeing you here."

"Hi yourself. I'm glad I caught up with you before the meeting this afternoon."

"The meeting... with the production team?"

"Yes." Errol's eyes questioned her as he held open the door for her and they passed into the lobby of the glass-fronted building. "I've been offered a freelance job with the programme."

"*My* programme?"

"Yes."

Errol was amazed. It was already a small world, and as far as Anne-Marie Simms was concerned it was getting smaller.

"Well..." She shrugged. "It wasn't easy. I've been sending my CV to organisations all over, including newspapers and broadcasting authorities. Being a qualified psychologist and author isn't all it's cracked up to be. I wanted to branch out."

"And Channel Five offered you a post?" They stepped into the lift. Before pressing for his own floor Errol asked Anne-Marie which she wanted.

"That's okay, I'll follow you. I'm early. It seems we could be working together on a couple of proposed shows. It makes me feel so good that I'll already know someone on the team."

As the lift rose, Errol began to suspect that this was a little more than mere coincidence. Or was he becoming paranoid? All right, so was Colin's ex, she happened to know Marion, and now she just happened to get a job on his show's production team. Coincidence?

But Errol wasn't so full of himself to think that this woman was deliberately interweaving her life with his own. They stepped out on to the smoky blue carpet and headed down the corridor. "I'm going straight to studio two to do a voice over," he said.

"I've got half an hour to spare. You don't mind if I sit in, do you?"

"Well ..."

"I promise I'll be as quiet as a mouse." She gave him that half-smile again, and Errol relaxed. She was one of the friendliest people he knew. It seemed she could fit in anywhere. What was his problem?

The studio was a small, beige-coloured room divided from the technicians' booth by a glass wall. It was crowded with sound and VDU equipment, and in its centre, the desk faced four TV monitors. Two male technicians were busy testing the microphones and recording equipment when they walked in.

"Hi, guys."

"Errol!" Anton turned from his task. "Punctual as usual – I like that. We're almost ready for you."

"This is Anne-Marie. She's a researcher, just started today. Is it okay if she sits in the booth for a while?"

"Sure, no problem."

Errol swung his briefcase on to the desk. After having read through the manuscript for the voice-over commentary this morning, he knew there was no way he could have memorised it, so he had brought it with him. Lifting the papers out of his briefcase, he realised he had only half of them with him. Anne-Marie was standing by his elbow, watching as he frantically flipped through the pages in his hand. "Something wrong?"

"I've left the second part of the manuscript at home. I was reading it through as I had my coffee this morning. How could I be so stupid? I have to do this today."

"Well, has no one else got a copy?"

"That's it! My agent e-mailed it to me." He flipped open his mobile phone and speed-dialled the office. "Is Harvey there?'

Anne-Marie watched as he nodded, said a few more words, then hung up, looking despondent. "He deleted it yesterday. There is just no way I'm going to be able to get back home and do this today."

"I've got an idea. Why don't you give me your keys? I could go back there and pick it up while you're recording the first half."

"Would you?"

"I'll be going against the traffic... and you could start you work straight away."

"Anne-Marie, you're a saint!" He whisked his keys out of his pocket. "This one's for the deadlock, and the code for alarm is..." He whispered, "one-seven-four-five."

"Okay, ladies and gentlemen. The *Do the Wright Thing* editorial meeting is now in progress. Good morning, everyone..." John Everett smiled briefly, took his seat as chairman of the meeting, and opened the folder in front of him. The meeting was being held in a small conference room. The wood-panelled walls and threadbare beige carpeting made the whole affair seem much less glamorous than the world the viewers thought Errol lived in. Around the long table sat the production assistants who had made the show the success it was, the researchers (including the recently recruited Anne-Marie Simms), and Errol Wright.

Anne-Marie was exceptionally nervous. She had been late, because she'd spent ten minutes in the ladies' getting her look just right. She'd wanted to look her best, to make an impression at her first meeting, and also to catch Errol's eye, of course. Just yesterday she had relaxed her hair and bought some new make-up. She had power-dressed in a short red dress and suit jacket. Her hair was worn straight to her shoulders with a side parting, and she had ventured to wear heels. She had to admit she looked extremely confident.

"I sincerely hope this time that you have all had a chance to read the agenda, which you should have recieved a week ago." Everett scanned the faces around the table as all eyes dropped to the open documents in front of them. "Anyway... We have Cassie taking the minutes today, and I won't ask for a volunteer to chair as I do it so well myself." He laughed at his own joke.

Anne-Marie leaned towards Errol. "Isn't sarcasm supposed to be the lowest form of wit?" she whispered.

Errol smirked but didn't say a word. He'd noticed Anne-Marie's transformation when she'd entered the room, and he had to admit that the woman had style and taste. Anyone could see it.

John continued. "First of all I would like to introduce to you the newest member of our research team, Miss Anne-Marie Simms. She has accepted a post starting today, and she will hopefully be with us for some time." He paused while everyone gave her a wecoming round of applause. "Anne-Marie's speciality is psychology, and she is the author of a book called *Internal Bleeding* which is based on the effects of painful relationship break-ups..." This was acknowledged with sounds of approval from round the table, and John steered smoothly to the next subject. "... Which brings me to the topic we are going to discuss today. For a while the idea has been floating around to do a programme on the effects of being in love." There were a few giggles from the table. One person who didn't find the subject amusing was Jack, a production assistant, who was tapping his pen impatiently on the table.

John looked at him pointedly as he continued. "With all the news in the media at the moment about stalkers, I thought it would be interesting to go with a theme of something like, Is Love a Disease? We could look into people whose lives have been dominated by it, who have become obsessed with a partner, who have had crushes... We may even dabble into cures, and look at the difference between healthy relationships and damaging ones."

There were nods from the team. Anne-Marie was smiling. It had been her idea. She saw herself as the resident psychologist on the show.

"Aren't we just covering old ground here?" Jack whined, still tapping his pencil annoyingly. "Other talk shows have done the love angle over and over."

John looked at him. They were all looking at him. Anne-Marie swallowed nervously. She wasn't the only one aware of the undercurrents in Jack's tone. Somehow she'd imagined the idea would have the same thrill for all of them that it had for her. "Actually it hasn't ever been approached as an illness on a talk show," she said, "it's always been seen as something sacred. Some shows have skirted around the issue of the hurt it sometimes leaves people with, when their love is not reciprocated, but never in any depth."

"I like it." Errol spoke up. "We could bring on the normal couples to start with, do some homie shots – love at first sight, romance – then live interviews with people who it went sour for, both the loved and the in love – and the obsessed. For audience sympathy we could do one of those in-depth interviews with someone who wants to remain anonymous, throw off a bit of emotion..."

"Are you supposed to fit all that into forty minutes?" asked one of the researchers, a woman with very frizzy red hair and glasses. "We've done it before, Tracey," John countered.

"Okay, what about an author?" another production assistant asked, looking pointedly at Anne-Marie. "A psychiatrist, maybe, and one of those people from marriage guidance – a counsellor. I've seen a book called *Women Who Love Too Much* – the author may be available."

"Yes!" John brought his hands together excitedly. "You're getting it. We'll leave it to the research team to dig up the appropriate guests. Anne-Marie will definitely be one of them – she has the right background."

"I do have quite a bit of material on the subject already," Anne-Marie said, trying to keep her expression neutral even though she was bubbling inside. "I could probably dig up some old clients who have helped with interviews in the past."

"Great! Theresa, can you get on to the other potential guests straight away? Errol, are you okay with this?"

"Sure, John, this is exactly what the show needs. It certainly won't do the ratings any harm."

Anne-Marie gazed at him as if he'd just given her the honour of a pay rise. John talked deadlines and dates for the next meeting, then the team filed out, full of chatter, most of them making their way to the kettle. Anne-Marie waited by the door as Errol finished a conversation with John.

"Hi," she said, flipping her hair over her shoulder deliberately.

"Hello," Errol said gently. "How are you settling in?"

Anne-Marie swiched her folder to her other arm and they walked towards the lifts together. "Pretty good. They seem a very organised team."

"Only the best. And you know you wouldn't have got the job if they didn't feel you would fit in."

They joined the small queue by the elevators. Anne-Marie was looking at his strong chin, and as he turned to face her she averted her eyes, suddenly unable to take the full force of his weakening gaze.

"How are you fixed for tommorow night?" she asked.

Errol flipped open the organiser he was carrying. "I'm free," he said, somewhat surprised. These days the words "free time" hardly ever entered his vocabulary.

"Well, how about that dinner you promised me?"

She was asking him out; this time there was no mistake. Errol actually froze for a few seconds as his brain processed this information. He'd be going against the lessons he had taught himself. "Tommorow night ..."

"I thought we could discuss the programme. You could fill me in on what it entails – you know, from first-hand experience. If it's too short notice—"

"No. No, it'll be fine." It was work. he told himself. Work, dinner, and good company. No problem. "You know where I live. Shall we say seven thirty?"

"Great. I'll bring a bottle." The elevator arrived and Errol stepped in. Turning round, he smiled at her. "See you then."

She waved her fingers at him as the lift closed, leaving her staring at her own reflection in the door.

Yvette looked across the dinner table at her son. Tyrone was shovelling spaghetti bolognese into his mouth and hardly chewing before swallowing.

"Tyrone, I got a call from your school today."

The boy looked up from the comic by his plate, one eyebrow raised in question.

"You know why, don't you?"

Tyrone sighed, and then continued to chew indifferently.

"Tyrone, I'm talking to you."

"Yeah, I know."

Yvette dropped her fork on to her plate. This wasn't like her son at all, being so unresponsive and rude. She grabbed the comic from under his eyes and dashed it towards the bin. "Then explain yourself!" Tyrone wasn't sure how to respond. Torn between continuing with his dinner and leaving the table, he stared stubbornly at his mother.

"You've been hopping classes. Why?"

He shrugged. "Boring."

"Boring! I want to know exactly what you find so boring."

He shrugged again.

"You have a nervous twitch or sump'n?"

No response. "Tyrone!" his mother warned.

"I just can't take some classes."

"You can't take them? What's stopping you?"

"I just don't like them."

"Are you being bullied?"

He looked at her as if she were asking him if he'd wet himself. "Course not."

"Then I don't care how boring the classes are – you have no choice in it. If you're having trouble with what you're being taught, or the teacher, then talk to someone. Your househead, for instance—"

"He's a batty man."

Yvette raised an eyebrow. "Don't use that language in front of me! I don't care if he's from Mars and sleeps with sheep. He's been employed to oversee and teach the pupils in your school, and he must be doing his job properly because he's concerned about you."

"Yeah, well ..."

"Well what?"

"I won't skip any more classes, okay?"

"You promise?"

He nodded.

"Good, 'cause I don't want to have to follow you around school to make sure you go. But if I get any more calls like this, that's exactly what I'm going to do."

Tyrone knew his mum wasn't messing. She never made threats; she promised – and never broke her promises. "Can I go now?"

"One more thing. I've asked Mr Peters to send home the work you've missed over the past month, which means extra homework."

"Mum!"

"What? Did you expect to get away with it?"

He stamped his way out of the kitchen. "Make sure you do your homework before you do anything else," Yvette called after him. "I want to see it before you go to bed!" She started to clear the table. Bringing up a young man on her own wasn't easy. Tyrone was very moody and withdrawn these days. Also he was shooting up in height. She had no idea how she was going to cope with him when he became a teenager, an adolescent, a man...

She would just have to take it in her stride; after all, she was his mother.

Errol gave his evening squash game his all, and by the end of the session he was aching. It felt good, though; he'd needed a release of tension, and that was what he had got. His partner Chris Stevens always gave him a good match. He was a fitter player than Errol, and tonight he was surprised at his opponent's vigour. "I know you said you was feeling good tonight, but you really had me running back there. Something happen today?"

"I'll give you one guess."

"It's a woman, ain't it?"

Errol looked at his friend as though he were a mind-reader. "This is between me and you, okay?"

"Okay. You know I was planning to call the tabloids up as soon as I left this place," Chris laughed. "You still seeing Yvette?"

"Yeah, and everything's going good."

"Yeah, so it's Yvette that's given you a high?"

"I ain't saying I'm seeing someone else ..."

"So what *are* you saying?"

"There's this woman – at work. She's got a body that is so ... I don't know, feminine, you know. She has this air of vulnerability, but as well as that she's cool, detached. All we've done so far is have lunch and talked, but I feel so good around her... and it's not sexual. She makes me feel special."

Now Chris was intrigued. "What – we talking falling in love here?"

"Hey man, you know me better than that."

"Then we're talking sex?" "No... I don't know." Errol knew how it must sound. He was still confused about how Anne-Marie affected him. He knew it was something he hadn't felt before, not even with Yvette. It was weird. "I'm not saying I wouldn't sleep with her. She's *fine*! But I'm seeing Yvette. This woman is just going to be a friend, a colleague. She's coming to dinner at my house, and nothing is going to happen."

"You know how many times I hear guys say that? 'We just gonna chat.' Next thing you know they're getting married."

"Chris – listen to me, man. I can't read the future, but you know my motto ..."

"Yeah, yeah: never get involved with colleagues. But I know men, like you know women. You can't 'just be friends' with a woman. It might happen by accident – you know, your arm brushes against her breast, you both bend down to pick something up and accidently come into contact, you fall asleep with each other and wake up naked..."

Errol was shaking his head.

"I'm serious!" Chris insisted. "Once it's happened – if it was any good – there's no reason why it shouldn't happen again. I think you should find out exactly what she wants from you before you make the assumption that all she wants is to be friends." He slapped Errol on his bare shoulder. "Why do you keep trying to be friends with them, man?"

"Because I *know* them, I listen to them. I know what a woman wants, and they can sense that. Why shouldn't men and women be friends?"

"If you succeed in this new venture of yours, you should write a book: *How To Be 'Just Good Friends'*. You could be rich, man..." Chris pulled his shirt down over his torso. He could already see the outcome of this little liason: "tears and swears" was what he would call it, the swears being the man swearing he'll never get involved again, the woman providing all the tears.

Daddy, where's all my toys gone? I can't find nothing." Errol wiped his hands on his striped apron and put the wooden spoon down in a saucer. He turned to his seven-year-old son. "Aaron, I told you. I have bought you a toy box – the one shaped like a bench, with the clowns on it. They're all in there."

A grin spread on Aaron's face and he shoved his hands into his jeans pockets before replying shyly, "Thank you," then turning and dashing up the stairs to his room. Fair-skinned, like his mother, with the miniaturised figure of his father, Aaron was a very handsome boy. And he was always dressed in the most up-to-date fashion. Money was nothing when it came to Errol Wright's son.

Aaron had been dropped off by his mother an hour ago, even though Errol had told her he had a date tonight.

"Are you actually going out?" she'd demanded.

"No," he had answered.

"So why can't you have him? It's not as though he'll be any bother. Jus' make him promise to keep out of the way. I do." Tanya was being her usual self-centred self. Errol had agreed to look after him for the night and take him back in the morning. It meant that the boy would have to eat with him and Anne-Marie – which was really no problem, since they were doing nothing more than having dinner and a pleasant evening of conversation.

He could have done without the extra work, though. It had been a hard enough day in the studio, recording another show. He'd gone back to his dressing room afterwards, and had frozen in the doorway. There, on the counter cluttered with tubes and jars of make-up, boxes of tissues and cotton wool, paper cups and bottles of water, had sat a huge bouquet of flowers. Errol had smiled as he'd slowly opened the envelope, thinking they had to be from an admirer, maybe Marion or Yvette. Two words. That was all. No signature, no name. "Soon, Errol." He'd dropped the card in the bin and left the flowers there. Maybe one of the cleaners would appreciate them.

Errol removed the lid from a pot of meat, and the steam escaped as the memory faded. So, he had a fan with money. No problem. The doorbell rang, and as Errol looked at his watch he heard Aaron's feet on the stairs.

"I'll get it, Dad!"

"Aaron! You don't know who it is." He untied his striped apron and hung it on the hook behind the kitchen door. Rubbing his hands together, he went to let his guest in.

Anne-Marie turned to face him as he swung the door open. "Good evening."

She wore a long overcoat and matching hat. Errol stepped back to let her into his home and she handed him the bottle she held in her gloved hands.

"Thank you. I'm afraid we have an extra guest for dinner. This is Aaron, my son."

Aaron was now standing behind his father, trying to get a good look at Anne-Marie before she spotted him. With surprise in her eyes, Anne-Marie stretched out a hand to the little boy. "Hi! My name is Anne-Marie."

Aaron looked up at his dad, waiting for the nod that said it was okay to shake.

She helped Errol prepare the vegetables for dinner while she chatted about her relatives' cooking and her own cooking skills. Over dinner Errol quizzed her on her interviewing skills. "Well, one vital ingredient is to be prepared – know the subject inside out."

Errol swallowed a mouthful of wine to wash some of the salmon starter down. "Good one. I learnt that from John. I always try to do a little research myself, however many assistants I have on the show." Then he indicated with his hand that she should continue.

"You have to have good eye contact. Listening – that's another vital one, you have to be interested – or at least appear interested. What else?" Her eyes studied the ceiling as if the answer was there, then she turned back to Errol, grinning. "Okay… Ask lots of why questions, and never questions that can be answered by a simple yes or no."

He was nodding, and Anne-Marie felt very pleased with herself. She couldn't think of any other points – her brain was too distracted – but Errol looked as though he was waiting for her to continue. "Anything else I should be thinking about?"

Errol put his fork down and picked up his glass, resting his elbow on the table. "Yes. You've got to *like* people – or find something about each person to like. I think that's the key. Once people know you like them it comes across. People will forgive you even the toughest questions, *and* they will answer them. Have enthusiasm, curiosity, and the ability to laugh, especially at yourself. And be as open as possible. I occasionally reveal bits of myself on screen…"

Anne-Marie giggled.

"… Not physical bits, of course, but personal things. Look at Oprah's empathy. She's accessible. It's the same with Ricki Lake. They're like friends; people tell them things."

They had been so deep in conversation that they hadn't noticed Aaron nodding off. His face was nearly resting on his half-empty plate. Errol looked at his watch. "It's well past his bedtime."

He told the sleepy boy to go and get ready for bed, and to give him a shout when he was ready.

Anne-Marie touched her napkin to the corner of her mouth as she watched the youngster make his way out of the room. "Can I read to him? He likes bedtime stories, doesn't he?"

"Of course. Although his mother and I don't get too much time to read to him."

"My parents were the same. You don't mind, do you? I mean, you can sit in on it if you like."

"No, that's okay. He'll enjoy it – you go ahead." Errol began to clear the table and loaded the dishwasher.

Anne-Marie was gone for half an hour. Every now and then Errol would hear Aaron laugh. He smiled, glad that his son was taking to Anne-Marie. She was turning out to be a good friend to have – and she wasn't bad to look at.

Relaxing in the living room after Aaron had gone to sleep, they started to talk more personally as they finshed off a second bottle of Chablis.

"He's a great kid. Just like his dad."

"Thank you. Did he do that kiss thing he does – where he pretends he's going to kiss your cheek and then smooches you?"

"Yeah, he did." Anne-Marie smiled. "I suppose you taught him that one."

Errol laughed, giving away nothing.

"Do you remember your first kiss?" she asked, her legs stretched out on the sofa, her stockinged toes pointing to the ceiling.

"Yes, as a matter of fact I do," Errol said from his spot on the floor, his back against the armchair. "It was with a very young-looking two-year-old with pigtails. My mum made me kiss her so she could take picture of us. I was about four or five at the time."

Anne-Marie giggled and jabbed a finger at him in jest. "You cad! Taking advantage of the young, even at that age…"

"Who me?" He laughed with her. "No, but seriously – my first teenage kiss was with Tracey Cole, at about… thirteen. I'd fancied her for ages, you know, since we'd started secondary. She was one of these girls who was the leader of the gang." Errol's eyes turned to the ceiling as he reminisced. "Always had the latest fashion, family had two cars, she wore about three gold chains round her neck, fastest on the track… You know the type – the most popular girl in school."

"I know the type," Anne-Marie said with feeling. It had been that type of girl who'd bullied her and made her an outcast. She remeembered her schooldays well. "And I suppose you were the school's most popular boy?"

He smiled coyly, "Wel,l you know… not far off it."

"So, how did this first kiss happen?"

"You know, we used to hang out together after school. I'd wait outside the gates with my boys and she would come along with her girls and we would all walk together, catch joke, check them out, you know."

"But all the while you were trying to get close to her?"

"Yeah." He shook his head and smiled at the memory. "One night I casually asked her to meet me outside the chippy after dinner. She asked if she should bring a friend, and I said no. I remember I had this real serious look on my face, you know, like I was trying to psyche her into reading my mind. Well it must have worked, 'cause she came alone."

Anne-Marie turned over on her side to face him.

"We just went for a walk round the park. I bought her chips and a Coke and boasted about what my family had. We had that in common, at least – our families were both professionals. By the end of the night, standing at her front door, I knew I wanted to kiss her, that I couldn't let her go without kissing her."

"Did you ask permissson?"

"Naw, man! That woulda been death to my credibility. She turned round to say goodnight and I just dived at her face, nearly breaking both our noses."

They laughed together as Errol refilled their glasses. "What about you? When was yours?"

"Oh, I was a lot older than thirteen. I kissed my first man at the ripe old age of twenty."

"*No*! What – a looker like you?"

"It's nice of you to say so, but it took hard work to get to look this good. Mum wouldn't let me wear make-up or relax my hair. She wouldn't let me out if she suspected I was seeing a man."

"Strict upbringing. Exactly how I would bring up my daughter."

Anne-Marie grabbed a cushion and threw it across at him. "Luckily I had no brothers, so I couldn't judge whether I was being treated unfairly by my parents. But when the other girls at school or at college would brag about their dates and their boyfriends buying them gifts, I would become insanely jealous.

"Describe your first kiss."

"Do I have to? I promise you it was nothing spectacular."

"Have you ever had a spectacular kiss?"

"Of course! Anyone who as been in love has had a spectacular kiss."

"Then describe that one to me."

"Errol Wright! What is this – research for your show?"

He shrugged, his face now serious. "Maybe. Stand up for me."

She gave him a look of curiosity, but stood up anyway. He followed. "I am going to describe a perfect kiss to you. Just how a first kiss should be. Do you trust me?"

"Errol, you're a man, I'm a woman, practically alone and drunk... Of course I don't trust you."

"Then pretend to trust me just for a couple of minutes." He took her hand and led her to the middle of the floor. She wondered what he was up to but didn't want to break the spell. Something was happening here, and if he was feeling what she was feeling she wanted it to carry on happening.

"Close your eyes," he told her.

Anne-Marie giggled. "Why, what are you going to do? Walk out of the room and leave me standing here?"

"Trust me. Close your eyes – or I'll have to find a blindfold." Anne-Marie breathed deeply, feeling a chilling excitement. She did as she was told with a sigh.

"Okay. Ready?"

She nodded.

"It starts here," Errol said, gently touching her lips with his fingers. "And here..." He placed the palm of one hand on her heart, just above her nipple. "And here..." A glancing touch against her belly. His voice was low, persuasively calming. She could feel his breath on her face, sweetly scented with wine.

"Think about a kiss..." He moved closer, so close his body was almost touching hers.

"I am," she replied. God, was she thinking about it. His warm hands cupped her face, fingers gently stroking the curve of her cheeks. She shivered, wanting to press herself closer to him. "When a boy wants a girl, when he wonders if that girl wants him, he kisses her first with his eyes, tests the texture of her skin, the shape of her lips, matching it mentally to his own..." His hands moved to her neck. "Kissing your body with his eyes, tasting you in his mind..." His hands were on her shoulders. "Exploring you..." His hands moved down her arms, so impossibly lightly through the satin of her blouse that it was somehow more erotic than if he were touching her skin. She could feel the hairs on the back of her neck rising.

"He's wondering what lies underneath," Errol continued, "picturing your breasts, sucking them in his mind, feeling your nipples harden to the touch of his imagination." She couldn't see him, but Errol had a wicked smirk on his lips and an erection that was aching in his pants. He remained, however, firmly in control. His hands, now on her hips, began to rise again, retracing his steps: over her upper arms and shoulders, just missing her nipples. He could feel every tremor of her body. The vibrations coming from her felt almost like electricity. Anne-Marie's breathing was deep and erratic. Her fingers clenched and unclenched, wanting to reach out for him – but this was his game, he played the lead. He had barely touched the silky satin over her breasts, but her nipples were hard, aching for his mouth. She could feel herself getting wet, a swelling heat between her legs.

"He'll be teasing you just a little, daring you..." His hands moved down, flirting with the waistband of her trousers, roving lower to the swell of her sex. "... tonguing you with his eyes, finding the curves your clothes hide, wondering how you will taste when he finally licks you..."

Anne-Marie audibly moaned and pushed her mound into the palm of his hand, but he was already moving on. His hands ran over the swell of her hips, then slipped gently away to trace the line of her thigh, the slender length of her calf. He knelt down in front of her, his head now level with her belly, his mouth so close she could feel his breath on her skin. He watched her face from where he rested on knees. His voice was so soft now that she had to strain to hear it. "... Screwing you with his eyes before he kisses you with his mouth."

She felt a sudden impulse to reach out and touch him, draw his head between her thighs, knowing that his whispers against her sex would be enough to make her come instantly. Almost as though he was reading her mind, Errol rose and took her hands in his. They stood with their lips almost touching. She could sense the heat of his body; she knew that the first touch of his lips would have the same effect as if he had gone down on her. "See? You can get all those things from a single glance, a look."

She was shivering with physical intensity.

"So that's it," he said matter-of-factly. "A first kiss. Open your eyes, Anne-Marie."

She did as he asked, suddenly too aware that he wasn't going to complete his demonstration. He was smiling ironically as he walked across the room and sat down, crossing his legs. Seething with frustration she took a sip of wine and excused herself to go to the bathroom.

Did he *know* what he'd just done? Was this a game – his form of foreplay? Because if it was, he was very good at it and she couldn't wait to get back downstairs for more. She splashed her face with water, dried it and freshened herself up. Thinking Errol would be waiting in anticipation for her downstairs, she exited the bathroom to find him waiting in the hall. "I've put the electric blanket on in the spare room, and put towels on the bed for you." Noticing the puzzled look on her face, he added, "You're welcome to stay; I wouldn't let you have to wait around for a cab." He kissed her cheek. "Good-night. I'll see you in the morning." And he was gone before she could even reply.

The next morning Errol woke slowly to the smell of cooking. He made his way downstairs, pulling on his short white dressing gown, and experienced a curious feeling of *déjà vu* as he entered the kitchen. Anne-Marie had her back to him; she was wearing the shirt he'd had on last night, and was singing as she cooked eggs. She must have taken the shirt from the bathroom. Her relaxed hair had been brushed smooth so that it hung straight to her shoulders, the morning sun making it appear lighter in colour. His eyes travelled down past her buttocks to her very strokable bare legs. He was tempted to creep up behind her and put his arms round her, but he knew by now that he should fight temptation. "Good morning," he said, leaning against the door jamb.

"Good morning! How do you like your eggs?"

"None for me, thanks. Look, I think you ought to go. You know – with Aaron here I don't want him to get the wrong idea."

"What possible idea could a seven-year-old get? Besides, can't a friend cook a friend breakfast now?"

"Yes, but—"

"No buts. You cooked me a delicious dinner, and I want to repay you."

"That's not necessary. Besides, we had a late night and I'm sure you want to go home and freshen up… before work, I mean."

She stepped seductively towards him. "We both know you don't want me to leave."

This wasn't what he'd intended. He should give up the drink – sometimes it made him a little too loose. He knew he had been giving off the wrong signs last night. Maybe Colin was right: you couldn't just be friends with a woman. "We both have work…" he said.

"Okay," she laughed, "then why don't I fix us a packed lunch? Cooked meats, cold salads, French bread…"

"Sounds more like a picnic to me."

"It can be whatever you want it to be. And Aaron would love it."

Errol sighed and took a step back. She was obviously after more than a platonic friendship. "I'm taking him home today. I'll drop you off after I drop him if you like." Anne-Marie's face clouded over. "I don't think your being here is a good idea."

"Too much too soon?"

He shrugged non-committally, though he knew he was hurting her feelings.

"No problem," she said, and left him to get dressed.

Throughout a man's adult life he has to put up with rejection time and time again. Any man who has had to ask a woman for a dance in a nightclub knows the feeling. The women who do the rejecting seem unaware of the harm they are doing, and yet when it comes to their turn they can't handle it. It is as though the man should feel so honoured to be offered her body that he shouldn't be able to refuse. Well, sometimes things don't happen that way. Errol wished he had put Anne-Marie in a cab last night. What had he been thinking?

They drove most of the way to Tanya's home in silence. Errol stayed in the car as he watched Aaron knock on the front door and wait. A minute later the boy's mother answered it. Errol waved his son goodbye, and the door closed behind him. Anne-Marie tried to make conversation as they drove on, but Errol wasn't in the mood. He liked her – she was a good conversationalist, and they had some laughs together; it also helped that she got along with his son – but there was Yvette to consider.

Y ou hear 'bout Predator?" Dean looked up from his cards. "Went to Nations laas week…" Fits of laughter from Colin. "… Come out wid six numbers and t'ought it was 'im lucky night!" He rolled about on the sofa.

"Nations! Naw, you know what dem call dat place, innit? Dungeons and Dragons!"

"Me know, me know! De guy called t'ree a dem an all were mashed, guy!" Colin licked wood.

"What'd I tell you about that place? Only desperados rave in Nations. Night pretties' paradise." Dean threw his legs over the side of the armchair. "One gyal I know was boastin' how she come out wid nuff numbers. I turn roun' and show her how easy it was. Called this gyal over from 'cross de road, y'nuh? Didn' even bodder wid any chat, an she han' over her number quick-time. Soon as her back was turn I dash it weh. Easy, man. Nation!" He wrinkled his brow in disgust.

"It's true! You ever hear of anyone meeting their woman in there?"

"No! A ride, yes – but you could nevah tek one out seriously."

"You know Predator. The guy's probably still trying the other t'ree numbers."

"He needs to fix himself up and tek care a dat bad breat' before he even t'ink about checkin' woman." Dean never minced words. If you wanted an honest opinion, just ask him. There had been times when his down-to-earth, blatant comments had lost him friends, but he didn't care; as far as he was concerned, if they didn't want to hear the truth they shouldn't ask.

Dean's flat was a cosy bachelor pad in Elephant and Castle. The living room and kitchen took up one space, separated only by a counter. The other rooms in the flat were the bathroom and bedroom. Still, it suited him just fine – he was planning on living on his own for as long as possible.

His apartment had seen more women come and go than hot dinners. Standing six foot one, with a caramel complexion, perfectly squared jaw and elongated almond-shaped eyes (he described himself as a Chinese black man), Dean knew he was irresistible to women even before they heard his deep, gravelly voice. Unfortunately his attitude occasionally got the better of him, and women sometimes didn't stick around for very long, whether he wanted them to or not.

He poured himself another shot of Cockspur and leant back against the sofa. "So, Errol seh he's coming tonight?"

"Yeah, man."

Dean picked up the remote control and started the CD playing again, and the cool tones of Adina Howard floated through the room. "Y'know what he said to me the other day? The reason he don't rave too tough now is cause he's always getting noticed. He can't relax." Dean, who had known Errol since school, missed the old times. He had enjoyed their old kick-back-roll-a-spliff-and-check-gyal days. Everyone seemed to be pairing off, meeting their soul mates, getting important jobs, buying property, taking on responsibility and cutting themselves off from their old lives. And soon, he surmised, he'd be raving alone – unless *he* met a soul mate too.

"He's bullshitting," Colin said. "He loves all dat. He's still raving, jus' moving wid a diff'rent crowd." He took a gulp of wine, shaking his head. "No, man. Errol ain't into that high-and-mighty t'ing. He's still my homie, y'know what I'm saying?"

"He may be dat, but my man ain't checking de punnany no more."

"Who tell you dat?" Colin's tone showed he was ready to defend his long-time spar against any derogatory remark.

"You don't hear what people are saying? He ain't sticking it to women." Colin shot straight up, rum spilling on to his fingers from his glass. "I know my man. He's got a woman!" Dean laughed, deep and resonant. "You should see your face!" He swung his legs to the floor. "Boy oh boy!" He shook his head, still chuckling as he crossed to the kitchen area.

Colin visibly relaxed. Dean was always winding people up. He swung the peak of his baseball cap to the back of his head and breathed out. "Errol's checking all right. He's just keeping it under cover 'cause of his career." Dean pulled open the fridge. "You wanna sandwich?"

"What you got?"

"What you t'ink this is, a restaurant?"

"I don't eat everything, you know, not like you guts," Colin retorted. Dean wasn't a fussy eater, and he ate plenty. But dressed in a string vest and boxer shorts he showed not an ounce of fat. "Ham, cheese, or both?"

"You doin' it in that toasting thing?"

"Sandwich maker, yeah."

"Gimme ham and cheese den." Colin reached for the cable control, but before his fingers could touch it Dean blasted him: "Leave it deh! How many time I haffe tell you nuh touch me t'ings!"

"I was only—"

"I don't care! Anyt'ing goes wrong wid it I've gotta replace de damn t'ing, so leave it!"

"Bwoy, you're worse dan a woman…"

Dean didn't give a damn about Colin's opinion. He'd grown up in a house with three elder brothers, and everything he'd ever had had belonged to all of them before, including his clothes. Now he had his own possessions he made sure no one took liberties with them.

The intercom buzzed and Colin looked to Dean before even thinking of answering it.

"Get de door nuh!" Dean slapped a slice of ham on top of a slab of cheese and completed the sandwich with another slice of bread. He heard two men's conversation as they came back into the living room: Colin's excited and full of news; Errol's cheerful, laughing. Errol appeared in the doorway dressed in a cream sweater and black jeans, jacket slung over his shoulder. He looked ready to go out. "Dean…" He nodded at his mate before hanging his jacket on the back of the door.

"Awright, man. Long time…"

"You know how it goes."

"I wish," Dean humphed.

"Hear dis, brudda. You t'ink what I do is easy?"

"Easier than lugging wood all day. You get paid to ponce about in a suit and chat to heartbroken people. Gimme dat any day."

"Jus walk t'rough de door an dis is what I get!" Errol threw himself on to the sofa. "So, what we having for dinner?"

"Dinner! I jus' done tell dis brudda dis ain't no restaurant. De only reason he's getting food is 'cause I don't eat without offering. You come too late, man." Dean put Colin's sandwich on a plate and chucked it on to the counter, signalling his friend to come and get it.

Errol let it go. "Bring us a glass when you coming – I might as well get a drink. By the way, whose turn is it to drive?"

"It ain't me!" Dean said, sure of himself. "Since we ain't bin nowhere wid you fe months, you can." He watched Errol's hand drop from the bottle of rum, his face drop with it. "Naw, man. You can't do this. I need a drink."

"Look, jus' cool. I'll drive, all right?" Colin offered.

"You pussy!" Dean spat. He handed Errol a glass and resumed his favourite chair.

"Wha' you dissing de man for? If he wants to drive, let him. You gonna argue wid that, you drive!" "You know he's only doing it to suck up to you."

"Suck up... Wha'!" Colin spluttered. "Errol an me go way back! He'd do the same for me."

"Yeah, whatever, man. Cho..." Dean bit into his sandwich and swung his legs back over the arm of the chair.

"Why don't you get a recliner?" Errol suggested.

"You payin' for it?"

Errol cocked an eyebrow but didn't answer. He knew Dean well enough to recognise that, despite his brash attitude, he was a good mate. They were guaranteed a good time with him in tow. When they were at college together, Errol and Dean had found that between them they made one massive talking machine. The both of them were tall, good-looking and intelligent, with sex appeal that didn't need turning on. While Errol had studied hard, Dean had studied woman. He'd had no problem in getting them, and he had taken advantage of his God-given talent... until he'd met Pauline. Pauline had been hard to land, and when he'd finally got her she'd told him that their affair was to be no fling. She'd heard about his reputation and wasn't planning on being just another lay. Before long he was totally hers. After a year or so his friends had started telling him he'd got it bad. He'd brushed their comments aside. Two years, and he'd begun to realise that he was in love. Three, and they were living together. Eight years, and Dean's life fell apart. Pauline's best friend had told him that his girlfriend was having an affair. She'd said she liked Dean too much to carry on lying for her.

Dean had confronted Pauline, she'd admitted it, and he'd moved out. Her best friend was the first bedding of his new, swinging bachelor life.

"So, where's this place we're going?" Errol looked from one man to the other.

Colin licked crumbs from his lips. "Earl's." "The wine bar?"

"Yeah. It's a nightclub and restaurant. It's all right, you know. I was dere about a month ago."

"Yeah, I hear it's kicking some nights." Errol leant back and studied Colin's profile. His friend was thirty, married, and he looked good on it. Not that there's anything wrong with the way I look, he told himself – but it just showed that settling down doesn't do you any harm. "So, Mister Superstar, nice to see you still 'ave time fe we likkle people," Dean teased.

"Time! The only thing I know 'bout time is dat I don't have any to myself any more."

"I hear dat," Colin put in. Dean cut his eye after him.

"You know," Errol continued, "it's like I get up, grab two food, then head out. I got meetings, rehearsals, recordings, interviews, photo sessions, more meetings... plus I gotta find time for my women and my son. My whole life is one big schedule."

Dean chuckled sarcastically.

"You wanna say somet'ing, D?"

"No, not really... but I'm just making an observation here, right?"

Errol opened his arms as if to say, "Go on."

"You're living in a three-bedroom house in Mitcham, right? You drive a brand new car, you have over ten set a suit an' a pair a shoes fe go wid each a dem. You're wining and dining models and TV stars, you 'ave woman ready fe drop dem baggy fe you. Correct me if I'm wrong..."

"Yeah – so?"

"What de hell yuh a worry 'bout time fa?"

Errol had to laugh. Looking at his life from someone else's perspective was a great exercise. He had to admit he enjoyed his work, and the money was giving him and his family a life of luxury. For the first time in his life he had something in the bank. If his only worry was finding time to sit and think, then compared to most people he had none.

"I know what Errol is saying." Colin, who had been quietly taking it all in, knew what not having time for yourself felt like. "When me and da guys were touring with the football team, I had two evenings a week to myself, that is nothing. An' in those two nights all I wanted to do was sleep."

Errol was nodding.

"I didn't want to call up my spar or woman to come keep me comp'ny; all I wanted was my bed."

Dean snorted. "People like you don't deserve to have money and fame. You cyan't handle it. Now, if it was me, I'd be on the ball twenty-four-seven wid me stamina and t'ing. I wouldn't care if I never see my bed again, 'cause all it would mean is dat I'd be sharing someone else's."

Errol and Colin shared a laugh. Dean was jealous. It was so obvious it was pitiful. But they couldn't tell him that – he'd only twist it up and throw it back at them.

The countdown had reached five minutes. Dressed in a short red velvet dress, the woman poured two glasses of wine then replaced the bottle in the refrigerator. On her way through the hallway she checked her hair in the mirror. She liked it this way; she'd noticed that other men liked it too. Every Wednesday was her day at the hairdresser's. Her appointment gave her enough time to get back home so that she wouldn't miss him. Satisfied that she looked good, she entered her living room. The curtains were drawn against the night, and the only light came from the television screen. The commercials were still running – yet another advert for yet another fast car. The type of car *he'd* drive.

Her favourite armchair was directly facing the TV. A small cocktail table stood on the floor next to it. On to this she placed a glass of wine before sitting in the empty chair and curling her legs into its warm comfort.

Holding the stem of her glass between two fingers, she sipped the chilled liquid. Impatiently she watched yet another gimmicky ad, then finally the multi-coloured trademark of Channel 5 came on to the screen. She reached for the remote control with a delicate hand, holding down the volume button until the surround sound engulfed her.

The signature tune of *Do the Wright Thing* sent goosebumps prickling their way over her bare arms. Then there he was. Still shots of the man she craved flickered on the screen, smart visual effects making them spin, flip over and change in an instant. She hadn't realised, but her pulse rate had quickened and her breathing had become a touch heavier.

The show started. The studio audience, not realising how lucky they were to be in the same room as him, applauded, whistled and cheered as

Errol Wright appeared on the stage.

She shivered with anticipation. Here was the man of her dreams, everything she had always wanted. He was heartbreakingly handsome, caring, sensitive, mature... and with it, humorous and open. His body was that of an athlete – finely toned, the skin smooth and fresh looking. He was smiling modestly as he sauntered across the screen to greet his audience. The camera came in for a close up, and Errol Wright raised the microphone to his mouth.

The woman found her throat had gone dry, and she lifted her glass to sip again from the wine.

"Good evening... and thank you..." Errol Wright addressed both studio audience and camera. "... Thank you for joining me once again on the most talked-about show since Oprah." His voice was that of a trained journalist and entertainer: demanding, coercing his audience's attention with ease. If only he knew how much she wanted him. She stood slowly, almost like a snake uncoiling and moving in for the kill. Her glass still in her hand, she smoothed her dress over her hips and padded barefoot across the room until she was standing in front of the screen, where Errol Wright had begun to introduce his guests.

She knelt, her nose a few inches from the glass. "Tell me what you like, baby," she whispered. "Tell me what you want from me. I want to be your everything."

Oblivious to his admirer's lust, Errol was chatting to a young black man who was about to confess to his best friend that he was gay.

Tears formed in her eyes and trickled down her cheeks. A single drop fell into her glass, causing no more than a tiny ripple.

"I'll make you notice me!" she wailed. "Why can't you see me?"

"Bobby, I've got something to tell you," the young man was saying. He swallowed and looked to Errol, who reassured him with a nod and a smile. "Bobby, the reason you never see me with no women is 'cause... I'm... I'm gay." Bobby jumped away from the young man as though it was catching. Gulping the rest of her wine, the woman screamed at the television, where the audience had gone wild: "Love me, damn you! I... love... you!" Finally, exhausted by her emotions, Anne-Marie crumpled into a sobbing heap in front of the television, ruining her new hairdo, and the glass fell from her hands.

The scenario had been the same ever since Errol's first show. It had originally started with a photograph in the *Voice* newspaper. Anne-Marie recognised the handsome new TV personality and had racked her brain to remember where from, becoming more desperate to meet him the more she tried to recall where she'd seen the guy. When it had finally come to her it had all seemed so easy: she simply had to get in touch with Colin, tell him how lonely she was, and remind him that she wasn't doing anything at weekends, tell him she was available for parties, get togethers... oh, and whatever happened to that friend of yours, Errol Wright?

From the moment she had set eyes on him she'd known he was destined to be part of her life. And it was up to her to make it so.

The weekend had passed with thoughts of Errol never far from Anne-Marie's consciousness. Her moods had swung from joy to confusion to pure lust. She had to know what was going on. Was he or was he not interseted in her? She knew how she felt. Marion had taken her out on Sunday night – dinner with an old friend and guests. It had been so... pally. Marion was a very friendly person who had decided to make Anne-Marie part of her circle of colleagues and friends. She'd introduced her to a couple of people in the same line of work, and everyone had seemed interested in her... and yet all she had been able to think about was Errol. Why hadn't he been invited?

She'd slept badly, and woke at seven with her eyes puffy and red from tiredness and the amount of wine she'd drunk the night before. She rose slowly, feeling unusual aches and pains in her back. Was this what getting to thirty meant? She knew she should exercise, start going to a class or swimming. Did Errol swim? Maybe she'd ask him – they could go together, make it a regular thing.

Breakfast was black coffee and toast, eaten alone in her living room with the TV on. She always watched television with a pad somewhere nearby. It was a habit from her days at college. Being a researcher, there was usually some piece of information she found useful. Even if she didn't realise it at the time, it might come in handy later on.

She was still thinking of Errol as she went to buy her morning paper. Another stalker story had stolen the headlines. She folded it and stuck it into her bag as she headed for the station.

Maybe she needed to make the first move with him. She had been too subtle so far. Play the right moves with a man, any man, and no matter if he's gay, married or committed to the church, you can get him to want you.

Women are used to being pursued, to having their bodies invaded; men aren't, and so they struggle against it more. But Anne-Marie's philosophy was that persistence pays. She was passing the florists when the idea came to her. She'd send him flowers. He'd like that.

Y ou know what we need round here?""A swimming pool?" Yvette suggested sarcastically.

"Where would we put a swimming pool?"

"On the roof." Yvette and her brother were sitting in her office. She was casually draped over a soft cloth armchair, dressed in her work gear – Lycra leggings and a crop top. Her brother Conrad, her silent partner, had been going through the books as he did once a month, making sure his money was being put to good use and that they weren't losing profits. A man of slight build with quick, inquisitive eyes and a sensuous, small mouth, Conrad was always smartly dressed, had his hair neatly trimmed once a fortnight, and also had a brain that never seemed to rest. Everything he did had a purpose, and he was constantly on the look-out for opportunities. When people asked him what he did, they regretted it when half an hour later he'd still be telling them.

When she had first decided to go into the beauty and fitness business, Yvette had had no idea what an enormous undertaking it was going to be. She soon understood what Conrad had meant when he'd talked of building a company out of your own sweat. Now she had done it, and she was making it work.

"No, I'll tell you what we need," Conrad said. "Men."

"We get men in here. They use the gym every day of the week, especially the weekends."

"But we don't want them just using the gym. The gym costs one price and they use it for hours. And why do we only have female instructors and trainers? Men can do step aerobics too; why don't we have a male instructor?"

Yvette shrugged and frowned. She felt as though she was being attacked for being sexist, but she knew she was nothing of the kind. Conrad quickly hid a grin. He recognised the sulk that had settled over his little sister's face. She saw this as her business, and didn't want to hear that she could possibly improve it with someone else's help. He knew she was good at her job, but another perspective never hurt anybody. "The idea came to me when I was at the black youth achievement awards last week," he told her. "They had this guy there on stage – a fitness instructor, black guy with bleached blonde hair, and he was toned until he couldn't be toned any more…"

"So you chatted him up, got his number and promised him a job. Now you want to install him at my club." Conrad was a closet gay. The only people who knew were his sister and his closest friends. Their mother had her suspicions, but would never voice them.

"No, sis, this isn't personal. I didn't even talk to him. But this man did a routine that was out of this world. There was six of them on stage, each with a step. I'm not talking one-up-one-down – this was a routine with attitude. They were twisiting, spinning, jumping, doing the shimmy and clapping all at the same time. This was like no step routine I've ever seen in my life."

Yvette hadn't seen her brother so excited about anything since they'd made their first thousand-pound profit on this place. "Better than mine?"

"Eve, you know you're good. But this guy—"

"All right, I get the picture. But if you didn't talk to him how am I supposed to contact him?"

"I got you the name of the organiser, he can put you in touch." He whipped a folded flyer out of his pocket and passed it to Yvette. She slid out of her chair and took it between two fingers, going back to her chair to unfold it. Now she was smiling. "Goldie? That's the aerobics guy?"

"That's him."

"And you don't fancy him?" she asked studying his face.

"Yvette, he's not my type," Conrad said honestly. "I think they call it step-cardiovascular funk."

"Okay. I'll get in touch, give him an audition."

"Good. I'm not saying it will just have more men doing aerobics; I think your female clientele will be flocking in here too to get a look at him. Only they'll have to pay to do it."

"You know, sometimes, Con…"

"What?"

"I think you really care about me."

He threw his head back and laughed.

Anne-Marie sat at her desk and sighed, the computer's monitor casting an eerie glow on her features. The report in front of her was entitled "Is Love an Illness?" She was planning to submit it to the executive producer on Monday. She was thinking about the other night at Errol's house. The photo she had "borrowed" from his son's room sat in a small wooden frame on the desk. Staring at it, she found her concentration lapsing and she daydreamed.

As she stared at her computer she imagined Errol appearing behind her. She could see his reflection in the screen, standing behind her. He bent to kiss her neck and she shivered, feeling goosebumps prickle all over her body. Then he unzipped her dress and ran his tongue down her back, stopping every now and then to suck and kiss her flesh. She shifted to the edge of her chair. In her fantasy he sank to the floor in front of her, turning on to his back as he shuffled under her chair, his body between its legs. His head came up between her parted legs, he looked once into her eyes, and then focused on her swelling lower lips. He took her clitoris between his lips and lightly sucked. She gasped. He was manipulating her to orgasm, sucking her to ecstasy. He was feeding on her juices like a thirsty man. She reached down and ran her hands through his hair. His head wasn't bald any more; it had tight, wiry hair, and her fingers were getting wet. Her pulse was racing and she breathed heavily as she exploded into orgasm.

"Oh Errol…" It wasn't enough. Anne-Marie wanted the real thing. She got up and put her coat on.

The phone rang just as Errol was about to leave the house. He actually had the door open, but swung it shut again. Yvette had been on his mind all day and, although he didn't usually turn up without calling first, tonight he wanted to surprise her. He opened the living-room door and picked up the reciever. "Hello?" he answered wearily. Silence. "Hello?" he said again.

"Errol Wright?" a nondescript female voice asked.

"Yes, can I help you?"

"I'm watching you."

Errol held the phone away from his ear for a moment and glared at it, as if his anger could somehow be silently transmitted to the caller. When he listened again he could hear soft breathing."Who *is* this?"

"I'm watching you."

"Oh yeah? Then what am I doing?"

"You'd just switched the lights off and were making your way out of the front door when the phone rang."

This time Errol's response wasn't so swift. He looked towards his curtained windows. Other colleagues had recieved calls like this. Somehow the weirdos had got hold of their home numbers. It was almost like an occupational hazard. He was about to say something when the caller got in first.

"I'll be waiting for you, Errol," and there was a click as the line was disconnected. He was left with the dial tone. Slowly he replaced the reciever and decided to forget it. Probably a one-off; he wasn't even sure if it was a man or a woman. He wouldn't let it bother him. Not yet. If he had been a defenceless woman he wouldn't set foot outside the door., but Errol Wright could take care of himself.

Hidden in the shadows across the road, a woman pulled her coat tighter around her and slipped her mobile phone back into her pocket.

Yvette was playing cards with Tyrone in the kitchen when the doorbell rang.

"I'll get it!" Tyrone rushed to open it, his cards still in his hand.

Yvette looked up at the clock. She wasn't expecting anyone. She heard Errol's voice before her son announced, "Mum, it's Errol!" Turning back to Errol, the boy showed him his hand. "Look at this."

"You're in big trouble, Mum." Errol grinned wickedly at Yvette as he made his entrance to the kitchen.

She rose from the table, smiled, but was clearly not pleased. "We weren't expecting you, were we?"

"No. I just got the urge to be here," he said, one hand reaching for her waist. This woman never ceased to look sexy, even when she wasn't expecting company. She was dressed in blue: a short cut-off top and a tight mini. Tyrone was tapping his cards impatiently.

"We'll pick the game up later, Ty'," Yvette said, removing Errol's hand from her body.

Tyrone breathed heavily in exasperation. "But I was gonna beat you!"

"Later, okay? Look, why don't you do the dishes for me? I'm gonna take a break."

Tyrone dashed his cards on the table and threw Errol a truculent look.

Yvette glared at Errol. "See? All that could have been avoided if someone knew how to use the phone." They went into the living room. "Maybe I should have called first," Errol said. "But I thought Tyrone would be doing his homework or something."

Yvette sucked air through her teeth. The liberties some people take! She had him that under no circumstances was he to turn up at her house unannounced. She like to be prepared. "So? I might have been busy." She left no doubt to what she was talking about; after all, they were supposed to have an open relationship.

"Well *are* you?" Errol asked, taking a seat as she poured some drinks.

"No," she said over her shoulder. "Tonight I'm spending quality time with my son." "I'm sorry."

She croosed the room and stood in front of him. "A woman has needs," she said. His head was level with her most intimate spot, and he looked up to meet her eyes, sensing a new game. "Tell me about it," he said, pulling her down to him. His voice was low and sexy, a tone she knew very well.

"Hey, my son's in the next room," she said, gently pushing him away and handing him his glass.

"I want you," he whispered, reaching for her buttocks with his free hand.

She smiled knowingly. "Maybe. But I'm not performing in front of my son. Now, if you'd called, we might have had the place to ourselves..."

Errol sighed and let his hand drop away. He looked like a sad puppy. Yvette was sure he needed her for something, but what was it? "So, you came round on the spur of the moment for sex?"

Errol shook his head, taking a sip of his drink. "No, I came round to be with you. The sex is a bonus." His eyes followed her as she crossed the room to the armchair.

She changed tack. "So – how was your day?"

Totally surprised by the question, Errol didn't answer.

"I know you didn't come here to talk about work," she sighed, "but we have to have some kind of conversation."

He got up and walked across to her. "Why would you want me to talk about work? This is about us."

"I just feel as though we don't have interesting conversations any more. You must lead such a glamourous lifestyle, and the most I hear about it is in the papers or by watching your show."

"Why didn't you say so?"

"I *am* saying so. Sometimes I feel you only want me for one thing – just a playmate."

He touched her chin, raising her face to meet his eyes. "I do want you as a playmate – we have fun together – but that's far from being all I want. I just don't want you to become what Tanya did. She got hungry for the celebrity life and the power, the money and the glamour, and she stopped caring about us." He was staring at her intensely. "When I'm with you I want to leave all that behind. I spend enough of my life belonging to everyone else; I just want to be yours."

Oh boy, this man had a way with words! Yvette grabbed the back of his neck and brought his lips down to hers, thinking, You don't know how much I want the same thing.

Symptoms: rapid heartbeat, stomach cramps, breathlessness, emotions swinging from ecstasy to melancholy, weak knees, erratic behaviour..." Errol came down the steps in the audience area, microphone in hand. He wore a light-blue satin waistcoat over a collarless navy-blue suit. "Not only that, but it urges you to spend money you ain't got, including running up your phone bill. Does this sound like an illness to you? Well, that's what we're here to discuss: the topic 'Is Love a Disease?'"

The audience applauded as the title spun on to the screen.

"We have with us today two couples who are in love, a single man and a single woman, both of whom say they have been bitten once and never again, and our resident psychologist, who knows what can happen when it all goes wrong: Anne-Marie Simms, author of *Internal Bleeding*. Let's give them all a good welcome to the show!"

Errol let the audience applaud the guests, who were already seated on stage, before continuing. "First, I would like to introduce Mark. Mark was hit by the thunderbolt ten years ago. He says the moment he laid eyes on Letitia he knew she was for him..." He paused as women whistled in the audience. "Mark, tell us about it."

Mark wasn't a very tall man. He was stout, with a tidy haircut and cute baby cheeks with dimples. He wore a red sweatshirt under a black leather waiscoat and black jeans. "I met Letitia at college, and when I first saw her, she was looking at me, you know, like watching me." He grinned at the memory. "I was hit here..." He pounded a fist on his chest. "I just knew, and I told her that on our first date, which was the next day. She didn't take me seriously, though. But now we're engaged, and as soon as we're both financially stable we'll get married."

Errol clapped and the audience whistled, stamped their feet and applauded.

When the noise had died down Errol turned back to his guest. "How'd it feel to bare your soul to a woman on her first date? I mean, I'm a man – I know how difficult it is to say things like that, even to my mum." He glanced round to the audience who made sympathetic noises, beforeaddressing Mark again. "Now, you didn't know this woman from a serial killer. So how did you know you loved Letitia enough to tell her that? Describe it for me."

Mark shifted uneasily in his seat, clasping his hands in his lap to stop from fidgeting. "It was just there, like I said before. It hit me. There was something like a magnetic force, a chemistry... I know they say opposites attract but we're actually a lot alike. Our birthdays are a day apart; we're aquarians with the same surname…"

There was a murmur from the audience.

"… We're a year apart in age; we want all the same things in life. She sometimes finishes sentences for me, or I'll answer a question she was just about to ask me. We can be in the same room doing our own thing without feeling the need to communicate that so many couples think is necessary. There's no pressure, because we'll know when the other needs that cuddle, a chat, togetherness…" Mark gave a huge dimpled smile that immediately endeared him to the audience. "It's like fate brought us together."

"That's amazing! And since you've been together you still feel the same? Knowing Letitia hasn't changed that … magnetism?"

"No. If anything the feeling has become deeper. Anyone who knows 'Tish knows that you can only grow to love her. She's a fantastic human being."

"There's a man in love!" The audience took their cue and gave Mark a warm round of applause, until Errol motioned them to stop and started speaking. "Later we'll meet Mark's intended, Letitia…" The camera panned to the seat next to Mark, where a young woman with gelled hair sat. "… But next we have Cheryl. Cheryl is living with her boyfriend, Curtis. Curtis and Cheryl say they love each other, but they can't stop arguing…" The audience laughed. "It's a case of can't live with him, can't live without him for Cheryl." He turned to his second guest and gave her a warm smile. "Cheryl, tell us about it."

"Let me just put you right there first, Errol. Curtis only lives with me when he feels like it, okay? When we have a disagreement he runs back to his mum's house…" Again the audience erupted. "But, Errol – I love the man, you know? We been together t'ree years but he's jus' so stubb'n."

"How's that?"

"I'll give you an example, right? When I wanna go out I tell him, an' he says, 'Well where do you wanna go?' So I says, 'Surprise me – you choose.'" She kissed her teeth and slapped her hands on her big thighs. "Then he tells me to choose, and we end up going nowhere… And he's always sulking…"

"Don't you ever feel that these arguments might be *your* fault?" Errol asked, raising an eyebrow.

"Naw, man! I'm into discussing t'ings, you know? I give the guy so many chances, 'cause I love him. All I get back is sorry! What good is sorry when he goes and does the same t'ings again? When we first met he used to always turn up when he said he would, he'd never come empty handed. He used to always say, 'Anything you want, just ask, I wanna take care of you...' Anyway, we made love, including foreplay ..." The studio now filled with whoops of laughter, as the women in the audience dug their boyfriends in their sides. "... now we 'ave sex, see? It ain't nuttin'."

Errol was laughing too, but remained professional. "So why do you put up with him? Why not just dump the man and start again?"

"I been there," she said, lifting her hands. "Better the devil you know... It's like a drug to me, bein' with 'im. Even though he has his faults and I complain about him, bein' with him is like a fix and I can't live without it."

Errol turned to Anne-Marie. "Anne-Marie, before we meet the other halves of our couples, would you care to say a few words on what you've heard so far?"

"Well, Errol, it looks as though Mark knows exactly how he feels. But what I find interesting is that, ten years on, this whirlwind affair is still little more than an affair." She turned to Mark. "You love each other, you must have a home because you're living together... Usually after this long a couple that have made the commitment to get engaged are making plans to get married. Also you haven't said anything about children; finance seems to be more important to you both. I would be interested to hear Letitia's side of the story."

"And Cheryl?" Errol asked.

"As with Mark, I would have to hear the other side of the story... But how do you live with someone you're constantly arguing with? Doesn't the love and caring suffer? Maybe you need to look for someone you're more compatible with, someone who wants to be no more than a part-time lover..." The studio erupted in agreement. "But – and this a big but – if you two decide that you really want to be together, I'll give you some tips on constructive arguing. Yes, there is such a thing!"

Under Errol's guidance, Letitia walked on confidently and took her seat next to Mark. He immediately grabbed her hand and held it in his lap.

Errol asked her to tell her side of the story, and she looked at Mark with a hint of apology in her eyes before she started.

"I love Mark – and it's true what he said about us being soul mates – but I do think that Mark loves *too* much."

Mark's mouth fell open and he turned sideways in his chair to glare at her. The audience was silent.

Letitia continued. "When we first started going out I loved all the attention. He was always there on the other end of the phone, ready to cheer me up when I felt down – and he still is. But now that we live together it's sometimes claustophobic—"

"Hold on," Mark interrupted. "What do you mean 'claustrophibic'? I give you all the space you want!"

Errol jumped in before Letitia could answer. "Now, this is where communication comes in. Letitia, do you tell Mark when you feel like this?"

"Well, I try. The thing is with Mark, because he feels so strongly about me he thinks I feel exactly the same. He wants us to do everything together. If I'm going out he wants to go too; even if it's a girl's night out, he'll get his mates and turn up at the venue, like he doesn't trust me."

Mark was now sullen. He'd let go of her hand and was staring at his shoes.

"I'm a very independent person, and although I love him and want him in my life for ever, I don't necessarily want him in my life twenty-four-seven."

The audience was loving it; the women were nodding and even some of the men were whispering to their girlfriends, "You see?"

Curtis, Cheryl's boyfriend, came on next. His view was the same as Letitia's: Cheryl wanted more than he was offering, but thought she could change him or make him want her more by being the perfect woman. "And there isn't any such thing," he said.

When it was her turn to speak, Anne-Marie was ready with advice on how to exorcise relationship anxieties. "First off, never, never believe you can change someone. We are all brought up differently; each of us has our own set of values. What might make someone happy doesn't necessarily mean that, just because his partner loves him, she'll be happy in the same way.

"Cheryl argues with Curtis, even in public. Don't do it. For one thing it's unfair. Do it behind closed doors. I'm sure it's a lot of fun for people to hear how much sex you've had recently, but it's not fair on the partner, who doesn't want his or her dirty laundry aired in public. And don't make personal attacks – it makes your partner defensive and doesn't get you anywhere except deeper into an argument. Concentrate on the main point of the discussion, not on him personally; because if it's him you don't like, then what are you doing with him?"

Anne-Marie was enjoying herself. She could now tell why Errol was so confident on the screen: the whole atmosphere just gave you a high, you were on television with people listening to you. "When you bring a point up to be discussed, when you're unhappy about something, it's important to keep calm. And get to the point – don't start way in the past when it began to fester. Never let it fester anyway. Have it out while it's fresh and clear in your mind. Learn to compromise, to recognise your differences, and learn to concede that you'll never have all your needs met. Realise that your relationship is not worth wrecking over one silly disagreement.

"I'd just like to conclude by saying to Mark and Letitia, you've stayed together this long because Letitia doesn't want to hurt your feelings, Mark. She loves you, but she needs her space. Now that you know this, maybe you could give her some. It may be hard, but try asking her ocassionally, 'Do you want to… ?' 'Is it all right if… ?' Believe me, you won't lose someone who truly wants to be with you by giving them a little space."

Goldie stepped into the gym and stood just inside the doorway. Yvette stood across the room from him, watching, hands on hips, one leg stuck out to the side, foot pointed. Like a vision from the eighties, Goldie reminded her of those body-poppers from California. He was wearing a bandanna around his head, a tie-dyed jacket, and trousers so baggy that MC Hammer would have been jealous. His skin was dark, in stark contrast to his bleached-blonde hair. She couldn't see what his body looked like under all that material, but so far he had her imagination going.

"So, are you as good as your reputation?" she asked suggestively as she approached him.

He smirked, dropping his gym bag to the floor and shrugging off the cotton jacket. "Put me to the test."

Her eyes drifted over his taut chest and the sinewy skin on his muscular arms. "I intend to." She turned to the tape machine and started the instrumental tape she used for her classes.

"I brought my own music," Goldie told her.

She raised an eyebrow, but stretched her hand out for the tape none the less. A mixture of James Brown funk and hip-hop sprung forth. Behind her, Goldie had removed his track-suit bottoms so he was down to short shorts stretched over tight buttocks and a thin, athletic vest. He positioned himself balletically on the step in front of the two-way mirror.

"You ready?"

She stepped beside him, gave him a sideways look in the mirror, and said, "Okay."

"First we're gonna warm you up a little, and then a lot, until you're feeling hot, hot, hot!"

Yvette rolled her eyes as he took her through the first steps of the warm-up. They stretched thier necks, shoulders and arms. Easy stuff. Then they used the step to warm up their legs and calf muscles, keeping their arms moving up and down from the elbows.

The second stage was a little more rigorous, and before Yvette realised it they were dancing and using the step at the same time. It felt great, energetic and fun. There was bum slapping, clapping, triple sequences... Every now and then Goldie would add a "Woo!" to his instructions.

"Oh yeah! Keep it going – step off, and kick!... I know you're feeling hot now. Stay with me. I know that feels good. Let me move ya!... Oh yeah! Now we got a change coming up – you're gonna do a three-count repeater, knee up, hamstring, then a kick..."

By the end of the hour Yvette was glistening with sweat. Goldie was no different, but he certainly looked less out of breath. He mopped himself down with a towel. "That was the beginners routine. Shall we go for the advanced?"

"Are you kidding?"

Goldie put his hands on his hips and rolled his head on his neck. "I thought you were a fitness instructor."

Yvette immediately jumped up off the bench. "Bwoy, that sounds like a challenge to me. Get back up here. Give it to me."

So they went again for a second hour. This time the pace was faster, not so sequenced, and they were up and down quicker than yo-yos, arms doing windmills as their bodies twirled on and off the bench.

When they finished Yvette sunk to the floor where she stood, struggling to get her breathing back to normal, while Goldie paced the hall keeping his muscles going while he cooled down. She had had a hard time keeping up with him. She hadn't realised how much of her training she had forgotten over the years, how stale her routines had become.

"Yeah!" Yvette shouted almost like an halleljah. "I found my man! When can you start?"

She had a mischievous look in her eyes." You do date, don't you Errol?" she asked.

"Meaning do I go out with women? If so, the answer is yes. I'm just not into seeing anyone seriously at the moment." The moment it left

Errol's lips, he wondered why he had he said that. What would Yvette think of being nobody serious? Anne-Marie smiled into the telephone's handset. "I know. Listen, I enjoyed the other night so much I was wondering if we could do it again. On neutral ground this time. I'll drive." There. She had made the first step and asked Errol Wright on a date. He hesitated, and it threw her for a moment, but eventually he came through. "Fine – so long as you understand we are just friends. Where are you taking me?"

"I know the very place. We can have a chat, a drink, a little food… and the waiters are very friendly."

"Right pick me up at … say eight?"

"Great. See you then."

Errol replaced the handset and a little frown creased his forehead. He wasn't so sure this was a good idea. Picking up the phone again, he dialled Marion's phone number. After a few minutes of chit-chat, he got to the point. "Are you and Paul doing anything tomorrow night?"

"Why? You wanna borrow our place for a wild party?"

He laughed nervously. Marion was his closest female friend, but she was also a woman. Could he trust her? "I need a favour."

"I thought so," she chuckled.

"I wouldn't ask, except … I'm running out of excuses."

"Excuse me?"

He sighed. "It's Anne-Marie. She's been phoning me at least twice a day since I invited her round for dinner last week. When I told her I was tired she offered to come round, run a bath, wash my back and curl up with me… Well, now I've kinda promised to go out with her tommorow night."

"You made your bed, boy…"

Errol went silent.

Marion agreed to a double date. If it took that to get Anne-Marie off Errol's back, then it would be worth it. She had suspected there was more to the girl's intentions than simple friendship, but had he listened? No. Just like a man, he'd thought he knew what he was doing.

She put the phone down and sipped at her lukewarm coffee. Errol was a level-headed man – maybe he was working his way up to dropping her gently.

It was Friday night, and the busy wine bar in Paddington had its usual trendy crowd in. The four of them walked in together, girls first, boys following. The women went to find a table while the men bought the drinks. Anne-Marie shrugged her jacket off and hung it over the back of a chair. Marion immediately noticed the garment she wore underneath. It was the shirt she had bought for Errol last Christmas. Blue silk. What right did she think she had to wear it like some kind of prize?

"Nice shirt," she said with a smile that was almost a grin. "It looks exactly like one I bought for Errol.

Anne-Marie took the seat opposite her and smiled warmly. "*You* bought it? Well, you have good taste. Errol lent it to me." Her eyes flitted up to meet Errol's as the men came back to the table.

Marion's eyes were also on him. The look on his face confirmed that he hadn't known she'd borrowed the shirt until just now. What was she up to? Marion waited for Errol to make a scene or to pull Anne-Marie aside, but it never happened. He simply gave her a questioning look and sat down, placing the drinks on the table.

They were sitting in a quiet corner, out of the way of passers-by. Paul and Errol quickly got into a conversation about America and Americans, with Anne-Marie anxious to join in, while Marion couldn't get her mind off the fact that this woman – who was presumably Errol's "new friend" – was wearing the shirt *she'd* bought him. No – not only was she wearing it, she had *stolen* it!

"Well, let me think ... I did want to be a fireman when I was five years old," Errol was saying. Paul and he laughed, bringing Anne-Marie back to the real world. She had been daydreaming about what it would be like to be undressed by him. She was finding it difficult to concentrate on what he was saying, more interested as she was in trying to find out whether his friendliness was masking lustful intentions, rather than being simple professional courtesy. He was *so* masculine, so astonishingly attractive, so at ease with himself. He looked more like a male model than a talk-show host.

"What did you want to be?" Paul asked her.

"Oh, I ... a nurse," she laughed.

Paul smiled. "I bet you dressed up as a nurse a lot when you were a kid."

Anne-Marie smiled coyly. "How did you guess?" Then her expression became serious. "Of course, I had no idea then how far it would go. Eventually I graduated in clinical psychology, my special interest being psychopathic behaviour. That was when I began making notes for my book. I've always been interested in researching the human psyche, and so I decided that the way women's minds work was to be my first study."

"I guess being a woman helped," Errol joked, showing his attractively dimpled smile once more.

Anne-Marie wanted to run her fingers along his silky eyebrows. "I still had to interview a lot of others. I hadn't lived as much as some of them. Being in your job, you must get into so many people's minds. Don't you find that interesting?"

"I guess it is. Sometimes it can be a little scary too – you know, when we have murderers or child molesters on. You don't wanna go into those people's minds, in case it rubs off ... But then you get people on with a zest for life, like the show we did on over-fifties acting like twenty-year-olds ..."

Once Errol had started discussing his show, it was difficult to get him to talk about anything else. Anne-Marie was captivated by his enthusiasm, his clear-cut opinions, his likes and dislikes. After about twenty minutes they ordered the food. Marion had lost her appetite and Anne-Marie ordered just a salad, but the men tucked into steak, fries and side salads. It was the first time Anne-Marie had met Paul, and she liked him. Marion was being unusually quiet. But that was all academic; what she really wanted was to get Errol alone. As yet, nothing had been mentioned about their personal lives, and Anne-Marie was a little at a loss over how she could weave it into the conversation. Finally she thought of an innocuous opening line. "You seem to be putting in a lot of hours, Errol," she observed. "Whenever do you get time for a social life?"

"I'm here, aren't I?"

Paul slapped him on the back. "You can make time for drink and food, but when was the last time you were at my club?"

"I'm getting there, man. I'm making time slowly. This is just the start of my career, and I think I need to make a good impression." He shrugged his irresistible shoulders. "I can see the admiration in the eyes of the research assistants and journalists, and I know I've achieved an all but impossible task. Eventually I know I'll have time to go away on holiday, safe in the knowledge that I can still come back to a job."

"And just what kind of holiday does Errol Wright take?" Anne-Marie crooned.

He gazed shyly into his drink. "Naw, you'd laugh..."

"Oh, come on! This is me you're talking to. I want to know all about what makes you tick."

His eyes rose to meet hers, and for the first time that night Anne-Marie got the distinct feeling again that there was a spark of attraction between them. This man was ideal fantasy material, and she hungered for closer contact with him.

"You really wanna know?"

"Please."

Errol shook his head and smiled into his lager. "I want to go mountain climbing and then lock myself away in a secluded cabin somewhere." His eyes took on a faraway look. "Somewhere with lots of snow and nothing else for miles."

Paul and Marion both rolled their eyes and laughed, but Anne-Marie was watching him seriously, her eyes widening and her mouth dropping open.

This man was more man than she could have guessed. She had to have him.

"See! You're too stunned even to laugh."

"No! No. God, that is just so ... I don't know. What a perfect holiday! I mean, you cut yourself off from everything, everyone. Give yourself time to think, to recuperate and plan. Perfect... And from the lips of a man ... Well, you amaze me!" Anne-Marie could have sworn that he blushed as she stared at him adoringly.

Marion made a face and mimicked Anne-Marie's breathless voice: "... from the lips of a man... you amaze me!"

Errol – and Anne-Marie – ignored her. "Thank you," he said. "Coming from a woman, I'll take that as a compliment." And they laughed together. She wanted to reach out and touch his dimpled cheek, and had to sit on her hands to control them.

Marion kept throwing Errol glances across the table. He seemed to be enjoying himself, but he wouldn't meet her eyes. As everybody finished their meal and chattered away, having a good time, Errol's arm found its way behind Anne-Marie and rested on her chair, and every now and again her hand would drop below the table and on to his leg. Outside the restaurant, Anne-Marie said she was feeling energetic and suggested they go dancing. One of her favourite nightspots wasn't far away. Marion and Paul said they had to get back for the babysitter, quickly adding that they had enjoyed the night out. Errol was a little unsure, but after Anne-Marie challenged him there was no turning back. Marion stood and watched them hail a cab, anger at his stupidity boiling up inside her.

As soon as she was alone with Paul she let rip. What the hell did Errol think he was doing? If he didn't want anything to happen between himself and Anne-Marie, why was he playing up to her like this – straight into her hands? And why had he sat throughout the meal next to a woman who had stolen his shirt – and heaven knows what else! – when he already had a girlfriend?

"What was he supposed to do?" Paul said in his defence. "Argue with her in front of everyone?"

"Why not? I bet if it was me or you he would've. Now she's got away with that, there's no telling what she'll do! I mean, taking her out with two of his closest friends—"

"Are you jealous?"

Marion threw her hands up. "Me! Jealous!"

"Yes, you! She's a colleague, Marion. I know you and Errol are close—"

"You know perfectly well that I care about Errol like a brother. I don't want someone like her getting her claws into him."

"You're overreacting. They just enjoy each other's company. Maybe Errol's looking for a change. What is it specifically that riles you about Anne-Marie? I liked her. He could do a lot worse…"

Marion had clammed up, so Paul continued. "She's well spoken, intelligent, attractive …"

Men! They all stuck together when it came to attractive women! "Leave it, okay?" She didn't bother to mention the fact that Errol had told her he wasn't interested in Anne-Marie, then turned round and done the complete opposite. This girl was a lot more powerful than she was letting on.

By three in the morning, after spending hours on his feet in a hot, smoky atmoshere, Errol was open to any suggestions. "Why don't you come back to my place? I never did get a chance to give you that signed copy of my book."

"Well …" he began, knowing that Yvette was expecting him to go back to hers tonight.

"Oh, come on. I promise I won't bite."

Almost a challenge. Errol went along with it.

She led him into her spacious lounge. He followed numbly, having had a little too much to drink, stupidly commenting on the weather they'd been having.

"What can I get you to drink?"

"Coffee would be fine, thanks." Errol took a seat on her cream leather sofa. She smiled. She could sense his apprehension from across the room, and took it as a sign of an imminent conquest. His nervousness would make him just that little bit more vulnerable, easier to handle, more susceptible to the powder…

Errol watched her move about in the kitchen from where he sat on the sofa. Her every move was made with sinuous grace. He shook his head again at the injustice of not being able to have this woman.

"You live here alone?" he asked, for the sake of something to say. "Yes. After my mother passed away I wanted a place of my own." She removed a sachet of powder from a small metal container and carefully shook the contents into his coffee cup before pouring on hot water and stirring. Then she poured herself a glass of wine and brought the drinks into the living room. "Here. It's quite special. I hope you like it."

"Thank you. You're not having any?"

"No, I still need something a little stronger." She placed the silver tray on the coffee table and helped herself to handful of nuts. Errol sipped the coffee and repressed a shudder. It was terrible stuff. How could so sophisticated a woman have such terrible taste in coffee? No wonder she was drinking wine. Oh well, he would have to drink it to show his appreciation.

"To us," she said, holding her glass aloft.

"If you like." Errol followed her action, and was forced to take another gulp of the vile brew before placing it on the table between them. "This is nice, don't you think?"

Errol raised his eyebrows in question.

"The two of us – here, alone. Dimmed lights, jazz music, intelligent converstaion…"

"Yeah, it is nice," he said. He reached for his cup and took a swig, forgetting momentarily how awful it was. He winced, and decided to down the rest quickly without tasting it. "Why haven't you got a husband already, a boyfriend at least?" he asked as he replaced the cup on the table.

"I did … have a boyfriend, I mean – until a month ago."

"Oh?"

"I finished with him. I'd been trying to ditch him for ages. Every time I tried he would threaten suicide. Once he slit his wrists; another time he took a load of Paracetamol and sleeping pills, I caught him in time and had him pumped out. Then he drove my car into a tree – wrecking the car and the tree but walking away without a scratch. Emotional blackmail…" She sighed and shrugged. "Now I'm young, single, and available again."

Errol nodded, turning his attention to the aquarium at the other end of the room. "Seems you've been through a lot."

"I suppose so, but I'm a fighter. Always have been." She paused.

"Marion is very protective of you. Did you know that?"

"Marion?"

"Yes, she seems to think that you're delicate."

Errol laughed hollowly. Was it getting hot in here? He could feel an undefined warmth snaking through his veins and centring in his groin. He crossed his legs. "I can't think why. Ah, she might ... feel..." He stumbled a little over his words.

She finished for him. "That you need protecting?" "Well ... we do know a lot about each other..." As he spoke he was removing his jacket.

"You're warm. Maybe I should open a window."

Errol's eyes roamed over Anne-Marie's body under his shirt as she stood and crossed to the window. He took in the way her breasts pushed out the material, her nipples straining as if wanting to be noticed, the lean, flat stomach, situated just above her—

"Errol, are you okay?" He was swaying a little and undoing the top button of his shirt. "I ... I'm not sure. Maybe I could get a glass of water?"

"Of course."

It was becoming increasingly difficult for him to think of anything but sex ... sex with Anne-Marie. He wanted to touch her, to feel her skin against his, to press himself against her.

"There you go." She handed him a glass and sat beside him on the sofa. Errol gulped it straight down. Her body was so close he could smell her perfume, the wine she'd been sipping, even the soap she had used this evening. Every sense on his body seemed to have been heightened. An erection ached and strained against his trousers. Suddenly he needed to be naked.

Anne-Marie studied him, trying to control her delight. "How do you feel now?"

"Sensations ... so hot." Had he said that out loud? He couldn't be sure.

"I think maybe you've had too much to drink," she said lightly.

Legs tightening around his waist... shivering... beautiful, bobbing breasts... "Why, Errol, I'm surprised at you!"

He barely heard her as he reached for her, his senses on fire. He slipped a hand under the shirt, *his* shirt, and touched her shoulder, squeezing the warm flesh. "You... *do* something to me..." Her skin was as smooth as he had imagined it. Leaning forward, he grabbed her and drew her closer. Gently, tentatively, he touched his mouth to her neck. His lips felt hot, tingling, but numb. His breath was warm against her skin. She sighed deeply. Hadn't she dreamed of this very moment over and over again, ever since she had first met him? "Errol, are you sure you know what you're doing?"she said.

He was beyond listening, beyond caring. Swiftly he caught her in his arms, stood up and pressed her against the length of his body. Restless, impatient hands roamed all over her body, her throat, her arms, her breasts her back and buttocks. Anne-Marie couldn't believe how good it felt. This was one of her night-time fantasies come true. She warmed to his touch, becoming loose and pliant under his fingers. She knew it was just the effect of the powerful aphrodisiac, but why not enjoy it? One of his hands was tracing a pattern through the silk of his own shirt, glancing off her nipples, moving slowly down to her belly, while his other raised her short skirt, found her thighs and then her crotch, teasing the flesh there until it quivered.

Errol dimly realised he was out of control, but he was beyond turning back. It was as though his life depended on seeing this through to its climax. His mouth hungrily nibbled an earlobe, then he traced the outline of her ear with his tongue, his pelvis thrusting against her groin, mimicking penetration. She followed the motion, rubbing herself against the massive bulk of his erection...

Until suddenly he pulled back. Summoning the last pieces of his flagging self-control, he looked directly into her eyes. To Anne-Marie his eyes looked glittery, unfocused, almost as if he were looking though her. The warmth of her arousal was chilled a little from the look he gave her. This wasn't the Errol she knew. It was as if some devilish, dangerous stranger had taken over. But she told herself it was just the drug. She forced his head back towards hers, mouth opem, waiting for the touch of his lips. And he responded again, bruising her mouth with his urgency, forcing his tongue around hers as though he was dying for the breath from her body.

She was aching all over now, a liquid ache that throbbed between her legs. She gasped for breath. "Errol, I'm—" "Now!" he growled, cutting off her words. "I need you *now!*" Her shirt and skirt were loosened it seemed in one movement, and she let them fall to the floor. Instantly his mouth was on her breasts. She held his head to her as he suckled like a hungry infant, breathing heavily. She groaned with the jolts of electricity coursing through her, the pressure in her groin now close to pain.

His hands were rough as he tugged at her skimpy panties and threw them aside, the expression on his face intense as he threw her body on to the sofa and stood above her, throwing off the clothes that had hindered his release.

Anne-Marie was now powerless to slow him. As he climbed on top of her she arched towards him, the heat of his skin welcome after the cool friction of silk and linen. He found her wet and ready as he drove into her without hesitation. He was massive, almost too big; she could feel him in her belly, filling her lungs, her thoat.

Harder and harder, deeper and deeper, his rhythm was powerful and relentless. While she squirmed and bucked under him, her nails clawing his back and shoulders, she felt herself rushing towards orgasm. Suddenly he stopped again. His head was buried in her neck, his breathing was erratic.

"God, we were so close," she whispered. "Not finished yet, big boy…" She slid from under him and rolled him on to his back. Now it was her turn. "I'm in control now, Errol…" She climbed astride his supine body. "And I'm going to drive you over the edge."

She closed her eyes and pushed against him. Errol groaned as she impaled herself on to his shaft, his groping hands clamped on to her breats.

"Oh, Errol. Errol…" Within moments she was arching her back as she began to quiver with the first tremors of an orgasm. So she increased her pace until she was bouncing furiously, impatient for the climax she could feel rippling through her.

Errol's hands moved to grasp her firmly by the the hips and he matched her rhythm with his own, thrusting upwards to her every plunge. Finally she sank down on to him with her full weight, and with his hot, thick length buried deep inside her she came in a flood, spasming and shaking. He felt her throb and tighten around him, and it sent him spiralling over the edge in a dark frenzy. With a cry he shot into her, spurting out his warm fluid in great jerks before collapsing and falling into unconsciousness.

Anne-Marie sighed contentedly, the aftershocks of the orgasm still shuddering through her. She lay perfectly still for several minutes before she opened her eyes to look at him. "Errol? Errol, honey?" Even in sleep he was irresistible. She placed a kiss on his mouth before slipping off his limp body. She bent to retrieve the garments he'd tossed to the floor in haste. As she picked up his jacket his wallet fell to the floor. She picked it up and flicked it open. Inside was a picture of a little boy, about six years old, she guessed: his son. She scanned the other pieces of his personal property, committing certain items to memory before returning them to his pockets.

She neatly layed out his clothes on the seat, then fetched a pillow and a sheet from the airing cupboard in the hallway, making him comfortable before retiring to her bedroom.

The next morning she woke to find herself alone. On the coffee table was a hastily scribbled note: "I'll call you. Errol."

He had made some mistakes in his life, but sleeping with Anne-Marie would probably be his stupidest. He worked with her, she was his best friend's ex, she was an acquaintance of Marion, his best female friend... All the way home Errol scolded himself. How could he have let this happen? If there was one thing he knew, it was that he would make it up to her – somehow... but at the same time he would have to make it clear that it would never happen again, and that nobody was to know about it.

He had woken up aching all over and with a splitting headache. Disorientated, he'd had no idea where he was until a faint memory of a date with Anne-Marie Simms had come to him. Lifting the duvet, he'd found himself naked. Slowly he'd got up and realised what must have happened. In less than five minutes he had dressed himself, quickly scribbled a note and left, closing the door noiselessly behind him.

When he got home he headed straight for the kitchen and made himself a cup of strong coffee. He sat at the table clutching the mug, trying to remember what had happened – but even after the coffee everything seemed a blur. No wonder she'd left him on the sofa. Shit – he hadn't even taken her into the bedroom! They'd done it right there, on the sofa. He could still smell her on him. He had to wash all traces of the night away. He felt ashamed, embarrassed by his actions. It just wasn't like him.

Standing under the shower, he heard the phone ring. The answering machine was on. He wasn't expecting any important calls today. Later he would have to go and pick up Aaron for the weekend. Maybe he could forget all about this incident in the company of his son. Maybe he could postpone it all until Monday morning... when she came in to work.

After his shower he fell across the bed and closed his eyes. The phone rang again. This time he picked it up without thinking.

"What happened? I woke up and you weren't there."

"I'm sorry ... I didn't want to wake you. We had a very late night..."

"And wasn't it worth it?" He could hear the smile in Anne-Marie's voice. "I don't know. I can't remember much after we got back to your place. I'm sorry... Boy, I didn't realise how much I drank! And... er, what happpened shouldn't have. You know I try not to mix business with pleasure..."

More answers to questions not asked. She knew it, and ignored it. He was *there*. Here. His voice was putting the image of him in front of her. "We were great last night. It's this morning that's the problem."

"This morning I wasn't thinking clearly. I apologise for the way it looked—"

"Why do you keep saying sorry? Are you trying to say it was all a mistake?"

"Anne... Anne-Marie, I don't know what to say ..." He transferred the phone to his other ear.

"You could say that you enjoyed it too and want to do it again."

"I think we should meet and talk about this... But I can't this weekend. How about I call you tomorrow night?"

He couldn't see it, but Anne-Marie was grinning. "Okay. I'll talk to you tomorrow."

Errol held the handset to his chest and breathed out deeply. He couldn't see Anne-Marie again because he was seeing Yvette... In fact, he was seeing her tonight... How was he going to face her? Should he tell her? Get it out of the way and let her decide whether she wanted to go on? It wasn't as though they were engaged... Holy shit, what had he done?

Karen shut the bedroom door and placed the tray on the desk by the window. Yvette was stretched out on her double bed, watching the television. Karen handed her a drink, then reached for her cigarettes. "I know you're only watching this for that black surfer guy..."

The programme was *Sunset Beach*, and Yvette tried to catch it whenever she had a chance. On Saturdays they broadcast the whole week's shows in one long omnibus. "He's a lifeguard. And no, I don't need to ogle a fictitious man – I've got one of my own—"

"Please! You've got *half* a man..."

"Don't start on me, Karen."

"What – reality too much for you? I seem to remember a ceratin woman calling me and cussing the man she's sleeping with because he won't talk commitment."

Yvette's eyes stayed on the televison. "It's not easy, Kaz..."

"Why not? You have a mouth, don't you? If he won't bring it up, then *you* do it." Karen dropped heavily on to the bed beside Yvette, spilling a little of her drink.

Yvette kissed her teeth. "Has it ever occurred to you that this was *your* idea? We could be making a mistake. Okay, we've been seeing each other long enough, but we've never spent any kind of time together. Living together... it's a big step."

"Is that what *he* said?"

"No! You don't know him like I do. Errol has a way with words. He always manages to say the right thing – we talk, and then it isn't until after he's gone that I realise I didn't get the answer I wanted. I don't know how he does it..."

"Actions speak louder than words. Don't let him get away with it. As soon as you realise he's wormed his way out of an argument, pull him up on it."

Yvette sat up on the bed and threw her extensions off her shoulders. "Let me give you an example. The other night, when I asked him why he never takes me to any of his functions at work but has escorts arranged by the studio instead, he says..." and Yvette put on Errol's voice: "'Baby, you wouldn't enjoy those things... A lot of air kissing, hoity-toity luvvie darlings patronising you and then forgetting you once they find out you're not in the business. Besides, you'd be too distracting for me...'"

Karen shrieked with laughter, rocking back and forth on the bed. "I love that bit on the end! Boy, he's slick!"

"You see what I mean, though."

"Okay... Let's do a role-play! I'll be you..."

"*What?*"

"Humour me." Karen sat up straight and threw imaginary extensions over her shoulder. She cleared her throat and put on Yvette's assertive voice: "'Now, Errol, you remember a couple of weeks ago I asked you if you would buy a house with me...?'"

"'Aah.'" Yvette slipped swiftly into character. "'Yes... yes I do...'"

"'Are you still interested?'"

"'Of course, baby. I mean, we have to talk about it sometime. I'll have to come see the place. Of course, I'll have my own place to sort out...'"

"'How about we view the house tomorrow?'"

"'Tomorrow? Oh, I have work tomorrow.'"

"'In the evening,'" Karen pressed, still in character.

"'I'd rather see the place in the day... Does it need any work?'"

"'Some...'" Karen was beginning to crack.

"'That will mean decorators, estimates... We have plenty of time.'"

Unable to keep it up any longer, Karen laughed. "I see what you mean! So... I suggest we plan it out now."

"Plan what?"

Karen hopped off the bed and came back with a pen and pad. "What questions you're gonna ask him: when he's free to view the place, what date… Then all you have to do is make sure he keeps it. If you decide to go ahead, get him to put his place on the market a.s.a.p. Go with him if necessary—"

Yvette laughed. "You don't think that's being just a little pushy?"

"No! He's had time, Yvette. If he cares for you at all he'll give it a go."

Yvette sighed. Karen was always right. Why couldn't she always be there to hold her hand? They would certainly get through this mess a lot more quickly.

To be, or not to be, that was the question.

Errol grabbed a trolley and strolled into Sainsbury's in his 'regular Joe' disguise: black track-suit bottoms, cream sweater, expensive trainers, baseball cap turned backwards and sunglasses. He would be picking up Aaron later, and wanted to make sure he had all his son's favourites in. Usually he would leave a list for Helen or Mrs Stewart, but occasionally he took a perverse pleasure in walking among his viewers without being recognised.

Besides, he needed time to think. He had a decision to make – a decision that would affect not just his own life but those of a woman and her son as well. He didn't want to lose Yvette. He realised she meant a lot more to him than he'd ever let on. She was more than a lover, more than a friend. And Tyrone was like a younger brother to him; he often came to him for advice. Errol had gotten used to being with them, to them being part of his life. He needed that constancy, that stability. It grounded him, helped him to stay normal.

He wished there was a way he could find out if it would work before moving in with them. After all, he'd already made mistakes in his life – Anne-Marie, for one. He'd never stayed with Yvette longer than a night, leaving early in the morning, making sure that no attachments were made. Now, all of a sudden, they were supposed to become a full-time family, bound by the commitment of buying property.

Not only that, but being a full time father… He wasn't even that to his own son! Every time he'd spoken to Yvette over the past few days he'd avoided talking about the house. Sometimes he was sure he could feel her wanting to bring the subject up, wanting *him* to bring the subject up. But he wouldn't. Maybe she'd get the message from his apprehension; maybe she'd have second thoughts and go ahead on her own. But if she did that, would she still want him, knowing that he found it hard to make big decisions? Would she see that, in the long run, he was probably doing her favour? After all, he had a past history – Tanya and their son – she would have to take that on. And heaven knows how Tanya would take the news that every time he took Aaron it was to stay with another mother figure. His career wasn't exactly stable either. The show could be cut at any time, leaving him redundant... Now a new thought occured to him. He was well known all over the country. Women wanted him, temptation lay on every corner. If he chose to, he could forget about Yvette altogether, date a socialite instead... Hell, he could marry one and be made for life!

But would anyone else be able to make him feel the way Yvette did? He realised that, if he said no to her now, he could lose her for ever. Finished!

She had turned a corner in her life. She was ready to move upwards, and she wanted to take him with her. He should feel honoured. She was looking for long-term commitment. Could he, Errol Wright, give it to her? The only thing he'd been committed to over the past few years had been his own career.

And could she cope as a celebrity wife? She was a working-class girl from Streatham. Okay, so she was also a business women. But that didn't prepare her for being photographed and hounded...

As Errol queued at the checkout, he knew he had been making excuses. This matter could be resolved only if he talked to Yvette about it. Talked to her, that is, without hurting her feelings – one thing he didn't want to do was hurt her feelings.

Errol reversed the car into the only parking space on the narrow street. Only five doors away from her house tonight. There had been times when he'd had to walk back two streets or risk getting a ticket.

The house was lit up, as if it were warding off evil spirits, the lights shining on to the dark street from the windows upstairs and downstairs. Didn't she realise electricity costs money? There were only the two of them in there. He supposed she'd be asking him to pay for it in extra maintenance. Ever since the show had taken off she'd expected more money; all of a sudden things had needed replacing and Aaron had started growing a lot more quickly.

He rang the bell to the right of the newly painted front door. He could see a distorted image of his face in the gloss. More money. Not that Errol begrudged giving to his son – it was *her*. Tanya knew nothing about money except how to take it and hand it to a hairdresser, or a boutique or a furniture retailer.

The door was answered by an extremely attractive fair-skinned woman, dressed in a figure-hugging body suit and ski pants. Her long, jet-black hair was pulled back into a ponytail. She had a face that needed no make-up and a figure that needed no exercise. Tanya had men begging for her attention, and she knew just how to play them. She'd had Errol eating out of her hands... until his money had started to mean more to her than he did. Then, suddenly, her spell had broken and he had seen her for who she really was.

"On time – for a change." She turned her back on him and sashayed down the hallway.

Errol entered his ex-home and closed the door behind him. The hall carpet was pathed with see-through plastic walkways, an effort to prolong the life-span of the expensive carpet.

"Is Aaron ready?"

"He's getting changed." Tanya entered the living room. "Don't forget to take your shoes off before coming in here."

"I won't come in." Errol stood uncomfortably in the doorway, glancing around the room. Nothing new caught his eye. This made a change – over the past six months the whole room had been altered beyond recognition. Tanya had gone for the art deco look – and an interior decorator friend of hers had designed the layout: uplighter lamps, obscure prints, unusually shaped shelving. Now the room looked like an ad for Ikea. The suite was made entirely of pine and leather. The floor, which had been concrete and carpet before, was now a polished wooden expanse with expensive rugs strategically placed to give warmth. The television was a massive screen built into its own cabinet. Exotic plants stood sentry-like each side of the patio doors, which Yvette had had built in to open out to the garden. "Looking for anything in particular?" Her tone was frosty.

Errol threw her an annoyed gaze. "Just looking at the luxury I'm helping you live in."

She immediately went on the defensive, her big Spanish eyes catching fire. "I work too, you know..."

"Yeah, but a shop assistant's salary wouldn't pay for all this in six months."

"All you have to worry about, Mister Superstar, is that your son is being fed and clothed properly. He's getting everything he needs."

"I suppose he's banned from this room now. Am I right?"

Tanya stepped forward, hands on hips, and started him straight in the eyes. "He has his own TV, right? His own room. And we have a dining room." She poked a finger at him, her black eyes flashing. "So don't come into my house trying to make me feel bad about having something for myself, right?" "Who said I was trying to make you feel bad? I just wanted to see how my son lives. You've been squeezing me for cash, and all I can see it going on is this house..."

"This house, in case you'd forgotten, is where your son lives! I ain't spending it on nothing he ain't sharing! Ask 'im yourself – anything he wants he gets... And d'you think dat does 'im any good?" she screamed.

"What you raising your voice for? I'm not arguing with you. Unless you've got a guilty conscience, we've got nothing to argue about any more."

Tanya's mouth opened thcn shut again, as if she'd been about to counter-attack and changed her mind.

Errol turned away to see his son at the top of the staircase in his baseball cap and his yellow denim outfit.

"All right, son?"

"Yeah, Dad." Aaron looked past his father at his mum, then back to his dad again. "Are we going out?"

"Course – like always. Your granny wants us to call her..."

Tanya's mouth drew into a tight line at the mention of Errol's mother. She turned and headed for her easy chair in front of the TV. Aaron skipped down the stairs to stand next to his father, his rucksack hanging from one shoulder. "I'm going then, Mum," he said. He knew he couldn't cross the threshold of the living room in his shoes, so he waited for her attention.

She got up and bent down in front of his him. "Bye, baby. Have a good time, yeah?"

Aaron was already heading for the door. "All right, Mum." Errol turned to Tanya. "We'll be back around eight tomorrow."

"No later, Errol. Remember—"

"He has school on Monday – I know that."

Again the hostile air. Every fortnight it was the same thing. Whenever he took Aaron on a Sunday she reminded him that the boy had school the next day – as if he didn't know. What was her problem? Whatever it was, it had stood in the way of Errol making Yvette his wife. They'd had everything; they'd been a stunning couple, meant for each other physically. It must have been the physical attraction that had made it last seven years. But Tanya didn't know the meaning of compromise. Whatever she had wanted, she'd had to get. And she was always right.

He'd had to tell her he loved her, but she hadn't had to say it because she'd shown him by giving birth to his son. No wonder he was unsure about getting into another relationship.

Errol was already seated at the table when Yvette walked in. She was wearing a short black dress, and a choker with three rows of mock pearls adorned her long, graceful neck. Her two-tone hair extensions were piled loosely on her head. The look was simple but highly effective, and heads turned as she crossed the floor to join him.

Errol stood, a wide smile on his face. "You look good enough to eat," he whispered in her ear as he kissed her cheek.

"Yeah, well you don't look too bad yourself – but then you can afford to."

Errol grinned, pulling out her chair for her before resuming his own. "I've been thinking about you all day."

Yvette indulged him. "And I bet I know what those thoughts were."

"Actually, you're wrong."

"You mean you *weren't* thinking of my body?"

Errol smirked. "Well, you know – that as well. But mostly I thought just of you being you." He was telling the truth. Ever since the call from Anne-Marie and the realisation of what he had done, he could think of nothing else but being with Yvette. He'd felt an incredible urge to talk to his mother, and had called the USA and spoken to her just before she left for work. She'd sounded so good that it brought home how much he missed her, how much he missed having a woman in his life who cared about him, cared for him. His mother was a very young looking fifty-year-old, in the league of Shirley Bassey or Diana Ross. He realised now, as he looked over at Yvette, that she and his mother were the fittest women he knew.

She spread a napkin on her lap and picked up the menu. "It's a coincidence, but I was thinking about you too," she said from behind the raised card.

"You can't look me in the eyes and say that?"

Yvette met his gaze and held it. "I've been thinking about you too."

He smiled. God, she was so sexy. He signalled the waiter. "Let's eat."

Yvette ordered steak with two different salads and fries. Tonight she felt she could eat everything in sight, but being the lady she was she controlled her appetite. "So, do we have the whole evening to ourselves?" Errol asked.

"Mm-hm." Yvette had dived into her salad the moment the waiter had put it on the table, and she answered through a mouthful of food. "Now we just have to decide what to do with it."

"I've missed you, Eve."

She looked up at him, licking her lips, but said nothing. Secretly she was extremely pleased. Errol rarely said anything that gave her a clue about how he felt about her; it had always been a meeting of bodies, not minds. This approach was new, and she found it quite exciting...

"I want to devour you." He rubbed her leg under the table. "This is what I'm hungry for."

But this was more like it. She put her fork down and picked up her glass of wine. She could feel the ache between her legs instantly. "You sex maniac. You'll have us arrested."

"Handcuffs and uniforms... That might be fun," he said, his eyes dancing, his voice low and seductive.

Yvette laughed. "You should be ashamed of yourself."

"The only thing I'd be ashamed of would be not pleasing you."

Yvette slipped her shoe off and found his crotch with her toes. "Don't worry. I'm pleased. You've just bought me steak, and later I'm gonna have some more meat, hopefully ..." She lowered her voice. "... deep inside me."

The waiter approached their table again. "Everything fine?"

Yvette straightened up in her seat self consciously. "Yes... yes, very good." Behind the waiter's back, they giggled like schoolkids.

"He knew what you were up to."

"You think so?"

"Yes, and I bet he's as jealous as hell – just like all the other men in here."

"You're too much!" she laughed through a mouthful of food.

"How about testing me right here, under the table? We could put on a dinner show, give these people some entertainment..."

"Just let me eat this and you can give me a private showing," she said quickly.

They passed the rest of the meal almost in silence, each knowing exactly what they wanted to do to the other, then they left the restaurant in something of a hurry.

Errol's house never ceased to surprise Yvette. It was filled with expensive furnishings and unusual antiques that she would not have expected a bachelor to own. In the living room, the overstuffed leather two-seater sofa and its two armchairs were surrounded by sculptures and art objects, every item in its place. In the centre of the room was a glass table, four sculpted marble mermaids forming its legs. He'd told her the piece had cost him two and a half thousand pounds. He kept the place immaculately tidy. No glass stood around without a coaster, no dirty dishes were heaped in the sink, no unmade beds, no towels tossed on the floor...

As soon as they arived, Errol bustled about creating the mood. He lit a fire in the fireplce and went to open a bottle of wine. Yvette yawned as he re-entered the room. "Didn't know I was away that long. You need some sleep?"

She kissed him as he sat beside her, tasting the wine on his lips. "You're what I need."

"Oh really?" he said, massaging her back through her dress. He loved a woman with a strong back. "You feel so good," he said into her neck. Gently he pulled the neckline of her dress down until her shoulders were exposed. Then he kissed each one and ran a finger along her collarbone. "I love this body: your skin, your bone structure, your nose..." He kissed her nose, then her lips. "Your mouth..."

Yvette moaned and leaned back, letting him work on her. She hadn't worn a bra, and soon she was nude from the waist up, the fire's warmth against her back. She fumbled with the buttons on his shirt, so excited she couldn't open them fast enough. They stared at each other in the dim light of the fire, then stepped closer until their chests were pressed together.

"Beautiful breasts," Errol said, reaching to take one nipple in his mouth while his hand roamed over the other. And in one easy moment they were on the plush carpet, her dress tossed aside, leaving her in her navy-blue g-string. Errol had bought her underwear before; he loved watching her parade about in silk slips and panties that always left something to the imagination. Now he ran his eyes over her body. "Beautiful," he said again.

She lay on her back as his hands roamed, her eyes closed, listening to the fire crackle a few feet away, the wine heightening her senses, loosening her reserve. A handsome, exciting man was making love to her, and nothing else mattered. As he spread her legs and bent his head between them her whole body tensed, knowing what was coming and preparing to be taken to the heights of pleasure. He held her in place with his arms, and her body responded, arching up to meet the downward strokes of his tongue. After a minute of his caresses she felt she couldn't take any more, so close was she to an orgasm. She tried to pull him on top of her but he resisted.

"I wanna do you like you've never been done."

The pleasure was overwhelming, building deep inside her body. She was out of control, powerless, high, and yet ecstatically aware.

"I need to feel you inside me. Please, Errol..." she begged.

Finally he came up for air and stretched out on the floor next to her. Instantly she was upon him.

"Ride me," he said hoarsely, his eyes filled with lust.

She let him plunge deep inside her, his hands gripping her buttocks, forcing her to rock with him. Her inner muscles were spasming, gripping him tightly then releasing him, over and over again. She would rise, so that they were nearly disconnected, then push back down and backwards, arching her body, making him gasp aloud. His hands flitted over her nipples, then moved down to her hips, her flat, hard stomach, and finally found her clitoris.

"Oh, God. Oh, man..." she cried out, riding him fast and hard, their bodies wet with perspiration. "I love you..." As the tidal wave of her first orgasm washed over her she collapsed on his chest, spent. He rolled over with her, still connected, brought her legs up and draped them over his shoulders, plunging inside her again and again. His eyes were shut, engrossed as he was in the power of the moment. His breathing came in shorts pants as he finally climaxed, body trembling, gripping her arms as he slowed, lowering himself, still moving inside her but gently now, back and forth... until at last he stopped.

They lay quite still for a time as their breathing slowed. Then Yvette gently eased herself from under him. He rolled on to his side, facing her. "You sapped me, girl. Don't think you're getting any more out of me tonight.'

Yvette laughed, cuddling up closer. "Old age catching up with you?"

"So I'm getting old. Leave me alone."

She laid her head in the crook between his shoulder and his neck. "Errol, you remember I said I was looking for a house?"

"Mmm." He stroked the back of her head.

"What would you say to buying it together? I've found a place, and it's beautiful – perfect. For us. And Tyrone. And even Aaron would love it when he comes to stay. So... what do you think?"

Errol was on the brink of sleep. "Sounds nice..." He sounded far away. "Are you in, then?"

"Whatever makes you happy."

"You want to live with me?"

"Who wouldn't?" He kissed her forehead and drew her closer. "We'll talk about it later."

Yvette grinned in the dark. He was going to be hers. They were going to be a family. She sighed, taking the scent of thier lovemaking deep into her lungs.

She was thirty, and had been in control of her life now for two years. Her previous existence had been one of prescription and routine. The most important rule then was "Take your time". But now she was a woman of thought, a woman of shrewd premeditation – you don't earn a degree in psychology by being emotional. One thing that had got her through therapy was finding the ability to start viewing humans as specimens again, a species to be studied.

Over the two trouble-free years she had befriended many men. But she had come to the conclusion that it was only when she was with other people that she got hurt. She knew she was better off staying alone, staying free. Deep down, though, she needed company, the warmth of a fellow human being. Which is where Errol Wright came in. She knew if anyone could heal her completely it would be him. But she needed him to fall for her too.

Anne-Marie Simms stood up in the bath and held out her hands in front of her, palms up. The scars on her wrists and forearms criss-crossed each other; some had been deep cuts while others were merely scratches, probably from her own fingernails, although it was hard to tell the difference. The marks were no more apparent now than thin stretch-marks. Her self-mutilation had been the only way she could think of dealing with the lack of attention she'd recieved from her parents. Cutting her arms had made them notice her. Errol, she knew, felt the same. His mother and father had been far too busy to devote any time to him. She wondered how he had dealt with it.

Sometimes, when she sat down and thought about her past, she wondered if she had subconsciously invited the bullies to pick on her at school. Had they really wanted to hurt her, or had she deliberately made herself different, distant and unfriendly, to provoke them? It had certainly got her attention. Painful memories.

Her training had taught her that girls were usually closer to their fathers than their mothers, that female teenagers would often leave home rather than stay in the same house as another woman. But it hadn't been like that for her. Daddy had always been there, but for all the attention he'd given her he might as well have been a visiting distant relative. He'd never acted as though he had anything to do with her creation, never taken the time to find out what was happening in her life, was never proud when she brought him things she had made – drawings, models, baking… He would just put them aside with a nod.

Trying to please Daddy had not been easy. Anne-Marie realised there must have been a deep sadness inside him. She had thought when she was about ten that his resentment stemmed from the fact that he'd wanted a boy child, and so she'd tried to be that little boy, dressing in track suits her mother hated and occasionally getting him to take her to the park with a football. Moments like these were rare, but she always remembered them as the happiest. They would kick the ball around and laugh and cheer when one of them got a goal. Sometimes she'd get carried away and run up to him and he would lift her in the air; she'd try to hug and kiss him, to show her love, and that would be when he'd tell her to put her things away and take her back home. Daddy left the house around her twelfth birhday and never came back. Anne-Marie blamed her mother at first, and then herself for not being a child any more. She was developing a woman's body by then, and Daddy had always been telling her to cover herself up. She had begun hurting herself soon after that. Men had been leaving her ever since.

But this time, with this man, she would not lose control. This time there would be no unconscious, reckless action. She had set out to get Errol Wright, she had had him, and she was going to keep him.

It was another weekend. God, how she hated weekends! Saturday night. Couples would be going out together, holding hands, laughing, being close, then going home and getting into bed together, making love… And where would she be? At home in her tiny flat, in front of the television, alone.

There was a note from Marion tacked to Errol's dressing-room door when he came into work: "Congratulations – you passed me in the ratings once, now watch your back!" He sighed contentedly. Everything seemed to be working out… Well, that wasn't quite true: everything except his private life. Apart from the little problem of his infidelity, he was a success.

Another bunch of roses sat on the dresser. This time he knew who they were from, and he was not amused. The note said, "You're mine. What was meant to be can't be undone." After the morning's recorded interview, Errol left the studio hurriedly. He was pacing through the foyer with his head down when the voice that he had been dreading all day called out from somewhere above him.

"Errol! Errol!" Anne-Marie ran down the stairs. He turned slowly to face her and forced something resembling a smile on to his lips. "Anne-Marie ..."

"I waited for your call," she whispered, looking around as though they were being watched.

"I'm sorry..." He shook his head, touching his temple. "I had my son until late, and when I got home I just crashed out. I never got—"

"I just want to know where I stand."

"I don't know what to say... It shouldn't have happened—"

"You're all the same, aren't you?" she hissed.

"Now don't try to put that one over on me. I never once tried to seduce you before—"

"And why not? Wasn't I good enough?"

"You are one of the most sensual creatures I know, but..."

She put a hand on her hip and tapped her foot impatiently. "I knew there'd be a 'but'."

"You know my lifestyle... I've been trying to avoid this happening for nearly a year." He was pleading with his eyes for her to let it drop.

"Can we go somewhere and talk?"

Errol looked at his watch. Maybe they should get it all out now. "Okay, I've got a few minutes." He led the way. Anne-Marie followed, her heels clacking on the pavement. He found a deserted wine bar and selected a table far enough away from the ears of anyone passing, where he sat and clasped his hands on the table in front of him. Anne-Marie sat opposite him, smiling. She shrugged off her coat. "It's really good seeing you again. I missed you."

Errol opened his mouth to speak but clamped it shut again. He ran a hand over his shaved head nervously, feeling light perspiration at his temples.

"We should start again." She was still smiling. "How are you?"

"I'm fine. You know, the usual... busy."

"I always said you worked too hard." She touched his hand with warm fingers and he drew away as if she'd stung him.

"Look, Anne-Marie, We can't see each other like this," he blurted out.

"Like what?"

"I don't know. What happened the other night... Maybe it was too much drink, maybe it was a mixture of the mood and the drink, I don't know. But what I do know is that I can't have a relationship with you."

Anne-Marie visibly bristled and sat up in her chair, her eyebrows drawing together. "It's *me* you don't want, not just any woman. Is that what you're saying?"

"Not exactly, no. I like you, I have since I first met you... I'm just not ready for something so intense with someone so close to home." He thought about another way to put it. "Relationships are just too much hard work right now."

"Ours wouldn't be, Errol. I *more* than like you. In fact, I think I love you..." He shook his head disbelievingly. In love? She was smiling again, and he recalled briefly how he had been unable to drag himself away from that smile. "You can't be. You haven't known me very long."

"Errol," she said, slowly, as if to a child, "time is irrelevant. This is an emotion, a feeling beyond our control. You know I can't sleep at nights, wondering who you're with, what you're doing. I want to be with you..."

"I'm sorry. I don't feel the same way." He wanted to tell her he was already seeing someone, but he knew she wouldn't believe him. He'd already said he was single and free. Besides, wouldn't that make him not only a liar but a cheat as well? "I don't see the point in pretending to save your feelings. This simply isn't going to happen."

"Oh, but it already has..."

"What?"

"You may not remember the other night, but I do. You wanted me then. You came on to me, in fact; I think I've still got the bite-marks. You took advantage of my feelings..."

"Feelings?"

"Don't try and tell me you didn't know how I felt. I'm not a cardboard cut-out with a stone heart, Errol. You knew what you were doing."

"*Knew*? I don't even remember touching you."

Anne-Marie let her head drop, making her appear suddenly smaller. She spoke in a quiet, moody tone, as though chastising herself. "This is getting ugly. I didn't mean for this to happen. I only have myself to blame. I have this habit of going for men that are unavailable..."

He wrinkled his brow, thrown off guard by the sudden change.

She stood up. "So, a sexual relationship is out. Can we be friends?"

He lowered his eyes. "I don't know. The way you feel, I think it would be better to have a clean break."

"You know that's impossible," she said, throwing her coat over her arm.

Errol jumped up and faced her. "Impossible? Have I no right to my own life now?"

She smiled, and spoke calmly. "I meant – we work together."

"Oh! Oh, I see what you mean... Well," he regained some of his earlier resolve, "we'll just stay out of each other's way then. Okay?"

"Whatever you say, Errol. I must be going. I'm supposed to be in the library."

"Acquaintances?"

"Yeah."

She held out her hand and he shook it. Then she stepped closer and threw her arms around him, embracing him. "I knew you were a bigger man than most," she whispered.

Then she walked away, leaving him standing there, dumbfounded.

Yvette had woken early – Errol was still snoring gently – and had decided to have a quick work-out in her mini gym to start the day. She was half-way through her cool-down when he came in, scratching his head.

"What's wrong with you?" he said. "You need to burn energy, why didn't you wake me?"

She grinned. "Why don't you join me?" "You know, I haven't had a better offer all day." In seconds he was stripped down to his underwear and on top of her. She pushed him off. "I think you've got to cool down, boy. You know what they say about a good exercise routine."

"No, what?"

"You should always warm up first and cool down after."

"What about the middle bit?"

She smiled seductively. "Let's get dressed and go for a walk – we'll discuss it."

Errol was used to Yvette's intrigue and unpredictability. It was one of the biggest attractions of her personality. He never knew what lay around the corner. He pulled his track suit back on and Yvette dressed in a long skirt. They took the short-cut up to the park, laughing and sharing experiences and memories as they walked. It was still very early, and the lack of people around made them feel as though they had the streets to themselves. Yvette bent forwards from the waist at one point, trying to entice a squirrel to take a cashew nut from her fingers. Beneath her skirt Errol could see the smooth outline of her deliciously perfect buttocks, ripely inviting, made for his hands, and he knew he was ready to accept her challenge. "Well? Do you want to?"

His hard-on pulsed and pushed for escape. "What – here?"

"Yes, here. Now do you want me or not?"

Did he want her? There was smoke coming out of his ears! He wasted no time in showing her how much. He reached out for her and pulled her, half laughing, half protesting, through the taller shrubs and greenery that surrounded the rose garden, running his hands up her thighs to to her naked buttocks as they went.

"You've got no panties on!"

"Oh!" she said in mock astonishment. "Was I going to need them?"

"You could get arrested for going around without them." He drew her close and pressed her mound against his thickening erection.

"You could get arrested for carrying such a lethal weapon – but I won't tell if you won't," she giggled. Helping him to drop his trousers, she eased them over his buttocks and his erection sprang forth. She turned her back to him so he had a clear view of the tight, dark globes that had been inviting him all morning, placed her palms against a tree trunk, and splayed her legs. His penis throbbed with anticipation as he eased it steadily into her vagina, where she was wet, warm and ready for him.

Brockwell Park was unusually quiet at this time of day. Except for the couple making love in the shrubbery and the ocassional dog walker and the squirrels, the only other person braving the chilly morning air was the woman in the trenchcoat and dark glasses. Twenty minutes previously she had been sitting in her car outside the woman's house, to which she had followed Errol the night before. She had dozed on and off through the night, but had been awake for two hours when at seven o'clock the front door had opened and the woman had come out. Errol had followed her, and they'd linked arms and made off up the road. After they had passed, their observer had considered following them in the car, but thought it too conspicuous, so she'd left the car and followed them on foot, down Acre Lane to central Brixton.

She stopped beneath a low sycamore tree and wiped her dark glasses on her coat, scanning the park and the path she had just come down. There was nothing. Up here even the traffic was barely audible.

The couple had turned a corner ahead of her and the trees had appeared to close behind them. An illusion, a trick of the curving path. She quickened her step, but walked with caution as she didn't want to come face to face with them.

Suddenly there was a squeal from the slope to her right and she stopped again, cocked her head and waited. Now all she could hear was the rustling of the leaves and the roar of a bus on the distant street. She took another step and there was more noise: a thrashing of branches and then a whispered conversation, none of it loud enough for her to hear what they were saying.

She crept silently into the shrubbery beside the path. Now she could see them, could see what they were doing. She crouched down and watched, not moving a muscle until their muted moans of ecstasy told her that the show was over. Then she crept away, a plan already forming in her mind. If only she had thought to bring a camera. But maybe actual physical evidence wouldn't be necessary.

The weekend had passed quickly, but for Errol it had been a memorable one, and he carried these memories into work with him on Monday morning. The internal phone rang as he was getting ready to leave his dressing room for the studio. He picked it up and said casually, "Errol Wright speaking."

"Errol?"

Damn. She had been put through to his dressing room from the switchboard. He must have a word with the receptionist. "Anne-Marie."

"I'm alone for lunch today. If you're not busy, why don't you join me?"

"Well, actually I do have a business lunch today…"

"Well then, how about dinner?"

Errol searched his mind for another excuse. "I don't know…"

"It's really important that I talk to you… and soon."

"Right," he said, resigned. They fixed a time and a place and Errol rang off, putting his head in his hands. He hoped she wasn't still playing games; he'd had just about enough of them, and his life was full enough as it was.

Errol arrived at the restaurant ten minutes late, but there was no sign of her. Recognising him, the waiter rushed over and led him to the reserved table in the window, where he could be seen by the other diners and any passers-by. He didn't complain; she would be here soon, and he'd make sure they got out as quickly as possible. As he sat down he realised the waiter wasn't the only one to have recognised him. Some of his fellow diners were turning to give him a smile or a nod; others were more guarded, and whispered to their partners who glanced at him from the corner of an eye.

He had worked out a golden rule for dealing with autograph hunters and fans: never catch anyone's eye in public. Look ahead when you're walking, and always have something to read when you're sitting down in a public place. So he picked up the menu and pored over it with mock concentration. He ordered a mineral water and waited, glancing at his watch every few minutes. At twenty past eight he was getting ready to leave when Anne-Marie arrived, smiling. She had dressed seductively for the occasion in a short, red swing dress and a choker of peearls, her hair tied up with a few ringlets allowed to hang free, framing her face. "Sorry I'm late. I had to sort a few things out." She kissed him brazenly on the cheek, and he noticed that most of the eyes in the room were upon them. Obviously the word had got around. He glared at her as the waiter came to their table. "Can I get you a drink, madam?"

"It's mademoiselle. Yes, you can: I'll have a white wine spitzer," she answered, never breaking eye contact with Errol. Thens he glanced quickly round the room. "I keep forgetting how famous you are. I shouldn't have left you alone for so long." She reached across the table for his hand, which he drew back.

"What is this, Anne-Marie? What do you want from me, money?"

She laughed. "Of course not! Can you imagine if someone got photos of us together? We'd make the front pages of the tabloids. I can see it now…"

He stared at her. Was she stark staring mad? "You haven't told anyone about us, have you?"

Anne-Marie twirled a finger in one of her ringlets. "Relax," she smiled, "I'm not ready to go public yet."

"*Yet*! Cha! I'm leaving," He half stood and quick as a flash she had grabbed his wrist.

"I don't think so, Errol." She looked round the restaurant again. "Unless you want me to make a scene you'll sit down and have a meal with me."

Slowly he took his seat again, shaking his head defeatedly. A little vein in his temple pulsed.

"Don't give me a hard time, Errol. I can make life very difficult for you and those who care about you."

"Why would you want to do this, Anne-Marie? What have I done to you?"

She picked up a menu and leant towards him, ignoring his question. "You enjoy fucking like an animal in the woods, don't you?"

His throat closed. He said nothing. A shadow of vulnerability had crept into his eyes, giving her confidence and a little extra knowledge of his weakness.

"Photographs leaked to the press of your little liason in the park wouldn't do your career much good, would they? Just think about that before you turn me down again."

He held her eyes defiantly for a minute. She didn't allow her gaze to drop for an instant.

"Let's eat," he said finally. The sooner he got this over with the better. He'd just have to make sure she never put him in this situation again.

During the meal she gave him a gift. She'd seen it in a shop, she enthused, and just had to buy it for him. She insisted he open it straight away. It was a blue silk tie, exquisitely made, the pattern running through it composed of capital Es.

She managed to manipulate him into giving her a lift home. He sat behind the steering wheel in stony silence, wanting her to know beyond any doubt that he was not enjoying himself.

"I hope you realise that this is just the beginning, Errol," she said as they sat in the car outside her flat.

"Your threats don't frighten me, Anne-Marie. You can't force me to feel for you."

"Wanna bet?" She got out of the car and walked quickly to her door. Errol didn't wait to see her inside. He was angry, and determined not to be manipulated again.

The phone rang at midnight. Errol had been in bed for over an hour, but he was still awake. Even the hot Milo hadn't helped. "I want you, Errol."

"Yvette?" he said, sitting up, the sheet dropping from his chest.

"When am I going to see you again?"

He sighed. Anne-Marie. "Are you still there?"

"Yes. I'm disappointed in you, though, Anne-Marie…"

"Disappointed?"

"From the strong, independent woman I met, to a woman who can't let go of a man she had sex with once…"

"I thought that was what being a strong woman was about: going for what she wants and getting it by any means necessary."

"What will it take to get through to you that I'm not interested?"

"If you just give us a chance, a weekend away… Let me treat you. We could fly to Paris, take in a show, stay in an upmarket hotel. I could—"

Errol hung up.

The phone rang again a few hours later. Errol was almost asleep this time, and as he reached out for it he saw Bart Simpson telling him it was four in the morning. "Yeah?" he answered groggily.

"Mr Wright? Mr Errol Wright?"

"Yes, that's me."

"Mr Wright, this is Dr Kate Trimble from King's College Hospital. We were given your name by your fiancé a few minutes ago—"

"My *fiancé*?" He bolted upright.

"She has been admitted into our accident and emergency. Could you get down here as soon as possible?"

"Is she all right? What happened?"

"She's stable, but I really do think you should get here as soon as possible…"

Errol had already dropped the phone and was dragging his clothes on. Yvette, in hospital. What had happened? They didn't tell you anything. And what about Tyrone? God, this time of the morning the boy would definitely have been with her.

He was out of the door within five minutes, his mind racing ahead of him to the hospital. He could picture her lying on one of those cots, bandaged, weak, moaning, calling for him.

Parking the car haphazardly he dashed into the hospital's reception and blurted out the information he'd been given on the phone.

"No, we don't have anyone by the name of Yvette Barker registered," the young man behind the desk told him.

"She's here, I tell you! I was called a few minutes ago by a… Dr Trimble."

"I'll get the doctor for you."

Seconds later Kate Trimble came to reception and led him to a row of cubicles. "She's doing okay, a little sleepy… but fifteen minutes later and she wouldn't have made it." She drew back a curtain and he saw her in the bed, lying on her side with her back to him. He rushed to the bedside, and at his touch she turned round.

Anne-Marie smiled weakly and reached out a hand to him. Both her wrists were tightly bandaged.

"I'll let her explain," the doctor said in a tight voice, "but she's going to be fine." She walked away, pulling the curtain closed behind her

Errol slapped a hand to his forehead. "What the *hell* are you playing at now?" he hissed angrily. "I thought…" He broke off and started pacing up and down beside the bed.

Easing herself up on the pillows, she stared at him. Half asleep and with a frightened look in his eyes, he was still the most gorgeous man she knew. "You thought what?"

He nodded towards her bandaged wrists, curious. "What happened?"

She lifted her arms. "I cut my wrists," she said, almost proudly. "Only I didn't do it properly. I was in agony for half an hour before I dialled for an ambulance."

"You're pathetic," he said, a look of scorn on his face.

"I didn't mean to put you through this. But I needed you, Errol…"

"You don't get it. You just don't get it, do you?"

Her eyes filled with tears. "I know how I feel…"

"You're sad, you know that? Lonely, and very sad." He leant on the bed with his knuckles and stared into her face. "I pity you."

"Is that why you slept with me?" "Don't give me that. You drugged me and you know it."

She grinned. It was a parody of a smile. "But you still care about me. You're here, aren't you?"

"They didn't give me your name. They just told me my fiancé was in here."

"Do you have a fiancé?"

"That is none of your business."

She reached out and touched his jacket. "I don't think you do. Maybe a lover, that tart I saw you with in the park …"

Errol dragged himself away. "You're sick! Why don't you do us all a favor and see a doctor?"

"Oh, it would suit you to think I'm crazy, wouldn't it?" she screamed at his retreating back. "I couldn't simply have been foolish enough to fall in love with you!"

He was gone, and Anne-Marie knew what she had to do. She had warned him she would go public if necessary. He obviously didn't believe her, saw it as just another threat. Well, she'd show him. She would show him all right.

Two men stepped out in front of Errol as he exited the hospital. One switched on a glaring light, the other aimed a camera at his face. The press! How did they know he was here? Did they know *why*?

"Errol Wright?" The cameraman took several shots.

"Can we have a few minutes?"

Errol, who usually had plenty of time for journalists, was in too much of a hurry to get away. How the hell had it got out that he was here? No doubt some unscrupulous porter had tipped them off.

He was backing off as quickly as he could. "I don't have anything to say to you." "What have you got to say about the attempted suicide, Errol?"

"That is none of your business."

"That's our job to decide. Who is she – a mistress, an old girlfriend, a relative?"

He slammed the car door and the camera flashed a couple more times as he put his foot down and took off. He knew enough about journalism to know that these hacks had nothing unless they talked to Anne-Marie.

For most people, a day at home usually means relaxation and living the life of Riley, but for Errol Wright it was nothing less than work on another level. Today though, after a sleepless night, he was having trouble arranging his thoughts. He'd tried to sleep, but last night's fiasco had left him too wary to be tired. Sitting at his desk, he stared absently at Helen's empty chair opposite. He wanted to be able to talk to someone about it, about Anne-Marie. Get some advice. Helen came back into the room, and for a second he entertained the idea of telling her. She was used to dealing with things confidentially. But this was too personal; besides, she was a woman – she might not see things from his point of view.

"Here, you look like you could do with this." She passed him a steaming cup of coffee and one of her blueberry muffins, then took her seat.

He had opened a book on the desk in front of him, which he now pushed aside. He'd read the first paragraph at least ten times, but still couldn't remember a word.

"Are you okay?"

"I think I've got a headache coming on."

The phone rang and Helen answered it automatically.

"It's for you," she said after a moment, and handed the receiver to him.

He answered distractedly. "Hello?" "I was expecting a call," Anne-Marie said. "You knew I was all alone in the hospital and you never called."

"Why would I do that?" Errol leant his elbow on the table and cradled his chin in the palm of his hand.

"I needed you, and you just left me there."

"What do you want from me? I've been totally straight with you." Remembering Helen was in the room, he looked up and caught her watching him, a look of concern on her face. She dropped her eyes back to the keyboard. "Put this call through to my room, will you?" he asked her. "I'll pick it up in there."

In his bedroom he took a deep breath before picking up. "Well?"

"That was your secretary, was it? Or is *she* there with you?"

"You seem to know everything about me – you tell me."

"Don't play games with me, Errol. I know you're sleeping with someone else. You lied to me about it."

"I sleep with whoever I damn well please! I don't have to justify my actions to you."

"You're such a dog, Errol. A fucking animal who can't control his own dick. You used me and now you seem to think you can just throw me aside. I won't let you do that, Mr Wright." Her voice had lost its pseudo-politeness now. She sounded angry and frustrated.

"Then tell me what you expect from me. I can't *make* myself feel something for you. We could have been friends, Anne-Marie…"

"God, you are so full of shit!"

He felt his own anger rising. "Can't we handle this like experienced adults? Can't we just agree that it was a mistake and move on?"

"Why should I?" she screamed, and then suddenly her voice was quiet, almost a whisper: "How can I? I love you."

Errol positioned his finger over the button on the phone. He could hear her sobbing as he disconnected. He suddenly felt very empty, vulnerable. He needed nothing more at that moment than a woman who cared for him – Yvette. He wanted her warm body, wanted sexual healing, but he knew she was working, and he couldn't have it… Abruptly he jumped up. Maybe he couldn't have Yvette, but he could have a work-out. Shouting out to Helen that he was disappearing for a couple of hours, he stuffed his kit into his bag, grabbed his mobile, and headed out.

Sweat poured down his forehead as he lifted the weights to shoulder height one last time. The gym was almost empty this afternoon. Christmas was just weeks away, so was no wonder that people were forgetting about keeping fit and devoting themselves to spending money elsewhere. The door to the gym swung open, and Errol looked up and smiled.

"Chris! Over here, man!" "All right?"

"Glad you could make it." Errol tried to sound casual but there was a hint of sarcasm in his voice.

"Boy, you're in a good mood. What's up?"Chris dumped his gym bag by the wall and bent at the waist to begin warming up.

"Domesticity."

Chris took his place on a bench beside Errol and threw him a quizzical look. "Come again?"

"You hear about the call of the wild, but it's the call to domesticity that I don't understand. You know, guys hanging up their boots to become domesticated…"

"Don't knock it until you've tried it," Chris grinned. "You're just feeling hard done by because all the lads have settled down and you're still between girlfriends."

"Get outta here! If… *when* I decide to settle down, I won't let it interfere with me catching up wid my bredrin."

"You're an inspiration to us all," Chris chuckled, shaking his head.

Errol frowned at his friend's sarcasm. Yes, he had two women after him, as well as all his unknown admirers, and still he felt unsatisfied. What was missing? Devotion? Maybe Chris was right; maybe he was jealous that his friends were able to make the decision to stay with the woman they loved. It was weeks since Yvette had asked him to move in, and he was still undecided. He'd cheated on her, for one thing. And she had a son who was nearly a teenager – could he be a father to him? Would his career allow it? And a shared mortgage – that was a commitment.

What did he have to lose by making the decision? From his point of view, too much. He put his weights down and joined Chris on the rowing machines. "I've been thinking about this settling down business, you know."

Chris threw him a look but said nothing.

"I been spending more time with Yvette and Tyrone lately, and… well, you know, it's nice."

"Nice! Cosy and welcoming…"

"Yeah, all of that… But I've got a problem…" What the hell? Errol thought. He had to tell someone. Another man. "You see, there's this one girl…"

"Woman?"

"Yeah, all right, a woman. She started work at the station, so I saw her kinda regular, you know."

Chris was staring at him intently, already knowing what was coming next.

"Nothing sexual– we were just hanging out. Then one night she got me drunk and slipped something into my drink. The next thing I know I'm waking up naked on her sofa the next morning."

"You did the dirty?"

"I guess we did. But the weird thing is I can't remember actually doing it."

Chris was shaking his head, bursting to say "I told you so".

"Don't laugh, man, this is serious."

Chris could even guess who the woman was. He stopped rowing and twisted on the seat to face his friend. "Do I know her?"

"You know *of* her. You remember the colleague I told you about?"

"How could I forget? I warned you…" There was a smirk on his face that Errol didn't like. "Why'd you do it? A moment ago you were saying you might be ready to settle down."

"Believe me, I didn't know what I was doing! You know me – would I ever touch a woman I work with? Especially when she's my mates ex…"

"What'd she do? Blackmail you?"

"Not financially, but she's done something…"

"*What*?"

"She's following me around, sending me stuff. She's on the phone every day. Just before I called you today she called me."

"An' what'd she say?"

"How she loves me, can't let me go… I don't know."

"Sounds to me like you've got a nutter on your hands."

"But she seemed so… sure of herself."

"Nutters are pretty good actors."

Errol stopped rowing and rested his arms on his knees. Now that he'd started talking he couldn't stop. He could do that with Chris. He was the only friend who'd listen objectively without judgement. "She slit her wrists the other night and called me to come and see her."

"What!"

"No joke. We had one night together – that's all – and I can't get rid of her. I wanted the friendship thing; we got on all right, you know. I thought maybe she was a little star-struck at first, going out with a celebbrity was probably a boost for her—"

"She needs a doctor."

"You're not wrong. She's a seriously disturbed fan."

"Fatal Attraction Part Two," Chris chuckled, trying to add a touch of levity to the matter at hand. But Errol wasn't smiling. "There's something else," he said quietly.

"What? She send you a birthday cake with a knife in it?"

"No." Errol was deadly serious. "She told me she's taken stuff from my house."

"Shit! What did she take?"

"She took a few things, but the only one she'd tell me about was a photograph from of Aaron's room. And I know she stole one of my shirts because she wore it on a double date I took her on with Marion and Paul."

"Lawdy, Lawdy, Lawdy!" Chris sighed. "You get it back?"

Errol shook his head. Even Chris was quiet now.

"I don't know what to do, man. I want to report it to the police but I don't want the papers getting hold of it. I can't let this affect my career or what I have with Yvette."

"You mean Yvette knows nothing?"

"I could hardly tell her, could I? But I'll have to do something soon, before Anne-Marie does."

The pavement was packed with Christmas shoppers, and decorations adorned every shop window. Anne-Marie checked her watch before continuing her pursuit on the other side of the street, dodging pushchairs and pedestrians laden with baggage as she went. Why there were so many people shopping in Woolwich escaped her. Most of the stores round here were temporary pound shops, which sold useful but cheap goods that would invariably break after the first month or so – nothing suitable for a present.

Last night had left her feeling so bad she'd nearly put herself in hospital again by stepping in front of a car. Luckily the driver had been alert. She hadn't been able to understand why Errol was being so mean. He liked her – she knew that. They'd had passionate sex, which they'd *both* wanted. So what was the problem? It could only be that bitch he'd fucked in the park. She had competition for his feelings. So, she had to eliminate the competition for him to be hers. Simple.

The optician's was quiet, and the girl on the reception looked almost grateful to have custom as she looked up from the magazine she pretended not to be reading under the counter.

"Good afternoon. Can I help you?" She smiled the smile of a toothpaste advert: clean, shiny, healthy teeth surrounded by cherry-red lips.

"No, thank you… I'm just looking for new frames."

The assistant nodded. "Let me know if you need some help."

Anne-Marie pretended to browse, picking up frames every now and again. There was no sign of the woman she'd been following, yet she'd swear she'd seen her walking in here a minute ago. Maybe she was in one of the back rooms… An eye test?

A moment later the woman with the braided hair came out of a room to her left. She studied a rack of frames for a while, then selected a blue pair and tried them on. "Not me at all," she muttered, placing them back where she'd found them.

Anne-Marie smiled. She felt as though she knew this woman. She

113

admired her bold style of dress, such a contrast to her own conservative appearance: the short leather mini-skirt, jacket and knee-length boots, her make up… She exuded confidence; she could only be a beautician. The woman must have felt Anne-Maries' eyes on her, because she turned to look directly at her. "You fancy me?" she said.

Anne-Marie immediately averted her eyes. How awful! Surely the woman didn't think she'd been appraising her! Thankfully the optician walked in at that moment with her results. "Miss Barker…" She spread a prescription on the counter as Yvette approached. "It seems you are slightly short-sighted in your right eye. Nothing serious at the moment. This prescription is for mild correction, but you should have your eyes tested again in maybe two years."

"Really? Short sighted!"

"Believe me, it's nothing to worry about. Will you be paying cash?"

"Mm-hmm. Hold on, let me just find my purse." As Yvette fumbled in her handbag Anne-Marie approached. "I'm sorry, but do I know you?" she asked.

Yvette frowned. "Pardon me?"

"I'm sure I know you." Anne-Marie touched a finger to her head. "Colin's wedding – right? You were there?" Yvette visibly relaxed; she recognised her now. "Right. Yes, I was." Then she remembered what she'd just done. "Oh! Listen, I'm sorry about what I said just now. I just didn't—"

"You were Errols' guest, right?"

Yvette was delighted to be recognised. "I know, I'm unforgettable. How are ya?"

"Fine."

Yvette handed some cash to the receptionist. "Christmas shopping?"

"Not really, I haven't any family to shop for."

"You lucky bitch… Oops! Excuse the French. There I go again." Yvette flipped her plaits over her shouler with one hand, and Anne-Marie caught sight of her long, scarlet fingernails. Yvette made to leave. "Well, it was nice seeing you again…"

"Are you going home?"

"No. Actually I'm meeting a friend for lunch."

"Oh… I see…" Anne-Marie turned back to the frames she'd been browsing.

"Well… look, if you aren't doing nothin', why don't you come with me?"

"Oh, I wouldn't want to intrude…"

"Rubbish! It ain't *that* kind of friend."

Despite their differences, Anne-Marie found herself strangely drawn to this woman. There was a friendly vitality about her. Her wilingness to talk to complete strangers was intriguing. Anyway, she had no intention of turning her down.

"Why not?"

"Good on ya! Just hold on while I find out about contact lenses. I've always fancied those coloured ones…"

They spent the afternoon in Lewisham, leaving dismal Woolwich for better climes. They were sitting at a café in the middle of the shopping centre when Karen walked by. "I've seen you somewhere before, haven't I?" she asked Anne-Marie after brief introductions were made.

"Joan's wedding," Yvette answered for her new friend.

She took a seat, and they ordered salads all round. "So who'll get married next, then?" Karen asked as the waitress disappeared. "First Jennifer Edwards, then Joan and Colin… I suppose the next impossibility would be me and Phillip!"

Yvette laughed. Jennifer Edwards and Joan had both had difficult relationships with their partners before they'd decided to take the plunge, and Karen was a die-hard independent woman who had just moved in with a boyfriend.

The food appeared, and they stopped talking as the waitress put down plates. Anne-Marie already felt comfortable in the presence of her new companions. She was itching to probe into Yvette's relationship with Errol, but she controlled herself. The time would come. When they were alone again, she resumed the conversation. "No, the next one to get married would have to be Marion," she said. "She and Paul are engaged."

"You know Marion too?" Karen asked through a mouthful of lettuce.

"We went to school together," Anne-Marie said, reaching for the butter.

"Right. And how long have you known Yvette?"

Yvette looked up. Karen was always this blatant when she wanted information. For her, subtlety didn't exist. She was feeling Anne-Marie out with her eyes, checking where she was coming from.

"We just met… properly," Anne-Marie replied. "We were introduced at Joan's wedding reception, but you know how those thing are, you never remember names." She put down her fork and lifted her glass of mineral water. "How long have you two known each other?"

"A coupla years," Yvette answered. "We met t'rough a friend – Elaine.

She works for me."

"And what do you do?" Anne-Marie asked Yvette.

"I run a health centre. A small one, but I'm gonna expand one day. Got big plans, man."

Anne-Marie smiled. Yvette was probably thinking of using Errol's money to finance it. The leech.

"What d'you do, Anne-Marie?" Karen asked, rubbing the rim of her glass with an index finger.

"At the moment I'm a researcher for a TV show," Anne-Marie said smugly. "*Do the Wright Thing*. You know it? I was on it the other week as the resident psychologist. You might have seen me..." Neither of them had. Karen caught Yvette's wide-eyed expression but didn't let her friend speak yet. "So you know Errol?"

Anne-Marie became coy. "Well of course we see each other at work..." This wasn't the right time to come clean about her relationship with him. Not, at least, until she knew who Yvette was.

Yvette was still staring in barely concealed amazement. This latest revelation shed a new light on the mystery girl. Was there something going on here? Errol hadn't mentioned her. Well he wouldn't if he was seeing her on the sly.

But as the three women chatted, any anxiety she'd felt about Anne-Marie and Errol quickly faded. She liked the girl. When they'd finished eating Anne-Marie insisted on paying the bill. She was grateful for Yvette's invitation to join her, and had gleaned enough information to be fairly sure that she posed no real threat. Karen admired the soft leather wallet Anne-Marie pulled from her purse. It was emerald green, almost like snakeskin. "Can I feel it?" she asked.

Anne-Marie handed it over, and Karen ran her hands over it. It was beautifully made, must have cost a packet. "Expensive?"

"Unfortunately, yes. But my mother left me her house and her savings when she died, so I can afford to treat myself occasionally."

Karen found herself popping open the catch, and was stunned when she came face to face with Errol. She showed the photograph to Yvette, but before her friend could open her mouth she jumped in. "Er, why have you got a picture of Errol Wright in your wallet?"

Anne-Marie looked at the purse and bit her lip, as though she'd forgotten the picture was in there. Then she looked at Yvette and gave a sheepish grin. "You may find this silly," she said, taking back her wallet, "but I really do admire him... you know, as a black man who is going places. Who knows – one day he might return my admiration."

Karen screwed up her mouth. "Girl, you're tripping!"she exclaimed.

Anne-Marie smiled, and shook her head slightly as she spoke. "Sorry. Do we have a problem here?"

Yvette was by now simmering just beneath the surface, but she remained outwardly calm. "Do you suffer from delusions? 'Cause I have to tell you, you're having one right now."

Anne-Marie was still smiling, looking from one to the other. "What are you talking about?"

Karen half stood and leant towards her innocent-looking face. "Errol's her boyfriend, fool."

Yvette touched her friend's hand. "Karen, keep out of this."

"Oh!" Anne-Marie looked down her nose at Yvette. "That's funny. He never mentions you."

"Whether he does or not, I'm telling you now: hands off."

Anne-Marie gave a patronising little laugh. "I think that's between myself and Errol, don't you?"

Karen, unable to help herself, stood up and slammed her palm on the table, and one or two other diners looked up, hopeful for some entertainment. "Listen, bitch, she just told you—"

"I think you should know something," Anne-Marie interrupted. "Errol and I have been intimate."

Yvette gasped. "Since when?"

"Two weeks ago. Look, I think this is something you should really discuss with Errol. Obviously you've got something going for him, but he can't possibly feel the same way about you. You do realise there are probably dozens of women like you, don't you?"

Karen was practically crawling across the table. She couldn't believe this. She had known Yvette a long time; she knew her friend could open her mouth when necessary. So why was she speechless now? The two of them could take this woman outside and give her what for and the problem would be solved. She couldn't let it go on any longer. "What's wrong with you, Eve? You can't just sit there and take that! Slap her one! Errol ain't cheating on you…"

But Yvette wasn't so sure. No wonder he couldn't give her a straight answer about the house. No wonder they hardly ever went anywhere he thought he'd be spotted. No wonder he always left her place so early in the morning. No wonder… no wonder.

"Why don't you call him and ask him if you don't believe me?" Anne-Marie was saying, waving a mobile phone at her.

As Yvette seemed too stunned to react, Karen snatched it out of her hand. "Yvette, call 'im nuh! You know you're right, girl…"   But Anne-Marie and Yvette were staring each other out, challenging each other. Anne-Marie looked too confident for Yvette's liking. She didn't want to be the one to get the bad news – not in front of Karen, she would never hear the end of it.

"You want me to make the call?" Karen pushed.

"No, leave it, man." Yvette took the phone from her and handed it back to Anne-Marie, who rose to leave. "Well, it's been nice meeting you both," she said. "I must go."

"Stay away from Errol," Yvette warned.

Anne-Marie threw her a superior look. "Listen, let's be reasonable about this. Obviously he is attracted to something in both of us. But he can't have us both. So why don't we let *him* chose his Mrs Wright?"

Yvette's jaw dropped.

"Scared he'll choose me?"

Yvette shut her mouth and narrowed her eyes. "No!"

"Then we're rivals."

Karen kissed her teeth. "I'll rival your backside."

"Okay…" Yvette stood up and stretched her hand across the table towards her rival. "May the best woman win."

Colin phoned at ten o'clock on Tuesday morning. He rarely called during work time, so Errol knew from the start that it had to be something important.

After they had exchanged pleasantries Colin asked, "You get the *Voice*?"

"I have it delivered. Probably be there when I get home. Why?"

"Then you bes' go and find a copy."

"Am I in there again?" Errol asked. Occasionally he would do a piece for the paper, and his name was always cropping up in there.

"You're in there all right, but I don't think you're gonna like dis one."

"Why?"

"Go and get the paper. Page twenty-seven."

As soon as he had a chance Errol hurried up to the library, found a *Voice*, and turned straight to page twenty-seven. And there, near the bottom of the page, was a photograph of him and Anne-Marie, her hand on his, staring intently into his eyes. The caption was a question: "The Wright Woman?" With mounting irritation, Errol read the short piece that went with it: "*Do the Wright Thing* presenter Errol Wright, 34, was spotted having a very intimate dinner with his attractive research assistant Anne-

Marie Simms last week. Word has it she could be the new woman in his life..." So that was why she'd reserved the window table; it was all a set up.

The telephone in his dressing room was ringing as he walked back in. "Errol, it's me."

"Yvette."

"Have you read the *Voice* yet?"

She'd seen it. Errol sighed. "Yeah, I did—"

"Is it true? Are you seeing her?" Yvette asked before he could start making excuses.

"Yvette, she's a colleague, we were having lunch..."

"I thought it was dinner."

"Lunch, dinner... It was food," he said matter-of-factly.

"And she needed you to hold her hand to eat, I suppose."

"Eve, I wouldn't lie to you." Errol sat down. "She's a friend. As we were about to get up and go she touched my hand. That was all. They've got it wrong, they always do."

Yvette was furious, but she was tamping it down. She knew he was lying. "Karen called me up and told me. I haven't seen it yet. You gonna sue them? They made it sound like you're planning to marry her."

"They haven't said anything incriminating. They've just insinuated."

"It may not mean anything to you, but how stupid d'you think it makes me look?"

"Ignore it. Anne-Marie probably set it up herself for the publicity. Listen, honey, I've gotta work. I'll see you later."

Errol sighed as he hung up. He sat in thought for a moment, then got up and crossed to his window. Not many dressing rooms had a window, but his occasionally doubled as an office and he liked to have natural light. He gazed out at the road, and thought about Yvette.

He had been completely faithful to her for almost a year. He'd never been tempted to sleep with another woman. Could that be love? Could he love one woman? Whether it was possible or not, Errol knew that was how he felt. Now decisions had to be made, and for the first time in his life Errol Wright was confused. Did he follow his heart or his practical mind? He was about to move away from the window when he looked directly down to the car park and saw a woman in sunglasses leaning against a dark car. Like the car she was quite motionless; her head was tipped back, and she seemed to be looking straight at him, though he couldn't see her eyes behind the shades. He tightened his grip on the window ledge. Was she watching him? It sure looked like it, and felt like it too. What could she possibly see from down there? First at home, and now here...

Errol left the room and hurried down the hallway to the lifts, his heart pounding. He'd get to the bottom of this, make her see that this sort of intimidation wasn't working. But by the time he got to the ground floor the parking lot was empty. Taking a deep breath, he began to calm down. Had it been Anne-Marie? Now he wasn't so sure he had seen her at all.

"Something smells good."

"Must be my perfume. You bought it for me."

He nuzzled her neck and mumbled, "You *always* smell good. I meant the food." "New recipe." The door closed behind them. Yvette cringed, twisted away from him and headed back to the kitchen. She couldn't help it. An image of Anne-Marie had come into mind just as Errol had tried to hug her. Did he do that to her too? "Make yourself at home," she said. "I'll be right there."

Errol watched her walk away from him. "Very nice." He entered the front room. "Where's Tyrone?" "With my sister. I thought we could do with some privacy."

Yvette had set a table in the living room and the lights were dimmed. Errol inspected her efforts and smiled. What had he done to deserve this? Yvette wasn't a very good cook and so they tended to eat out a lot. He knew that whatever she was cooking it was out of a recipe book. He helped himself to a drink and took a seat on the sofa.

Yvette brought the food in dish by dish, and served him first. Everything looked delicious. The main dish was a cheese bake, which they ate with pasta and various vegetables. The meal was going fine until Errol started to choke a little. He took a swig of wine to wash down his food.

"Are you okay?"

He placed his glass back on the table and tried to swallow, but his throat felt as though it was constricting. Suddenly his mouth began to salivate. "I'm not sure," he replied hoarsely, coughing again.

"I'll get you some water." Yvette got up and walked to the kitchen while Errol continued to open and close his mouth like a fish gasping for air. By the time she had brought the water back he was pacing up and down, wheezing, retching and looking distinctly red in the face.

"Errol, what is it?" Yvette handed him the water and rubbed his back, gently forcing concern on to her face. As if she didn't know.

"The food, the little pieces of meat... what was it?"

"In the bake?"

He nodded.

"Pork..."

Errol collapsed into the armchair. "I'm allergic."

"Oh God..." Yvette faked mild alarm by flapping her arms up and down. "What can I do? Have you got medication?"

"At home."

Her mouth twisted sadistically and she took a deep breath. "Oh God, I'll call you a cab." *Bastard, I hope you die painfully.* There was nothing she wanted less, but she was so angry.

"No. No time," he gasped. "You'll have to drive me."

Driving him home was the last thing she'd intended. "Well... okay." She went back into the hall for their coats. They took his car, and arrived at his house half an hour later. Once Errol had taken a couple of shots from his inhaler his breathing began to settle. Yvette was standing motionless in the hallway as he came out of the kitchen. She wanted him to know it had been a punishment, but how could she? He would hate her. Errol let her take the car back – he would cab down to pick it up tommorow, he said. She apologised under her breath for the ruined evening, and after kissing his cheek lightly made a hurried retreat.

Anne-Marie sat in her car outside Errol's house and cried. She knew she was out of control again. Several times she had picked up the phone to call the clinic. She would dial a few numbers and then stop, as flashes of buried memory resurfaced. The waiting rooms with "really sick people" in them; the sterile white or pastel-painted rooms where she was spoken to like a child; the admissions to hospital when she cut herself; the medication that turned her into a zombie.

She couldn't, wouldn't go back to living that way. She was in the normal world now, where she worked with people who respected her. She was an author. Back then she'd been a patient, she'd had a label she didn't like, didn't ever want again.

Besides, this time it was different... wasn't it? She was in love with Errol Wright. She didn't want to hurt him. She just knew that they had to be together. So, if it took a little manipulation, it was worth it. And they had looked so *good* together in the photo.

Errol stopped the car at the traffic lights and saw Nyam Food, a Caribbean takeaway, just up ahead. Suddenly he realised how hungry he was. He smiled at the thought of Errol Wright, television celebrity, calling into the local takeaway for curry goat and rice and peas, but it was exactly what he fancied now. It had been a hard day. He'd been suffering from a persistent headache, and lunch had been nothing more than a salad sandwich. Anne-Marie had called his office three times before he had finally returned her call.

She still hadn't got the message. Apparently ignoring her didn't work either. She seemed to find a thousand excuses to visit him on set, was forever asking to come round and cook him a meal or take him out somewhere, offers on which Errol always took a raincheck.

The other woman in his life had been exceptionally quiet. When he'd made his regular call to her this morning, Yvette had apologised again for the pork. He'd been quite forgiving. He'd had trouble before with his fish and pork allergies. Usually just the smell of the potential danger was enough to warn him off it, but this time the pork had been so heavily buried in cheese that he hadn't even tasted it, much less smelled it. He'd tried to make her laugh on the phone, but had felt as though somehow she wasn't really there.

What he really needed now was a long, hot bath, some good food and a cool, strong drink. He was going to pamper himself tonight, he decided. Parking the car outside the takeaway, he locked the doors and set the alarm and went to get some food. Of course, he was recognised as soon as he went inside, and he recieved extra food on the understanding that he would give the shop a mention on TV.

He drove home without the radio on, determined to keep this rare moment of solitude untainted by outside influences. All around him people were going about their business: normal people, with their own individual lives, all different, yet all the same. As he pulled up outside his house he waved to two of his neighbours' children. The boys grinned back at him before darting indoors. These lads were young and carefree, each wanting to grow up before his time. At their age Errol had been the family entertainer; even back then he'd had a talent for attracting the grown-ups' attention. "Mr Brighty", his Uncle used to call him. He'd always had a cheeky grin, an idea for a game, a joke to tell. He would perform his impersonation of Michael Jackson for friends and relatives – his party piece. His parents had always been sure he'd end up as some sort of entertainer, although never in the kind he had finally turned out to be. It had been so easy to please people, to be Mummy's pride and joy, to make her smile when she was tired or feeling down. He was always a natural listener, a child with genuine concern for those close to him.

Wearily he opened his front door and dropped his briefcase just inside. He put the food in the kitchen before going up to shower. He took the stairs like an old woman, dragging his feet up heavily, praying there wouldn't another day like this for a long time. Days like this came only once in a while: every minute of his time occupied, travelling from one location to the other for meetings, interviews, recordings...

He drew the already loosened tie from round his neck, draped it over the back of a chair, and stared at his face in the mirror. Looking back at him, he saw a weary black man. "Boy, you need a holiday..."

Then out of the corner of his eye he saw in the glass something out of place: a big, striped box on the bed, tied with ribbon. Spinning round, he nearly gave himself whiplash. It was a gift box! Not unusual in itself, but Errol knew that no one else had a key to his house – the cleaner and his assistant only came in when he was here. Maybe Yvette had taken his spares to surprise him... As he approached the bed he suddenly wondered if he should call the police first. After all, it could be a bomb. It could have been sent by some psychotic fan. But surely nobody wanted to kill him...

Very carefully he picked it up. It barely weighed a thing. Probably not a bomb, then. He gave it a gentle shake and heard the rustle of tissue paper. Frowning, he pulled at the bow and let the lid fall on to the bed. Inside was a smaller parcel with the word "SURPRISE!" written on it in big red letters. It had to be from Yvette. Now excited as a little boy at Christmas time, he ripped the wrapping paper away. A note dropped out, and in his hands he held a silk shirt. Picking up the tiny white envelope, he removed the card and read the handwritten words:

> Errol, my love,
> This is a replacement for the shirt I borrowed. I've become so attached to it, but I know I had no right to just keep it. Hope you like it. I love giving surprises. Miss you, see you soon.
> Love you
> Anne-Marie

Errol's skin broke out in instantaneous goosebumps. He dropped the shirt and the note as though they were contaminated. She hadn't broken into his house, so she must have let herself in. She must have copied his keys. He walked around the house, checking every room and storage space. There was nothing apparently missing, no one hiding in the house, so he locked the door on his way back to the kitchen, when the phone rang. He picked it up and held it just away from his ear. "Errol?"

Her voice was like a switch, turning on his anger. "Anne-Marie – what the hell do you think you're doing breaking into my home!" he yelled. "I could have you charged—"

"Did you like it?"

"Damn you, stupid woman! Didn't you hear what I just said? I'm calling the police!" He slammed the phone down.

But what would he tell the police? That he was being given presents by a beautiful woman? She hadn't broken in, she hadn't stolen anything or done any criminal damage... He stumbled back into the kitchen, defeated, tired and hungry. Maybe it was better just to ignore her. Surely she would eventually get the message. All he had to do was change the locks and his phone number tommorow.

Yvette stepped out of the health centre and walked towards Errol's car. She had on a red two-piece suit, the skirt nearly reaching her red court shoes, with a cream blouse underneath, and her braided hair was tied back in a bun. Errol watched her from the car. She looked extremely uncomfortable, confined. At first he hadn't recognised her. "What's up with the suit?" he asked as she opened the door. "You got an interview?"

"Don't you like it? It's my new image."

"It's nice, but..."

She sighed as she got in. "It's not me."

"Got it in one. Why the change?"

"You know... Coming up to new year I thought I'd try a new, more executive image. To tell the truth I thought you'd like it."

He leant towards her. "Why would you think that? Have I ever complained about the way you dress?"

She shook her head, meeting his eyes only fleetingly.

"I love the way you dress, the way you wear your hair..." He buried his head in her neck. "The way you smell..."

Yvette gently pushed him away. "Let's get home first."

Errol frowned and studied her face. "Something wrong?"

"No," she replied, much too quickly. "I just want you to myself." That was no lie. She'd hardly slept for the past two nights, thinking of him and that woman together, doing it, laughing at her behind her back. The outfit had been to see if his attitude toward her would change. He'd taken Anne-Marie to bed, so he must think her sexy, Yvette had reasoned, and this was the way she dressed. Confident. That was what Anne-Marie was. A lot more confident than Yvette, who at the moment felt little more than confusion. Errol had slept with someone else, and yet he still treated her the same. He didn't look or smell any different; he still took her out, the sex was still overwhelming. He still seemed to want her – or was he just biding his time? What the hell was she doing wrong? She wanted to scream.

They listened to jazz and ate smoked salmon with garlic bread, home-made by Errol. The light was dimmed and they lay on huge floor-cushions in Yvette's living room. Yvette was now feeling frustrated as well as anxious. She had spent the last few days tamping down feelings that she felt she shouldn't have to hide, and now the pretence was getting the better of her. It was make-or-break time. To hell with Anne-Marie's competition. She knew she couldn't keep up this charade any longer.

"Errol, we have to talk…"

He met her eyes questioningly. "I thought we were."

"No. Seriously."

"About… ?"

"About us. I'm making plans for my future, and I need to know if you're going to be part of it."

"I'm here, aren't I?"

"You're here *now*. But in a few hours' time you'll be back at home, at work… or maybe with someone else." She hardly dared make the suggestion any more forthright.

"*What*? God, why would I want someone else?"

"That's a good question – but then you could also ask yourself why you want me."

"What kind of question is that?'

"A question you can't seem to answer. Aren't I intelligent enough for you? Is my career not good enough, not glamourous enough? Are you ashamed of me?"

Errol propped himself up on an elbow and took one of her hands in his. "I don't know what's provoked this outburst, but it has nothing to do with you."

"Obviously not!"

"Eve, I'm thirty-four and very ambitious. I haven't recently had as much time with you as I'd have liked. Because of this it's hard for me to build a loving relationship. I don't want to end up hurting you… You know that when I settle down it'll be for life."

"So what now?"

He stroked her hand. "What?" "Is this all there's ever going to be to our relationship – dates and sex? I feel as though I'm still having some kind of sordid affair; we haven't moved on from that. I mean, how many times have you invited me to your house?"

Errol knew she'd been inside his house only a few times, had slept in his bed only once. But he liked his privacy. Irritated and restless, he pulled his hand away. "Do we have to discuss this now?"

Yvette sighed. She should have guessed this would be his reaction. He hated being cornered. Any minute now, she thought, he's gonna say "This is getting heavy".

He stood up and lowered himself on to the sofa."This is getting heavy." Yvette sat up on the cushion. The knowledge that she knew him so well made the situation more intolerable. Anger was bubbling up inside her. She desperately needed to know what she meant to him, yet she was having such difficulty confronting him about his other woman, this woman who seemed so convinced that he was her man, so confident that she was willing to compete for him. Well, Yvette wasn't prepared to play that game any more. She wanted Errol to decide which woman he wanted to be with now. "I've had enough of this…"

"I know what this is about. It's about the house, isn't it? I was supposed to give you a decision—"

"Oh, fuck the house, Errol! This is about *your* infidelities!"

He stopped in his tracks. "My what?"

"I know about Anne-Marie, okay?"

"*What* do you know about Anne-Marie?"

"Don't tek me for no fool, Errol! I bumped into Anne-Marie by accident while I was out shopping. I recognised her from Colin's wedding. She told me all about your undercover affair."

Now Errol was sure. Nothing ever happened by accident with Anne-Marie. He was beginning to wonder if she ever encountered an unplanned incident in her life. He sank slowly to the floor by her side. "It's not like that," he said, barely audible.

Tears sprang to Yvette'seyes and she wiped them away furiously. Errol would only see them as a sign of weakness, and she most definitely was not weak. She was a woman scorned, and the tears were the result of her frustration and anger. "Then what *was* it like? Don't tell me she carries your picture around in her purse because she's your number-one fan."

The look on Errol's face showed he was every bit as surprised as she had been.

"What's going on, Errol?"

He leant forward on the sofa and took her hand again. "Yvette, I don't want to lose you. This woman's been coming on to me…"

"Coming on to you?"

"Yes. Trying to seduce me. Hear me out, okay? I did go out with Anne-Marie on purely a platonic basis. We worked together, had a couple of the same friends, and I just thought… well, I didn't see any harm in it."

"If you were just friends why couldn't you tell me about it?"

He shrugged. "I don't tell you about all my friends, do I? I don't come round and say, 'Hey, guess who I had lunch with today… Ben!' She was just someone in my life. I didn't find her particularly fascinating, so I didn't see it as important to tell you about her."

"So nothing happened?"

Errol forced sincerity into his eyes and voice. "Nothing. I wouldn't risk what we have."

"So she's been pestering you?"

"Yeah. She fancies me." He shrugged.

"And you haven't touched her?"

"No!"

"Do you… like her?"

"Yvette, I'm not going to lie to you. When we first met, I did find her attractive. You've met her – she *is* attractive. But she was one of Colin's exes and one of Marion's old school friends – I wouldn't dream of touching her… You don't believe me, do you?"

They fell into a silence that Yvette found impossible to break. That was the big question. Was he worth her dignity? The fact that he was accusing Anne-Marie of lying about it intrigued her. Why would she do that? But Errol was good. When he turned on the sincerity he always had her begging for more. She wanted to believe him. But being Yvette, she wasn't letting him off that easily.

"I need some time to think it over. It could have happened that way. But then again…" and she let the end of her sentence drift away.

"You're honestly willing to let our relationship go because of some lie from a stranger?"

"I don't know…"

"Eve, I love you."

Her head sprang up. This was the very first time he'd said it.

"Is it too late for you to buy your house?"

"I think it's still on the market. But it's beyond my reach."

"Not if we go into it together."

"Don't try to blackmail me, Errol—"

"We're good together. Good for each other."

"How can I be sure *she* won't tempt you?"

"Baby, I wouldn't do anything to hurt you."

The look in his eyes and the feeling in her heart told them both all they needed to know. They kissed.

"But no more part-time lover," she warned. "This is going to be a commitment. You're either mine exclusively or we have nothing."

"Fine by me. I don't want anyone else."

As he pulled her towards him, the emotional distance that had stood between them seemed to melt away to be replaced by passion. Suddenly they were kissing, stroking, pushing away all the unanswered questions that remained, each feeling only the smell of the other. And that was the only answer Yvette needed.

He became her lover again, her gentleman, the man she knew she was in love with.

In the bedroom they made slow, sweet love like never before. Later, before Errol fell into oblivious sleep, a deep realisation came over him. He bent his head to kiss her neck and whispered, "Why didn't you tell me I was in love with you?"

She turned her head so she could see his face in the semi-darkness. "It happened to me a long time ago. I was just waiting for you to catch up."

"I think I realised it then. I just wasn't sure what it was... how to go about putting it into practice."

"And you know now?"

"I think... no, I *know* I do. Believe me, this is just the beginning." Errol didn't know how right he was.

She got back into her car and started the engine. It had taken her almost forty-five minutes to finish her task, and it would be a couple more hours before anyone saw them. She sighed a little at the thought. It could be a whole day before Errol knew anything of it. But when he did... She smiled to herself and set off, suddenly feeling light of heart having almost completed a job well done. Now she had some sleep to catch up on. She still had about half a dozen examples of her handiwork left – maybe she'd stop off at the local police station or the library on the way. The thought amused her so much that she laughed out loud. He would take her seriously now. She was certain of that.

Yvette woke up two hours after Errol had left for work and smiled, satisfied, even happy about waking up in his bed. He finally trusted her alone in his house. She wasn't the snooping type anyway. She took a leisurely shower, trying out two of the shower gels she found because she'd never seen them before. They made her skin feel supple and soft, and their scent was intoxicating.

She heard the newspaper drop through the door as she stepped out of the shower, and within five minutes she was sitting down to read it with a breakfast of muesli and orange juice. Just before she took her first mouthful the doorbell rang.

A uniformed delivery man stood on the porch with a clipboard under his arm, "I have a parcel for Mr Wright. Will you sign for it?"

"Yeah, yeah – bring it in." Yvette held the door open. She was dressed only in her dressing gown and her wet hair was wrapped in a towel.

The man went back to his van and returned with a large, flat package that looked like a framed picture, which he put down in the hallway. A gift? Maybe it was a surprise from Errol for her. If she hadn't been here today there would have been no one to collect it. She signed for it and the man left. Then she took a few moments to stand back and look at it, intrigued. There was an envelope attached, addressed to Errol Wright and written in big, florid handwriting. The writing of a woman – no doubt about it. Maybe he'd bought it and had had it delivered instead of carting it home himself. Of course. It *would* have his name on it, and the writing could belong to someone at the delivery firm. She left the package to get dressed, but her mind kept going back to it. There was no return address, no company name or sticker: it didn't say "Personal" or "Private"...

She descended the stairs again and paced in front of it. Curiosity getting the better of her, she peeled the envelope from the side. Definitely a woman's writing. What would be her excuse be for opening it? "I thought it might be urgent, and that you might have forgotten it was coming." Something like that. Before she could talk herself out of it she was ripping the envelope open as carelessly as a little kid at Christmas. The words she saw burned themselves on to her sight.

"To Errol, in endless admiration..." the note began.

Her heart dropped to the pit of her stomach. This was a gift for the man she was planning to live with. A gift from another woman. Immediately she thought of Anne-Marie. Errol had played down the amount she was pestering him, so why then would she go to this much trouble? That was it. She dropped the note and stalked to the kitchen, where she pulled a sharp knife from a drawer. Newspaper and polystyrene beads spilled out on to the floor as she slit three sides of the package, pulling it open. It was a painting, a canvas of a semi-nude woman whom Yvette thought she recognised. The more she looked the more she became sure: it was Anne-Marie, the woman who had boasted about sleeping with Errol. The woman Errol had denied having any involvement with.

Her mind raced. What the fuck was Anne-Marie whatsername doing sending her man a portrait of herself? Why would she think he would like it?

Yvette found the note again. "This is for you," she read, "with my love. Every time I sat for it I thought of you. Can you see it in my eyes? At every stroke of the brush I was creating something endless, everlasting, in memory of our love. Always, Anne-Marie."

Yvette zoomed in on the crucial words: love, everlasting, always, endless...

Anne-Marie and Errol were lovers. Or was Errol telling the truth? Was she just coming on to him?

She had fallen for the oldest trick in the book. She had believed a man because she'd wanted to, and because she loved him. You fool, Yvette.

She called a cab and got dressed quickly. She was getting out of here – now. Ten minutes later the cab still hadn't arrived, and Yvette decided to walk to the nearest bus stop. As she left the house and walked down the path she felt the curious sensation that she was being watched. Every time she looked up at a window it looked as if it had just been dropped or pulled closed. Was Errol's paranoia rubbing off on her? She almost laughed out loud. She'd believed that story about him being stalked – she had actually felt sorry for him – and now it looked as though he'd been having an affair all along.

Her thoughts raced. She found it impossible to make sense of the situation because she had no idea who was telling her the truth.

Maybe the affair was over now.

Maybe.

But what if it wasn't? She couldn't take the chance that she was being made a fool of.

As she hurried down the road she became aware of the yellow posters. First one caught her eye, then another, on the next lamppost. As her eyes focused into the distance she saw that every lamppost and tree along this side of the road had a yellow sheet of paper stuck to it. They'd caught the attention of other passers-by too; Yvette watched as they stopped and read them. Stopping by the next tree, she squinted in the bright sun to read the bold printed notice:

RESIDENTS OF WILSON AVENUE
&
CONCERNED CITIZENS OF BRITAIN

I FEEL IT IS MY DUTY TO INFORM YOU OF WHAT IS GOING ON IN YOUR MIDST. ERROL WRIGHT, OF NO. 30 WILSON AVENUE, IS LIVING IN A DEN OF SIN CREATED BY NONE OTHER THAN HIMSELF.

I MYSELF WAS LURED THERE UNDER FALSE PRETENCES A COUPLE OF MONTHS AGO, SEDUCED AND ABUSED SEXUALLY, THEN THROWN AWAY LIKE RUBBISH. MAYBE I WASN'T KINKY ENOUGH FOR HIM.

OTHER WOMEN HAVE NO DOUBT BEEN TREATED THE SAME. JUST A FEW DAYS AGO I WITNESSED HIM OPENLY HAVING SEX WITH A WOMAN IN A LOCAL PARK. ANYBODY COULD HAVE SEEN THEM, EVEN YOUR CHILDREN.

THIS IS A MAN WHO SPEAKS FOR OUR COMMUNITY, A MAN WHO IS SUPPOSED TO UPHOLD MORALS AND BE A ROLE MODEL TO OUR YOUNG.

PERSONALLY I THINK HE SHOULD BE CASTRATED. I LEAVE THE DECISIONS UP TO YOU.

Yvette felt faint as the blood drained from her face. How had she managed to do this? When? Obviously when Errol left this morning he'd not seen it… but most of the neighbours must have done by now.

Yvette felt a range of emotions, but predominant was disgust. She knew now that Anne-Marie must have been watching her house that morning, must have followed them to the park. With blind rage she tore the paper from the tree. Then she ran along the road, ripping, tearing, scratching the posters down. This was pure spite, the senseless degradation of the man she loved. No one deserved to be publicly ridiculed like this. First the portrait, and then this… Her brain was on overload, her life falling apart around her. How was it possible to feel totally happy one moment, and then total despair so soon afterwards?

When she was sure she had all the posters she walked back to Errol's house and posted them through his door. There was bound to be some comeback about this; she felt she ought at least to let him know what was coming.

Anne-Marie sat at the back of the studio, far enough away that he wouldn't see her but not so far that she didn't have a good view. The auditorium was getting busier and more crowded as people began to arrive and move about, preparing for the show ahead of them. She sat next to a young lack man and his girlfriend, who were chatting animatedly about the show and their opinions on the guests. He kept grabbing her hand and stroking her cheek; embarrassed, Anne-Marie tried to keep her head facing the stage. This was her first time as a member of the audience, though she had stood in the wings on several ocassions, watching Errol as he performed, even done her guest slot as the resident psychiatrist. Either way, the experience was awesome – nothing like watching him on a television screen along with millions of others. It was actually being there as history was being made. She imagined what he would be doing right now. Would he have some beautiful make-up artist powdering his nose? Would he be sitting nervously in the wings, waiting for his cue? Would he be reading his lines, sipping something to relax his nerves? She remembered seeing an interview in which he'd said that that was what he did, that even after months in the TV business he still got nervous before each appearance.

Last night Errol's enchanting smile had stayed with her as she'd wandered aimlessly around her flat, drinking wine and staring out of her silent home through the dark living-room windows. With her he had sunk into the bottle of her favourite claret and eventually into her bed, and had stayed as she'd slept restlessly, and had woken with her and her headache on a dull, cold morning.

That had decided her to come. Today's show was about five young men who had set up a new organisation called the Men of Vision, and who intended to change the way black men were perceived in society. She hadn't told Errol she was going to be in the studio; she didn't want him to be any different just because she was in the audience. It would be a surprise if he saw her. But if he didn't then no big deal – she worked only a floor away from him, she was only ever a phone call away. Her phone bill was now two hundred pounds above its usual figure, but it was worth it to bring him closer, even if it was only his voice. She was wondering if Yvette ever came to see him live, when there was suddenly a ripple of excitement and a few cheers from the crowd around her, and she looked immediately to the stage. There he was, wandering into the studio. He raised a hand in acknowledgement, and Anne-Marie was already raising hers, before realising he couldn't see her behind the lights and letting it drop again.

He had a script, a pen and notebook in his hand, and was discussing something with the floor manager...

Errol had tried several times during the day to call Yvette. She wasn't at his place, she had called the gym and told them they'd have to manage without her today, and her answering machine wasn't on.

He walked back to the comparative calm of the hospitality room for a last-minute read through and to greet his guests (whom he always made a point of meeting before a show to put them at ease). Feeling ready as he ever would, he returned to fetch a handkerchief from his dressing room. The phone was ringing as he walked in. It was minutes before the show and he almost ignored it, but he knew a missed call could mean trouble later on, so he impatiently snatched it up.

"Yeah?"

"Errol?"

"Yeah?"

"Errol, have you been home today?"

He gripped the phone tightly. "Anne-Marie?" "Do you like surprises, Errol? I do."

"Anne, stop this..." He heard a click and then the station's internal dial tone. "Shit!" He threw the reciever violently against the wall and dug his fingers into his temples. "Don't do this to me! You have no right to do this to me!"

At precisely six thirty the warm-up man began his routine in front of the seated audience. Errol stood behind the set, listening, deep-breathing. A few minutes after the call from Anne-Marie he'd tried without success to call Yvette again. After last night he felt an overwhelming need to hear her voice. Maybe she'd gone out shopping. This wasn't unusual for Yvette, who loved treating herself to new outfits whenever she felt good.

"Stand by," the floor manager called, and Errol looked around for somewhere to stash the now redundant notes he was holding. His dresser rushed up to him with his jacket still on its hanger. "Man, you've got the wrong jacket on!" He handed Errol the correct item of clothing, grabbed the notes from his hand and disappeared.

"Silent studio, please..." The countdown began. Errol took two more long, deep breaths, flexed and released his shoulders and gave each leg a shake. "Fifteen seconds to recording... ten..."

The walk to his chair on the set got longer each time.

"... three... two..." The signature tune swelled, an out-of-vision voice boomed, "Ladies and Gentlemen, would you please welcome your host for *Do the Wright Thing*, Errol Wright!" and he was on, in the spotlight. The audience applauded, whistled, cheered, and his mind suddenlycleared. His smile was real. This part of his life was untouchable, all his own.

"Thank you... thank you. I am in good company tonight! Thank you... Now, not only am I gonna be in the company of you all..." He waited while the noise died down. "... but tonight my special guests are: the one and only, unpredictable, sensational author of the best-selling book *Baby Mother*, Andrea Taylor!" More applause. "And also a group of young men who wanna say 'Stop looking at the past and look to the future' to the youths out there. And they're here now, so without further ado please welcome my guests, Tyrone, George, Michael and Ricky, the Men of Vision!"

The four men walked in and raised power fists to the audience as they took their seats. They wore black suits, the jackets zipped from bottom to top, and on the back of each were written the words "Open Your Eyes, Men of Vision".

The interview went down extremely well. At the end of it the audience got a chance to throw a few questions in.

"What about women? Don't you think there are young women who need putting on the straight and narrow? What are you doing for them?"

Michael, a light-skinned guy with a very low fade cut, stood up to answer. "Sister, that is for you to take care of. See, if we went into girls' schools and started telling women how we thought they ought to act we would get dissed for not knowing what we're talking about. There is nothing stopping women getting together and doing what we are doing for young men."

"Is what you do religious?"

"What we do is tell young people what's wrong and right." George rose as Michael sat. He was dark, bulky, and wore sunglasses. "Good and evil is the same thing, but we don't want to preach to you all. We're not militant and we're not dictators." A middle-aged black man stood up with his hands on his hips. "But is it working? I mean, don't the kids just go out an' carry on the same way once you're gone?"

"We try never to do one-offs. We are running programmes here. We set up groups to come into the communities, the schools, and teach. We help the teachers to understand where our young black men are coming from. We help the young black men to feel good about themselves, to respect women. 'Cause dat's where they coming from – they want to respect the law and society; they want to know that, no matter what any man do to them, they don't have to be affected unless they want to be affected."

"What are you doing about the ones already in trouble – on the streets, or in prison?"

Ricky, small and light-skinned with thin, silver-rimmed glasses (and looking to Errol more like a member of a male swing group than a new black man), stood and addressed the questioner. "We're working on that. The only thing at the moment that is stopping us is a lack of access to these men in trouble. In prison we have to get permission to go in, so we write to the governors and the local MPs, but usually we'll get an unsatisfactory reply. The trouble with men is that they don't talk about their feelings enough. Who knows when we need help... ?"

Errol couldn't help feeling relieved when finally he ushered the men off the stage in preparation for the arrival of the next guest. He gave a brief, glowing introduction, then faced the main camera. "Please welcome the baby mother with attitude – Miss Andrea Taylor!" He turned to greet his guest. Andrea Taylor walked on to the stage, smiling, head held high, dressed in a long black dress. Her hair was cut in a short, layered crop that emphasised her cheek bones and dark, catlike eyes. She shook Errol's hand before taking a seat. Errol had read her book and was looking forward to this interview. He gave her his sexiest smile. If this woman is a feminist, he was thinking, let's see if I can just charm her...

"Andrea, I've heard a rumour that you're now a single woman out of choice. Is this true?"

She laughed modestly. "I am single, Errol, and I'm single because I haven't met a man who matches up to my criteria: ambition, good looks, charm, generosity, sex appeal, sense of humour, an air of authority..." She was counting the points on her fingers. "... a man who will let me be myself, who will have a willingness to love my children as his own—"

"You don't ask a lot, do you?" Errol joked, and the audience laughed. "So, your book, *Baby Mother* – was that based on your own experience?"

"Every author puts a little of himself or herself into a novel. *Baby Mother* needed my experience to give it credibility. I've raised two children on my own since their father walked out on me. Like my lead character, Jennifer Edwards, he left while I was pregnant. So, yes, I can identify with the story, and I used my own experiences and those of my friends and family to create the characters."

"Was it painful to write – because I know you've been single now for seven years? Dredging up the past must have made you feel some

135

bitterness."

"It was actually hard to remember the bitter feelings," she smiled. "Mostly because I am happy now, and my children are happy and healthy. Although at times it's hard, trying to explain to them why they haven't got a father around, they have adjusted to being in a one-parent family pretty well. I've achived an ambition that I held since the age of fifteen; I'm a published author now, and the bitterness has gone. Sometimes I even thank him for leaving me, because I don't believe I would have had the inspiration to write if we'd still been togterher."

"You actually work full-time too, don't you?"

"Yes. I work a nine-to-five job, raise two children, and I'm now writing my second novel."

Errol clapped and the audience joined him, a cheer going up from the women. "So, what is your secret?" he asked. "How do you fit it all in? Tell us about a typical day in your home."

"Well, my alarm goes off at five forty-five a.m., I get up at six and do half an hour of step aerobics, then I get washed and dressed and get the kids up. I drop the children down to my mum's – she's my child-minder – then I go to work. After work I pick the children up and get them dinner. Then I start writing. How much I do depends on whether I have a deadline to meet and how the story is flowing."

"A pretty packed day!" More applause. "So, when people tell you they want to write but can't find the time, what do you tell them?"

"I'll usually ask them what they do with their evenings and weekends. If they say thinks like watch TV, sleep, shopping, housework, take care of the children, then obviously writing isn't for them. When you want to write, you *have* to write. Sometimes to me it's more important than sleep; it's like a therapy..."

By the time he got home Errol was almost frantic. He'd tried to call Yvette three times on the way, without success. As soon as he opened the front door he had an idea why. Somehow, even before he picked up the scraps of yellow paper that littered the hallway's carpet, he knew that Anne-Marie had her finger in this, if not her whole hand. Slowly he pieced some of the larger pieces of poster together until he had the whole message. Now he understood Anne-Marie's phone call earlier.

Then he saw the torn paper, the polystyrene beads, the painting...

He sat in his living room and stared at the four walls. He started off feeling guilty, then angry, then he wanted to punch glass. For the first time in his life he was feeling rage, and he had no idea how to vent it.

Yvette sat at Karen's kitchen table, her hands wrapped around her cup of coffee. Tyrone and Karen's two kids were watching television in the front room. Yvette had been badgered into spending the night and she had agreed, knowing that Errol couldn't possibly contact her here.

She was in a worse state than she'd thought. She seemed to be filled with adolescent emotion that she was unused to.

"Men!" Karen said, half filling her glass again. "Why the hell did we think Errol would be any different? Damn! Give them a bit of fame and it goes straight to their damned cock."

"*Why*, though? Shit, I shouldn't have let him get under my skin. I thought I was giving him all he wanted..."

"What are you, blind *and* stupid?" Karen touched Yvette's hand, not wanting her friend to take affront. "I can say that, 'cause we're soul mates. But men *never* have all they want. There's always something missing in their lives."

"But what is it, though? Karen, you know I'm no pushover. I waited with Errol. I wasn't carrying on like no love-sick teenager. I was making grown-up plans. He didn't even know how I felt until a few days ago..." She faltered in her speech. "I still love him, you know..."

"Then, when he knew he had you where he wanted you – under his thumb..."

Yvette looked up from her coffee. "Maybe I should have given him a chance to explain."

"Now you're sounding like a pushover!" Karen got up, turned her chair round and sat backwards on it, resting her arms on its back. "Baby girl, you did that when you came clean about knowing about her. And what did he do in return? Lie through his teeth! This bitch basically told you she was shagging him. But you chose to believe him."

"So that's it? It's over?"

"Of course it is! Leave him to all them celebs and models, them television people. They're not for us, an' he's one a dem."

"We had it good, you know. I can't just forget him—"

"It was sex, babe. You told me yourself." Karen looked steadily at her through a haze of cigarette smoke. "It's not love. It might have been good, but you'll get over it."

Yvette was silent. Her friend watched her, wondering how the woman she knew so well could get into a situation so alien to her nature. "You're not getting ready to forgive him, are you?" she asked sternly.

"I suppose I did overreact..." Karen opened her mouth to say something.

"No – let me finish. He told me this woman was deranged – you even thought the same thing when we met her. I've had one-night stands, you know – cheap thrills, irrestible circumstances. He never promised to be faithful to me. Neither of us promised that."

"Just 'cause you don't say it doesn't..." The telephone started to ring and Karen got up to answer it.

Yvette watched her. It could be Errol trying to track her down.

"Jennifer!... Girl, you calling from abroad?... No! Really?... Course – we got to get together. Where you staying?... Donna's... Okay. I'll catch up with you tomorow. I'll call you... Yeah. Listen, got to go. I've got company."

She looked at her watch as she hung up. "It's nearly midnight. She must be in another time zone!" She came back to sit by Yvette's side.

Yvette yawned and stretched. "Speaking of time, I'm tired..." "Time to walk away from Errol the Irresistible."

Yvette straightened her back suddenly. "You're right. We have different ideas about how affairs should be conducted."

"You wanna go to bed..." Karen smiled. "Or we could open some Haagen-Dazs with loads of canned whipped cream."

They both laughed.

"What'd I do without you, Kaz?"

"You'd manage. Not very well, mind you. But you're strong. When he finally finds you and you have to speak to him and hear his excuses, that's when you'll really feel it." Karen got up to get the ice cream.

Yvette breathed deeply. Tommorow was another day.

Two days later, Errol woke to find that he'd overslept. It had taken him until four in the morning to drop off, and it was the only the sounds of Helen starting work in the study that had woken him.

He had spent the previous day undergoing excruciating mental torture. Yvette's colleague at the gym had told him she'd taken leave at short notice, and she wasn't picking up the phone at home. When he'd called Karen's, she'd told him that if Yvette wanted to call him she would call him and to stop wasting her time. So he'd decided to let it go for a while. Let her cool off.

Maybe she simply didn't love him. Could she have been like all the rest, those who just wanted him for him his money and fame? Yeah. Maybe that was it. Perhaps, when she thought she might have to share it with someone else, she didn't want to know any more. He didn't want to believe this, but if it was true he couldn't blame her for reacting the way she had. And now she didn't trust him. He was hurt by that realisation.

He stood in the shower for almost half an hour, the barrage of water like fingers, digging, kneading. Some of this time he spent thinking over the past few weeks, but for most of it he was just blank.

Later, he shuffled through his mail while eating dry toast. Another love letter from from Anne-Marie – he recognised the handwritng. He didn't bother to open it, but left it aside to go into the file.

Most of his calls that morning were business, except for one from his mother, which perked up his day. She still cared. Nothing from Yvette.

That night he dined with his good friend Chris Stevens, the only man he felt that understood him.

The waiter poured their wine, then left them to study the menus. "I think I'm in love with her."

"You! In love?"

"I dunno. Now I've said it, how do I know what love is?"

"Boy, don't ask me, you know. 'Cause I been caught in that is-it-love-or-is-it-lust triangle too many times."

"It's definitely not only lust." Errol took a gulp of wine and leant his elbow on the table lowering his voice a little. "I think about her almost constantly; I have to hear her voice at odd times during the day or night; she makes me feel good…"

"Yeah, you been bitten."

"It just hit me. Like one day I was fine being single, doing my own t'ing…" His vocabulary always seemed to slip around his closest friends. "And now, whenever I'm at a loose end, the first person I think about is her. Her opinion matters to me…" He shrugged his shoulders. "I dunno. I guess I was so out of practice, I didn't even realise it was happening."

Yvette had her head in the clouds. Walking was a favourite pastime of hers. Walking on her own, walking with Errol… It helped clear her head. When Tyrone had been a baby she would often walk for miles, pushing the pushchair. Cheapest way to keep fit, and the baby always slept well afterwards.

She was approaching their restaurant. They'd started to call it "ours" because he'd taken her there many times. They even had their own special table, a glass partition separating them from the other diners. God, how romantic it used to be… and they would go home and make love, and it would continue all night long. She shivered with the memory. She still loved that fool.

She stopped by the restaurant door, wanting to go in, to sit at their table, order food and reminisce... No. She was being stupid. About to walk away, she caught sight of a very familiar back. He was getting up... to pull out a chair for a very stylishly dressed woman.

Yvette's mouth fell open and then clamped shut as the blood rushed to her temples. "You really are something, Mr Wright!" she hissed. "Two women not enough for you?" Arms pumping, she barged into the restaurant. She didn't wait to reach the table before she started to vent her pent-up anger. "Didn't take you long, did it! Got bored of Anne-Marie already?"

Errol's companion, expensively dressed and way too old for him, looked up in astonishment. "Excuse me—"

"Do you *know* about him? Can't keep his dick in his pants longer than a couple of hours."

"Yvette..." Errol started.

"There must be some mistake," the woman gasped.

"I'll give him a mistake." Yvette siezed a nearly full pint-glass of lager from the table and threw the contents over his head. He collided with his chair, which clattered to the floor behind him, causing muted gasps from inquisitive diners.

Yvette turned and stalked out, still cursing.

Chantelle Wright, Errol's companion, sought an explanation. "Errol, what is this all about?"

"It's okay, Mum, I'll sort it out." He followed Yvette's lead, and caught up with her as she threw the door open. She came to a halt outside the restaurant. Breathing heavily, she could feel his presence at her back. She turned to see him mopping lager from his head and face with a handkerchief that was already sopping wet. "Your mother?"

He loosened his tie as he answered. "My mother. Arrived this morning. I didn't expect her, she called from the airport..."

Yvette's hands flew to her head in embarrassment and she backed away from him. "Oh my God! What did I just do?" she gasped. "I just went completely insane in front of a TV celebrity's mother – and not just *any* TV celebrity's mother; the woman could have been my mother-in-law! It's a good thing we're not still together. I'll never have to see her again, or those people in the restaurant. All those people..." she added breathlessly. "I think I'm going to pass out..." She spun round, almost head-butting Errol in the process. "What the *hell* was I thinking of? I *wasn't* thinking, was I? I was about as crazy as your bloody stalker." She looked at his ruined suit. "Look at you... God, I'm sorry. I mean, I'd better go – let you get back to your mother." She turned away as she felt the tears stinging her eyes, not wanting him to see her bawl.

Errol grabbed her arm and she turned back and looked into his eyes. He pulled her to him. "No, *I'm* sorry..."

Yvette twisted out of his grasp; it wasn't difficult as he wasn't trying to restrain her. "I don't want to do this. Just let me walk out of your life now..."

"What are you talking about? Walk out of my life? I don't want to lose you."

She held her hands up, palms towards him in an attempt to stop him saying the things he didn't mean. "No. It's not happening, Errol. You're not getting the chance to twis' me up again."

He looked pained, his eyes filling with concern. "I don't want to do that. I wouldn't do that." He glanced back to the restaurant. "Come back inside with me. I want you to meet my mum."

She gave him an are-you-crazy? look.

"Then let me bring her out to meet you. She's only here for four days..."

Yvette now started to feel a tinge of anger resurfacing. She crossed her arms and tapped one foot, breathing hard to hold on to her emotions. "And what about your other woman? How are you going to explain there being two of us?"

"There *is* no other woman. Only you." She let him pull her into his arms this time, and she sobbed into his chest for a minute. Then she turned her back to him. "Maybe another time, eh? I have to go." She started to walk away.

"Yvette!"

"I'll call you!" She started to trot and then broke into a run, tears streaming down her face. Their worlds were just too different. She should never have attempted to be something that she wasn't. Errol Wright's wife? Yeah, right!

As Errol watched the warm-up man's routine on the monitor beside him he recalled how he'd felt just a week before. He'd been so happy. He'd finally decided he had found the woman who could keep him that way. He wasn't after any upper-class snob who couldn't go out unless she had a new designer label. He wanted Yvette Barker: simple, down-to-earth, sexy, ambitious in her own right... and in love with him.

Now he felt completely changed. The happiness had susided, leaving him feeling vaguely distraught, wishing he'd made firmer decisions about Anne-Marie.

His dresser came up and whispered in his ear. "Got a visitor for you. I got her a drink and put her in the box. Let me take your notes." He whipped the script out of Errol's hand and disappeared.

Errol was left standing with his mouth open. He called out, as loud as any whisper could be: "What visitor?" but the man was already on the other side of the door and didn't hear a word.

Joanne, the make-up supervisor, rushed up with a powder compact in her hand to dust his nose.

Errol brushed her hand away irritably. "Leave me alone, will you!"

Joanne, looking totally flustered, backed off. "Sorry. You had a bit of a shine…"

Errol realised he was being totally unreasonable. The woman was only doing her job, and there he was practically assaulting her for it. He touched her arm. "Forgive me, Jo. I'm a little on edge. Must be nerves." He tried a smile, which he hoped looked convincing.

She lowered her eyes shyly. "You'll do fine – you always do." He was so charismatic – and more. Errol could make a ninety-year-old grandmother blush.

"Thanks." Errol knew his reaction had been caused by the fact that it might be Yvette – or, wors,e Anne-Marie – waiting for him in the control box. The evening stretched ahead of him dauntingly.

The recording didn't go well. He couldn't concentrate. he forgot lines, missed scripted camera angles, and basically blew his cool image. The studio audience was getting restless with the constant takes and retakes. They began to shift in their seats; some got up and left for the lavatories or to get refreshments. The floor manager attempted to settle them down.

Joanne rushed out to retouch Errol's make-up, and someone was sent to check on the reformed drug addict he was about to interview. Then recording continued. The *Do the Wright Thing* theme tune played him in, and he announced the guest and stood to greet him. Errol's heart sank to the pit of his stomach when the young white man stumbled and giggled as he took the single step to the podium. Errol hastily put his hands out for him to steady himself.

"Yikes!" He giggled again. "Who put that step there?"

The show didn't get any better. Errol knew they could bleep out the language afterwards, but his guest was either stoned, brain-dead or had an attitude problem. It was hard work getting a coherent word out of the man at all. A few minutes before the final music, the floor manager began to make signals for him to wind up the interview.

The man was retelling a tale of the night he'd broken down his girlfriend's door while she was out, and stolen anything valuable to get money for drugs.

"Well, Tony, that's a terrifying story – and I'm sure the viewers and our audience are glad to hear that it's all behind you now…"

"Yeah." Tony rubbed his eyes. "Yeah, I… I lef all of that now, man." He stood and swayed on his feet. "The only drug I take now is caffeine."

Errol frowned and the audience gasped unanimously.

Errol moved swiftly to regain control. "Well, Tony, the clocks have caught up with us." He truned to the audience. "Time for me to say thanks to our fascinating guest, Tony Collins!"

Tony was trying to get off the set. He tripped on the step and fell in a tangled heap to the floor. The music started to play the show out, louder than usual to cover up the mutterings of the audience, and two medics rushed on stage to help the guest off.

"Last time I deal with druggies…" Errol, forgetting all about his supposed visitor, headed for his dressing room where he immediately poured himself a stiff brandy.

He held his head in his hands for a few moments, and when he looked up his mother was standing in the doorway.

"Mum!"

"Hi, baby. I saw what happened. You're not having a very good day, are you?"

"Not having a very good life. Period."

Chantelle Wright came into the room and stood behind her son, placing a manicured hand on his shoulder. "Sounds to me like you need a love life."

"I had one – until I ruined it with one stupid mistake."

"We all make mistakes, baby. And each of them is a learning experience. But the only people who learn are the people who do something about making it right again, the people who don't let those mistakes ruin the rest of their lives."

Errol met her eyes in the mirror. His relationship with his mother, a thing of such distance in his childhood, had become stronger and warmer throughout his adult life. Chantelle held the hair off her face and bent to kiss him on the cheek. "You love that girl, don't you?"

He nodded.

"And she loves you?"

His voice caught in his throat. "She did."

"Boy, don't give me that," she said, gently but firmly. "She's hurt – and she's waiting for you to show her that you're ready to give her devotion and commitment. I don't know what went on – that's none of my business – but I don't want to go home knowing you are unhappy. You go get her."

Errol swivelled his chair to face his mother and circled her waist with his long arms. She was so trim that his arms doubled over, his fingers reaching his elbows. She held his head to her stomach. "You don't need me to tell you where your heart lies, Errol. Remember, never stop trying for the things you want in life."

He felt so secure in that moment, nestled in his mother's arms, that he wished briefly that the rest of the world would just evaporate and he could stay like this for ever. No woman had ever made him feel this secure. Except Yvette. She cared.

Marion sank against the wall outside Errol's dressing room. Finding the door slightly ajar and voices coming from inside, she had waited silently in the corridor, and had overheard the last part of their conversation. She had seen the elegant older woman earlier, and had assumed she was working for the studio until she'd been shown into Errol's dressing room. She didn't know her, but hearing the advice she'd given Errol, Marion felt a resent growing for her. For the last few days he had come to Marion for advice on relationships and women – one woman in particular: Yvette. She thought he was much better off staying single, and had told him so. Yvette couldn't possibly be right for him. As soon as the going had got tough she'd left. She hadn't stood by him. She couldn't possibly put up with the celebrity pressure and the long hours. Errol needed someone stronger.

As soon as this other woman was out of here, Marion decided, she would have to get him on his own again. First that Anne-Marie and now Yvette screwing with his head… Why couldn't they all just leave him alone?

Errol sat in the car outside Karen's house for fifteen minutes before he had the courage to get out and face the music. The door was answered by Karen's ten-year old-daughter. Errol bent down to speak to her.

"Hello. Is your mummy in?"

Without answering she turned round and walked back into the house calling, "Mum! Errol's at the door!"

In the living room Karen put a finger to her lips, indicating to Yvette that she should stay there and keep quiet. "I'll handle it," she whispered.

Yvette got up anyway, and pressed her back to the living-room door so she could hear everything. The children watched this little act, bemused for a couple of seconds before turning back to their video game.

"Good evening, Errol. What can I do for you?"

"Hi, Karen." He shoved a hand in his pocket and put on his brightest smile. She didn't invite him in. "Is Yvette here?"

"Errol, you asked me dat yesterday *and* dis morning, and I told you she doesn't want you to contact her."

"If you just let me see her, I might be able to persuade her otherwise."

Karen crossed her arms. She knew he wanted to make amends – but did he have a right to? Yvette was her friend, and she had a duty to protect her.

Errol could see all of this going on through her eyes. It looked like she wasn't going to give in. He pulled an envelope from his pocket. "Do me a favour, then. Give this to her. Please."

Karen took the envelope and glanced at it. "You got it. Anything else?"

Errol started to go and then turned back, looking into Karen's eyes. "Tell her... tell her I love her."

Another sleepless night. Yvette lay on her back on Karen's sofa-bed, Errol's crumpled letter still clutched in her hand. Karen was a good friend, but there were some decisions a woman had to make on her own. He said he loved her – and Yvette knew how she felt about him. Even after she'd made such a fool of herself in that restaurant, and then the tears afterwards, he cared enough to seek her out and give her this. How many men did she know who could write a real love letter?

What would he be doing now? Thinking of her? She doubted it. But all of a sudden she felt she had to know; she needed to feel wanted. On impulse she got out of bed and picked up the phone. Dialling his number was hard, but necessary.

"Hello?'

Yvette held the phone to her ear and listened. Are you alone? she wanted to ask. Are you missing me?

"Anne-Marie, is that you?"

Yvette suddenly felt sick. It was *her* he expected to hear. It didn't even occur to him that it could be someone else.

"Haven't you caused enough trouble? I warned you, woman, and I'm not playing any more. You keep out of my life or…"

Yvette hung up and started to shiver, so she lay down and pulled the duvet up around her head. He had sounded so unlike himself… He had been enraged. That wasn't her Errol. What was this woman doing to him?

Finally she managed to sleep, only to be woken up again by a sudden realisation about her situation. As she lay in the dark her thoughts assembled, and she knew she was right. This was exactly what Anne-Marie had wanted: for Yvette to walk out and leave the coast clear for her to move in on her man.

"Well she's messing with the wrong couple," she said out loud. Yvette made up her mind to go back, to see Errol and talk. There was a lot at stake here. Too much of her heart was invested in their relationship. They had a home to get ready to move into before Christmas. She was going to fight for her man. He meant too much to her. But first she had to build up the courage to face him and lay down some rules.

The club was packed, which was usual for Nightmoves on a Sunday evening, and being ladies' night there was an unusually high proportion of women in the room. The men certainly had their pick. But there was only one woman Errol was interested in. He was acting on information that she would be here tonight, and he didn't care how much she protested, he was determined to make her see the truth.

He walked tall through the dimly-lit club, trying to look as casual as possible. He was aware of the stares of recognition and the girls whispering to their girlfriends; it was an occupational hazard he had become used to.

The first hour was uneventful, but then as he was about to go back to the bar for another drink he saw her. She was swaying to the sound of the gentle soul music, her eyes half closed. The feeling in his chest was so strong, he thought for a moment he was about to have some kind of seizure. He approached her as quickly and carefully as he could – no way did he want her to make a bolt for the door. She didin't notice him until he was standing in front of her, devouring her with his eyes. The music throbbed and pulsed, as did his whole body. The beat was almost hypnotising. Errol registered the shock in her eyes. She had stopped dancing and now faced him square on, her eyes challenging him in her own way. He accepted the challenge. He reached for her, gathering her in his arms. She melted into them, kissing him hard and deep. He held her by the back of her neck, kissing her with equal vigour. Their bodies pressed hard, as if sealed together. His hands roamed her bare back, her tight bottom through her tiny satin skirt. They seemed to be barely moving, but where their hips were pressed together they were moving, winding so slowly it was like making love. The track came to an end and Yvette met his eyes once more.

"Let's go," she said.

And they left, leaving Karen watching with amusement. "That girl's got it bad," she said to herself.

The phone woke Errol just before seven o'clock the next morning. He let it ring until the answerphone picked it up. Yvette was snuggled up beside him. He looked down at her, gently removing a few strands of hair from her face. She was back in his life. Last night their lovemaking had been intense, as potent as before, but without the game-playing. It had been the soothing, pacifying love of true lovers.

He kissed her forehead lightly and she woke up. They squeezed each other for a few minutes without saying a word. Then she whispered, "What are you thinking about?"

He kissed her again, rubbing her bare forearm. "About you – us."

She breathed deeply, inhaling the scent of his body. "Me too."

"I can't believe how blind I"ve been. I didn't realise what I had before now."

She smiled sleepily. "It happens."

He tipped her chin up so that their eyes met. "You won't leave me again, will you?" "Are you planning to sleep with another woman again?"

Errol tensed and sunk a little further into his pillow. "Never. I don't wanna be a player no more. The only woman I want is you, Eve."

"I'm glad. 'Cause that's what you got."

As he left the house that morning he marvelled at how freakishly warm it was for late November. He'd got behind the wheel of his car before he saw the note on the windscreen. He looked back towards the house and saw Yvette coming down the path, so he scrambled back out and retrieved the note, stuffing it into the glove box before letting Yvette into the car.

Anne-Marie hadn't given up yet. He hoped that if he ignored her enough she'd finally stop, seeing her manipulation wasn't working. His mind soon turned from her and back to Yvette, who slid into the seat beside him, tying the belt on her leather swing jacket. They were going to view the house. Yvette hadn't cancelled the sale, but was waiting to hear from the bank about whether they would increase her loan. Errol had assured her that if he liked it, they could forget the loan.

His eyes were still apparaising her as she turned towards him.

She giggled. "What's up?"

"Just admiring my rib."

"*What?*"

"'Eve, I'm thinking of changing my name to Adam."

She laughed out loud, punching his arm playfully as he started the car. Occasionally he could surprise her with his romantic streak.

Errol looked around the empty room. One wall was completely dominated by a huge window overlooking the rooftops of houses and buildings for miles. He could imagine the view at night, twinkling city lights.

Yvette watched him, her hands in her jacket pockets. "Well?"

"Well… It needs a lot of work. A few gallons of paint, miles of carpeting and expensive curtains. To heat this place is gonna break the bank. We won't even be able to move in until we've had all the essential rooms decorated…" Yvette smiled coyly. "But you like it though, don't you?"

"Elegant squalor."

"You gotta admit it's got potential. It's exactly what I want."

"Home sweet home, hey?"

Her shoulders dropped with relief. He liked it, she could tell. She did a twirl in the middle of the wooden floor. There was a huge brick fireplace dominating one wall and she danced over to it, stretching her arms along the length of its mantel.

Errol, who had been watching her every move, moved quickly towards her and pinned her arms in place. "Okay, we'll buy the house, turn it into a palace…"

She licked her lips, her eyes fixed on his steady stare. "I love it – the house, the view. the garden…"

"Me?"

"Of course you, rude bwoy."

He pressed closer. "How 'bout we christen this room as ours?"

"Oh no, big boy. You just control yourself. We're not doing anything in here until I have my four-poster bed and a shag pile carpet and a fire burning in that grate."

"You drive a hard bargain." He released her hands.

"Only way to keep your man under manners," she said.

Later, after dropping Yvette off at home, Errol remembered the note and removed it from the glove box. It was a single sheet of A4 paper folded in half, typed with large, bold letters. It said, "LOVE HAS NO BOUNDARIES."

Kissing his teeth, he screwed it up and dumped it in the street. The sooner he moved out of here and in with Yvette, the better.

Anne-Marie was searching for aspirin, paracetamol, Nurofen – anything. She always had something available; her long hours of concentrated reading required it.

Giving up, she went back into her living room and stretched out on the sofa, her dress riding up to reveal her soft, feminine thighs. Waiting. She was waiting for the call. It *would* come, wouldn't it? A few words, just some contact… She glanced at the telephone. Why didn't the damn thing ring? She didn't necessarily want to talk to him, but she passionately wanted to hear his voice. But deep down she knew he wouldn't phone. She tried to think of something else. Work – that subject always brought her back to thinking of Errol.

Family – she had none. She wanted Errol's babies…

It was no good. It was impossible to think of anything else. She needed him. To hear from him. Just to see him. He should have got her messages by now. If not the phone messages, then the one on his car. Trying to get hold of him at work was getting harder, he placed as many barriers in her way as he could. He hadn't even called to bawl her out about the posters; surely he knew about them by now. The phone rang and her body jerked upright. She dashed across the room, knocking her ankle painfully on the coffee table as she went, and grabbed it on the third ring.

"Hello?" she answered breathlessly.

"Anne-Marie?" A female voice.

"Yes."

"It's Marion. How are you? I haven't heard from you in two weeks." Marion sounded so cheerful, it was sickening to Anne-Marie's ears.

"Oh, Marion," she sighed, and sat cross-legged on the floor.

"Well? What's been happening?"

"Happening?"

"You know – the new job."

Anne-Marie summoned up all her expertise to disguise her disappointment. "Oh, everything's been great. Errol and I have worked on a couple of programmes together. You know, researching, interviewing techniques…"

Marion was fishing for information. Before she took sides, she knew it was good practice to get both angles of the story. "Oh? He never said."

"Well… He's trying to keep our relationship… you know, under wraps."

Marion felt her heart sink to the pit of her stomach. Just who *was* telling the truth here? "Relationship, is it now?"

"We've been seeing each other… intimately."

"You *have*? You and Errol?" Marion asked incredulously. He had only just got back together with Yvette! Marion couldn't believe, with the amount of work he'd spent on doing that, that he would already be two-timing her. "Is that such a surprise? You know we've been getting on pretty well. In fact when the phone rang I thought it might have been him. We're going out tonight… or staying in, as the case may be…"

Marion was flabbergasted. This woman could also tell stories – was there no end to her talents? "Well… congratulations! I guess you finally got your man." She tried to keep her voice neutral. "Although I must admit I'm surprised."

"I told you, all he needed was the right woman. Now I think he loves me. I know I love him. But, Marion, remember: don't say anything. I would hate for him to get cold feet. We've come so far. He doesn't need any pressure right now."

"Yes… Well, it's none of my business. I really called to ask you to a dinner party to celebrate my birthday. Errol, of course, is also invited. I suppose you could come together."

"When?"

"Next Friday night."

"I'll try. Can I let you know after I've talked to him?"

"Sure."

"I'd love to be there, but Errol's schedule has been a little hectic recently. We may decide to stay in."

"I've already left a message on his answerphone. He never misses my parties."

"We'll be there then."

"Good. I'll get off the line in case he's trying to get through. See you next week."

Anne-Marie's false smile fell from her face as she put the receiver down. Her heart-rate was erratic and her throat felt dry. A couple! She and Errol – a couple? What had got into her? She laughed out loud. Such a good actress! How the hell was she going to pull this off, if the actor was refusing to accept the script? Well, she had until next week. A week, to become Errol's other half. It wouldn't be that hard. He had already taken the first step.

The blinking light on the answering machine told Errol that he had five messages. He had no interset in playing them back, but somehow, as if magnetically drawn, he pressed the playback button.

Every message was from her. She had started by simply asking him to call her, and ended up screaming that she needed to talk to him urgently.

Anne-Marie had drifted off, but being a light sleeper she was fully awake on the second ring. She picked the phone, and before she could finish saying hello Errol's voice cut her off, cold and insistent.

"I got your messages. And as I've said before, don't call me. Don't send me nothing. I won't be returning your calls. It's over. Take care of yourself. Bye."

The line went dead. Anne-Marie stared at the reciever, then slammed it down and burst into tears

By Monday Errol was feeling better emotionally, but his workload was giving him no time to enjoy it and he had a dull, persistent headache. He rubbed his eyes with his fingertips and closed the folder that lay in front of him. His eyes drifted to the roses, dumped unceremoniously upside-down in the dustbin in the corner of his dressing room. They had arrived earlier that day with a card from Anne-Marie: "Marry me, Errol, and I'll make you the happiest man on earth." What the hell was she playing at? He'd thought they had it all sorted out. She must have sent these before his orders to her last night. Luckily her stint on his show was over for now, and they didn"t have to work together for a while – although she was still hanging around the studio.

He had issued a notice to his assistant that day: "If Anne-Marie Simms calls I'm very busy, okay? Meeting, script conference, whatever. Tell security she's not allowed up to this office. Understood?"

"Any reason I should know about?" she had asked.

"No." He'd turned his back then, dismissing her.

The phone rang, making him jump, and he was tempted to let it go, but as usual his hand found itself reaching out and picking up the reciever hesitantly, steeling himself against Anne-Marie's voice should it be her.

"Errol?"

"Marion, thank goodness! How are you?'

"Fine. Good to hear that someone's glad to hear from me…"

"Who wouldn't be glad to hear from you?"

"When was the last time we had a quiet drink together? We used to do it all the time. Anne-Marie wasn't too happy when I called her last night."

That name again. "Yeah?"

"Why didn't you tell me, Errol?"

"Tell you what?"

"That you and she were seeing each other."

Errol was no longer surprised by any revelations concerning Anne-Marie Simms. What did surprise him, though, was that she hadn't given up. "Because we're not. What's she been saying?" "Errol, I know this is none of my business, but she told me you were, in her words, 'Intimate'. She also said that you were keeping your relationship a secret."

Errol moaned, sagging visibly in his chair. "It's not true."

"That's not what she thinks. The other day she was wearing a diamond ring. I asked her about it and she said you'd given it to her after she spent the night at your house."

"She stole Yvette's ring!"

"That's not how she tells it. I didn't think anything of it at the time – I know you have spare rooms, so she could have slept over – but now—"

"Marion you don't know the half of it! The woman's obsessed. All right, I admit we had one night… You know, it was nothing. You know Yvette and I are back together?"

"Does she know about your one-night stand?"

"Unfortunately that's what caused the split – but she believes my side of the story. Yvette trusts me. I can't lose her now. And I couldn't tell you about it; you were just too close to home."

"Errol, as I said before, this is none of my business. But Anne-Marie seems to think there's something going on. Maybe you weren't clear enough when you said you weren't interested. I know you men; you probably told her you'd call her sometime and now she's sitting around waiting for that call."

"It wasn't like that! From the start I told her nothing was going on." Errol's headache suddenly throbbed painfully. "Look, Marion, just stay out of my business, okay?" He hung up and instantly regretted letting off on Marion like that. But why were all these women all of a sudden trying to tell him how to run his life?

As Christmas loomed inexorably closer, Errol fould himself relaxing more and more into his relationship with Yvette. For the first time in months he was feeling extremely loved and pampered. Yvette had convinced herself that the affair – or whatever it was had gone on with Anne-Marie – was over, and now at last she felt happy to be in love. She bought them sexy underwear (even though they were for her she was wearing them for him) and spiced up their already spicy sex life. Massages became a regular thing – she was doing *all* the things that women are told they do when in love: cooking, cleaning, rushing home to be with him, constantly picking up the phone when they weren't together.

"You know, there's something about your body in dungerees that's got my mind wandering…" he was saying.

"What?" Yvette carefully half-turned on top of the step ladder, a paint roller in one hand. She was wearing a pair of denim dungarees over a plain white vest; her hair was caught up in a bushy ponytail; a shaft of winter sunlight caught her face sideways on. Errol thought he had never seen her look more beautiful.

"The dungarees… leave a lot to the imagination."

"Turning you on, is it? Maybe I'll start a whole new fasion trend. Painted baggy dungarees." It was a grumble, but her eyes were twinkling.

Errol cocked his head to one side, one paint-splotched hand on his chin. "You know, you could have something there…"

"Look, you – are we supposed to be decorating or admiring each other's bodies? At this rate we'll still be painting at Christmas."

"What, no ravishing today?" He made a puppy dog face.

Yvette kissed her teeth and turned back to the wall. She was enjoying watching her home take shape. And she found it doubly satisfying to be doing it with her partner – the partner she hoped to have around for the rest of her life and had come so close to losing more than once.

Some of the walls needed to be stripped and filled, and the skirting boards replaced. The floorboards, they had both agreed, would look wicked sanded and polished. At the end of each "decorating day" they would massage away the aches and pains from thier necks, backs and arms. Although they weren't living together yet, they were spending a lot more time together on the house project. In the time they had for breaks they would laugh, hold hands and kiss and cuddle just like newly-weds.

The house was slowly but surely taking shape. Errol had wanted to get professionals in to do the whole lot – the renovations and the decorating, including the interior design – but Yvette was having none of it. This was her home, and she intended to make it exactly as she wanted it. Of course the renovations had to be done professionally, but the

153

decorating... ! Errol's mother would never have allowed him to take part in this sort of activity. Whenever his childhood home had been decorated, a team of designers would swoop in and usher the family out until the job was completed. Now he wondered what his mum would think if she'd seen him the other night, down on his hands and knees sanding the wooden floor, or now, covered in paint, his head dusty with plaster.

A few minutes later he dropped his roller back into its tray. "Finished!"

Yvette looked across the hall at the smooth, still wet expanse of wall. "How the hell did you finish before me?"

He threw back his handsome head and laughed. "Jealous?"

"You sure you done it good? I'm gonna check, you know..."

"Sore loser, eh? Want me to finish yours for you?"

"How would you like to be coloured blue from head to toe?"

"What'd I tell you? Sore loser."

He ducked when Yvette turned on him, roller in hand, aimed for flicking, then held held his hands out in appeasement. "Okay! Sorry, babe.You're a good loser. Satisfied? How 'bout some coffee?"

Yvette didn't answer. She dipped the roller into the tray for the last time, and watched the last bit of plaster disappaear beneath the cool blue paint. "Perfect!"

It had been a long day, and Errol couldn't wait to get home. But before he called it a day he had a report to write up. Soon they would be making the last recording of the show this year. The phone rang, and he cussed in annoyance as he reached for it, saving his document with the other hand.

"Anne-Marie Simms calling again, Mr Wright," the operator told him.

"Again? I thought you told her I'd call back."

"I did, but she's quite insistent."

"Okay, put her on..." He heard the click of the call being put through. "What is it with you?"

"I dreamt about you last night."

A vein throbbed in his forehead. "I'm really not interested in your dreams." She continued as though he hadn't said a word. "I was watching you on TV. I had this incredible urge to touch you. So I held out my arms and you stepped right out of the television and into them."

"I'm sorry, Anne-Marie, but you're not leaving me much choice I'm going to have to get legal advice on this."

"You shouldn't have thrown away those roses. How do you think it made me feel? I was furious, Errol. So furious I almost forgot how much

I love you."

"Goodbye, Anne-Marie."

A few minutes later there was a knock on his office door, and before he could look up Anne-Marie had let herself in and closed the door behind her.

"So. You won't take my calls, you leave me little choice."

"I have little respect or time for women who continue to throw themselves at me after I've told them I'm not interested. Now will you kndly leave?"

"I'll teach you about respect, Mr Wright." She strolled over to his desk and sat on the edge.

Errol pretended to be suddenly engrossed in the computer screen.

"There's a party at Marion's on Friday night. I was wondering if you'd like to go with me."

"No." The single word was sharp and stern.

"Actually I wasn't asking you – I was telling you. We *are* going together. I've already told Marion. I know Yvette won't be there…"

Now she had his attention again. "How the hell would you know that?"

"I know all about you. She found out about us and dumped you, didn't she?"

Errol's ran his right hand over his head and down to the nape of his neck. "For your information, Yvette and I are back together. Marion invited me in my own right as her friend. And I shall be taking my woman. Now get your ass off my desk and go and do some work. That's what you get paid for, I presume…" he added with a hint of malice.

"I think you're making a big mistake, Errol. Kiss-and-tell stories are very big at the moment. How would your loved ones feel to open the Sunday papers and be faced with pictures of us together?"

"*What* pictures?"

"Meet me tonight and I'll show you."

"You're bluffing. I'm not buying it, Anne-Marie."

She slid off the desk and undulated out of the room, slowly turning at the door to blow him a kiss. "We'll see." Errol was shaking with rage. He slammed his palms down on the desk so hard that he was still feeling the sting an hour later, as he sat across from his producer, waiting for him to come off the phone. He thought about what he was about to tell him and the repercussions it could have. This was going to be hard. He was hoping that, by being honest, things would go in his favour. Anne-Marie Simms had to realise she was not playing with a boy here. John Everett finally put down the phone and reached over to shake Errol's hand. "Errol, my boy! What can I do for you?" Errol sat up straight and leant towards him, elbows on knees, fingers twined in front of him. "Can I be frank?"

"Sure." John raised his shoulders in a shrug, hands spread. "I'm always frank with you."

Errol breathed out heavily, wondering where to start. John leant on the desk, subconsciously mimicking the position of Errol's hands. "Trouble?" he asked.

"In a way. It's Anne-Marie Simms. Things aren't working out with her on the team."

"In what way?"

"She's become obsessed with me, is the only way I can describe it."

A quirky smile touched John's lips. "Obsessed?"

Errol cleared his throat and fiddled with the knot of his tie. "I had sex with her, a one-off, and now she won't let it go. She spends more time following me around and calling me on the phone than doing what she's being paid for. I've spoken to other members of the research team, and they've told me her work has become slap-dash and ill thought through."

"You want her off the team?"

"I was thinking of something a little more permanent. She's got to be as far away from me as possible."

"You want her fired because she's an ex-girlfriend?"

"John, she was *never* a girlfriend, not in the real sense. No – I want her fired because she isn't behaving professionally; she is, in fact, incompetent at this kind of work. Yes, she is harrassing me, but if she isn't doing her job as well I feel we have good enough reason to let her go. This is affecting my work too, John..."

"I'll look into it," John placated. "If there's one thing I won't stand for here it's sexual harrasssment. I'll do what I can."

As Anne-Marie made her way towards Catford in her black Fiesta, her face was set in grim determination. Her eyes, though, were expressionless. She passed the house and parked the car fifty yards away, turned off the ignition and the lights, and waited. The windows were dark and Errol's girlfriend's car wasn't there, she didn't seem to be home – but if she had to confront them both she would. She kept her eyes on the house in the rear-view mirror, imagining the rooms. Expensively furnished. Everything picked out by that no-mark girlfriend of his. A thought flitted through her mind: how many times a week did they make love in their four-poster bed?

At around eleven o'clock a taxi pulled up. Anne-Marie peered into the mirror and saw Yvette and her son stepping out. There were no words exchanged between them as they hurried into their home and the taxi pulled away. The front door slammed, and then it was quiet again. Anne-Marie wondered where Yvette's car was. An accident? In a garage? Sold, even? Maybe she was taking advantage of the fact that she didn't have to drive now she could afford taxis.

She only had to wait half an hour more before Errol's car pulled into his drive and he almost seemed to leap out of it. He seemed excited, as though he couldn't wait to get inside. He wouldn't feel so good when when he saw her, though. He mustn't be allowed to get away with treating people this way. She was no more disposable than he was. She got out of her car, slamming the door.

Errol looked up to see a woman in a brown suit walking hurriedly and anxiously towards him, her long flapover skirt flying in the breeze. "Hello, Errol."

"Miss Simms. What can I do for you now."

"I lost my job."

"Is that so?" He turned away from her and walked towards the comfort and warmth of his own home.

"Did you have something to do with it?"

He stopped and turned slowly on his heels. There was a smug smile on his face as he looked Anne-Marie up and down. John had come through for him. "What makes you think that?"

She suddenly came alive and leapt forward, her eyes blazing, voice screeching, "You can't treat me that way!"

Errol's voice remained calm as he grabbed her wrists, her fingers flexing like claws. "I haven't done anything to you, Anne-Marie."

There were tears in her eyes. "I love you! I want to take care of you, and you just keep pushing me away! Why?"

After all this time, after all she had done, Anne-Marie had never ceased to amaze him. "If you had just backed off when I asked you to, maybe you'd still have a job. You're an adult, not a schoolgirl with a crush on the teacher. Give it up!" He dashed her arms away from him and she was thrown a few steps backwards. "If there's one thing I don't need, it's you going round telling people we're an item."

"We were lovers—"

"Lovers!" He laughed in her face.

A look of scorn came through her tears. "You can't have forgotten how good it was!"

"Forgotten! Forgotten *what*?" He tapped his forehead. "It's all in your head, Anne-Marie. There was never anything between us. Now this has gone far enough. It has to stop, or I'll go to the police.You're infringing on my privacy, you're harrassing me, and you're making my life hell. What would it take for you to leave me alone, a court order?"

The door flew open behind him and Yvette marched out. "What the hell is going on out here?"

Anne-Marie glared. "Keep out of this." Yvette marched down the steps towards them. "I shoulda given you a slapping from time. Come here telling me what to do!" Yvette flew at her, fists at the ready.

Errol grabbed her and held her from behind. "Leave her! She's not worth it," he said with contempt. Then he turned back to Anne-Marie. "I'm calling the police."

Defeated, she turned and headed back to the car. She looked back just once, in time to see Errol stroke Yvette's face as he guided her back to the house. Hatred and nausea making her head spin, she leant over at the kerb, bringing up her lunch, and what was left of her dignity.

It was two days since Anne-Marie had been given her marching orders. The whole office had known she had a crush on Errol Wright, and now the gossip was ripe, everyone adding their own details to the tale of a love affair gone wrong.

"What did he do – make a formal complaint?"

"I don't know. He could have had her arrested, though. If anyone was stalking me I'd do anything to keep him away from me."

"Oh, she's so pathetic! I almost feel sorry for her."

"*Sorry* for her? It was Errol she was harrasssing. The woman was detached from reality! Anyway, we can do without her kind in here…"

Wearing red for confidence she didn't feel, Anne-Marie walked into the office and was aware of her ex-colleagues' heads turning back to work, an abruptly terminated conversation. Under one arm she carried a cardboard box folded flat, over her other shoulder a handbag that matched the shade of her suit. Her hair was pulled back into a loose ponytail. She straightened her back and walked to her desk. The phone began to ring. She looked at the faces of her ex-colleagues. Most of them were looking away, some in embarrassment, and a couple gazed at her in sympathy. She swallowed hard, and for what seemed like a long time she couldn't make another move. The phone continued to ring unanswered.

Just as quickly as the paralysis had come over her, it left.

"Will someone answer that phone?" she said loudly and a lot more confidently than she felt. She began to sort through the things on her desk. She fought hard to control her breathing as the whispers started behind her back and all around her. It's all right, she told herself. A job's just a job. It wasn't as though she'd lost everything. A shadow fell over her desk and she looked up at Roger, who was holding a card out to her. "We were going to post it, but as you're here..."

She reached for it and, slipping it out of its envelope, she scanned the short messages and signatures. "Thank you..."

"Errol would have signed it, but we haven't been able to get hold of him." Roger watched her face intently.

The mention of Errol's name, so casually used, was like a bullet to Anne-Marie. She tensed with the memory of her last encounter with him.

"We didn't know about you and Errol," Roger continued tactlessly. "I mean, I hope you don't mind me mentioning it. Of course it's none of my business..."

"No. You're right – it isn't."

Roger shifted uneasily from foot to foot, aware of the glances from his workmates. "Well, I'll leave you to it. If you need any help getting them down to the car, just give me a call."

Anne-Marie raised her heavy eyelids to him and smiled a sickly smile that said she couldn't care less. Half an hour later she left, clutching her box of belongings.

Errol left his guests in the green room and walked with his usual strut towards the staircase. He felt so good that he wanted to run. Anne-Marie was off the programme. He was free.

When he reached the next floor he saw her standing in front of his dressing room and froze on the spot. For a moment the two of them stared at each other, neither speaking a word. Then Anne-Marie's gaze slid away from Errol's face and she began walking towards him, but her eyes were staring through him, past him. Errol didn't move, unsure whether he could or should say something. Then she brushed past him. He heard the door to the staircase swing open and her footsteps going down. She'd been so cold, detached... Giving himself a mental shake, he continued down the hall and into his dressing room. He unbuttoned his jacket and slung it over the back of a chair. The Donna Karan suit he was wearing for today's show was hanging on a rack at the other end of the room. He pulled it from its hanger, gasping as it fell into pieces at his feet.

Rain, sheets of it, blown erratically by the wind, slanted down on to the almost deserted street. It was dark, except for the misty orange glow of the high street lights shining weakly onto the road.

Yvette clung tighter to Errol's arm. "I feel like singing!" Errol swapped the umbrella to his other hand so he could take Yvette's. "Now there's a cue for a song…"

"I'm si-nging in the rain…" Yvette warbled.

"You'll get us arrested with that voice! They'll think we're mad enough as it is, walking in the rain when we have two cars."

"Well, you know, if I wasn't mad we wouldn't be together."

"Hey!"

Yvette had called him from the station an hour ago. She had been out for a drink with friends, and was feeling in such a good mood that she'd wanted to walk in the downpour. She had instructed Errol to leave the car at home – it was more romantic that way.

Romantic. That was what she'd said. He had given her his mac, and now he could feel the cold through to his skin, but he had to admit that thit was romantic. He squeezed her hand, and when she looked across at him and smiled he sent a silent, thankful prayer to whomever it may concern.

There had been times when he'd thought he would never feel like this about anyone again. He'd thought that he would spend the remaining evenings of his life with his little black book in his hand, dating women he didn't really know, let alone like or love. "So, you got any energy left for me after your night out?"

Yvette smiled up at him. "Always, baby."

Errol bent to kiss her lips.

"You know…" Yvette curled her hand into the palm of his. "There are still things we haven't explored."

Errol raised an eyebrow. He knew that tone of voice. "Are there? Enlighten me."

"You know, rain…" She twirled a finger. "Remember that film *Nine and a Half Weeks*?"

When a flash of lightning was followed by rumbling thunder, Errol thought it was time to get a move on. Grabbing Yvette's hand, he glanced to his right and they stepped into the road. He hadn't heard the engine, but now there was a car heading straight for them without its headlights on. "Jesus!" he shouted, stepping back instinctively, the umbrella falling to his side. Yvette, however, hadn't registered the danger and for a split second she stared at the speeding car with disbelief. Reflexes quick as a cat's sent Errol springing into her back, knocking her forwards across the road and out of the way of the car. But there wasn't enough time for him to swing himself clear. He felt a sharp, explosive pain in his side as he made contact with the metal and was sent somersaulting into the hood of a parked car. Blackness spilled like blood across his vision, and the sound of the car's engine roaring away receded into nothing. Errol was unconscious before his body slid to the ground.

He was sure he'd opened his eyes, but everything seemed unreal. Everything was too bright, too misty, unstable... I must be dead, he thought. "Errol?"

He could hear a voice, a familiar voice, and he turned his head slightly to where he thought it was coming from.

"Errol?"

Now the cloudiness cleared enough for him to be able to make out a figure by his side. It was Yvette. He wasn't dead after all.

"Eve."

She took his hand and placed a cool palm on his forehead. "Hi, lover..." She struggled to keep the emotion out of her voice. "How you feeling?"

Errol thought about the question. He really didn't know the answer. Not only that, but he wasn't sure who or where he was. Everything faded out again.

The next time he opened his eyes he could focus. He could feel pain this time around; it hurt to move even a fraction. He was in a white room with yellow curtains. A private room – there was no other bed. A television was bracketed to the wall ahead of him. He turned his head to look at the figure sleeping in an easy chair by the side of his cot. Her head was almost touching her shoulder. He watched her for a few minutes, remembering why he was in here – the rain, their romantic walk, the car... and then the pain. He didn't know how badly he was hurt. All he knew for certain was that he was.

Yvette woke up and looked at him through red eyes. She pushed the concern from her face to show a smile of bravery. "Errol," she breathed out with relief.

"You been here all the time?" he croaked, surprised at how weak his voice sounded. She poured him a glass of water and held it to his lips as he raised his aching head a little from the pillows. "Where else would I go when my man's in hospital?"

He found it hard to concentrate on remembering what he needed to ask. Things were slipping out of his mind as quickly as they appeared. "Are you okay?"

"A little bruised, mostly on my backside. That was some tackle you dropped 'pon me."

Then memory came back more clearly, the scene flashing before his eyes: the car, speeding towards Yvette, and his instinctive reaction. "God, my head..."

"That'll be the concussion."

Errol closed his eyes. "How..." He licked dry lips. "What's the damage?"

"You've got two fractured ribs, one broken... oh, and the head. Any pain?" "All over." He opened his eyes again and regarded her with suspicion. "Why are you smiling?"

"Cause you're still here, talking to me." She leaned closer and kissed him full on the lips. "Scared the life out of me, the way you just went out again last time you woke up. Anyt'ing's better than the things that ran through my mind when I saw you lying there not moving."

"Come here..." He raised an arm to her, wanting to feel her as close as possible, then howled in pain as the pressure on his ribs reminded him why he was there.

Later the police came to question him about the incident. They had already spoken to Yvette and declared that they had very little to go on. There had been no headlights, it was raining, and Errol's main concern had been Yvette. So they knew nothing for sure. Although they both had their suspicions, they decided not to leap to conclusions and incriminate Anne-Marie. This was to turn out to be the wrong decision.

On Saturday morning Yvette rose slowly. The space next to her was still empty, but Errol would be discharged tomorrow. She had already planned to stay at home with him for a few days until she was sure he was over the worst. Men! When they weren't well they were worse than babies.

As usual on a Saturday, Tyrone was out playing football. Errol would normally take him and bring him back, but the boy wasn't spoiled: he had volunteered to go on a bus. The house felt extremely quiet and empty. Dressed in a shortie negligée she tied her hair up and descended the staircase. She picked up the mail from the door mat and, placing the phone bill aside, began to sort through the cards and letters. Probably more well-wishers. They'd had more than enough get-well cards over the past couple of days. Errol was well loved, and missed at the studio. Marion had sent flowers and cards, and visited Errol every day. He was as bored as anything in that place, and needed his friends around him. Chris had turned up with Dean and Colin, bringing with them enough alcohol to knock an elephant out. Errol had had to sit and watch them without touching a drop because of all the pills he had inside him.

One by one, Yvette opened the letters addressed to her. The last came in a lavender-coloured envelope and was a single folded sheet of notepaper. It was all typed, including the signature.

Dear Yvette,
I thought it was time we had a little chat. Woman to woman, sister to sister. You don't know what you're living with. Errol doesn't really want you, you know. At the moment you've got him hooked on your sex, but it won't last.
Errol is in fact in love with me, right now he is in torment. The only thing stopping us being together is you. After meeting you, I think he's scared of you but then that's just my opinion.
You're not the kind of woman for him. He needs a woman with an education, a woman who knows how to take care of her man. He needs a woman with no ties, not a single mother looking for a meal ticket. And believe me he's going to realise.
Whatever it is he thinks he's getting from you is only because you've brainwashed him. By now he must be showing signs of restlessnesss. I know his kind so well. He is not the settling down type. He needs a free spirit like me.
I'm only telling you this as a woman who understands, a woman who is trying to save you the pain of an awful breakup when the time comes. I urge you to let him go now, if necessary throw him out, he'll always have somewhere to go. Let real love blossom.
Your sister in spirit,
Anne-Marie

Yvette had to read the letter again before it really sunk in. A shiver went down her back and she began to tremble, and she screwed the letter up in her clenched fist. Tears had already to begun to trek down her cheek. Her man was in hospital. He could have been killed by that bitch, and yet she still wouldn't leave them alone. She had to be the devil.

Breathing deeply, Yvette swept the hated tears away from her face, she had let Anne-Marie get away with enough. Yvette was not going to allow it again. Errol was hers, and she was going to fight for him. She stood up and walked deliberately to the telephone. Errol kept a small book of contact numbers on the table there – it didn't take her long to find Anne-Marie's. Several other numbers were scribbled or Tippexed out, but not hers. Yvette, however, did not have time to think about this. She picked up the phone and dialled.

It rang four times before it was answered. "Hello?"

"Don't you 'hello' me, you bitch! How could you do what you did and still be sane? Where the fuck do you get off sending me a letter like that? My man is in hospital in serious pain." Yvette sniffed back tears. "I think I told you before: stay out of my face, out of my life, and out of my – you hear me? *my* – family."

"Yvette, what is this?"

"Woman, you're asking for a good slapping. You show your face anywhere near me again and you're going to get it. I have a long memory."

"Errol's in hospital! Where?" Anne-Marie sounded convincing, as if she didn't know. Errol had said she was a good actor.

"Everyone in the country knows that. I ain't playing with you. Why don't you just kill yourself and get it over with quickly, 'cause believe me it'll be a lot less painful than me getting my hands on you!" Yvette slammed down the phone.

Miles away, Anne-Marie replaced the reciever and picked it up again. Her finger pressed the numbers 1471. Ex-directory! I don't think so.

She was still in bed, alone as usual, but now she rose, her brain whirling. Over the past couple of days Anne-Marie had stayed out of circulation. Something strange had happened to her. It was as though a piece of her recent memory had been renoved, wiped clean. She had done something she couldn't remember... and now Yvette had told her that Errol was in hospital... She picked up the stack of newspapers that had been delivered over the past three or four days (she had lost count), carried them into the living room and switched the television on before sitting down and finding the oldest edition.

She scanned every column. Nothing.

The next paper, however, screamed at her: "ERROL WRIGHT IN HIT-AND-RUN MADNESS". There was a picture of an amblance, a figure being lifted on a stretcher. Holding it close to her face she could see it was Errol, and Yvette in the background, a blanket around, her being helped into the ambulance.

They revealed no clues to who had done it or how badly he was hurt.

Quickly Anne-Marie turned to the next day's paper. This time there was more information on page four. The accident had happened at around midnight: a car without its headlights on had pulled out and sped towards the couple as they were walking home. The car was discribed only as a small black hatchback, no make, no registration number or driver identified as yet. The police were appealing for witnesses...

Anne-Marie walked on shaky legs to the window and looked down to the street below. Her black Fiesta was parked at the kerb, just as it had been for four days, or so she thought...

If there was one thing Yvette hated, it was waiting – for anything: a man, a bus, food, time to pass... A few minutes ago the tannoy had announced a twenty-minute delay before the next train to Ladbroke Grove. Along with at least a hundred other commuters, she had mumbled disgruntedly. It was cold, and she paced the Baker Street platform impatiently, looking at her watch every other minute. She was going to be late for the start of the course.

The platform gave her the creeps. It looked like the set of a gothic Victorian movie with its dark-green ironwork and dull orange light. She shivered and pulled her leather coat tighter round her body, almost expecting to see Dracula come stalking out from the tunnel, looking for his next victim. If only she had company. She could have done with Karen on this trip. That woman could chat. If it wasn't dissing men it was cussing kids, bitching about women with perfect figures (who'd obviously had plastic surgery) or recounting her latest exploits with her boss, whom she loathed with a vengence. They had their laughs. In fact, no matter what Karen was talking about she made it funny. She was the one Yvette would pick up the phone to call when she was feeling down.

It was about time they had a holiday. A girly holiday. So what if they were both in their thirties with children? They also had men who could take care of the kids.

This trip was going to keep her away from home for two nights and three days. It was a new course in health and beauty, which Conrad had booked her on to so she could ease herself back into work after Errol's accident. She had wanted to travel home in the evenings and then back to Ladbroke Grove in the mornings, but Errol wasn't having it. To him, it was bad enough that she was going at all. So he'd booked her into a hotel instead. So, the next three days was a break: a break from work, from her son, even from Errol.

Their life together still seemed like a dream. It was wonderful having him in her bed every night and every morning... but sometimes – only sometimes – she missed having her own space again. Her space to think, to listen to her music at full blast, to watch what she wanted to watch on television, or to have perfect silence. Sometimes she wanted to be able to drop her clothes where she pleased, to work out in her underwear, even when they were old ones held together by a few threads.

Of course this weekend wasn't going to give her all that, but at least she would have her own room for three days.

One person she was definitely glad to get away from was Anne-Marie Simms. Just thinking about that woman made Yvette clench her fists. The nerve of her! It was months now since her one-night stand with Errol, and she still couldn't grasp the idea that he was never going to belong to her. The phone calls had started again – somehow she had got their new number – and more and more times Yvette had caught Errol taking his mail out with him in the mornings, or taking it into his study to open in private.

At last the display was showing that her train was approaching. The whole platform came alive – feet shuffled, cases and bags were hoisted off the ground, belongings secured – and Yvette walked a little further down, hoping to get a carriage that wasn't so packed. She wanted to sit down, even if it was just for a few stops. She could see the lights of the train as it rolled down the tunnel into the station. "Thank goodness," she breathed. Why in the world had she chosen to wear these boots? They were half a size too small... but they looked good.

Suddenly a shove from behind threw Yvette off balance; her arms windmilled and she dropped her holdall, but she couldn't stop the momentum. She was heading for the tracks, and the train was still coming towards her.

Then she felt the grip of a hand on her arm, dragging her back to the platform, and safety.

"Easy! Are you okay? You could have been killed."

Her heart was beating extremely fast, but she nodded and straightened her coat. "Some bugger pushed me!" She craned her neck to look around.

Walking away from the platfrom, in the opposite direction to everyone else, was a woman, a scarf tied over her hair. Yvette didn't have time to see any more, she was bustled on to the train. The man who had saved her life had taken hold of her arm to make sure she was got on safely this time.

Yvette felt tears of frustrated anger beginning to erupt. The realisation dawned like a revelation. Anne-Marie – it had to have been her. She's following me, she thought. Trying to kill me!

Three days later Errol, out of his bandages now, was sitting in traffic. He knew he was running late. Yvette was due back into London in fifteen minutes, and he was stuck. He'd tried the back streets and they had led him right back into the jam.

He arrived at the tube station five minutes after the train had arrived, rushed frantically to where she'd said she would wait, and sighed with relief as he saw her pacing, looking around for him.

She smiled and began to walk towards him. "Boy, I knew you'd be on time. Never let me down yet," she said, kissing him.

He took her bag from her hand and drew her into his arms. "You look good enough to eat. I missed you."

"I can tell." She hugged him back. "So, how are you? Any pain?"

"Only an ache that I know you can cure," he said meaningfully.

"Ooh. We'd best get outta here then." She discreetly grabbed his hardening member as she stared into his eyes.

"Let's do that."

In the car she relaxed. One hand on his leg, she inhaled the smell of him and his car. She had missed him with a passion, never realising until they were apart how much she had got used to him being by her side in bed, or being there to give her a cuddle, a back rub, or to chat into the early hours.

After a few minutes of driving Errol pulled the car into a side street and took it all the way to the dead end, where they were surrounded by disused garages and industrial units. Before Yvette could open her mouth to say anything he was on top of her, hands scrabbling for her underwear, lips all over her face, sucking her lips into his mouth, biting his way through her dress. She gasped for breath. Slipping her shoes off, she raised her legs to the dashboard, allowing him easier access. Together they worked his trousers down to his knees, her drawers hanging off one ankle by now, and he plunged himself deep inside her. Yvette's bare feet were on the windscreen, her head at an awkward angle as she pushed her buttocks towards him, feeling him hit her g-spot time and time again. "Oh God, yes!" she screamed. Errol's perspiration was dribbling down his cheek and she reached her tongue out, licking the salty liquid from his face. His breathing became faster, his thrusts deeper, as she felt his penis engorge and shoot into her. They came together in a simultaneous blast of passion that took them both by surprise. "Oh, boy, did I miss you!" he breathed, collapsing on to her heaving chest.

After a few minutes of recovery he stepped out of the car to straighten his clothes. He had to stop by the studio. On the way, he switched the car's humidifier on, which also produced an air freshener, and by the time they arrived he was calm and collected again. "You want to wait here or are you coming up?"

"I might as well stretch my legs."

Errol asked her to wait for him by the set while he ran to the dressing room. She walked on to the deserted stage. So, this was where it all happened... She looked up at the audience seating area, now dark and empty. How did it feel to be so famous? She strolled over to the sofa and sat opposite Errol's armchair. "Welcome to Barker's Hour..." She giggled at the instantly made-up name, then stopped suddenly.

Were those footsteps she'd heard? She stood up, trying not to look as silly as she felt. The studio was quiet. Too quiet.

"Errol?' She barely raised her voice. Supposed someone caught her in here? Get out, a little voice in her head told her.

Again she heard a noise, and this time she spun towards its source. It had been a rustle from behind the set.

"Errol?" This time her voice was a little louder, with just a hint of nervousness in it. She walked up to the brightly painted backdrop. Made of wood, it was at least fifteen foot high. A loud creaking sound suddenly filled the air. She looked up and realised too late that a large weight, the shape of a bolster, had come loose and was whizzing towrds her. It brushed her shoulder and sent her reeling as it crashed to the floor, but she was still on her feet. The weight, however, was still rolling. It hit the edge of a huge flat, the size of a small house, and there was a loud creak as a section of scenery teetered, then started to fall towards her. She turned and ran, but not fast enough, and pain exploded as she saw the carpet flying towards her face and she was suddenly flat on her stomach, the weight of the flat on her back and legs. Groaning, she struggled to wriggle out from under the wooden wall.

Several people must have heard the noise, because she heard running footsteps and raised voices approaching. She touched a finger to her head and it came away with blood on it. A lump was already rising. Her shoulder throbbed painfully.

"What happened?"

"Are you okay?"

"What were you doing here?"

Hands were reaching for her and pulling her free while other faceless bodies lifted the set.

"I'm fine," Yvette croaked, looking around for Errol.

"Anything broken?" A tall woman with wild brown hair was bending down to feel her legs.

"I'm fine," Yvette insisted. "Has anyone seen Errol?"

"Errol Wright? You're here with him?"

"Yes." Yvette tried to stand and a big man dressed completely in black rushed to her aid, lifting her as though she was as light as a feather.

"Hold on, I'll get someone to page him for you," the woman said. "Anton, can you do that, please? I'll get... Sorry, what's your name?" she asked Yvette, who told her. "I'll get Yvette to his dressing room."

She was made comfortable in his dressing room while she explained what had happened.

"It wouldn't just fall," the woman, who had introduced herself as Jayne, said. "Those weights are always secured. Okay, that particular piece of the set was new, but I'm sure it's had all the safety checks. Someone had to have undone the bolts and used force to shift it."

Yvette felt as though she was being accused of meddling. But she didn't say another word. She wanted Errol, and she wanted to get home as quickly as possible. She'd had enough brushes with death for one week.

Errol was by her side ten minutes later. They only had to look at each other to know what had happened.

Jayne hovered by the door. "You want me to call the police?"

"Only if it's studio policy to do so, otherwise we'd rather not get involved."

"I'll need Yvette to fill out an accident report."

"Okay, okay, get one to me later."

Jayne knew when she wasn't wanted.

Christmas came round with startling suddenness. Only a few weeks ago Yvette had thought she and Errol were finished. Now they had the house she wanted. There had been no hold ups with chains or the motgage, and the place was theirs. Errol had bought a Christmas tree which touched the ceiling, decorated by the men of the house in silver, with the tiniest of twinkling lights. Presents lay in abundance at its base. They had bought each other at least four each.

Tyrone was the first person down the stairs that morning. He might have been closer to a teenager than a six-year-old, but Christmas still meant little more than presents to him – especially when his mum's boyfriend was a celebrity, a black man of means.

Errol and Yvette followed, after giving each other their first Christmas present, which didn't involve spending money. They ate a cooked breakfast Jamaican style, compliments of Mrs Stewart, who had no one else to take care of at Christmas time.

Once they were washed and dressed, Errol announced, "Wait – there's a present missing…"

Tyrone looked at his mother, who shrugged and smiled back at him.

"Damn!" Errol slapped his head and looked at him. "I left one of your presents in the car! You wanna come and get it with me?"

"Safe!" Tyrone knew Errol always had something up his sleeve.

Yvette watched them leave the house, Tyrone in the lead. Errol was dressed casually in dark blue trousers and a satin high-neck waistcoat, over which he'd thrown his leather jacket. Tyrone was in a Fila track suit and brand new trainers that were one of his presents.

"So, what'd you get me?"

"Have patience." "For what? You might as well tell me. I'm gonna see it now anyway."

"Not so fast. We've got to drive a little way to pick it up."

Tyrone looked up at him, studying his face with a mixture of curiosity and impatience. "You do know the shops are closed today innit?"

Errol just smiled. "We are not going to a shop." They got into the car and Errol headed for Marion's house. It was while they were driving that he noticed the boy scrutinising the windsreen. He looked at the glass. A pair of smudged but still clear footprints had materialised on the steamed-up glass.

"Why… ?" Tyrone began, but was instantly silenced as Errol switched on the fan.

"Don't ask," he was warned. Tyrone studied the roads they were driving down. They turned into Marion's street, and he knew that this was obviously the hiding place for his present. If he'd searched for it at home, he wouldn't have found it.

Paul answered the door. Tyrone was standing behind Errol, his hands shoved into his pockets.

"What's up, Ty?" Paul greeted the boy with a slap on the shoulder. "I don't know where this one is stretching to – soon taller dan me!"

"All right, Paul?" He shuffled into the flat behind Errol.

Errol made his way into the living room. "So where is it? You two haven't gone and sold it, have you?"

170

They all looked at Tyrone, who frowned back at them. Something weird was going on here.

Marion sat with Diallo, her son, on her lap. She nodded towards the Christmas tree. "No, it's right where it belongs."

Errol shoved Tyrone forward. "Go get your present, son."

Tyrone took his hands out of his pockets, a smile breaking on his worried face. "Which one is it?"

"You'll know when you see it." Errol was grinning wider than Tyrone now. Marion and Paul were just looking amused at the whole fiasco.

Why the hell was his present here? Did Errol have to get Marion to buy it for him? Why the big runaround?

Tyrone saw why soon enough. Lying by the Christmas tree in a huge basket, previously hidden by the armchair, was a grey puppy. A great dane. Tyrone looked at Errol enquiringly. "Mine?"

"Yeah, it's – or I should say, *he's* yours."

Tyrone wrapped his hands around the sleeping dog, who yelped and woke up to look into his new master's face. A few months previously, Tyrone had complained to Errol that his mum wouldn't let him have a dog where they'd lived because it was too small, and they could never afford the dog he wanted anyway. Errol hadn't forgotten. Tyrone loved it instantly. As they left with their new family member, Errol turned to Marion. "Don't forget Yvette's present when you're coming."

"As if I would…" She smiled sweetly.

"Just leave it on the doorstep and I'll get her to go out and pick it up before we sit down to dinner."

"Don't worry, I've got it under control." They kissed cheeks and Errol took his family home.

Tyrone sat in the back with his new pet. "I can't wait to take him out. He can go out now, can't he?"

"Yeah, he's had his jabs. We'll take him out tommorow, so long as it's not too cold."

Later that evening Marion and Paul arrived bearing more gifts. As promised, Marion left the present from Errol on the doorstep, rung the doorbell, and she and Paul hid around a corner. Errol sent Yvette out to see who it was, and when she came back she carried a box in her hands.

She looked radiant, in a gown made of sequins and beads which fit her every curve, her chest pushed up high, her hair wrapped into a French plait. "You got me a surprise present, didn't you?"

Errol looked surprised too. The box was a lot bigger than the one he'd given Marion, who appeared in the doorway behind Yvette. When he looked questioningly at her, she just smiled back at him. Errol had a funny feeling in the pit of his stomach as he watched Yvette tear the gold paper off. Inside the box was something smaller, wrapped in red tissue paper. Yvette reached in like an excited child and pulled it out. Then, surprising them all, she grimaced, gasped and dropped it.

Yvette shrieked. Her hand was covered in blood – blood that had dripped from a still warm dead rat, its head now protruding from the tissue paper at her feet.

The next morning Errol took Tyrone and the puppy to Blackheath Common. Yvette was sleeping at home. She'd had a pretty rough night; their Christmas day had been ruined. Errol had tried to stay awake with her through the night, talking constantly about anything else except what had happened. In the morning Tyrone made them breakfast in bed, then they had left her in peace. Errol had decided to get Tyrone used to walking and training his new puppy – a great dane would grow fast and need plenty of exercise and discipline. Besides, after the amount Errol had eaten over the last few days he could do with a little himself. They had decided to call the dog Charles – Sir Charles to be exact, because he looked so distinguished.

Errol parked at the edge of the common and they got out of the car, Tyrone holding tightly on to Charles's new lead as they jogged on to the grass.

Anne-Marie waited in her hired car until they were far enough away not to notice her, then she followed at a distance. The young boy obviously respected and loved Errol. He followed his instructions with a patience and admiration rarely seen in boys that age. And Errol looked well; the accident hadn't crippled him – indeed, there were no visible signs that it had even happened. She still couldn't recall whether she had been involved or not, and the news hadn't reported any updates. So, for the time being at least, she was safe. They were totally oblivious to her as they trained thier new pet.

The puppy was just as excited as Tyrone, and jumped, ran and yapped as they threw a frisbee between them. Ocassionally the dog would catch it and dash off with it in his mouth.

Unable to take this show of family solidarity any longer, Anne-Marie returned to the road. She looked at Errol's Saab. It looked so flash, so expensive, so perfect, so Errol Wright. She remembered the small knife she kept on her key chain and, looking around her, she pulled her keyring from her pocket, released the knife, and very quickly stabbed two of his tyres. Let him try to get home in that. She almost laughed, but she was crying. No matter what she did, he still didn't want her. So now she wanted him to hurt like she did.

It was three hours before Errol arrived back home. He'd had to call out the RAC, and then they'd had to call out a specialist tyre company for the tyres. On a bank holiday that was no easy feat. Errol had paid, grudgingly, and by the time they pulled up outside the house he was not in a good mood. Tyrone took Charles straight upstairs while Errol went into the kitchen to make himself some hot chocolate. He was surprised to find Yvette in her dressing gown at the kitchen table. She had her head down and was sobbing.

He pulled a chair up beside her. "Eve, honey, what's wrong?" In her fist she held a crumpled note. Errol teased it from her hand and unfolded it.

> Did you have a good nap, Yvette? I hope so, because you're going to need your strength. By the way, blood red's the perfect colour for you. Someday soon you're going to be covered in the real thing. That's a promise.

It was unsigned.

New Year's Eve, and outside a cold wind blew. More snow, Yvette predicted as she sprayed Eternity into her cleavage. So far the night was clear, but there had been frequent, heavy falls over the past two days. What a night to be going to a party! She'd have been happy curled up in front of the fire with her men by her side. A moment ago a car had sounded its horn outside her house. The limousine Errol had arranged for her had arrived. She was to meet up with him at the party, held at a country mansion in Essex. He'd told her about the do two weeks ago, and she'd had a frantic fortnight trying to find a dress that would be appropriate. It had been the hardest shopping trip ever. She threw on her cashmere coat, a present from Errol, and left the house. The car was parked at the kerb, a silver grey model with tinted windows. So often she had seen this type of limo passing her on the streets of the West End and wondered which celebrity sat behind that darkened glass. Now she would be the one whom people would be wondering about. The thought made her smile indulgently.

She tapped the window, and when there was no sign of anyone getting out she opened the back door and climbed into the warm interior. She had no idea exactly where she was going, but the chauffeur had his instructions, it had all been arranged. He was blocked from her view by smoked glass, and the side windows were tinted so all she coud see outside were vague points of light. She settled back and enjoyed the luxury of the leather seats, helping herself to a drink from the bar.

Half an hour later, Yvette was bored and a little tipsy. That driver must be just as bored as I am, she thought. What does he do all day, sit around in a car waiting for the rich and famous to hire him? She tapped on the dividing glass and waited. Nothing.

"Hey!" She tapped harder. "Driver, I want to talk."

Still nothing. She knew they were on a motorway; there was hardly any other traffic noise and she could feel the speed.

"Can't you just tell me how much further?... Hello?... Hello?"

Maybe she was supposed to pick up a phone. That's it, she thought, they must have one of them intercom systems in this buggy. After a brief search she found the phone behind a leather panel. She picked it up, listening for a dialling tone. There was none, but she jabbed at the buttons anyway, shouting into it.

That was the moment when the first little alarm bell went off inside her, like a quiet bleeper. She tried pushing down on the door handle. It didn't budge; the other was the same – central locking.

"Driver!" she shouted, then opened an assault on the dividing window again. The panic bleeper was turning up its power now. Her breathing speeded up, her stomach muscles tightened. "Oh my God," she said aloud, "I'm being kidnapped!"

No, this can't be happening, she told herself. I've just got a deaf driver. She collapsed back against the seat. That's it. I'm the prisoner of a deaf driver. Kidnapped, indeed! Who did she think she was? So long as the deaf guy got her where he was supposed to, why panic?

But as she sat back and tried to make out some detail beyond the tinted windows, a slow but sure feeling of claustrophobia crept over her. She struggled to suppress it, but it escalated until she couldn't bear another minute. Just as she was about to try breaking the glass with the heel of her shoe, the car came to a stop. She heard the locks click open and slid her foot back into her shoe, using her fingers to get her heel in. Now she prepared to give the chauffeur a piece of her mind. There was no way he was getting away with this behaviour, deaf or not. He hadn't checked on her once during the journey. Whatever happened to common courtesy?

She grabbed her bag, jumped out and stormed round to the driver's door. That proved to be a big mistake. The car took off immediately, the rear door jolting shut.

"Hey, where the hell are you going?" she screamed. The car didn't even slow down. Yvette looked around her. It was pitch dark, she was standing on a snow-covered dirt road, with woods on one side and a wide open field on the other, and it was freezing. She wore sandals on her stockinged feet, and nothing but a light wrap over her evening dress. She'd left her cashmere coat in the car. No headgear, no scarf... Last night's snow still lay in clumps everywhere. She looked... and wasn't that snow she felt touch the tip of her nose?

What was this? Some kind of sick joke? Who would do this to her – or to Errol? The answer came to her, crystal clear.

Anne-Marie.

Yvette screamed, but there was no one to hear it.

The jazz music in the background was mellow, and complemented perfectly the mix of people in the room. Everyone here had something to do with the media. Errol was deep in conversation with a script-writer when suddenly he had the sensation of eyes watching him. He glanced up from his conversation and saw Anne-Marie beckon to him. He excused himself from the group, his face set rigid, his jawline punctuated by drawn-in cheeks, and walked purposefully towards her.

"What the *hell* are you doing here?" he hissed.

"I was invited." Anne-Marie smiled. "Errol, darling. Am I late? I had *such* a job deciding what to wear..." Her voice had deliberately risen, and a few of the closer guests and waiters had turned to look.

Errol, confused and furious, clenched his teeth. "Where's Yvette?"

"Well how should I know? I'm here to be with you, not her."

Errol caught a glimpse of Marion Stewart entering the room and made a huge effort to smile nonchalantly. Marion dropped her eyes and turned away. Damn it, Errol thought. She really believes there's something going on here. How many of the others think the same thing? Another hour of mingling and networking passed before Errol suddenly realised that Yvette had still not arrived. They were less than an hour away from midnight. Where the hell could she have got to? He knew she was never on time, but he had sent a driver for her. There is no way the car would have been late, not this late. To make matters worse Anne-Marie was following him around like a lap-dog, and he was having great trouble controlling his temper. Again he excused himself and went to find a phone.

Marion watched him leave the room and, telling Paul she was going to the ladies', followed him out. In the huge foyer she spotted him and gently called out his name.

Taking a deep breath, he put on a smile. "I was just trying to find a phone. Yvette should have arrived by now, and I'm getting worried."

"If there was a problem she would have called you."

"No – she couldn't, you see. She doesn't know where this place is; it was supposed to be a surprise. A car was bringing her."

Marion touched his arm. "I'm sure she's okay. Have you called the car company?"

Errol silently fumed. "I left the number at home. I was just about to call there, see if Yvette's still waiting." He paused, as if deciding whether he should reveal his suspicions to his friend. "Marion, I'm convinced Anne-Marie is behind this, but I can't prove anything, not here…"

"I doubt it somehow. But I'll go talk to her – you make the call. Yvette's probably sitting at home waiting for it. Come and find me when you finish."

"Thanks, Marion."

She smiled reassuringly and made her way back to where she had last seen Anne-Marie.

The phone rang seven times before the answering machine picked up. "Eve, it's me. If you're there, please pick up…" He waited a few seconds, then left the number of the house. "Call me as soon as possible. I just hope you're on the way… Anyway, I'll see you soon."

He hung up and pressed his back into the nearest wall. He knew she'd had doubts about fitting in at one of these functions. She'd told him this morning she would have preferred to stay in tonight… Maybe she had decided to go clubbing with her friends instead… But no. This was their first New Year's Eve as a couple – she wouldn't do that. So where was she?

Yvette was shivering with the cold. Yet somehow, as she walked, she could feel herself getting colder. It snowing quite heavily now, the fresh fall covering the previous day's slush and whiting out everything she saw. Her feet and fingers were numb, and as she took each faltering step she had to keep blinking to stop the liquid in her eyes from freezing over and blinding her. She had been trying to follow the dirt road that her kidnapper had brought her along, but some time ago she had lost it under the new snow, and was now walking through a field. The ground here was soft, and she sunk into it up to her calves with each step, having to stop and rub her legs every few feet with fingers she couldn't feel, to try and keep the blood flowing. She exhaled with her mouth open, to let the warmer air touch her face briefly before it was whisked away. She was almost panting now anyway; whenever she tried to breathe more deeply she couldn't seem to get enough air into her lungs.

She was passing out of the field now, into some woods. She couldn't feel her feet at all but she continued to move, looking straight ahead and trying not to panic. Despite the cold her fingers felt hot – burning cold, if there was such a thing.

At least the snow gave her enough light to find her way through the woods. Her wrap covered the bottom half of her face and her hands were balled under each armpit as she emerged the other side into another field. After a few shaky paces, her legs refused to move any further and she found herself on her hands and knees in the snow. She willed herself to stand, to get back on her feet before it was too late, but she sank to her elbows, her hands clawing at the sodden turf. Suddenly her elbows gave out too, and she found herself face-first in the snow. She thought of Tyrone: Tyrone as a toddler, his smell, sitting in front of the TV with his Nintendo, his smile and his laugh. She thought of how he would feel if she never came back.

Against the judgement of her heart's slow beat she somehow hauled herself back up on to her knees. But it was too hard. She felt pain, ferocious pain, as she tried to move a body she couldn't really feel. And then, quite suddenly, it didn't matter. It seemed so startlingly clear to her: she didn't have to go on. She could give it up, throw in the towel. She had had a good and full life, she'd cared for those whom she'd loved, she had no regrets. She had been very happy – and she had brought Errol and Tyrone together...

Mum and Dad – they would be heartbroken. The thought cut through everything. She felt tears try to come, but nothing happened.

Her clothes were now soaked, and it felt as though the material was freezing to her skin in the chill wind, becoming one. She was becoming a part of the ice and snow, a part of the frozen landscape. To be at one with nature, she thought. Someone, take care of Tyrone, she prayed, and Mum and Dad. Errol, I love you.

Just before she closed her eyes she thought she saw clouds coming towards her, heard the tinkle of bells. Clouds and bells. She was going to heaven. She smiled before she fell unconscious.

For the second time in as many months Errol walked down a hospital corridor. But this time there was no pain, just a deep-seated numbness. He didn't hurry. He took steps that reminded the nurse accompanying him of a pall bearer.

He had arrived home from the party just before two a.m., and had called out for Yvette, hoping she had stayed at home for some reason. After a search of the bedroom he'd gone to the living room and found his answerphone blinking.

Two messages: one was his own, which he fast-forwarded immediately; the second was from a hospital, who asked him to call and ask for a Dr Turner as soon as possible. He knew it was Yvette even as he dialled the number. He almost sensed that she was hurting somewhere. Another certainty was that it was down to Anne-Marie.

As soon as he had confirmed it with the hospital he'd called Yvette's brother and let him know what had happened, promising to call again straight after he'd seen her. He'd been told that Yvette was in intensive care, suffering from hypothermia. She had been found unconscious in a field by a farmer who'd been rounding up his sheep from the bad weather. Errol's name and contact number had been in her purse. From the description of her circumstances Errol pieced together what must have occurred that night. The way his heart was beating erratically he knew that, if Anne-Marie were to appear right before him at that moment, he would quite happily throttle her, smiling as the life was squeezed away.

Errol hesitated in the doorway to the intensive care unit. There she was. She had the room to herself. There was a chair by her bed, and Errol slumped down into it, weary with guilt and anger. The nurse left them alone as he took Yvette's hand and bent his head to kiss it.

"Yvette… honey?" He tried to raise some kind of reaction from her but she lay still, eyes closed, unconscious. The doctor had said she was stable, but she might lapse in and out of consciousness for a while before coming round completely. Even then she would be drowsy for a couple of days.

"You don't know how sorry I am that I let this happen." Errol raised her warm hand to his cheek. "It's all my fault – and I promise I'll make it up to you. I've learnt a valuable lesson…" He swallowed hard and shut his eyes wearily. "You can't trust anyone, sometimes not even yourself. If anything good has come out of this, it's that you are going to be my wife – sooner than later – 'cause tonight I have realised that, if I lost you, I couldn't go on. Of course I'd have to, for Tyrone's and Aaron's sake, but it would be the most difficult task I'd've ever undertaken." Watching her face, he was sure he saw her eyelids flicker – or was that wishful thinking?

An hour later he was being woken up from a deep sleep.

"Mr Wright, Mr Wright…" The voice was coming from somewhere above him. At first he thought it must be a tannoy, then he recognised his own name and opened his eyes.

He'd only left the room to get coffee and sunk into a chair while he waited for the queue to go down. He must have drifted off, his fatigued mind recognising an escape route.

"Ms Barker is now conscious, Mr Wright. Her temperature's back to normal."

Errol jumped up, and a smile emerged through his exhaustion.

The sister followed him back to the room. "She's still very drowsy and a little confused… Don't expect too much."

"She's going to be okay then?"

"As far as we can make out, Yvette never actually stopped breathing the whole time. There is no apparent brain damage."

The heart monitors were bleeping steadily as he entered the room. Her eyes were still closed, but her chest was moving up and down regularly. Errol experienced a fresh surge of fury, tempered only by the sentiment of pity. His voice was a hoarse whisper. "Eve? Eve, what happened? What happened to you?"

Yvette's eyes opened.

It was past midday by the time Errol left the hospital and made the diversion towards Streatham and Anne-Marie's block of flats.

Outside, he sat in the car for a few minutes looking up at her window. How many times had she done exactly the same thing to him – sat outside his home and watched him going about his business? Crept about in the night, posted letters through his door, left him unwanted gifts… Instead of abating, his anger grew. Yvette could have died last night. From the hospital he had called the limousine company hired by the station. Their car had arrived a few minutes late and there had been no one in. Anne-Marie must have hired another car, picked Yvette up and kidnapped her, leaving her in the middle of nowhere to freeze to death.

He stepped from the car, his jaw rigid, cheekbones standing out clearly. He rang the intercom to her flat and waited. About thirty seconds later it was answered. "Yes?"

"It's me."

"Me who?" came the reply.

"You know who it is," he hissed loudly.

"What do you want?"

"I want to talk to you."

"Oh, so *now* you want to talk?"

"Open the fucking door."

There was a buzz as the door was released. He swung it open and took the stairs to her second-floor flat, where she stood smiling in the front doorway. She was wearing work-out gear: a cropped top and leggings. "I wasn't expecting company – especially not yours. But you're welcome." She stepped into the flat, eyeing his attire as she let him pass. "Where did you sleep last night? I can see you haven't been home—"

"You make me sick!" He spun round, his eyes flashing, fists clenched at his sides. "Why Yvette? Why couldn't you leave her alone?"

"What are you talking about?"

"Don't play the innocent with me." He couldn't even look at her for fear of losing control. "She could have *died* last night, being left out there…" His voice broke in anger on the last word.

"Left where? I have no idea what you're talking about, Errol." She walked away from him and into her kitchen. "Can I get you something to drink?"

Errol ignored the question. "Why couldn't you just go and get yourself some help when I asked you to? You don't know what you're doing to us!" His voice was almost a sob as he thought of the usually strong Yvette lying in a hospital bed.

"I haven't touched Yvette. If you remember, the last time I saw her she tried to attack me…"

"Are you telling me you didn't kidnap her last night and take her place at the ball?"

Now Anne-Marie laughed, throwing her head back theatrically. "*Kidnap*? I turned up at the party because I was invited… and to be with you." She walked round the counter, a glass of wine in her hand. "I couldn't care less if she was there or not… although I wouldn't have had you all to myself if she had been." She stoped in front of him, allowing her hand to creep up his shirt to his shoulder. "Don't you think I've shaped up pretty well?" She kissed him on his lips and he pulled away, a revulsion so violent rising from the pit of his stomach that he couldn't stand to be close to her. Before he could stop himself, he swung his arm and knocked the glass out of her hand. It rose in the air, spilling wine before shattering on the edge of the counter and falling in splinters to the floor.

Anne-Marie's brown eyes become black with anger. "There was no need for that! What – don't I kiss as good as Yvette?"

"Don't even utter her name!"

"Errol, look at me…" She raised her crop-top over her head and quickly unfastened her sports bra, exposing her firm round breasts. "I'm no different to other women. I have needs…"

Despite himself he felt his penis jump and lengthen He turned his back. "Cover yourself up. I didn't come here for that."

"Why? Having trouble getting it up?"

"You're not well, Anne-Marie. Don't come near us again. I won't be responsible for my actions if you come anywhere near my family." And with that he spun round and headed out of the flat, slamming the door behind him.

The drive from London to Devon had taken them five hours, but as they finally neared the beach cottage Yvette smiled. At last she could hear the sound of the sea, and a salty, fresh smell filled the car.

She put a hand on Errol's leg and breathed in. "I'm feeling more relaxed already."

Errol looked over at her and forced a smile to his lips. He had been far away in his own thoughts. On one side of them was the ocean, white-tipped waves lapping up to the beach then rippling away to nothing. On the other side were hillsides and fields, and every now and then a guest house or cottage.

The orangey twilight shone warmly through the glass of the windscreen, and Yvette closed her eyes and sank lower into her seat. "Yeah, man…"

Errol knew he'd made the right decision to get her away from everything that had been going on since he'd made the mistake of getting involved with Anne-Marie Simms. She had been out of hospital a week now, and ever since he had kept her cocooned at home – on her own during the daytime, but in the evenings Tyrone and Errol hadn't let her lift a finger. They would do the cooking, cleaning, ironing, running baths, giving massages, fetching her drinks…

He still blamed himself, but felt he couldn't apologise enough verbally, so he had made up for it by showering her with affection, by surprising her with little love notes left in places around the house where he knew she'd find them. A single lily had arrived every other day.

Yvette was strong, and felt she was well on the way to recovery, but she had enjoyed being pampered by her men. She'd kept herself busy around the house during the daytime, indulging herself occasionally by dropping in at the gym for a full body massage – well, that was her excuse, but really she was checking on her business. Conrad was running things well, but she knew her clients liked the personal touch, and she didn't want to lose them.

But what she really wanted more than anything else was revenge. She tried to tell herself that Anne-Marie wasn't important, that Errol loved her and was here by her side. But that woman had made it personal; it wasn't about keeping her man any more, it was about showing Anne-Marie she didn't need a man to keep her under wraps and protect her. She could take care of herself, and she wanted to demonstrate this to Anne-Marie. In short, she wanted her right where she could lay some licks 'pon her body for messing with her life.

Every day she regretted not having given her a few blows on the couple of occasions she had been face to face with her. Now the woman who had the means and the motivation to have killed her several times over was still out there somewhere, free, living her life while others had had theirs turned upside-down.

The car turned on to a narrow dirt road and ascended a hedged path up the hillside. Yvette opened her eyes and could see the cottage they would be staying in. It was like something out of a fairy tale: stone-clad walls, two chimneys – which meant open fireplaces, log fires... She looked up to see French windows leading on to a balcony.

She hopped from the car as soon as it pulled up at the back of the house, and with the excitement of a child she rushed round to the front. She gasped at the breathtaking view. The sun had reached the horizon, and the sea was ablaze with oranges and reds. A pathway led from the front garden down to their own private section of beach.

Errol's mouth was against her neck as his arms circled her from behind. "Hey, you," he whispered.

She leaned back into his body as he pulled her close. "How did you find out about this place?"

"I have my sources. Now, are you going to help me unpack all that food? And then, if you feel up to it, we can go for a walk along the coastline."

"Feel up to it? Boy, you couldn't stop me!" She turned and clung to him as she looked out at the sea. "It's perfect..." She looked up into his smiling eyes. "I love you."

"And I love you – more than life itself."

They kissed deeply before walking back to the house, arms around each other. The inside was as she'd imagined. Even the dining room had a log fire. The bedrooms had four-poster beds, with white cotton and lace bedding and curtains, and en suite bathrooms.

After unpacking and taking a walk by the sea, which now looked like Tango, complete with bubbles, they settled down on the sofa in front of the log fire in the living room. Their glasses held pink champagne; the rest of the bottle cooled in a bucket of ice by their side. The room was filled with the gentle glow from the hearth, and a soft soul CD played on the portable machine Errol had brought with them.

"Could this possibly get any better?" Yvette sighed.

Errol smiled. "I'm sure it can."

"That's impossible."

"Nothing's impossible when I'm around."

He proposed to her that night. The setting was their private beach, their only witnesses the moonlight and the stars, a table set with crystal and an electric lamp. Dinner was delivered and served by a lone, uniformed waiter, who looked as though he was used to working in unusual places; he didn't bat an eyelid as he brought the food and wine across the pebble and sand beach.

Yvette's ring was served on a silver tray in a polished oyster shell. As he took it and slipped it on her finger, Errol recited a poem he had composed from his heart. It was a night Yvette knew she would never forget.

"You were right," she whispered as she accepted the proposal with a deep, deep kiss.

"I was?"

"It did get better."

When they arrived back to face the new year in London, they both wanted the romance to carry on. Announcing their engagement was top on Errol's list, and he set about making arrangements for a party immediately. Helen took care of sending the invitations and arranging the catering; Yvette just had to supply her with a list of guests.

Marion's gift was an enormous crystal chandelier, which she had delivered and installed before the engagement party. Yvette looked upon

Marion as a new friend. Errol loved her, and so it followed that she should too. The message in the accompanying card made Yvette smile: "I suppose someone had to tie him down one day. Glad it's you. Enjoy every minute it lasts. Look after him for me, Marion."

Errol turned his car into the driveway, and was about to press the remote control for the garage door when he saw Tyrone coming up the road, not alone. The boy was arm-in-arm with a young lady. Could this be the Charlene that called him every evening – the calls he had to take in his bedroom? The boy was only twelve going on thirteen, what did he know about dating?

Charlene looked a like a woman dressed as a thirteen-year-old schoolgirl. Her hair hung in two short bunches and she she had a side-parted fringe. Errol had to admit even at his age that his eyes were drawn to her bosom – the girl must have been chased around the playground by every adolescent in the school.

His school bag slung over his shoulder, Tyrone must have seen Errol's car because he and his girlfriend stopped a little way up the road and talked.

Errol, curious, left the car on the driveway and got out to wait for Tyrone, who kissed the girl's cheek and called out as they parted that he would see her tomorrow.

"All right, son?"

"All right," he answered.

"Was that your girlfriend?"

Tyrone looked at him. "Dat's a bit personal, innit?"

"Sorry…" Errol remembered back to his schooldays: you don't tell your parents that kind of thing. "So tell me, how was school today?"

Tyrone shrugged and hitched his bag back on to his shoulder. "It's all right."

Errol made a mental note: never ask the boy questions which can be answered with "It's all right". Their conversations these days were definitely getting shorter. It seemed that since Tyrone had moved up a year at school he had left behind half his vocabulary. Errol intended to give the kid a little more attention. Tyrone was definitely not going to be another statisitic…

Errol pulled his door keys out of his pocket. "So, you cooking dinner tonight?" Tyrone gave him the exact same look his mother had ofter used on him. He called it the are-you-crazy? look. Then the boy smiled as he saw the amusement in Errol's eyes. "Only ribbing you, Ty. But you know it won't be long before I have you in that kitchen." Errol swung the door open, and immediately they both knew something was wrong.

"Charles!" Tyrone called. Dropping his bag in the hallway, he went into the living room and called again. "Charles! Here, boy!"

As he looked back at Errol there was concern in his eyes.

"Maybe Mum took him out with her." Errol knew this was most unlikely; Tyrone knew it too, and climbed the stairs in leaps, calling his pet.

Errol walked through to the back of the house and the kitchen. As he pushed open the door a smell hit him with some force. A rotten smell – and another: dog's mess. He scanned the floor, then rushed over to where the dog was lying by the back door.

"Tyrone! Tyrone, call the vet!" At first Errol had thought he was dead, but on closer inspection he noticed the dog's eyes were only half closed. In a feeble display of loyalty, the animal tried to wag its tail and get up. It barely managed to move at all.

Tyrone skidded to a halt behind him. Errol turned and reassured him with a smile and a nod. "He's gonna be okay. You go and call the vet. You know where the number is?"

Tyrone barely nodded; there was shock and hurt in his eyes as he stared at the weak animal. "What's wrong with him, Errol?" His dog, the strong beast that had chased him around the park since Christmas, the pet that always welcomed him at the door... He felt tears in his eyes and turned away quickly to make the call from the living room.

A few minutes later he had taken Errol's place by the dog's side as they waited for the vet. He was talking to the animal and Errol was relieved to see Charles's reaction to his voice. Every now and then a whimper would accompany Tyrone's voice. The vet was prompt, and collected Charles plus samples of faeces and vomit from the floor. He said he would call and let them know as soon as he had any news, but from the evidence it looked like some kind of poisoning.

Poisoning! The words hit Errol like a blow to the stomach. Where would the dog have found anything poisonous? The answer was obvious: he was fed it.

Errol finally went to the police. The situation had become too serious to ignore. He now knew he couldn't just sit by in the hope that Anne-Marie would just go away. She had tried to kill the dog, and, more seriously, himself and Yvette. At the police station Errol was taken into an interview room by a young officer who opened a pad and began to make notes.

"Okay, Mr Wright, what is your complaint, and who is it against?"

"Her name is Anne-Marie Simms, and she's been harrassing me for several months now," he answered.

The PC's pen hovered over the pad. "Forgive me, but… would this happen to be a lovers' tiff?"

Errol was taken aback by the inference. "Not exactly, no," "Then what, exactly?"

Errol leant forward to tell his story. "I met this woman sometime last year, in the Autumn. A few weeks after we met… well, I slept with her . It happened once only. I thought we both understood that it wasn't to happen again. You see, I have a girlfriend; she's now my fiancée. We were good friends before… you know, before the sex. But ever since… well, she calls me, sends me letters, gifts…"

"Hardly a reason to complain, sir. I mean, we can hardly arrest someone for being in love, can we? What evidence do you have that this woman means you harm?"

Errol was surprised by the officer's attitude, but continued calmly. "If you'll let me finish… Recently she has become irritational. She's tried to harm my girlfriend, left out in the middle of nowhere on a freezing night. She's had us both in hospital on different occasions – she tried to run us down in her car. She's slashed my tyres, and tried to poison our family pet."

"Are you sure it was she who did this?"

"Yes! Yes, of course…"

"Any witnesses?"

"No. None that I know of."

The officer put his pen down. "There's not a lot we can do without evidence, sir."

"I just want her to stop. She's harrassing me and my family. There's no telling what she might do next."

"We can't arrest someone for what they *might* do—"

"I don't necessarily want her arrested – just cautioned. Someone official to talk to her. I want it to stop."

"We could talk to her, but it might make things public – and I'm sure you don't want that, being a celebrity an' all…"

Errol met the policeman's eyes. He had recognised him.

"It might even aggravate the situation," he continued. "Why don't you apply to the courts for a restraining order?"

"Can I do that without evidence?"

"Unfortunately you will still need evidence, catch her at it…"

Errol left the police station with a new purpose. He had to catch her in the act – but how, when he never knew what her next move might be?

Errol sat in first class, opposite Marion Stewart. A pair of reading glasses was perched on the end of her petite nose, and a magazine was spread on the table between them. The train was bound for Manchester, and a recording of a celebrity quiz show. They chatted amiably in between periods of quiet reading. Marion's series was over, and so she was constantly in touch with her agent to get small jobs like this one to do. She was thinking of going back into journalism.

Suddenly she looked up from her magazine. "I saw the show you did with that drug addict."

Errol laughed, then looked rather embarrassed. "I can laugh about it now, but I hate it when disorganised things like that happen – it doesn't do the show any good. They didn't tell me the guy had gone cold turkey only the day before."

"Believe me, it didn't do your ratings any harm."

"Sad world, isn't it?"

Marion leaned towards him and lowered her voice. "Are we allowed to talk about Anne-Marie Simms?"

Errol raised his eyebrows. "Who?"

"That bad, hey?"

Errol suddenly seemed exhausted; he gazed out the window at the passing fields. "Can we *not* do this?"

Marion reached over and placed a hand on his knee. "All right. But if you ever want to talk – or even if you don't, but have to – make sure it's me you bell, okay?"

He nodded, and gazed out of the window again. "Yvette's actually coping better than I am."

"Is that so?"

"I'm a total wreck and she's like a solid rock."

They were interrupted by the show's director who had lurched into their carriage to explain the finer points of the quiz game to them. So, Anne-Marie was definitely out of bounds, and Marion would have to fight the urge to find out more about what she was up to – her journalistic instict, she told herself.

The hotel had a leisure complex attached, and Errol had decided to make the most of it. With a towel thrown over one shoulder he entered the swimming area and suddenly stopped, watching the lone swimmer. The woman was doing laps so smoothly and quietly that he hadn't heard a sound, and had expected the pool to be deserted. She was athletic, dark-skinned, and for a crazy moment Errol thought it was Anne-Marie. He almost began back-pedalling to the changing rooms, but as she pulled herself to the edge of the pool for a breather he could see it wasn't. She was pretty, even dripping with water, slender, not as muscular as Yvette, with long arms and even longer legs. She had jet black hair which was tied with a band; she pushed a few stray strands off her face and briefly glanced up at him before turning and dolphin-diving back under the water. Her stroke was effortless, strong and rhythmic. It would be a shame to disturb her, Errol thought, so he lay his towel on a bench, climbed into the opposite end of the pool and started a quiet routine, washing away the stresses and tensions of the day. It was the first time he had loosened up in ages, the business of the past few months having hung heavily on his conscience. He did five widths before coming up for air. He shook water from his head, and when he looked up he saw the woman sitting on the side, staring at him.

Used to being recognised, Errol swam over, ready for the usual "Don't I know you from somewhere?"

"Only five laps!" she laughed, her voice a musically lilting West Indian. "Cha, a fit young man like you mus' can do betta!" Errol stopped just in front of her, sculling the water with his arms to stay afloat. "I'm only just warming up," he quickly pointed out, irritated at this slip of a woman belittling him.

She was grinning mischievously. Pulling her ponytail forward she squeezed water from the end of it. "Maybe…"

"That sounds like a challenge to me."

"Men! Cyan' tek criticism without seein' it as a challenge! You in good shape, though. I'll tek yer on."

Now it was Errol's turn to laugh. "You serious?"

"Are you?"

She was too up front to resist. "You're on. Fifty laps?"

She slid her brown body into the water and came up beside him. "Your call, mister."

"After three?"

She nodded.

"One… two… three!" They took off together but, even though he'd had the advantage of being the caller, the woman soon started inching ahead. He'd underestimated her. He caught up on the second lap and stayed with her for ten, when again she pulled ahead. After thirty he was feeling the strain in his shoulders. But his competitor was apparently feeling no such fatigue, and made the fifty laps well before him. She climbed out and waited for him to finish.

Breathless, Errol dragged himself up beside her and they sat on the edge, dangling their legs in the water. "You're good," he said. Up close she was even better – he could see every muscle that had prompted her to win.

"I know it," she laughed. This lady was not modest. "I'm Jazz..." She held out her hand. "I t'ink I ought to know who I jus' beat."

"Errol," he replied, shaking it. She hadn't recognised him.

"You know, you're not bad – jus' not as good as me. You got to learn to move with the water, not against it."

"I was doing the best I could."

"Never min', darling, better luck nex' time." She patted his back and they both laughed. She was funny. It felt good to laugh for a change. Real good. Real necessary.

"So, do you come here often?" he asked.

She shook her head, her hair dripping little crystals of water on to her skin. "Dis pool, a couple a times a week. I work part-time for a print comp'ny up de road. You?"

"I'm a visitor. Staying in the hotel. I needed a relaxing work-out... and that was nothing like a relaxing work out."

They laughed again. "You need a challenge every once in awhile. Get your blood boiling, y'know."

"Yeah, but I've had my share of blood boiling recently. So, how come you're so good at this?"

"I used ta swim fa me school back home. It's one t'ing I hold on to fram me yout'."

"It shows."

"An' what do you do?"

"I..." he stopped himself. He'd made the mistake of getting too friendly with strange women before. Never again. Besides, this was nice – just chatting without talk of his career and being a celebrity. "I'm a mechanic," he lied.

"Mmm. So dats where you get dose muscles." She ran a hand over his shoulder. It wasn't a caress, more like testing a piece of furniture for firmness. "You're strong, but a real clumsy swimmer... On de other han', you do look good in swimming trunks."

Errol blushed and automatically moved his hands to hide the bulge in his trunks.

Jazz suppressed a giggle. "You hungry? I was gonna pop in to my favourite Chinese restaurant on de way home."

Errol hesitated. But what was he worried about? Tommorow night he would be on his way back home to Yvette. And this Jazz woman hadn't even recognised him. "Chinese? Sure. I'll join you."

They met in the lobby of the restaurant. She wore jogging bottoms, a V-necked body suit and squash trainers. She'd brushed her hair back and clipped it at the nape of her neck. Over dinner they chatted about their past and ambitions. She was good at drawing him out, and he eventually succumbed. Usually he would be the questioner, inquisitive about what made someone tick, but he found Jazz so easy to talk to that by the time they'd finished eating he had told her much more than he'd expected. However, he had managed to skirt around his television role, making up the story of his life as he went along. She was a graphic designer – freelancing at the moment, after being made redundant. Her name was Jacintha, but everyone she knew called her Jazz and she had adopted it.

Two hours had passed so comfortably that they were both surprised when the waiter, after hovering for fifteen minutes, told them that the restaurant was closing. It was eleven thirty. They paid the bill – going Dutch, she insisted.

"Can I give you a lift home?" Errol asked, before remembering he had no car but could always call on the stand-by driver.

"No, I 'ave me own car."

"I'll walk you."

They walked to the car park. "That was a most enjoyable evening," Errol said.

"De food or de comp'ny?" she asked, watching his face.

"Both."

"You know, Errol, you're all right. Guys like you are usually married and will still try somet'ing."

"Don't think I haven't thought about it... and as for getting married, I *have* found the right woman. We just haven't got around to it... yet."

"This is me," she said, stopping by a red Metro.

"Thank you... for your company tonight."

"My pleasure." She kissed his cheek. "Maybe we'll meet again."

Errol watched her get into her car, and was about to reach for one of his cards when he rememebered they had his profession printed on them. Instantly she would know he had lied. She could also turn out to be another adoring fan, or a maniac. So he stood helplessly, and waved as she drove out of his life.

He thought about Jazz as he made his way back to his room. He had the curious feeling that he knew her from somewhere. In fact, she reminded him of Marion. Lying on his bed that night, he felt extremely proud of himself. In the old days he would have charmed his way into Jazz's bed. Now he had Yvette, all that was behind him, and he had no regrets.

He turned over and picked up the phone, dialled home, and grinned as Yvette answered on the second ring.

"Hey, you…"

The next morning they were up early to start recording. He had to share a dressing room, but it wasn't the first time, and the other guy was a brother. He introduced himself as Roy, a comedian, also up from London. "Another hole in the wall," he sniffed as they were pointed in the direction of their room. It was a narrow, windowless cubbyhole with a long counter bolted to the wall. A mirror ran above the counter, surrounded by bare bulbs, half of which had blown. There was a small pile of envelopes on the side. Errol ignored them, but his roommate scooped them up. "Mail," he said, sorting through them. "Looks like people know you're here – they're all for you."

Errol's brow creased. He took the letters Roy handed him but didn't look at them. His eyes were riveted to the far end of the dressing table, where a single red rose stood in a clear vase. A small card was taped to the side of it.

Roy followed his gaze. "I guess that must be yours too."

Errol couldn't believe it. This had Anne-Marie stamped all over it. But how could she have known he was here? Another sweet-smelling, blood-red rose. He didn't even read the card. He wouldn't give her the satisfaction. He snatched it off the counter and dashed the whole thing in the bin.

"Hey, don't you want to find out who it's from?"

"I have a pretty good idea."

"But all the same…" Errol watched as Roy retrieved the rose and the card. He took it out of the envelope and handed it to Errol, who sighed and accepted it. As he read it a strange smile curled his lips upwards.

"Errol. Can't get you out of my mind, Yvette." She'd had it sent to him.

Errol laughed with relief, took the rose from Roy's hand and placed it back on the counter. "It's from my girl. She's missing me."

During a break Errol finally caught up with Marion. "Hi there, got time for a coffee?"

Marion grinned. "For you, I can probably spare a few seconds."

Errol laughed, and she was glad to see it. This was the real Errol shining through again.

Over coffee he told her about the rose. "Freaked me out at first, but..."

"You thought it was from her?"

"Yes. Silly, huh? I'm getting so paranoid."

"Considering what she's done I wouldn't say so. Look, I'd better get back on set, I have to redo my make-up."

Smiling to himself, Errol trotted back to his dressing room, a spring in his step. But the smile froze on his lips when he glanced at the long mirror, and his heart thundered in his chest.

Scrawled across the glass in red lipstick was a message:

MISS ME YET? I'M CLOSER THAN YOU THINK, ERROL.
WE'LL BE TOGETHER SOON.

Before leaving Manchester Errol called the police station where he had reported Anne-Marie's misdemeanours. He needed to find out if they had talked to her, maybe even arrested her.

"Mr Wright... Yes, we did talk to Miss, er... Simms."

"And?"

"She admits sending you letters and calling you, but says that's all she did. She claims she's in love with you, sir, and wouldn't want to hurt either you or your family."

"She's lying!" Errol barked. "I know I have no proof, but she is."

"I don't blame you for being upset, Mr Wright," the officer said. "If what you say is true, someone has made an attempt on your life. But we can't arrest her for sending you letters or flowers. We did give her a warning, though. A pretty strong one. But without evidence connecting her to the other incidents, there's not much else we can do."

"Well, your warning didn't work." Errol was trying hard to keep his temper under control. "I'm up in Manchester, and she's been here – in my dressing room, writing on my mirror in lipstick."

The officer's voice became a little more alert. "Did you see her, sir?"

"No, but... how many stalkers do I know?"

"Listen, sir, as soon as you have some proof, something we can *use*, we'll be happy to help you."

"Sure," Errol replied, and hung up. At least she wasn't in London causing Yvette any grief. It was a consolation that did little to help the way Errol felt. He would have to be on his guard.

Two days later Anne-Marie Simms was still on Marion's mind. She reached forward and pressed the intercom on her desk. Her assistant answered. "Mike, can you come in here with a pad, please?"

The door opened seconds later.

"Can you find out all you can about a woman called Anne-Marie Simms? She's a psychologist and author of a book called *Internal Bleeding*. We should have her on file somewhere – I was going to use her for a show before the cuts. Use research if you have to."

A few hours later there was a knock on her office door, and a file was dropped on her desk. There was a part of her that dreaded what she might find, but nevertheless she leant forward and read.

Anne-Marie stepped from her car and took a deep breath before looking up and down the residential street. So far so good. It was three thirty. Any minute now he would be coming to the gates.

The school was comprised of four single-storey buildings, and because Anne-Marie wasn't sure which one Aaron would emerge from she tried to keep a vigil on them all. Anyway, there was only one exit to the road.

Two hours ago she had called the boy's mother and pretended to be Errol's secretary. From what Errol had told her about Tanya, she'd known she wouldn't question a change of plans if it saved her a journey. She had told Tanya that, instead of picking Aaron up from her home, Errol would be collecting him from school. Asthe children started to flood out of the buildings, Anne-Marie smiled at the waiting mothers and nannies – some with other children, toddlers, babies in prams... Of course Aaron would be no problem. He knew Anne-Marie, and she was certain Errol wouldn't have concerned his child with the recent goings on. He would go with her. She recognised him waiting just inside the gates, and approached slowly. "Hello, Aaron. Remember me?" Sshe smiled her most friendly smile; it wasn't hard – she genuinely liked the little boy.

At first, she could see, he had trouble placing her face. "Anne-Marie," she reminded him. "I'm a friend of your dad's."

"Oh yeah!" He smiled back, revealing a cute dimple.

"He's asked me to come and pick you up and keep you occupied for a few hours."

Aaron cocked his head one side, and for a second he looked just like his father.

She took his arm and began leading him towards her car. "Would you like that? Just the two of us…"

Aaron grinned, and in no time they were driving towards town and the Trocadero, where she hoped to exhaust him and, of course, give him a treat.

Errol knocked impatiently on the front door again. This time a light came on and Tanya opened the door, holding it to her body, just her head appearing in the gap. "Did you forget something?"

"Sorry?"

"Look, I'm busy – what do you want?"

Slightly confused, though quite accustomed to Tanya's abrupt manner, Errol controlled his voice. "I'm here to collect my son. Remember – Friday night?"

Now it was Tanya's turn to be confused. "But didn't you pick him up from school? I thought that was the arrangement."

Errol placed a hand on the door. "What arrangement? You mean he's not here?"

Panic took over in an instant. "Oh my God!" Tanya's hand flew to her throat. "I… I got a call… from a woman who works for you – an assistant… no, secretary. She said you were picking Aaron up from school as you wanted to surprise him. I just thought… I mean, how could I know—"

Errol had stopped listening. "You stupid, selfish cow! You know I would never let someone else call about my child!" He whirled back down the path towards his car. "How was I supposed to know? Errol! Errol, wait!"

But he was already back in his car and heading towards Anne-Marie's flat, holding his mobile in his left hand and dialling 999. He was thinking about what she had done to their dog. It didn't bear thinking about what she might do with his child.

Finally put through to the police, he blurted out a few details of the kidnapping and where he thought she may have taken his son. Too many questions started firing back at him… and Errol was hardly thinking straight as it was. He switched off, cutting off the officer mid-sentence, and dashed the phone on to the seat beside him. He put his foot down, threading dangerously through the traffic in his haste and panic. When his son's welfare was at stake, his own safety was a lower priority.

Screeching to a halt outside the private flats where Anne-Marie lived, he jumped from the car and tapped out her number on the intercom pad. It rang eight times, Errol agitatedly hopping from one foot to the other, before he punched the number again. It rang once more before the door was opened by someone leaving the flats.

Errol didn't wait for the lift to take him up to the second floor; he dived up the stairs and was soon hammering on her front door. Still no answer, and now he began to get very frightened. There was no noise from inside the flat – no television, no radio, no voices. A middle-aged white woman came out of the flat opposite as Errol began to call through the letterbox. "She's not there. I think she's gone away for a few days – she had suitcases with her this morning."

Not even thanking the woman, Errol dashed back down the corridor and headed for the stairs. Now he knew this was premeditated – if she had packed she could be anywhere. Her way of getting back at him, once again. Back in the car his mobile was ringing. "Yes!" he answered.

It was Tanya. "Errol, what's going on? Have you found him?" "No I haven't. Look, have you called the police yet?"

"No. I thought you—"

"Well call them. I'll let you know if I hear anything."

He speed-dialled Marion's number. She might have some idea where Anne-Marie could have gone. "Marion, it's me."

"Errol! How are you?"

"Look, Marion, I think Anne-Marie's got Aaron. She's taken him from his school," he said breathlessly.

"*What*? How?"

He explained all he knew so far. "I thought you might have some idea where she could have gone."

The line went quiet. Then, "Her mother's house. She still has it; it was up for sale, but—"

"Do you know where it is? An address?"

"Meet me outside my house."

She hadn't realised how much fun a seven-year-old could be. Aaron was a happy child, and Anne-Marie found she could easily make him laugh. And what a laugh! What a smile – just like his father's. They had gone to the Trocadero, played on the virtual reality machines, and she'd watched him laugh with delight on the mini rides. He'd beaten her easily on the video games, even though she was trying her hardest.

The train ride back was bliss. They hugged, Aaron sitting on her lap with one tiny hand hooked around her neck. She breathed in the little boy's scent and felt tears in her eyes. She had no idea what she was going to do with him. *Could* she take him away – just leave the country? She hadn't thought that far ahead; she'd just wanted to scare Errol a little. But how could she take him back safely and avoid capture? She closed her eyes. She needed to think.

It was eight o'clock when Anne-Marie finally turned into the road where she'd grown up. She held Aaron's hand. He was dragging his feet – he had fallen asleep on the train – and she realised how tired she felt too. Mum's house would be cold – she'd forgotten to put the heating on – but there would be food. Earlier she had cooked for them both, knowing the boy would be hungry. She had made up a bed on the sofa too. She would decide what to do with him tomorrow.

"Anne-Marie, I'm hungry."

"Not long now. We're nearly there. I've cooked you some chicken. You like chicken, don't you?"

"Yes," he nodded.

Such a well-behaved boy. She would miss him – almost as much as she missed his father.

She had just put the key in the front door when she was grabbed from behind and Aaron was whisked away from her side. She uttered a yelp and turned to face Errol Wright. Marion held Aaron against her shoulder.

"What did I tell you? What did I tell you?" Errol yelled.

Anne-Marie gulped air. She had never seen him look so mad. Even before, when he had threatened her. There was a wild look about him, all the coolness gone; there was also fear in eyes. Fear of being out of control.

She looked from Marion to Aaron, and back to Errol. She didn't dare open her mouth, afraid of the reaction it could provoke.

"*Why*? Why *us*? You have brought an innocent child into this madness. You must have some sense of right and wrong…"

"I didn't want to hurt him…"

She was right. Her voice got the reaction she had feared. Errol grabbed her by the throat and shoved her up against the wall. She struggled, trying to free herself.

"Errol, no – let's get out of here. Let the police deal with her," Marion coaxed.

For a second it was as though he hadn't heard her. Then Marion grabbed his arm and pulled him away from Anne-Marie. Gasping, she slid to the ground.

"I'm warning you, Anne-Marie – stay away from my family or I'll kill you!" He started to walk away, then turned and pointed his finger like a gun. "That's not a threat, this time it's a promise!"

Yvette heard the front door open and close, the beep of the alarm being disarmed and set again. She shook her head, her expression sombre.

Her dream home was becoming a prison. Every time they opened a door or a window they had to remember to disable and reset the alarm. Convenient control boxes had been installed in most of the rooms; the perimeters of the house had been heightened by railings and barbed wire. There was no way in or out of the back garden any more, apart from the back door.

"Hi." Errol entered the living room and dropped into the seat beside her.

A faint look of amusement touched her eyes. It was hard these days. "What, no kiss?"

Errol leaned towards her wearily – almost grudgingly, she thought. She turned to meet his lips and recieved a quick peck before he slumped again into the seat.

Yvette used the remote control to lower the volume on the stereo and lifted her eyebrows slightly. "Headache?"

"I don't know. Not enough sleep, I think." He stood abruptly, staring straight ahead, his eyes hooded with memories. "I think I'll just take a bath and get an early night," he said, walking towards the door.

"Want me to come with you?"

There was the tiniest pause. And did she see an expression of strain crossing his face? "No. I just need to relax, Eve. Come up when you're ready."

She stood at the doorway as he took the stairs. "Can I get you anything?" "I'll be fine. Let me fall asleep before you come though, yeah? And remember to set the alarms."

She watched him drag himself upstairs, his head hung low. This was not the Errol Wright she knew – the world knew. His bounce and vitality had gone. She looked at the clock – it was barely six. Before all this, Errol would work until about eight at night, then go on to visit friends, stop for a drink, meet business contacts or play sport. He had been an active man. Now he would rush home, having called her several times during the day, and was fast becoming the most knowledgeable man in London on security systems.

Even when Tyrone left the house he had to have his mobile phone on him, had to call in regularly to let them know where he was. The order hadn't come from Yvette, but from Errol, who was becoming obsessive about knowing where his family was going to be at any given time.

Yvette, who had found the situation quite amusing at first, was now beginning to resent it. Tyrone was only twelve, and he was being made to carry a mobile! Anne-Marie had a lot to answer for. And yet, she was nowhere to be found. She had vanished, ever since Errol and Marion had rescued Aaron from her clutches. Errol had hired a detective – he wasn't after her arrest, he just wanted to know where she was and what her movements were. He wasn't going to be taken by surprise again.

But now Yvette was afraid it was getting out of hand. He'd even made her install security cameras inside and outside the gym. So if Anne-Marie turned up there they would have it on tape.

Errol skipped easily down the step and faced his audience. "Thank you…" he said, but they continued to clap so he gestured for quiet. "Thank you… thank you to our guests – Lennox Lewis and Rianna Scipio!" In the midst of further applause he bowed. "Thank you – and goodnight," he said, then straightened up. And then he saw her. She was standing in her seat, applauding with the other viewers. Watching him. Him, and nobody else. His heart pounded, he felt light-headed, and then something inside him snapped. He dashed towards the auditorium. "Errol, what's going on? Errol, your mike!" the floor manager called after him, but his words fell on deaf ears. Errol was still moving. He unclipped the mirophone from his waistcoat and scanned the crowd as they shuffled into the aisles. They were turning into a sea of bobbing heads.

"You're in for a surprise, Anne-Marie," he muttered under his breath. "Excuse me!" He squeezed past two women who, realising it was him, tried to get his attention, one grabbing his sleeve. But he pulled away and slipped his way through the smiling faces, the people chatting about the show and what they would be doing next. The lobby was packed. "Excuse me, please! Excuse me – I'm in a hurry…" Faces turned towards him, startled at first, then annoyed, then softening in recognition. "Great show, Errol. I wonder—"

"Thank you!" He was already past them. He craned his neck as he reached the stairs to the front door, and saw her again – the back of her head, heading down . "Coming through!" He barged past a group of teenage girls.

She was wearing a red sweater, a long brown skirt. She'd stopped to read a poster.

Got you, Anne-Marie. I've got you now…

He marched right up to her and grabbed her arm. "You don't give up, do you!"

He spun her round to face him, and found himself looking into the startled brown eyes of a complete stranger. "Hey! What do you think you're doing? What is this – some kind of joke?" The woman pulled her arm free and backed up a step.

"I… I'm sorry." Errol's hand flew to his head. "I'm sorry – I thought you were someone else."

The woman shot him a look to kill and hurried towards the exit, looking back every now and again to make sure he wasn't following her.

Errol turned to face hundreds of eyes, some of them shocked – obviously those who had witnessed his pursuit. The chatter that had filled the lobby died down as he approached, then started again as soon as he had passed. Embarrassed, he made his way back to the set and the dumbfounded faces of his colleagues.

Errol passed the phone to his other ear. "*How* much? Well you might as well get him a new one. I'll put a check in the post for two hundred – get him a decent one with ten gears. Can I speak to him?"

Yvette walked into the room and curled up on the sofa with a magazine, donning her headphones, which she had to wear so the television noise wouldn't interfere with his surveillance. Errol had arrived home agitated, unable to sit still for more than a minute. Every noise would have him out of his seat, checking all the systems. He patrolled the house, not even trusting the lights that indicated everything was secure. And to make matters worse he had taken to phoning Tanya every night.

Yvette lowered her magazine and gave him worried looks every few minutes. When he finished his call he got up to check the locks on the windows for the thirteenth time.

"Can I get you something to drink?" she asked, putting her magazine aside. "Herbal tea, brandy…"

He barely glanced at her as he pulled the curtain aside."Brandy sounds good. Ice, please," "Are you expecting anyone?"

He looked up as though she had asked a stupid question. "No. Why?"

Yvette shrugged. "I dunno. Could be the fact that every couple of minutes you look out the window."

"Well… I thought I heard something," he replied.

"Like what? I've been sitting right here and I heard nothing."

His eyes were full of scorn. "That brandy sounds real good, Eve," he said pointedly.

She breathed out heavily and forced down a temper that had been threatening to explode. Her lips puckered, but she said nothing. She would get his brandy, with ice – he sure as hell needed it. Then she would go upstairs, change into her work-out gear, turn Biggie Smalls up to the fullest. and have a long, invigorating step workout. Goldie had certainly trained her well enough.

Errol turned back to the window as she left the room.

There was that black car again. In the last eight minutes it had gone past slowly three times. He pressed his face against the window pane, his eyes following the vehicle until it disappeared from view.

"It's going to come back, I know it…" he whispered.

Sure enough, the car reappeared a minute and a half later. Yvette was coming back from the kitchen when Errol dashed past her and bolted out of the front door.

"What… Where are you going now?" she called after him as he hurtled down the front steps.

"She's here! She's still out there!" she heard him yell back.

Yvette left the drinks on the hall table and took off after him. He was pounding along the pavement by the time she got to the front door. There was no one else around apart from a solitary black car, its brake lights on, double parked a little way up the road.

Yvette watched with horror as Errol caught up with it and proceeded to hammer on the driver's window. She ran to see what was going on.

The cab driver looked up, startled, then vexed. "What de…?"

Errol shuffled backwards as the man got out and loomed large. He looked about seven foot tall. Yvette stepped in between them, grabbing Errol round the waist. "I'm sorry," she said, now backing off as well. "We thought you were someone else…" Much to her relief, the cab driver squeezed himself back into the car and sped off. As he drove away he glanced at the two figures in his mirror. "Couldn't fin' de bloody address anyway," he muttered. "People can' get addresses right and nutters runnin' loose attacking innocents on de street…

He decided to go straight home to his bed and his wife.

They lay in bed that night, their arms around each other. Yvette could hear his heart beating steadily in his chest.

"I've been so wrapped up in protecting you, I forgot that part of that protection should be shown to you physically."

Yvette sighed. "You've been here, Errol. That's more than a lot of women get."

"I may have been here, but my mind hasn't. My mind has been hunting for that bitch. I just didn't want her to harm you or my boys. I just couldn't bear for that to happen again; for me not to be there when you need me."

Yvette leant up on one elbow. "Errol, none of what happened was your fault. Not one thing. The woman isn't well. Anyway, she's gone now. Maybe she's finally looking for help. Maybe she realised how much she was hurting people – and still not getting what she wanted."

"If it wasn't for me she would never have been anywhere near us in the first place."

Yvette had had enough of this self-pitying guilt. She wanted her man back – the man she had fallen in love with. "Why don't you get away from here for a while?"

"Not all of us?"

"No, you. Remember you told me about that opportunity to record in LA?"

"Montell Williams's show?"

"Yeah. Why don't you go for it? You'd only be gone a month. And the Americans would love you; it'd build up your confidence again."

"I couldn't leave you, Eve – she's still out there somewhere…"

"Errol, I'm a woman. I'm big enough and bad enough to take care of myself. Tyrone's here, Karen's down the road, and anyone else – including you – will be only a phone call away."

"If you're sure… ?"

She squeezed him. "Baby, I know how hard this is for you… but it's been harder on me watching you go through it."

"You want me to go, don't you?"

She laughed. "Yes, I do. For both our sakes."

Yo, baby!" a voice purred down the phone line. Yvette smiled. He'd only left the country this morning but she missed him already.

"Hi, honey," she purred back.

"You know where I'd like to be right now?"

"No… Tell me." She grinned.

"I don't have to tell you – you know."

She knew all right; only this morning he had been right there, making love to every inch of her body. Her grin widened as she remembered the orgasm. "So, are you there?"

"Yes I am."

"And what's it like?"

"Babe, I only just got here. Give me a chance to look around, get to know some people... How's everything at home?"

"I'm on my own. Tyrone begged to go and stay at Anthony's."

"And you let him go?"

"Errol," she warned. "I'm a big girl now."

"I tell that boy to look after you while I'm away and what does he do? The first day, and he leaves you alone for the night."

"Look, I'm glad of the break. I'm a lady of leisure for the weekend. Everyone I need is at the other end of the phone."

"If you're sure... Talking of numbers, I've got one you can reach me on."

Yvette took it down. "I miss you already," she said.

"You too. Make sure you lock up – and switch the alarm on before you go to bed, okay?"

"Of course. Will you call me tommorrow?"

"Yep. I gotta go. Love you."

"Love you more." And he was gone.

She put the alarm on, double locked the door, and on her way up the stairs flipped off the hall light. She felt suddenly quite exhausted. It had been a long day, and it would be an even longer night without her men around.

She crossed the thick carpet to her bathroom and began to fill the tub, knowing she'd probably fall asleep in the soothing water. Thoughts of the past weeks tried to crowd her head, but she didn't want to think about it. The worst was over. The police would find Anne-Marie and put her away. She was a seriously sick woman. Walking back into the bedroom she dropped a Johnny Gill cassette into the stereo and undressed lazily in front of the mirror, tossing her clothes across the foot of the bed. Her eyes fell to her breasts, then continued down to her flat stomach and pubic hair, her taught thighs and the curve of her calves. "I am woman," she mimicked, laughing, then turned to get a view of her backside. Wicked body. Never needed silicone or plastic surgery. "Errol, you are one lucky bastard..."

She turned off the water, tied her braids into a loose bun on top of her head, and stepped in. Sighing, she sank slowly into the perfumed water, feeling it lap soothingly over her skin. She closed her eyes, stretched her legs out, and let herself drift off to the sound of Johnny telling her nobody can love her like he could.

After a few minutes she opened her eyes, and was sure she'd been woken by a noise downstairs. She tensed, straining to hear the rest of the house over the sound of the music. Nothing. Shit, she was getting jumpy. The house was locked and double-locked and alarmed: a fly couldn't get in here.

She closed her eyes again and thought of Errol in the water with her, and suddenly felt extremely turned on. She thought of the vibrator in the other room. What good was that when she didn't have the energy to use it?

The water was starting to cool. Not wanting to end up cold and wrinkly she grabbed the soap, washed quickly and stepped out.

Skin smoothed and scented with cocoa butter, she went back into the bedroom naked and slipped into a long silk nightdress that Errol had bought for her on their first night here.

Ready for bed, she thought a drop of brandy was just what she neded to aid restful sleep. She didn't drink often – but a comforting glass of brandy just before bed isn't really drinking, she told herself.

She checked the alarm again as she walked past the front door. All the little lights were lit on: armed and dangerous. She poured herself a drink in the dining room, then switched lights off on her ascent.

With only her bedside lamp on she slipped between the cotton sheets and sipped her brandy, the liquid burning its way to her stomach. Still a little too awake to go straight off, she picked up a book from her bedside table.

Minutes later the book slipped from her hand. Yvette didn't even wake up as it thudded on to the floor.

"Yvette..."

She turned over and pulled the covers over her head.

"Yvette... Can you hear me?"

That was her name. Someone was calling her... No... must be dreaming. The house is empty. Sleep...

"Yvette!" Sharper this time. A woman's voice.

Yvette bolted upright, her eyes wide open. "Oh shit," she hissed. Anne-Marie Simms had managed to get into the house, past the alarm system! Impossible... No, it wasn't. Yvette remembered the rush they'd been in that morning, the frantic pressing and last-minute packing of clothes, Tyrone getting out of bed late... They had forgotten to set the alarm; by the time they remembered it had been too late to go back and do it. That's when she had gotten in. Which meant that she'd been in here with Yvette all evening.

She started to tremble and her stomach tightened. Where the hell was the woman?

"Answer me, Yvette. You know I know where you are. I've come to claim my home, my rightful place." The voice was coming from downstairs, and didn't seem to be getting any closer. She probably wanted Yvette to come to her.

Then it all made sense. The keys had been in her coat, New Year's Eve... the cashmere coat she'd left in the limousine. "Here I come, ready or not. Do I sense fear, Yvette? Are you all alone without your Mr Wright?"

So, she wanted to play games. Silly, childish games. No. That was wrong: what Anne-Marie wanted was a murderous game. Cat and mouse. She wanted her rival out of the way for good.

The house was suddenly totally silent, the voice gone. Yvette didn't realise she'd been holding her breath until she let it out. She could hear her own heart, feel sweat beginning to bead on her forehead. Somewhere in her house was a mentally disturbed woman, bent on her annihilation.

She moved slowly off the bed and slid her feet into her slippers. What the hell do I do now? She reached for the phone. The police – she had to get the police. Her eyes were trained on the doorway as she dialled 999.

"Emergency – which service do you—" The line went dead.

"Hello? Hello!" Yvette stabbed at the buttons with a shaking finger. Nothing. She'd cut the fucking line! Okay. Deep breaths, Yvette. She's only a woman. A sick woman, but still human. I can take her. She tried hard to remember all she had learned in self-defence classes. But those had been months ago, nearly a year. She really should have paid more attention.

She looked towards the bedroom window. She was three storeys up. She would injure herself severely if she jumped... then Anne-Marie would come along and finish the job.

She froze, listening. Still nothing. What in hell was she doing down there?

Looking around frantically for something to defend herself with, she threw up her hands in despair. She was in the bedroom. A coat hanger, a toilet-brush handle from the bathroom – what choice did she have? She dashed to the bathroom and unscrewed the wooden handle from the brush. Then she moved slowly towards the open door. Staring down the landing, allowing her eyes to adjust to the dark, she could see nothing – no shadows, nothing out of place. Her heart felt as though it was in her neck, which felt like sandpaper. She swallowed and heard a dry click in her throat.

She edged along the wall. "Where are you, Anne-Marie? I know its you," she called, risking revealing her position in an attempt to locate that of her rival.

Her slippered feet were soundless on the carpet as she took the top step. Why didn't I just lock myself in the bedroom and wait this out? she suddenly thought. But that would have been stupid. She would have been trapped, a sitting duck. She found herself thinking of all the horror films she had seen. The victims all went looking for danger, didn't they? You never saw them sitting around waiting for the killer to come and get them. No, they heard a noise and went to check out what it was. And didn't they always get killed, Yvette? Come to think of it, they did. She could probably kill Anne-Marie with her bare hands. Poke her eyes out, reach down her gullet and yank out her tongue...

She saw the movement before she heard the menacing snarl. A pair of hands was reaching for her, floating in the darkness up the stairs towards her. She dropped the brush handle and threw her arms up to defend herself, but lost her balance and fell on to her back, a stair digging uncomfortably into the middle of her back. She heard the brush-handle knock inoffensively against the banisters.

Then she dared to look up, and in an instant she knew the truth.

This woman wasn't Anne-Marie. Yvette's brain registered Marion's features, but she had trouble equating the fact that she was being attacked by her. For this reason she didn't fight back – that is, not until Marion lunged at her face with her nails outstretched. Yvette caught her wrists when those claws were just inches away from her face, the fingers clenching and unclenching. Mustering up the kind of strength that is brought on only by fear, she wrenched her assailant to one side and managed to roll on top of her. With the momentum of their movement she brought her knee up and caught Marion just below the ribs, winding her. Now Yvette registered that she was dressed entirely in black: black roll-neck top, black leggings and trainers. Like a shadow.

"Marion, what the hell are you doing?" she screamed.

"Surprised? Ha! You mean you didn't know?" she rasped. "You *really* didn't know?"

Yvette just stared and shook her head, her grip loosening on Marion's wrists. "It was *you*! You've been trying to kill me? All this time it's been you—"

Marion had ceased to struggle. "Not all the time. I guess you could say Anne-Marie was my inspiration." She was breathing heavily. "Had to get you out of the way, Eve. You took him away from me." Her hand was slowly slipping down to her waist band. "Once he had you, he... I hardly saw him. He didn't want to know when I asked him to stay late with me, to go out with me... I *loved* him, Yvette – for so long." She held Yvette's attention with her eyes as she spoke. "It was always me he came to when he was down... Until you came along..." Her arm suddenly flew up and Yvette saw the glint of the knife just in time. She screamed, swinging her body up and against the wall. Marion was trying to stand up. Ignoring the knife, Yvette reacted quickly. She grabbed Marion's hair, lifted her, and threw her headlong down the stairs. Yvette didn't run. She kept her back pressed flat against the wall as she watched Marion tumble to the bottom and land a heap, groaning. "I don't know what bit you, Marion," she whispered, "but I hope that bump on the head just cured it." Then she moved. She hurdled over the banister, losing a slipper on the way. She wanted to go for the front door, but knew that, by the time she had the locks undone and the bolts open and the chain off, Marion would be on top of her. So she headed instead for the back of the house and the kitchen. Turning the corner in the hallway, her thigh smashed into the telephone table, knocking the vase of flowers to the floor. Pain shot up her leg, but she was oblivious to it. She could hear sounds behind her, as if Marion was trying to stand and had fallen back against the wall, and before she slammed the kitchen door shut and jammed a chair under its handle she turned to see Marion's head coming around the bottom of the stairs, the glint of the long silver blade. She's crazy! Crazy and armed. And all this time she was supposed to be a friend— Move – fast! her inner voice was telling her, and instantly she obeyed. One foot bare, she headed for the back door and outside, knowing that as soon as the door was opened it would trigger an alarm at the police station – if the line hadn't been sabotaged, that is.

She was outside before she realised that the garden was now totally sealed off. She was still trapped. "Now what?"

She ran towards the trees at the end of the garden. Maybe she could hide, dodge her attacker until the police got there. There was no moon; maybe Marion wouldn't be able to see, or she'd fall into the pond, break her neck and drown.

Where are the bloody police? If she could just keep out of her way long enough...

She hadn't seen Marion coming out of the house, although she'd heard the chair collapse as she'd forced the kitchen door open. She looked back at the door now, straining her ears, pushing all her senses to the limit like a hunted animal. She heard a movement – somewhere on the path. Lowering herself to the cold ground, shivering, trying to muffle her breathing, she prayed.

She was controlling the urge to jump out and rush her. Take the consequences. Wake up, Eve. She's got a knife.

"Yvette?"

She couldn't tell how close the voice was and she couldn't see her. Afraid to move in case she drew attention to herself, Yvette swore silently as she thought of the lost chance she'd had to arm herself in the kitchen.

"Yvette… come now. We're grown ups; can't we talk?" She sounded very reasonable. It was a negotiating voice, the kind that says, "You do me a favour and I'll do one for you." Then she laughed. "I can't believe you didn't know it was me! I didn't mean to hurt Errol, you know. The car should have hit you, he just got in the way. Such a hero!" She laughed again. "Anne-Marie – the perfect cover. Her mistake was just wanting Errol; hardly thought about you at all… But I did."

Yvette heard a rustle of leaves to her right and lifted her head a little, straining to see in the dark.

"Yvette…" The voice was closer this time. Where were the goddamn police? It seemed like an age since the alarm should have gone off. Probably dozing over their cups of cocoa… A second too late Yvette realised that Marion had found her hiding place. She was grabbed by the hair and dragged to her feet, the knife inches from her face. Instead of fighting back Yvette focused on the blade.

"How about I scalp you, Yvette? How would that be?" Marion giggled like a child. "Show you how sharp my blade is. I sharpened it myself."

"Marion. please… maybe we *can* talk about this…" Yvette's eyes switched back and forth between the knife and Marion's face. "You want Errol? Okay – well, he could still choose you… if he knew how you felt."

"He slept with Anne-Marie," Marion sobbed. "He could have had me, and he chose her and then you. Every time I saw you together he did nothing but drool; if he had a tail he would have been wagging it… No, I'll *never* have him, not with you around!" she shrieked, and she sliced through Yvette's extensions in one swoop.

But it meant that Yvette was free, and she got hurriedly to her feet and yelled in the darkness, her shortened braids bouncing on her head: "Bitch! Why can't you just leave me alone?"

"You've got my man! I want him back – and if that means getting rid of you—"

"You know the police are on their way?"

"Yeah?" Marion said with mock surprise. "Can't hear the sirens…"

Yvette's breathing was heavy but she tried to stay as quiet as she could, backing away in the dark. This game was living torture. She still felt that if she talked to Marion, tried to reason with her, she might snap out of it, realise what she was about to do. "Listen, Marion – I've got a son, so have you. What about him? What is he going to feel like when he finds out what you did? And Paul… finding out you did it for another man. He's already put up with a lot from you – could you really hurt him again? Do you want to make your son motherless? Come on, girl, give it up…"

"He won't be. Yours will, though – such a shame." Marion leered, her eyes sweeping the dark garden. "But you're right – we don't have much time…"

Yvette was moving away from the voice. Marion wasn't coming straight for her; her voice seemed to be weaving from left to right as though she were leaping from side to side. This was the moment. Yvette turned to run back to the house and stepped on something that flipped up and slammed into the side of her ankle. She skipped her next step, feeling pain shoot up to her knee, before reaching down for the object.

It was Tyrone's tennis racket. She gripped its handle and felt its weight. This was like landing on a safety-net after free falling. Finally she had a weapon. The kitchen door was a few feet behind Yvette when Marion loomed out of the inky darkness into view. She knew that if she turned to open it Marion would have her.

"Hi, Yvette. We meet again!"

Marion was grinning, slicing the air with the knife. Suddenly she yelled and rushed at Yvette, lunging with the blade, her face twisted into a grimace of murderous intent.

"No!" Yvette hollered, and her left hand joined her right on the handle of the tennis racquet. To her, it seemed like slow motion. In the split second that followed it was as though all the survival techniques she'd been taught at the gym combined with an animal instinct she didn't even know she had. She bent her knees, planted her back foot firmly on the path, and, starting low, she swung the racquet up… and through.

WOMEN BEHAVING MADLY by Marion Stewart
Naomi Campbell has one, Whitney Houston and Madonna too.
What am I talking about? Stalkers.

And just to prove that it doesn't only happen to women, U2's Adam Clayton, Chris Evans, Trevor McDonald and more recently Errol Wright have all fallen prey to these menaces. These days you don't even have to be famous to have someone obsessed by you as the recent news stories have indicated.

What is a stalker? People who terrorise another with a barrage of relentless harrasssment. This can take the form of stalking, following their victims around, sending gifts, abusive letters, pictures, newspapaer cuttings, nuisance phone calls, threatening behaviour.

But what turns these seemingly normal people into the pathetic creatures they become? Love, revenge, the thrill of the power it gives them, most of these people are loners, could that be the reason?

A close friend of the talk show host Errol wright told me, "Errol is very alarmed. When it first started he just shrugged it off. But now it has escalated to the point where he is living in fear of what might happen next."

Trevor McDonald who gets more fan mail than any of the other ITN Newscasters' put together said, "I feel very sad and sorry that someone is desperate enough to do this sort of thing."

Errol Wright's stalker was a colleague of his, up until a few weeks ago. Anne-Marie Simms lost her job because she spent more time harrassing Mr. Wright than doing her job.

She claims she did nothing wrong but fall in love. "I didn't want to hurt Errol. I felt very deeply for him and still do, I tried to make him see this, in the hopes that he could love me back."

To 'show her love' Miss Simms will call Errol on the phone up to twenty times a day sometimes more. Sometimes leaving messages over and over again, and not taking any notice and his rejection. she sends love letters daily and follows the TV celebrity and his family around, even camping on his doorstep. Her gifts range from flowers to items of clothing she wants him to wear for her. There is now an injunction out against her.

Jealousy, fury and an attempt at self destruction were just some of Simm's symptoms. Other stalker's such as the ones who preyed on Julia Sawalha, Chris Evans and the Wonderbra model Caprice Bourret have threatened murder; the crazed woman threatened to 'ruin her looks'.

These people by their very nature are devious and resourceful, they use everything at their disposal to get to their victims. The modern day phone nuisance has even been known to use the Internet.

In the past the law has failed to recognise the deep psychiatric harm suffered by the victims, until the reported cases escalated to where the law could no longer ignore it. Often all these perpetrators needed was therapy, and even then the system failed them.

So who do we trust, even that charming, attractive, well groomed guy at work could turn out to be an obsessive maniac. There's just no telling is there. Or is there?

EXCLUSIVE: 'I'M NOT MAD' SAYS MAZ

Marion Stewart, digraced ex-presenter of TV chat-show Mantalk, last night accused her male counterpart Errol Wright, presenter of rival show Do the Wright Thing, of wanting people to think she was mad.

Speaking for the first time about her current troubles, she said it suited Mr Wright and his 'comrades' to get her out of the way — because they don't want anyone to know the truth about their illicit affair.

Ms Stewart was sectioned after attacking Errol Wright's fiancée Yvette Barker with a butcher's knife. She is on police bail while she is treated in a psychiatric hospital in Kent.

At an impromptu press conference outside the central criminal court, Ms Stewart also claimed that her common-law husband was in league with the Wright clan in a conspiracy against her. Last week's attack was the culmination of a campaign of harassment that has allegedly lasted months. It was originally thought that Anne-Marie Simms, a former colleague of Mr Wright's, was the perpetrator. Ms Simms admitted in court that she had sent him love letters and persistently telephoned him.

Marion Stewart, however, turned into a copycat stalker.

The trial continues tomorrow.

They held hands in the back of the limousine, while around them the streets of Hammersmith buzzed. Yvette kissed Errol's cheek, then removed a long white silk glove and rubbed the lipstick off with

manicured hands. She'd always wanted to wear silk gloves to a function.
"Hey, lover, stop shaking. You're starting to scare me."

"I'm not shaking, am I?"

"Baby, you've got no competition."

He wished he had Yvette's confidence. The Black British Entertainment Awards was being held tonight at the Palais. In the chat-show-host category Errol knew he really didn't have any competition, but that knowledge didn't allow him to control his nerves.

A month ago they had found a new home in Finchley, North London; The contracts were going through at the moment. Tyrone would have to go to another school – which he wasn't too happy about – but it would be too much of a trek back to South London.

Yvette was on the look-out for new premises. Commuting to and from Woolwich to thegym was becoming a drag. She didn't need to work, but there was no way she was giving up her independence and the business she had sweated to build. No, she was going to build it bigger. The new premises would include, a pool, saunas, jacuzzis and toning tables :

Errol was thinking about Marion. She would have been his main rival tonight, if…

She had sustained injuries to her jaw and a fractured skull from her fall. He hadn't been allowed to visit. It was recommended that, until the treatment was seen to be working, he stay away from her completely. Paul kept him up to date on developments.

Errol had wondered time and time again why he hadn't noticed the signs. Marion had seemed such a sweet, loving person to him…

The Bentley pulled up outside the venue and Errol waited while the chauffeur walked round to his side and opened the door on to the red carpet. The streets were jam-packed with fans, curious to see what their idol looked like in real life. The queue for tickets stretched out of sight round a corner of the building.

The cameras flashed as Errol, dressed in a tuxedo that made the women gasp with adoration, turned and put out a hand to help Yvette out of the deep leather seat. Her exceptionally long, curvy legs attracted the attention of the photographers, who surged towards her. She was sheathed in a clinging black silk creation, off the shoulder, that exposed a cleavage many women would give a year's salary to have. She had relaxed hair now, with the help of a weave, shoulder length. Bernard Evans, celebrity stylist to the stars, had spent hours on her this afternoon. She was truly striking – and she was Errol Wright's fiancée. The thought gave her a powerful high as they walked arm-in-arm, smiling and waving, through the glass doors and into the theatre.

"The nominations for the best talk-show host are..." Brenda Emmanus opened the gold envelope in her hand and read out the list. When Errol's name was mentioned the cheer that rang through the hall was louder than the applause the other nominees received.

Junior Simpson then opened another envelope. "And the winner is..." There was a drum roll. Errol was squeezing Yvette's hand so hard she would have screamed, were she not holding her breath. "... Errol Wright – for *Do the Wright Thing!*"

The audience shrieked its approval. He was releasing her hand and standing up. The theme tune to his show blasted out and she saw the cameras spin towards him as he kissed her on the cheek and trotted towards the stage.

"Thank you," he said, accepting the trophy, and when the cheers had died down he began his speech. "I would like to thank my producer, John Everett, for his support and encouragement over the past two years. Also the production crew, all of you behind the cameras, thank you, and please forgive me for making your lives so miserable..." This brought some laughs and a few wolf-whistles. "A special thank you to my fiancée, Yvette Barker, who has stood by me through the good times and the bad. I love you, baby." Now the audience was in rapture. It took Errol a minute to calm them down enough for his conclusion to be heard: "And finally to my viewers, especially those of you who came to the studio week after week. The show wouldn't have been the same without y'all." He held the trophy in the air as he walked triumphantly back to his table.

A handful of celebrities was waiting outside for their cars to brought round. The majority of the public audience had headed home hours before, but some die-hards still hung around for autographs or photos of the stars.

Errol and Yvette clung together, the trophy grasped firmly in Yvette's gloved hand. She still thought she was dreaming.

"Can I have your autograph, please, Mr Wright?" The girl had obviously been waiting for him to come out. She stood there, about five foot seven, wavy brown hair cut level with her jawline, her creamy skin blushing as he met her eyes. She held out a pocket book.

Errol knew a few people who had a problem with signing autographs, thought it was an invasion of their privacy or something. But he always enjoyed it. It put him in touch with his public, and if it made others happy... He pulled a photograph of himself from his inside pocket. "Of course. What's your name?" he asked, producing a marker pen with a flourish. Her eyes twinkled. "Angie. I'm a big fan of yours, you know. I wouldn't watch *Do the Wright Thing* if it wasn't for you."

END

Baby Mother

ONE

Jennifer Edwards sighed deeply. "Sod's law," she muttered before dashing the laddered pair of tights aside and searching her drawer in vain for another pair. She had only been home half an hour — straight from the courtroom and into the shower — yet had succeeded in doing her hair and make-up with minutes to spare. Everything had gone smoothly, except for the tights.

Panicking, she rushed out of the bedroom in her lacy bra and panties and called to her sister. "Donna!"

From across the landing the other bedroom door opened and Donna appeared, dressed in the rude gal's uniform of tight, coloured jeans and a top that just skimmed her belly button. "Yeah, Sis?"

Jennifer often wondered what her sister would look like in a classic cut suit. Getting her into one voluntarily would be nothing short of a miracle. For once Donna wasn't modelling a hat or that bandanna she'd taken to wearing. Her hair, tied back at the nape of her neck with a shiny cotton band, was relaxed and easily came to her shoulders.

"Tights D, tights. I've just laddered my last pair."

"I've got a couple of yours, hold on."

Donna disappeared into her room leaving the door open for Jennifer to face the life-size poster of a bare-chested Tupac Shakur - tattoos and all - on the opposite wall. Written large in gold ink across Tupac's torso was the legend, 'MINE.' Jennifer shook her head disbelievingly before returning to her pine-mirrored wardrobe to find something suitable and ready to wear. Nothing except her work suits. It had been so long since she'd been out raving that she no longer possessed any party dresses. One of the suits would have to do. She pulled out the least formal two-piece then went to her other wardrobe for a blouse.

This reunion had better be worth it. Jennifer had had to break sweat to get home from court in time. It was an open and shut case, but for the over-enthusiastic foreman, the jury were only expected to retire for an hour or two. In the event, they were out for four hours. Then on her way home in the taxi, she ended up in a roadblock. Well, the main thing was that she'd won the case. Sometimes that was all that mattered.

"Here," Donna handed her two pairs of black tights.

1

"Why do you never replace my things? Come to that why don't you ask if you can borrow them first?" Jennifer snapped, snatching her tights from her sister.

Donna flicked a few wisps of hair over her shoulder and waved away her sister's complaint. "Don't stress me, man." She sloped back to her bedroom, shutting the door behind her.

Kids! Donna was lucky she was her sister and not her daughter.

Jennifer sat on the edge of the bed and eased the tights onto her smooth legs, before slipping into the lilac suit. She stood briefly in front of the mirror to straighten her clothes and admire herself. She looked good and felt good. Her hair, clipped to perfection by Splinters of Mayfair, was cut mid-length into a chic bob and caressed the back of her neck sensuously. Her linen suit, obviously expensive, was worn over a silk blouse; its skirt, nearly touching her ankles, was cut to fit her waist and curve naturally and smoothly over her hips. Below the skirt, her black-stockinged legs peeked out briefly before ending in shoes with two inch heels and just a shade darker than her suit. Yes! Tonight, she was going to show her class that she had class. Snatching a handbag from the shelf in her wardrobe, she pressed the 'off' button on her cassette player before skipping out of the room.

"D, I'm gone. Okay?"

The reply came back to her through the closed door, "Right Sis, enjoy yourself."

Downstairs she went through her day-to-day handbag, taking only the essentials: keys, money, credit cards, pen and address book. She'd left her lipstick upstairs. Clattering back up the wrought-iron spiral staircase, she grabbed her lipstick from the dressing-table in her room and headed again for the stairs. Her white Volkswagen cabriolet stood in the driveway. Damn! She had forgotten to lock the door and set the car alarm last night. She scolded herself as she eased into the comfortable front seat. That wasn't the kind of mistake you could afford to make in south London, or north London for that matter. She glanced at her watch. She was late. At least the drive from Honor Oak to Crofton Park wouldn't take long. As she slipped the car into gear, her mind drifted to the evening to come. She couldn't wait to see her old school friends again. Apart from the odd chance meeting she hadn't seen most of them since she went to college almost ten years ago. She backed the Volkswagen into the road, wondering what her old friends had been up to all these years.

"*...This is how we do it,*

It's Friday night and I feel all right,
the party's here on the west side..."

"Go, Montell!"

Dressed in an off-the-shoulder blue lycra dress, that showed every movement of her well-toned muscles, Elaine Johnson waved her long, sinewy arms in the air, trying to get the party moving — preferably onto the dance floor. She was fit, energetic and disliked spending her evenings sitting down.

A young man in a silk suit stood watching the ladies from the nearby bar, propping up the counter with his fine self. Karen was the first to notice him and she was sure he was staring in her direction. She was one of Elaine's closest friends and had a lusty sensual look which men rarely failed to notice. He had the biggest, brightest eyes she had ever seen. Discreetly, Karen coaxed up the front of her short black velvet dress to make her tiny bosom look larger.

"Get back in your chair, girl, before you shame the lot of us," she told Elaine. "Anybody'd think Montell Jordan was singing live and direct right here beside us." Then she turned her attention back to the handsome stranger and gave him the full come-on through her grey-green contact lenses. He smiled back. Karen wet her lips.

Beverly, who had spent two days trying to find something in her wardrobe to fit before admitting defeat and buying a cheap, size sixteen rose-printed dress, was gazing expectantly towards the entrance door. "Look who Cynthia's with!"

Her friends' heads swiveled in Cynthia's direction. Elaine's mouth fell open. "Isn't that...?"

"Jason Adams!" Beverly finished.

"The year below us at school." Elaine reached for their bottle of complimentary wine, her eyes following the couple as they made their way to a table near the centre of the hall.

Karen screwed up her pretty mouth, and shook a cigarette from the Benson & Hedges packet. "Oh yeah. Wasn't he... y'know... gay?"

Beverly slapped one chubby hand to her ample chest. "Get outta here!"

Elaine patted her beehived hair with slim fingers, the nails carefully manicured and crimsoned. "He most certainly was not gay. I can personally vouch for him."

Karen leaned back in her chair, lighting the cigarette that hung between her lips. "Eh-eh! You can personally vouch for him!"

3

A knowing glance passed between Beverly and Karen, followed by a burst of laughter around the table.

"He was simply obsessed with his looks back then. The relaxed hair, precision pressed clothes, he was immaculate from head to toe. Apart from his hair, the man don't look like he's changed a bit."

The most mingling was going on inside the huge hall. The guests walked tentatively from person to person, unsure of identities or reactions. Smiling, chatting, sipping alcohol, swapping phone numbers, business cards even, from those who looked like they had made it big time. Elaine scanned the crowd, pausing only to flirtatiously eyeball the nattily-dressed Jason Adams.

"I suppose you wanna say hello?" Karen asked her.

"We-ell…"

"Come nuh. We can pass his table on the way to the buffet." Karen got up without waiting for an answer, stubbed out her cigarette and pushed back her chair. She smoothed her short velvet dress over her hips and made her way across the hall, followed by her friends.

The hall was rapidly filling up with Crofton School's students of yesteryear. Some were already at the bar where the food and drink was, while others were checking out the dance floor. Most had already secured seats and tables for their old crews. Tonight was going to be a good reunion rave.

"Don't get Cynthia jealous now, it looks like she's put on a bit of weight!" Karen had to shout to be heard above the music as they neared the dance floor and the speakers.

Elaine heard, but chose to ignore the advice of her homegirl. When the threesome sauntered over to Jason's table, she immediately leaned over between him and Cynthia. "Hi Jason, remember me?"

Cynthia caught Elaine's eyes and the two women stared at each other impassively.

"Blast from the past!" Jason was quick to jump up and give her a hug. "How are you girl?"

She looked him over and memories of the cold brick wall she had let him thrust her up against all those years ago came rushing back to her. He had smelt good then too.

"Can't you tell?" She did a slow twirl, showing off her aerobic instructor's taut body. Cynthia, a sour look on her face, ignored her completely.

Jason could hardly believe the female body builder physique before him. He whistled despite himself, then remembered who he was there with. "You know my wife?"

Elaine raised an eyebrow. "Do I?"

"Cynthia."

Behind Elaine, Karen laughed hoarsely.

"One wedding I didn't get an invite to," Elaine said.

"Sorry about that." Jason took her hand. "Before you go let me have your number, maybe we can get together."

Cynthia shot her husband a disapproving glare. If looks could kill...

"I might just do that," Elaine said, loud enough for Cynthia to hear.

"Later, yeah?"

Elaine pouted her lips provocatively and let her hand slip out of his. Married men were the worst flirts. She hoped Allan would never turn into one once they were married.

The women set off again through the crowd and took their place in the queue for the buffet. Elaine bopped her head to the music. Karen greeted several people she knew and went over briefly to talk to a man who had waved her over. An assortment of cold meats, curried chicken, savouries and salads, with several variations on coleslaw, awaited them when they got to the front of the queue, not to mention the free drinks already sliding down their throats. The crew were getting into the party spirit.

"Is that all you're eating?" Karen stared at Beverly's plate of a single leaf of lettuce, a spoonful of coleslaw and half a tomato.

"It's healthy, isn't it?"

"It's only healthy when you eat enough to stay alive."

"I'm dieting. I mean look at the size of me. Since I had Jerome I've put on two stone. Remember at school, I was the one who could eat anything without gaining a pound. Now I only have to look at a cake and I put on half a stone."

"You know what works for me?" Elaine waited until she had both their attentions. "Ginseng, lemon tea and aerobic exercise at least once a day."

"Really. Ginseng? Isn't that the root that makes men stay hard longer?" Karen asked.

"I heard that," Beverly grinned.

"You'd have to ask Allan about that, I don't know about men, but it sure keeps me going," Elaine said with a mischievous glint in her eye.

"Bwoy, you look good girl. Whether it's the ginseng or the man, you're a walking advert for it," Beverly complimented. "I can't afford no expensive herbs or aerobic classes. I haven't even got time for exercise."

"Listen Bev, even if you lose weight you've still gotta tone up."

"But you don't wanna end up like Elaine, pumping too much iron and not enough men," Karen laughed.

Elaine thumped her friend's arm but laughed anyway.

Karen speared a piece of chicken with her fork. "When was the last time you had a man, Bev?"

Beverly pushed the half tomato around on her plate with her fork.

Elaine glared at Karen. "Nuh mind her, me dear," she said, touching Beverly's hand. "Karen thinks that having a man is the be all and end all. Believe me, you don't need them."

"Give over Elaine. You're only saying that because you've got Allan."

"I'm just saying Beverly is a good woman, she doesn't have to search for a man. Lose a bit of weight and start fixing herself up and the decent men are bound to flock to her. But in the meantime she needs to put the whole ah dem outta her mind and concentrate on her baby."

"Jennifer was good at banishing men from her thoughts. Remember?"

"Yeah... Jennifer Edwards, now she was a sister with sense," Elaine agreed. "Anyone know if she's coming tonight?"

"She is," Beverly said. "First letter I got from her in years was to say, 'Looking forward to seeing you again at the reunion.' I was going to write back but never got round to it."

"How come I didn't get one?" Karen whined.

Elaine consoled her. "You've moved around so much since we left school she probably hasn't got your address."

"Oh look, there's our old drama teacher. What was her name?"

"Barry. Mrs Barry. Remember that time Maureen squirted invisible ink over her blouse?" Beverly giggled.

"Yeah, the whole class burst out laughing and she burst into tears. We got a real ticking off at registration."

"God, I remember now. It was April Fools Day and her husband had just told her he wanted a divorce. She broke down and confessed the whole thing to us," Elaine joined in.

"Bwoy, we felt so guilty afterwards we chipped in to buy her flowers."

"She was alright, Mrs Barry. Gone a bit grey now though, she must be at least fifty odd," Beverly said watching their former teacher laugh at a joke.

"So Elaine, why didn't you bring Allan with you?" Karen asked.

"Allan wouldn't come to one of these things. He doesn't know anybody and he hates people asking personal questions. He's a very private person."

"Shy is he?" Beverly asked.

Karen smirked. "Not in the bedroom though, I'll bet."

"That's why I didn't bring him. D'you think we could talk about men like this with him sitting here?"

"Did Jennifer ever get married?" Karen asked Beverly.

"There was no mention of a husband in her letter."

Elaine crossed her supple legs, waxed smooth just yesterday. "The few times I've seen her she's always been Miss Single Black Female."

"After all these years?" said Beverly.

"Don't look so shocked," Karen said. "It doesn't mean she ain't getting any. I haven't got a husband either, but I've got a man who services me regularly and my kids have got me."

Elaine looked concerned. "Your kids, yes. Do they ever get to see their father?"

"Once a fortnight, once a month. When he feels like it. Sometimes he even sends some money," she said ironically.

"I know Allan would never do that to me. When we decide to have kids we'll be married and the kids will be planned."

"Y'know that's exactly what Charles said to me when I met him," Karen said.

"Well he was obviously just saying that to keep you interested," Elaine replied tactlessly.

"He stayed with me for five years! Natasha had a father for the first four years of her life," Karen snapped back.

"Alright, girl, calm down. I'm not blaming you. It was Charles who decided fatherhood and domesticity was not for him."

"Men! I wonder how many of the women here are in mine and Karen's position. Baby mothers."

"How can you call yourself that?" Elaine said. "That's just a phrase invented by today's black man to claim you as his property."

"It's true, Bev. Once a man starts calling you his baby mother it's like he's putting you in a stable. Part of his harem," Karen chuckled.

Elaine laughed at the idea, but it was true. The first woman to have a man's child was his baby mother and, as long as she was the only one, she was special. But once the man has more children with other women, everything changes. Then, the one with the most children earns the most respect.

"Besides, no disrespect intended, but you can't call yourself a baby mother when the man did dig and lef' you before the baby was even born, in fact as soon as he found out. He can't lay no claim on you or your child."

7

"What goes through those guys' heads? I mean one minute they love you, can't get enough of your sweetness. Then you tell them you're pregnant and WHAM! It's like everything they saw in you was never there," Elaine said.

"Nah, that's not how it goes. It's not you they run from, it's the fact that money haffe start coming outta dem wallet to pay fe de chile. That's why nowadays I'm just out for what I can get. Why d'you think I haven't got a regular boyfriend? Because I'm not setting myself up to take that shit again."

"But what about mental stimulation, you telling me you prefer sex to that?" Beverly asked in disbelief. Her bed had been empty for almost a year and she would take either without question if it was offered.

"Yeah man, every time. That deep emotional stuff only leads to trouble. I don't want a guy getting to know me inside out, because before you know it he thinks he owns you and starts taking liberties. I play them at their own game. If I was a man I'd be the Don, my spars all bigging me up. My lifestyle's ideal. First sign of any of that 'You're my girl shit,' and he's out the door. Treat 'em like dirt."

"Karen, how can you say that? I know Allan and he knows me, we've been going out for two years and neither of us is taking liberties."

"Okay that's you, right, but look at Beverly. The man was around even through her putting on weight, health problems, and her parents dissing him, right?"

Beverly nodded. Behind them the atmosphere was buzzing as old school friends reminisced and caught up on lost years and exchanged telephone numbers to the sound of *21 Seconds To Go*.

"Okay, then she tells him she's pregnant," Karen continued, "and the man couldn't be seen for dust. There are millions of women out there with the same story."

Karen had only just finished speaking when she noticed someone waving at them from across the hall. She waved back, embarrassed, and Elaine and Beverly looked round.

"Who the hell is that?" Elaine wondered.

"Jackie Palmer," Beverly whispered back. Jackie was coming over, red high-heels clicking and a red leather mini-dress tight around her waist. Her brunette-coloured weave hung down to the middle of her back and she wore make-up so thick it clung to her face for dear life.

"Karen love, how are you? Lovely to see you again," she screeched, planting imaginary kisses on either side of Karen's cheeks.

"Jacks, long time no see," she faked a pleasant surprise. "You

8

remember Elaine and Beverly."

"Elaine, yes you were in Mrs White's class too, weren't you?" She reached for Elaine's hand with a handful of red-painted false nails.

Elaine rubbed her chin thoughtfully. "It's coming back to me now," she said, shaking her hand. "You were in Mr Dixon's class, used to move with us when your best friend wasn't at school."

Flustered, Jackie giggled nervously and moved on to Beverly. "So how are you Beverly? You look... well..."

Beverly pursed her lips sulkily. It didn't take a genius to figure out that Jackie was referring to the extra weight she was carrying. "I've just had a baby," she said by way of an excuse.

"How lovely," Jackie clapped her hands together. "How long have you been married?"

"I'm not."

"Oh..." Jackie hastily turned back to Karen. "So what about you? You have to be married. One of the most popular girls in school you were."

"Married no, kids two, boyfriend no, lover yes, job part-time. Did I miss anything?"

Elaine and Beverly stifled laughs as they rose and, leaving Karen with Jackie, headed towards the ladies.

The toilets were surprisingly clean and empty.

"Can you believe that Jackie?" Elaine said, heading for the mirror.

"I'm surprised Karen even bothered to give her the time of day."

"That's the trouble with reunions, everybody pretends they were friends from time. It ain't until afterwards that you remember you either couldn't stand the person or never really knew them in the first place."

"Mmm," Beverly said from inside the cubicle, "I didn't see many of the black boys from school out there."

"Saw a few of the white guys from the sixth form. You know how black man don't reach until after midnight."

"It finishes at one."

"Well they don't know what they're missing," Elaine said flatly. She opened her purse and took out a lip pencil and looking in the mirror, she outlined her well-shaped mouth carefully and re-applied her dark brown lipstick. "I could've brought Allan, you know, someone to dance with later..."

Her last words were drowned out by the sound of the lavatory flushing. Beverly emerged and washed her hands. "What did you say?"

"We're gonna be short of men to dance with." She moved away from the small mirror and watched Beverly re-adjusting her bra.

"I'm not bothered about that. Shit, I knew I should have worn the white one, damn thing keeps digging into me. I don't know what bra size I am since I've been breast-feeding. I've been three different sizes already. I usually feed Jerome at this time of the evening, that's why I'm so full." She lifted her heavy breasts with both hands.

"Perks of the job, Elaine laughed. "Geddit? Big breasts… Perks?"

"Oh yeah," Beverly laughed with her. Elaine's chest was high and firm, along with her bottom and could hardly be described as big.

"Karen hasn't changed though, has she?"

"What d'you mean?" Beverly squirted her neck and chest with *Soft Musk* perfume.

Elaine wet her fingers under the tap and slicked down one of her sideburns. "Well, you know, still blatant. I bet she still flirts like mad."

Beverly seemed to remember it was Elaine who was the flirt, always jealous of Karen's popularity. "She isn't a flirt, she doesn't have to. Especially since she started going out with Charles in the sixth form. That was love, she didn't even look at another man."

"Still dressed like a tart though."

"Elaine!" Beverly thumped her gently on the arm.

"I'm only saying…" Elaine shrugged innocently. "I love Karen too."

They opened the door that led back into the hallway and re-entered the party atmosphere.

"I wonder if Charles will turn up," Beverly said above the music.

"No, not if he thinks *she's* going to be here."

When Beverly and Elaine arrived back at their table Karen had already dispatched with Jackie, been to the bar and refilled their glasses. Next to her was a man neither of them recognized. Elaine took in his silk suit and the heavy gold around his neck and wrist.

"Girls, this is Roger. Apparently he was in the sixth form and he recognizes me."

"Hi, Roger."

"Hello, Roger."

He smiled at both of them, his eyes mesmerized by Elaine's chest. Elaine's chest always had that effect on people, even women. She had that 'perfect' chest from the dirty magazines that schoolboys drool over behind the bike shed. "Roger just happens to be single and on the lookout for a wife," Karen announced rapturously, her eyelashes fluttering in his direction. Could he see the colour of her eyes in this light, she wondered?

"Good luck, Roger," Elaine said coolly taking her seat again. "I'm engaged, Beverly here has just had a baby, and I guess you already know

10

about Karen."

Karen's mouth dropped open as Roger announced that he had just remembered something that needed attending to urgently on the other side of the hall and hastily said his goodbyes before sloping off. "What d'you do that for?"

"Karen, he's a no-hoper. Any man who has to go around telling women he's looking for a wife is looking for a meal ticket."

"And how d'you work that out?"

"Experience." Elaine sipped her Malibu and pineapple. "Anyway Karen, you've got a man."

Karen kissed her teeth. "How many times do I have to tell you, he's not my man, he's my bed companion. They're easier to replace." She turned to catch Roger's behind disappearing across the dancefloor.

"What happened to your friend Jackie?" Beverly asked.

"Gone back to her husband." Karen mimicked Jackie's squeaky voice, " 'Better get back to Johnny, he'll be missing me.' Jeeze, I can't believe we used to let her hang around with us."

"She always had gossip and spare change, remember?" Beverly said.

"She's married! Where's the poor victim?" Elaine asked.

Karen swiveled around and pointed to a table against the back wall. "There they are, Mr and Mrs Price."

Elaine squinted her eyes to peer across through the dimly-lit hall. "The white guy?"

Beverly shook her head. "You're having us on. He must be nearly fifty!"

"As sure as I'm sitting here, that old white man is her husband. Big diamond and gold wedding ring on her finger. Dat ain't all either."

Elaine and Beverly turned back to face her.

"She's pregnant."

Elaine nearly choked on her drink. "Bwoy, you'd think ten years would change a person. But she's still a bimbo."

"At least she's married," Beverly said wistfully.

"To a white man!" Karen added.

"At least she won't end up being called 'baby mother'. You can't call a white man 'baby faada' can you?"

Karen and Elaine laughed at the image of Jackie's husband as a polygamous yardie in string vest and baggy jeans.

All of a sudden the music changed and Elaine felt herself being transported back to their school days. "Rufus and Chaka Khan...!" She stood up, dancing on the spot. "You guys gotta get up now. Come on, they're playing our music."

Karen raised a disapproving eyebrow. "How many drinks you had?"

"Don't tell me you've come here to sit down all night. Let's party."

Happened so naturally didn't I know it was love
Next thing I felt was you, holding me close
What was I gonna do I let myself go
Now we're flying through the stars
Hope this night will last forever…

"Come on they're playing tunes," Elaine hollered as her fit body bounced.

Ain't nobody, love me better
Makes me happy, makes me feel this way
Ain't nobody…

Elaine's enthusiasm was becoming too much for her friends. Karen took a swig of her Bacardi and coke and got up. "Okay, let's show 'em we ain't no old timers yet."

"Go girl!"

Beverly's breast milk had started to flow and she felt too uncomfortable to dance. As her mind drifted to thoughts of ducking out early her eyes wandered to the exit. "Hold on, isn't that Jennifer?"

All eyes turned towards the door as the silhouette of a tall woman stood just inside the doorway, underneath the bright red, 'EASTER REUNION — CLASS OF '86' sign.

Karen waved Jennifer over. As the newly-arrived woman crossed the dancefloor, the eyes and heads of the gathered guests turned and followed her to her seat. Certain men didn't even realize that their tongues hung from their mouths as they ogled, while more than one pair of women's eyes burned with envy.

"Jen, you look wicked," Karen said, hugging Jennifer with true affection.

"Karen," Jennifer's voice was deep, sophisticated, cultured. She noticed Karen's green eyes, but wasn't sure if she was supposed to. "You haven't changed a bit."

"Don't lie to me now," Karen laughed.

"Jen, remember me?"

Jennifer turned to greet Elaine who was standing behind her. "How could I forget the one person who was always rational when the rest of us were seeing red. Hi, Eileen."

The look on Elaine's face told her she had got it wrong.

"It's Elaine. How you doing?"

"Good, thanks. I don't even have to ask you, you look terrific." Jennifer's gaze swept over Elaine's trim figure.

"Believe me, I wasn't even this healthy as a teenager," Elaine boasted.

"And Bev..." Jennifer walked around the table, arms outstretched. Beverly stood to greet her. There were real tears in her eyes as Jennifer's arms embraced her.

"Let me look at you all," Jennifer said, stepping back to admire her old friends. "If it wasn't for the fancy clothes I could imagine we were all sixteen again."

They all laughed.

"Bwoy, have we got some catching up to do," Karen said, rubbing her hands together. "First, what do you want to drink?"

"Oh... ah, Southern Comfort and lemonade, please."

Karen disappeared towards the bar. From there she watched Jennifer gesticulating in animated conversation with the other two. Back in their schooldays Karen had always been the centre of attention, not least because she always wore the latest fashions which her friends could not afford and regularly had her hair relaxed at the salon. It was Karen to whom most of the boys flocked when they all started dating seriously because she was allowed to stay out as late as she wanted and had always been good for a laugh. *Looks like being serious paid off for Jennifer Edwards,* she mused with self-regret.

Back at the table, Jennifer was definitely the centre of attraction.

"Yeah," Beverly was saying when Karen returned with the drinks, "by the looks of you, you're making a good living as a lawyer."

Karen sat herself down sideways on her chair and crossed her legs. "Either that or you're making a good living on the game," she joked.

"Has she been like this all evening?" Jennifer smiled, an appealing dimple appearing in her left cheek.

"Does a fish live in water?" Elaine said, her head still bobbing to "Joy and Pain", bubbling through the speakers. "So what's it like being a solicitor?" Elaine asked, curious as to what you had to do to look as good as Jennifer. It was one thing to be able to stop traffic with your figure, but Jennifer could do it with her aura alone. That was something special.

"Actually, I'm a barrister."

"Eh-eh," Karen said, obviously impressed. "You mean one of those that wear a gown and the wig? Like on the telly?"

"Something like that," she smiled. "I'm aiming to be a QC — a Queen's Counsel — only another ten years or so to go."

"Go girl!" Elaine said, playfully punching her arm. "More power to the sistas."

"Had any juicy murder cases?" Karen asked, green eyes almost catlike.

"I've assisted on one or two, but I mostly get domestics." Jennifer felt real warmth from Elaine whereas Karen seemed to be cold towards her. "Enough about me, so what are you all doing now?"

"I'm an aerobics dash afrobics instructor, not that you needed telling," Elaine jokingly boasted, throwing her muscular arms open dramatically to show off her trim waist.

"Shut up about your body already. Bwoy, Allan must be half dead having you work on him every night," Karen teased.

"Allan? Are you married then?" Jennifer asked. "Strike one," Elaine chuckled.

"Neither am I," Jennifer admitted. "Sometimes a woman's got to stay single to survive. Sometimes that's the only way to achieve your goals."

"But I am engaged though," Elaine stretched out her hand showing Jennifer the ring, "to Allan of course. No date yet though."

"So what about you two?"

"I came close, but it turned out he didn't deserve me," Karen replied flippantly.

Everyone waited for Beverly's answer.

She looked up meeting their eyes, shrugged her shoulders. "I just haven't met the right man yet."

"Aaah, the old cliché," Jennifer empathized. "Not one of us?"

Karen placed a comforting hand on Beverly's shoulder. "Children are what we have. Children with no fathers." Her voice was deep and slurred.

Jennifer waited for an explanation.

"Beverly here has a beautiful baby boy of six months — Jerome."

Beverly reached into her handbag for the photo album she always carried around with her. She handed it to Jennifer while Karen continued.

"You heard of Amway?"

Jennifer nodded. They were a firm with agents all over the world selling their everyday household products at tupperware parties for commission. Some did it part-time, for others it was their full-time job.

"Well, I work for them, and I have two children Natasha and Kyle.

14

Five and nine."

"We're planning to have children after we're married," Elaine added.

"That's the only way, girl. Especially in this day and age," Jennifer said, then qualified herself when she caught a glint of fire in Karen's eyes. "Only a man can make a child fatherless, so tying him down seems like a good idea to me."

"Whatever happened to your younger sister, what was her name again?"

"Donna. She's living with me now. Pure worries, believe me."

"Worries? But she must be, what, how old now?"

"Seventeen."

They each nodded sympathetically, remembering the age well. The killer years.

"It's like Donna's always got something to prove. She's got to prove she's independent, that she's a woman now. Behind it all she's still a child of course. She doesn't realize that I've been through all that before."

"You talking housework or men?"

"Men. Every time she stays out all night it worries the hell out of me."

Beverly empathized, she was the eldest of five children. "You don't need to have a child when you've got a little sister living with you."

"Don't I know it."

"But your sister was so quiet at school. Used to get the mickey taken out of her because she had to go church every Saturday, Seventh Day Adventist wasn't it?"

"Mmm-hmm. Those were the days. She raves every night now and wears little more than her underwear to clubs. Skirts barely skimming her bottom, fishnet stockings…"

"Me dear!" Karen exclaimed.

"…Thigh high boots, a studded bra with sequins and see-through blouses and jackets. The amount of times I've told her that the way you dress is the way you're treated."

"Especially by men," Elaine added. "The other day I saw her with that Fitzroy Lucas. You remember, the one who got a girl pregnant before we even left school."

Karen exhaled deeply, shaking her head slowly. "Fitzroy, bwoy he was sweet."

Beverly was taken aback. "Karen, you didn't!"

"Well… he was offering," she replied deadpan.

"But the guy was a slag," Elaine grimaced.

"Maybe, but he always made a girl feel like the one and only."

That had to be the attraction, Jennifer thought. Sweet talk and sex was all guys like that knew about treating a woman. "I don't want him around my sister. He's too experienced and Lord knows how many children he's fathered."

Elaine took her compact from her purse and dabbed the shine from her nose. "I'm sure somebody told me he'd settled down about a year ago."

"You know, I saw him with a woman in Lewisham only a couple of months ago," Karen clicked her fingers in the air. "Yeah, yeah he was pushing a pram."

"Looks like you've got nothing to worry about then," Beverly consoled.

"You don't understand," Jennifer was becoming more and more anxious by what she was hearing, "they're more than just friends. She's even stayed over at his house."

"Oh boy. Looks like Fitzroy's hooked another one," Karen whistled, looking around the hall for any stray unattached men. "I don't think he can afford to get another girl pregnant though. From what I heard, the CSA are looking for him to pay maintenance on at least five kids already."

"Alright girl, don't give our Jen a heart attack," Elaine said, clocking Jennifer's expression.

"I know how she feels though," Karen said, returning her attention to the table. "Look how many young girls you see pushing prams with no man beside them and no ring 'pon dem finger. Simply because guys like Fitzroy have had their fun and done a runner. Jennifer wants to spare her sister the kind of prejudice we single mothers have to put up with."

Jennifer nodded.

"Both of my children were planned," Karen continued, "Charles wanted me to have the first baby when I was only seventeen," she kissed her teeth. "You see what love do to yuh?" She looked up in time to see a familiar face from the past swerving towards them.

"Yaow, sis!"

A can of Tennants came crashing down on the table between them. Jennifer caught her breath sharply and looked up at Lloyd Campbell's leering grin. He was six foot three and hairy, a fact he was proud to display by wearing his shirt open down to his belly button. He sported an unfashionable mini afro and what looked like the same jacket he'd worn back in school, the sleeves now grown back to the elbows. "Hell fire!" Karen blurted, sitting up straight in her chair. "Yuh nuh 'member me, Miss Sweetness?" He leaned closer breathing lager and cigarette fumes over everyone.

Jennifer leaned back, a look of distaste on her face. "I remember." Lloyd had plagued her last year at Crofton sixth form. He was the type of admirer that every woman dreaded. He was rude, brainless, untidy, and when he had the hots for a woman, he never gave up. In her final year, Jennifer just happened to be that woman.

His grin widened, groggy eyes ran down her body. "I was hoping I would see you, y'know…"

"Well it's good to see that some things don't change, eh Lloyd?" Elaine looked at him mockingly with one delicately raised eyebrow.

He ignored her and resumed his flattery of Jennifer. "You look good, yuh know… still fit… yuh know how me mean?"

Jennifer felt like gagging and was about to get up and move when someone tapped Lloyd on his back and he stood up straight to challenge the intruder.

The ladies sat with their mouths open. It was Jonathan. Only five foot nine to Lloyd's six three, but somehow he managed to seem more imposing. He was dressed in an up-to-the-minute style suit, a khaki green cut to fit a man of class — a man who had the body to carry it off. He wore a very low fade haircut and a ring on his little finger was his only jewellery. His friend, a taller dark-skinned man, stood just behind him. Jonathan's natural hazel eyes met Lloyd's mean ones.

"This man bothering you ladies?"

"You could say that," Jennifer breathed a sigh of relief. How long had she gone out with Jonathan, she wondered to herself. A mere two months before finishing it because of other women throwing themselves at him. He had too much temptation in his way for her liking. *Looks like he's doing well.* She always knew he would.

"What's it got to do wid you?"

"Look Lloyd, we don't want any trouble. The ladies are here to…"

"Fuck you!"

Jonathan's friend stepped forward so that the two men flanked Lloyd on either side. Karen licked her lips in anticipation of a ruckus.

"Come on, man." Jonathan picked up the can of Tennants and handed it to Lloyd. "Go drink yuh drink somewhere else."

Lloyd looked up at the tall friend and then back at Jonathan. There was a loaded pause. He reckoned he could take this little squirt, when he was sober, but the two of them? Lloyd backed up shakily. "Later Sweetness… I comin' back fe me dance."

Jonathan and his tall friend touched fists before turning back to the table.

"Jennifer, long time no see."

"Were you looking?" "I'm looking now."

He leaned closer to Jennifer and a waft of fruit and masculine spice aftershave tickled her nose. Jonathan looked good, smelled good and still had that same penetrating look that used to go through her like a blow torch. "Didn't your mother ever tell you not to stare?" Jennifer couldn't resist flirting. She leaned back casually so that her wrapover skirt flapped back revealing tight long calves.

"It's more polite than doing what I'm thinking…"

"Oooh, gimme some ah dat," Karen oozed.

Natural hazel eyes met contact lense green. "Hi…" Jonathan said, a quizzical look on his face.

"Karen," she filled in, giving him what she thought was her most appealing smile. Why was he pretending he couldn't remember her name?

He smiled around the table, shaking the other's hands, "Jonathan."

"We know, " Elaine purred holding onto his hand a little longer than necessary.

His eyes met Jennifer's again. A profound silence followed… a cool silence.

"I would join you but a group of us have come down from Luton… where I'm living now," his voice was wistful.

"That's a shame," Jennifer meant it. "What are you doing now…?"

"I'm an accountant… freelance. You?"

Jennifer's eyes were filled with admiration. "A barrister," she said with airy modesty. He raised an eyebrow, equally impressed.

Karen's green eyes watched the intimacy between her friend and the man she knew would never be interested in her no matter what. *Let her have him, he's probably a stuck-up snob anyway.*

Jonathan kissed Jennifer on her cheek like a cautious man would if he thought a lady might be offended by it. "I'll see you later maybe…?"

"Maybe." Jennifer watched the two men walk away and wondered how she had let Jonathan get away. All the ambition in the world couldn't change the fact that she was a red-blooded woman and still had an eye for a charming man. Was there a whole life out there she had missed while she'd had her head stuck in books and spent all her spare time in libraries? She shook her head, no, if she had ended up with him she wouldn't be where she was today. *Sometimes a woman's gotta stay single to survive*, she reminded herself.

On their route to the bar for more drinks Elaine and Karen engaged in a game of 'spot the face' as they eased their way past the growing crowd of ex-pupils and teachers from yesteryear wanting to know what they were now doing. By the time they weaved their way back to the table, a group of guys had noticed that sistas were thin on the ground and wanted to join up. But they looked too desperate to even contemplate.

Jennifer leant her elbows on the table. "Is it my imagination or is it getting weirder out there... I mean, being single?"

"We're just getting older."

"It's a new era," Elaine offered, "romance is a thing of the past."

"Bullshit... It's just that men are fucked-up! There aren't any good men anymore," Karen said. When she thought about how seldom she got to go out because she was now strapped with bringing up two young children on her own, and in a job that didn't offer her the luxuries of life, she became bitter. Her life was fucked-up because Charles had decided he wanted to be a single man again. He couldn't even keep his promise to contribute regular money for the kids. Arsehole!

"Let's change the subject," Beverly intervened. "We were both going to go to college together, remember Jen? Instead you went while I had to go to work to support my family."

"I know," Jennifer frowned. "Did you ever think of going back to school? You could still do it, you know that don't you?"

"Not with Jerome and no money to pay for child care."

"Study at home if you have to. There's nothing stopping you except yourself."

Beverly knew that Jennifer was right. Years of menial cleaning jobs and temporary clerical were all she thought she was good for. So many years wasted at the service of others, while her goals lay abandoned by the roadside. She could have been Jennifer Edwards. Elegant, confident, rich... unburdened. She could still be Jennifer Edwards. Easier said than done.

"*...Going to a show tonight, after working hard nine to five.*
Not talking 'bout a movie no, on a Broadway stage, show with lights..."

"Oh my God! "Encore"! Elaine jumped up, "No way am I sitting here through this. Cheryl Lynn! Remember going to Nations when this came out...?" She was already dancing her way onto the dance floor.

"I guess we bes' follow her for her own safety," Karen said and they all got up together and made their way after Elaine's gyrating figure.

It was as though the entire party had chosen to get up and dance at the same time. The dancehall filled quickly. "Encore" was followed by "All This Love That I'm Giving" by Gwen McCrae, and Jocelyn Brown's "Somebody Else's Guy".

Elaine was singing along and strutting her stuff. For Jennifer this brought back memories of her youth. She had to learn all over again how to "shock out". Jennifer mopped the light perspiration from her forehead. The memories were bittersweet. What had happened to these women, she wondered? In the sixth form they all had ambition. They all wanted careers. Elaine had been an athlete and they had all thought that one day she would run for England. Karen was going to run her own restaurant, and Beverly was going to study for a degree. All they had to show for the passing of the years was that two of them were now single parents and, as far as Jennifer could see, Elaine might be next, despite her engagement ring. So much talent gone to waste. The more she thought about the old days and what could have been for her sisters in spirit, the more Jennifer felt depressed. And what they had told her about Fitzroy didn't help either. The question mark hanging over his head was how many baby mothers he had out there. A sudden panic flared in Jennifer's chest. Like her old school mates, Donna had dreams. She wanted to be a graphic designer, but Jennifer couldn't see how Fitzroy Lucas could possibly assist her in that ambition.

She made a mental note to fill Donna in on 'Mister Loverman' just as soon as she saw her next.

The reunion was over. Endless choruses of "Auld Lang Syne" had been sung and those who could remember the words had even added a verse or two of the old school song. Karen ran to catch up with her friends as they waited by the exit.

"Got his number did you?" Elaine asked.

"Might come in handy," Karen waved the slip of paper at them. The cold air hit them as they walked out of the school building in a huddle and the women pulled their coats around their bodies as they walked up the pathway towards Manwood Road and Jennifer's car.

"Jerome must be missing me," Beverly said throwing her scarf over her shoulder. "This is the first night I've been away from him."

"I'll bet he hasn't even noticed," Karen yawned.

Jennifer removed her car keys from her bag and began to cross the street. "He's her baby, course he will."

"Babies need a break as well, you know. It's good for you to do your own thing every once in a while," Elaine wrapped an arm around Bev's huge shoulders.

"Karen!"

"If one more person calls my name I'm gonna slap 'em silly."

They all turned to see a man running up the road towards them, his jacket flapping behind him.

"Looks like you've got another admirer," Elaine giggled.

Karen frowned, "Mmm."

Just a bit taller than Karen with a dark complexion and friendly smile, the man came up to them. Karen was clearly embarrassed.

"Karen, I'm glad I caught you."

Karen's green contacts smouldered. "Philip, what are you doing here?"

"I came to give you a lift home." He looked over at the huddled group of bemused females. They were wondering who the fit-looking stranger was.

"Evening ladies."

"Evening," they chorused.

"Philip!" Karen called back his attention. She didn't bother introducing him. "I told you I'd call you tomorrow."

"I know, but I don't see why you should have to wait on a cab and pay a stranger when I've got a car," he caressed her shoulder softly. "I've been waiting out here for two hours."

Elaine giggled. Beverly poked her in the ribs.

Karen's cheeks felt hot despite the bitter wind that had blown up. "Why?" she said simply.

Philip shrugged. "They wouldn't let me in, 'cause I didn't have an invitation."

"Look Karen, it's okay," Jennifer moved forward, "We'll meet again soon. I'll call you."

Karen threw Philip a dirty look. "I'm sorry girls. Looks like certain man can't wait to get their daily 'slam'."

They all laughed. "I'll call you tomorrow," Elaine kissed Karen's cheek. "Don't wear him out," she whispered. "Looks like you've got a real loverbwoy there." "Bev, kiss Jerome for me." They embraced.

"Will do."

"Any of you going our way, I could drop you?" Philip offered. Karen threw him another dirty look. What the hell was he was playing at? First he offers to babysit the kids for the night, now this. He had better not be getting serious on her. It would be a shame to say goodbye so soon, besides she was enjoying being waited on hand and foot.

"No, no, we're fine," they agreed. The girls said their goodbyes and watched Karen and Philip walk away arm in arm.

They held their tongues until they were in the car and then let rip.

"Whoy, looks like we've just met Mr Karen."

"Naaa," Elaine shook her head. "She jus' told us, she only want a man for one t'ing. She'll use him an' dump him. She's probably putting him under manners as we speak for not doing as he was told."

Elaine was right. She knew Karen well. But love, true love, has a habit of finding a way.

It was almost two o'clock Saturday morning when Jennifer returned to her maisonette on the top two floors of the large Victorian four-storey house overlooking Honor Oak Park. As late as it was, the first thing she did when she stepped through the door was call out for her sister.

"Donna!"

Still no answer. She shed her outdoor clothes, hanging her coat on the classic wooden stand by the front door, and climbed up the wrought-iron spiral staircase in the middle of the lower floor living room up to the bedrooms above. She went straight for her sister's room.

"Donna!" she called again, this time louder. "Donna! Are you in there?" Still no answer. She let herself into her younger sister's domain. The bedroom was filled with the normal hoardings of a seventeen-year-old. Records and CDs sat atop the stereo — a Christmas present from Jennifer. Her jackets, ranging from denim to padded puffa, hung on the wall-mounted coat rack. Her college books, folders and papers littered her desk, the parquet floor, bookcase and the bed. Tupac steered down at her from the life-size poster, a leery look on his face. A poster of ragga queen Patra caught Jennifer's eye. Another one of Donna's role models! Jennifer sighed. Donna's dressing-table showed signs of a hurried make-over. A hair magazine propped up against the mirror, her tongs, brushes and comb were left where they fell. An open tub of gel sat on the floor by her chair over which hung discarded garments.

The bed in the middle of the room had clearly not been slept in. Donna's teddy bears were lined up against the pillows exactly as they were every morning. Where was she? She hadn't mentioned going out. But then again, a phone call from one of her ragamuffin friends was usually all it took to tease Donna out of the front door.

Jennifer went down to the living room to call Donna on her mobile. Cordless phone in hand she sat in her favourite armchair. Favourite because her fax, two telephones, desk and filing cabinets were all within easy reach. On either side of her stood bookshelves stacked with law books. This corner of the room was designed for work and study. She dialled quickly and held the phone to her ear. Engaged! She pressed redial. Still engaged. She was beginning to feel anxious about her sister and king rat, Fitzroy. What did Donna see in him? As she paced the floor of her newly fitted kitchen she wondered how mothers of teenagers managed.

Only this week they had received a letter from their parents in Jamaica. Mummy wanted to know when they were coming to visit next. She missed them and always worried about them not eating properly. But most of all she worried about her daughters going out with 'wotless' men. The only thing that eased her fears, she said, was knowing that they were together and watching out for each other, especially where men were concerned. She wanted to be kept informed, of everything, and told them off for not writing enough. At the bottom of the letter she had again written their Jamaican phone number in large bold print. Jennifer grimaced. There was no way she could tell her mother about Donna's new man. She'd probably have a heart attack! No, she'd have to make Donna see sense. The streets at night were no place for a girl her age. That, however, was not her main concern. The thought of her sister ensconced in Fitzroy's flat... in his bedroom... him, barechested and horny... ragga music playing on his stereo and God knows what happening on his bed... With that nightmare vision in her head, Jennifer took her drink back to the living room and dialled again. This time she got the voice box answering service and had to endure the intro to "Undercover Lover" before her sister's bubbly voice announced, "You have reached the voice box of Donna Edwards... You know what to do and when to do it."

"D, it's me... your sister. It's after two in the morning, where are you? Call me as soon as you get this message... I'm at home."

Sighing, Jennifer walked over to the stereo system and flicked it on. The tuner was pre-programmed to her favourite, Choice FM. The sweet and sultry vocals of Jenni Francis oozed out of the speakers giving a shout to, "...all those women out there who are on their own tonight... this one's going out to you all, sistas."

Jennifer flopped onto the huge five-seater sofa as the sounds of Barry White's "Practice What You Preach" filled the room. She was so tired that before she knew it she had slipped into a deep slumber.

23

Donna Edwards had spent the night having a wicked time! Fitzroy had a car and had insisted on visiting five parties for the night. By the time they came home, Donna's feet were killing her, she couldn't wait to pull off her new knee-length leather boots. On the way back she'd complained to Fitzroy how much her toes were killing her.

"Wha' me tell yuh? Ya doan wear new boot out ah dance."

They were exhausted, drunk, high on each other's company. They giggled all the way up the communal stairwell. Fitzroy was feeling good and could barely keep his hands off his woman. If he wasn't tickling her, he was whispering into her ears teasingly. Donna did try to hush him, but it did no good. He was in a playful mood and couldn't bring himself to consider anyone else in the building who might be trying to get to sleep when he was having so much fun with his girl. Outside the flat Donna struggled to line the key up while Fitzroy tickled her. It slipped in eventually and Fitzroy made a joke about fitting a key in her lock. Giggling, they fell into the darkened living room.

"Quiet Fitz," Donna hissed, "you'll wake Jen up."

"Ah wha' dis, you nevah worry 'bout making noise before," he whispered back, nibbling the back of her neck.

"Yeah, well, we weren't on our feet then, an' we weren't in my sister's flat neither," Donna hissed, running a hand over his short twisted locks.

"Cho', dat sister ah yours, she's going on too stush if you ask me. Just 'cause she's a lawyer. Ah nuh she one live yah, y'know. Jus' tell her dat Fitzroy seh she haffe settle an' cool, seen?"

"Why don't you tell me yourself?" The voice came from the other side of the room and made both Donna and Fitzroy jump into each others arms.

"Ah wha' de blood...?!!" Fitzroy exclaimed, his head spinning in the direction of the voice.

Donna hit the light switch by the door and illuminated the room. Jennifer was standing over by the bay windows, her arms folded and a pissed-off look on her face.

"Oh Sis. Didn't know you were still up. Did you fall asleep on the sofa again?" Jennifer took in the short lycra dress her sister was wrapped in and the way Fitzroy's hand slipped to her backside. "I must have done. Which is just as well, otherwise I wouldn't have heard what your friend thought of me."

"Heh... heh... hey!" he stuttered not liking the way she put him down with that single word 'Friend'. "Didn't you get my message on your mobile?" Jennifer asked.

"Oh yeah... the message. Yeah, I got it. What about it?" her sister replied.

"Well why didn't you call me back?"

"'Cause we were almost home by the time I got it. I figured it could wait until morning. What was so urgent anyway? Has somebody died? Don't tell me that something's happened to Mum and Dad."

Jennifer exhaled. Her lips twisted into an angry pout. Wasn't it obvious what was wrong? The child comes in here six o'clock in the morning. The sun is up, the milkman has done his rounds. Did she even think to leave a note to say where she was going? No! That would have been too easy. Then she doesn't come home alone, but with this... this degenerate, who looks as though he's wanted by the police.

"Well... what is it?"

"It can wait for now." Jennifer's stern attention was now focused on Fitzroy Lucas who had unzipped the heavy leather coat he was wearing to reveal a limp string vest over a well-toned, slim torso and unbuckled baggy jeans. He threw himself on the sofa, his legs splayed out in front of him. "We'll talk about it in the morning," Jennifer said bitterly, making her way to the spiral staircase.

"I thought it was urgent," Donna said.

"It was," Jennifer replied. "And it still will be tomorrow morning. But it'll have to wait. I'm tired, I'm going to turn in. I'd appreciate if you told your guest to keep the noise down. It is, after all, nearly dawn." With that Jennifer climbed up the staircase to her bedroom, leaving Fitzroy stuttering, "Eh... eh... eh," after her.

Jennifer awoke later that Saturday morning, her head feeling as though she had spent the night in a cement mixer. She had only had two glasses of wine and was well within her limit. But wine and worries don't mix and right now she had a trailerload of worries in the shape of an unruly little sister and the company she kept.

Jennifer glanced across the landing. Donna's bedroom, its door wide open, was empty. She heard noises coming from the kitchen downstairs. She secured her silk dressing gown at the waist and went downstairs for some juice before her morning jog. She sensed Fitzroy's presence even before she entered the kitchen. He was dressed in baggy jeans which hung at the hips, revealing the red and white striped boxer shorts beneath. He stood over the stove barechested, cooking himself a fry up. The kitchen was awash with the smell of oils and fatty food. After all, what did someone like him know about a luxury such as an extractor fan.

Jennifer cleared her throat to alert him to her presence.

"Yuh awright, Jen?" Fitzroy turned with the frying pan in his hand, and a grin that showed off his two gold teeth. Jennifer ignored him and crossed to the fridge, pulling out a carton of grapefruit juice.

Fitzroy kissed his teeth. "Cho', some people need to learn manners more than adders."

Irritation gathered within her. "If you're referring to me, just remember whose house you're in."

He turned to her and leant against the counter. "What 'appen to yuh, eh? One time me did t'ink seh you was criss. Now you so stush I man cyant even 'ave a decent conversation."

"Tell that to one of your baby mothers." "Ah wha' you ah seh?'

"Don't act ignorant," she said. "I know all about you and I'm going to make sure Donna knows too."

"Know wha'?"

It was all a game to Fitzroy. Even though he hadn't been back to the Caribbean since he was thirteen, he spoke as though he'd just stepped off the plane from back-a-yard.

Jennifer walked towards the spiral staircase. "Just make sure you clean up the kitchen when you finish doing whatever you're doing."

She heard him kiss his teeth again as she climbed up the steps. Fitzroy needed babysitting. Where the hell was Donna? Jennifer had things to do and didn't want Mr Loverman in her home when she got back.

Jennifer sat patiently in her Volkswagen with the roof down. The Lewisham Centre's three car parks were rammed to capacity. Usually she would have waited until Sunday to do her shopping, but she couldn't bare to stay indoors a moment longer with HIM around. He was still there when she got back from her morning jog, going through her record collection, a spliff in hand. She had to talk to Donna and soon. She didn't want Fitzroy in her home, no way, no more.

The streets of Lewisham were going through reconstruction. Lewisham 2000 they called it. The old clock tower had come down the previous year, and was now replaced by a new one. The old Army and Navy store had vanished. Knocked down to the ground, along with the glass overhead walkway that had joined the department store to the shopping centre. The actual shopping centre hadn't changed much over the years. A lot of the shops had been around since Jennifer was at school. Boots the chemist, Argos, Our Price, Etams, where she used to buy her school uniform (come to think of it didn't she get her first bra from there too?) The commonly known 'Black market' was just that, a market that sold goods for black people. There was a black hairdresser, a black hair care shop, a greeting card shop, that also sold posters, black dolls, incense and books. Finch's sold patties, hard dough bread and bun, and competed with the hair care shops with it's own stock of beauty products. There was a black man who sold kids' and baby wear, mostly socks, vests and pants, he always had a smile and a joke for everybody. Jennifer remembered that someone had told her Errol used to be a famous boxer, and now here he was years later selling baby's knickers.

Jennifer bought herself a patty and browsed around. She checked out a pair of leather boots in River Island and eased her earlier tension by purchasing a stack of books from the Black Writers section at Wordsworth Books on the High Street. Then she went back in the Centre, deciding to treat herself to some new clothes. She was so engrossed with comparing outfits in Marks and Spencer, that when a hand tapped her on the shoulder it took her by surprise.

"Jen! Bit jumpy aren't you? Did I catch you doing something you weren't supposed to?" Elaine, her hair pulled back into a bun, dressed in jogging bottoms and leotard with a jumper casually draped over her shoulders, stood grinning beside her.

Jennifer laughed and hung the tartan skirt she had been considering back on the rack. "Elaine, I don't see you in years and then bump into you a day after the reunion."

"Funny how life works out, isn't it?" Elaine admired Jennifer's casual weekend style. Lemon lambswool jumper tucked into black denims, ending in a pair of polished black ankle boots. Her short leather jacket looked and felt as soft as rose petals. Quality. Even her hair looked as though she had just stepped out of a salon. Elaine, in contrast, had dressed minimalist and her fit body was barely concealed by the tight-fitting leotard.

"What are you doing out dressed like that, it's only spring."

"I'm taking an Afrobics class down at the Riverdale. You should come along one day, they're fun plus you get a body like mine thrown in for free."

Jennifer smiled. Elaine did look good, but Jennifer preferred her body to look a little more feminine. In her book, rock hard muscles were for men. "I will when I get a chance. I don't have a lot of spare time. And when I do I find myself having to watch out for Donna. Who'd have thought that at the age of twenty-seven I'd be playing mother to a seventeen-year-old?"

"What?"

"It doesn't matter."

Elaine remembered last night's conversation. "You mean your sister?"

"Who else?"

They walked together, pausing outside Ravel's to browse at shoes.

"You'll never guess who I've just seen."

Jennifer seemed less than interested. There was a pair of pink and cream platforms in the shop window that reminded her of shoes her mum was wearing in one of the photographs they had at home of their parents taken in the seventies.

"One of Fitzroy's baby mothers!"

Elaine immediately had Jennifer's attention. "Where?"

"In Sainsbury's. She's got their kid with her. I only know her because she don't live that far from me."

Jennifer was immediately gripped with an overwhelming urge to meet this woman. "Show me," she demanded urgently.

"You're joking aren't you?" Elaine regarded her with jovial concern. "What are you going to do, go up to her and ask how she's living?"

Jennifer shook her head. "Elaine, I just need some questions answered. This woman... What's her name?"

"Celia."

Jennifer grabbed Elaine's arm, leading her back towards Sainsbury's. "She might have some answers for me."

"Alright woman, you don't need to kidnap me," Elaine protested as she was whisked away.

They entered Sainsbury's through the main entrance and weaved through crowds of shoppers with shopping trolleys and baskets and children. The pair kept their heads high and searched up and down each aisle. Jennifer pointed to a woman with a young boy by her side. Elaine shook her head. They were just about to give up when Elaine spotted the woman in question and directed Jennifer towards the tills at the far end of the supermarket. They barged towards the front of the queue.

"Celia!" Elaine called. The young woman looked up, her brow furrowed at having her name shouted out in a public.

Celia was a big woman. Not big in the fat sense but she looked like she could have held her own in a wrestling match. Her large black leather jacket covered most of her bulk, but still she was an imposing figure. Her hair gelled to her head in Marcell waves, she wore gold sandals on her feet. Jennifer was only too aware that this was a woman from the streets.

"Elaine, whatcha running me down for, man? Didn't I jus' see you?"

"Celia this is a friend of mine, Jennifer. You have something in common."

Celia looked Jennifer up and down as though she couldn't possibly have. "Yeah?"

"I'm a…" Jennifer struggled to find a word to describe her relationship with the man they knew in common, "…an acquaintance of Fitzroy's."

Celia's son grinned cheekily up at Jennifer. A familiar grin. Celia turned to Elaine then back to Jennifer and screwed up her mouth, pushed up her chest and set her feet in a fighting stance. "You want trouble?" she challenged.

"No, you don't understand," Jennifer turned to the little boy, two years old at the most. "Is this his baby?"

Celia still wasn't convinced Jennifer was a friend and not foe. "What's that got to do with you?"

Elaine stepped in. She could see a situation developing here that could leave Jennifer lying flat on her back. "Easy nuh, C. Jen's just trying to get some information for her sister."

"I'm not no advice bureau, y'know."

"Fitzroy's seeing my sister, okay? I just want to make sure she knows what she's getting into."

"What Fitzroy does is his own business."

"I don't want to interfere with whatever you and Fitzroy have. I'm just trying to make my sister see that he's no good."

"You know where he is?"

"Yeah, at the moment I do."

"Well you can tell him from me he is a no good dirty bastard who owes me three months' money. His son needs new shoes and a coat that fits an' if he don't find his raas down my yard by weekend gone, I'm sending my bruddas for him…"

"Well Celia, nice seeing you again, we'll make sure he gets the message," Elaine said, dragging Jennifer away. "Them kinda people you don't mess with," she advised.

" 'Them kinda people', as you put it, is who my sister's already messing with. But I'm not going to let Fitzroy turn my sister into that woman," Jennifer replied forcefully. Her blood was boiling. As she walked Elaine back to her class at the Riverdale, Jennifer resolved that she would have to make Donna see sense one way or another.

Four shopping bags later Jennifer arrived back home and found that her sister still wasn't there. Fitzroy had made himself at home on her sofa and was eating lunch. "Jen, remember these programmes?" he said through a mouthful of bun and cheese.

Jennifer looked over at the TV screen. He was watching Batman. The original action series. "Don't you have anything better to do?"

"No, but if yuh 'ave sup'm in mind…" Fitzroy had one hand down the front of his jeans.

Jennifer shook her head with disgust. "Why don't you go home?" She moved around the living room clearing up his mess. Newspaper pages scattered on the floor. "Don't start taking my place as a doss house."

"Me ah wait fe Donna. Yuh 'ave one serious problem, y'know," he said sitting up straight, crumbs fell from his chest into his lap.

"Yes. You."

"See how I mean?" he gestured. "Frustration, man. Pure frustration. It nuh good fe yuh," he stood up and came up behind her as she plumped up the cushions.

"What d'you think you're doing?"

"Jus' easing yuh mind," he touched her shoulders and was immediately pushed aside.

"Don't play those games with me Fitzroy, I'm not my sister."

With that she left him and climbed the stairs to her room for some peace and quiet. When Donna eventually showed up, Jennifer still didn't get a chance to talk to her because Fitzroy stayed for tea and even supper and emptied the fridge of every can of Red Stripe. By nightfall he was too drunk to leave and Donna said he might as well stay, much to Jennifer's chagrin.

The clock radio woke her up at exactly 9.15 when the voice of Alaister Cooke with his Letter From America filled the bedroom. Jennifer opened her eyes to the bright and beautiful Sunday morning. It looked like it was going to be one of those lazy ones. For a busy barrister who didn't have time to listen to the radio as much as she would like, Radio 4 on a Sunday morning was the perfect review of the week. Listening to Alaister Cooke, the Morning Service and the Pick Of The Week put her in the right mood to enjoy her day of rest. But this morning, her attention was only partly on the broadcast, because her mind kept wondering back to the current problem in her life. Donna was next door in the bedroom with Fitzroy and while they were there together, Jennifer couldn't help being tense and uptight.

She got up hurriedly, and went next door. She stood outside Donna's bedroom for a moment, with her head against the door, listening. She couldn't hear anything. She wanted to wake them up and get Fitzroy out of the house so that she could get a chance to finally talk to her sister woman to woman about the man in her life. She knocked loudly on the door.

"Donna! Donna, are you awake?" There was no response. She put her head to the door again. This time she could just about make out a deep, guttural snore — the kind that could only have come from a man. Jennifer grimaced and went back into her bedroom where she climbed out of her pyjamas and changed quickly into her track suit. She slipped on her new Nikes and headband, the one with just the logo on it, before skipping down the stairs, out of the flat and out the main entrance of the house.

The route wasn't always the same, depending on the weather. Dry weather would see her tracking the slopes of Honor Oak Park. Wet mornings would take her down Devonshire Road, its hills were just as steep as the park's. Distance was always the same, two miles every day. Then after her circuit, she would jog over to the newsagents down the road and pick up a copy of each of the broadsheets.

She walked back leisurely to her place. The sun was shining bright and there wasn't a cloud in the sky. She filled her lungs with a deep breath of air which made her feel charged enough to face the rest of the day.

Back at the flat, Fitzroy and Donna were still not up. Jennifer slipped out of her running gear and into the bathroom for a leisurely shower, after which she dressed in a simple cotton dress and went downstairs to read the papers over a bowl of muesli. She turned first to the business pages as usual. Even though she was making a steady climb in her career as a barrister, she had ambitions for bigger things. Criminal and civil law was not where she wanted to be in five years time. She saw herself more as a company lawyer. That was where the real money was and in the hierarchy of things, that was where all the kudos was. So now she made a point of keeping abreast of all the business news and kept herself aware of all the little changes in company law, so that she would be prepared to make the move when she was given the opportunity.

After browsing the business pages, she turned to the Home News sections. There was an article on how the CSA were getting tough on absent fathers. Apparently, they were now offering rewards for information leading to the successful apprehension of any of the 100 absent fathers on their 'Britain's Most Wanted' hit list. They had also hit upon the novel idea of putting up the 'Wanted' posters of these fugitives in pubs, bookies and football grounds up and down the country. Jennifer couldn't help thinking of Fitzroy and whether or not his name was on that hit list. She mentally calculated how much she would get for turning him in. The horrible thought entered her head that it might already be too late. Donna could after all already be pregnant. If so, she couldn't see Fitzroy making any contribution to a child. Not ever. He didn't work and seemed to have no inclination to get up off his backside to find a job. Even though she had previously presented him with the Evening Standard's classified jobs pages, Fitzroy had failed to get the message, saying only that there wasn't no job out there which could pay him what he was really worth so therefore it was better that he just took time to set up something for himself. He was working on it, he said. Working on it just like he had over the years since leaving school with no qualifications. What did her sister see in this guy? She just couldn't understand. It had to be the sex.

Almost on cue, she heard the quiet giggling from the bedroom above, followed by the rhythmic squeaking of the bed springs. Her heart began to beat fast and furiously. She got up, her face contorted in anger and her nostrils flaring. She climbed up the stairs fast, taking them two at a time. Almost before she realized it, she was outside Donna's room. She paused for a moment to catch her breath. The heavy breathing was more audible now. Jennifer winced and started knocking loudly on the door. She heard herself call, "Donna! Are you awake yet?!"

A faint "Bumboclaat!" came from within. It was Fitzroy's voice. Undeterred, she knocked loudly again. "D, wake up, I need to speak to you. Urgently!"

After a moment she heard her sister's breathless voice. "Yes…? What is it? What d'you want Sis?"

What did she want? Such was her haste in running upstairs to do what she could to break up any tenderness between her sister and Fitzroy that she hadn't even prepared an excuse. And now when she had to conjure one up, she couldn't come up with anything. She scanned her imagination for a good one, but the best she could do was say, "I just wanted to ask if you fancied going for a little picnic in the park a little later? It's such a beautiful warm day, there isn't a cloud in the sky."

Again she heard Fitzroy's exasperated voice from within: "Picnic?! Wha' de bumboclaat! She ah mek noise 'bout picnic?!"

She heard Donna's whispered giggle, "Shush!" Then her voice rose to reply, "Are you serious?"

"Well, what d'you think?" she couldn't believe she was doing this. "Shame to waste the day away in bed."

There was a silence before Donna shouted back, "I'll be down later."

"You want to go out then?"

"Leave it out, Jen. I'll be down soon."

Jennifer heard the whispering of their voices behind the door and then laughter. They were laughing at her! She felt like a fool. What could she do to save her sister from this dangerous liaison? She stomped down the stairs making as much noise as possible.

Five minutes later she heard the two of them come out of the bedroom having a conversation about some ragga DJ they were on different sides of the fence about. Then their voices faded into the bathroom. Half an hour later they emerged downstairs smelling fresh and dressed casually. By the look of things Fitzroy had every intention of enjoying the hospitality further. He acted like Jennifer wasn't even in the room.With both remote controls in his hand, he spread his body out on the sofa. The telly went on in one corner, the stereo in the other.

"Don't you have a home to go to, Fitzroy?"

"Yeah, an' if Donna want me fe go, me will go."

"We could always go back upstairs if you want your peace," Donna suggested. A look passed between her and Fitzroy which meant exactly what Jennifer thought it did.

"No, that won't be necessary. I want us to spend some time alone D. How often are we both at home on a Sunday?"

Fitzroy pulled his girlfriend closer. "You want to spend time wid yuh sister?"

Donna giggled. "I want to spend time with you."

"Me know dat a'ready."

One of those looks again.

"I'll make us some breakfast." As Donna stood up to go to the kitchen Fitzroy smacked her bottom playfully.

Jennifer had had enough. As soon as Donna was out of the room she got up and switched the stereo off, leaving the church choir singing on the television.

She stood in front of it with her arms crossed, "Don't you have a church service to attend Fitzroy?"

"Wha' you mean?"

"It is Sunday. Didn't your mother always tell you to repent your sins in church every Sunday, I'm sure you've got a lot to catch up on."

"You don't know me, y'know. Talk to yuh sister, man, she will tell you she don't want anyt'ing else from me, but me," he threw his legs over the arm of the sofa and reached for one of the Sunday supplements on the coffee table.

"I'm sure there are others out there who don't want anything else but your money. N'est-ce pas?"

"Why yuh always haffe talk in riddles fa?"

"I bumped into a woman yesterday whose name was..." Jennifer paused, a finger on her chin for effect, "...Celia..."

She watched Fitzroy's expression, but he was still nonchalant, "Yeah, and...?"

"It was funny really, because she got very excited when I mentioned your name. She said something about you not bringing her any money for three months. When I told her I knew where you were she got even more excited, said something about her brothers wanting a word with you. Does any of this mean anything?"

Fitzroy's eyes suddenly came alive. "De 'ooman, she did 'ave a pickney wid her?"

"A boy, yes."

"Yuh nevah tell her weh me deh?" He shot up now, studying Jennifer anxiously. Jennifer shrugged. "I did as a matter of fact, told her that this afternoon would be a good time to call around." She had to turn her back to avoid him seeing the smirk bubbling up from her belly.

"A lie yuh ah tell!" He jumped up from the sofa and rushed to look out of the window in case the woman's arrival was imminent.

"I would have told you earlier but you were in bed so late that it slipped my mind..."

"I... I jus' remember, me 'ave sup'm fe her, y'know. Maybe me will... uhm... jus' drop by, y'know. Save her de trouble..." Fitzroy was already at the doorway before he finished the sentence. "Yaow D," he called, "me gawn, seen?"

Donna came to meet him in the passageway wiping her hands on a tea towel.

"I jus' remember me 'ave some bizness to tek care ah. Is a'right. Me will call you, seen?"

Fitzroy hit the road, his shirt tail full of wind.

Alone at last the sisters sat at the kitchen table while Donna ate her breakfast.

"How about the picnic? The sun is still out." Jennifer asked tentatively.

Donna gave her sister a look that told her what she thought of that idea. She swept her hair off her face with one hand. She had what people back home called 'good hair', Jennifer thought, not for the first time.

"Get real, Jen. I can think of better things to do on a hot Sunday."

Jennifer stared into her cup of warm coffee. "We should do more things together. Then you wouldn't have to spend so much time with Fitzroy."

"Sorry Sis, but you can't do for me what Fitzroy does," Donna bit into her buttered toast and smiled cheekily.

Jennifer winced. She hated the way Donna made a joke of everything. They'd had the argument about having sex under her sister's roof a year ago. Donna had asked her if she'd rather she did it on the streets. Jennifer couldn't argue with that and had little choice but to accept that her baby sister was going to bring boys home and that they were going to be using her bedroom for their carnal knowledge.

"I know that, but I'm not going to get you in trouble the way Fitzroy will."

"What makes you so sure that Fitzroy is going to get me in trouble? You don't know him."

"You wanna bet? Donna, he's ten years older than you. He's got three women pregnant that I know about and God knows how many more."

"I suppose you've got proof that the kids are his, right?" Donna tilted her head in question. "Fitzroy told me that ever since school women told lies about him because he didn't want them. They'd get pregnant and blame it on him because he was an easy target."

"And you believed that?"

Donna shrugged. "I can't see what the problem is. Even if it was true, do you think I'm stupid enough to let myself get pregnant?"

"No. I'm saying he's devious enough to make you pregnant."

Donna got up from her seat and paced the kitchen. "You're never gonna let me make my own decisions are you? You're never gonna trust my instincts, my judgments. You know what, Jen, why don't you just live my life for me?"

"If you would only listen to me..."

"What, like you listen to me?"

"Don't raise your voice to me young lady. Sit down."

Slowly, Donna sat down at the dining table and faced her sister sulkily.

"I know women who, years ago when they were your age, thought they were grown up enough to make their own mistakes. No matter what people told them they never listened, as far as they were concerned they knew what they were doing."

Donna sighed, expressing her boredom. "Mum and Dad had you at my age."

"That was in those days…"

"That wasn't all that long ago, y'know. Or what, are you saying you're an old woman already?"

"This isn't about Mum and Dad. These days you're on your own. And if you can't deal with it your kids end up in crime or in care… And then when the father reappears fifteen years later he can have rights to the kid and can upset any kind of relationship the mother has managed to establish with the child. I've bumped into old school friends who ended up as single mothers and they all regret it and wish they had their time again. They would rather be out clubbing than at home every weekend because they've got no one to help them. These are women who wanted to travel the world as teenagers, yet hardly travel further than the corner shop now and who have to juggle benefits to make ends meet."

Jennifer rested her arms on the kitchen table and made Donna meet her eyes. "You've got to realize that there's no future in a relationship with Fitzroy. All someone like him can offer you is a life in menial jobs with no career prospects, or a future raising children on your own. He might turn up at Christmas with a twenty pound note for you and the kid, but nothing more."

Donna picked at her fingernail, seemingly unconcerned.

"Mum and Dad cared about us enough to make sure we got a good education," Jennifer continued. "The least you can do is carry on the way they brought you up. Whatever happened to the baby sister who used to follow me around everywhere and want to be like me?"

"You really want to know? I grew up. Look, I'm not Jamaican, I'm British. So there was no point in Mum and Dad bringing me up like they would have in Jamaica."

Jennifer sat back in her chair, ready, listening. She could hear the kitchen clock ticking away behind her.

Donna continued. "When you moved out, I was left at home with them. You know how old-fashioned they are, I always had to wear your hand-me-downs. And they still cooked food for four after you left and made me eat extra because they couldn't understand why there was food left over."

Jennifer chuckled at that.

"It's true. So not only was I wearing hand-me-downs and my Dad's old glasses, but I was also getting fat just so that Mum wouldn't have to waste any food."

"I'm sorry, D," Jennifer laughed, "but that is funny."

Donna laughed too. "You don't understand why I enjoy how Fitzroy makes me feel because you didn't lead my life. When I wanted to go out with my friends after school, Mum and Dad made me come straight home and do my homework. I wanted to relax my hair and style it myself, but Mum plaited it in them cornrows every week from primary until they went back to Jamaica."

Jennifer's expression was thoughtful. "So what you're saying is that you're rebelling against what they taught you."

"I don't see it that way. The way I see it, I've finally got the chance to express myself and that's exactly what I'm doing."

"Don't you think I've heard that before from women who are now single with babies coming out of their ears?"

Donna stood up abruptly. "Jennifer, I love you, but you've got to trust me. I know what I'm doing. I can handle Fitzroy."

Jennifer mumbled. "Let's hope so."

"Pardon?"

"Beware of young men that give so little and take so much."

"Yeah, right Sis," Donna shook her head in mirth.

Jennifer decided to give Donna a couple more days to come to her senses about Fitzroy. After that she would start laying down the law. That was her prerogative because she paid the bills and her sister's expenses which enabled her to go to college. Maybe the only way to force Donna to get rid of Fitzroy would be to cut her weekly allowance. It had worked for their parents when they were kids.

TWO

By ten o'clock Monday morning Jennifer had already taken four paracetamols for a headache that just wouldn't go away. The senior clerk Julian Holland, a small grey-haired man with a Greek nose, was the first to greet her when she arrived at chambers.

"Good morning, Miss Edwards," he handed her fax messages and mail.

"Morning, Julian."

"Miss Edwards, I've placed a brief in your tray, an industrial injury case we're considering. Let me know as soon as you've read it and I'll arrange a conference."

She smiled a thank you at the clerk and walked on to her room to be met by a pile of early morning phone messages placed in the centre of her desk. There were two messages from a Mr Harvey who was claiming to be a lawyer from some society. He wanted to meet with her. She threw it into her pending tray. The others were from lawyers and clients who wanted follow-ups, or updates on their cases. As she was due in court in fifteen minutes she delegated the calls to the clerk.

The woman took the stand in disguise. No one would have guessed that she was recently nominated Businesswoman of the Year by a black newspaper.

The first time she had met Mrs Matthews, Jennifer had asked where she had purchased the beautifully made beige three-piece suit she was wearing. Now the woman who took the stand looked as though she was on benefit and had to borrow her mother's clothes for her day in court. She wore a long, flowery, oversized dress with a grey cardigan and an old coat that might have been fashionable twenty years ago. She wore no make-up and her hair was simply brushed back off her face.

Mrs Matthews coughed timidly into a white hanky, before speaking. "He walked out on me an' the children eighteen months ago," she sniffed. Jennifer's 'learned friend' Patrick Wilson, representing the plaintiff, was a tall thin man with a beard, who wore his gown like a tent. He faced the witness on the stand. "And have you seen Mr Matthews in those eighteen months?"

"He came by last year to ask me for his share of our house."

"The house that you no longer own?"

"That's right."

"What happened to your home, Mrs Matthews?"

Mrs Matthew clutched her handbag tightly. "Had to sell it, couldn't afford to stay in that big house no more on only one salary."

"And the proceeds from the house, Mrs Matthews, what happened to that?" "It's all gone... I had debts to pay and the kids needed stuff and when the council put us in that flat we had to buy furniture and stuff."

"But the house was worth half a million. Do you expect the court to believe that you simply spent the money on furniture?"

"Yes, sir... I mean no, I put some into my business... and... I donated money to a gipsy settlement... but they've moved on without trace." She paused and looked straight at the barrister. "Money don't last forever, y'know."

"Does your husband have any rights to that money, Mrs Matthews?"

"No sir, the house was in my name."

"But wasn't the mortgage being paid out of his salary until he left you?"

"That's right, but then when he ran off with his slut he stopped paying... nearly had us thrown out on the street." Mrs Matthews crossed her fingers behind her back, "I even turned to prostitution to pay the mortgage before the house was sold."

"He is still the father of your children, of which he now has custody, do you not feel that he has a right to his share from the sale of your home?"

"No!" she said adamantly. "I slaved for that man for years. Years of washing, cleaning, sexing him..."

"Thank you, Mrs Matthews," the judge interrupted. "Any further questions?"

"Yes, Your Honour," Jennifer stood while Patrick Wilson took his seat.

Mrs Matthews looked increasingly uncomfortable, her fingers were clenching and unclenching her handbag, controlling her anger.

"Mrs Matthews, would you please tell the court why the family home was in your name only."

Mrs Matthews visibly relaxed. "It was because Victor... Mr Matthews, always said that if we ever divorced then the house would belong to me and the children, that we wouldn't have to go through this..." she indicated the courtroom.

"And why do you believe Mr Matthews changed his mind about this arrangement?"

"Because without my money he had NOTHING!" Mrs Matthews threw a look of scorn across the court at her ex-husband.

Jennifer smiled at her reassuringly, though deep down she was beginning to regret having this case assigned to her. "No further questions," she said and sat down.

"Any further questions, Mr Wilson?" the judge asked.

The senior barrister stood. "No further questions, m'lud."

The judge turned to the witness box. "You may step down, Mrs Matthews."

The next witness for the prosecution was a detective whom Mr Matthews had hired to prove that Mrs Matthews still had the money and was living wealthy from it.

The detective took the stand. A black man! And a Denzel lookalike! Jennifer did her best to hide her amazement as she listened to this cool operator's testimony. Then she began her questioning.

"Mr..." she referred to her papers, "...Carnegie, my client is a small business woman, with a struggling business I might add. She now lives in a council-owned maisonette on the Peckham North estate. Does this strike you as the lifestyle of a woman who has half a million pounds at her disposal?"

"That's simple, Miss Edwards, Mrs Matthews has chosen to live this way ever since she realized that her husband was going to claim half of the house's worth." His voice was youthful and almost musical.

"How would you go about proving such a claim, Mr Carnegie?"

"I've followed her, watched how she spends her money, where she spends her money. I've observed the way she dresses, what transportation she uses to get around..."

Jennifer looked up from her notes and was sure she detected a smirk on his face. She began to take a dislike to this ruggedly handsome witness. He was too smooth by half and she had a sudden urge to cut him down to size.

"Mr Carnegie, you say you saw my client, Mrs Matthews, shopping in town recently. What exactly did you see?" The private investigator, Tony Carnegie, unbuttoned his jacket slowly, like a male stripper about to go into a routine, and pulled out a leather bound notebook from his inside pocket. He flicked through it until he came to the relevant page. "On the morning of April 12th, Mrs Matthews walked into the Croydon branch of Dorothy Perkins and browsed for approximately fifteen minutes. During this time she picked up five items of clothing, a skirt, a pair of trousers, two dresses and a blouse."

"Did she purchase any of these items?"

"Yes," he turned to the next page. "Mrs Matthews purchased the two dresses, the skirt and the blouse on her credit card. A total of one hundred and fifty pounds altogether."

Mr Matthews let out a loud whistle of astonishment. "Coulda fed the pickney fe a month on dat."

"Are you sure," Jennifer continued, "that the purchases were for herself?"

"Yes. Definitely," he said with another smirk. "They were in her size, she paid for them with her credit card."

"Are you in the habit, Mr Carnegie, of purchasing women's clothing?"

Tony Carnegie jumped back defensively. "No!"

"Then I put it to you that the items of clothing Mrs Matthews purchased could possibly have been for someone else. A present? A purchase for a friend with the same size in clothes? It's not unusual."

"Miss Edwards," Carnegie said suavely, his head tilted a little to the side, "I assure you that I know women, sometimes better than they know themselves. I could look at a woman and tell which shops she buys her clothes from, how much she spends on clothes, whether she does her hair herself or pays an expensive hairdresser. That's what I do for a living — study people. Especially women." His eyes looked her up and down. "I've been trailing Mrs Matthews for two months and in that time I've learnt her clothes size, shoe size, her tastes in food and men, and her desires and aspirations."

Jennifer hated the man's arrogance. Next he'd be telling her he knew what she fantasised about while she lay in bed at night. "Also..." he referred again to his notebook, "Mrs Matthews wore one of the dresses purchased on the date of April 12th to a luncheon at a restaurant called 'Chez Noir' where she again paid by credit card."

"M'lud, as self-employed, Mrs Matthews does have a business expense account. I'm sure you will find that her restaurant bill is noted in her company's books."

The judge referred to the account book he had in front of him and waved the proceedings on. Jennifer walked back to the desk and picked out a sheet of paper from her file.

"Mr Matthews left his wife a year and a half ago, leaving her to raise their two children, Donna and Jason, alone. A year ago Mr Matthews came back into their lives and threatened to file for custody on the grounds of neglect. Mrs Matthews let him take the children because she accepted they needed to spend more time with their father and because she wanted to pursue a life-long dream of setting up her own business. In the time that the children were living with their mother Mr Matthews made no contribution to their parenting, financially or otherwise. Or do you have any evidence to the contrary Mr Carnegie?"

"Urr..." Tony Carnegie swallowed. "No." He wasn't sure he knew where the questioning was heading. The judge raised his mallet. "Miss Edwards, I must remind you of the reason Mr Carnegie is on the stand. He is here to give us evidence of his investigation into Mrs Matthews' expenses and finances. Not to give evidence as to why Mr Matthews did not pay maintenance. Are we clear on that?"

"Yes, Your Honour. I was coming to that." Jennifer sucked her cheeks in and her lips pouted. "It is my belief that Mr Matthews only sought custody of the children because he felt it was the only way he could get his hands on the proceeds of the house. That is the only reason he employed you to tail his wife, isn't it Mr Carnegie?"

"That is quite possible, Miss Edwards, but then, who would you say had the greatest need for that money, a struggling unemployed single father, or a successful businesswoman?"

Jennifer's chest heaved, she sighed internally. "Do you have any more evidence as to Mrs Matthews' financial status, Mr Carnegie?"

"As a matter of fact, I do." He proceeded to reel off a series of spending sprees that included parties, presents for a boyfriend and redecoration of her flat, plus modernisation of her work premises. Holidays abroad.

In the middle of it Mrs Matthews, who had restrained herself as best as she could throughout, jumped up out of her seat and ran over to her estranged husband and grabbed him by the throat. "I gave you everything a man could ask for: a beautiful home, two beautiful children. You bastard, what did you do in return? Dump me for an eighteen-year-old slag and now you're trying to take my money too..."

Her outburst was too much for the judge and as Mrs Matthews was dragged away yelling by a court guard, he ruled against her and ordered Mrs Matthews to pay Mr Matthews his share of the house — two hundred and fifty thousand pounds — and his court fees. Jennifer shook her head and sighed as she put her things in the leather briefcase her parents had bought her on graduation. Monogrammed with her initials, it was one of her most treasured possessions.

She hurried out of the court room, the sound of her high-heeled stilettos echoing as she went along. She had a case at another court in the afternoon and would only have time for a quick snack.

"Excuse me... Miss Edwards...?"

Jennifer turned in the direction of the voice. It was the private investigator.

She looked him up and down as he swaggered down the corridor towards her. There was something about him... she couldn't put her finger on it. Something...? She didn't have time to sum it up, however, before he stood right in front of her smiling warmly, the kind of smile that expected to be reciprocated. He had a small scar in one eyebrow and the cutest smile she had ever seen on a grown man. "I just wanted to tell you how much I enjoyed your performance in court," he said, the smile broadening.

"I'm sure you did," she replied brusquely, walking on towards the exit. "After all, you won the day."

"Yes, but no matter what the judge says, I think that your arguments were really a lot better. What does the judge know," he said, following her.

Jennifer felt his presence behind her. He was patronising her, winding her up. She was sure of it. She just kept walking, her stilettos sounding a little tap dance with every two-step combination.

"Hey!" Tony Carnegie called after. "No hard feelings. Just because you lost the case. That's how it goes in life, there are winners and losers. I thought you would know all about that, being a barrister and all. Today for me, tomorrow for you."

Jennifer stopped momentarily and turned to look Tony dead in the eyes, trying to see if he was laughing at her, but all she could find was a charming twinkle in his eye. She thought that he must have been a real rascal as a youngster. However, she had better things to do right now than stare into his eyes. She carried on towards the exit. Tony stepped ahead enough to reach the exit before her. He smiled holding the door open, catching the scent of her perfume as she stepped out of the building. Class. The single word was like a price tag in his mind. "Well," Jennifer addressed Tony when they were both outside, "I'm sure we won't be meeting again, so I'll say goodbye." She turned to go.

"No wait," Tony called after her. "If we won't be meeting again that's all the more reason to give me the pleasure of joining me for lunch."

"Thanks, but no thanks," she told him politely but firmly.

"No… don't tell me you're turning me down…"

"It was nice of you to offer, but I'm otherwise engaged. I need to get back to chambers. Thanks anyway."

"I should have known," said Carnegie almost dejectedly, "you put one over on a woman and she won't forgive you," his voice held a distinct edge of sarcasm.

" 'Put one over'? Excuse me, you gave a testimony in a court case, that's all. If you want to kid yourself into thinking that you put one over on me go ahead, but I think that's taking it too far."

Tony looked pleased with himself. "But you have to admit that if you had won that court case or if I was testifying on your behalf, you wouldn't be so averse to lunching with me."

"Look, I've got better things to do with my time than to shed tears over a case. I really am busy and I need to get back. Anyway, I'm surprised that you have time for lunches, I thought you'd be too busy stalking some poor woman somewhere, on behalf of her ex-husband."

Tony seemed unfazed by Jennifer's wit. He looked as if he had heard comments like that about his profession many times before and, indeed, he had. "I don't only snoop after women, I also investigate men… on a professional basis that is," Tony reminded her. "My services are open to any members of the general public." He smiled charmingly. "Anyway, I see you're not interested in any of that and as you would rather die than have lunch with me, I'll say goodbye."

With that Tony Carnegie made his way slowly down the steps at the front of the court house and looked up and down the road for a taxi. Jennifer remained standing on the top step, staring at him. She was thinking… Something he said was sticking in her mind.

Tony had flagged down a black taxi and was just about to climb in when Jennifer called out: "Wait…!"

Tony turned around, looking Jennifer hard in the eyes.

"I've changed my mind… I see that I have got a few minutes to spare for lunch… maybe just a snack."

"As you wish," he replied with that inviting smile.

"But I insist, I'm taking you to lunch," she said.

"I wouldn't dream of it," he smiled. "The only women I allow to buy me dinner are clients."

"Then I'll have to become a client," Jennifer said with an equally inviting smile. Tony held the cab door open as she stepped in, then he climbed in behind her.

El Montenegro's was crowded as usual. It was one of the favourite City haunts for people in the law. Situated on Fleet Street, it used to be popular amongst journalists on the national daily newspapers before they all moved to Wapping. Now it was a popular watering hole amongst the barristers, solicitors and clerks of the law who congregated around the Old Bailey and the Central Criminal Court. Jennifer returned from the bar with a dry white wine for herself and a Mexican bottled beer for Tony.

Taking a sip of his beer, Tony raised the glass in a toast. "To adversaries and all who sail in them," he said smiling.

"Quite," said Jennifer stiffly. "Now, what I want to see you about…"

"Whoa! Do we have to rush into this business thing straight away?"

Jennifer looked at her watch hurriedly. "Yes, if you don't mind. I don't have much time."

"How do you know if you can afford my fee?"

"Because, I suspect that you probably couldn't afford mine," she replied quick time.

"Touché!" Tony knew when he was beaten. "Nuff said."

"Back to the matter at hand. I want you to do some investigating for me. Do you think you can handle it?" "That's my business… you have a problem and I take care of it."

"Well, it's not me exactly who needs the help. It's someone I know… she's in trouble. She's got a man who she doesn't know if she can trust.

She wants to know if her man's got any children by any other woman. Or other women, as the case may be. And if so, how many?"

Tony studied her critically, "Who is this friend of yours exactly?"

"I'd rather not say," Jennifer sipped her drink.

Tony leant forward on the table. "Sorry. No can do. I need to know the facts."

"Okay, if you must know, it's my baby sister," she said frankly.

"Let me get this straight... your sister's got a man who you don't trust?"

"I didn't say that, I said she suspects..."

"Yes, but what people say and what they mean aren't necessarily the same thing are they, counsel? You're a lawyer, you know that... So you're the big sister and you want to stop this man being with your kid sister by any means necessary. You don't trust him."

"Okay, I admit it. I want you to check this man out. My sister's young and naive. He's taking advantage of her."

"He is from your point of view."

"He is from anybody's point of view. It's quite obvious to everybody but my sister. You know how it is when you think you're in love."

"How is it?" Tony said with a glint in his eyes.

Jennifer felt self-conscious, his eyes were almost undressing her. "Well, you know... you fall in love and suddenly you become blind to what's really going on around you. You believe that the sun shines out of your lover's backside."

Tony sighed. "Yeah, I've been there... but it's been a while. It's only a fading memory now... So he's taking advantage of her and it's obvious from everybody's point of view except baby sister's. Am I right?"

Jennifer nodded. That's exactly how it was. "Look, I wouldn't be asking you to check this out if I didn't already have some proof. I've personally spoken to a woman who has had a baby for him, but from the gossip that's reaching me he's got a whole army of kids out there that he's not admitting to."

"And you think that your sister will drop him the moment she finds out exactly how many children he has?"

"Well, I hope so."

"Let me ask you one thing, you're a barrister, an attractive sista. I'd say you were between twenty-six and twenty-eight years old, about five feet nine inches tall and around ten stone in weight, you speak well, you've got an air of success about you plus the kind of looks that many men would describe as 'criss'..."

"Please!" said Jennifer, embarrassed. "Go easy on the sugary stuff."

"No, but seriously... why are you so concerned about your sister's man? Why not let your sister make her own mistakes?"

"She's seventeen for goodness sake. I'm not going to let her throw her life away before she even knows the meaning of it."

"But maybe she's really in love... maybe it won't make any difference what I find out about her boyfriend. Maybe your sister's just crazy about this guy."

"I'll cross that bridge when I come to it."

Tony sat pondering as he took a long slow swig from his glass of beer. He pondered too long for Jennifer's liking.

"Look," she said getting up to go, "maybe this was all a mistake... you're obviously not the right person for this job."

"Woah... hold on. I didn't say that I wouldn't take the case. Sit down. Please relax. I just have a couple more questions to ask you. I need to know the facts."

Jennifer considered it a moment before easing herself back down on the seat.

"Are you sure that this isn't all about jealousy on your part?"

Jennifer was about to explode inside, but she restrained herself. "I consider that question to be out of order," she said simply.

"I could say that about some of the questions you were asking me in court. But I didn't. In fact, standing in the witness box and testifying, I ended up enjoying them and looked forward to your next question."

Jennifer looked at him hard. What was his game? Was she wasting her time even bothering to discuss her problems with this man? "Look," she said, "I've told you the situation as best I can. I want you to find out some information about Fitzroy that I may be able to use in preventing him from turning my sister into yet another single mother statistic in a world full of baby fathers. It's as simple as that. If you can find me any useful information on him you could be saving a young black teenager from ruining her life by one careless night of passion with 'Johnny-too-bad'."

The private investigator smiled admiringly. "Fair enough. That sounds reasonable to me."

"Jen, could you do my hair for me please," Donna called out.

Jennifer put down the legal papers she was reading. The sound of swing music floated out of her sister's bedroom and down the staircase. "Fitzroy coming round is he?" she called back.

Donna came down the spiral staircase, her blow-dried hair sticking up all over her head. "Fitzroy's not the only person I try to look good for, y'know. I'm going out with Shanika."

Jennifer sighed. Shanika was just as bad as Fitzroy. Either of them could get Donna pregnant. One directly, the other by leading her to it. "But it's a week night. Haven't you got homework from college to do?"

"Nothing that can't wait until tomorrow. Look, if you don't want to do my hair just say so. I don't need a lecture." "It's all right, I'll do it," Jennifer followed her back upstairs.

Donna sat on the swivel chair in front of her dresser mirror. "By the way, what's all this?" Donna held up a small blue and white cellophane wrapped packet.

Embarrassed, Jennifer avoided her sister's gaze. "Condoms," she replied.

"I know that," Donna rolled her eyes. "But how did they get under my pillow?"

"Look D, I put them there because I wanted to make sure you would always have some. I was in the chemist anyway, so I thought... When they run out I've got more."

"Jen, they give them out free at the family planning clinic." Donna pulled open her bottom drawer and opened an old chocolate box stuffed with an array of different coloured condom packets. "I have plenty, thank you very much. And I use 'em."

Jennifer now felt like the naive schoolgirl she was taking her sister for. "Sorry. I just thought..."

"All right, jus' don't do it again," Donna grinned.

"Do you still want me to do your hair, or do you just want to embarrass me?"

"I want you to help with my hair," Donna said turning back to her dresser. Containers of hair gel, combs, brushes and make-up were laid out in front of her. Her curling tongs were already heating up on a flannel she'd placed on the table.

"So what style do you want?"

"See that magazine on the bed..."

Jennifer picked up the magazine. It was open on a page full of glamorous women wearing various extensions. "You want one of these?"

"Don't say it like that. It's what's in now. You see that one with the ponytails and the sideburns?" Jennifer stood by her side and Donna pointed out the style she wanted. "That one."

"I can't do extensions."

"I'll direct you, Sis. I just can't do it myself without it looking naff. It'll be quicker with four hands."

Jennifer looked at the picture again. "If you're sure."

Teenage girls certainly were more daring these days. They dressed in baggy jeans half the time and shaved off their hair like the boys with all sorts of patterns cut into it. Otherwise they were adding extensions and colouring their hair several different colours. Donna had even toyed with the idea of having an earring in her nose!

Half an hour later, Donna's hair could have featured in Black Beauty and Hair Magazine. With a zigzag parting, multi-coloured spiral extensions creating two high ponytails either side of her head and slicked down waved sideburns, she couldn't help but get noticed. Jennifer had to admit she was proud of her effort. Then she noticed Donna's outfit hanging from the wardrobe door and decided that her sister had either bought the hair to match the outfit or vice versa.

"Good job, Sis. Betcha didn't know you had the talent in ya."

Jennifer chuckled. "If I ever need a sideline to pay the bills I'll open up a salon."

The doorbell rang. Jennifer went down the stairs knowing it had to be for her sister.

Shanika was eighteen and had gone to the same school as Donna. Of course she hadn't even noticed Donna until she'd started to change her image. Since then, Shanika had been a bad influence, in Jennifer's opinion. Shanika had had a well-developed body since early in her teens when she was often mistaken for a more mature woman. Her mother had brought her and her sisters up alone. Three sisters, three different fathers. None of these facts endeared her to Jennifer.

Tonight Shanika was dressed in a yellow puffa coat that reached her knees. She wore lace tights and knee-high boots identical to the ones Donna had recently purchased. Her hair was cut short, the front lengthened with the help of a row of weave-on hair. Stripes of red and gold went through it. Jennifer turned from the front door and called up the stairs. "Donna, your friend is here. She's just getting dressed," she told the girl. She wished she could pick and choose Donna's friends.

Shanika followed her into the living room. "All right, Jen?" she asked.

"Yes. You?" She sat down on the sofa and picked up one of Donna's beauty magazines absentmindedly.

"Yeah man. We're going to rave tonight."

"Where are you going?"

"What! Donna didn't tell you?"

"Does she tell me anything these days?"

"Granaries, man. They have this male stripper every Friday. You musta heard of Friday Night Raw." Shanika threw herself down in the armchair opposite Jennifer and shrugged off her puffa jacket, revealing a very short black leather skirt and see-through lace body suit.

"Friday Night Raw! Male strippers? You must be desperate."

"Chill, Jen man. We ain't gonna rape him or not'n," her mouth worked on her chewing gum. "It's a laugh."

"Isn't there an age limit in that club?"

She popped her gum making Jennifer wince before replying. "Yeah, so?"

Shanika had grown accustomed to pushing up her chest in bouncers' faces to prove her age.

"And how's your baby? Naomi, isn't it?"

"Naomi's safe. My mum's got her."

"Her father not around anymore?"

"Him? He comes round. He's all right though, y'know, 'cause anything she wants she can have."

"What about you, do you get what you want from him?"

"I'm getting enough. I'm not his woman anymore, but I'm still his baby mother."

That phrase again. So many black women were beginning to use that to describe themselves. But Shanika wasn't fooling her. Jennifer had heard Donna's conversations with Shanika, and knew that anything Shanika got from Delroy, her baby father, she had to beg for.

Donna came down and rescued her friend. "Shan why didn't you come up, man, I was waiting for you?"

"I was keeping Jen company. Weren't I, Jen?"

"Something like that." Jennifer turned to see what her sister was wearing. The black lycra catsuit wasn't too bad until she turned to the sides, made out of yellow lace, and you could tell she wore nothing underneath. Jennifer bit her tongue to stop herself nagging. "D, have you got enough money?"

"Well actually, Jen, I am a bit short. Don't want the others to think I'm scrounging off 'em."

Jennifer got her handbag from the desk and gave Donna a tenner. "If you need a lift home, make sure you call me."

"Sure Sis, but we'll be all right, Val's driving."

The girls left and the house was suddenly quiet. Jennifer felt an emptiness, like she was an old maid, alone, her children grown up and gone and all she was left with was the television and her thoughts for company.

She tidied and cleaned the kitchen, half-listening to the radio in the background, dipping in and out of the angst of the soap characters as the programme drifted on, but too worried about Donna to give it her full attention.

Was it always going to be like this now that Donna was old enough to stay out all night? The two of them used to enjoy sitting together in front of the telly, watching videos. They would eat ice cream, their legs covered with a duvet, watching horror films. Some evenings they would get the old photo albums out and look and laugh at themselves as children. Plaited hair and missing teeth. Flared trousers, tank tops and frilled collars. Platform shoes and plimsoles.

She missed those simple evenings with a vengeance now. She gazed at the phone, it remained silent. She hadn't needed a social life of her own before, Donna had always been there when she needed a chat, a hug, a laugh, someone to go out with. She needed to get out more, meet new people. Most of all she needed to take her mind off family matters. She found a half-empty bottle of wine. That would be her company for the rest of the evening, she decided, curling up on the sofa with the latest issue of Essence at her side.

As Friday night turned to Saturday morning, Jennifer found comfort in a tub of Haagen Dazs at the bottom of the freezer. The ice cream went down smoothly. She hit the television remote control. An old film on Channel Four was the best option, and for a while she watched James Stewart in Vertigo. Soon her mind drifted to thoughts of her parents in Jamaica. She hadn't written to them in weeks and hadn't made a phone call for months. The sudden urge to speak to Daddy made her reach for the phone without bothering to work out the time difference. The phone rang unanswered. They were probably on the beach, swimming in the beautiful Caribbean sea together, she figured. Jamaica at this time of year was made for romance.

Jennifer had been in love only once in her life. Kenny had been her knight in shining armour. It had been so good. She was twenty-one and he was ten years her senior. She found she had little in common with men her own age. Her independence always seemed to challenge them. Kenny was a banker, the kind of success story she had had fantasies about marrying throughout her teenage years. They had met in a wine bar in the city. He told her about his climb to the top and she told him about her dreams to get to that same status. After two wonderful years together she had fallen so deeply in love with the fairy tale that even when his ex-wife, whom she knew about, turned up at her front door with the son she didn't know about, she refused to drop him. She hadn't realized the kind of man he really was until she told Kenny that she wanted them to get married and have children and the very next day he turned up with a pre-nuptial agreement for her signature. She blew her top. The agreement required her to give up all rights to anything and everything. It was stalemate. She wasn't going to sign the agreement and he didn't intend on marrying without it being signed.

The relationship had gone steadily downhill from there. He had eventually given her an ultimatum that left her no choice but to let him go. Whenever she thought of how worthless he had made her seem, it still hurt. Since then she had had nothing but what she called brief encounters. She kept men as acquaintances and stayed at ease with herself and reminded herself often that, 'Sometimes a woman's got to stay single to survive'.

Jennifer knew what she was worth on the market. The more success she had in her career the more men, of all shades and colours, wanted her. The City was full of fortysomethings searching for Miss Right. And she still had an interest in men, she just didn't trust them with her feelings. It was going to take a lot for a man to sweep her off her feet again. She fell asleep in front of the flickering television with dreams of a wedding that never happened.

Monday morning at chambers. There was another message from Paul Harvey: 'I don't know if you've received my last two messages. Please call me. We could be an asset to one another.' 'I don't know if you've received my last three messages. Please call me. We could be assets to one another.' What was that, a chat up line? Jennifer picked up the phone and called a colleague, another female barrister, and asked her if she knew of Paul Harvey. Angela knew a lot about Paul Harvey and filled Jennifer in on his reputation. He was an up-and-coming black barrister who fancied himself as every sista's dream in a profession where the black women outnumbered the men. He knew people in power and ran the Worshipful Company of Black Barristers, a networking group. The rumour was, Angela added, that Paul Harvey had an extremely large penis. "Hung like a horse, apparently," she giggled.

Hung like a horse or not, Jennifer was always interested in meeting powerful professional contacts. She dialled his number. It was answered by a husky voiced black woman.

"Oh Miss Edwards. Yes, Mr Harvey has been trying to get hold of you for days. I'll put you through."

There was a click on the line.

"Hello, Ms Edwards," a male voice came on the line.

"Mr Harvey?"

"Yes. Thanks for returning my call."

"I was curious, Mr Harvey."

"Please call me Paul."

"Okay, Paul. What can I do for you?"

"I've seen you in action. In court. But when I checked we didn't appear to have you listed on our network. The Worshipful Company of Black Barristers I mean."

"Right. I'm already a member of the Society of Black Lawyers and the Association of Women Barristers."

"Ah. But why limit yourself? You'll find that the Worshipful Company of Black Barristers is altogether different from those organisations. And that's why I'm calling you, I've heard some good things about you and your work. Can we meet, say over lunch?"

"Sure."

"Tomorrow, if you're free."

"I'll just check my diary," Jennifer flipped over two pages of her diary knowing full well that she was free. "Tomorrow afternoon? That's fine."

"Great. I'll pick you up at one."

"Fine."

Jennifer hung up, feeling intrigued. He didn't seem too bad. A lunch date with an intelligent black man would make a refreshing change.

At a corner table in an upmarket restaurant Jennifer found herself in deep conversation with a man she'd met for the first time two hours ago. She had dressed formally to imply that this was strictly a business lunch. She wore a navy trouser suit with Chinese collar buttoned to the neck.

Paul Harvey towered five inches above her, with a body that already showed it was succumbing to the excesses allowed by a generous expense account. Nevertheless, he was a striking figure of a man. His skin complexion was dark chocolate and though his recently trimmed short hair was thinning on top, overall his look was manicured. His expensive suit set off the look and complemented his immaculate moustache.

They'd started off with drinks and then moved onto the restaurant for their meal. Paul was leaning towards her, his chin resting on a bridge he'd made with his hands. His engaging brown eyes contained a powerful mixture of impudence and assurance. Right now they were fastened on her face as she spoke.

"It's not even the fact that I'm a woman that isolates me," she was saying, waving her wine glass back and forth, "it's the fact that I'm a black woman. They look at me and I know that they're thinking this woman obviously got where she is today because of positive discrimination, positive action and every other employment act under the sun. And you know why? It's because of this old boy network that still exists in the legal system."

Paul shook his head as she held out her glass for a refill.

"You trying to tell me I've had too much?"

"Let's put it this way, the tablecloth is starting to see a lot more of your wine than you are."

"Point taken." She placed her glass back on the table and leaned back in her chair. She must have made such a bad first impression. Going on about discrimination in the legal system and about her baby sister. He must be bored silly. She'd told him all about her climb up the career ladder and he had sat there charmingly taking it all in. She didn't meet many black men who she felt equalled her, status wise. Paul was an exception. If she was looking for a male companion she could do a lot worse. "I'm sorry Paul. I've been a little uptight recently. I really do need to unwind."

"No, it's okay," he flashed a killer smile. "I've had a delightful time and I happen to know what you're feeling."

Jennifer seriously doubted that he did but she let it go.

"We've all been there," Paul continued. He reached for her hand and laid his own over it on the table. "I do a good line in massages."

She raised her eyebrows at him, "Excuse me?"

Paul smirked, "Did that sound too forward? I apologize. All I meant was it's a good way to relieve tension… but then you probably have someone to do that for you," he said, meeting her eyes over the burning candle.

He was fishing and Jennifer knew it. It might have been the fact that she'd had too much to drink for a lunch time, or the fact that she actually felt a strong attraction to this man, but she wanted him to know that she was available.

"No," she ran a finger around the rim of her glass, "there is no one to relieve my tension."

Paul squeezed her hand meaningfully. For a while his eyes locked with hers in a disconcerted gaze. It was as though the rest of the room had vanished. There was just the dining table and the two of them. Jennifer broke the look and as an excuse she took her hand back to beckon the waiter with.

"We shouldn't have to wait this long for coffee," she said to Paul whose gaze had not wavered.

The waiter came over, took their order and left again. Jennifer started feeling that the sooner this lunch was over the better. She had felt things she had no right to feel at this stage. But it had been so long since she had had anyone special in her life.

"Jennifer."

"Mmm," she replied picking up the menu from the table, she scanned the pages without reading them.

"Can I have your attention for a moment."

"Of course Paul," she smiled her 'Buddy' smile and tried to forget the way she had tingled at the touch from his hand. "Today has been very special to me. I feel so foolish saying this but I have this feeling that the two of us were brought together by fate."

Jennifer's menu closed and she laid it flat on the table. Her brow creased into a frown. "Yes?"

"Yes. You told me before how few black men there are in our profession..."

"Black women too," she interrupted. She had an idea where this was leading and was trying to avoid it.

"Yes, granted. But my point is that very rarely would you find two people so clearly made for each other within our profession."

"And which two people might that be?" Jennifer was completely serious.

"Why, us of course," his smile widened.

Jennifer did not believe in the saying, 'Flattery gets you everywhere.' She was worth more than flattery. Paul would have to work harder.

"Paul did I say or do something to lead you to that conclusion? Because if you feel that I did then there's been a misunderstanding, and I apologize."

Unfazed Paul continued his quest. "This isn't about actions or words, Jennifer," he said her name like no one else. It flowed off his tongue like treacle. "Can't you feel it? I want you in my life. I'm even willing to let you choose the terms."

Jennifer couldn't believe what she was hearing. She wanted to laugh, she wanted to curse. She wanted to get up and pour her wine over his head and leave him sitting there embarrassed, like in the movies. She had to admit that she was enjoying the idea of a simple business lunch turning into a flirtatious rendezvous. Paul Harvey was having an effect on her; whatever it was, they had it going on. "Paul, we barely know each other," she told him placing her napkin on the table. She chuckled, "I mean, for a minute there I thought you were going to propose."

He smiled. "You're right, Jennifer. We're two professional people. In our early thirties, years ahead of us. Why rush?"

Just then the waiter came back with the coffee. Then he whisked away the menus and left them alone.

Paul stirred cream into his cup as he talked. "Okay, forget the relationship. But why sleep miles apart. Why sleep with a cold empty space on the other side of our double beds? Aren't we allowed to fill that space with someone who we feel is special? Someone we want to touch..." his voice dropped to a seductive whisper.

"Mr Harvey, I think... no... I know you are being far too personal. I thought we were having a business lunch, then you turn up with flowers, bring me to an exclusive restaurant. Your touch is too familiar and you're talking to me as though I've known you for months instead of hours."

"Well, that's the way I feel."

"I can't help your feelings, Mr Harvey. Let me tell you one thing about me that you haven't noticed. I know what I want in my life. I'll know when I'm ready to settle down. Meanwhile I can control my lustful cravings. I suggest you start learning." With that she stood up and grabbed her bag and coat and strode towards the door.

"Jennifer, please."

"I believe our meeting is over, Mr Harvey," she said over her shoulder.

They were all the same. Give a man the time of day and he'd think it was his cue to try to get you into bed. Paul Harvey was no different. If she had a pound for every man who had try to get into her knickers she'd be a rich woman.

Jennifer waved down a taxi outside the restaurant and sat in the back, full of disappointment.

She'd hoped Paul would be different. It had been a long time since anyone had stirred up her orgasmic juices. Stirred! He could have had them boiling, but he'd blown it. Talking dirty didn't work on her anymore. What Jennifer craved was sweetness. Paul could have told her over the phone that he wanted to get her into bed and saved them both a whole lot of trouble.

Three quarters of an hour later the cab pulled up outside her home and was greeted by the heavy bass of jungle music coming from the direction of Jennifer's flat.

The noise, because that's exactly what it was, was coming from the living room. Jennifer ran up the steps and flung open the door to her flat. "Donna!" she screamed.

Two faces peeped up to meet hers from the sofa. "Oh God, Jen!" Donna leapt up from the sofa clinging to her unbuttoned blouse. Fitzroy got up fumbling with his jeans and pulling up his flies nonchalantly. "Awright Jen?"

"What you doing home?" Donna asked.

Jennifer glared at Fitzroy. "It doesn't matter what I'm doing, I live here, but it looks as though I was just in time."

"We weren't doing nothing. Jus' mucking around."

"Don't," Jennifer held up her hand to stop the excuses. Her head was thumping and she could feel heat rising from her neck up to her eyes. She turned to Fitzroy. "Get out of my house."

"Jennifer! What d'you think you're doing?"

Fitzroy was already getting up and pulling on his jacket, "Me nah budda wid dis, seen? Donna, call me when yuh ready."

"Hang on, jus' stay there," Donna stood between her sister and her man. "We both live here and when I moved in you told me that this was our home. How can you walk in here and diss my friends like that?"

"Exactly, this is our home, but every time I come home lately, this layabout is here eating my food, messing up my front room..."

"Ours Jennifer, ours. You can't treat me like no baby no more. I'm seventeen for God's sake. You know what, I get the feeling you're jealous," Donna said snidely. "Jealous because I've got a man who makes me feel like a woman; what have you got? You're still a woman y'know, feelings and flesh. You can't do nothing about me having a man, so you may as well go and get one of your own."

Jennifer stepped forward raising her hand to her sister. Fitzroy stepped forward. "Hey..."

Donna flinched and held out a hand to stop Fitzroy, but stood her ground. "Slap me nuh."

Jennifer hadn't realized her hand was in the air until her sister pointed it out. Had things between them got so bad that she was willing to beat sense into her? Her hand came down slowly.

"Me gone, seen," Fitzroy, a man of few words moved around Jennifer to the door.

" 'Ole up Fitz, I'm coming with you."

"Donna, you're not leaving this house with him. Not until you hear what I have to say," Jennifer followed her into the hallway.

"No? How you gonna stop me?"

Fitzroy handed Donna her jacket and stood with hands in pockets sizing up Jennifer. He was enjoying her loss of control.

"Donna you don't know what you're doing. Are you expecting him to look after you? He can't even look after his own flesh and blood."

"I can look after myself, Jen. An' you know what, I'm gonna prove it to ya." Donna grabbed Fitzroy's arm and the two of them left, the door slamming behind them.

The jungle music still hollered in Jennifer's ears as she ran a hand through her hair and slid slowly down the passage wall. "Shit, shit, shit."

Paul Harvey's clerk called the very next day to make apologies for their misunderstanding. He was having a social gathering on behalf of the Worshipful Company of Black Barristers this evening, would she be interested in coming along? Mr Harvey expressed himself so well through his clerk that Jennifer was tempted to say yes straight away, but she told the clerk she would have to check with her secretary and get back to her. Socializing was the last thing on her mind. Donna hadn't called. She had no idea where she was or even where Fitzroy lived. She'd waited up until after midnight. By then it was too late to start calling round all her friends.

That evening Jennifer found herself parking her car in the underground car park at Lauderdale Tower, one of The Barbican's skyscraping residential tower blocks. She wore a long black satin figure-hugging dress, with a lime green shawl draped across her bare shoulders. Other upwardly mobile black men and women were making their way to the same entrance, and Jennifer felt conspicuous going in on her own. They made their way up to the second floor where they had to sign a guest book before entering.

Inside, Billie Holiday was playing just loud enough to be heard but not to hinder conversation. Jennifer marvelled at the perfection of the flat's interior design. Pine contrasted with stark black. To her right was a fake log fireplace with a black chimney piece bordered by a real pine wall. The floor was polished parquet and the double sofas were a midnight blue. Two sculptured lamps and Art Deco statuettes stood on a heavy marble and glass coffee table. Uniformed waiters circulated, carrying trays of champagne. Jennifer spotted Paul almost immediately. He was looking casually fine in a navy blue wool suit with a black polo-neck shirt. Jennifer made her way over to his side of the room without being too obvious. Her plan worked. Paul spotted her and paused to pick up a glass of champagne before approaching.

"Good evening," he greeted. His eyes took in her well-groomed hair and the way her dress fitted her curves like a second skin.

"Hello again," she said.

"I'm sorry…" he began.

"I apologize…" they said in unison then smiled at one another. "Paul, there's no need for you to apologize. I was having a bad day. It didn't end too well either."

"Be that as it may. I did come on too strong," he handed her the glass of bubbly.

"So did I. With the ticking off I mean."

"Well, enjoy the evening. Let me introduce you to a few people." They crossed the room together and Paul presented her to a woman around her own age who had just passed her law degree. "Jennifer could make a great mentor for you," he said leaving them to talk. Paul Harvey's sixty or so well-heeled guests sipped champagne and manoeuvred to get their share of the vast buffet. Jennifer was not interested in either. She was conscious of only one person in the noisy throng. Although she made a deliberate effort to avoid looking at him, they still made eye contact from time to time. Paul Harvey wore the confidence of a man who was definitely making it. He was great at mingling, moving smoothly from one person to another without leaving anyone standing alone. He would introduce someone to someone else, then leave them to get acquainted. Or he would join a conversation and complement it, adding his own point of view whilst flirting with the many intelligent and attractive women there.

Jennifer had been cornered by a man she had no interest in whatsoever. He was boring and told stale law jokes. "What haven't you got if you've got three lawyers buried up to their necks in sand?"

"Enough sand," Jennifer answered drily. She spotted the legal representative from The Mail and took the opportunity to excuse herself from the bore. The only thing she could remember about him was that he was a law student.

Every time Paul came near her Jennifer felt hot and was sure he had to be feeling it too. She wasn't surprised when even before all the guests had left he asked her to stay behind until after the waiters had packed up and gone, for a chance to talk quietly.

Jennifer sat on the firm sofa and relaxed. Paul said he hadn't had a bite to eat all evening and went off to put a plate of food together. Jennifer had been in bachelor pads before but nothing like this. It was hard to know just what type of man lived here, apart from the fact that he had to have money. A mix of bachelor with a hint of the soul of a woman.

"More champagne?" he offered, coming back in.

"Thank you."

He disappeared again. She heard the low pop of a cork before he came back carrying two glasses, the bottle and his plate of food. He placed them on the coffee table and sat in the adjacent armchair. They had a table between them but there was body heat in the air. He poured for both of them and passed her a glass.

"To us and a bountiful relationship," Paul toasted.

Jennifer raised her glass. He tucked into his food, commenting occasionally about how well the night had gone. Every now and again he offered her various morsels from his plate saying, "Do try this. It's wonderful the way it slides down your throat." It was too tempting to refuse, even though she wasn't hungry.

They debated on everything from politics to why black women wore weaves. She found his conversation refreshing. He didn't think it unusual that she agreed with those women who were against the principle of marriage. After all, he said, it wasn't the piece of paper that mattered but the bond between the two people. He was curious about her and she had to think hard about her responses to his questions. It had been a long time since she had conversed with a man about what she was feeling deep down in her soul.

Paul was well-read and quoted lines from poetry effortlessly. He sympathized with her lack of free time but warned of the dangers of only mixing in like-minded professional circles. "You end up losing touch with the rest of the world," he said.

To emphasise a point Paul would touch Jennifer's hand or arm, leaving his fingers a second longer than was necessary. Jennifer was bewildered by the mix of apprehension and excitement running around in her mind. She was actually longing for each touch of his hand.

She discovered that he had lived on his own for ten years now, though he had not exactly been celibate. He had bedded many women, this much was obvious without him saying so. After all he was an unmarried, attractive, eligible bachelor.

Paul told her that when he met a woman he was attracted to she had to pass certain criteria before he would take it seriously. He was very quick to point out that the criteria had nothing to do with what shape body the woman had. It was more to do with the meeting of minds. His heart always told him when something was right. Like now.

They were onto coffee when the music from the stereo stopped and Paul got up to change the CD.

"What's that?" Jennifer asked cocking her head to one side. She could hear a musical tinkling coming from one side of the room.

"You mean the chimes."

"Windchimes?"

"Yes, I collect them on my travels. Would you like to see my collection?"

She smiled delightedly. There was so much to this man that she had yet to find out. "Yes please."

He took her hand as the music started again and led her to the back of the room where he drew back a ceiling to floor curtain to reveal a huge balcony which had remained concealed throughout the party. The door slid across and he lead her outside. The night was warm. The chimes hung about a foot apart around the perimeter of the overhanging roof of the balcony.

Miniature African masks, delicate oriental petals, silver crafted planetary shapes, tiny sea shells, multi-coloured discs and crystals were among the feast of windchimes before her. While she marvelled at their beauty Paul ducked back inside to bring out their coffees.

"Impressed?"

"You have an eye for beauty."

"Handcrafted or made by nature," he stated his eyes meeting hers.

Jennifer felt she'd walked straight into that head-on, but she didn't mind, she had already made up her mind that she was going to allow Mr Paul Harvey to seduce her.

"I've had a terrific evening," he said.

"Me too."

Keith Washington's "Make Time For Love" was playing in the living room. Jennifer breathed in the scent of spring from the flowers in the hanging baskets on the balcony.

"Look at that sky," Paul said, pointing up at the star-studded velvet above their heads. Jennifer followed his gaze. "Superman's a lucky guy," he said.

Jennifer laughed, "What?"

"To be able to carry his woman up into the stars," he explained. "Couldn't you just imagine riding on a cloud through a night like this?"

Jennifer was enthralled. Speechless. Her heart was racing and when he put his hand on her shoulder and turned her to him a warmth tingled its way through her body. She wanted him to kiss her so badly that she nearly made the first move. Paul kissed her gently on the cheek and said. "It's late," he glanced at his watch. "Four in the morning already. I apologize for keeping you so late."

"No apologies needed. I've enjoyed your company," she moved closer so that their chests touched.

But Paul was already leading her back into the flat, straight to the coat rack where he retrieved her shawl. "Will you be all right driving home this late?"

Jennifer was confused. Was it so long since she'd had a man that she was mixing up the signs? Hadn't the whole evening been constructed to seduce her? "I'll, be fine. Thanks for a wonderful evening."

"We'll do it again very soon. Maybe we could go out sometime?"

"I'd like that." They kissed cheeks again and Paul waited by the door as she got into the lift. Downstairs and feeling as horny as she ever had, she climbed into her car and drove away quickly.

For six weeks Jennifer and Paul dated. He was always the perfect gentleman and Jennifer began to wonder if this was the real Paul Harvey. He never laid a hand on her unless it was to kiss her good night or to show friendly affection. He seemed a very different man from the guy who had laid it on thick the first time they'd gone out. It probably normally worked too, but not with this lady. They dined out, dined in, went to the cinema and theatre and spent the evening at his flat watching videos, worked out together and gave each other healthy eating tips. But they never made love. They never even got near making love, much to Jennifer's disappointment.

She had even gone so far as to pretend to fall asleep in his flat one night. Paul had given her his bed and slept on the sofa in the living room. All night she had lain awake waiting to hear him creep into the bedroom, but her fantasies remained unfulfilled. Despite the setbacks she was determined to get her man. There was no way she was going to give up on him. He was the perfect type of black man, someone who always paid when they went out. Jennifer would always make sure she offered, but Paul insisted it was his pleasure. There was no mistaking what she was feeling. A mixture of hot, passionate lust and the beginnings of love, she was sure this was it. There had to be a way of making Mr Cool hot, and it was about time Jennifer found out what it was. She called his office early on Wednesday and invited him round to dinner for Friday evening.

"Come into my bedroom, baby, don't you know you belong to me, ah yes you

do.

Come in, close the door baby, your body belongs to me, tonight..."

Jennifer smoothed cocoa butter over her waxed legs and then reached for her new bottle of perfume. Tonight would be the night. She began to feel like a mistress waiting for the married man to turn up so that she could seduce him into thinking she was the one he should be with and not his wife. The whole house smelt of her expensive perfume, she'd sprinkled a little on the furniture, curtains and carpet. What the heck, it was only money! She hoped she hadn't forgotten anything. Wine, flowers, music, a drop-dead outfit, plus she had the place to herself with Donna still too stubborn to come home. When the doorbell rang she took her time walking to the door. Didn't want him to think that she had been waiting for him impatiently. Although Paul was dead on time, Jennifer had been ready and nervously waiting a good half an hour earlier. Jennifer opened the door wearing the nearly see-through chiffon blouse and loose flowing trousers, that had set her back more, much more, than a bob or two. Paul stood there, a bunch of flowers and a bottle of her favourite wine in his arms. His hair had been waved with some kind of texturised perm. It looked good.

"Good evening," he planted a friendly kiss on her cheek and handed her the wine and flowers.

"It will be." Jennifer placed the wine and flowers on the narrow table by the front door and helped him off with his jacket. She stood on tiptoe to kiss the back of his neck.

He shivered and turned to her with a surprised look in his eye. "What did I do to deserve that?"

"You're here aren't you?" She gave him her sexiest smile and they embraced.

"New perfume?"

"Mmmm, Champagne, I treated myself."

Paul took a seat on the sofa. On the centre table was a flower display to rival a professional florist's. Roses and orchids, just as Paul had on his balcony. She knew he liked them but he didn't comment.

"Dinner is nearly ready, can I get you a drink?"

"Mineral water please, I'll save the hot stuff for dinner."

Jennifer skipped back to the kitchen singing along to the Keith Sweat CD. He was still acting cool, hadn't commented on her outfit but she was determined to warm it up. It may have been a long time between relationships but not so long that she had forgotten how to turn a man on.

She returned with his water and a glass of wine for herself and sat next to him on the sofa. "So here we are again," she clinked her glass to his.

"Cheers."

She admired the charming, attractive man beside her. For some reason she found herself wondering whether there was any truth to the gossip about the size of his penis. To have that kind of gossip hanging over him he had to be a ladies man. But why was he not making a move on her? She hoped that the gossip had been started by women and not men.

"It's been a long day," he said catching her eye.

Jennifer sipped her drink. "Has it?"

"You know when you think you're just about to reach a goal and something jumps in and halts your progress..."

"Ye-es."

"My career in law is becoming that barrier," Paul sighed and took a sip of water.

Jennifer waited for an explanation.

"I've got bigger ambitions than the legal profession can offer. I want to be where the real power is. I want to be part of the decision making process in this country. And that's politics."

Jennifer listened intently.

"But it's just not happening at the moment. All I need is a break, a foot in the door and I'm there."

"Nothing happens that quickly. Not without hard work."

"Ah, but it can," he raised a finger in the air. "Look how many of our colleagues and acquaintances have made it to QC or MP on the old boys network." He fingered his tie. "You attend the right public school and all it takes are a few words to the right people."

Jennifer nodded, she knew all about it. That was what kept most women back in the professions. "But where's the satisfaction in that? Wouldn't you rather know that you got to where you are because of merit, hard work?"

"You're missing the point. Whether I got there on merit or by climbing on the backs of others the result is the same."

Jennifer disagreed but didn't say so. "I'll check on dinner, it should be about ready now."

"The food smells delicious, I hope you haven't gone to a lot of trouble. I'm not a big eater anymore, as you know."

Paul was referring to the diet he had recently embarked on after the embarrassment of being puffed out after a mere five minutes of squash.

"I've cooked all your favourites. Tonight is your night. You've given me so much." Hearing that seemed to please him. He patted her knee endearingly. Over a candlelit dinner and soft music, Paul talked of his wish to get into politics and of becoming an MP. He saw himself becoming Britain's first black Prime Minister.

"You never mentioned this passion of yours before."

He placed his fork on the side of the plate. "Somewhere along the line it became buried." His eyes searched hers. "Occasionally we start out to do one thing and it ends up as something else, but that's okay because it's along the same lines… and then you realize it's not as fulfilling as your original plan."

"And which party would you run for?"

"Well, obviously I'm a Tory by nature, but I'd consider any party that would guarantee me a safe seat. You see it's all about getting your foot in the door, then after that I can switch my allegiance like the wind. 'By any means necessary' as Malcolm the Tenth once said."

Jennifer laughed. Paul had never been quite this witty before. She was seeing a new side to him that he hadn't revealed before.

"This old boy network you mentioned before… imagine if black women got together and started their own networks."

"I don't see why not," Paul resumed eating.

"You know what my ambition is now?"

"To marry a rich man…"

She watched his face and a smile broke that told her he was joking. She wagged her finger at him, "I was about to come down hard on you, don't run those chauvinistic jokes in front of me."

"I'm sorry," he smiled, "I know you're not the type to marry for power or money."

I wouldn't go that far, she thought but kept it to herself. "My ambition is to start my own good ol' sistas network, bring in other women behind me. All I'd need to do is to learn the old boy's network game."

"That would take forever. It's much simpler to marry for status."

"I wouldn't do that. I might marry because that person is my equal, but not to elevate me into something I'm not."

"It's not about that. If you marry someone that gets you into the right circles, complements your ideals, it's like taking advantage of a good thing. It's about giving, sharing, balancing. What's the problem?"

Love, Jennifer wanted to say but didn't. She wanted to avoid being seen as a romantic. Her career was more important to her than marrying for status. Paul's mind seemed to dart from one subject to the other, but she still hadn't got the drift of the evening. Since the candlelit dinner and smouldering eyes hadn't worked, Jennifer decided to be a little less tactful. She knocked back another glass of wine and unbuttoned the top two buttons on her blouse, revealing a little cleavage. But all Paul did in response was loosen his tie a little and undo the top button of his shirt.

They talked some more about law and their futures, the future for black professionals in this country, everything except their relationship. Every time Jennifer brought up couples and relationships, Paul managed to steer the conversation back to work. But as she emptied another bottle of wine and the subdued lighting lulled her into a relaxed warmth, Jennifer found herself confiding in Paul about her fears for her sister, and her worry that there would never be time for love in her own life. Paul nodded and empathized. He moved over to the sofa and took her hand. "I understand. Some of us make sacrifices for our careers, others make sacrifices for our families. It's a matter of priorities."

He was the closest he'd been all evening and Jennifer decided this was it. She moved up closer so that their lips were almost touching, then suddenly Paul looked at his watch. "It's quarter to one," he announced, "I've done it again, haven't I? Kept you up late…"

"No, it's quite all right."

"No," he pushed her gently aside. "I wouldn't want you getting a bad reputation with your neighbours… you know, seeing me leave late at night." He stood up straightening his clothes.

Screw the neighbours, she wanted to say. "I wish we had more time together. The night just seems to go so fast," Jennifer said, standing facing him. The look on her face should have told him what she was thinking, but Paul either didn't see it or chose to ignore it.

He kissed her cheek as he would his mother's. "We are so alike aren't we?"

"You noticed it too."

"Like minds…"

Jennifer touched a finger to his lips. "I thought it was opposites attract."

"I don't want to ruin our friendship."

"How could it?"

"How could what, Jennifer?"

"It doesn't matter." By this time they had reached the front door.

"Pity," he said.

Jennifer felt desperately tired as the adrenaline ebbed away. Perhaps he was only teasing her, but then why? He must know what she was thinking and she was sure that he was thinking the same thing. Did she have to make all the moves? Jennifer reached for the front door. "Yes it is. Two people in our position couldn't possibly get sexually involved could we?" There, she'd said it. She turned her back to him, so she didn't see when his hand went into his inside pocket and removed the small leather box.

"But there is one way…"

Jennifer turned around to him, and before she saw the glint in his eyes she noticed the jewellery box. Her mind was thinking 'ring' but she was too confused to make sense of it.

"What's that?" was all she could utter.

Slowly, Paul opened the box and revealed the diamond cluster ring. "Jennifer, will you marry me?"

One hand flew to her throat. "It's… it's all a bit sudden… unexpected…"

Paul dropped down on one knee, taking her left hand in both of his, he asked again, "Miss Jennifer Edwards, will you be my wife?"

She looked down at him, tears of joy welling up in her eyes. "No!" she said breathlessly, "…I mean yes" Paul kissed her hand before scrambling to his feet and easing the diamond ring onto the appropriate finger. He was delighted. "Thank you, you have no idea how happy you've made me. From the moment we met I knew we could be an asset to one another. A match made in heaven." He held her face in his hands. "What advantages our children will have."

Jennifer was grinning too much to reply. Had she just said 'yes' to marrying a man she'd known for only two months? She had. Why? Because it was right, it felt right. She fell into his arms and as they kissed passionately, she couldn't help wondering about those rumours… She stepped back from him just long enough to savour the moment.

"Are you okay? This is what you want isn't it?"

"I think… I'm scared."

"Don't be," he filled the space between them again. "Leave everything to me."

His lips caressed her neck. She clung nervously to his shoulders.

"Paul…"

"Mmm," he sucked the flesh on her neck so gently it made her weak at the knees.

"Will you still respect me in the morning?" she sighed dreamily.

He met her eyes and held her face in his hands, gently. "My darling, you're mine now. Everything I have is yours…" he kissed her lips,

"...including my respect."

"Oh Paul!" a husky cry escaped her lips. At the same time she felt his strong hands holding her by the waist, pulling her towards him, belly to belly, chest to chest. They walked backwards into the seductively-lit living room and to the sofa where he flopped on top of her, surprisingly aggressive in his need. His lips were filled with hunger. This had to be love!

She felt his weight on her legs as they fumbled to remove clothes. He undid a couple of the buttons on his shirt hurriedly, loosened his tie some more and unzipped his flies before abandoning the job half done.

"Paul, slow down, I'm not going anywhere." "I can't help myself," he mumbled as he took one firm breast in his hand and with eager long fingers, pushed aside the flimsy material of her lacy white bra. "You are so adorable." He showered her cheeks, neck and chest in tiny urgent kisses. He kneaded a nipple into hardness before devouring it like a hungry infant. Without missing a beat he turned to the other one, covering it with his hot saliva and licking it to a firm peak.

Jennifer gasped as she was carried away on a tidal wave of emotion and lust. Their clothes hung from their steaming bodies. Paul had suddenly now become hungry for everything the evening had promised. Jennifer felt as though she had fallen from a great cliff and instead of going down she was rising to dizzy ecstasy. It was a rush like nothing before. She opened her eyes and he was looking straight at her, the raw intensity of his need burning through her. This wasn't how she had imagined the first time with Paul Harvey would be. Was this the same calm, controlled gentleman she had got to know or had he transformed in the heat of lust? He was tracing a path down her hard stomach, sucking on that tender hip erogenous zone that not many men seemed to know about. He's in love with me, was all she could think as she abandoned herself to his wild kisses. He was all over her... wanting her... needing her. And God, she wanted him right back. He rose again to take her lips passionately, finding her tongue and engaging it in a tantalising dance. He pressed two fingers into her vagina, touching her magic button with experienced precision, causing her to arch her back and groan. His erection was pressing into her thigh and, moaning with excitement, she reached down to help it out of the confines of his suit trousers.

Jennifer purred with pleasure, and clawed his back as he pressed himself inside her just a little, then pulled out again and as he entered her again everything else in the world disappeared. Donna, Fitzroy, work, the room she was in, the sofa underneath her, all her worries — none of them mattered. She sought his lips and whispered, "I want you... all of you."

In reply, his hips thrust upwards driving his penis deeper and deeper. He was giving, she was taking. They were made for each other, he'd said and he was right. Physically, mentally, two pieces of the same puzzle. Him, her fiancé. The passion started exploding inside her first and an overwhelming feeling of joy burned with a heat that swept from her genitals to every part of her body.

"Ohhhh, you feel soooo good... Aaahh...!!" she heard him groan and his orgasm seemed to collide with her own, as they thrust their groins towards each other simultaneously with a final burst of energy.

Jennifer cried out as her orgasm completely dominated her. His groan accompanied hers and he pushed deeper one last time before shuddering to stillness. They lay exhausted, breathing heavily, holding each other close as their chests heaved in syncopation. His penis became soft and limp inside her.

"I hope you enjoyed that as much as I did," he breathed into her neck.

Her arms were under his shirt, her fingers now relaxed and spread out like starfish on his back, her head was bent at an awkward and uncomfortable angle against the sofa's arm. Her blouse tangled around her arm, one breast hanging over the top of the cup of her bra. She reassured him with a squeeze, not wanting to say it had all been over too quickly and that she would have preferred it if they had at least taken their clothes off, even taken it into the bedroom perhaps, and made love instead of just having sex. She didn't say any of those things because all in all she had enjoyed herself and it was enough to have the satisfaction of having reached orgasm on her first time with the man she was going to spend the rest of her life with.

They lay like that for a long time, Paul dozing off and his body becoming dead weight. Jennifer wanted to drift back to reality 'sloooowly', but the magic of the moment was beginning to wear off as she developed a cramp in her neck. She tried to move but she couldn't shift him. She cleared her throat, hoping to rouse him, praying that Donna didn't walk in just now. Paul groaned but didn't budge.

"Paul, could you..." She shoved and he rolled off the low sofa onto the carpet, his eyes still closed and a blissful smile on his face. She raised herself up on her hands. Her chiffon blouse hung loosely from her shoulders, one white button was stuck onto her naked skin, ripped loose in the heat of the moment. She looked down at the face of her new fiancé. Her eyes travelled down to his crushed sweaty shirt and shrivelled cock, his trousers tangled around his ankles. Jennifer stood astride him, looking down. He was so vulnerable. Holding her left hand up she looked at the ring and smiled smugly to herself. It had all happened so quickly. She was now an engaged woman. She ran a hand over her hair and felt the untidy peaks. Her hair was a ruffled mess!

Sitting up at last, Paul's eyes opened. "Jennifer…?"

She pulled her blouse closed over her chest, suddenly embarrassed. "Why don't you make some coffee, I'll be down in a minute." Quickly she gathered her clothing and headed for the hallway, climbing the stairs as though she were on a cloud. She had just broken her two year drought and as she remembered the act she shivered. It had definitely been worth it. She felt happier than she had ever felt before and decided that nothing, nothing was going to spoil it.

The warm water of the shower cascaded over her taut body and she again felt rejuvenated. She couldn't stop admiring the ring. Emeralds and diamonds set in a beautiful circle. Doubts had no space in her mind now. Jennifer wanted to be Mrs Paul Harvey. 'A woman's gotta stay single to survive!' Her own advice echoed back to her until she succeeded in banishing it from her memory. Lost in her own thoughts she lost track of time.

The knock on the bathroom door startled her. "Yes?" she gasped.

Paul's voice came back to her through the wooden door. "I'll take our drinks to the bedroom shall I?"

He was planning to stay! There hadn't been a man in her bed for two years, how was it going to feel?

"That's fine," she called back, "it's the door opposite the bathroom."

Paul wasn't just any man, he was her fiancé, the man she was going to marry and spend the rest of her life with.

"Okay."

She heard her bedroom door open. He would be lying in bed between her cotton sheets waiting for her when she entered with just a towel wrapped around her naked body. Would he be ready to go again?

She needn't have worried about Paul waiting hungrily for more because by the time Jennifer got to the bedroom he was snoring peacefully under her duvet. One thing she had learnt tonight, the rumours about his size were just that. It wasn't its size that was special, but its shape. It was a 'hit the G-spot' shape and she should know. Rumours!

In the city a couple of weeks later, a damage lawsuit that had dragged on for months, came to an unexpected and gratifying end. The plaintiff agreed to settle out of court for an amount nothing short of stunning. Jennifer wasted no time in getting her clerk to prepare the settlement document and had it signed by the plaintiff the same day. The plaintiff's lawyer had stood by shaking his head in dismay and disbelief, while Jennifer sat behind her desk with a strong, silent look on her face. The good guy had won. Victory tasted so good! Jennifer had called Angela at her chambers and arranged to meet for lunch.

"Darling," Angela kissed Jennifer on both cheeks.

They sat in the bistro style restaurant by a tinted window overlooking the street. Jennifer glanced at the passers-by. Were any of them as happy as she was? The waiter poured Frascati for them.

"Congratulations on the case, but what I want to know is how are things going with Paul?" Angela leaned towards her and whispered conspiratorially, "Are the rumours true?"

Jennifer feigned innocence. "Angela! I don't know what you mean, I'm sure."

"I'll bet you do," Angela grinned.

Jennifer's face cracked into a smile too. She decided to lie. "The rumours are most definitely true, and I'm going to be the very last woman to testify to it."

But Angela didn't get the drift, which was just as well because Jennifer wanted to tell Donna the big news first.

"Go on," Angela squealed with delight and brought her hands together. "Tell me all." Jennifer did.

A call from Donna awaited Jennifer when she got back to chambers that afternoon.

"Hi Sis."

"Hello Donna. How are you?"

"I'm good…"

"And Fitzroy?"

"I suppose he's fine."

Surely that sounded like disenchantment. Rejoice! It had been nine weeks since Donna moved out.

"So when am I going to see you? You haven't called in two weeks."

"I was planning on coming round tonight… We could go out, eat, talk. How about the pictures?" "I suppose I'll be paying for the pleasure of your company?"

"You stopped my money remember? If you don't want me to come round then…"

"Don't be silly. We'll go to the pictures."

"It's a date then."

They confirmed that they would meet at home for seven o'clock.

"Oh, and I've got some BIG news to tell you," Jennifer said.

Donna arrived back home, wearing a micro-mini denim skirt with opaque black tights and a long shirt with her hair braided, short and two-toned. Because the argument that led to her moving out had never really been resolved, she hovered in the hallway, words hanging in the air, feeling uncomfortable carrying her overnight bag.

Jennifer noticed the bag. "You're staying?"

"Just the night, I'm seeing Fitzroy tomorrow night." She looked away and picked at the scarlet varnish on her long fingernails.

"So everything's just fine with you two."

"Yeah," Donna insisted a little too quickly.

Jennifer drove to the cinema. On the way, Donna informed her that Fitzroy had taught her to drive and that she was going for her test. Jennifer told her that was wonderful. "How are you going to afford a car though?"

"I've got an interview for a job next week."

"Doing what?"

"A holiday job. In Tescos, Lewisham."

"Haven't you got exams to think about?"

"It won't interfere with that. I'll only be doing seventeen hours a week."

"Seventeen hours!" Jennifer shook her head. She felt a pang of guilt about her sister's allowance, but decided that Donna could have it when she finally came to her senses.

They drove past McDonalds on Peckham Rye. Donna waved to a couple of boys, both wearing yellow and navy Michigan puffa jackets and baggy jeans. The current gangsta lick.

"So what's it like being an independent woman?" Jennifer asked as they queued outside the huge multi-screen cinema.

"Awright, sometimes. Fitzroy's got some nasty habits..."

Jennifer could imagine.

"...He needs a mother not a lover."

"Let's not talk about him. Let's just have a good time and then when we get back tonight we'll sit up all night chatting."

Donna smiled and they went into the cinema to see a box office smash that the black community had raved about for months.

After the film the sisters bought fried chicken. Back home they changed into their night clothes and, like little girls allowed to stay up late during the holidays, settled down in front of the television to watch a romantic comedy video. In the 'intermission' Jennifer opened a bottle of wine while Donna warmed up chicken, corn on the cob, fries and coleslaw. A late night feast accompanied the rest of the film. Then they lay on their backs on the polished parquet flooring, facing the ceiling.

"Remember Aunt Iris's parties?" Donna giggled. "I was about eight years old and used to hide under the table and, when no one was looking, I would reach up and drink the drinks."

"Mmm," Jennifer said through a mouthful of chicken, "and you got sick, I remember that. Dad took you home and made you sleep in the bath in case you were sick again in the night." She laughed at the memory.

"I don't think I was myself again for a week."

Jennifer felt Donna was relaxed enough now for her to tell her about Paul. "Donna… you know that when you left… I was single…"

"You still are, aren't you? Unless you're hiding him in the wardrobe."

"A lot has happened since you left…"

Donna turned sideways on the floor, with a glint in her eye, she looked at her sister. "You got laid didn't you?"

"Donna!" Jennifer kicked her sister's leg lightly. "I wouldn't quite put it like that. I started seeing another barrister. His name's Paul Harvey. He's thirty-five, single and he's asked me to marry him."

"No!" Donna sat up excited.

"And I said… yes…"

Donna's jaw fell open. She leapt up and with arms wide open threw herself on her sister who was still lying flat on her back. "You work faas eeh?" she teased.

Jennifer frowned, her sister was beginning to sound more and more like that ruffneck boyfriend of hers. She only just managed to push Donna off her and sit up. "Sis, it wasn't like that. I mean, we didn't do… anything for weeks nearly two months and then he asked me to marry him before we did… He's perfect, trust me."

"You fell in love and got engaged in two months?"

"It happens."

No one had yet asked Jennifer whether she loved him or not and she declined to bring it up. It didn't seem to matter to anyone. She was getting married, that was blessing enough.

"I can't believe this. So why didn't you say anything?"

"I wanted it to be special. Just us, here."

"So you're going to marry him?"

"I'm going to marry him, yes."

"Well... what's he like?" Donna was on the edge of her seat.

"He's attractive, very professional, ambitious, caring and he is very interested in me..."

Donna twisted her mouth dubiously, "So does he make you laugh?"

"We laugh together."

"Is he fun, sexy, exciting..."

"D, I'm not going to marry a male stripper." Donna reached up to the coffee table for her glass of wine.

"So what do you think?"

Donna swilled her wine in her mouth a little before turning to her sister thoughtfully. "I seem to remember someone saying to me over and over again 'a woman's gotta stay single to survive'," she furrowed her brow. "Was that by any chance you?"

"Donna, you know why I said that?"

Donna looked at her and shrugged.

Jennifer continued. "A woman can't achieve her goals once a man becomes a part of her life. Her only goal then is children."

"So why are you getting married?"

"Because I've reached my goals. I'm what I set out to be — a barrister. Plus, my fiancé..." she liked using that word, "...shares my goals; we couldn't be more perfect for each other."

Donna seemed to be considering it. "And where will you live?"

"I don't know. I suppose we'll buy somewhere together..."

Donna sighed and when she looked up at her sister her eyes were glistening. "I get to be bridesmaid?"

Jennifer grinned back at her. "If you're good you can be chief bridesmaid."

Donna smiled broadly. "Congratulations, Sis," she said as she hugged her.

Donna still had reservations, that much was obvious. All those questions. Why was it that kids were so cynical?

"I do want the best for you, y'know."

"You too, D."

It was almost morning, but neither of them felt like sleeping. It had been so long since they last talked like this and, as it was a weekend, they had all day and all night. They switched on the stereo and listened to sweet soul on Choice FM and talked about everything. Almost. Donna didn't mention that she had spent the past week on her friend Val's sofa since she caught Fitzroy chatting up another girl at a dance they had gone to together. The closest she got to bringing it up was to say that she was thinking of asking the council for a place of her own.

Talking with her now, Jennifer realized how much she missed not having Donna around, missed telling her off for leaving the butter out of the fridge, not washing out the bath after her or for leaving crumbs on the living room floor after she'd had a snack. There were, she had to admit, advantages to not having Donna around. She now realized that she had been so caught up in her sister's life because nothing was happening in her own. But now spring had turned into summer and with it Jennifer floated on air. Now when she put something somewhere it stayed there. Now when she tidied up she was the only one who messed it up again. And she could work at home without having to put up with a jungle or ragga bass as accompaniment. She didn't find hairpieces in the bathroom, or false fingernails on the kitchen table. And, most importantly, she didn't have to put up with Fitzroy sprawled all over her home. Still, she wished there could be many more long nights together with Donna like tonight, but it seemed like they were slowly drifting apart.

The sun was streaming in through the living room windows when they finally decided to wearily climb the wrought-iron staircase up to their bedrooms. When they woke up several hours later Donna went back to 'Fitzroy's' and Jennifer was again left in peace, perfect peace.

A few weeks later Jennifer was unpacking Marks and Spencer bags when she opened the refrigerator and her attention was drawn to the empty space where only this morning there had been a tub of yoghurt. Donna had been home again and had helped herself to the food in the freezer. Little sister had a habit of sneaking in, like a thief in the night, to feed herself while big sister was at work.

Over the last few weeks Jennifer hadn't really had the time to worry about Donna because Paul had literally taken her breath away and swept her off her feet with style and charisma. He was a man who knew where he was going and he was taking her with him. He had chosen her to be his lifelong companion. She focused on the coming evening. Tonight she would get the chance to show Paul off. She had invited her girlfriends around to announce her impending nuptials. She wanted to shout it out loud to her old schoolfriends. Nobody knew yet. They knew about Paul Harvey but not about the engagement. She had wanted to let it sink in first, relish the fact that this was for real.

She continued unpacking the pre-packed meals. Perfect, the vegetables only needed to be popped into a saucepan and heated. Good old M&S always came to the rescue whenever Jennifer didn't have time to spend on anything so mundane as cooking a meal.

She set the table for eight. The tablecloth was brilliant white, the glasses sparkled. Candlesticks shone and the silver gleamed. It was perfect, set to impress. Satisfied with her preparations, she poured herself a Bacardi and coke with ice and took it upstairs with her to get ready.

Eight for eight thirty she'd told them. At eight o'clock precisely, just as she was putting her earrings in, the doorbell rang. Hurriedly she fastened the gold hoops and zipped up the back of the red halter neck dress she was wearing. She hurried to answer it, hoping it was Paul. It wasn't.

"Angela, as punctual as you are in court," Jennifer took the bottle of champagne from her.

"But of course, that's how I got my reputation," the petite brunette stepped over the threshold into Jennifer's hallway, her eyes flitting around. "My husband, John," she introduced him without turning around as he followed her in.

John was the living model for Barbie's Ken doll. A fine dark-haired version. "Nice to meet you."

"Likewise," he replied. "Are we early?"

"No, perfect timing. Let me take your coats and you can go on through to the living room."

Angela unbuttoned her dark camel-hair coat and handed it to Jennifer. She wore a simple black V-shape swing dress and had dressed it up with gold jewellery, a choker and bracelet. Simple but effective. "You look fabulous Jennifer, bit different from the old wig and gown, eh?" Angela smiled through cigarette-stained teeth.

Jennifer caught the hint that Angela wanted a compliment back. "Just something I threw on, but you… that outfit must have cost more than…"

"Please," Angela pushed back her perfect hair, "a lady never reveals how much her clothes cost in front of her husband," she laughed and John and Jennifer laughed with her.

Jennifer hung the coats up before following them in. "What will you have to drink?"

"My usual, G&T please, Jennifer."

Jennifer turned to John. "Whisky and soda's my poison," he said with a trace of a Welsh accent.

"Mr Harvey hiding upstairs is he?"

"No," Jennifer felt a nervous twinge in her stomach. "He isn't here yet."

"He's cutting it fine isn't he? Oh I know, he wants to make an entrance."

Jennifer giggled. "Yes, that must be it. Lemon?"

"Please. You have a lovely home. Maybe I can have a tour later."

"Sure, when you're too drunk to notice the cracks and rising damp," Jennifer joked.

She handed them their drinks and made small talk. John appeared to be preoccupied with the CD collection and was making no effort to join in the conversation.

The doorbell rang and they all looked towards the door. Jennifer put her drink down and excused herself. Please let it be Paul.

It was Elaine and Allan.

Jennifer tried to mask her disappointment and greeted Elaine with an awkward hug, both women trying not to smudge their make-up.

"This is Allan." Elaine grinned at her fiancé.

He was a lot darker than Elaine with big eyes that looked as sensitive as a child's. He looked like a body-builder and had an air of purpose and control about him. Even though he was wearing a suit, the defined outline of his well-toned pecs bulged through. Jennifer took his hand and shook it lightly. "I've heard so much about you," she said.

"You too, but Elaine's obviously not too good with descriptions," he smiled. He had lovely teeth that shone out of his dark face like beacons. "Nice to meet you."   "You too. Angela and John are inside, introduce yourselves while I check on the food."

At this rate everyone will be here before Paul. That wasn't how she wanted it. By now Paul was supposed to be mixing their guests' drinks and introducing himself, while she served canapés and looked beautiful.

Karen and Beverly arrived together at half past eight. Paul still hadn't turned up. Jennifer had dialled his office and home numbers but neither answered. Jennifer started to panic. Everyone else seemed to be getting along fine. Angela and John saw nothing wrong with Karen and Beverly bringing up their children on their own and if they did they hid it well. Beverly told them of her plans to go back to school and study law and they encouraged her to go for it. Elaine and Allan revealed that they had now set a date for their wedding in August, two months away. It would be a small church wedding, with only one bridesmaid and a best man — Karen and Allan's brother respectively. The reception would be held at their flat. Everyone congratulated them. Elaine's news made Jennifer even more anxious about Paul showing up.

By nine Karen had started to complain about how hungry she was and Beverly was saying the babysitter was only staying until midnight.

"He's bound to turn up soon," Angela said reassuringly.

Jennifer nodded, but her heart sank. She shrugged and began to remove Paul's place setting. Then she lit the candles on the dining table. "Need a hand?" Karen came into the kitchen behind her.

Jennifer was decanting the food from the plastic cartons into serving bowls and looked embarrassed as she saw Karen's smirk.

"Good old M&S, eh?" she said, indicating the packaging. They laughed together. "Thanks. There's the vegetables to drain and put into the green bowls."

"Been stood up?" Karen had a way of saying what nobody else dared to. "I don't know where he is. He's ruined my surprise..."

"Surprise?"

"Yes..." Jennifer leant against the counter. "I was going to make an announcement, about us."

Karen came closer, her lively eyes fixed on Jennifer's. "Yeah?"

"I should wait and tell you all together..."

"Naaah... you can't leave me hanging like this. What?"

"Paul asked me to marry him."

"Aarrgh!" Karen screamed, rushing forward to hug her friend.

"I take it that's congratulations."

"You lucky dog. Shit, I knew you'd be the one to get married. Gonna be a big one an' all innit?"

"Well we haven't got that far yet..."

"So why didn't you say something when Elaine was going on about her little wedding?"

"I wanted Paul to be here when I announced it."

"But you still gonna do it, ain't you?"

"Well..."

"You've got to. You've got us all here, your other friend Angela and her husband, the food and drink..."

"You're right, I will."

Together they carried in the plates and food and drink, and invited everyone to take their places in the dining room. The aroma of the food made Jennifer forget her disappointment and reminded her that she had been too nervous to eat all day.

Jennifer had to rearrange the seats so that she wouldn't be facing an empty chair at the other end of the table. She began to unscrew the cork of a wine bottle, but Angela stopped her.

"Let John do that, it's a man's job. You don't mind, do you darling?"

John took the bottle from her hand. "Of course not." Jennifer got the feeling that he felt slightly uncomfortable in a room full of black people, but he was coping.

"Hold on, before everyone starts eating and drinking and stuff, Jennifer's got an announcement to make," Karen said standing up. She looked at Jennifer encouragingly.

Jennifer stood up nervously, all faces were turned up towards her. Some looked concerned, others excited, the men were just hungry.

"As you've noticed Paul hasn't managed to make it tonight. We were planning... I was planning on having all my friends here so that I could announce my engagement to the man I've been waiting for all my life... and this evening..."

For a second no one moved, then mouths dropped open and eyes opened wider. Elaine, Beverly and Angela stepped forward and showered Jennifer with kisses, hugs and congratulations, while the men poured champagne into everyone's glasses.

Then the questions came. "When?" "How have you kept it so quiet?" "Let me see the ring." "Why didn't you tell me sooner?" "How and where did he ask you?" "I can't wait to meet the man who managed to conquer Jennifer Edwards." Excitement vibrated over the table.

Jennifer's heart danced around in her chest throughout, beating madly, wildly. Paul still hadn't turned up but in the euphoria of the moment she couldn't feel angry with him. He was bound to have a very good reason for his absence. He was probably tied up with a client or finishing important paperwork. She'd been there herself often enough. As they sat down to eat, Jennifer answered all the questions and told the guests of her future plans. She had had two days to think about it and decided she wanted a spectacular wedding that would make the society pages of the national papers.

THREE

Jennifer was late for her tennis lesson. She jogged out onto the court where her coach waited. He was not pleased. "I'm sorry Carl, had to make a stop off on the way." Carl was a short, muscular, fair-skinned black man who wasn't quite good looking, but not exactly ugly either. "You're paying, Jen."

"I'll pay Carl, let's get going."

After a hopeless year of squash, Jennifer had decided to try another racket sport. Athletics had been her forte at school, but her arms needed exercise too. Angela and John often played tennis and had invited her over to one of their lawn parties. She didn't want to appear to be an amateur, hence the lessons.

She stood with a serving stance, her calf muscles already aching. The ball whooshed towards her racket. She made a half-hearted swipe at it but missed.

"Jennifer," Carl complained, "concentrate."

"Sorry Carl, my mind must be elsewhere."

"Well call it back will you," he walked slowly back from the net. Carl had hairy legs with rigid thigh muscles that disappeared into white shorts. Jennifer found herself wondering if his buttocks were just as hard and immediately scolded herself. She was soon to be a married woman. Thoughts like that were for single swingers. She adopted an athletic stance and returned the next oncoming ball gracefully.

"That's good, keep it coming," he encouraged.

Grinning, she lobbed the ball back a second time and darted nimbly across the court for another volley.

An hour and a half later it was over. Sweating and aching Jennifer made her way back to the changing rooms. Carl patted her on the back. "You doing good, girl."

It was the way he said it. Now she was sure he was gay.

Jennifer climbed into her third shower of the day. She felt tired and just a little queasy. She wondered if the ginseng and multivitamins were doing her any good. They were supposed to give you energy, stop colds, improve your skin, your eyesight, oil your joints, but she felt wrecked.

She had arranged to meet Paul for dinner tonight, he was going to explain why he hadn't shown up for their engagement announcement, but now she just wanted to go home, fall into bed and sleep until tomorrow evening.

She dried herself and climbed out of the shower, then dressed in a light cotton dress and slipped her trainers back on over her ankle socks. No, she was in no condition to go out to dinner, she felt completely exhausted and needed to sleep. She would call Paul and cancel dinner, he could explain things another time. She yawned loudly and stretched her arms.

Jennifer turned over in bed and focused her bleary eyes on the alarm clock. It was five past four in the morning and still dark. She threw back the duvet and dragged herself to the bathroom. She felt terrible.

After emptying her bladder she leant against the sink basin, a wave of nausea overwhelming her. She retched and spat into the sink. Light-headed and breathless she sat on the lid of the toilet bowl and breathed deeply. She was hot and needed air, but her legs shook when she tried to stand again. It had to be that summer flu bug that was going around.

It was time she saw a doctor. A week of this was too much. Bile rose in her throat again and she quickly raised the lid of the toilet and heaved into the disinfected water. It was too late or even too early to call a doctor. She would have to get a replacement to stand in for her in court in order to make a trip to the surgery as soon as they were open. Five minutes later the nausea had passed. After rinsing her mouth with Listerine she ran the shower.

She woke up early and called Julian Holland to arrange for one of the other barristers in chambers to cover for her. That sorted, she flopped back on her bed and slept until well into the afternoon. When she finally lifted herself up, a message on her answering machine awaited her from Paul. Shit! She forgot to cancel dinner. The message was brief. He apologized for missing her dinner party, said that he had been trying to get hold of her since yesterday because he had been invited by America's Black Attorney's Group to replace the Society of Black Lawyer's Peter Herbert at the last minute on a mini lecture tour of universities over there. He was leaving on a flight from Heathrow in a few hours. He said he would call her from Washington when he arrived. Jennifer's heart sank. He was leaving the country, already she missed him.

Jennifer went downstairs and rustled up a bowl of cornflakes for a late late breakfast. She decided that she probably wouldn't be able to get an appointment with the doctor at this time of day and anyway, she felt much better this morning, all the sickness of the night before had disappeared. She was going to take the rest of the day off. She felt like going out though and, impulsively, she dialled Beverly's number and asked if she fancied a shopping trip to the West End. Beverly agreed so long as she could bring Jerome.

The sun beamed down on the three of them as they crossed Regent Street. Jennifer fanned herself feverishly with the magazine she had just bought, glad she had worn the full-length summer dress. It kept the scorching heat off her legs and fanned her body with it's swaying as she walked.

"Are you okay, Jen?" Beverly asked, strapping Jerome back into his pushchair. "Yes, why?"

"Oh, nothing… your cheeks look a little flushed, that's all." Beverly's ample bosom heaved under the yellow sun dress. "People used to say that I looked flushed all the way through my pregnancy. Really pissed me off."

"Really." Jennifer's forehead and cheeks felt a little warm, but then so did the weather.

Nine month old Jerome was chewing on a teething biscuit. He was Beverly's burden, the millstone around her neck, and made every simple trip to the newsagents seem like a major expedition. Beverly complained that with Jerome, her work was never done. It always took forever to get him to sleep and when she finally succeeded she would be stuck indoors for the duration because there was no way you dared disturb a dozing child who had problems sleeping at the best of times.

They crossed over to Old Compton Street. Everywhere Jennifer looked she saw babies. Babies in push chairs and carried in pouches. There seemed to have been a baby boom while she was asleep.

"I hadn't noticed," Beverly said, "but then, when you've got your own to concentrate on you haven't got time to be looking at other babies," she gazed lovingly at Jerome. "Do you and Paul want children?"

Jennifer fumbled for the right answer. "I suppose so, but not right away, we both have some career goals to fulfil first."

"But you won't have to work when you're married to him, will you?"

"I may not have to, but I will." Jennifer played her motto over in her head again. 'A woman's got to stay single to survive.' She would have to modify that a little after she was married. 'A woman has to stay focused to survive,' or 'a woman's got to stay childless to survive.' She would work on it. They came to a gift shop and Jennifer waited outside with the pushchair while Beverly rushed in to buy something that she knew her mum would love.

"What a lovely baby boy." Jennifer looked up at the sound of the American accent. She smiled at the white woman who came up and gazed at Jerome.

"He's so cute. Looks like his Momma."

It took a moment for Jennifer to register that the woman mistook her for Jerome's mother. "Oh... No, he's not mine."

"But you are expecting aren't you? I can tell, you got that look aboutcha."

Jennifer threw her a dirty look. Woman doesn't know what she's talking about. She caught her reflection in the shop window. What was it about her today? Earlier, a pregnant woman holding the hand of a toddler had come up alongside her and started going on about how expensive babies were and had even asked her when hers was due. Maybe it's a sign. To warn her about Donna. Could baby sister be pregnant? Jennifer felt tears come to her eyes. How many times had she told, warned her sister to be careful? How many times had she given Donna the facts and figures of careless sex. Fitzroy Lucas had a lot to answer for. The only thing that would cure a persistent baby father such as him was a 'Bobbit' and Jennifer wished she had the bottle to do it herself. Men like him didn't deserve to have a sexual organ if he couldn't be responsible for it.

Donna sauntered in around six o'clock, wearing a new red felt hat, her hair still braided and looking good.

Jennifer cooked dinner, her sister's favourite curry goat, rice and peas.

"Sup'm smells good," Donna said.

"I'm glad you think so."

"I'm starving..."

"D, do you have something important you want to tell me?"

Donna thought about it. "No, I don't think so."

"Something about Fitzroy?"

Something flickered in her eyes. "How did you find out?"

"Instinct," Jennifer lied. "Do you want to tell me about it?"

Donna rested her head against the back of the sofa and sighed. "He didn't like the way I cussed about his kid. I told him I didn't want them living with us..."

"You didn't want Fitzroy's baby?"

"Well he didn't have to let her stay did he? I mean, was I wrong to get upset?"

Jennifer frowned. "Who?"

"Fitzroy's baby mother of course. Come crying on his doorstep a few weeks ago. Her mum chucked her out telling her to find someone else to look after the baby and she comes running to him."

Jennifer stared at her. "That's all you had to tell me?"

"Well... yes. What did you think?"

"I... I..." her voice died away. Jennifer shook her head and said, "I just knew something was wrong and I needed you to tell me... that's all."

"You thought he was beating on me or something?"

"Well, maybe not that serious, but I was concerned."

"We argued... he got rid of her. I couldn't have that woman sleeping on the sofa with her toddler running around the flat with no leash."

"I understand," Jennifer touched her sister's hair affectionately. "You see what I told you: that woman should have stayed single..."

"...To survive," Donna added.

They laughed together as Jennifer dished up the hot food.

"And is there any chance you might be pregnant?" the white-coated doctor asked.

The question took Jennifer by surprise. She had been feeling sick again but had managed to avoid that option. "It's a possibility, but I'm usually very careful."

The doctor looked over his glasses at her. "Have you had unprotected sex within the last few months?"

"Yes," she replied, feeling like an adolescent being scolded.

The doctor huffed exasperatedly. "Okay then," he put his pen down and stood up. Behind his desk were two white, wall-mounted cabinets. One, glass-fronted, contained empty vials, tissues, medical swabs, syringes and spatulas. The other locked one was probably where the doctor kept the drugs.

He produced a small white-capped sample bottle from the glass-fronted cabinet, filled in a label and stuck it on the container before handing it to her. "Take a urine sample first thing in the morning and bring it in to reception." He didn't look up again as he filled in her notes. "We'll have the results within a couple of hours after that."

"It's not gastric flu, or something then? I've had that before you see."

"These things happen…" he looked at her name on the records, "… Miss Edwards. But why don't we just wait and see?"

Patronising old man, she thought, putting her sample bottle out of sight inside her handbag. She got up and left, stepping out of the surgery and into a heavy downpour.

Pregnant indeed! She unfolded her telescopic umbrella. It was impossible and the test tomorrow would prove that smug grey-haired fool wrong beyond a doubt, she told herself, hurrying across the road to her car.

Nevertheless the thought followed her. When had she had her last period? She had forgotten, they were so irregular these days. Then she remembered she'd had a period last month, she hadn't missed one. Jennifer breathed a sigh of relief, climbed into her cabriolet and slipped in the Keith Sweat cassette. She smiled to herself.

Tuesday, Wednesday, Thursday passed with Jennifer working hard. She picked up one single white envelope in the mail on Friday. Inside was Elaine's wedding invitation:

Mr and Mrs Reginald Johnson
request the pleasure of your company

at the marriage of their daughter Elaine
to Mr Allan Goulden
at St. Mark's Church, Ladywell

On the back was the address of the flat they shared where the reception was being held. Jennifer felt happiness well up inside her. She went into her living room and propped the invite up on her mantelpiece.

Dressed in her favourite navy suit, the skirt just covering her calves, the jacket fashionably dropping past her hips, her jewellery was understated but elegant, she began her weekly handbag clearout when the clear sample bottle rolled off the table and onto the floor. The pregnancy test! She'd completely forgotten. Girl, sort yourself out, get the test done. Today! She ran a hand below her stomach, her bladder felt like it was about to explode.

The wedding was small, family and close friends only. The newlyweds were saving for their own house and wanted a white wedding, but not an expensive one. The reception was held in Elaine's front room and she wore a modern off-the-shoulder, knee-length, layered white lace dress with a matching hat. She had a glow that didn't falter all day.

Her father, a small bald man in his fifties, was in tears as he made his speech. Holding his daughter's hand he told of how close they were and he was proud to have played a part in producing such a beautiful successful daughter. He then turned to his wife and kissed her saying, "Thank you." Tears filled Jennifer's eyes as she watched this touching family scene, and when Allan's voice broke as he told of his love for Elaine, there was no holding back, Jennifer mopped tears of joy from her cheeks.

Monday morning. A message from Paul on the answering machine. He was back from the States but even that failed to raise a smile. The call from the doctor's surgery was totally unexpected. Jennifer had been so preoccupied with other things she had forgotten about her test result. Sitting behind her huge desk she put the phone down, threw her head back and sunk into her swivel chair. How could this be? She had to get out, get hold of Paul. If there was anyone she had to talk to it was him.

She dialled his work number. "Hello, it's Jennifer Edwards, is Paul Harvey available?"

"Miss Edwards... please hold."

A few seconds later Paul's faithful clerk came back on the line. "Mr

Harvey's in conference, Miss Edwards. Can I take a message?"

"Just ask him to call me as soon as possible will you."

"Certainly. Goodbye."

She replaced the receiver. If he was busy, he was busy. What the hell was she going to say to him anyway? 'Hi Paul, guess what I'm pregnant... we're going to have a baby... how do you feel about kids? I know we said we wanted to have kids one day, so how about in seven months time?' Somehow she didn't think it was going to be that easy.

She could always bawl her eyes out and blame it on the pill that she wasn't on. Would Paul feel deceived and leave her? Then she'd have to tell Donna and her parents and that was the hardest part. Maybe she was being too pessimistic. Paul might actually love the idea of a baby right now.

She rubbed a hand over her belly. Why me and why now? How was she going to juggle her career and a child? And after all she had said and the way she had behaved, how could she admit to her little sister that she had got pregnant?

She got her coat from the coat stand by the door and her handbag from her locker and stepped out into the adjoining office. Catrin, her pupil, stopped typing and looked up inquiringly. "Can I get you something?"

"I'm not feeling too good. I think I'll go home."

"Sure. You haven't been looking too good lately. There are no more appointments this afternoon and I can handle any calls so don't worry."

With that Jennifer departed. On her way out she checked that her mobile phone was on and entered the hubbub of the London streets, walking towards the tube.

She got off at Oxford Circus and was soon in Hennes department store. One of her favourite places to shop.

She flicked disinterestedly and automatically through a rack of clothes and wondered bitterly why buying herself a new outfit didn't have the same thrill anymore. She felt the warning sting of tears behind her eyes. She felt so alone. Fine example she turned out to be. She was staring at nothingness when she felt someone watching her. She turned her head to find a sales assistant hovering uncertainly.

"Everything all right?" the assistant asked.

"Everything's just fine," Jennifer sniffed.

The assistant in her stiff navy blue uniform tidied the rack beside her. "I'm pregnant."

"Are you?" The assistant looked at Jennifer's flat stomach. "You look so slim."

"Two months," she replied, wondering why she was telling a complete stranger her business. Was she looking for sympathy?

"What do you want, boy or girl?"

That was the furthest thing from Jennifer's mind. She was beginning to feel sick again.

"Girls are easier," the assistant went on. "My sister's got one of each and she says girls are easier. Hers always slept through the night, even at one month old."

Jennifer looked at her watch, hoping the woman would get the message.

"You ought to have a look at the maternity wear upstairs. They don't look like maternity these days, you can even wear them afterwards."

Obviously she couldn't take a hint.

"Most people don't get their figures back straight away, they stay baggy," she continued. "Everything just drops. My sister put on a stone with each baby."

Jennifer imagined herself being blown up slowly and unwillingly like a balloon. A tight and painful process. Then, when she could expand no more, the air being let out quickly leaving her body like an overstretched balloon, all the tightness gone.

She leant down to pick up her handbag. "Thanks," she said.

The assistant looked surprised. "You're welcome."

"You've made me decide to get rid of it."

When Karen had received the call from Jennifer on that afternoon, the first thing she'd thought was, good. It was a chance to get out of work for a couple of hours and have a good old chin wag. They had arranged to meet in the cafe at the Crofton Leisure Centre, a convenient meeting place for both of them.

Karen hadn't been expecting the look of a worried woman sitting on her own by a window overlooking the tennis courts.

"Bwoy Jen, you don't look too good, y'know," Karen said, taking a seat opposite her.

"Nice to see you too, Kaz."

"Wassup?"

"We should have met in a bar instead. I need a drink."

"Hold on, I'm sure we can get a glass of wine in this place." She left her friend gazing out of the window and went to get them both a drink.

"I bribed him into giving us some Bacardi," she grinned on her return.

"Thanks," Jennifer said, taking her drink.

"So, what's up, girl?"

Jennifer couldn't even bring herself to say it. Why had she picked Karen to tell anyway? Why did she need to tell anyone when she had already decided not to have this baby?

Karen watched all the confusion in Jennifer's face and became even more intrigued. "Is it yuh sister? I know how dat gal gets to you. You must be a saint to put up with her. If I was in your place I'da kicked her arse out long time... She's got no gratitude. I tell..."

"It's not Donna..."

Jennifer reached inside her handbag and produced a card which she handed to her friend.

Karen took the card from Jennifer's shaking hand. "An ante-natal appointment card," she said falteringly.

"Exactly."

"With your name 'pon it."

Jennifer gulped the Bacardi down. Their eyes met across the table. Jennifer's sad and devoid of feeling, Karen's incredulous and searching.

"This is a joke, right Jen?"

"Does it look like I'm laughing."

"Eh-eh!" Karen's hand flew to her mouth stifling a laugh. Jennifer Edwards got knocked up! She never thought she'd live to see the day. For all her upper class hoity-toity, Jennifer, the big-shot barrister, was on the same level as her.

"Karen!"

"I'm sorry, Jen. This is just so unreal."

"You're telling me!"

Karen crossed her forearms on the table and scrutinized Jennifer's face. "Bwoy, this hit you hard didn't it?"

Jennifer nodded.

"So how did you let yourself get knocked up?"

"It was the night when he proposed. I was walking on air. I guess contraception was the last thing on my mind."

"Your fiancé... Paul?"

"Yes, it's his. My first sexual encounter in two years and I mess up big time."

"Mmm-hmm. These men with money and charm are the worst. They mess you up man." Again Jennifer wondered why she had chosen Karen, the least sympathetic of her friends to confide in.

"So does he know?"

"No, not yet."

"Are you going to tell him?"

"I'll only tell him if I decide to keep it."

"If?"

Jennifer stared down at two men on the badminton court below. "I didn't plan for this to happen. I have absolutely no idea what to do with a baby." She threw her hands up in despair. "I never wanted this."

"Who does? At least you're not going to be left on your own. You're getting married in two months, remember. It's not the end of the world."

There was a silence between the two women. A group of school kids came up the stairs, rowdily discussing a punishment they were about to incur from their teacher.

"That Mr Baxter needs a slap, y'know."

"Needs more dan dat. I should get my uncle down here with his shotgun, man. Sort him out quick time." The boy clapped his hands together for effect.

"Y'know whose fault dis is, it's dat Kevin. You wait 'til I ketch up wid 'im, he ain't gonna show his face around for months." If only those kids knew that their problems would seem petty compared to the real troubles that awaited them in adulthood, Jennifer mused.

"I don't want you thinking that I'm on the side of the opposition, but I think you should tell the father."

Jennifer shrugged. "Well, you still haven't decided whether you want to go through with it or not and I think the father's attitude could sway your decision."

"What a mess... A child's life in my hands."

"You manage all right with Donna."

Jennifer half smiled. Donna was a separate problem. "All the times I warned her about getting pregnant..." she swallowed the rest of her drink.

"You got a lot of thinking to do. Go home Jen, call Paul and talk to him."

Karen was right. Sooner or later Paul would have to be told.

Jennifer leaned across the arm of the sofa and picked up the phone on the third ring. "Hello."

"Jennifer," Paul's deep tones came down the line.

"Paul, you got my message then?" she asked casually.

"Yes, eventually. Listen, can I see you tonight? I've some good news."

Bemused at the coincidence, Jennifer replied, "Yes of course. I have some good news for you too. Why don't you come over."

"Great. I'll see you in an hour."

"I'll be waiting." She hung up and immediately started to make herself presentable. She took the ponytail out of her hair and combed it into it's usual bob haircut, retouched her make-up and changed into a casual dress, showing off the best of her smooth athletic legs.

Paul was always punctual. An hour later he was on her doorstep, a bunch of red roses in his arms. He kissed her full on the lips. "I can't believe it's been so long."

"Good trip?"

"Perfect, I can't wait to tell you my news."

They went into Jennifer's sitting room and he unbuttoned his jacket before making himself comfortable on the sofa. Jennifer had already popped the cork on a bottle of champagne and placed it in an ice bucket.

"What a day I've had," Paul breathed deeply, spreading his arms along the back of the sofa.

"Wait until I tell you about mine." She filled two glasses with bubbly and cuddled up beside him. "But you first."

"Well it all started with a chance meeting about a month ago. I was sitting in chambers going through piles of paper work, when my secretary buzzed me to say there was an old friend in reception to see me. It was somebody I hadn't seen in months and, to tell you the truth, never expected to see again. Anyway, to cut a long story short, after several meetings and telephone calls, we've come to an agreement." Paul fidgeted excitedly.

"Well, come on tell me."

"I am now halfway up the ladder to my new career," he grabbed her arms. "Can you believe it?"

"Paul, I'm overjoyed, but what are you talking about exactly?"

"Politics, my love. That good old boy's network really does work!" He clapped his hands together.

Jennifer was becoming irritated. "Yes, *and*…?"

"I've always said it's not what you know but whom." He leant forward, elbows on his knees and clasped his hands. "…Jennifer, we may have to postpone the wedding."

Jennifer shot him a cold look. "I don't think so, Paul, you see there's a tiny complication to our plans… I'm going to have a baby."

Paul's face remained expressionless. Maybe it hadn't registered. She knew the feeling.

"Ah," was all he said.

"Our baby, Paul..."

He seemed to come out of his shock. "But of course," he removed his hand from her knee, smoothed his moustache nervously and stood up. "I'm terribly sorry Jennifer. How could I have been so careless... In this day and age you would think a man my age would be more responsible."

"Paul, I'm not accusing you..."

"I know, honey. Next you're going to tell me it takes two."

"Well... yes."

Jennifer's eyes followed her fiancé as he paced back and forth. Her heart was beating much too fast. Could you get a heart attack from giving somebody bad news? Paul finally stopped his pacing. His arms fell to his side and he smiled.

"Jennifer," he breathed deeply, "Jennifer, Jennifer, Jennifer..." His voice rose higher and his smile broadened with each mention of her name. "You know something... this really isn't a problem." Paul sat beside her on the sofa and took her hands in his.

Jennifer was surprised but glad at his reaction.

"In fact, this is an added bonus to my astounding good luck."

Now Jennifer was flabbergasted. "B... But..."

"No, my love," he touched a finger to her lips, "what more could I have wished for, a wife and child, at the same time as my star ascends careerwise. You are beautiful, did you know that?"

Paul kissed her tenderly and Jennifer forgot all the angst and agony she had been through. He wanted her and he wanted their baby. Life couldn't be sweeter.

Despite morning sickness Jennifer floated on air over the next two weeks. She felt as happy as she could possibly be. She was engaged and pregnant and had a man who wanted her that way. Karen warned her to keep her feet on the ground when she told her.

"Yuh t'ink he's still gonna want you when you look like a baby elephant compared to the Naomi Campbell lookalikes out deh?"

"Paul doesn't look at other woman in that way. Paul appreciates women with brains."

Karen kissed her teeth. She had known too many men, it would take a lot to convince her that Paul Harvey was some other species. But Jennifer knew it. He hadn't even mentioned abortion!

The wedding was brought forward. They would still marry in a church but the reception was going to be limited to a reasonable two hundred guests. Preparations were stepped up. She enlisted the help of her friends and her sister to help organise and go shopping with her. The wedding buzz even seemed to enhance her performance in court.

"It's like this, you see…"

Paul had come around to Jennifer's flat late that night after standing her up yet again. He had an apology to make. She'd waited on the other end of the phone for him to make it, but he'd insisted on seeing her. He hadn't even kissed her when he'd arrived. He avoided her gaze and refused any refreshment, saying he wasn't staying long. Something was wrong.

"More good news?" she asked.

"For one of us," he replied solemnly, rubbing his hands as he paced the living room. "This new career I've been telling you about… Well, it's more than a job."

"More than a job?" Alarm bells sounded in Jennifer's mind.

"The post was given to me under false pretences," he paused, cleared his throat and smoothed his moustache nervously. "I don't quite know how to put this… I told them that I was unattached. They are totally against… attachments as it were."

"What kind of antiquated criteria system is that?"

"That's not quite it," Paul glanced at her out of the corner of his eyes before focusing on the ceiling. "You see, the person who put me forward for the post was a woman…"

Jennifer's mouth clamped shut as if she knew what was coming.

Paul continued. "When I first started out in law I was introduced to a beautiful, intelligent, well-off young woman whose father just happens to be a powerful Tory politician. At the time he was a judge, one of the most powerful in the country. I strived to get close to her father, I strived to get her, but I was never good enough," he swallowed and began pacing again, a little smile touched the corners of his mouth.

Jennifer sat rigid, feeling empty and numb, while swirling in her guts was a volcano about to erupt.

"…Then she comes back into my life, she's heard of my accomplishments and hands me a proposal on a plate, a proposal I've been waiting for all my life. She offers to practically grease my career path into parliament. I would get selected, win a safe seat…" he was ranting. Jennifer sat impassively on the sofa. "…After a few years a government post and, who knows, maybe even my own department eventually. In twenty years from now I could become Britain's first black prime minister. You wouldn't want to stand in the way of all that, would you?"

"I'm sorry, did I miss something...? " Jennifer cleared her dry throat and narrowed her eyes. "I'm sure there's a message for me somewhere in all of this but I didn't quite catch it."

Paul ran an itchy finger around the inside of his collar. "I... I," he coughed and turned his back to her, "I can't marry you, Jennifer."

"What?" Jennifer suddenly felt hot and dizzy as the living room seemed to spin round fast.

"I'm sorry..."

Jennifer raised a hand to her forehead. "What you're saying is that you're pushing me aside to take up with this woman?"

"No! Not exactly. It's a career move. Being pregnant you're not in a position to understand. But if you weren't, maybe we could have still..."

"Still what?"

"Well, I have to be unattached at the moment, unmarried, no dependents... but once I make it to government... It's just that I couldn't possibly leave you hanging on, never knowing when I'd be coming back, or whether we were still going to be married some day. It just wouldn't be fair to you or the baby."

Jennifer stood slowly frowning. "And this woman, she's the reason you don't want anything to do with me or my baby?!" Her voice rose without effort, she didn't even realize she was shouting.

"Jennifer! Come now, we don't need to get hostile over this. It's nobody's fault, it's just the luck of the draw. Career comes first, you know that. You'll be okay, women like you have so many options nowadays."

Jennifer winced, feeling like a volcano about to spew lava. "You mean abortion, kill my child?"

"If you wish. Look, this woman is my passport to the very top. One silly mistake on my part is all it would take to wreck the opportunity. I can't afford to let that happen."

Jennifer glared at him. To Paul it was nothing more than a game of musical chairs. But this was her life he was juggling, and the life of her baby. "You know what, Paul? I should have followed my first instinct."

"And what was that?"

"To kick you in the balls and make a run for it!"

Paul chuckled nervously. "Jennifer, darling, one thing I always loved about you was your ability to stay in control. Don't disappoint me. Who knows, maybe when you've sorted yourself out... I could visit... stay over occasionally."

The eyes he looked into were as hard as bricks. Jennifer wanted to scream. Become his mistress! Did she come across as desperate? He must think he's speaking to a child. Jennifer's right hand took the initiative and before Paul could defend himself she had slapped him so hard in his face that her hand stung.

"Jennifer!" Paul's hand went to his injured cheek.

She was shaking with hurt and humiliation. "Don't even utter my name from your filthy mouth again. I trusted you, I gave you everything and this is how you repay me..." She suddenly remembered that she still wore his ring. She ripped it off her finger and threw it in his face. "... Treating me like some old garment that has lost its use!" Tears rolled down her cheeks.

Paul moved towards the door his eyes widening. "I... I think I'd better... leave. I'll call you in the morning when you've had a chance to calm down."

"Go, yes, by all means but don't call me or show your conniving, disrespectful face anywhere near me or my family again."

Paul hurried out the flat. "I thought of all people you would understand how much this meant to me, Jennifer..." he called back.

"Get out! Just get outta my house!" She slammed the door behind him and collapsed against it.

FOUR

Jennifer sat in Beverly's front room making a paper plane out of a till receipt. Beverly was babysitting for Karen, whose two children were proving difficult to contain in the modern flat in Lewisham. Toys littered the small front room — teddies, building bricks and a plastic tricycle. Jerome was walking now and was trying to reach a porcelain clown on a shelving unit. Jennifer watched as he cocked a leg up trying to get some leverage and then fell back onto his backside. Undeterred he tried again.

Nobody knew the wedding was off yet, but unprofessionally, she had taken the whole week off work to rest. The clerk for her set, Julian Holland, had not been happy. "Who am I supposed to get to cover you at such short notice?"

"I'm sure Terence can handle it, he was assisting on the Mellows case."

"Mr Childs will also need an assisting barrister," Julian pointed out.

"Do what you can please, Julian, I really need this break." She burst into tears after hanging up. She had spent too many nights laying awake, just thinking about things and she now felt it was time to get it all off her chest. She waited patiently for the right opportunity to tell Beverly her story.

"Sorry about the mess, Jen. Children!" Beverly handed her a cool glass of pineapple juice.

Jennifer took the drink and looked around the room as if noticing it for the first time. "It's not that bad."

"I've just started a college course in the evenings and when I get back I just about drag myself to bed. I don't know how Karen manages to do so many things. And she's got two kids. I can't find the energy to follow Jerome around, clearing up after him."

Beverly had decided to dedicate herself to self-improvement. The college course was just the start. Maybe she would stick at it and maybe she wouldn't, but life was too short to waste sitting at home playing with her son every day. When she had her qualifications and could provide for him a lot better they would have ample time to play together, Beverly reasoned.

She stepped over a squeaky toy and flopped down on the sofa beside Jennifer. Jerome had given up trying to scale the unit and noticing the women's drinks began to bawl for one too. The only way he knew how to ask for something was to open and close his fist in a beckoning gesture. "You want drink, Jerry?"

Jerome just bawled some more. "I'll be right with you, Jen." The toddler followed his mother out of the room.

"Look Bev, if you're busy, I'll talk to you another time!"

The large woman popped her head back in the doorway with a carton of fruit juice in her hand. "Don't be silly Jen, sit down. Jerome will probably have a nap soon." She filled the baby's feeder cup, pressed the lid on and handed it to him. Beverly sat down again, and looked over at her friend. "Karen always tells me when she hears from you. We really should get together more often."

"I know," Jennifer said wistfully. "Time is so precious nowadays, isn't it?"

"Especially when you're about to get married."

Jennifer met Beverly's eyes. "I'm not… anymore."

"Not what?"

"Not getting married. It's over."

Beverly moved up on the sofa closer to Jennifer and took her hand. "You're not wearing your engagement ring."

"I gave it back. I had no choice. You see, he…"

"Jennifer, you don't have to tell me this if you don't want to." Those were Beverly's words but her tone said, let it all out, I want to listen, lean on me.

"I want to. Bottling things up makes me unwell."

"I hear ya," Beverly nodded. Jerome snuggled up to his mother and pushed himself up onto her lap.

"Paul and I broke up because of another woman."

"Oh Jen, poor thing. That's always the way. And pregnant too?"

Jennifer's head whiplashed in Beverly's direction and as their eyes met, Bev realized too late that it was Karen and not Jennifer who had told her about the baby. "I'm sorry…"

Jennifer related the events of the other evening to Beverly and was soon in tears. She had felt numb for days but was feeling it now. Beverly had been there herself. Devon had left her pregnant. Hadn't even been back to find out if he had a boy or a girl. And even though his family had told him he still hadn't visited.

Beverly was truly sorry for Jennifer who had always been so sensible at school, always knew where to draw the line with boys and stuck to her studies. Jennifer who had succeeded in her chosen career, bought her own home, brand new car and had everything going for her including one of London's most eligible black men, yet now… Beverly looked down at Jerome sleeping in her lap and realized that Jennifer would soon, as she herself had done, learn that the world is full of possibilities and opportunities when you don't have to bring children up on your own.

"Couldn't you call him, try and make things up?"

Jennifer dried her eyes. Beverly obviously didn't understand or else she wouldn't be suggesting that things might not be as bad as they seemed. Things were bad. Really bad. Worse than they seemed, because she had decided not to keep the baby, but she couldn't bring herself to tell anyone.

"So what are you going to do?"

Jennifer shrugged. "I'm going to have to cancel everything…"

Guests would have to be notified. The dresses had already been bought and paid for, but the caterers would have to be called and the food orders halted. It was too late to cancel the cake, so maybe she would throw it at Paul instead. At least she'd get some satisfaction out of it.

"Imagine getting this close and then this happens. I can't say I know how you feel but I know how I'd feel."

Jennifer felt humiliated.

The early October sun beamed through the window onto the chintz armchairs. The clinic was private, homely and civilized, yet Jennifer was unable to relax. The sun was giving her a headache. Was that a flutter of movement she'd felt in her abdomen? She poked her stomach spitefully. Turning on her heels she made towards the small coffee table where a kettle, cups and individual packets of coffee stood waiting. She poured herself a cup.

"Jennifer Edwards?" the female voice called from the doorway.

"Yes." She picked up her handbag and somehow her trembling legs carried her into the consulting room. This was the real thing, she thought looking around. An examination bed and a trolley laid out with a blood pressure monitor and a stethoscope, kidney-shaped bowls and plastic gloves. Jennifer sat opposite the doctor, on the other side of a huge desk, unsmiling.

"Relax Jennifer, this is just an examination. We tested your urine, it's positive," she smiled. "You're definitely pregnant."

That much was already certain. Three tests and no period for three months left little doubt. Tears of genuine self-pity welled in her eyes nonetheless.

"I thought you knew..." The doctor handed her a box of tissues.

Jennifer felt for the box and pinched out a tissue, dabbing her eyes carefully. "Yes, but every time I hear that word it hits me again."

"Bad news has a habit of doing that. When was the date of your last period?" The doctor raised her eyebrow when Jennifer told her. "Left it late, didn't you?"

"I thought I was getting married up until recently," Jennifer explained.

"All right, just take your pants and stockings off and lie on the bed for me."

Jennifer did as she was told, lying stiffly on the unyielding surface. The doctor advanced, pulling rubber gloves on and examined her inside and out. She shook her head doubtfully. "You can get dressed now." Jennifer got off the bed, pulled her underwear on slowly. The doctor scribbled in a file. Jennifer stared at her, trying to read her face for clues. "Well?" She took her seat again.

The doctor's hazel eyes were clear, but her eyelids dropped and she shrugged. "I'm sorry Jennifer, you're too far gone. Maybe if you had come a few weeks ago..." The doctor smiled, a smile that said there was really nothing to smile about. "You knew already, didn't you?" Jennifer was already putting her coat back on and heading for the door.

"Jennifer, any doctor will give you the same opinion, you're nearly five months pregnant..."

Thoughts, all kinds of thoughts, were running through Jennifer's head. One thought especially... an option... a dangerous one... but at the moment, she was a desperate woman clutching at straws and it seemed that any option would do.

"Look, I know what's going through your mind," the doctor looked at her wistfully. "I know because I've seen hundreds of women in the same situation as yourself. And the same thoughts have gone through their minds. All I can say is, don't even think about it..."

Mind readers! Jennifer hated every one of them. She slammed the door behind her and walked the path of no return.

The candle flickered as hot wax dripped down the sides of the Chianti bottle. Jennifer looked around the small Italian restaurant. More than one male diner had his eyes on this stylishly-dressed attractive black woman sitting alone. She hardly noticed them. She had more important things on her mind.

It wasn't the kind of place she cared to be seen in, far less spend the most nerve-racking evening of her life, but Tony Carnegie, private investigator, had called to say he had some good news for her and she desperately needed some.

"Anything to drink while you're waiting, madam?"

"No," she said, dismissing the waiter with a wave of her hand. She glanced at her watch. He was late. A moment later the waiter was on his way back to her table, followed by Tony Carnegie. "Your guest has arrived, madam." He pulled out the chair opposite for Tony to sit on and handed them the menus. Tony smiled warmly at Jennifer.

"You're late."

He grinned. Tony looked confident and, dressed casually, seemed younger. He placed a box file on the table to his right and placed his menu open on top of it. "I know," he said studying the menu. "Have you decided?"

"Just wine please, I'm not hungry."

"A bottle of dry white, please," Tony said to the waiter.

"This isn't a bar, sir, you have to eat..." the waiter held his small writing pad in front of him pointedly. Tony pulled a funny face, Jennifer stifled a smile.

"What do you recommend?"

"Spaghetti?"

"Whatever..." Tony handed him back the menu and the waiter turned to Jennifer. "Twice," she answered before the question was asked. Then turning to Tony as the waiter walked away, "Now, tell me the news."

"You mean we're not going to eat first?"

"Mr Carnegie, I really didn't come here to socialize."

Tony's smile disappeared. "Fine," he mumbled. He placed his hand on the file and pulled it in front of him. "As I've said, it's good news from your point of view," he looked up from the papers in his hand. "Fitzroy Lucas is no more a criminal than I am, but he's also not as much of a private dick as I am," Tony grinned wickedly, expecting at least a smile from Jennifer, but her face remained blank. "Okay," he continued, "he's given ten women pickney in Birmingham, Manchester and London. A few concentrated in the Lewisham borough. I went to Somerset House, had to go through the registry of all the children born since Fitzroy was fourteen. His name crops up a dozen times."

Jennifer was stunned. She had suspected at least five women, but ten, and twelve children! Tony turned over another few pages in the file. "Young Mr Lucas is one of Britain's most wanted men. The CSA are after him, he owes them £300,000 in unpaid child maintenance!" He laughed. "The guy's a rude bwoy, a ladies man, but the only crime he's guilty of is smoking weed and I'm sure you already knew that."

Jennifer was still reeling from the revelations. "Mr Carnegie, how can a man just walk out on his children without any guilt? Answer that. Okay, I agree about safe sex, but it's both persons' responsibility and thereafter also. If you think you're responsible enough to have sex, then you should be equally responsible for the consequences."

Tony shrugged. "Don't look at me. I'm not my brotha's keeper."

Jennifer turned to his report and muttered, "I could have done better myself." She pushed the file away from her. "I should get my money back."

"You haven't paid me yet."

Good judgment on my part, she thought shrewdly. Tony Carnegie was just another arrogant cocksure man. Her first instincts were always right but why was it she never followed them?

The waiter appeared, carrying two steaming bowls of spaghetti on a tray. Jennifer felt her stomach juices rising.

"Pepper? Parmesan?" the waiter was asking.

Jennifer leaned across the table and told Tony very softly, "I'm sure you know what you're doing, you're probably very good at your job, but this time you just haven't helped."

"It wouldn't be the first time," Tony requested more parmesan over his spaghetti. Jennifer sipped her wine, watching as he chopped up his spaghetti with a knife.

"My sister is everything to me. I have to save her."

Tony looked up from the bowl he was twirling his fork around in. "We should all learn by making our own mistakes, my mum always said."

Donna had said exactly the same thing. Maybe they were right. Tony looked up from the last mouthful and raised his eyebrows at Jennifer's untouched bowl of spaghetti.

"You're not eating that?"

"I said I wasn't hungry."

"Can I have it?"

Jennifer couldn't get mad at him even if she wanted to. There was something touching about the way he asked.

"Help yourself," she slid her bowl across to him. She watched as he gave the spaghetti the sauce treatment. He wound some spaghetti onto his fork and shoved it into his mouth. There was a certain intimacy in having your food eaten by someone else, Jennifer felt. It took her back to the first time she had been in Paul's apartment. He had fed her from his own plate then. Tony was cute, almost little boy cute, unlike Paul's manly look. And Tony didn't put on airs and graces to impress. With him what you saw was what you got.

After spending a couple of depressing hours alone in a bar, Jennifer was not looking forward to spending yet another solitary weekend alone with her gloomy thoughts. When she stepped through the front door, however, she was greeted by the smell of a spicy hot Indian takeaway and a jungle track on the living room stereo. Donna was home again. Walking wearily into the hallway she half-expected to see Fitzroy sprawled on her sofa. He wasn't.

"Jen!" Donna rushed at her from the kitchen, her braids flying behind her and greeted Jennifer with a hug and a peck on her cheek, like a long lost friend.

"You're back home then?"

"For good this time. Can't get rid of me that easily." Donna headed back to the kitchen. "Did you miss me?"

Jennifer followed. "If you gave me a chance to, I might have."

The washing machine was on and a holdall on the floor contained more of Donna's dirty clothes. Jennifer put the kettle on. "So what happened to what's his name?"

"It's finished innit," she shrugged. "Expected me to be his personal slave... tidying up, washing his briefs, dragging bags down to the laundry... I had enough. No way, no more."

Jennifer couldn't suppress the smile. "So you're completely finished?"

"Yeah man," she said as she ate her curry. "Been living on junk for months. I need some home cooking."

Jennifer had to laugh. "That's good news, D." The saying 'learn by your own mistakes' came to mind again. Tony Carnegie's investigations had been meaningless after all. All it had taken to cure Donna of her infatuation was for her to spend more time with Fitzroy, not less as Jennifer had believed.

Donna winked at her sister. "Thought you'd be pleased. An' something else…" she pulled a sheet of paper out of her back pocket and waved it above her head. She couldn't control her proud smile as she handed the certificate to her sister.

"You passed your test! Congratulations. First time as well."

"Yeah man. Fitzroy was good for summink after all… Shanika's coming round later, we're gonna celebrate."

"You're going out tonight?"

"Yeah, probably only local though." Donna popped a spoonful of rice in her mouth.

Jennifer grimaced. She needed to tell Donna everything tonight before she lost her nerve. The kettle clicked off behind her and she turned to the cupboard to get a mug for her coffee. "Any chance you could stay in tonight?"

"You did miss me," Donna giggled.

If it meant she stayed in… "Yes, I missed you."

"I ain't seen much of Shan lately, y'know."

"I know, but you haven't seen much of me either," Jennifer sipped at her coffee. "It's just that there's uhmm… something I've got to tell you as well."

"You split up with that lawyer geezer, I know."

"How did you know?"

"Saw Karen in Lewisham."

Jennifer's heart leapt into her throat. "Did Karen say anything else?"

"Like what?"

"Well… uhmmm… there are going to be a few changes around here."

"Oh yeah?"

Jennifer clasped her hands around her mug on the dining table in front of her. She mumbled, "I'm pregnant."

"What Jen?" Donna leant forward. She hadn't caught the important word. Jennifer made her eyes meet her sister's just long enough to repeat herself. "I'm going to have a baby."

Donna jumped up. "You?! Whose baby? I know you gotta be

adopting."

Admitting this to her little sister was the biggest hurdle. Shame engulfed Jennifer, unlike any shame she had ever felt. Seeing her sister's reaction Donna sat down again, her eyes becoming serious. "You're pregnant, Sis?" she asked gently.

Jennifer nodded. There was a few seconds of silence as it sank in.

"Backside!" The laughter escaped unexpected and Donna didn't try to stop it. She slapped the table, rocking back and forth in mirth. "Wait 'til I tell Shanika bwoy, you're lucky I'm not even talking to Fitzroy, he'd never let it go."

Jennifer was shaking her head. "I'm sorry, D…"

"What you sorry for? I'm not having the pickney, you are! God, d'you realize what that means?"

Jennifer looked up at her sister. She thought she could guess what was coming. Donna was going to say that her sister was going to be a baby mother.

"I'm going to be an auntie, 'bout time too." Donna continued eating. "Mum's going to freak, probably come flying back to England to look for her grandkid."

Don't. Jennifer didn't need to be reminded that she had yet to face her parents when she would have to admit that every lesson they'd ever taught her… Oh, the shame of it!

"The kid can have my room. I'll sleep in the living room. "

"D, how do you really feel about it?"

Donna tilted her head to the side. "Bwoy, Sis," she shook her head, "what can I say, man? You messed up big time. Big career woman like you, couldn't even find a decent man to have your kids with — times are hard, guy." A cheeky grin spread across her face. "Remember how you used to say I should find a man like Paul?" Donna laughed again, slapping the table.

Jennifer lowered her head.

"Jen, man, it's tough… all right it's happened. You thought about abortion?"

"Too late. Baby's due in February."

Donna shook her head again and sucked air through her teeth. "When you mess up you mess up big!" She took her plate to the sink and ran hot water onto it.

Jennifer began to sob.

Donna dropped what she was doing and and rushed to her sister's side.

"Jen, it's not that bad. It's not like you're a kid. You're an independent woman. Okay, you ain't got a man, but you've got me." She punched Jennifer's shoulder playfully. "I'll be Daddy, yeah? Since I wear the trousers in this house anyway."

Jennifer smiled despite her feelings. Donna poked her stomach gently. "I thought that was just wind," she said.

They laughed together. Standing in the middle of the kitchen, the two women hugged each other tight.

FIVE

I knew I was going into labour. Knew it. Didn't think it. Didn't wonder if this was it. I, Jennifer Edwards knew. Four weeks early, in court, in the middle of the biggest case of my career. I felt a contraction that was nothing like the ones I had been having for the past week. It gripped me around my middle like a vice, taking my breath away for the few seconds that it lasted. Like a fool I thought it was better to conduct myself in a professional manner and I carried on summing up the evidence against my client.

It was at this point that my waters broke. I doubled over in pain. It was obvious to everyone what was happening. The court was immediately adjourned, an ambulance called and I was dispatched to a couch in the judge's chambers.

The embarrassment and humiliation of it all. Didn't these things usually happen in the middle of the night? I'd spent months building up this case. Had witnesses and a detective waiting to give evidence and I go into labour!

Strange men were asking what they could get me. Water? Tea? Whisky? All I really wanted was to go home and sleep. Oh why did I have to be a woman? Why did I have to get pregnant? And why hadn't I listened when everyone had warned me about cutting it fine?

I got someone to call Donna, who had agreed delightedly to be my birthing partner. Fortunately she was at home studying and knew the drill off by heart. She got to the hospital before I did.

I was shaking uncontrollably by the time I got into the ambulance. Suddenly I was scared. I felt so alone. Alone and in pain. The medic who accompanied me in the back of the ambulance turned around and said, "You'll be alright love, got hours to go yet."

Thank you very much. I grinned through gritted teeth. Hours more of pain and frustration and being so damned out of control. I could feel the child aching and dancing in my belly.

Unfortunately, the ambulance driver was right.

Donna was at the hospital waiting for me. I'd never been so happy to see anyone in my whole life. By the time Donna had helped me to wash and change into night wear, the midwives had wired me up to the monitor, the labour was in full swing. The baby was on its way.

I had been through this moment a hundred times in my mind. I had imagined the pains and the anxiety, but never really felt them.

I found myself thinking of the good times I'd had with past boyfriends. Those who I could, perhaps should, have had kids with. Would I be here by myself if I had got it together with one of them?

I remember saying to the midwife, "I think I've made a terrible mistake." Hours later, drowsy under the influence of pethidine, I was still repeating the same thing as an army of doctors, nurses and midwives examined between my legs. Neither they nor the drugs could stifle the wave after wave of unbearable pain. Donna simply stared at me, punctuating my every scream with, "Oh Gawd. Thanks Jen, you've put me off getting pregnant for life, guy. I'm never going t'rough dis."

I could have slapped her, but I was too busy panting, gritting my teeth and pleading, "It hurts, get this thing out of me!!!" It was unbearable. How women go through this again and again I'll never know. All those months of antenatal clinic appointments and literature should have prepared me for this, but no. Somehow they managed to miss out the words, extreme and pain. The pain was in my back, in my sides, in my abdomen, in my chest for Christ's sake. I hollered, and breathed. Breathed just like the midwife told me to.

From the time I realized I was going to have to keep this baby I had planned a natural birth. No painkillers, I wanted to be able to walk about, crouch, stand, listen to my favourite music, 'Computer Love' by Zapp. How comforting was fiction. Donna had remembered the music but I couldn't hear it. Forget the alternative childbirth, I just wanted to lie there and push. I couldn't believe that just lying there was as painful as this. At one stage I held my breath to see if it would take the pain away but that just gave me a headache.

I wondered what Paul was doing now, probably sipping iced tea on a balcony overlooking the beach with his bitch rubbing sun block into his shoulders. Bastard! Despite the pain and the way I felt about him I found myself screaming out his name.

"Who is Paul dear? Your husband? Do you have a number, I could call him for you?"

"Nooo!!!" I screamed, sounding just like the possessed girl in 'The Exorcist'.

The midwife patted my hand and turned to Donna, "This is quite normal. You should hear some of the things I get called. Remember your breathing, Jennifer, nice and easy..."

Thank you, ma'am. I've been breathing all my life and this baby isn't changing anything.

By three o'clock that afternoon, the contractions went from every ten minutes to every two minutes. I was sick until I didn't have any sick left. I pushed when I was told to. Pushed until it felt as though a team of horses was dragging my vagina inside out.

Disjointed voices floated around the room. "I can see his head," Donna screamed. His head! How did she know what sex it was?

"One more push and we'll have his shoulders," a doctor ordered.

"Nearly there, it's coming, keep pushing."

It's coming and I'm splitting in half. It felt as though a watermelon was being forced out of me. A hole that had had trouble accepting a penis was now expected to open its doors to a baby's head. I noticed the red weals on Donna's forearms, recognized each digit of my fingers. Finally, the head was within reach and the midwife brought the child into the world... "It's a boy!" The doctor held up a tiny, wailing creature covered in white slime.

"A boy, Jen!" Donna kissed my cheek. "My nephew. Wicked!"

I closed my eyes, I didn't want to look, I was exhausted. A moment later I felt a hot, slippery body on my bare stomach and, I swear, I screamed. My eyes flew open and for a split second I saw Paul's face on that baby's head. My nightmare became reality. I blinked and felt a sigh of relief deep down within me. He was all right... he had been born with all his little fingers and tiny toes... both his eyes and ears and legs and arms. I swear, I felt like I wanted a tall glass of whisky, straight, no chaser.

Donna was the first to hold him after they'd cut the cord and cleaned him up. When she offered him to me I pretended to be too tired. Just when I thought it was all over, I felt another contraction. "Nurse, it's starting again! Oh God, not twins."

The midwife came to my side. "It's the afterbirth dear. One final push and it'll all be over."

The worst was over but, still, I had to control the urge not to strangle the cause of all my pain when he was placed on my chest to suckle my sore nipple. He sucked so hard I was sure it would come off in his mouth. But my milk wasn't coming and the baby began to scream, and kept screaming. I saw the rest of my life dissolve into one long high-pitched scream and I burst into tears.

The hospital staff were all sweet and condescending over the next two days. I was patronised by midwives telling me what a good little mother I was going to be, and that child birth had its teething problems... I was never alone. Doctors checked up on me several times a day, paediatricians checked on the baby and an endless flow of medical students studied me as though I was part of a biology lesson. And as well as the other new mothers in the adjoining beds, I had to share the ward with their families and friends who came to visit. Every time I tried to get a bit of privacy from the lovey-dovey mothers and fathers and doting grandparents by pulling the curtain around my bed and putting my headphones on, a member of staff would come along and whip the curtains back. "Sorry, it's not allowed unless you're actually indisposed."

Motherhood! From where I was lying, it seemed like a farce. Wasn't I supposed to be bonding with this infant because of all we had been through together? But I couldn't bring myself to love him. I had no feelings for him other than that he had come to ruin my life and the more I thought about it the more determined I was that he wasn't going to succeed.

The next day Jennifer's milk came in full force. The baby was still having trouble sucking, and the doctors advised her to stay in for a couple of days until he was settled, they even coerced her into trying him on the breast again, despite the pain. By now Jennifer's breasts were so full that between feeds she would have to go into the bathroom and squeeze them to let the milk go. Sucking, she discovered, seemed to only produce more. Jennifer felt numb.

She shared a ward with four other women and so far she'd kept to herself, just sitting on the sidelines listening. Josey, a bleach blonde, wild haired white woman was a chain smoker and kept having to "pop out for a fag." Her baby had been born premature and spent most of its time in an incubator. Her husband was a bricklayer, who had a habit of coming to visit with his jeans hanging halfway down his backside and his belly hanging out from the bottom of his jumper.

Janine was a small cockney brunette, at fourteen years of age a mere infant herself. She was still pregnant and was to be induced any day now. Not that she could possibly understand. Janine spent most of her time walking around with her headphones on and gazing out of the windows. She never had any visitors.

Maureen was about the same age as Jennifer. A nervous looking black woman who was always gazing adoringly at her baby girl. She had plenty of visitors but not the baby's father.

Lorraine was middle-class, white, married. Her husband always wore a suit no matter what time of day he visited. She'd had a caeserian section and walked as though she had a disability. She didn't talk much to the others. She bottle-fed her son and dressed him in the same colour clothes she wore every day. Unlike the others Lorraine didn't walk around in her nightie, but went to the trouble of getting dressed every day, in clothes that still looked like maternity wear.

Jennifer got up to make herself a cup of tea from the tiny kitchen along the corridor. She carried the coffee into the day room where three of the women from her ward sat. Josey was smoking as usual, Janine was nodding to her headphones, and Maureen was knitting a baby-sized cardigan.

"Hiya," Josey raised her cigarette. "Come and join us, love. Good to see ya up an' about."

Jennifer smiled uneasily and took a seat as far away from Josey as she could without being rude.

Maureen looked up from her knitting. "Your sister coming back today?"

They had obviously picked up bits of information about Jennifer by eavesdropping as she had. "Yes, I expect so."

"It's good that she comes isn't it?" Maureen leaned forward whispering. "Janine doesn't get any visitors, parents threw her out and boyfriend didn't want to know."

Jennifer nodded. She didn't want to discuss her business with these people, it was enough that she had to share a ward with them.

"You not married then?" Josey asked, placing her cigarette into the clay ashtray on the worn-out surface of the small wooden coffee table.

"No."

"Boyfriend?" Maureen leaned in.

"No."

"Poor cow," Josey puffed, pulling her mass of bleached hair back off her face.

"Are you married?" Jennifer asked Maureen out of politeness.

"Not yet, my boyfriend's overseas. Training in Germany for the T.A."

"The T.A.?"

"You know, the territorial army. We'll get married when he gets back."

Josey rolled her eyes, showing Jennifer that she didn't believe a word of it. Janine took her headphones off and studied Jennifer sceptically.

Jennifer gave her a friendly smile. "Hi, I'm Jennifer."

"Awright. You don't look the type to not be married, don't sound like it neither."

"Well," Jennifer shrugged, "nobody's infallible."

"Hey?"

"Everyone can make mistakes."

"Oh."

The day-room door swung open. Jennifer turned to see the midwife who staffed their ward. She carried a cup of hot beverage and made her way to the only vacant chair in their circle. One of those ageless black women, there were few signs of the passing years on her Caribbean face. She was tall and slim and her attitude alone betrayed the fact that she was in her mid-forties. "Good afternoon, ladies."

They each greeted her in their own ways.

"Just taking a well-deserved break. You lot better mek de most ah your free time," she advised.

"I know all about not 'aving free time, I got three o' the bleeders already," Josey puffed.

Jennifer winced at how crude the woman was and wondered at her bringing children up to be just like her. She shuddered.

"So yuh becoming acquainted?"

"Kind of," Maureen chirped in, "Jennifer just joined us."

"How are you, Jennifer?" the nurse asked.

Jennifer got the feeling that the question was asked just for the sake of it and not because the woman really wanted to know. "Tired, if you must know."

The nurse chuckled. "What me tell yuh? You will haffe get use to it cah it ah go be a long time before you get to sleep when you feel like it."

"Wha' d'you do for a livin', Jen?" Janine asked.

"I'm a barrister," Jennifer replied proudly.

Janine's mouth hung open. Josey stubbed her cigarette out. "A barrister! What, in all dem gowns and wigs an' stuff?" She fished another cigarette out of the packet.

"Yes."

"That's like a dressed-up lawyer innit?"

"I suppose so… Do you work?"

"Did. Used to do night shifts at the local cabbies."

Jennifer couldn't think of anything encouraging to say about that. "Right…"

The nurse sat on the edge of her chair and turned her stern face towards Jennifer. "How a woman like you manage to end up pregnant and alone?" "The usual way — sex," Jennifer said flippantly. All the other women, except the nurse, laughed.

"Don't ask me that, I was at school, see," said Janine, before waiting to find out if she was going to be asked. "Got pregnant on my first time… well, unless you count those times in the back of the car, or under the stairs…" she giggled, "…babysitting at my mum's friend's house… kissing, sucking, biting," her eyes had a far away look and for a moment Jennifer thought she saw Donna's face in Janine's.

"…Let him in just a little, just the tip, but not all the way, that's what he said. Said he was just going to come in a tiny bit, but not all the way, but before I knew it he was inside, the whole of him! Before I knew it he'd come hadn't he?"

"Where's he now?" Josey asked her.

"Who?"

"The kid's father?"

"Gone off, couldn't take it when I told him…"

"Off where?" Maureen sounded more concerned than Janine was herself.

"Fuck knows," she joined her hands together like a bird, "Evaporated into thin air."

"Wass his name? I might know him," Josey dusted ash off her cheap kimono.

"Can't remember."

"Oh come on, don't be a spoilsport, we're all in the same paddling boat, travelling down the same river…"

"He was a black guy, alright? He din't wanna know…"

Josey rolled her eyes again. "White guys are just the same as black guys when it comes to bed, love."

The black nurse kissed her teeth. "See where all your lust and feelings get you? Is not me having to hide away, too ashamed to face people," she shook her head. "Why couldn't you have waited for someone nice and respectable to come along. A real man who wasn't just looking for a bed companion."

"It weren't like that… I loved him."

"Love! If he loved you, he'd have married you… what you did was a sin. You're not'n but a baby yuhself."

"Love isn't a sin, it's the most religious act there is," Maureen put her knitting aside and decided to stand up for Janine.

"Love is not an act, it's an emotion, and sex is a sin in my church. It's a sin… what she called love was nothing but lust, no matter how ole you are. Unless of course you're married, and even then yuh only supposed to do it to start a family, it's a sin to do it fe fun."

Josey glared out of the corner of her eye at the midwife. "I take it you're a virgin then."

"I tek it yuh should mine yuh own bizness." Maureen cleared her throat, cutting through the sudden tension in the air. "I hate this being alone, don't you?" she said to Jennifer.

"I'm not really alone. I live with my sister."

"Yes, but your sister doesn't share your bed or wrap her arms around you and make love to you when you're feeling the need."

Jennifer hid her eyes behind her cold cup of coffee as she took a sip.

"When I get outta 'ere I'm going back to school," Janine boasted.

"And who will look after your baby?" Jennifer asked.

"I'm not keeping it. Din't you know? I thought that news would 'ave got round."

The midwife took it upon herself to explain Janine's situation. "Janine was going to have an abortion, until the boyfriend's mother said she couldn't let her kill her grandchild. Told her to go ahead an' have it an she would tek care ah it."

Janine interrupted. "Only they move away, don't they? No forwarding address. By then it's too late to get the abortion an' so I went for the next option, adoption. Abortion, adoption, sounds the same dun it?"

Jennifer felt a tinge of empathy with the girl. Their experiences were quite similar in a funny sort of way. They had both made mistakes, but at least she had Donna to lean on. Janine didn't have anyone.

"I've decided to have my tubes tied," Josey lay her head back in the huge worn armchair, the cloud of blond hairs falling over the back. "Jus' gotta get Steve to agree."

"Three children already and you're going home with a fourth, how can you stay so calm? I'm tearing my hair out trying to figure out how I'm going to manage with one," Jennifer marvelled.

Josey's laugh bordered on a smoker's cough. "I'm calm 'cause I have to be. What's done is done."

"I'll be alright when my Geoffrey gets home. We're going to have a big church wedding. He called yesterday, you know, couldn't talk for long but he says he's written to me, I should get it soon."

"How long has he been away?" Jennifer almost envied Maureen. Her man so many miles away and phoning to remind her how much he loves her. Damn Paul Harvey!

"Two months, due back any day now."

The nurse stood up, regarded Maureen with a shake of her head and a look of sympathy. "Right ladies, doan feget yuh have kids out deh." She left them to go back to work.

"She's got a problem that one. Her an' her Christianity. Needs a good seeing to more like it," Josey laughed again and this time she coughed something up from deep down in her throat.

Janine stood up and stretched.

"Can't wait to get rid o' this lump."

Jennifer smiled to herself as she stood to go back to the ward. The lump, that's just what she'd called hers.

I'd given Donna a list of things to bring for me and when she struggled in carrying my small suitcase, I almost laughed.

"Was there really that much on the list?"

"Your portable telly, your laptop computer, hairdryer, curling tongs and make-up. More baby clothes, nappies, nighties, and clothes so that you don't have to go around in your nightie all day."

"Did you remember my mail and that casebook...?"

"Yes, Sis, I ticked it all off. There's even some chicken and rice and peas in there from Aunt Iris." Donna went over to the crib and looked down at our new relative. She took her coat off and hung it over the back of the chair by the bed. *"Why's he always sleeping?"*

"Because he spends the whole night making sure that I don't get any sleep."

"Really," she grinned. *"Can't wait to get him home."*

Home. I had almost forgotten that I had one. Donna lifted up the baby and peeled back the shawl he was wrapped in. Why was it that I was the only one who could resist the urge to pick him up? Why? I didn't want him to be woken up because as soon as he started to cry they would immediately hand him over to me. Donna stayed an hour before getting up and embracing me and promising to come back tomorrow. I picked up my laptop after she left and started writing. There were so many feelings I needed to get out of my system. I needed someone to complain to and my good old Powerbook was the perfect listener. And when I started 'talking' I didn't stop until I had re-lived the embarrassment of going into labour in the middle of a courtroom and my murderous emotions towards Paul Harvey as I screamed with pain in that delivery room.

An hour later I realized the lights were going out and our evangelical midwife was doing her rounds again checking up on our repentance. She stopped by my bed and pulled back the blanket covering my baby's head. "He'll get too hot yuh know. It's not good fe dem skin."

"He sleeps longer covered up."

She raised her eyebrows at the computer on my lap. "Working already? You can't wait 'til you get home?"

I closed the laptop. "I made a promise to myself, Mrs Thompson, that I wouldn't let a baby disrupt my life. I'm a professional."

"You may have made that promise but did your baby?"

I squared my shoulders, "Look, I didn't plan this baby, but even when I found out I never, in my wildest dreams, imagined that I would be a single mother. How do you think I felt when I told my fiancé I was going to have his baby and all he could say was 'sorry'? Well I'm sorry too, but I can't be expected to give up everything in order to bring up a child on my own. My life is too important to me to let it come second to anyone."

There was fire in her eyes. All of a sudden I was terrified. "Women like you mek me sick," the nurse lowered her voice so that only I could hear. "You're in a position to give your baby everyt'ing he needs in dis world. So what if he doesn't have a father? You should still be strong and do it all on your own... if he doesn't want to know, then fine. Look at all these other women... they really got sup'm to moan about... they've got nothing to hang on to. Even Maureen who goes on about her man comin' back, maybe he will one day but she doesn't know where he is or when she'll see 'im again. And he's the only thing she's hanging on to." Her hands clenched into angry fists. "I want to tek your world and shake it. You don't know is better yuh lose yuh time than yuh character?" she said through clenched teeth, "Put yourself in their place — no money, no house of their own, and no man."

The other women were coming back in from the day room. "Why don't you just go ahead and sign the adoption papers?" Janine was saying to Maureen as they walked back to their beds. "No I couldn't do that... I could never..."

"Auntie giving ya a lecture, is she, Jen?" Josey bounced in, the scent of cigarette smoke trailing her.

I smiled at her humour. Mrs Thompson shot me a look that wiped it off my face.

"Let me tell you somet'ing," she scanned all of us. "You t'ink dat you're the first people to have gone t'rough dis... you all t'ink dat your private hell is de worse... but believe me, I seen hundreds of gal like yuhself in dis situation. You t'ink t'ings so bad, because you've given birt' to a chile and your man's not around, the faada's disappeared..."

Maureen clung to the neck of her dressing gown as if protecting her chest. Josey just rolled her eyes. She had a man around even if he was a no-good layabout.

Mrs Thompson continued. "Well, imagine if it had been twins, or worse, triplets? How would you have coped then?" I looked around at the other women and we all had the same expression on our faces, what the hell was she talking about?

Mrs Thompson walked away from my bed to the window that covered one whole wall from the waist upwards. "I been t'rough the same t'ing meself," the nurse continued. "Believe me..."

We must have all gasped at the same time, even Lorraine who pretended to be reading her book suddenly looked up aghast. Mrs Thompson looked and talked *like a spinster who despised younger women still able to have children when opportunity had long past her.*

There were many rumours about her background. One had claimed that she had once been in love herself, long ago, but had been abandoned at the altar by her betrothed and that since then she had remained a spinster. Another was that the guy she loved and was about to marry had been killed in an accident and since then her heart had refused every other possible suitor. No one knew for sure whether there was any truth in the rumours, only that they had been passed on from one group of women in the ward to the next.

"…Yes, I been t'rough the same t'ing," she continued, gazing absentmindedly out of the window, "it was many years ago. When I see all you women going t'rough the same t'ing, my mine can't help remembering. Yes, I had a man once!" she almost shouted. She looked at each of us accusingly before turning back to the window.

"He was a musician, a very good saxophonist… a jazz musician. Travel de world wid dat saxophone, I even went wid him once or twice… to Paris, to Amsterdam, Copenhagen. It was wonderful. I loved him. He could lighten up my day wid a flash of his eyes and his smile never cease to warm my heart and, when he laughed…" she smiled and we got a glimpse of what she must have looked like as a twenty-year-old. "…the angels blew their trumpets in praise. He could make a rainy day sunny and he could make a sunny day warm… When I was with him, I had no worries, everyt'ing was just perfect. I was as happy as I could be and he was as gentle as de summer breeze. And when he had to go away to play wid his band, wherever it was, he would always call me at night to tell me how much he was missing me." We were all sitting on our beds in hushed silence like attentive primary school children at story time.

"…And before long I was pregnant," Nurse Thompson sniffed. "I couldn't help it, this was the man I wanted in my life and I knew that he was going to tek care of my baby. He watched my stomach get bigger and bigger, day by day and made me promise many times over that if anyt'ing happened to him I would tek care of his baby. Ah course, I didn't want him to speak like dat. Not'n was going to 'appen to him and we were going to bring up baby together, that I was sure of." She looked over at Maureen who held her eyes for a few seconds before breaking the gaze.

"I even got ready to marry him. He had insisted that we should do things properly and I had chosen a white dress and was getting everyt'ing prepared. The day before the wedding we had arranged to meet at our favourite spot, under a large blossoming tree by de stream. But he didn't show up. I tried to call him all day, and the next day, but it was like he had vanished completely…"

By now tears were streaming down Nurse Thompson's face. I wanted to go to her, to put my arms around her, but at the same time I didn't want her to stop talking. I wanted to hear the rest of the story.

"...A week later, my son was born. Even when I lay there in the maternity ward, just like you are now, I hoped, expected that he would show up. I had left messages for him everywhere I could think of and I prayed that he would get one of dem. Even if he didn't, he knew I was due, he had no excuse. Okay, he missed the wedding, but how could he miss the birth of our child which he had often talked about being present at? Well, I didn't hear a word from him an' you know how not'n soon stretches into not'n. By the time I accepted that he wasn't going to ever show up, my son was already on the way." She produced a tissue from her pocket and mopped tears from her brown cheeks.

"I bought myself a wedding ring and went away for a few weeks to give birth to my baby. When I returned I told everyone my husband had drowned on our honeymoon. I became a widow, so dat people in the church wouldn't have to keep asking me questions as to where the child's faada was. You see, it was different back then. In those days, you could bring shame on top of the whole family by giving birth out ah wedlock. It's different nowadays. Some of you women even get praise, but not from me, be sure ah dat... Because I've paid for my hot moment of passion many times over. All that's left for me to do now is to work hard and look after my child as best as I can. That's what you ladies should be doing." The hard opinionated side to her personality returned. "You all fill in yuh breakfast menus yet?"

Speechless, we simply nodded. "Good, You know where I am if you want me." She marched out of the ward taking deep breaths and straightening her starched uniform as she went.

How can life be so unfair? If men could see the devastation they left in women's lives when they betrayed them, wouldn't they become more responsible? If it were their lives that were turned upside down, inside out, never to be the same again, wouldn't they all become celibate? Maybe not. The only guaranteed way to get a baby father to understand the pain of a woman is to hang him upside down by the balls.

I lay there the next morning listening to our silence. The baby on my chest, lulled to sleep by my heartbeat, blew a saliva bubble. I rose slowly and placed him back in his crib. I still haven't felt this bond that I'm supposed to. And I'm hardly likely to, because every time I look at him I see his father and all the other men who have ruined women's lives.

The other sounds of the hospital floated in to me, breakfast being served, the shifts changing over and medication being given out.

Maureen was sitting on her bed folding a letter.

"From your boyfriend?"

She looked up. "Uh… yes," she quickly unfolded it and handed it to me.

I put a hand up to stop her. "Oh no, I didn't mean to be nosey."

"No, that's okay I'd like you to read it." I took the letter from her outstretched hand. "He'll be home in a week, says I might as well go home and wait for him."

I scanned the letter not really reading it. "That's great." I felt pity for this woman with her delusions. She still couldn't believe that her man didn't feel the same way about their child as she did.

"I'm leaving today." She was glowing, but it seemed like a mask covering a sadness. I wanted to change the subject, I wasn't too good at acting. I looked over at the bed opposite mine. "Where's Janine?"

"Her labour started an hour ago. They wheeled her away to theatre. Poor kid. She's going to go through all that pain and not even get to see or hold her baby."

I wouldn't see Janine again. They put her on a ward with no babies and no pregnant women. I lay on the bed, all my dreams and hopes had burst like bubbles in front of my eyes. Where were my dreams of walking down the Champs-Elysee with a panther by my side, just as Josephine Baker had done, and of flying my own private jet across the ocean? The longer I stayed in the maternity ward, the more I was reminded that I was nothing more than a baby mother. For my sanity's sake, I had to get out.

The next day, without warning, Elaine, Karen and Beverly strolled into the maternity ward, eager to give the new baby the once over. Jennifer put her laptop down when she saw them and they each showered her with hugs and congratulations.

Karen peered into the crib. "Bwoy 'im small, eeh?" She shrugged off her coat, revealing her tiny belted waist and pulled up a seat. Jennifer looked on enviously, she hadn't been able to wear a belt for months. Karen's hair had also recently been seen to by a hairdresser and she wore it short with a feathered cut. One of the first things Jennifer promised to treat herself to when she got out of the hospital was an appointment at the hairdresser's to take the extensions out of her hair.

Beverly, still big, maybe bigger than ever, was already lifting him out of the crib. "How much did he weigh?" she said, smiling down at him.

Why do people always ask that? Jennifer wondered. "Seven pounds, four ounces." How come when Beverly picks him up his head and arms don't flop the way they do when I pick him up?

"My two both weighed nearly nine pounds," Karen quipped, "but then they were both a week late too."

"You know why that happened, Karen?" Elaine asked taking off her scarf. She had a dark red love bite on her neck which she had obviously forgotten about. "Because your baby heard you cussing and decided to stay in a while longer to buil' itself up first. Nuh true?"

"Don't budda mek me start 'pon you an' dat excuse for a man you 'ave deh," Karen retorted. 'Cause if he was any kinda man he woulda had you knocked up by now."

"Oooh," Beverly chimed, "you gonna let her get away with that?"

Elaine was about to say something when Jennifer cut in. "Ladies please, you're in a maternity ward."

Elaine held her peace. Beverly turned her attentions back to the baby. "He looks nothing like you, Jen. Do ya," she cooed, "look nothing like mummy."

Cheer me up, Bev, why don't you. Jennifer sighed, "I know." She moved up on the bed to let Elaine sit down and felt her stitches strain. She immediately straightened her legs again. Sucker had torn her flesh just coming into this world. "You never met Paul but you see that determined little mouth? It's his."

"Bastard! Never mind Jen, what goes around comes around, he'll find out the hard way."

Jennifer wished she could agree, but in her experience it was always the shits that prospered.

"My Natasha's like that, she has her damned father's eyes. She even gives me his stare when she's upset," Karen shuddered. "Spooky."

"God knows who Jerome looks like. He certainly doesn't look like either of us — his parents." Beverly rocked the baby in her arms, as he started to wriggle. "I sometimes wonder if they mixed the black babies up in the maternity ward just for a laugh."

"I hope my baby looks like Allan, he is just so handsome. The baby's got to have my teeth though 'cause Allan's leave a lot to be desired."

The other three women all stared at Elaine as if waiting for an announcement. "Well, you pregnant?" Karen snapped finally.

"No... not yet but we've decided to try... properly. Now that we're married."

"You've been married nearly six months, what's the hold up?"

Elaine ignored Karen and took the baby's little ski cap off his head instead. His hair was his best feature in Jennifer's opinion.

"You haven't said what you're gonna call him."

Jennifer didn't have a name for him yet and she was in no hurry. Names bred familiarity and she couldn't risk being too attached to him. "I haven't decided yet." Her friends looked at her like she was crazy. "But I'm open to offers."

"You 'ave nine months to mek up yuh mine an' nuh do it yet?"

"You know how it is," she protested, "you don't know if it's going to be a boy or a girl…"

Beverly nodded her head understandingly. "I didn't pick Jerome's name until he was a week old. I had a list of girl and boy names and when I knew it was a boy I just picked one that suited him."

The baby was now in Karen's arms. She sat by the window with him on her lap, his legs curled up towards his stomach and sucking on his fist noiselessly.

"Uh-uh, you know what dat means? Breast-feeding used to make me so horny, I'd have to jump on Charles as soon as I finished feeding."

Jennifer forced a smile, but felt deflated. He needed feeding again? Where the hell did he put it all? She preferred to wait until he was actually crying for it, but Karen was already handing him back to her.

Even as the thought of feeding came into her mind Jennifer's breasts filled up with milk. Now she was ready to do almost anything that would get rid of the feeling of carrying around two lumpy rugby balls in her bra.

Her friends stood around the bed engrossed with the process of his feeding. Jennifer ladled one rock hard breast from her white maternity bra and gingerly guided the tender nipple to his gaping mouth just as she'd been shown by the midwife. Oh God! It hurt, her toes curled and her buttocks clenched as he sucked his mother's flesh eagerly.

Jennifer assured herself that she was only putting up with this now because she had been told it would stop him being a sickly baby, no colds or sniffles. Apparently breast-feeding was also good for the mother because it helped to contract the womb muscles. She could definitely do with some of that.

"I breast-fed Kyle for six weeks and then stopped," Karen offered. "I didn't have time to sit around for hours with my tit stuck in the kid's mouth."

"Exactly," Jennifer agreed. "Every time he wakes up he's hungry."

"That'll settle down," Beverly said. "Don't worry, motherhood has its ups and downs but you deal with it. I'm still breast-feeding Jerome, y'know."

They all stared at her horrified. Her son had to be nearly eighteen months old.

Karen slapped her arm, "No!"

"The milk's still coming. It's our bonding time, while he's on the breast I read to him."

"Fuck that!" Karen said, then immediately slapped a hand to her mouth. Other visitors and mothers had turned to stare. Jennifer shared her sentiments exactly. There was absolutely no way that this child was going to have access to her nipples once he had teeth in his head.

Elaine stroked one of his tiny brown hands. "Babies. They're so precious aren't they? I mean, who'd have thought that a simple act like sex could create another human being?"

"It's been happening for millions of years, El," Beverly chuckled.

"I know that, but…" her words died away.

"Anyway," Karen interrupted, "we should have brought some champagne… wet de baby head, plus welcome Jennifer to the club."

"What club?" Jennifer asked.

There was a mischievous glint in Karen's eyes. "The baby mother club of course."

A shiver ran down Jennifer's back.

SIX

The day Jennifer was due to leave the hospital it was snowing. Donna had gone out and bought a baby seat and arrived at the hospital in her sister's car on time. Jennifer felt strange carrying her baby to the car park, Donna beside her carrying her personal effects. She felt totally alienated to the woman she had become. Since being in hospital she had put on ten pounds, rather than lost it as she assumed she would once she gave birth, she had a chest which looked like it belonged to a Swedish masseur and she was still having to wear a maternity dress, which only added to her feeling of unease.

The journey home was like a sentimental journey down the streets she used to know in her former life. Looking out the car window she noticed a young woman outside a newsagents, noticed the way she flicked her hair off her face as she chatted to her boyfriend, noticed her youthful body, noticed her taut, size ten denim-covered buttocks, a behind like she used to have before all this. Jennifer was filled with dismay, depression oozed into her mind. She knew what she had to do. She would renew her membership at the health club and start going to Elaine's Afrobics class. She would even invest in an exercise bike to snatch some extra workout time at home. Pretty soon no one would even suspect that she had been pregnant.

To Jennifer's surprise the flat was actually tidy when they got home. Donna had even cleaned the cooker, which was a first, mopped and polished the floors, and there wasn't a single dirty garment in the wash basket!

Jennifer handed the baby to her sister as they climbed the spiral staircase to the bedrooms. Donna had prepared her room for him. She had put sheets in his cot and hung a musical mobile up over it. Everything was perfect. "You better put your feet up while Junior's asleep. I'll make you some tea."

It was good to be home again. Her own bed, own food, her own privacy. Jennifer had made up her mind that he could have breast milk but she had no intention of going around with a baby attached to her nipple. She would buy one of those machines to express her milk. That way Donna could feed him sometimes. After putting the baby down and switching the intercom on, Jennifer went downstairs to the living room for the tea. She sat down on the comfortable Chesterfield sofa, picked a magazine from the stack in the wicker basket and flicked on the state-of-the-art widescreen television. In the middle of her desk was a pile of letters already opened. She looked around the room, considering its potential. She had already set her sights on her home as an office.

"D, this mail, have I seen it all?"

"A couple came this morning, Sis," she called from the kitchen.

She picked the new ones off the top. The first envelope contained a card, the front of which showed a black woman and her husband holding their baby proudly between them. Intrigued, Jennifer opened it. When Donna brought in the tea, Jennifer was frozen stiff, a ghostly look on her face. "What's up, Sis?"

"He sent a card... with some guilt money inside." Jennifer handed the card to Donna. It was signed by Paul and contained a cheque for two hundred pounds.

"I suppose he feels this makes up for everything..."

"I don't want it." Jennifer was already opening the other envelopes.

"Don't be silly, Sis, it's money and you and Junior deserve it."

"If I accept it he'll think everything's all right, as though I was saying the money makes up for it all."

"But he says here that he'll be sending you a cheque every month."

Jennifer was silent, reading a letter from the office. The case she had had adjourned because of her untimely labour was coming up again in three weeks. She had just three weeks to fill herself in again, contact the witnesses and read up on her briefs.

"Damn, I'm going to have to start working immediately," she said reaching for her laptop.

"Sis, you've just got out of the hospital. Don't you wanna ketch some

Zees."

"I'm fine, D, couldn't wait to get back."

"What should I do with the cheque?"

"You have it… or better yet open an account for Junior with it."

Donna shrugged, "Don't stay up for too long y'know. The baby's gonna need you when he wakes up. I read up on it, you're supposed to rest when he does, so that you don't tire yourself out."

Jennifer knew this but she had things that needed doing now. Not later or tomorrow. Now. She carried a file back to her desk and picked up the phone. There were more important things in heaven and earth than her son's sleeping habits. If she and 'Junior' were to agree he would quickly have to become an asset instead of a ball and chain.

Junior, as Donna had named him, woke up an hour later and cried until I was forced to stop work. I'd been so engrossed in my work to even notice that the pizza Donna had laid out for me was now cold. In that hour I had almost begun to feel like my old self again. Not Jennifer Edwards, the single mother, but Jennifer Edwards, barrister. Donna's fallen in love with the baby and talks to him as though he can understand. Every little noise, she's jumping up to see to him. She doesn't seem to mind carrying him around the house all day whispering to him, cuddling him. She's even taken a week off college to help me look after him. Sis is better than a husband — she's a lot more helpful and she doesn't insist that I have sex with her when I'm exhausted. Like I always say: 'A woman's gotta stay single to survive'. Without a man around I can do as I damn well please.

At bedtime I ran up the iron staircase, while Donna carried Junior. It felt so good, I ran down and then up again like a child. Donna just shook her head. She had no idea what it felt like to be free of that unwanted lump. Thank goodness! Pregnant, I was breathless walking ten feet, climbing stairs had been like climbing Everest. Now that I had been given a list of breathing, pelvic floor muscles and stomach exercises to do, I intended to start them all right away.

"I want to go for a jog," I announced.

"Are you mad? Get upstairs to bed now."

My goodness Donna was starting to sound more and more like the old me. The old me? Had motherhood changed me? I hoped not.

There was no point in Donna sleeping on the living room sofa, so that night she shared her old bedroom with Junior. But as soon as he needed feeding she brought him in to me. It didn't take long for me to fall back asleep with him sucking on my breast. Roll on tomorrow.

The next day the three of us went out. Junior was now nine days old and I badly needed to get out and about. Top of my list was the breast pump, then to the town hall to register my son. The trouble is he still didn't have a name. Donna and I deliberated and decided to carry on using Junior, we could always change it by deed poll later. Of course I called him Edwards, he was definitely not having 'Bastard' as his surname like his father. Donna had started carrying Junior in a baby pouch. I had told her that I couldn't manage that much weight putting a strain on my back. The truth was I wasn't ready to be seen in public with a baby and no husband. On the way into Lewisham shopping centre two handsome young men nearer Donna's age than mine grinned at us. Donna ignored them and walked on, but I was stupid enough to turn and give them an inviting smile. It was the first time a man had looked at me in that way in months.

"You have a nice backside there, ya know!" one of them shouted after me and then I heard their laughter.

Yes, I told myself. I have got a nice backside. It's for sure you'll never see it though. Peasants!

The shopping centre was overflowing with women and their new babies. In Mothercare we bought Junior some proper baby boys clothes to make a change from all the yellow unisex babygrows he had. Donna was carrying on like a kid in a sweet shop.

"Jen, look at this," Donna held up a navy blue corduroy suit with matching hat. "We've just gotta get one… Sis, you see these?" It was a pair of lemon bootees with bows. "Junior needs some, can't be taking him out in socks all the time. An' we'll have to get him a christening outfit soon. Innit, Jay-Jay?" she warbled at the baby. "Does Junior want some stush christening outfit…?"

We put them in the basket anyway while I looked for practical things to make my job as a mother as effortless as possible. A baby rocker, breast pump, feeding bottles and electric steriliser, breast pads to stop the infernal milk stains on my clothes. Bibs, disposable nappies and dummies/soothers to shut him up. A couple of maternity bras.

Junior soon started to whinge, so we headed for home. There was absolutely no way I was going to breastfeed in public.

On the way I picked up a copy of Essence. The magazine is just made for me, written by professional women for professional women. Women who have the same tastes in clothes, hairstyles, careers. But what do I find? Page 50 was a true life story about a woman reporter who got pregnant on holiday. The father-to-be wanted her, but thought neither of them was ready for a kid. She didn't feel ready either but against all odds decided to keep her baby and was telling the world that it was the best decision she ever made. How could having an unexpected baby be the best decision a dedicated career woman could make? I didn't understand. Why didn't I feel like her? Later that day I started to take the plaits out of my hair. I'd had them in for four months and my hair had grown thick and long. My *hairdresser appointment was for the next day, until then I wouldn't start to feel like myself again. I missed the hairdresser's. Missed the people, the gossip. The proprietors of Hair Shack in Camberwell were more like old friends and I always received a warm welcome, good advice and a delicious cup of coffee. Maybe then I'll start to feel more like the old Jennifer Edwards.*

After two weeks of working from home and adjusting to the life of a housewife/mother Jennifer was becoming restless for the outside world again. The first week had seen people coming and going, visitors asking stupid questions about the labour and the weight of the baby. She hadn't realized how tired she was until Junior stopped sleeping through the day as well as the night. Cooked meals had become a thing of the past and Jennifer survived on take-aways unless Donna was around.

Hiring a nanny became a priority. There was no way she could work from home, and she needed to get back to work as soon as possible. She needed someone who was not overly expensive and didn't mind doing housekeeping as well. Qualified nannies only need apply.

Jennifer interviewed the candidates over the next two days, with Donna at her side for a second opinion.

"So you've been child-minding for five years now," Jennifer referred to the paper in her hand.

The woman opposite her was fortyish with hair just beginning to grey and tied back in a bun. A very matronly figure. Her skin was already wrinkling even though her face was like dumpling dough. Her huge arms were crossed under her hefty chest and she sat on the edge of the sofa, feet spread in front of her. "Yes. An' me bring up eight pickney ah me own." She pulled the red cardigan she wore over her bosom.

"Eight! Goodness," Jennifer swallowed.

"Dem faada was a no-good layabout, but 'im did bring in de money somehow, yuh know."

"Right. How did you find time to study?"

"Study?"

"Your qualifications."

"Me have me firs' aid."

Jennifer waited for her to continue.

"Yuh don't need no certificate to chilemine yuh know. I run my home wid a heavy han' an' a tongue of fire. Let one pickney step outta line an' he will know nuh fe do it again or else, nuh fe let me fine out about it."

Jennifer smiled nervously. A look passed between the sisters.

"You young people dem nowadays cyaan stay home an' bring yuh pickney dem up properly. I tell you," she pointed an accusing finger at Jennifer, "if me was nevah home fe me pickney, dem woulda end up skylarkin' 'pon street. Dat's another t'ing... when I was young a man's family was 'im priority, yuh understan'?"

Jennifer saw she was getting nowhere with this one.

"Bwoy pickney need a man aroun' de place," the woman continued. "Anyhow my son was to get a gal in trouble he wouldn't dare lef' her, 'cause he would have me to answer to."

"Right," Jennifer forced a smile. "Tea?"

"You 'ave coffee? Me only drink coffee."

"Okay, I'll be right back."

Donna followed her sister into the kitchen. "There's no way I'm going to allow you to let that old battle-axe look after Junior."

Jennifer sighed. "I know you're right, but I've seen five already and I'm getting worried that we won't find a suitable person by the end of the week. I really need to get back to work next week."

"We've still got time. Besides, if you can't find someone qualified, Shanika will do it, she ain't got not'n better doing and she's at home all bloody day with Naomi anyway."

Jennifer had no intention of allowing any such thing, Shanika wasn't exactly her idea of a responsible person. The idea wasn't even worth considering. "I can't burden your friend with another baby and besides she's not qualified. If anything happened we wouldn't be able to complain to the authorities."

Donna just gave her a look and mumbled, "She brought up her own child, didn't see no harm coming to her."

"I know she's your friend, but Junior's my baby and it's my duty to make sure he's looked after properly."

Donna lifted Junior in the air. "Did I say anything?"

The kettle boiled. Jennifer made the coffees and carried them through to the living room.

"Yuh nuh 'ave no biscuit...?"

Jennifer could hear Deborah's laughter through the walls.

The next candidate arrived an hour later. She was tall, slim and reminded Jennifer of a primary school teacher she'd once had.

"Tell me more about your experience please, Mrs Gregson."

"Well, I went to school around here and studied child development, child psychology, human biology, and sociology," her voice was soft and somewhat soothing. Almost like a hypnotist. "I then went on to work at a nursery as that was where I felt my talent lay."

Jennifer nodded. All of this was already on her CV.

"I was at a nursery in Camden for three years before going on to be a child-minder in my own home and then a nanny in other people's homes," she giggled.

It was such a strange reaction that a chill ran down Jennifer's spine. There was something not right about this one. If she could bore you to death just telling you about her career, heaven only knows what she could do given the chance to tell her life story.

One more candidate to go.

"I absolutely adore children. Could just eat them up if they were edible. Couldn't have any of my own you see," she leant forward to whisper to Jennifer, "Men, dirty creatures the lot of them. Couldn't bear to be touched by them."

Jennifer laughed nervously. Junior had begun to cry upstairs.

"Aah, is that the little tyke now? Perhaps I should meet him."

"Not right now, Mrs Gregson," Jennifer stood up and held out her hand. "I've got your number, I'll be in touch."

Donna was coming down the stairs with Junior as Jennifer shut the door behind the man-hater.

"Okay, give me Shanika's number."

SEVEN

I remember someone saying to me that because I had money my job as a mother would be so much easier, because at least I could afford to pay for full-time childcare. True, I can still afford expensive holidays, I can give my child all the material things he needs, but there's more to bringing children up alone.

Junior is now three months old and has colic so bad that no amount of hugging, feeding or lullabies will calm him down. I usually get home around seven every night. By this time Donna has relieved Shanika and is taking care of him. I used to love spending a bit of time when I got home checking my work schedule, reading or preparing briefs, then taking a glass of wine up to the bathroom with me and immersing myself in scented hot water and bubbles for an hour at least. Then I'd slip into a silk negligée and watch television or listen to the radio until I was ready to sleep. This is how things go now: I get up at six thirty, exhausted after only about a couple of hours sleep. With every bone in my body aching, because of all the awkward positions I've had to sleep in to accommodate him, I ease baby off my chest, put him in his cot and tiptoe cautiously out of the room.

Even before the invigorating effect of a morning shower has worn off Junior is awake and hungry. If Donna's up by this time she deals with it, if not I have to throw a towel over my shoulder and bottle feed him. Unfortunately he's still not yet old enough to have a bottle propped up to feed from himself while I carry on.

I'm generally at chambers by eight so as soon as Shanika turns up, sometimes in her nightclothes, I'm out of the door.

I work harder on my cases than I did before to prove to everyone that having a baby has not affected my abilities. I'm still as sharp as I always was.

When I get home Donna's usually waiting on me to take over so that she can go out with her new boyfriend, who I haven't had a chance to meet yet, or raving with her friends. I envy them as they dress up, laugh and go out to enjoy their freedom, leaving me behind with a screaming child. I've complained to the nurses and midwives at the clinic that it can't be normal for him to carry on screaming all the time like this. They assure me that it is, he'll grow out of it. Lots of gripewater and cuddles. I spend the evening walking about with him strapped to my chest because every time I put him down he screams until I feel like screaming. I lie in bed at nights with Junior on his back beside me. I can't help thinking of his father. I remembered the nights we'd spent together in each others arms. I want so much for someone to hold me while I cry. To put their arms around me, a warm male body caressing mine. Whispering with a warm breath that he'd be there for me. That he loved me and, no matter what, was going to take care of me and our child. I wanted someone to share what I was going through and I wanted that person to be his father.

I've been forced into having a christening. I don't understand this tradition. The child was officially named when he was registered. Why go through this naming before God when I don't even go to church? If there's one thing I hate it's a hypocrite and that's exactly what I'm being forced to be. Seems like a waste of time and money to me. When I convey this to Donna or my friends they're all blasting me:

"Your child won't go to heaven if he's not christened."

"Mum would have a fit if she found out you weren't going to christen him."

"How's your son going to feel when he grows up and there are no christening photos in the album."

"You can't bury him on consecrated ground if he dies."

"Everyone needs a religion. You're Christian aren't you?"

Am I? The last time I was in church was for Elaine's wedding and even then I wasn't too happy about singing hymns that meant I was a sinner no matter what I did.

They were the ones who wanted a christening, they could organise it. Donna dug out our christening gown. The one we'd both worn at our own christenings.

I said I'd do the food for the reception. That was before the discrimination case came up and I was again deep in paperwork. Two days before the christening I called Karen for help with the cooking. The phone was answered by a man.

"Hello, is Karen there please?" I could hear the sound of kids playing in the background and unmistakable pop music.

"I'm afraid not. I'm holding the fort for a couple of hours," his deep voice said. "Kyle's birthday party. Who should I say called?"

"It's Jennifer." I was beginning to think that Karen was holding out on me. Had Charles come back?

"Jennifer, it's Philip." Philip? The same Philip who had come to collect her after the reunion? It must be over a year now. With one lover. From what I had heard of her affairs, this was a record for Karen. "Hi, Philip. Look, it's urgent that I speak with her."

"A problem?"

"You could say that."

"What's up?' He sounded genuinely interested.

"Well you probably know all about the christening this weekend."

"Yeah, I'll be there with Karen."

So Karen was even showing him off in public now! Boy, she had been keeping this a secret. "The problem is I haven't been able to prepare any food yet. I've got relatives coming in from all over the country and nothing for them to eat."

Philip laughed. "Sounds like one of Karen's dilemmas."

I didn't think it was so funny but I laughed anyway. "So can you get her to call me as soon as she gets back?"

"I can do even better than that," he said, "I can do the cooking."

"Sorry?" I thought I heard wrong. This was Karen's 'himbo' talking.

"I used to be a chef, owned my own Caribbean restaurant before we went bust. I could cook you up some curry goat and rice, ackee and saltfish, roti…"

"You're not pulling my leg are you, Philip?"

"No! I'm serious. I'll go out and buy everything and come round. You can pay for the stuff, but it's a favour, okay? Any friend of Karen's is a friend of mine."

No wonder he was lasting so long in Karen's home. Which woman would want to lose a man who cooked and looked after her children during a birthday party?

"Thanks, Philip but really, I couldn't…"

"I insist. I'll come over tomorrow."

What could I say? I backed down and let him do it. It was either that or go out and get tons of Marks and Spencers ready meals, crisps and peanuts. Besides I was alone with Junior and he had started to make noise. I was about to call out for Donna to get him, but remembered that she was out with her mates.

We recently started Junior on solids to supplement his formula milk. I wasn't with him enough to keep my own breast milk going, but it was almost impossible to get him to take a bottle from me. Donna seemed to have no trouble. It was as though he knew by instinct who should be giving him the breast milk and who gave him the bottle. By the time I got to his cot Junior had stopped crying but when he saw me he immediately started again.

"Oh, so now you're playing games."

Oh where was Donna? I picked him up and held him at arms length. I had learnt by experience to protect my clothes before picking up a baby. I reached for the towel at the end of his cot and draped it over my shoulder. Once placed comfortably against my body he settled down, opened his eyes and looked right at me. "I wonder what you're thinking, boy." I hadn't looked at him properly in a while. He had simply become that screaming tiny human I had to put up with. His hair had grown thick and was soft and silky. He had filled out and the wrinkles he'd had at birth were now just creases in his pudgy joints. He seemed to be watching my face as I opened his palms, stretching his fingers out. He had the same shape fingernails as Paul. How strange that I should remember the shape of his nails. I saw Paul in Junior's eyes, mouth and even his eyebrows. All he had of mine was my forehead and nose.

"It must be about time you were fed," I told him. Junior looked at me not understanding. He gurgled and stuck a fist into his mouth. The sooner he was fed, changed and put back in his cot to sleep, the sooner I could get on with my work.

True to his word Philip turned up the next day with two huge carrier bags full of provisions. When I answered the door I almost didn't recognize him as the dishevelled, but cute man I had seen over a year ago. Philip now wore Malcolm X style glasses. His hair was shorter and he'd grown a moustache and goatee. Wow!

He handed me the bill, donned an apron, washed his hands and set to work. While I chopped onions he browned the meat. While I added seasoning, he stirred sauces. This was true cooperation, Karen was a lucky woman. For the first time since I had split with Paul I began to feel the loss of a relationship. I had thought about the physical, but had not missed having a man around. I had been so consumed with the pregnancy, the baby and keeping my career afloat that I was often too tired to think about a male-female relationship.

Would I have time for one? What would my priorities be then? Would another man be interested in me once he found out about the baby? If I did find a man willing to take me on, how would he feel about living with my sister as well? Would a man be intimidated by my career? While I had a man in my kitchen I decided to use him to my advantage.

"Philip?"

He turned to me while chopping fish. "Yes, Jennifer."

He was cute, I could see why Karen had been with him for so long. Nice butt too. "Would you think I was a good catch... I mean, if you were looking?"

"I like women like you," he said. "You're intelligent, beautiful, a lady with her own independence and means and you're good company. I admire women like you. I don't know how you find time to fit in the demands of a career, friendships, family, and other commitments."

I was grinning with pleasure and tried to hide it behind my cup of coffee. "Thanks. But women like me also come with a lot of baggage, like a child for instance. What is it that frightens men off about going out with a woman who already has kids?"

"Firstly, men are afraid the children will start looking at them as fathers and the mothers will expect commitment. My parents always steered me away from getting involved with single mothers — not that I listened to them." He paused to fill the kettle with water. "Men are like free spirits and sometimes they like to make their own decisions, move from place to place without anything to hold them back. As we grow older, we want to settle down and have children and don't mind if they happen to be someone else's."

"Like you?"

"Ye-es. Although I wasn't thinking that when I met Karen... When we met she told me she just wanted one thing: someone to share her bed occasionally. Someone to take her out and give her a good time. Even warned me not to mix with her children or her personal life."

"How did you take that?"

"I wanted her. At first it was just sex. Then I started to spend more time, weekends and the odd couple of days. I'd fix things around the house, take the children off her hands..."

"You made yourself indispensable."

"Not on purpose. It's just the way I am and the way I feel about her. I wanted to do things to help her."

"How do you feel about Karen?" I pushed.

He smiled shyly.

"Go on, I won't say a word," I crossed my heart.

Philip scratched the back of his head then scraped the diced fish from the chopping board into the frying pan. It sizzled and the aroma of peppers and onions filled the kitchen.

I got up to switch the extractor fan on. "Do you love her?"

There was hurt in his eyes. "I do," he shrugged, "but I can't tell her that."

"Why not?"

"She won't let me."

That sounded about right. Karen fighting not to get hooked and messed up by a man again. I kind of knew how she felt, but here was a man willing to do anything for her and yet he had to keep his mouth shut about his emotions. What I wouldn't give for a man to feel that way about me. I touched his arm and he turned to me and gave me that smile that I had first noticed at the front door. Aah, the scent and closeness of a man. If he wasn't my friend's man I could have fallen in love with his honesty and kindness, not to mention his good looks, fit body and cooking skills. Whatever Karen was up to, she'd better wake up soon or he'd be gone before she realized what she had.

The day of the christening. A warm May sun beat down on the small entourage. Karen climbed out of the Ford Escort and opened the back door for Beverly and her son. On the other side of the car Karen's children Natasha and Kyle hopped out and ran towards Jennifer's house. Karen straightened her clothes under her coat. Behind them a Fiesta pulled up. Elaine stepped out, locked up her car and approached them. Karen slammed her car door shut. "Do you think she's getting any yet?"

Philip removed a cake from the boot and followed a few paces behind.

"Who?" Beverly was trying to iron out the creases in her skirt with the palm of one hand while keeping Jerome upright with the other.

Karen rolled her eyes. "Jennifer, of course."

"Wouldn't bet on it. The woman's never at home, she's either at work or sleeping." Having seen the other two children take off Jerome, now twenty-one months old, was struggling to be allowed the same freedom. Beverly let him down but kept hold of his hand.

"She should need some relief right about now, you know her baby is three months old. The man disappeared when she was around four months pregnant. I make that at least eight months without any nookie."

Elaine cracked up. "Karen you're disgusting. There is more to life, y'know. Maybe she's happy with a celibate life."

The women all looked at each other — Beverly who had been without a man for two years, Elaine, who was a married woman and Karen, whose lover still gave her goose pimples when he sucked her toes. "Naah," they chorused.

The smooth soul with a touch of hip hop was pouring out onto the street from Jennifer's flat. A group of youths, Donna's friends, hung around outside sipping cans of Dragon stout and, the new lick, Hooch and Two Dogs (alcohol which tasted like lemonade so you wouldn't feel too guilty). The women pushed through the group. A couple of the youths were about to make a move on Elaine when they spotted Philip bringing up the rear and decided otherwise.

The guests of honour made their way towards the tiny dining area crowded with relatives and old friends, many of them cooing at the baby.

In the midst of it all they could hear Jennifer's voice. "He puts on a pound a day, I swear. I don't need to go to the gym, all I have to do is carry him around for a few hours a day, enough to burn a few hundred calories." "Yaow, anybody home!" Karen called out. The rude stares she got didn't faze her at all.

Jennifer appeared from the centre of the gathering and came towards them, arms empty and open. "Where have you been?" Dressed in a long white twenties style dress with a fringe, she looked magnificent.

"Well we had to go home, have a nap, do our hair…"

"Again," Elaine finished.

"Your fault ya know, dragging us outta bed nine o'clock inna de morning fe go ah church."

"Your godson's christening! It was an exception."

"Well so is my Sunday morning lie in."

Jennifer embraced Karen. "You didn't bring your mother?"

"I told her you only wanted her for one t'ing and she said she ain't coming," Karen said good naturedly.

"So no Johnny cake?!" Jennifer put on a distraught face. Back in the day Jennifer had had a thing for Karen's mum's Johnny cakes, not to talk of her fried dumplings.

Karen poked her friend in the stomach. "Looks like you could do with losing a bit of weight anyway girl."

"You serious?" Jennifer examined herself.

Beverly laughed along with Karen. "She's ribbing you. You look great." Jennifer laughed with them and turned to Philip who was still carrying the cake he'd spent last night baking and this morning icing. Philip handed Jennifer his hard work. "Hi Philip, thanks for everything. It's beautiful. We've got enough food to last until next weekend."

"My pleasure," he said modestly.

"So where is our godson?" asked Beverly still holding Jerome who was no longer trying to escape his mother's reach. This was unfamiliar territory and maybe he was better off with mummy.

"He's somewhere in here," Jennifer said, handing the cake to a passing relative. "Where's Allan, you didn't leave him at home on his own?"

Elaine explained her husband's absence. "No, he had to work last night. Being a nurse he sometimes has to cover other's shifts. He'll be by once he's got some sleep."

Jennifer nodded. "Let me take your coats upstairs. Help yourself to drinks."

By this time Junior was becoming extremely confused with all the new faces coming at him from every angle. Donna, meanwhile, was busy socializing with her friends. A number of relatives had asked her if she had any plans to settle down and have pickney as well. She'd grown tired of explaining that that was the furthest thing from her mind.

"So now you 'ave de baby you t'ink you can fine a man?" Aunt Iris asked Jennifer. She was studying Jennifer closely so she could report back to her brother, Jennifer's father. This was exactly why Jennifer hadn't wanted to invite her family. Married for God knows how many years, she didn't understand how the youngsters of today could bring up children without a father. As far as she was concerned, if the baby father was not available it was the mother's duty to find a replacement and get married as soon as possible.

"You want to fix me up with your son, Auntie?"

Aunt Iris threw her hand up to Jesus. "Lawd me God. Yuh t'ink I want my son slaving for somebody else's pickney. Fine de culprit an' bring 'im before God, mek 'im face 'im mistake."

"Yes, Auntie."

"Yuh ah feed 'im yuhself?"

"I expressed my milk so he could have it in his bottle at first, now he's on formula and solids."

"Yuh a tell me yuh useta squeeze out fe yuh milk an put in a bokkle?"

"Yes, Auntie. I didn't have time to breastfeed."

"Chile, yuh miss out 'pon the pleasure an' happiness you an yuh baby coulda get from breast-feeding. Yuh nuh watch a baby breast-feeding an see how 'im lickle fingers and toes jus' a curl up wid pleasure?" she curled her hands into fists and let them go again.

Karen rescued Jennifer in the nick of time and dragged her away from Auntie Iris who was already turning to find someone else to share her views.

"Karen," Jennifer kissed her full on her cheek with gratitude, "I love you."

Karen wiped the kiss off quickly. "Don't mek no one see you do dat again, yeah?"

Jennifer laughed.

"Elaine's fawning over her husband enough to make you sick. Come mek we sort this deejay out."

Beverly came up to them. "Can't you get that deejay to play something else? Do we look like gangsta bitches?" Jennifer had been too busy talking to people she hadn't seen for years to notice that about twenty of Donna's friends, each with a drink in their hands, had taken over the living room and were distressing her Wilton carpet with a 'jump up' they called dancing.

"Excuse me!" Jennifer shouted above the music. No one paid her any attention. She moved closer to the deejay's set. "EXCUSE ME!"

The deejay, his baseball cap turned backwards, looked up at her feeble attempt to attract the crowd's attention. He smiled at her before turning back to his records, his head bopping in time to the hard core rap.

Jennifer was in no mood to pop style however, and grabbed him by his collar. "Hey man! Mine my garms," the deejay said, straightening his silk shirt and dusting down his trousers unnecessarily.

"I don't give a damn. I've told you once before, change that music NOW. Put on something decent, this is a christening."

"Awright, awright. Bwoy yuh touchy, eeh?"

As Jennifer walked back to her friends, Barry White replaced Biggie Smalls. Over in a corner of the living room, Elaine and Allan weren't seeing eye to eye. "Always the same t'ing," he said, raising his voice. "I can't even walk inna de house good before yuh start hassle me 'bout pickney."

Carrying Jerome on one hip, Elaine tried to reason with him. "I just want us to have the tests…"

"What did I tell yuh? I don't need nuh test. There's nothing wrong with me." Just then Philip appeared, providing Allan with an opportunity to escape. "Yaow Phil man, I been trying to reach you."

Elaine sighed and turned around to face a dozen or so people staring at her, including her friends. She shrugged and joined them as Allan sloped off for a chat with Philip. The two men were the only two in their age group and even if they hadn't known each other too well to start with they would probably have become acquainted just for the company.

"Everything alright, El?" Beverly asked, taking Jerome from her arms and letting him back down onto the floor.

"With me, yes. But the black man's ego could do with some therapy," she glanced over at Allan who was now laughing as though nothing had happened.

Donna, dressed in a long satin skirt and chiffon blouse, now had

Junior on her lap on the sofa which was pushed back against the wall. She was holding him under his armpits and trying to teach him how to dance. His strong little legs were pushing against her thighs and he was actually taking steps.

"Let me have him," Beverly begged. But Jerome wasn't having that. As soon as Beverly took the baby from Donna's arms he started to bawl.

"Best see to your jealous husband," Elaine took him from her arms and Beverly bent to pick up Jerome. It was as if they were playing musical babies.

Junior fell asleep on Elaine's shoulder. It had been a long day of being dressed, undressed, handed from one stranger to another and quick feeds. Jennifer and Donna would pay for all the disruption in his day later that night.

As it got darker and the guests got more drunk the music slowed down, and people began coupling for a dance. Elaine had disappeared, Beverly and Karen were talking old times, while their children played outside in the communal back garden. Jerome seemed to have more energy than the rest of them. Jennifer excused herself to go to the bathroom and climbed the stairs on legs that had been in heels all day. Once upstairs she slipped her shoes off, threw them into her bedroom and slipped on her comfortable slippers.

As she was going back downstairs she thought she heard someone choking in the bathroom. She knocked on the door. "Anybody in there?"

"Jen?" The word came out as a broken cry.

"Elaine, is that you?"

The latch was drawn back and the door opened. Elaine stood inside, her face tear streaked. "Come in will ya."

Jennifer did so reluctantly. Big women crying always meant big trouble. "What's wrong? Have you and Allan had another fight?"

Elaine broke down as though the world had come to an end. Jennifer pulled her over to the bath tub and they sat side by side on the edge. Jennifer put an arm around her friend's shuddering shoulders. "What is it?"

"My period," Elaine sobbed.

Jennifer slapped a hand to her forehead. "You mean you've missed it, you're pregnant?" she said ecstatically.

Elaine let out a wail and doubled over hugging her knees. Jennifer was confused. Hadn't Elaine been trying for a baby? Then it dawned on her. Of course, if you were pregnant the last thing you wanted to see was your period. "You haven't missed your period, you're not pregnant?"

"We've tried so hard, Jen," Elaine sniffed. "I've done everything the doctor told me to."

"I know."

"You don't, none of you understand how I feel. You all got pregnant with absolutely no effort at all. I want to and..." she broke off again sobbing. "Allan won't go for the tests. It's possible he's got a low sperm count."

"Is that what the argument downstairs was about?"

Elaine nodded. "If only he would come with me and get checked out, then we could be sure."

"You've still got Allan, don't force the point. Maybe the problem is that you're trying too hard."

"I was so sure," she said. "So sure this time. I was a week late." Jennifer reached for the spare toilet roll, ripped a handful off and handed it to her friend. Elaine stood and faced herself in the mirror. "Look at the state of me. Could I use some of your make-up, Jen?"

"Sure, come on," arms around each other they left the bathroom for the bedroom. By about eleven o'clock people started to leave. Jennifer made her promises to keep in touch and kissed so many wrinkled cheeks she made a mental note to get a stronger strength moisturizer as she got older. The remainder of Donna's crew had gone up to her bedroom, and the sounds of muffled jungle music drifted down the stairs.

Junior was asleep in Jennifer's room with the intercom switched on in the living room and kitchen. Exhausted Natasha and Kyle were stretched out on the sofa end to end. Jerome was laid out on his mother's lap in the armchair adjacent. Philip, Allan and Trevor, a husband of one of Jennifer's family friends were in the kitchen playing a three handed game of dominoes. Philip had even insisted on clearing up while the women took a break. "So did Paul get an invite?" Elaine asked sarcastically.

"Ha-ha." Jennifer laughed. She still received two hundred pounds a month from him, occasionally with an accompanying letter but most times just the cheque. The money was all in an account for Junior, but Jennifer never answered his letters and he never called.

Pat, a long-time friend of the family was now handing out christening cake from an oval shaped plate. She was self-employed, the owner of her own successful textiles business. Not one to miss a business opportunity she had brought a copy of her brochure with her in the hope of getting some orders.

Beverly accepted a slice of cake, and shifted in her seat a little. "I invited Devon's parents to our christening."

"And what happened. They turn up?" Elaine asked admiring a set of ruffled blinds from Pat's brochure, that would look great in her baby's room if and when she had one.

"Yes they did. Then they had the cheek to ask me if the baby was his."

"You lie!" Karen's cigarette nearly fell from her lips. The other women had turned their attention towards Beverly who immediately felt uncomfortable.

"They walked in, handed me an envelope with ten pounds in it for the baby and then his Dad said, 'He doesn't look much like Devon does he, you sure is his baby?'"

"Bwoy, I'da tear up the money and dash it back in his face," Karen said.

Pat was furious. "What right do these people have to come into her house and ask a question like that? Why the hell would she invite them if the kid had nothing to do with them?" "They were always really good to me when Devon and I were together, I couldn't leave them out of their grandson's life altogether."

"You heard from them since?" Elaine asked.

"Christmas card every year that's all."

"God that makes me so sick..." Pat sat cross-legged on the floor, listening.

"Do any of you still like your children's father?" Elaine asked.

Karen stood and reached for the bottle of brandy on the coffee table. She poured a large measure and swaggered back to her seat on the floor, "Him! I don't even waste my time thinking about him."

"I hate Paul. How else can you feel about someone who puts another woman and his career before his child. As far as he was concerned the child was my responsibility and my mistake."

"Trevor's a good father..." Pat's eyes caught each woman's in turn. "We didn't plan to have children until we were well-off and set up but when Iesha came along we were happy, Trevor takes just as much care of her as I do." Beverly remained quiet.

"Bev?" Elaine prompted.

"Hmn?" she pretended she hadn't heard the question.

"How do you feel about Devon?"

Dropping Jerome's hand she picked up her glass from the floor, but instead of drinking from it she twirled it between her fingers. "I try not to feel anything, but I was in love with him. Sometimes I feel that if he came back and said he was sorry and wanted to raise his son, I'd take him back."

"He left you pregnant, Beverly!" Elaine gasped.

"We were having problems before then," she sipped from the glass feeling the warmth of the alcohol burning its way to her stomach. "Sometimes I feel that I didn't try hard enough to help him with his problems. We never talked enough."

"Charles couldn't stop tell me dat me talk too much," Karen huffed. "He was seeing the children regular after we broke up. Bringing lickle money every now and then." She giggled unexpectedly. "You know what I used to do whenever he came round... I'd mek sure I wasn't cooking and any food in de cupboards or fridge I'd tek it all out, hide it in the hall cupboard. Then when he arrived an' asked if I needed anyt'ing I'd jus' show him the empty cupboard dem an' ask him if he see any food in de house. The man would hand over some money quick-time. Same t'ing wid the pickney clothes, show him all the ones wid holes in dem. If they see you doing well yuh don't get not'n'."

The other women nodded and laughed with her. Elaine slapped her thigh. "He stopped doing that when he caught Philip there though, innit."

"Damn right. He come in, saw Philip lying on the settee and walked out again. Change 'im mobile number an' didn't even leave an address to reach him at."

"Naaah, that's bad. What, did he expect you to live your life like a nun, while he spread his wild oats?" Pat asked.

"I don't care what he thought. It's his kids suffering for his own selfishness. You wait 'til dem grow big an' he can't explain where he was when they was growing up."

"No conscience," Jennifer said. "That's what makes women so different. Men have no conscience."

"At least when they're young they don't have no conscience," Pat leaned into the circle. "When old age ketch dem then they start to t'ink 'bout family and want to mek amends. By then the kids are big, grown up people wid they're own families, and couldn't care less about his lonely, sick arse."

"You go girl," Karen said. They all laughed.

"Mummy," Kyle woken by the laughter, raised his head from the sofa, a line of dribble sliding down his cheek. "Lay down, boy," Karen said almost harshly, "I'm only over here." The boy looked too much like his worthless father for her liking. Her mother had always said a child conceived from love will always look like the father, a child conceived outside of love will take after the mother's side. Kyle seemed to have proved his grandmother right. He rested his head back on the arm of the sofa and was gone again.

"Allan told me that when we have our children he's going to set up a trust fund for them," Elaine said. "So that if anything happens to him or our relationship they'll still have that money put by."

Karen looked at her incredulous. "What's he expecting to happen? And just how much does he think he's gonna be able to put away when you've got children to feed?"

"We're both working. We can afford children."

"Anyway, by the time you have your kid you'll have a nice lickle nest egg there," Karen snapped.

Jennifer met Elaine's eyes and saw the hurt in them. Sometimes she could just slap Karen. Even if she had guessed Elaine's problem correctly, it wasn't fair to tease her.

"I never realized how much a small baby needed until I had to shop for Junior," Jennifer said, changing the subject.

Beverly lifted Jerome off her lap and heaved her large body off the sofa. Elaine watched her. For some time now she'd been thinking that her friend could do with some afrobics classes and a calorie controlled diet. Even going out more or getting a job would do, anything that would stop her sitting around alone eating tubs of ice cream and chocolate. She had once spent an afternoon at Beverly's house in which time her friend had put away two portions of chips, four pork sausages, eggs and beans and still had room for dessert. Elaine could show her the right things to eat and how to tone up painlessly. And, perhaps, she wouldn't have to be on her own once she was looking trim. The men would flock to her.

"Out of a group of five women, three of us have children here and on our own. Why? Because our men are weak," Karen spat, lighting up another cigarette, she blew a stream of smoke into the air.

"I don't know about weak," Beverly said, "but they have no staying power that's for sure."

"Please! Charles was all right about having kids until they wanted his time and his money, then he couldn't hack it. What choice have I got?"

Jennifer sunk deeper into the armchair and sipped her drink, enjoying the company of women her own age and the chance to get a lot of her pent-up frustration off her chest. "Our choice was in the beginning when we first got pregnant whether to have the child or not."

"But should that be our only choice?" Elaine asked.

"What do you mean?" Beverly looked at her friend.

"Men tend to say, yeah have the baby, because they're not carrying it.

If they had to get pregnant would they still say, yeah we'll have the child?"

"So what you're saying is that a man doesn't see it as a living person until the child's actually born, so it's not a problem."

"Exactly, Jen. Do a role reversal, tell him when the baby's born that he'll have to stay at home with it, feed it, change its nappies, wash it, get up at least three times in the middle of the night. Tell him that every move he makes the baby will be the first thing he'll have to think about. Let him know exactly how much stress it will entail and then see if he still wants to have a baby."

"So wha'? We mus' siddung wid dem an' tek dem through child rearing step by step? Get outta here! Anyway, it still wouldn't work because so long as you're there to take care of the kid he can do what he damn well likes."

"That's another thing, Karen. Why are you treating Philip like a sex object when he's trying his hardest to make you see that he wants to take care of you." Jennifer couldn't help herself. Karen didn't appreciate the good thing she had going — one of the most loving men around.

Karen defended herself. "I came to a decision in my life that I'm not gonna sit around waiting for Mr Right or anybody else for that matter. When I grow old an' look back on my life I don't wanna see me sitting on my arse waiting for him to float through the door. I did that with Charles, I ain't doing it again. One day I'll have a Jag in my garage, minks in my wardrobe, and a jackass to pay for it all. Philip's only acting the way he does because he knows his place. Once I let him think he's got me, I'll never get it as good as I'm getting it now."

"You don't know that," Elaine reasoned.

"I'm telling you, girl. Charles was exactly the same, promising me this and that. When we first started going out I was sixteen. He would always turn up with something for me, a rose, a teddy, a packet of jelly babies…"

The women giggled.

"We were only kids, wid no money. Useta lay in each others' arms and dream of having our own kids, our own house and earning enough so I wouldn't have to work."

Beverly nodded in recognition.

Karen continued. "Two years after we had Natasha we bought the house, Charles got a promotion an' we were living large, man. We had money, jobs, and friends all over. Then the mortgage rates went up. He started to take out loans and things got harder." Karen sipped from her glass of brandy. "You know, we thought having another baby would ease the tension. I can't believe I was so stupid, or so in love."

"But what actually split you up?" Jennifer asked.

"A lot ah t'ings, but I feel his dick was number one. He had the damned cheek to call the woman while I was in the same room and chat her up. It wasn't even like he went for another woman, it was dat woman's lifestyle he wanted. Y'know, she was single, no kids, no stretch marks, an accountant, her family were all lawyers, doctors, police officers. She had freedom and money," Karen spouted bitterly.

"What's wrong with these men?" Elaine marvelled. "They get it good and yet they've still got to get it better." She wondered how she would feel if Allan ever did that to her. She trusted him so much it would kill her. Elaine wanted to console Karen and reassure her that Philip was not like that. In the short time Elaine had spent with him she felt sure he was sincere. But Karen wasn't having it.

There was no point in arguing about men, Beverly reasoned. It was hard enough bringing a child up on your own without spending all your spare time thinking 'if only I had a man'. They were all strong women who could raise confident, stable children into successful adults. That was the point.

Each woman thought about it for a moment, considering her own priority in life.

Beverly wanted to be married, have a house and garden. She had exams in a few weeks and she was using every spare moment to study and revise. This was important to her.

Elaine wanted children, but it seemed there was obviously a problem there that she wasn't ready to tell her friends about.

Karen wanted her independence, to show the world that she was tough, so tough that not even love could break her.

Jennifer just wanted her career, the only thing she'd ever really wanted. The thought of being pitched into a meaningless life made her nervous. Who would she be? The need for money, status and a useful role in society had kept her going all these years. She had struggled for success, worked hard for it and at last she had reached the pinnacle of her chosen field. There was no way she would give it all up to be a mother.

EIGHT

Things have worked out quite nicely for myself and my little family. I'm back into the swing of the legal world. Donna is putting her head down and is going to university to study graphics and interior design. I'm so proud of her. Junior's still being looked after by Shanika and so far so good. At first I was worried about what she would expose him to, but I've grown to trust her.

Remember Tony Carnegie, the cute detective I gave a hard time on a case last year? Well, he's blown back in my life like a blast from the past. I was coming out of court today, a million things on my mind when I walked straight into him.

"So you ignore old friends now," he says.

I had to look up to see who it was. I recognised the face right away. "Tony." I was glad to see him. We hardly know each other but I felt close to him, like he was a link to my old life. Dressed in a suit that looked brand new and a little stiff on him, he still reminded me of Denzel Washington. Dark, tall, edible. "How nice to see you again."

He looked surprised. "Well, Miss Edwards, this is a change from the cold efficient reception I received the last time we met."

I remembered our last meeting well. I'd really given him a hard time. I flashed him a warm smile. "I don't know what you mean."

His expression was unreadable. "I suppose you've got yet another meeting to rush to, or a court case, or piles of paper work back in your chambers."

"No, actually…" I was about to tell him that I was going home to relieve my sister of my son when something stopped me. I couldn't tell this man that I had a baby. I was afraid that the first thing he'd ask me was when had I got married, just like all the others had done. I felt at that moment that if I told him about my son I'd miss out on the chance of getting to know him better. One thing I've learnt from my friends about single men, is that, to them, a single mother is for one thing only. Sex.

"…I was just about to go for a drink, why don't you join me."

He turned around and looked behind him and then turned back to me, studying my face quizzically as if he wasn't sure I'd spoken to him. "No one else around, I suppose you must be talking to me."

I laughed.

"And I suppose you want to pay for your own drinks," he beamed and then winked.

"Hey, I'm a liberated woman, remember? You can pay for the pleasure of my company," I flirted mildly.

"Should we go now?"

I thought about Donna sitting at home with my six-month-old son, waiting for me to come back. "I have to make a phone call, why don't you meet me at the wine bar around the corner?"

"Montenegro's?"

"Yes. I'll be five minutes behind you."

"Don't stand me up now."

"Would I?"

He was backing away from me. "Be there or be square."

I laughed as he backed into a wall.

"I meant to do that."

I laughed harder.

"I did!"

I used the phone in the outdoor clerk's office. Donna answered almost immediately. *"Sis, you on your way?"*

I lied. *"I've been held up, D."*

"What?! You promised you'd be back to take him."

"I know but I can't help it. Look, take him round to Shanika's, I'll pay her."

"Jen, I'm going out with Shanika."

"Well, where is she leaving Naomi?"

"At her mum's."

"Can't you…"

"Are you sure you can't get back?"

I chewed my lip, considering. My options were to either go back to a teething baby or have a drink with a witty, good looking young man. It was no contest. *"I'll drop her mum a few pounds. Please D,"* I pleaded.

There was a deep sigh down the line before Donna said, *"Alright,"* and hung up. I renewed my make-up and headed back down the road. The guilt wore off as I walked up to the wine bar and when Tony stood to greet me with a kiss on the cheek it disappeared completely.

I spent the whole afternoon being entertained. Tony was not only funny but he was intelligent and caring. He told me of his family. Being the only boy with four sisters he felt he had an empathy with women that he got from watching his little sisters grow into adulthood. His mother and father had struggled to stay together for the good of their family and had instilled in him a deep respect for women and family.

He told of how he had been at the birth of one of his nieces and reminisced about the anticipation, the longing for it to be a boy only to find out that yet another girl had been born into his family.

He said if he had the chance to raise a son he would teach him how to treat a woman. How a woman is supposed to be loved and treasured for what she does for mankind. There was a sincere sadness in his eyes when he talked about the way boys thought that being hard and dominant was the way to go. He really seemed to know what he was talking about.

"So did your sister take your advice?"

"Eventually."

"She got rid of Fitzroy then?"

"Yes."

"And she didn't end up being another single mother statistic?"

"No, thank goodness."

Three hours later we were still talking and then I remembered I had a life outside of this liaison. I thanked Tony for his company, stood up and swayed on my feet.

"Never fear, Tony Carnegie is here," he grabbed my elbow. "My car is right outside. I'll give you a lift home."

"No...! That won't be necessary." I couldn't let him come home with me. I still hadn't told him about my son and I didn't want to spoil the past three hours with the revelation.

"Au contraire. Besides, what kind of man do you take me for? I wouldn't get a woman drunk and take advantage of her... Not unless she was well aware of what she was getting," he said, raising an eyebrow mysteriously. I giggled.

"Alright then, we're agreed. I take you home." I had no choice. I nodded and was led out to his car.

The drive home was uneventful. I couldn't concentrate on anything other than how I was going to get out of inviting him in.

In front of my house I jumped out of the car quickly and headed for the door, then I realized I'd left my handbag on the dash and my briefcase on the back seat. Tony was sitting there watching me through the car window with a grin on his face and my purse in his hand. I walked back to the car and he reached into the back seat, retrieved my briefcase and got out of the car.

"If I didn't know better I'd think you were running away from me."

"Ha!" I laughed, swallowing nervously. "Course not." I took my belongings from him. "Give me a call sometime I might have some more work for you."

"Ah so yuh treat me?" He put on a yardie accent.

God, this man was so irresistible. I fished my business card out of the handbag. "Call me." This time I let my tone of voice do the talking.

"You better mean that 'cause I will."

As I turned to walk up to the house, I felt his eyes on me. Even after I'd opened the door he was still standing at the gate, a smile on his face.

"I didn't get a kiss," he pouted like a little schoolboy.

I curled my finger at him, beckoning. He shuffled up to the door and I kissed him on his cheek. Just then we both heard the sound of Junior crying. I nearly bit my tongue. Why wasn't Junior at Shanika's mum's house? I didn't want to have to make any explanations but before I could pull the door to, he looked past me into the house. Donna was coming down the stairs.

"Hi!" he waved.

"Hello." Donna replied coming towards us. "I heard a noise," she continued,

"I was just making sure..."

I turned around and gave her my sweetest smile. "Everything's alright, Sis."

Donna looked at me nervously, then at Tony, then back at me. She got the message finally and made her way back upstairs.

"You have a baby living with you?"

Oh, why did I have to lie? I had completely forgotten that I'd previously told him Donna hadn't got pregnant when I replied, "My sister's."

He looked taken aback. "But you said, Fitzroy..."

"Yes, well it happened anyway. Another boy."

"Right," he nodded. "Must be tough having them live with you."

"They're family, what can I do?"

He nodded. "I'll see you around then."

"Bye, Tony."

I closed the door behind me and floated up the stairs and into the living room of my flat where I fell onto the sofa, wondering why it had been so easy to lie. It had come out automatically as if Junior really was Donna's son and not her nephew. He just seemed more hers than mine.

"So was he the business that held you up?"

I glanced up to see Donna standing in the living room doorway, Junior held to one shoulder. Dressed in shorts and a huge jumper she looked like a child herself.

"It was work, D. He's a detective I'm working with."

She came into the room, sniffing as she walked past me, and sat on the armchair opposite which was big enough for her to bring her legs up, cross them and place Junior in the cradle they made. "You stink of cigarette smoke and you don't even smoke."

I stood up wearily, "What is this? Am I suddenly on trial for going to a business meeting in a bar?"

Donna gave me a cutting look. "Shanika's mum is gonna call you for her money. She could only look after Junior for a few hours so I had to get back early." She began unbuttoning Junior's babygrow as he watched me through upside down eyes. I sometimes wondered who was the big sister when she carried on like this. All I had done was take a little time out for myself. Now I was feeling as if I had no right to feel good about spending time with a man.

To get rid of the guilt that was seeping its way into my psyche, I offered Donna some money to go back out and enjoy herself. A frown creased her pretty face. "Was he worth it?"

"Was who worth what?"

She lowered her lashes. "Forget it. Just remember, Junior's your baby and not mine." She unfolded herself from the sofa, handed me my baby and walked out. I heard her bedroom door slam shut upstairs. What had I done wrong?

"Come on, girls, you're not trying hard enough. Work it." Elaine Goulden, dressed in a two-piece leotard and leggings with matching carnival coloured headband, walked between the twenty or so hot, perspiring women who were doing the shimmy in the gymnasium hall of the leisure centre. Women who had decided this was the way they wanted to lose weight or get fit. She passed Jennifer in her cut-off top and jersey shorts and slapped her backside. "Go on, girl." The girl was good. If only most of the women that came were that fit, but then she'd probably be out of a job.

"Come on Elaine, man. I thought we were friends," Karen puffed, sweat dripping off her chin.

"That's why I'm doing this, honey. Gotta be cruel to be kind."

Beverly stopped mid star jump and bent double clutching her sides. Her chest straining in the leotard she had squeezed herself into.

Elaine rushed to her side. "You alright, Bev?"

Beverly could only signal that she had to sit down, she didn't have a breath left in her body.

"Alright girls, take ten minutes out," Elaine announced to the rest of the Afrobics class. There was a huge sigh of relief around the room as the women all stopped their exercises and walked off into groups. Elaine stopped the cassette player and joined her friends on the gym benches.

"Bev, I should kiss you. Thought I was about to have a heart attack."

"Karen you were doing great, especially that wine yuh waist, girl," Elaine slapped her on her back.

"Now she waan bruk me back!"

Jennifer was dabbing her neck and chest with a towel. "I don't know why I didn't come before. This is much more fun than jogging every day."

"You always used to say you never had time."

"Now she 'ave baby she 'ave time," Karen flung Jennifer a disbelieving look. "You better start talk 'ooman, tell us what we doing wrong."

Jennifer wrapped her towel around her neck. "I make time for myself that's all. Plus I've got a minder and a younger sister. It's not like Junior's a small baby anymore. He's nearly a year old now you know."

"Bwoy, where does time go?" Elaine whistled.

"I know, I took Jerome to his first day at nursery last Friday to kinda get to know everyone," Beverly laughed at the memory. "Boy didn't want to come home and then all weekend it was, 'When we going back,

Mummy?', or 'Can't you take me now?'"

"My two was exactly the same when they started. Now I have to drag them outta bed. Especially Natasha now she's in secondary."

"What's happening wid you an' that detective?" Karen asked, raising a bottle to her head and taking a swig of mineral water.

"Nothing's happening. We're just friends. I like it that way."

"You're not sleeping with him yet?"

"Maybe he can't get it up," Karen laughed.

Elaine winced.

"He's a nice guy, we get along really well and to tell the truth I would hate to spoil that with sex," Jennifer replied.

Elaine nodded, glad they had got off the subject of children. It had become like a thorn in her side. She and Allan still hadn't managed to conceive and even though they'd both been checked out and knew the problem was his, he wouldn't accept it. "Come on girls, back to your steps, we're gonna step it up!"

"Aah man," Karen dragged herself up from the bench and made her way out to the middle of the floor. Jennifer jogged back, while Beverly hauled herself up with as much enthusiasm as a man going to the gallows. After aerobics and steam baths the women went their separate ways. Jennifer picked up a leaflet entitled, "Beauty From The Inside Out" and read it on the way back to the car. The author, Toni Lee, was a black American who was in England running a series of interesting seminars for black women at the leisure centre. Before the baby, Jennifer had taken a keen interest in black women's support groups. But since having Junior the single item on her agenda seemed to be work. Now that Junior was a bit older it was time to start doing things that she enjoyed again. Maybe even go on a skiing holiday this year.

Later that night as Jennifer prepared her bath, she chided herself for allowing Donna to go out tonight. Tony had asked her to go bowling. Bowling! The first time anyone had suggested going bowling since her school days. She enjoyed his company and would have liked to have gone. Over the past few months they had begun calling each other regularly, to talk or invite each other out for drinks, dinner, a show. He had become one of her best friends. Still only a good friend, Tony was the break she needed from baby things, family problems, the hassles of work. He was the sunlight entering her prison. She wondered about their relationship as she lathered her body. She had never thought it possible, but now she noticed that she was developing muscles where she had never had them before. Did Tony like his women hard, or soft and pliable? A smile spread across her face at the thought of him answering the question. He would probably say something like, "Give me one of each, I'll squeeze them and then tell you."

She only thought about the future when she really had to, because it didn't look good. Each day for the rest of her life would be like a slap in the face. Each year would be saying to her, your son is a year older and still doesn't have a father. She had to admit that the older he got the more she worried about the lack of a father figure. The boy had plenty of 'aunties', but no male role models. Tony sprang to mind again..

She stepped out of the bath and briskly dried herself with a large towel. There was one problem with her getting together with Tony Carnegie. She had a son she had lied to him about. Lied! She'd told an untruth on the spur of the moment five months ago, and now it had caught up with her.

"Mamma!" The call came from her bedroom down the hall.

Jennifer's heart sank. She slipped into her satin nightie, the one with thin shoulder straps. A nightie made for seduction on a night like tonight. Instead she had to see to Junior.

"Smile, baby," Donna kneeled down with the camera and caught a toothy grin from Junior. Around them children ran back and forth from the living room to the kitchen. It was a shame it was freezing outside. January was grey and although it hadn't snowed it was cold enough to. Jennifer wished his birthday was in the summer then she could have sent them all outside.

Donna had spent the entire morning turning the flat into a toddler's paradise. Balloons hung around the front door with a huge clown face attached to the actual door. Junior had a squashed chocolate roll in his fingers. "He's going to ruin that suit," Jennifer fretted.

"It's his birthday, leave him. Besides Mummy can always afford to buy him a new one," Karen laughed. Junior was dressed in a white shirt, with pressed pleats in the front and one in the back, with a navy bow tie. He wore baby suit trousers, and with his fade haircut he looked for all the world like a half-pint-sized man. His first birthday and it seemed as though everyone was having more fun than he was.

Karen's daughter Natalie lifted him up and carried him out to the hallway where they had set up a small slide. Junior struggled to be put down and eventually became too much for the eleven-year-old.

"He's growing up so fast isn't he?" Beverly watched him try to crawl up the short ladder.

"He's growing up and I'm growing old," Jennifer frowned.

"You're gonna be twenty-nine this year. Girl, if you'd started when I did you'd feel like forty by now."

To Jennifer that was no comfort. Junior hadn't taken away her youth, as having Natalie had taken away Karen's, but he had taken away her freedom. Her choice. She often thought like this and hated herself for it because she knew it wasn't Junior's fault. If she had used her own common sense and taken her own advice Junior wouldn't be here now and she wouldn't have children running around trampling cake and soft drinks into her carpet and parquet floor. He was something, though, wasn't he? An accomplishment that had gone well so far without affecting her career either.

"I feel good!"

I had earlier bathed in jasmine aromatherapy oil and was getting ready for enlightenment, that fulfilling feeling that I was expecting from tonight's lecture. American lecturers were always the most enthusiastic, the most passionate about their subject.

I wanted to look like a sista, a sista that had found her roots, who knows where she's coming from and where she's going. I picked out an ankle length trouser suit with a long knee length blouson, in Kente cloth. There was even a scarf to match, which I wrapped my hair in. My make-up was very light, almost natural. These women don't go in for the Westernized look.

My drive to the leisure centre was accompanied by the gospel music of Sounds of Blackness singing "Black Butterfly". I felt free. My first leisure trip out without my friends, Tony, Junior, Donna or work colleagues. There'd be women there like myself. Women who wanted to be told that they had a right to be selfish. After decades of liberated slavery, they could now go to work, buy themselves expensive gifts, etcetera, without feeling guilty.

For the lecture the leisure centre had reserved the same hall I had taken my Afrobics class in. It was set out with chairs side by side in a large circle. In the centre stood a microphone stand. Women were milling around. Some had already chosen their seats, others were helping themselves to food and drink from the buffet, a few gathered around the stall tables selling books and self-help tapes written by Toni Lee, but glancing around it appeared that the speaker had yet to arrive. I walked over to the book stalls and browsed through the titles. "Treat Yourself To The Relaxation Experience", "Confidence, Composure and Competence for the Black Woman", "Self Empowerment", "Stress Skills for Turbulent Times", "30 days to Self-Discovery", "The Black Man: A Translation For Women". I was tempted by that last title but decided that I'd had enough of them for the time being. On another table I discovered products for black parents, "The Working Woman's Guide to Raising Your Child and Still Finding Time for Yourself", "Building Self-Esteem in Your Child". There was a tape and workbook set that claimed it would instill cooperation and respect in your child through songs and play and I bought them both. So that I wouldn't have to spend the whole evening alone I made my way to the makeshift bar and buffet. "Is Toni Lee here yet?" I asked a young black woman, dressed in jeans and a white t-shirt.

She looked up at me. "I haven't seen her but the whisper is that she likes to make an entrance."

I smiled, now curious to meet our mentor. I helped myself to a pineapple juice. "Have you been to one of her talks before?"

"No."

"Neither have I," the woman bit into a sausage roll before putting it back on her plate. "I can't wait."

I held out my hand to her. "Jennifer Edwards."

"Reverend Fay Turner," she shook my hand and then chuckled. I thought it must have been the look on my face and was ready to apologize.

"I know what you're thinking," she said, "my name sounds like an old movie star. I think that's what my parents intended."

I laughed with her. Reverend Fay Turner fitted in perfectly with what was to come for the rest of the evening.

We got into an easy conversation about what we did for a living and our reasons for coming tonight. It had been a hard day and I told Fay that this was my way of pampering my mind. She agreed and told me she would love to have me come by her church one day and give a mentoring speech for her girl guides and brownie groups. I handed her my card.

Suddenly, over the loud speakers came the sound of drums. The rhythm deep and resonating. Before the drums there had been no music, just the sound of people talking. We saw it as our cue to find a seat but, before we could make a move, in stormed a huge woman, clapping her hands loudly. The room full of women turned to see the extravagantly dressed woman wearing the type of African costume that you only saw on the television — the turban-shaped headdress, long, flowing multi-coloured cloak. Heavy wooden jewellery adorned her ears, throat and wrists. She was followed by another woman who was smaller, dressed in a business suit and carrying an armful of office files. Fay and I quickly found a seat together.

"I have arrived. I am woman and I have arrived," the accent was clearly American. It was loud and authoritative and she wasn't even using the microphone.

Fay and I looked at each other. Was this her?

"For those of you who have never met Toni Lee, let me ask you, which one of us is she?" She turned to her companion. "This neatly dressed office type with perfect make-up, or me, big, proud of being African, loud and domineering?" her eyes were scanning the circle. "You want it to be me…"

The other woman hadn't said a word. She placed her armful of files on the table behind her and stood in the background watching the leader. "The truth is it's neither of us." Everyone began to mumble among themselves. The big woman began to unbutton her cloak and as she undressed, handed it to the woman behind her. Underneath it was a padded body suit which her assistant unfastened from the back. She took her jewellery off and packed them away. "We all wear an outer image," she took the turban from her head and shoulder length relaxed hair fell free. Underneath the suit she was dressed in jogging bottoms and a long baggy jumper. "This is me. This is how I am comfortable." There was a vast outlet of breath from everyone around me and I'm sure mine was among them. She looked nothing like the woman we had all seen come in. Toni Lee now stood before us, dressed like any of us on a day out shopping. She was stunning nonetheless.

Toni introduced herself and then her assistant, Ashanta. She had begun by showing us just how an appearance can get a reaction, that she wouldn't have got by walking in as herself. "Would you have felt disappointed?" she asked rhetorically. She already knew what we'd have thought.

She didn't disappoint us, however. She talked of liberation and our struggle against racism, sexism and the manipulative controls of society upon the black woman. What she also did was tell us that although we wanted to rush ahead of our black men into the twenty-first century, we had to first ask ourselves why? What the satisfaction would be to ourselves. Were we still just being controlled, wanting to prove to others that we could do just as well, if not better, than the men? Or were we doing it for ourselves? We had discussions on literature, white feminist writers and how their writing compares to our own. How their experiences became so much different when tainted with colour. Toni told us how her seminars grew out of impatience. Impatience with the all too few women's magazines and women's liberation groups that were the half-hearted attempts by black women to copy white women's groups. And impatience with men trying to give us equality. Equality derived from their needs, their fantasies, their second-hand knowledge, their agreement with the experts, Toni explained.

By the time she passed us over to Ashanta we were all spellbound. If she had been a man I would have fallen in love with her. Ashanta was to teach us how to tap that beauty within.

"Let's turn beauty inside out!" she started.

"For black women, a personal commitment to take time out for you…" she gestured to the whole room, "…may mean reshuffling priorities. We have the *unique roles of being a homemaker, lover, wife, mother, confidante - if you're lucky, student, artist and career woman and sometimes all of the above at once, our schedules are already packed. How can we maximize our energies to nurture ourselves when there are so many pressures and so little time?" Unlike Toni's voice her tone was that of a mother speaking to her teenage daughter.*

"The answer to is to flex that self-esteem! Since we've so much to do it's your only choice. Girls, what do you do?" she threw her hands up indicating that we follow her lead.

"Flex that self-esteem!" we chorused.

"Louder, I don't think Toni heard that. Come again."

"FLEX THAT SELF-ESTEEM!"

"Because the woman that feels good about herself inside is the woman who makes certain she always looks her best outside. Whether you need to jump some emotional hurdle, schedule time for exercise, lose forty pounds, or pull yourself out of depression, self-esteem will pull you through every time."

Ashanta covered everything from weight loss to nutrition, psychology to exercise, make-up and hair to being a mother. The latter being the part I was most interested in.

Up on the screen from the overhead projector was a guide that we all laughed at. Ashanta questioned us as she read out each one, "Isn't that true?"

A mum has to learn to:
* *Do five things at once — and do them all properly.*
* *Shower very quickly.*
* *Enjoy tidying up.*
* *Only iron what's absolutely necessary.*
* *Like cold coffee.*
* *Plan the day's activities meticulously.*
* *Change every plan at the last minute.*
* *Shut doors on mess now and then and get out!*
* *Talk in shorthand when little ears are wagging.*
* *Guess the end of her friends' sentences.*
* *Fall asleep within seconds as soon as the baby does.*
* *Be selfish occasionally.*

The last one she had underlined. 'Don't be afraid to be selfish, just don't forget that sometimes you also have to make sacrifices.'

By the time she had finished I was ready to go out into the world and practice self-expression, openness, to show people that I am freer in the mind than I thought I was. I even wanted to get up there and share my story with those women, show them that I knew exactly what they were talking about. I was still full of Toni's parting words when I pushed open the front door and entered my quiet flat: "I leave you love, I leave you the challenge of developing confidence in one another, I leave you a thirst for education, I leave you responsibility for our young, I leave you desire to live harmoniously with your fellow black man, I leave you, power, faith and dignity."

The Savoy was full when they walked into the lobby that evening at just after seven thirty.

Tony was nervous and kept fiddling with his collar. He'd never been to these places socially. Once, on a case, he had to spend two nights in the Hilton, at the expense of his client. He remembered how uncomfortable he'd felt, despite the fact that everything around him was designed for the guests' comfort.

"Will you relax?" Jennifer slapped his hand playfully.

"I'm not used to this kind of place. Do you realize we'll probably be the only black faces in there. All ah dem looking at us and wondering who we are."

"If it bothers you so much we'll go somewhere else."

"Dressed like this?"

Jennifer smiled at him. He looked good in his black suit and had even been practicing his posh-speak on the way there in the car. The Savoy had been an old haunt for special occasions and Jennifer felt a thrill coming back again as she entered for the first time in two years.

"Evening, Miss," the familiar top-hatted doorman saluted her with a smile. They turned left in the lobby, walked past the grill room and up the thickly-carpeted steps into the American bar. She took a seat at a table. Tony sat down beside her, awkward and out of place.

"Should we have a drink first?"

Tony shrugged, looking around at the glamour. "It's your date."

"It might help to relax you."

"If it does, I'm game. Let's go for it."

A nod to the barman brought him to their side. "What can I get you Miss?"

"I'll have a vodka martini," she looked to Tony and he cleared his throat before answering.

"Whisky and soda please." The waiter walked away back to the bar.

Tony gazed at the woman by his side as she looked around the room. She was strong, intelligent and sensual. The type of woman he had only ever dreamed of dating. He often disgusted himself with the occasional one-night stands over the years. A quick lay, no real conversation, no meeting of the minds. Girls who thought that wearing a weave and tight, short skirts was the way to a man's heart. Together their IQs wouldn't match Jennifer's.

Yet there was something stopping him from making the move on her. Every time he thought of them together... alone... in bed... making love, he wanted to call her, turn up on her doorstep, take her in his arms. It was an ache that only one woman could cure. But was someone else in her life? Was that why she kept him at bay? Just good friends. Jennifer was more than just a passing diversion, a companion. Of that he was sure. The lifestyle she led, this place, he would never fit in. But he could learn to couldn't he?

Jennifer gave a cursory look around the room, and she too began to feel nervous. There was a time when she had fitted in here amid the talk of politics and law; expensive second homes on remote islands; universities, celebrities. Her eyes met Tony's. She smiled and touched his hand affectionately. "We'll just have our drinks and leave, okay?"

"Look if you really want to stay..."

"No, I want to have a good time. I guess I must have changed. This place doesn't impress me anymore."

She could see Tony visibly relax. They chatted briefly over their drinks, finishing them quickly so they could leave that much sooner.

They were walking back towards the exit when Jennifer suddenly stopped. She pulled Tony to a halt. "What's wrong?"

"...I've just seen someone I know."

Standing near the cloakroom was Paul Harvey. A middle-aged white woman standing just behind him. Deliberately Jennifer took Tony's arm and walked towards them. Tony was surprised by the sudden intimacy but followed her lead nonetheless.

"Good evening, Paul."

Both Paul and his date turned to face them. Paul made a croaking sound in his throat before coughing to clear it. "Goo... Good evening," he stuttered. His eyes flitting between Tony and Jennifer were filled with a kind of silent pleading that made Jennifer want to laugh.

She extended her hand and he shook it woodenly. She then turned to the woman beside him who was sizing her up and down.

"Ah... darling," Paul said, turning to her but keeping his eyes on Jennifer, "this is Miss... or sould I say Ms... I'm sorry, I don't remember your first name..."

Jennifer glared at him. "Edwards, Jennifer Edwards."

"Yes, Miss, ah, Edwards. She... uhm... joined the Worshipful Company of Black Barristers... last year wasn't it?"

"Nearly two years ago," Jennifer shook the woman's cold hand. "And you are?"

"Paul's wife, Hilary. It's good to see so many young black women joining the profession, isn't it?"

Jennifer felt her stomach tighten and her eyes became bleared with a sudden rush to her head. It was her! The woman who had greased his path to success - and he'd even gone as far as to marry her!

Jennifer wasn't sure what the look on her face conveyed as all she could feel was a nerve jumping in her temples. She ignored Hilary Harvey and again clung to Tony's arm. "My... my date, Tony Carnegie," she said introducing him.

"Nice to meet you," the Harveys said as one, shaking his hand in turn.

"Darling, we really must be off, we have a dinner engagement," Hilary said, tugging at Paul's sleeve. "Maybe you'll come to one of our dinners, Jennifer?"

"If I'm invited, I don't see why not." Her eyes never left Paul's.

"Good. Are we ready?"

Paul nodded. "Nice seeing you again, Jennifer. Good luck."

Jennifer's heart was beating so fast that she thought she would have a heart attack. Before she could say another word the Harveys were gone.

"An old friend?" Tony asked and then when she didn't answer, "Are you okay?"

Jennifer's jaw was hard and her eyes held such a look of scorn that Tony let it drop, for now.

"I'm fine let's just get out of here."

NINE

"What's this, Junior?"

The nearly three-year-old studied the picture in the 'open the flap' book thoughtfully. Then a cheeky, dimpled grin spread across his face. "Chicken."

Donna kissed him loudly on his cheek. "See, he can read."

Jennifer looked at her cynically. "He memorized it. Don't you know children remember pictures easier than words?" she slipped a file into her briefcase. Dressed in a beige, classic silk suit with a complementary shirt

152

and pearl beads, she looked her usual stylish, confident self.

"No he didn't," Donna stood up and took the book over to Jennifer. "You bought this book for him two days ago. He's known his alphabet since he was two."

Junior mounted his tricycle and weaved in between his mother and aunt. "Dee-daa, dee-daa."

Accidentally he brushed Jennifer's leg with his handlebar. With a tut of annoyance she immediately checked her stockings for snags. "Alright, so he's developing fast. I don't have time now, but I'll read with him as soon as this case is over."

" 'As soon as this case is over'," Donna mimicked. "Ever since he was born it's been as soon as this case or that case is over, 'I'll spend more time with him', 'I'll take him out', 'I'll take him to nursery', 'I'll pick him up'."

Jennifer stopped what she was doing and watched her sister's ranting. "He's doing alright, isn't he?"

"He may be doing alright but it's no thanks to his parents."

Jennifer took that remark like a slap in the face. "Thanks, Sis," she said drily.

"God," Donna threw herself onto the sofa. "Why am I always the one getting stressed out, when you can come and go as you please? I'm single, I'm not a mother and yet I feel like one. I have a life too, you know. Every time the chance of a job comes up I've got to check with you first that it's alright for me to go for an interview, or leave for a few days. Why is your life so much more important than mine?"

"I'm sorry you feel that way about my career. The career that is paying for you to live in luxury while you study. The career that pays for your food, clothes and raving…"

"I'm not talking about your career, Jen, I'm talking about your son. For most of the time since he was born Shanika, Naomi and I have been the only company he's had in this flat."

"Is it my fault that I'm out before he wakes up and he's asleep when I get home at nights?"

Donna met her eyes. "You want the truth?"

"Not having my permission has never stopped you before."

"You could make time if you really wanted to. You're not the only barrister in London. You don't have to work all the hours God sends. I see you making time to shop with your friends, to go to keep fit, or out with the detective.

How can you go out with a man who doesn't even want to meet your son anyway? I just don't think you care about your Junior enough."

If only she knew that Tony had no idea Junior was her son. She had managed to keep Tony at a distance, never letting him get closer than a kiss between friends. After all, that's all he could ever be now. She never let him come back to her house for fear the truth would come out and she was too afraid to go back to his because the temptation to let the relationship get sexual would become a reality. "Donna, how can you say that," Jennifer was indignant.

Donna placed her hands on her hips. "Action speaks louder than words." It sounded like a challenge. "All right. I'll talk to Julian when I get to work, I should have some leave due. I shall spend some time with my son."

"Damn right, 'cause as soon as you get the time off I'm moving out for a while. I need a break too, and so does Shanika. We might even go on holiday."

For a few moments Jennifer panicked. She was doing this deliberately to wind her up. Then she thought, what could be so hard about spending two weeks with an infant. He was her son. Many women before her had managed it and if Donna thought she couldn't then she'd show her.

The thought of being totally alone with her son dominated her day. She had never actually spent time with him as a mother. Junior was three years old and all she could remember about his baby years were the worst months. The painful breast-feeding, the colic, the struggle to stop him spitting out the solid food during weaning, the teething when she had spent whole nights pacing up and down with him. Sleepless nights because he wanted to play instead of sleep. Baby food or milk spilt on her homework or worse still, on important briefs for that day. Cancelled appointments due to the lack of a babysitter. The potty training that had meant having a potty in every room of the house and asking him every five minutes if he wanted to go. The times she'd been walking around the flat barefooted and stepped in something wet or soft and squishy.

Had that really been a skip of her heartbeat when he'd read the word 'Chicken' or had that just been her imagination? After three years of motherhood she had to admit that she was practically a stranger to the little boy running around her home. The cute, dimpled face that sometimes bugged her to play with him. The strong determined mouth like his father's that asked "Why?" over and over until you answered satisfactorily. But Jennifer knew he needed a man in his life for balance. But she could only give him herself.

Jennifer's son. The son she hadn't even bothered to give a real name.

Two weeks later I was on my way home to begin a fortnight alone with Junior. Donna had decided to go off on a holiday to Tenerife with Shanika. They would be leaving tonight after dinner. You know, I'm not even bothered about what the two of them are going to get up to. My worry is that I won't have anyone to call on. By the time I reached my front door I was hyperventilating. I barely made it to the sofa before Junior had come running in, nearly knocking me flying.

"Mummy, look," he said holding up a cardboard model he'd made and painted. It looked like… well, it looked like nothing ever invented.

"That's nice, Junior." I had heard that giving praise was very important to a child of his tender age."What is it?"

He opened his eyes wide at me and said with a huff, "An airplane."

I nodded and smiled, that was encouraging wasn't it? Yes, I'd learned that on a customer care course once. "It's for you," he said handing it to me.

I shook my head. "It's too good for me, Junior. And besides I don't play with aeroplanes so why don't you keep it and then I can come and see it whenever I want."

He liked that, he was beaming. Donna was upstairs I could hear her stereo and for once it wasn't shaking the house. "Let's go and see Auntie Donna, okay?" I suggested.

Before my sentence was finished he was dashing for the stairs. Did this child never walk? It was a miracle he hadn't broken some part of himself by now. I followed him up and we made it to Donna's door almost at the same time. Donna was folding a pile of clothes she had taken from her wardrobe into a suitcase. She'd had her hair plaited into extensions again so that she wouldn't have to be bothered with styling it on the holiday.

"Hi, Donna."

"Sis," she whirled around and her braids flew over her shoulder, "I'm nearly ready."

I went in and sat on the bed. "So I see." Junior climbed up on the bed and sat cross-legged, his cardboard model still in his hands.

"Auntie Donna gonna buy me present," Junior informed me.

"Is she now?"

He nodded enthusiastically. I felt my heartbeat speed up again nervously. In a few hours I would be left completely alone with this bundle of energy. I hadn't brought much work home for the two weeks, just one brief which I wouldn't have to read until I was ready to go back.

"What d'you think of this?" Donna held up a tiny bikini against her T-shirt. Well I never! The top part would just about cover her nipples. Not only did my baby sister have better hair than me she was also better endowed, if you know what I mean. "You're not going to wear that out on its own are you?" I gasped.

"Course," she threw it into the suitcase. "Cost me twenty-five, I'm not hiding it."

Junior bounced up and down on the bed, "I like it."

"You would, you're a man," I told him.

"Not man," he pouted. "Am a boy."

Donna and I laughed. He had a point, but boys turned into men and one day he might remember this conversation and know exactly what I meant.

"So, you going to be all right?" Donna asked me.

"What do you think I am, sixteen?" I wrapped a plastic bag around my travel iron that I was letting her borrow. "Yes dear, I'll be just fine."

"Well, you know," she stopped folding to study me, "you haven't really had to do this alone before. But I've left a list downstairs of what he eats, what he likes to do, where he likes to go, his favourite books..."

"Donna, I am his mother," I reminded her yet again, "I do know him, I live here too."

She touched my arm affectionately. "I know Sis, but..." her words drifted off and I suddenly felt incompetent. What was it that she thought I couldn't do? Communicate with him? Play with him, be his mother? I could do it. The hard thing would be the loneliness. Day in, day out of baby talk.

An hour later Shanika turned up and soon after that they were gone. Luckily by this time it was Junior's bedtime. I put him to bed and then went myself. Tomorrow would be the first day of being a real single parent.

Saturday morning. Jennifer settled herself in for a lie in. She didn't have to work, she didn't have to shop and she couldn't go for a jog now that Donna had left her alone with Junior.

She had only just drifted off when the door slammed back into the wall and a tiny body flung itself onto the bed on top of her. Jennifer groaned.

"Mummy, Mummy," Junior chanted and then not getting an answer decided to use her as a trampoline. Jennifer turned over and opened her eyes. She wished she could tell him to go and bother Auntie Donna. The child was just a blurry, coloured shadow. His Batman pyjamas made her dizzy.

"Junior, stop," she said hoarsely. The bouncing ceased, for a second, and then as she closed her eyes and relaxed he started again.

"Mummy, Mummy, Donna not in bed."

"Hmn I know, she's gone," Jennifer whispered.

"Gone where?" He stopped bouncing and crawled up beside his mother.

"Holiday."

"Where's 'oliday?"

Jennifer sighed and sat up, flipping Junior over onto his back with the motion of the duvet. "It's far far away, Junior," she swung her legs off the bed and slipped her feet into her slippers.

Junior kneeled on the bed, "Can we go wiv her?"

"No Junior, she's gone in an aeroplane." Drawing her arms through the sleeves of her dressing gown, Jennifer yawned and headed for the door.

"Why?"

It was going to be one of those never-ending conversations that Junior so much loved. If she indulged, it could carry on all day.

"Why don't we go and have some breakfast?"

"Yeah!" He jumped off the bed and followed his mother to the bathroom.

Jennifer helped him brush his teeth first and then while she brushed hers he stood on the toilet seat, watching. "I can sing, Mummy," he boasted.

"Can you?" Jennifer asked through a mouthful of toothpaste.

He nodded. "My teacher learn me song 'bout brushing teet'."

"Teeth, Junior."

"Yeah, I said teet."

"Teeth," she pushed her tongue between her teeth and pronounced it slowly.

Junior watched and followed. "Teetha."

"Not teetha, just teeth," she did it again.

"Teeth," he replied.

"Good, give Junior a gold star."

He smiled proudly puffing up his chest. "You want to hear my song?"

"Okay, sing it to me as we go downstairs."

He climbed down off the toilet seat and followed his mother down the stairs singing:

"Dis is the way we brush our teeth, brush our teeth, brush our teeth. Dis is the way we brush our teeth on a cold and frosky mornin'."

He applauded himself at the end and Jennifer clapped too. "I did that one at school too," she told him as he sat down at the dining table for his breakfast.

He looked at her quizzically. "You don't go school."

"No, but I used to. A long time ago."

"An den you got too big?"

"Yes," she smiled. This communicating with children was easy. Why, it was even easier than talking to an adult. She poured milk on his cornflakes and brought it over to the table for him.

Junior cocked his head to one side, then sat back on the pine chair and crossed his arms.

"Junior? What's wrong with it?"

"I din't want dat. You din't ask me what I want."

Jennifer screwed up her mouth and was about to tell him off and then thought, no, that's perfectly fine, he was right. Adults have a choice, why shouldn't children? If that was the way things worked for him then she would adapt. "Okay Junior, what would you like?" She opened the top cupboard where they kept the cereals. There were two rows of the individual serving boxes of Kellogg's and she brought one set out and laid them in a row in front of him.

"Uhm," Junior scratched his head looking for all the world like a professor trying to solve a difficult equation.

This was going to take longer than she thought. Jennifer pulled out a chair opposite and watched as her three-year-old son picked out one box, set it aside and then had a rethink and swapped it for another one. "Junior, if you don't hurry up and choose one we're not going to be able to go out later."

"A'right, dis one," he picked out a box of Coco Pops and handed it over. "An' I only drink warm milk," he informed her.

Cheeky! No, Jennifer. She was beginning to see why Donna had thought it necessary to leave her the list. Junior was a very fussy child. Things had to be done just so. How had that happened? There was no way she wanted a spoiled child. He had to know the difference between not having something, and getting something without earning or deserving it. He had to learn respect for other people and their time. Looks as though whatever he asks for he gets. And if he didn't get it right away he would keep on until he did. Did that remind her of someone? Paul Harvey. Yes, Junior was taking after his father even without having him around. But cycles could be broken, she had seen it happen often enough with families that had passed through her career.

Jennifer decided that they would spend today at play indoors. Tomorrow, if the spring weather stayed the way it was today, they would go out and then, starting Monday, they would begin to explore his education. Donna had pointed out that he was bright so it was about time she found out for herself.

Water was dripping from his glistening, taut body as he positioned himself on the diving-board for a second dive. He easily executed a complicated dive before his well-developed body hit the water. Junior was jumping up and down excitedly by the side of the pool, as Tony swam the width under water before emerging on their side of the pool.

"Tony, Tony…" Junior was heading for the side of the pool. Jennifer rushed to grab him.

"It's okay, I've got him!" Tony called out.

"I can swim."

"Can you?" Tony lowered the little boy into the pool beside him.

"He can't," Jennifer smiled.

"I can," he was indignant. "Auntie show me, she did."

Jennifer eased herself over the edge of the pool into the cold water of the swimming pool. What a break this had been. She had spent the whole morning trying to occupy the energetic toddler when Tony had called.

"I'm babysitting," she had told him.

"Need help?"

"From you?"

"No, Santa's elves - of course me. I'm chief babysitter in my family you know."

Jennifer had considered it and then thought better of it. She couldn't afford the risk of bumping into someone who knew that Junior was her son. Besides Junior had learnt to call her mummy now and that was the big giveaway, he was now a baby who could talk. It wouldn't take Tony long to find out the real relationship between babysitter and baby. Children this young didn't know how to lie.

Then Tony told her that taking Junior swimming would tire the little boy out, that was all she needed to hear. She went and got Junior ready and told him to call her Jennifer for the day. He was curious as usual and asked, "Why?"

"It's a game Junior. Just for today," she lied, trying to make the idea sound exciting. It seemed to have worked perfectly.

Now Junior was proving he could indeed swim. Jennifer watched them swim away from the side together. Tony staying above water and close to Junior's side in case he should need help. At the other end they hugged each other and Jennifer felt a pang of jealousy. When had her son ever hugged her like that? Only on the odd sleepless night when he crept into her bed. She never encouraged it. That wasn't the only reason for the pang of jealousy though. Jennifer also wanted to hug Tony like that and because of Junior she was holding back on her romantic life.

"Mu…" Junior caught himself, a twinkle came into his eyes, and then he continued, "Jennifer, see I did swim."

"Yes you did, didn't you?" She smiled, pleased that he'd remembered to call her Jennifer. He certainly was a bright boy.

She bobbed in the water watching them whisper conspiratorially. They were swimming back towards her, man and boy. Father and son. The thought had crept into her mind suddenly and she pushed it out just as quickly.

"Jen, you telling me you didn't know your nephew could swim?" Junior giggled.

"I've never been with them when they go swimming. He's Donna's son after all and I am a very busy woman."

"Sure, sure," Tony winked at Junior and they giggled again, completely throwing Jennifer for a second. "GET HER!"

Jennifer was soon splashed to a soaking, shivering screaming mess. She swam away and they came after her. In the end she gave in to the game and began to splash them back. The three of them played pool kiss chase, until they were exhausted.

Back at the flat, Jennifer again stopped Tony at the door. "We had a great afternoon Tony, thanks."

"It's me that should be thanking you two. Bwoy, I haven't played kiss chase since primary school." He winked at Junior who was yawning. "Pity there weren't more girls, hey champ?"

"Yeah," Junior rubbed his eyes.

"I'd better get him up to bed, I'll call you soon."

"You off for the rest of the week?"

"Yes, while Donna's away."

"Good, we can do something else in a couple of days."

"I don't think so Tony."

"And why not? Junior will enjoy it."

"I just don't think it's a good idea letting him get attached to a man. He's never had a father you see, kids this age make attachments…"

Tony looked offended. He shoved his hands into his jacket pockets and turned to go. "I'll see you around then," he said and was already walking away when she said goodbye. Jennifer closed her eyes. Tony didn't deserve that. She was sorry she had to do it, but she knew she wouldn't be doing him any favours by encouraging him. Hurriedly she closed the door, put Tony out of her mind and lifted her sleepy son to take him upstairs to bed.

"Never mind baby, you've got us," she kissed his head, surprising not only Junior but herself.

Monday morning, the first thing I did was turn the kitchen into a classroom. We used the dining table as a desk, the notice board as a blackboard and me as the teacher. Junior was excited at the fact he was going to get to play school. I had dressed him up as though he was going to school. And I dressed like I remembered school teachers dressing.

In front of him he had a pad of plain paper and a felt tip pen. I decided we would start by giving him some first words. To my surprise Junior already knew some six letter words. He was telling me that he could 'draw' the words, Cat, Dog, Rabbit, Pig and Donkey. I said, okay, so you know the farm animals, what about street words? I gave examples: Taxi, Road, Shops, Crossing.

Would you believe, out of those the only things he got wrong were Road which he spelled Rod, and Crossing.

I remembered the self-esteem tape I had bought for him and brought that down from the bookshelf. Together we listened to the moralistic story told by a black woman and a black man then sang along to the song:

"Now can you move right to the beat?
I can do that, I can do that.
Can you touch your head, your shoulder and your feet?
I can do that, I can do that.

Can you shake hands with a neighbour or a friend?
I can do that, I can do that.
Can you spread peanut butter and jam?
I can do that, I can do that."

We stood in the middle of the living room floor doing all the actions, laughing at the funny bits and dancing around the coffee table. God, I hadn't had so much fun since primary school. I promised Junior he'd have to practice what he was saying he could do. The song went on like that. Giving the child accomplishments, like tidying your room, dress yourself, right down to pedalling your bike.

By the time we settled down in the afternoon I had learnt so much more about my son and his potential. I'd been missing out on this and all because of my work schedule and my refusal to let him disrupt that.

It's his father I really feel sorry for. There is so much he is missing and unlike me he will never have the chance to catch up. He might have photos to look at and I could sit and tell him just how bright our son is but there is no way he could relive these moments in Junior's life: seeing his small milestones happening before your eyes and knowing that this little talented person had come from you.

No, Paul Harvey will never have what I have — the love and respect of his son, even despite the lack of time I have spent with him during his short life. I'm now determined that years from now my son isn't going to be able to turn around to me and say, "Where were you when I needed you, Mum?"

"Mummy?" Junior looked up and his face was illuminated by the television. I was busy typing up a record of my day on the laptop and as I looked up I noticed Junior was running a toy car along the surface of my glass-topped table. No matter how many times I tell him not to, he only listens long enough to forget.

"Yes, Junior," I looked up from the computer.

"Well, you know daddies, right…"

He sounded just like Donna. At some stage I would have to start correcting his grammar. "Fathers you mean."

He looked up at me with puzzled eyes. "Is dat the same?"

"Yes, Junior."

"Well, why come I don't have one?"

"A father?"

He nodded.

I should have seen this coming. I'd had months, years even to prepare an answer and yet I was speechless. "Why Mummy?"

"Not everyone has one Junior. Some mummies don't need daddies to bring their children up."

"Oh," he said and carried on scratching my table top with the toy car. I assumed he was satisfied with my answer so I started typing again. "Mummy?"

I sighed, "Yes, Junior."

"But don't kids need daddies?"

"Not always," I paused. What do you tell a child who was not yet four years old about the real world? The realities of relationships. The ups and downs. Money problems, careers, sex!

"Did you used to have a daddy?"

"Yes I did."

"Where is he den?" I remembered the photo album we kept in the storage cupboard in the kitchen. Donna and I occasionally spent evenings going through them. Photos of us growing up. Pictures of Mummy and Daddy, friends, neighbours. I went and fetched them. Junior followed me, and we came back to sit on the rug in the living room. I opened one that contained pictures from five years ago and it showed photos of the four of us one Christmas.

"This is your grandma and grandad, my mum and dad. We were having our Christmas dinner in this picture."

He looked up into my face. *"Where are dey?"*

"In Jamaica. I've sent them pictures of you and told them all about you."

He turned the page and studied the next set of photos closely. *"Does Auntie have a mummy and daddy?"*

We were getting awfully close to the truth now and I knew he wouldn't be satisfied until he got answers. *"Yes."*

He came right back with, *"So why don't I?"*

I sat back against the settee and pulled him to me. Junior was watching my face closely. I knew I couldn't lie. *"It started before you were born, your father was a man who wanted to be rich, and if he'd kept you it would have stopped him from getting rich and so he left us."*

"He wanted money more dan me?"

"He wanted his..." I stopped, suddenly realising that I really didn't know what he wanted. I was not prepared to make his excuses for him. I was also not going to make anything up about Paul Harvey. Junior would only know the truth about his father. I wasn't the one stopping him from seeing his child, it had always been his decision.

"Mummy, did you want money as well?"

"Why?"

" 'Cause I didn't have you for a looooong time," he dragged out the word.

"I know and I'm sorry." I felt guilty. *"I was so angry at your father that I became angry at you too... because you were a part of him. Do you understand?"*

It was obvious he didn't. He was turning the pages of the photo album. Images of my happy childhood family were planting themselves into his head. I felt tears in my own eyes at how much I had missed out on his life because of my own selfishness. My son had had to grow up without his father and without the attention of his mother, and for what? Money! Status! What is all that without the love of your family? Your own flesh and blood. I hugged him to me and he put one small chubby arm around my neck and we sat like that for the longest time.

Jennifer had been trying to shut off her alarm clock for several seconds before she realized it was the telephone that was jarring her nerves.

"You were asleep?" The familiar deep voice brought her slowly round to consciousness. Her heartbeat increased and her temperature shot up ten degrees.

"Tony... no, no not really," she stammered.

"Mmm. What does that mean? Could it be that you're in bed but not alone?"

She chuckled, this was just what she liked about Tony. The ability to make her smile in any situation. She was exhausted, after spending half the night with a fretful toddler. Junior had had a stomach ache and wouldn't sleep in his own bed, but even in hers she had to keep getting up to rush him to the toilet. Jennifer touched her head, her soft curlers were askew under her fingers. Her silk headscarf lay on the pillow.

"Of course I'm alone. Where are you?"

"In bed."

"In your own bed?"

"Of course I'm in my own bed," he mimicked her coquettish tone making her laugh again.

Jennifer imagined him laying on top of his duvet with nothing on but his boxer shorts. Before her imagination could go any further she rolled over to look at the clock. It was only eight o'clock, but usually she was up by now. Junior moaned and curled his little body up into a ball. "What are you doing up at this time of the morning?"

"I was woken by a dream of you in your swimsuit and couldn't get back to sleep." She was his closest female friend and yet he often found himself thinking about her in ways he knew he probably shouldn't. She had trim legs, a nice bust, the most remarkable eyes. Maybe he wouldn't mind taking her to bed, but would she mind being taken? And what would happen after that? More than once he had found his eyes wandering down to the V of her blouse and had to remind himself that your little head could often get your big head in a lot of trouble. It worked every time.

Jennifer was smiling, it was the first time Tony had made a sexual reference to her and she liked it. "Yeah?" If only he could see her now, with her bleary eyes and curlers he wouldn't be thinking what he was thinking.

"Mmm hmm."

"I suppose I should be flattered that I was your first thought of the day."

Now he laughed. "What are you doing for the rest of the day?"

"Sleeping, most probably. Junior was up all night with a stomach ache." There was silence on the other end. "I had a good time the other day with you and Junior," Tony chuckled. "Boy makes you want to have kids of your own doesn't he?"

"Yes he does," Jennifer replied meaning every word.

"So when can I take you two out again?"

"Tony…" she said hesitantly.

"Don't start with that 'not getting attached' business," he interrupted. "I don't mind being his uncle." There was a second's silence. "Don't you trust me?"

"Tony, it's not a matter of trust."

"You're a very protective auntie, I like that. But you don't want to rob your nephew of male companionship."

Jennifer thought about it. "I'll need to discuss it with his mother. I'll call you later, okay?"

"Mmm. Promise?"

She imagined his face, the way he pouted his lips and fluttered his eyelashes when he was teasing her. "Promise."

They finished the conversation with a jokey phone kiss and Jennifer leaned back on the pillow glowing from the conversation but still feeling exhausted. Junior woke up a few minutes later and Jennifer rolled out of bed, stood stock still in the shower, dragged on a long jumper and an old pair of leggings and moved mechanically through her new morning routine.

Junior seemed to notice her lethargy and decided to take full advantage of it. He dragged every single toy he owned out of their boxes and placed them in all the places she'd told him not to. Mid-morning, they did another self-esteem lesson. They were now onto feel-good-about-yourself songs such as "I Love You No Matter What", and "Positive Power". Each day they would sing one song together. It didn't always have to be at the same time of day either — morning, lunchtime, bedtime. Junior had even remembered one as they walked through the streets of Lewisham the day before and had begun singing happily to himself:

"I love you when you're happy, I love you when you're mad,
I love you when we disagree or when we're holding hands."

He'd squeezed Jennifer's hand then and she'd looked down into his sweet chubby face and had to bend down to give him a hug.

After their song she realized what a mess their home was and sent him outside with his bike while she tidied up indoors. She had taken to watching the afternoon soaps and chat shows with a cup of tea and a doughnut whilst Junior took his afternoon nap and she set about the task of cleaning so that the flat would be in order when she came to sit down. When the doorbell rang Jennifer was reluctant to answer it. Who could it possibly be? She hadn't even bothered to take out her curlers. Had Tony decided to overrule her decision not to see him and come over anyway?

She got up and looked down the stairs to the front door. What was she doing, she didn't have x-ray eyes? Tentatively, she walked down in her slippers and half opened the front door, peering through the gap, and immediately wished she had followed her first instinct not to answer it.

Paul Harvey stood there with a bunch of flowers in his arms. He was dressed in his business suit. "Jennifer?"

She didn't say a word, one hand went to her head. The curlers! The way she was dressed! Oh my god! Jennifer had always thought that if she saw Paul Harvey again she would be showing him how having his child hadn't changed her. She was still working full-time and living the life she had planned to live. But right now she looked a mess and felt like a cleaner out of Coronation Street.

"Aren't you going to let me in," there was a wry smirk on his face.

"I'm not dressed. What do you want anyway?"

"Jennifer…"

She shivered involuntarily, remembering how she'd loved the way her name rolled off his tongue. "Don't start with any explanations and you can keep your flowers, we don't need you."

"My son might feel differently."

"Your what?!" She pulled the door fully open, facing him in all her charwoman glory. "My son wouldn't want anything to do with you no matter what you were offering as a bribe."

Paul looked around disconcertedly, he coughed. "Can we talk about this inside?" Jennifer crossed her hands over her chest. "I have nothing to say to you, Mr Harvey."

"Jennifer, I have found a way to disperse our grievances," he told her, leaning closer to the door. "If you let me in perhaps we can discuss them."

Jennifer scrutinized him hard before letting him into her home. Junior was still out in the back garden playing, she hoped he would stay out there until she got rid of this intruder. "Well?" she asked, as he stood opposite her in the living room.

He looked around at the toy box in one corner, the pile of children's books on the coffee table and her mug and plate sticky with the jam from her doughnut. He cleared his throat.

"You said you had a way to stop me hating you?"

"Not quite the way I put it, but yes. May I?" He gestured towards the sofa. Jennifer nodded but remained standing herself. Paul still held the bunch of roses and orchids.

"How is… our son?"

"My son is doing just fine, healthy, intelligent and prosperous, like his mother."

"I see. And you received the money I've been sending?" "Yes, although I haven't touched a penny of it, you're quite welcome to have it back," she spat back at him.

Paul Harvey shot her a look, but it quickly disappeared as she stared him down with a look of her own. He clasped his hands around the stem of flowers. "I'm married now."

"I know," she sniped, "How is Mrs Harvey?"

"As a matter of fact that was what I came to talk to you about."

"Your wife?"

"In a way. My wife and I want to start a family. She is a little older than myself and we've encountered some... complications."

Jennifer breathed out exasperatedly. Get to the point.

She saw Paul swallow hard and then run a hand around the inside collar of his shirt. "Our son..." he coughed, "needs a father. You have no idea how overjoyed I was to find out I had a son." His eye met hers and she stared him down again.

"Just in case you'd forgotten, Paul, you gave up all rights to your son the moment you took up with that bitch for your career."

Paul placed the flowers on the coffee table, freeing his hands. "Let's not get heated, Jennifer," he held up his hand. "What I have to say may be to your advantage. I realized that when you fell pregnant with our baby..."

There he goes with that 'Our' baby again. Since when did he have anything to do with this child other than providing the sperm? She didn't seem to recall him going through pregnancy, labour, or sleepless nights in order to call himself a parent.

"...That you didn't want to go through with it on your own. I also realize what a terrible time it must have been for you to find yourself in that position. He must be a real handful now, about three isn't he?"

Jennifer was too angry to speak without screaming.

"Anyway, my proposition is this," he cleared his throat again, "I want to have custody of our son." Jennifer's mouth fell open, "Whaat...?!!"

"Please, hear me out first. Just think of the benefits to yourself. You wouldn't have to do this on your own anymore. I could let you have full visiting rights as agreed with my wife. I could even run to giving you maintenance when he comes to stay with you." Blood was pumping in her ears, her heart was beating way too fast. She felt so hot she was afraid she would pass out, then she heard the back door open and close. The sound of the little boy's footsteps raced up the stairs and stopped in the doorway to the flat. Jennifer turned and went to her son's side.

Paul stood up, a smile on his face. "This must be the little man in question."

Junior looked up at his mother questioningly, wrapping a hand around his mother's leg.

"And what's your name, son?"

Jennifer grimaced at his use of the word 'son', she wasn't finished with him yet.

Junior grinned because he knew the answer to that question, "June-ya Edwards," he said proudly.

"Junior, so your real name's Paul," he said, crouching down in front of Junior.

Junior looked confused. "No, my name's June-ya."

Paul looked up at Jennifer. "You named him Junior?"

"That's what he said, didn't he?"

"I can't believe you would do that," he shook his head and muttered. "Never mind, that's easily remedied." Paul turned on his smile again and touched the boy's shoulder. "Well, Junior, it's nice to finally meet you."

"Who're you?" Junior asked.

Jennifer tensed and was ready to stop him when Paul said, "I'm your daddy."

Jennifer felt Junior's arm grip her leg tighter. "No. You're not my daddy. I don't 'ave a daddy." Paul looked up at Jennifer accusingly.

"Junior, it's okay," she bent down to him trying to soothe him, his little cheeks had turned red.

Junior continued to shout at Paul, "You're not my daddy. Leave my mummy alone, we hate you, leave me alone!" He struggled out of his mother's arms and headed for the spiral staircase, climbing it as fast as his little legs could carry him.

Jennifer waited until he had gone before turning her wrath on Paul. "What the hell did you do that for?"

"He has a right to be told."

"Jus' like you think you've got a right to come in here and tell me that you think you and your bitch can raise my son better than I can."

"I never said that."

"You damn well did," Jennifer felt her street-self erupting, her hands flew in his face. "You can take your blasted self-righteous self back out that front door just like you did when you left me pregnant to marry for money." "You've turned my son against me..."

"What was there to turn against? He doesn't know you, and even if he did he wouldn't like you, Paul." She looked him up and down, eyes burning with hatred, dragging him down to something she would wipe off her shoe.

Paul approached her, "I know how you must feel..."

Jennifer was enraged, "You know! Know what? I'd be very interested to know exactly what it is you think you know," her head bobbed from side to side.

Paul's expression changed from fake compassion to a sneer. "I can see I'm wasting my time here. Don't think you've heard the last of this. I'll see you in court."

Jennifer ran up behind him as he reached for the door handle and as she did so she raised one leg and caught him square in the centre of his back. His head slammed into the front door with a thud. He let out a cry and when he turned back to her his nose was bleeding.

"You shall be hearing from me," he said through his hand, his voice muffled. "Maybe I'll add assault to my list of charges."

"In that case maybe I should make a good job of it," her hand went automatically to the vase on the table by the front door. Paul noticed this and he was out the door before the vase even left the table.

Jennifer shut her eyes and fought back tears of anger. Then she laughed. She laughed so hard that her sides hurt. Junior came down the stairs, watching his mother leaning against the front door laughing.

"What's funny, Mummy?"

"Nothing baby, nothing." Junior looked at her, his baby face puzzled and then he started to laugh too. "We showed him didn't we?" Jennifer said through tears.

Junior wiped her cheek with a chubby hand, "Yeah."

Just what makes a man think he has the right to walk back into a woman's life after three years and tell her how to run it? What is it with them? Yes, I had the hots for Paul. I wanted him body, mind and wallet, but that was nearly four years ago!

This is a new generation of women he's dealing with. Unlike our grandmothers and even our mothers before us, we don't need to wait around for a man to marry us, get us pregnant and turn us into his personal housekeeper and sex slave. Oh no! This generation is taking care of its own business. We're not standing for any of their macho crap either, because sometimes a woman's got to be a bitch to survive.

Paul Harvey obviously hasn't woken up to that fact, nor will he until he stops looking for an easy way to the top and wakes up to reality. If he thinks marrying a white politician's daughter will make him fit in and guarantee him status, he's wrong. They're still looking at a black man, no matter who he's married to or how he speaks.

Take my son away from me! Ah, if he thinks I'd stand by and let him be taken away by a complete stranger, he's got another thing coming. I would seriously consider murder before I let that happen. When I told Karen and Elaine the other night they thought I should get a hit man and just scare him a little. Between Karen and myself I'm sure we could come up with enough hard cases that would be only too glad to do it for a few pounds. But seriously, if he does come after my son he's got a fight on his hands. Anyway, that's enough about Paul. Over the past few weeks I've gotten to know two males a lot better, my son and Tony Carnegie.

Junior is just so bright, and loving. He's reading well, attentive, inquisitive and on the odd occasion he has a helpful streak. Don't get me wrong, he's as boisterous as most three-year-old boys but when I need a hug or a kiss he seems to sense it and comes to my aid. He's back at nursery now. I went back to work two days ago and Donna got back from holiday too. At the moment I'm trying to reschedule my work pattern and case loads so that I can spend time with Junior in the evenings, before he goes to bed. I miss him like crazy. I've got a photo of him and Tony together on my desk, it was taken the last time we were in the park together.

Tony, now he surprised me. Just last night he told me a well kept secret. He shared this with me on our first… romantic night together. After years of being just good friends and colleagues, Tony asked me out on a 'real date' as he put it. He told me to wear something sexy so that he could stop seeing me as Miss Edwards. He wanted to see the real Jennifer.

"So where exactly would the lady like to go?" he'd asked me.

"I don't know," I said, "surprise me… I just want to have a good time… take me where I can have a good time…"

So I asked Donna to babysit and spent ages trying to find 'the real me' as Tony put it. I parted my longer length hair down the middle and swept the front behind my ears, letting the back hang to my neck and then the ends were flipped up for that sixties look. I wore a short lilac sleeveless dress with a matching bolero jacket and fashionable platform silver shoes. Tony pretended not to recognize me when I stepped out of the taxi in front of the wine bar, then he twirled around and whistled. "Miss Edwards, where have you been all my life?" before putting an arm around my back. It felt exciting. We started off in King's wine bar in Dulwich, but didn't stay longer than it took us to finish two drinks. The atmosphere wasn't right. We then went back to his flat. I hadn't realized how much private detecting pays. Tony's flat was simple but tastefully furnished courtesy of Ikea. He put a video on and we settled down on the sofa, side by side, to watch 'The Last Boy Scout' over microwave popcorn and diet coke.

Tony was laughing so hard at one point that he spilt coke down the front of his T-shirt and without a care in the world whipped it over his head and threw it in the direction of the bathroom. He leaned back on the sofa dressed just in his black jeans and socks. How lucky men are. They could take off their tops in public, walk the streets in nothing but a skimpy pair of shorts, a woman doing that would either get arrested or whisked off to the local loony bin. Now if I had just taken my top off and sat there as normal, he would have thought I was getting fresh.

I hadn't really noticed his body before. Even when we had gone swimming I was too worried that Junior would forget to call me by my name, to take in his fine physique. Now as I took in his lean, toned frame, broad muscle-capped shoulders, I wanted to touch him. He smelt of cocoa butter and aftershave, a lickable smell. What I was feeling surprised me because, right at that moment, I wanted him to be mine. Every time his bare flesh brushed mine, I broke out in goose pimples.

This had never happened with Tony before. When we'd first met he was just an annoying PI with a cheeky smile. Then he'd become an arrogant self-assured MAN, then a witty companion and friend. But now... Now what? There was an electronic keyboard in the corner of his front room covered by a dust sheet. I asked him if he could play.

"I played a bit at school," he shrugged.

"Play for me."

"Now why didn't you just ask me to sing?"

"Because I've heard you sing," I said wryly. Tony had this habit of singing along to songs on the car radio as he drove. He sang terribly.

He whipped the dust sheet off of the keyboard and switched it on. "Well, you'll be happy to know that during my performance you will be so taken aback by the fact that I can't play that you won't even notice my singing." I laughed. Tony cleared his throat, cracked his knuckles and then played a couple of bars before starting a bluesy tune. I knew it, it was the intro to Gershwin's 'Summertime'. He was obviously being modest, because he could actually play the thing.

"Summertime, and the living is easy," he sang with a deep exaggerated Southern accent, "...fish are jumping and the cotton is high. Oh your daddy's rich and your ma is good looking, so hush little baby don't you cry." He chuckled to himself as he played on. A sweet shiver went down my spine. My heartbeat quickened. I was amazed. There were hidden depths to this man that I hadn't realized.

"You can play."

"I surprise myself sometimes," he said arrogantly. I knew he was joking.

"*Come sing with me,*" he said and opened the book on top of the keyboard. I went over and squeezed onto the seat next to him.

I sang the next verse on my own and when I'd finished we both started laughing while he played on through the chorus.

Afterwards Tony put some music on and we got talking. We talked about movies we'd seen, places we'd visited and ambitions. He always had amusing stories to tell about his work. Finally the conversation had come around to families, ex-relationships and children.

"I have something I need to tell you."

For a moment it took me back to when Paul had said almost the same thing. I wondered why I couldn't stop comparing them. "You know you can tell me anything, T."

He was playing with the gold bracelet he wore and then he stopped and looked me straight in my eyes with a look of sincerity that took me aback. "I'm not like other guys," he said in a high-pitched Michael Jackson voice.

I giggled and curled one leg up under me. "I know that you fool, you're a mad man."

He laughed too but kind of shyly, he really did have something to say. "You know how I feel about you don't you?"

"How's that?" I asked.

"Come on, you don't need me to spell it out."

"I think I do. Indulge me."

He laughed in that cute way he had, "I L. O. V. E. Y.O.U."

"Come again!"

"You wanted me to spell it out."

I placed one hand on his bare chest and pushed him, he fell back on the sofa, his legs came up and fell across my lap. A strategic move on his part. I was laughing with happiness by this point. He crossed one arm across his chest and reached for my hand with the other. I took it happily.

"That wasn't all I had to tell you," he said.

"Stop playing around. Spit it out man."

"There is someone else," he was dead serious.

Now I knew this had been too good to be true. I could feel my throat constricting and my eyes glazed over, but he was smiling and squeezing my hand tighter. "I didn't mean another woman silly," he sat up and kissed my forehead. My confusion must have shown on my face. Why was he doing this to me? A joke is one thing, but why did he have to be so good at winding me up.

"I have a son," he confessed. "Wesley is eight and I get to see him only when I make an appointment with his mother or when she needs him out of the way, so that she can go out."

I searched his eyes waiting for the, 'Gotcha', but it didn't come. "You're serious?"

"Never been more so… except for when I said I loved you."

That brought another smile to my face, but also a sense of guilt to my heart. "So why didn't you tell me before?" I wanted to know.

"I didn't want you to think of me that way. You were always going on about baby fathers and how the lot of us couldn't care less about our kids. I do, but I knew you wouldn't believe me."

I felt sad. He was right I wouldn't have. Although now that he had opened up to me I so much wanted to tell him the truth about Junior. I touched his face with one hand, his smooth youthful face, so trusting and open. I kissed his lips lightly. "I love you too. I'm glad you told me about Wesley."

He grinned at me. "So, do you have any secrets you wanna tell me about?"

"No," I said hastily, "Do you have any pictures of Wesley?"

He was up and had the pictures in his hand within a minute. He showed me pictures of Wesley from the beginning. His girlfriend had been pretty, was pretty still I presumed. When I commented on it he said that was all she had going for her.

Wesley looked more like her than Tony. He had a round face, but was tall, and lean like his father. "Gonna be a basketball player," Tony said proudly. Watching him talk about his son made me want to share all I'd discovered about my own, but I couldn't yet, not now.

"…One more chance, baby
Give me one more chance…"

Later we lay on the sofa together, my head on his chest, the CD left to repeat over and over. Just talking as easily as we always did, about everything and nothing, finishing each other's sentences. I could feel his breath tickling my forehead with each word. Our first kiss was unlike I'd imagined it would be. His lips brushed my forehead, settling on each eyelid so softly as I turned my face up to him. It was as though every nerve in my body were transmitting signals to each other. An R. Kelly track was playing in the background and our bodies were already moving to the beat of "Downlow".

"…You want me but he needs you.
Yet you're telling me that everything is cool,
Trying to convince me baby to do as you say,
Just go along and see things your way…"

He kissed my nose, then looked at me, "I want you, " he said. "Is that all right?"

"...Keep it on the downlow,
Whispering, nobody has to know, nobody..."

A shiver ran down my back to my toes and then burned its way back up the front of my body, setting my vagina alight and then sending burning little fires alight in all my erogenous zones. My lips found his, our lips touched for a whole minute before I opened up to him and our tongues met. I felt his mouth on my neck, sucking my flesh tantalizingly, I sighed with the new senses awakening. One of his hands went to the zip at the back of my dress. The little jolt of electricity began again and the tingling along the surface of my skin. We swapped places so that he was on top. I grabbed the back of his neck and held him to me while I lay back, his arms made struts on each side of my body, his body like a tent. I was kissing his chest, sucking his tight little nipples and he moaned as his body came down on top of mine. I could feel his erection strong against my groin. "You're beautiful," I told him, "Your body is so beautiful."

There wasn't the hurried passion I'd had with Paul. We were taking our time. Taking our time to remove our clothes bit by sensuous bit. Tony hadn't closed his eyes the entire time, which at first I found unnerving and then erotic. He was taking in every inch of me. Tony pulled one nipple into his mouth, and then the other, his mouthing so soft that I couldn't tell his mouth from my own skin, with little flicks of his tongue he had me digging my fingers into his hard back. His fingers found the moistness between my legs, he stroked lightly and I felt myself melting. I twisted to pull down the zipper on his flies to release him from his jeans and he grabbed my hand. Pulling me up from the sofa he led me into the bedroom. He didn't pull back the bed sheets, we undressed in the middle of the floor, still exploring, tasting each other's bodies. That night I discovered that the soles of the feet are one of our most erogenous zones, but Tony must have known this already. Before he pushed me back gently onto the bed, he took a packet of condoms from his dresser drawer and kneeled in front of me. He rolled it on so sensually making sure I was watching him that instead of being a passion killer it became a sexy part of the foreplay. At that moment I longed to be penetrated whilst the rest of me wanted desperately to hold onto that feeling, to memorize the warmth of being held, the ecstasy of being in a state of desire.

At last, he took me into his arms and laid me down. He brushed kisses onto my cheeks and neck and then across my breasts. As he entered me I remember saying all those things that lovers say that sound so corny afterwards. Already I was coming, but he waited for me to come again and again. Afterwards, laying dreamily in his arms, I knew this was what love was all about. So when he turned *around and said, "Jen will you marry me?" I almost said 'yes' straight away before reality crowded my senses again and I stopped myself.*

"Can I think about that one?"

He kissed my forehead. "Sure, as long as the answer's yes." I loved the shape of his jaw and chin and the way his lips always seemed to curl upwards. I realized I'd wanted to kiss those lips since the very first day I'd met him. So I kissed them now to my heart's content. Soon his arms were around me and we were off again.

The week passed quickly. Tony had called her every night. Sometimes just to talk and other times to ask if she had made a decision yet. She hadn't, and by Sunday night she had a permanent headache. Self-induced pain, she thought glumly. Thoughts of Tony came and went in her mind. Her moods would swing from joy and warmth to confusion and guilt. One moment she was willing him to call and the next, wishing he would disappear off the face of the earth.

She had told Elaine about her problem of owning up to disowning her son and Elaine had said, "Don't make fire where there's no smoke — tell him."

When she told Beverly, she said, "How could you do that? How would Junior feel if he found out you were ashamed of him? And what about Tony? He's proposed... Who would want to marry someone who lied about something like that?"

Okay, it had been foolish to lie. She hadn't thought he would ever have to know the truth. How could she have predicted the future?

After Beverly's reproach Jennifer decided not to mention her dilemma to Karen. She dreaded what she would say to her.

"So when are you going to invite him round?" Donna was asking.

"What?" Jennifer looked up from her computer.

Donna got up from the floor where she had been eating sausage and chips in front of the telly. Junior was sprawled out asleep on the sofa. "Tony. When are you going to invite him round to meet his new family?"

Jennifer frowned and turned back to the computer, her hair fell over one eye and she threw it back irritably. "It might not be his new family, I haven't made a decision yet. I've been thinking, maybe it's too soon to be introducing a stranger into Junior's life."

Now it was Donna's turn to frown. "What are you talking about? Junior knows Tony and he likes him, you told me that yourself."

Jennifer breathed deeply and evenly. "It might turn out to be a complete disaster. You know how quickly Junior bonds with people. What if it doesn't work out with Tony and we break up, what will that do to Junior? I don't want to risk it."

"Have you told Tony this?" Donna placed her plate on her sister's desk and leant against the wall to her sister's right.

Jennifer was suddenly angry. "I will, okay! Why is everyone hassling me nowadays?"

Donna's eyes widened, "Jen, what's the matter?"

Jennifer jumped up, pushed her chair back and made for the door, "Just leave it." Her life, it seemed, was in everybody's hands but her own.

Donna was shocked and wanted to go after her, but knew that when her sister was angry it was best to leave her to deal with it alone. She hadn't expected that kind of reaction from mentioning the man Jennifer was supposed to be madly in love with. It could be that Jennifer was just being careful because of what had happened with Paul. Whatever it was, she would find out eventually. Donna went over to the sofa and picked Junior up, hugging his cuddly, warm body against her chest. She lay back on the sofa with her nephew snuggled against her and turned back to watch the Eddie Murphy movie on the television.

Jennifer glanced at the clock. It was almost eleven o'clock on a Thursday night. She'd been in the office since ten o'clock that morning. There had been paperwork to finish. She dropped her pen on the blotter and stretched. Rubbing her eyes she poured water from the jug on her desk. There was a big discrimination case tomorrow afternoon and she hadn't been able to concentrate all week.

Tony had wanted her to go shopping with him on Saturday… for an engagement ring! He was still trying to convince her to say 'yes'. And Donna was excited at getting another chance at being a bridesmaid. Marriage! Her second proposal. Jennifer wished she had kept it to herself but she had been too excited when he'd asked her. She'd felt like an excited fool. The perfect opportunity for her to tell Tony about Junior and she had chickened out. All of this week she had managed to avoid seeing Tony, claiming that she had too much work on. To Tony it must have seemed as if she had second thoughts because of his son, but the truth was she was still trying to find a way to tell him about Junior.

After a moment or two of contemplative silence, she wandered down the echoing corridor to the ladies.

"Evening Miss Edwards," Ken Power, one of their regular security guards, was rounding a corner as she pushed the door.

"Evening Ken," she smiled tiredly.

"Working late again? Young girl like you should be home snuggling up with your boyfriend not sweating over dusty books."

"I know, Ken, maybe one day I'll find the time."

Life was a bitch. If this was a movie she could have the bit where she had lied to Tony edited out, but this was real life. Anyway, if Tony had told her about his son from the start she wouldn't have had to lie in the first place. Jennifer freshened up and made her way back to her office dragging her feet on the polished wooden floor. The office door was still open and as she walked back in her semi-sleepy state she didn't even notice the man in her seat until her chair spun around. Tony smiled broadly at her.

She was too startled to smile. "How did you get in here?"

"Your kind security guard let me in on my fake ID."

"God, you just can't get the staff nowadays," she said sarcastically, hands on her hips.

"Ready?"

Jennifer was somewhat bemused. "For what?"

"I thought you'd be hungry. We could get something to eat…"

She cut him short. "I'm tired, T," she walked over to the coat stand. "I just want to go home, maybe it's my time of the month."

"Why don't you come back to my place? If it's your monthlies we don't have to…"

"I just want to get home." Tell him, put him out of his misery.

He clasped his hands on the table and nodded, his smile fading, but still flickering on his lips. "Maybe Saturday night?"

She nodded, reaching for her coat, Tony jumped up and helped her put it on. He put one hand on her shoulder turning her towards him. He bent forward and kissed her, aware that she was keeping her arms by her sides. He frowned. "Talk to me Jen, what's wrong?"

"I told you," she turned her back to him again, "I'm just really tired. I've had all this work," she indicated her desk full of books and folders.

He followed her and standing behind her he pulled her close. "Jen, this is me you're talking to. I know you."

"You don't know anything about me," she pulled away walking to the other side of the desk out of his reach. "Tony… I can't see you again."

His arms dropped to his sides.

She glanced up and looked for a brief second into his sad brown eyes. "There's someone else," she lied.

"You expect me to believe that?" he placed his knuckles on the desk leaning towards her. "Last weekend we made love, I proposed to you. We've known each other for over two years…"

"I just can't have you in my life anymore."

He swiftly covered the space between them and stood directly in front of her. Jennifer's heart was pounding and she wanted to cry, but her lie wouldn't ring true. If she was really finishing with him for someone else why would she be crying over it? He was so close now she could smell his mouthwash. "Jen," he reached out and placed a finger under her chin, turning her face up towards him. There were tears in her eyes. "Jen... I know."

She sniffed. "What do you know?"

"I know about Junior. This is what this is all about, isn't it?"

Jennifer wasn't giving anything away. "What do you know?" she repeated.

"I know he's your son and not your sister's. I know who his father is and who he's married to. I know that you're paranoid about being labelled. I told you a long time ago, I know women. I'm a detective, it's my job to know these things."

She stared at him incredulous. He'd known all along and he'd let her carry on this charade! Had he been laughing at her? Was this supposed to make her feel better? Well it didn't. And what was all this detective stuff all of a sudden?

"You've been spying on me?" her voice was angry and husky.

Tony jumped back. "Don't you think I'm the one that's supposed to be angry here?"

"Don't give me that," she glared at him. "You've been digging up my past without my permission. God, Tony! How low do you go?"

He sighed, and his shoulders sagged. "I was curious, and then when I found out I figured it would only be a matter of time before you told me. I thought telling you about my son would get you talking to me, trusting me."

Jennifer lowered her eyes. "Touché," she said and walked into his arms. "How long have you known?"

"A year."

Her tears started afresh. What a fool. How could she have carried on that way for so long? What must he think of her?

Proving how close they were, he answered as if reading her mind. "I don't think any less of you. Remember I told you I loved you, I knew then and it doesn't make any difference."

He kissed her nose and then her lips.

Her lips trembled. "I'm so sorry, Tony," she choked. "As time went on I wanted to tell you..." she looked up at him "...but I just didn't know how." She rested her head on his chest and he caressed her face until her sobbing ceased.

"Come on, enough already. Big 'ooman ah bawl like lickle pickney." She laughed.

"That's better. I understand," he said softly. "So, your place or mine?"

"That's another thing, about us getting married…"

He had one eyebrow raised. "Yes?"

"How would you feel about us living together first?"

"I'm down with that."

"It's just that I feel Junior should have an adjusting period."

He let a breath out through his lips. "Bwoy, this is a big move… Are you sure?"

She looked up into his eyes. "The question is, are you?"

He nodded. "Never been more sure."

She hugged him before going to her desk for her briefcase and handbag. She wiped salty tears from her eyes. "Home, Jeeves."

He put on an American drag queen accent, he let one hand go limp and placed the other on his hip. "Girl, when we get home, we is gonna do some talking."

"Yes sir, or should I say, sista," she laughed.

He smacked her bottom lightly as she passed him.

She leant on his shoulder as they left the building, arms crossed behind each other.

"So, what are we having for dinner?"

"How about microwave lasagne."

"Mmm, my favourite."

TEN

Donna took a month to make up her mind about Tony moving in. We had told her together, sitting side by side holding hands like teenagers facing my parents. Donna had looked from one of us to the other and then said, "I'll have to think about it." It wasn't as if I was asking her permission, I just wanted to know what she thought of the idea. But as this would mean a disruption in our household, I felt it only right to hear her views.

Junior had taken to him from their first meeting and was impatient for Tony to move in with us. Donna said that, seeing as she would be moving out to live on campus in September, I could do as I pleased.

Tony wanted me to meet his parents.

"It's best that you meet them now before we start cohabiting, so you don't

chuck me out 'pon de streets afterwards." He was always joking around, I was never sure whether he was winding me up or not. He had given me a pretty good idea of his parents and their views on family so I basically knew what to expect. And I felt it was only right that I was introduced to his parents with Junior in tow. Tony said that was fine by him but he'd warn them in advance so that they could put away all their breakables.

We went in Tony's car. It was pouring with rain, the traffic was moving lethargically through the streets of south east London. As we turned off Peckham's Rye Lane I suddenly got nervous. I turned around and looked at Junior who had fallen asleep in his booster seat in the back of the car. Suppose they were fond of Tony's ex-girlfriend and had wanted them to stay together. Wouldn't they see me as an intruder? Would we end up with all those old arguments like, why did he run from one relationship and leave his son to raise someone else's? I hadn't voiced these fears to Tony because they hadn't raised themselves until now. Tony must have felt my anxiety too because he placed one hand on my knee and gave it a squeeze, I covered his hand with mine and our eyes met.

Tony was carrying a still sleepy Junior. I stood silently by his side and waited for that blue painted front door of his parent's home to open and reveal his background to me. It was still raining and memories of those old horror movies where the travellers turn up at a spooky house in the country came back to me. The door opened.

"Hello, Dad," Tony smiled at the man standing in front of us in a short sleeved shirt. He was as tall as Tony and thin, his eyes lit up at the sight of his son.

"Come in boy, we expected you later. Yuh madda's still cooking," he smiled warmly at me. "Come in, come in." He invited us into the narrow hallway and I followed awkwardly. The door closed behind me and my heart leapt. This was it, no escape.

"This is Jennifer," Tony turned to me. "And this is her son Junior."

"Hello, Jennifer," he took my hand and I looked at him properly for the first time. He was in his mid-fifties with very young lively eyes. His hair was still jet black and there was no bald batch. Which meant that Tony would hopefully be just as lucky.

"Hello, Mr Carnegie."

"Derek," he said. "Come t'ru, come t'ru," Tony was already heading up the staircase into the flat above. The smells of Jamaican cooked chicken were wafting towards us as we ascended. Junior's head rose and he looked around him and then at me. His inquisitive eyes were everywhere at once. Inside the flat stood the woman who had brought the man I loved into the world.

"Derek, open some wine, my son is home," the woman's voice was loud and confident. I almost stood to attention. She was a large imposing woman, streaks of grey hair were just beginning around her temple. Her mouth had the same cupid's bow as Tony's and her brows and eyes would probably look like his if she smiled. Instead, there was discontent etched in those eyes as she looked at her son. He turned, handing Junior to me before moving across to her. He folded his arms around her affectionately and they embraced.

"Hello, Mum." I met her eyes over Tony's shoulder. Had I just imagined that she was imposing because of the tension I'd felt? In Tony's arms, she was smaller in height than she'd first seemed. However, in every other detail, Tony really was his mother's son.

"Anthony, yuh not eating? Just like yuh faada, bwoy I can feel yuh ribs."

He laughed. "That's hard muscle, Mum. By the way, this is Jennifer and Junior." "Nice to meet you, Jennifer," her eyes passed over Junior and he clung tight to my neck. "Is he shy?"

"Not usually," I said feeling like a teenager all over again. She walked towards me, three steps and it was like it happened in slow motion and took the longest time.

"Would Junior like an ice lolly?"

Junior's face immediately lit up and he pushed to be let down. I put him down and he followed Tony's mum into the kitchen.

"Come upstairs, nuh," Derek called. Following Tony's lead I took the two steps up to their split-level living room. It was an overcrowded little room, filled with furniture that they probably couldn't bear to part with. Beautiful ruffled blinds hung from all three windows along one wall. I sat down on the dark leather couch, in the centre so as not to disrupt the plump yellow cushions in each corner.

"Move over," Tony said lowering himself next to me. "It's hard to believe, but two can sit on it."

Derek chuckled and handed us both a glass of wine. My throat was dry and I wanted to knock it back all at once but instead I sipped it ladylike. There was a glass coffee table in front of me, on top of which was a vase of nylon flowers. There were photos of the family all around us. Black and white ones of their daughters and son growing up as well as newer portraits of the grandchildren — Tony's nephew and three nieces. Everything was dust free. Junior came back in with an ice lolly and I immediately started searching for tissues.

"Relax Jen. Mum's had kids in here before, you know."

I breathed deeply, trying to relax. When his mother came in and took a seat opposite me, Tony got up and went to sit on the arm of her chair, taking one of her hands in his. I didn't know where to look. I felt lost, so I pulled Junior closer and said, "You've got a lovely home." Her smile widened at the compliment.

"You known Anthony long?" she asked me.

I looked over at Tony and he was smiling. He probably found this very funny. "About three years, Mrs Carnegie," I replied. "We worked together before we became… friends."

"Please call me Rose," she smiled. I know she was trying to put me at ease but I was still waiting for that punch line.

"Jennifer's a barrister," Tony said.

Derek raised an eyebrow and slapped his thigh, "Big time lawyer!"

"My son always did have an eye for quality," Rose said. I took another sip of my wine to avoid her eyes. "So, you're divorced?"

"No, uhm, Junior's father just didn't want to know."

They both nodded. "How is Wesley?" Rose asked her son, but was looking at me.

I watched Tony's face. "He's fine, Mum, why don't you phone him sometime and ask him yourself?"

"I shouldn't have to, you should be bringing him down to visit me," she slapped his hand lightly. "Have you met my grandson?" she turned to me. I knew it was coming, my test. "No, but Tony's told me all about him, I look forward to meeting him soon." Tony was looking at me with pride. I wanted him beside me not over there holding his mother's hand.

I had almost forgotten Junior while we were talking and when I looked around he was playing with a porcelain horse on the floor. His lolly-sticky hands leaving marks all over it. "Junior, can't you leave things alone."

"It's all right," Rose reassured me, "I can clean it." She rose from her chair almost regally and made her way to the door. "I'd better serve up dinner. Why don't you come with me, Jennifer." This was not a request but an order. I placed my glass on a coaster and glanced over at Junior who was admiring himself in their mirrored drinks cabinet. Tony saw my worried look "I'll watch him," he said.

"So, did he buy you a ring?" she asked as soon as we were out of earshot of the men.

"Yes," I held out my hand and showed her the emerald and diamond ring we had chosen together.

"Anthony knows how to treat women right. Some take advantage of it," she said giving me a look out of the corner of her eyes.

I faced her and mustered up the courage to put her mind at rest. "Rose… I can see that you and your son are very close. I love him too, how could I not?"

She smiled at me in a kind of, 'I know what you mean', way. "Tony and I fell in love after being friends for years, I wouldn't want to hurt him and if you're thinking that I might be trying to replace Junior's father, then you're wrong.

Junior has only had me and my sister all his life, there was never a father to replace. You can see for yourself how much they love each other."

"Jennifer... I like you," she wiped her hands on a tea towel and faced me. "You're honest and I can see you're not after Tony for his money, you have a career all of your own," she crossed the kitchen her arms open to me. "Welcome to my family. Just take care of my boy for me."

"Don't worry, I will." It was all I could wish for, but I knew she would be watching me still.

Rose got me to chop the salad while she finished off the cooking and we talked. She told me about Tony's childhood. How he was a spoilt child, being the only boy. She laughed as she reminisced about the girls dressing him up in their clothes and putting make-up on him. He was never short of girlfriends as he grew up because his sisters' friends often fell in love with his cute smile and his jokey ways. Tony had always been loving. One of his sisters, Denise, still regularly came to him for advice on her love life.

The mother of Tony's son was exactly the type of woman Rose had been scared of him meeting. She took advantage of his caring attitude, and knew she could get whatever she wanted from him without giving. Especially once she had his son. Rose had actually breathed a sigh of relief when Tony had told her he was leaving that woman, but he insisted he was still going to see his son as much as possible.

I had yet to meet his sisters and hoped I could give it some time. More women in this family of protective females would be too much straight after this one.

We left their home at around nine o'clock that evening.

"Don't leave it so long to come back and see us again Anthony," his mum kissed his cheek and there were tears in her eyes.

"I'll phone, Mum."

Both his parents kissed Junior and told me to feel free to come up and see them anytime and bring my son with me. I still felt more comfortable with Derek than Rose, but I felt that I would get to like her eventually and she would grow to trust me.

"You met his what!"

"His mum and dad."

"And?" Karen was eager to get the news out of her. Ever since Jennifer had told her about the engagement and the decision to live together, the couple had become big news.

Jennifer switched the phone to her other hand and crossed her legs. "Don't sound so surprised Karen, we are getting married."

"Me know. Yuh know how long I been seeing Philip and I've only met his brudda... once."

"Well that's your choice. Once you've met the folks it's like you're his wife, and I know how you feel about that."

"So how'd it go?"

"Dad's a real nice guy. I got the feeling he would have married me himself if he had the choice. Mum pretended to be a hard nut to crack but I managed it."

"Brave, brave 'ooman. By the way, Phil's moving in properly next week."

Now it was Jennifer's turn to be shocked. "Was that my fault?"

"Naw, I just thought it'd save on the bills, you know. He's here most time anyway," Karen deftly changed the subject. "You know Beverly's lost weight?"

Jennifer smiled to herself. Why did Karen find admitting getting close to a man embarrassing? "No, I haven't seen her for months. How much?"

"Ten pounds, you should see her. You can see it in her face."

Jennifer didn't want to admit that since she had been seeing Tony she had started to neglect her friends again. Maybe when Tony moved in they should have a housewarming. She'd get to meet his friends and family and he could meet hers.

"I spoke to Elaine the other day, she didn't say a word."

"Yuh lucky if you get anything out of Elaine these days. She nuh start dem test to get pregnant."

"I know, she said that much. Artificial insemination," Jennifer said, suddenly feeling sad.

"You see how God wicked? Gal can get pregnant in seconds by accident, but when it come to people who really want pickney, dem haffe suffer."

"Mmm."

"Look, Jen, I gotta go, catch you later."

"Take care, Karen." She hung up and was about to call Elaine but thought better of it. She called Beverly and congratulated her on her weight loss instead.

Jennifer was pleased with herself for taking the time to catch up with her friends. Just a simple phone call could make such a difference to the way people felt. She didn't want them saying behind her back how she never kept in touch now that she had a man. By the time she had replaced the receiver she realized her own life still had a couple of loose ends that needed tying up.

Tony, of course, knew of Paul's existence, but she hadn't mentioned the visit he had paid on herself and Junior, the threat that he had issued and the summons that had arrived by courier yesterday. Paul was going ahead with his case for custody. She had promised there were never going to be anymore secrets and she wanted to explain to him, tell him that Paul Harvey was a part of her life that she would rather forget. Over the months she had been seeing Tony she had all but forgotten the threat and at the time had thought it was nothing more than a vindictive jab at her. Just when everything had started to go so smoothly Paul shows his balding head and upsets the apple cart, throwing Jennifer's emotions into turmoil. The only weapon he had against her would be to win the right to her son.

The date was set for three months away. By then she and Tony would be cohabiting. Jennifer had tried enough of these cases to know that the most custody Paul would get would be weekend split custody, but even that could disrupt the new life she had planned for her family.

It was time that she spoke to Paul Harvey, person to person.

Jennifer raised her arms sensually and stretched. Getting up she crossed to the mini bar. She wore a cream loose fitting linen and wool mix top over navy slacks belted with a black velvet belt. She poured herself a brandy. Before she made that call she needed a drink.

Tony moved in in July. Between us we decided what furniture we'd sell. To be honest it was mostly his. I was comfortable with my home and so was Junior and I didn't want too many changes all at once. The first night Junior didn't leave us alone at all. He followed Tony from the living room to the kitchen, from the bedroom to the bathroom and decided he was going to help him unpack. Having a three-year-old help you pack or unpack anything takes almost three times as long as doing it on your own. He would take something from a box and ask, "What's this, Tony? What does this do? Can I play with it? Can I have it?"

Several times I told him to go play in his bedroom or the back garden but he kept sneaking back in. Tony seemed to enjoy Junior's attentions and spent time answering his questions and even having a break to play with him. Watching them together made me feel so content. Junior finally had a man around the house and he seemed determined to make the most of it. They were like kindred spirits, and that night we had to take him to bed with us too, until he fell asleep. Then Tony carried him back to his own bed.

"Hi, lover," he slipped back into the bed beside me.

"Finally alone," I whispered back. He folded his arms around me and we kissed. "Do you mind if we don't make love tonight?" I asked.

"Course not babe, so long as I can feel you next to me."

I snuggled closer if that was possible, and breathed in his scent. He was my man. *Handsome, talented, gentle, sensitive, humorous and he made me so happy. We loved each other and one day he wouldn't be just my man, he would be my husband and Junior's father. I could hear his heartbeat and feel his breath on my forehead. I was falling deeper in love with him by the second. As I fell asleep I was thinking... my man. Sunday morning he got up early. While I was showering I could hear him downstairs with Junior. Donna was still in bed. We wouldn't see her on a Sunday before midday. I arrived downstairs in my summer jogging gear. Junior was on Tony's lap tucking into a cooked breakfast. Bacon, eggs, beans and toast.*

"Morning, Mummy." "Morning, baby, and how are my handsome men this morning?" I went over to the fridge to get myself a glass of fruit juice. Tony's eyes were following me around the kitchen.

"We saved you some," he said.

I looked at the food and said, "You eat it."

Tony looked wounded so I went over and kissed him. "I'm sorry," I said in my baby voice, "I just never eat before my run and then never fry ups."

"Well neither do I," he eased Junior off his lap and stood up in front of me, grabbing my bare waist with his gentle hands, "but muesli and orange juice just doesn't look like hard work." He shrugged and I kissed him again just for being so cute.

"I didn't get a kiss," Junior pouted. So I picked him up, held him against me and planted a big wet kiss on his cheek making him giggle.

"Can I run with you?" Tony asked, flicking a stray hair off my forehead.

"Could you keep up?"

"Try me," he was already heading for the bedroom to change into his track suit. Junior was sent to go and bother Donna while we headed out. He wasn't happy about having his new companion taken away from him.

Three miles later Tony and I were back and panting against the front door frame. Okay, so he could run. He had good lung capacity and strong legs. I'd taken him on some of the toughest slopes I knew and he'd kept up.

"What d'you say to moving to the Caribbean when we're married," said Tony a little later, catching his breath from a kiss in the middle of the kitchen.

I looked at him. "Move... to the Caribbean?"

"Why not? What do we have holding us here?"

I pulled away returning to the dining table. "My career for one, Donna, your work, Junior's schooling..."

"Stop," he pulled up a chair opposite me. "Your career, you can practice something else. Donna is a big twenty-year-old woman she can take care of herself. Junior would have a much better education in the West Indies than here, even if we had to pay for it. I can get work out there doing exactly the same

thing…" his eyes glazed over. "Or we could open our own agency together, a law and detective agency."

"Get outta here!"

I waved him away turning back to the paper.

He gave me that wounded dog look. "Will you at least think about it… for me."

"Mmm," I said, through a mouthful of muesli.

"Great," he jumped up from the chair. "Junior, we're going to Barbados… Oh, we're going to Barbados," he sang. I glared at him as Junior came running and giggling into the kitchen and he whirled him around his head.

He was like a big kid! There was no way I was leaving, not after having had to struggle through so many obstacles to get where I am now. That was another of men's differences. They never liked to put down roots. A woman wants to find somewhere were she can settle and build, a man prefers to pack his clothes and his walkman and move on at the drop of a hat. Pick up some trade or other along the way to make a living. After all, they didn't have to work as hard as a woman to build a career, make a home for their family. Family ties meant nothing to them. What about his own son, Wesley? If we just picked up and left, he would never see him.

I had hoped that Tony would soon drop the idea but instead, he took every opportunity to remind me of how beautiful Barbados was. If there was a travel programme on we'd have to watch it. He brought home brochures that I would find under my pillow, in the fridge and wrapped up in the towels in the bathroom. Honeymoon shots taken on beaches or lush green mountains would find themselves into my briefcase.

He even went as far as to enlist the help of my son. Junior would come up to me and look up at me with his big eyes and say, "Mummy, I want to wear uniform like kids in 'Bados. Can we swim everyday if we went there?" I still stuck to my guns.

In the three months since Tony moved in Jennifer seemed to be living in perfect bliss. She had a man who was deeply in love with her and her son, living under the same roof. She loved Tony and saw how much he cared for her, their love seemed to grow and grow. Moving in with him was the natural progression, to give both of them the chance to find out if this was what they wanted or if he could handle bringing up someone else's child. She couldn't possibly marry him without finding out if he could cope with an inquisitive, time-consuming infant and an over busy mother.

Tony, true to his word, had done everything he promised and more. The panic about the invasion of her privacy, space and independence didn't disappear overnight though. There hadn't been a man in her life in a long time and nothing as intense as this. When he had first moved in there had been the dilemma of where to put his stuff. So she had had a clear out. Clothes and shoes that would never again see the light of day were given to charity, her dressing table was cleared enough so that they had a his and hers side, as were the shelves in the bathroom.

Then there were things to learn about him, such as what he liked eating — they would have to shop together. Did he do his share of the housework, washing, ironing? Did he have habits that would drive her mad? Rules had to be laid down as to who would discipline Junior. What Tony could do without referring to Jennifer, who would Junior ask permission from. Who was Tony to Junior anyway? All these questions and more raised their heads and between them they dealt with it.

Jennifer found herself rushing to get home in the evenings now, which she hadn't done ever. She liked the fact that he was there to share the load, he was there to give her reassurance, a hug, a compliment, a massage after a hard day, an ear to listen to her troubles. She could feel comfort in his scent. In the middle of the night she could reach over and touch him or snuggle up on the sofa, when the house was still and quiet, for heart to heart talks, or put on a smoochy record and rock together in the middle of the front room.

What a difference having a man around the house had made to Jennifer and Junior's lives. There had been a three foot painting of a black family — parents and three children ranging from teens to baby — having a picnic, painted by a young artist, which Jennifer had fallen in love with but had never got around to hanging. Tony knew all about it, she had shown him where she would hang it, and one evening she had come home and it was there, on the wall, facing you just as you came out of the living room. The embodiment of a happy family.

Junior had someone else to read to him, a male voice to add new perspective. He had a man who not only played football with him, but knew all the rules of football too. He promised to take Junior to judo classes where he would not only learn the art of self-defence but would learn the discipline of the power of the mind and physical fitness. But there was more to being a father than playing football with Junior, and Tony understood this. They had what Tony called their 'man on man day' which was Sundays. Women excluded, it was a day where Jennifer either had to leave the house or they would go out for the whole day, just Tony, Junior and sometimes his son Wesley. At home they would talk about growing up, doing things around the home, 'taking care of the women'

(Tony joked trying not to make it seem heavy). This was basically a talk about how females developed and were brought up, what makes them different. For Junior some of it went right over his head, but Wesley, who would be going to secondary school in two years listened intently and asked questions. For them there would be no men's work or women's work, just hard work. Outdoors they would go camping for a day, learn how to build barbecues in the woods, basic first aid, cycling and bike repair. They would talk about and play sport, climb and build, and most importantly, bond.

Jennifer found herself having to fight down jealousy when Junior would want to take a bath with Tony instead of her, when he wanted to play a game with him, when he would sit by the window just waiting for Tony's car to pull up and then dash to the front door to jump into his arms. It was only natural the boy would take to Tony, he was the most selfless person Jennifer knew. One day, Junior would be a man like Tony, a man who had character, ambition, determination, sensitivity and the intelligence to learn how to use the gifts he was born with as well as the ones she had instilled in him.

Of course she still had the worry that Paul Harvey would come back and undo all that she had managed to achieve with her son, but after talking it over with Tony she knew she had no worries. Tony was like her right arm, although she told herself over and over that she shouldn't become too dependent on him. She couldn't let love mess her up, she had to stay focused and in control.

Tony had taken to doing his case notes on my laptop computer. I came home one night and he was sitting at my desk reading something from the screen.

"Hi, honey," I said, dropping my briefcase and planting a kiss on his cheek.

"Mmm, oh hi," he turned back to the screen almost immediately. Curious, I walked back to the desk and looked over his shoulder.

"Tony, you're reading my diary!"

"Babe, why didn't you tell me you kept a journal?"

"Why didn't you ask permission to read it?" I swatted his head with the palm of my hand.

"Jen, this is really good, especially the parts about me," he grinned and I'm sure I blushed.

I stormed out and heard him pushing back his chair to follow me. I hung my coat up in the hallway and went to the kitchen. I swung open the cupboard where we kept the glasses and took one out. "I thought we didn't have secrets from each other anymore?"

"It's not a secret, you can read it," I slammed the cupboard door. "Why couldn't you have asked first?"

"Alright, you're upset," he came towards me and laid his arms on my shoulders. "I was looking for a disk to save my work on and came across the box of disks labelled 'journal'."

I looked up at his pitiful face. He was dressed in one of my big jumpers and his green track suit bottoms, and stood bare footed on the cold kitchen floor. "So you opened up the box that obviously did not contain blank discs and put one into the computer, and when you saw it did indeed have something on it, you proceeded to read it..."

"Caught red-handed, Guv," he put on a cockney accent and raised his hands in the air submissively.

I lowered my eyes laughing. "Silly. It's okay, I don't mind you reading it. You know it all anyway."

"You sure?"

"I said so didn't I?"

He kissed my nose and then my lips. "You ever thought of publishing it?"

"Now you are being silly. Who'd read the perils of being a single career mother?" I chuckled, but Tony was serious.

"Well if the perils of being a baby father can get two bestsellers, why shouldn't yours?"

"It's not fiction though, Tony. That's my life on those discs, it would be open to public ridicule."

"Well then we pass it off as fiction, change the names, places, dates, give you a pseudonym. Baby, I know someone in publishing, why don't you let me show it to him."

"No," I was already backing out of the kitchen. "It's not even worth considering wasting someone's time for."

"How do you know unless you try?" He was giving me that look again.

"Okay, do it, then I'll get a chance to tell you I told you so."

Tony spent most of that night with the lap top on his knees in bed. In the morning he woke up bleary eyed and told me he just couldn't put it down. I was bemused, I hadn't even read the thing back to myself. Twice a week I'd recorded my thoughts and feelings on my life without ever expecting anyone else to read it and now my fiancé wanted to have it published. I let him go ahead. Maybe it would take his mind off Barbados.

Tony came into the room and stood behind Jennifer's chair in the middle of their bedroom with his hands deep in his pockets. "Junior finally fell asleep after the fifth story," he grinned.

Jennifer applied her lipstick with a lip brush and sat back to view her made up face. "Thanks, T." Junior had been hyper all evening. At one stage Jennifer had suggested giving him a drop of brandy to knock him out. Tony had managed to tire him by first singing his self-esteem songs with him and then reading to him. Tony watched Jennifer getting ready for her date. "Do you have to do this?"

Jennifer met his eyes in the mirror as she fastened her gold droplet earrings. "Babe, you know I do."

He sighed. "Then let me come with you."

He cared so much. Standing there with his hang dog expression, his eyes were pleading, so full of love. Jennifer pushed her chair away from the dressing table, she stood up and her long black dress fell to her calves. She had to meet with Paul, once and for all, before this got as far as the courts making the decision. She wanted to lay down her feelings, spread her cards on the table so to speak. Tony could never bring Junior up the way he so much wanted to, as his real father, while Paul had rights to see him whenever he pleased.

When she had called Paul's office he seemed so surprised he was speechless. Then he went on the defensive, threatening to call his lawyers. Jennifer had remained calm and simply told him she wanted to see him to talk about their son. Paul was then flabbergasted, she could almost see him grinning into the phone. She told him where they should meet and when, and that it would be his one and only chance.

Tony felt awkward, like an outsider. He had no say in this situation. Choosing to move in with Jennifer and her son in the first place was a big decision. Whenever a man moved into a ready made family he had to prepare himself for the absent father turning up one day. Tony had thought about it and even talked about it with Jennifer but he had never felt any threat before until now.

Jennifer felt this was her business. Something she should have cleared up months ago. Tony shouldn't have to become involved. He loved her and Junior unconditionally and there was no way she was going to jeopardise that. Junior was her responsibility and any decisions concerning his life would have to be made by her.

"I know you want to be there for support, but honey, I know Paul. He'll see you coming along as a weakness and attack it. Plus neither of us would be able to say what really needs to be said with you there."

"You forgot to say 'no offence'," Tony smirked.

"I'm sorry..."

Tony's eyes fell on her dress. "I guess I'm jus' jealous. I mean look at you... You're beautiful."

Jennifer smiled.

"Look, I know how you felt about him, you wrote it all in that diary. He was supposed to be your husband, you had his baby. How could he not want you back?" He reached for her and she stepped into his arms.

"Tony, I love you. The way I felt for Paul Harvey is history. Did you ever once hear me mention love in connection with him? I have nothing but contempt for him, but he wants to try to take my son away from me. I want to make sure not one of us has to suffer. I want to make sure that any rights he gets will be with my consent and not one forced onto us by the courts."

"I know that..."

"But?"

"But look what he can offer you and Junior. He's got money, power and fame... Who am I compared to that?"

Jennifer could feel his uncertainty. Maybe it had been a mistake to let him read her journals. She had almost forgotten how she had lusted for that power and status that Paul Harvey had. She had acted like a child promised a trip to Disneyland. A dream come true. The real cost had been of no consequence, only the result. Thank God she had changed.

"Paul Harvey is not the man I'm in love with. He is not the man I want by my side raising my son. He is selfish and vindictive and the only reason he wants custody of my son is because he and his wife can't have children. He doesn't want me and he doesn't want Junior. What he also doesn't want is for people to think he has the problem."

There was a silence between them. They held each other and their eyes locked. Communication was the key here. There was a childlike quality in his eyes that said, 'I want to believe you, it's him I don't trust'.

"Don't let him sweet talk you into anything, y'know."

"I won't," she smiled.

"An' tell him if he so much as raises his voice to you, or lifts a finger in your direction he's got me and Junior to answer to." Tony's hand caressed her neck and hair.

That was more like the old Tony. God, it was good feeling this secure about a man. She was a lucky woman and if there was one thing the Toni Lee seminar had instilled in her, it was never to bemoan what you didn't have, but to appreciate the hell out of what you did have.

Before she left to meet Paul Harvey, Tony had hugged her so hard that, for a moment, she nearly changed her mind and stayed at home.

Paul still had his flat in Lauderdale Tower. The Barbican apartment was his private domain. His escape from the pressures of politics and his wife's socialite friends. Jennifer's heart was beating triple time as she rang the intercom buzzer and Paul's clipped voice came out at her. His old-fashioned charm and patronizing manner came flooding back to her, and she wondered how she could ever have contemplated marrying him. He stood in his doorway waiting for her as she stepped from the lift. They stood for a moment sizing each other up, sensing the mood, the attitude, the tone their conversations would take. Paul's thinning hair was now balding. He was dressed the most casual she had seen him, in a t-shirt which he wore over jeans. "Good evening," he let her in with a flourish of his hand. It had been nearly four years since she had been there and it hadn't changed. She suspected there was no need for him to make changes in an apartment where he no longer lived.

Silently, she stepped over the threshold and felt his eyes burning into her back. She turned to face him. "Can I take your jacket?"

Jennifer had wanted to impress him with her fit body. Wanting him to see that physically she hadn't changed a bit despite having a baby. After seeing the way he dressed, she felt overdressed. "No thank you."

He shrugged his shoulders and led the way into the sunken living room. "Can I get you a drink?"

"Water will do, thanks." Her palms were sweating. She pretended to study a painting on the wall until he left to go to the adjoining kitchen and then she sat down on the edge of the seat of one of the armchairs. Paul came back, carrying her water and a glass of wine for himself.

She took the glass and held it firmly in her hands, the ice cold glass cooling her palms. Paul sat opposite. "How are you?"

"I'm very well, thank you." It was the third time she'd said anything and the third time she had said 'thank you'. Her nerves were at breaking point but Paul looked as cool as a cucumber. But then he was a politician now, who knew what was going on behind the mask?

"You look fabulous." His compliment was met with an icy glare and he cleared his throat before continuing, "I'm glad you called... you know a lot could have been avoided if you'd talked to me months ago."

Jennifer took a sip of the water and felt her throat open up again. "Are you saying if I had let you walk out with my son, I'd have been a lot happier?"

"I'm not saying that... Look I don't want us to start out on the wrong foot. We are two civil people.."

"One of us is," she interrupted bluntly.

"Jennifer, please let me finish. I've thought about what I said, and I know I'm not the best when it comes to affairs of the heart. The way I came across may have been very callous and I apologize."

Jennifer silently watched him.

"I apologize for the way I treated you four years ago, leaving you with my child to raise alone. I thought money would take care of you both. Then when I saw you with that man…"

Jennifer's eyes glared at him, her jaw set hard.

"I felt a longing," he quickly held up a hand, "no, not in that way… I felt a longing for what I could have had. A son. I felt a longing for you too, but I knew I had lost you, but there was still a chance for me to be a father to my son."

Jennifer shook her head and imagined she could hear violins playing somewhere overhead. This was so sickening. Had Paul digested some soppy romance, or one of William Cosby's books on good parenting?

He continued. "I hadn't realized the extent to which you had come to hate me…"

Jennifer felt she ought to stop him before she puked. She held up her hand, halting him in mid sentence. "Paul, let's not pretend this is some kind of reconciliation. I'm here because you are taking me to court to get rights to see my son."

Paul's mouth clamped shut.

"All right, you are his biological father, but you are not his daddy. A daddy is someone who is around for his child through the good times and the bad, offering support and love, encouragement, a positive role model for the child to follow. A daddy is not an envelope containing two hundred pounds every month. Do you think you fit the bill in any way?"

He said immediately, "Given the chance…"

"Given the chance!" Jennifer interrupted once again. Oh, he was so full of it this one. He had probably sat up all night planning his little speech. "What did you get when I told you I was pregnant? Wasn't that your chance? When you had a choice between having a wife and a family of your own, you chose a white woman for status. I'm not going to bring your wife into this, I'm just using her to make you see what you've lost."

Paul swallowed the rest of his wine. "I am content with my life, except for not having my offspring beside me."

"Oh, so now you just need that one little accessory to add to your collection and your life will be complete?" she asked sarcastically.

"I do not see my son as an accessory. I want him to know who I am, I want to make up for what I've missed out on in his life."

"And what about him? Have you thought about what you are doing to him?"

"What? Giving him the father he hasn't had for three years, I hardly see that as a disaster."

"He has a father. I'm going to be married to him one day and he has already expressed a wish to adopt Junior legally."

Paul let out a hiss and got up. He stomped noisily to the kitchen and she heard the fridge door open and close. Sitting down again with a bottle of wine in his hand, she watched as he poured for himself and then offered it to her. Jennifer took the bottle.

"You can't do that." His voice was now low, not as confident as before.

Jennifer knew what he was talking about. He expected the world to stop for him. He could go on and live his life as he pleased but everyone else's life had to be held in suspended animation until he walked back in. "We can and we will."

"Where do I fit into your plan? As a visiting uncle? A long lost relative?"

"If you hadn't turned up and ruined that plan, yes."

Paul shot her a look, then looked down at the glass in his hand. He breathed deeply and then relaxed in the chair, crossing his legs. He looked hard at her. "I'm not some street thug who is going to cause either of you harm. I don't want to take him from you, I just want to be part of his life. Why are you so against me?"

Jennifer poured herself wine and coolly sipped before answering. She slipped her jacket off her arm, now warm and the wine was making her relax. Where should she begin? Did he want to hear about how he had ruined the life she had planned for herself and her son? Did he want to hear about her humiliation, her pain, her loneliness? Did he want to hear about how Junior had been registered without the signature of his father on his birth certificate, how they had to spend hard times making explanations and excuses for him? Did he want to hear about Junior asking why he didn't have a father? She didn't think so.

"You have no idea,"she shook her head sadly. "You left me pregnant, a week away from my wedding day. I didn't hear from you again until after Junior was born, when you couldn't even pick up the phone. For three years Junior had no father. I didn't trust another man in all that time until I fell in love again. Then you suddenly decide now that he is walking, talking, potty trained, feeding and dressing himself that you want in. He has a life of his own. He is settled, content, he loves Tony as I do..."

"What's to stop him getting to love me?"

"He'll ask questions you won't be able to answer. Remember it was you who walked out. I've never lied to him. No one stopped you from turning up as he grew from baby to child. We never moved or changed our phone number and yet you couldn't call. How are you going to explain that, Mr Harvey?"

All he could do was hang his head. What excuse could he offer? He was ashamed and had every right to be. Jennifer would have gloated if she didn't feel so wretched about the whole thing. This was the moment she had waited for, making Paul humble, wanting to hear him beg.

"I'm so sorry," when he looked up again his eyes were filled with water. "Haven't we all been punished enough?"

"It's up to you."

He searched her eyes. "You mean the court case."

"You want to punish me and Junior just a little more. You want to put me in court to tell the world why I can't have you disrupting this happy little boy's life."

"You think I haven't thought about him in all those years, don't you?" His voice was breaking on every other word.

"Prove me wrong."

He leaned forwards so that she could see his whole face a lot clearer. "Look, I didn't get a secretary to send those cheques you received every month. I sent them all myself. Not a week went by when he wasn't in my thoughts. I knew when his birthday was coming up, I followed his development stages in a book I hid from my wife. I wondered whether he thought about me. I thought about you after we... broke up," he shrugged. "I wondered if you kept the baby or not. I found out while having drinks with a colleague that you had gone into labour in court, turns out it was big news."

Jennifer remembered it all too vividly.

"I wanted to come and see you both, but how was I to know when the right time was? How was I to know what kind of welcome I would receive?"

"Turns out you weren't welcome at all."

"I know that now and I understand why, but can't you see my point of view?"

"Believe me, I want to see your point of view but I want you to realize mine and Junior's. How can you be so selfish?" "And you're not? By stopping him seeing me now, aren't you being selfish? If I have to live with the questions he's going to ask, then why don't you ask yourself if you can take the questions he'll ask you ten years from now, when he might want to see me."

Now it was Jennifer's turn to feel guilt. Yes, Junior might well want to find his father someday. Would she just cross that bridge when she came to it or sort it now? "It might never happen. I'm sure he'll see enough of you in the papers anyhow."

Paul laughed. He laughed real belly laughter. Jennifer wondered if he was becoming hysterical, or drunk. "Oh Jennifer, I remember why I fell in love with you. You have a knack of finding a solution to every problem. You must be an extremely successful mother."

"I am now," she swallowed. "It wasn't always that way, as I'm sure you'll realize."

Paul raised an eyebrow, "Am I to take it that you're giving me the chance to prove I can be a good father?"

Jennifer shifted in her seat. Was that what she meant? "I'll need to discuss it with my family first. There have been a few changes at home recently and I wouldn't appreciate any more."

Paul was grinning incredulously.

"Does your wife know about your son?"

"Of course," he coughed clearing his throat, "although only recently."

Jennifer nodded and poured more wine for both of them, "I didn't tell Tony at first either."

Paul watched her curiously.

"Well... I'm sure you can guess why. The stigma of being a single parent. It just wasn't me. I wasn't sure how men would take me." As the words left her mouth she wondered why she was telling him this, of all people. Then again, they had always been able to talk, she had once felt comfortable talking to him about most things.

"I'm sorry..."

"Stop apologizing, Paul. Saying sorry now means absolutely nothing to me. What would mean more to me would be you making things up to us by being a man now."

"That's what I'm trying to do..."

"And I'm trying to punish you. But I wouldn't go as far as taking you to court to fight this. I've seen too many families pulled apart by courts."

"Again you're right, and I'm wrong. I want to make it up to you. Just tell me what to do."

Power! Now she had him eating out of her hands. Guilt ridden, he was begging to ease things. Did he have sleepless nights, pangs of guilt everytime a child crossed his path, nightmares that he may never have another child, dreams that his one and only would grow up to hate him?

Jennifer stood up and felt the alcohol suddenly rush to her head. On her empty stomach she had only had to have three glasses of wine and she was feeling drunk. Paul saw her wobble on her feet and jumped up, lending her his arm to steady herself. Jennifer jerked away from it as though he was offering her a red-hot poker. "I'm fine."

"Look, sit down, I'll make some coffee."

Jennifer obeyed, not that she had a choice she felt suddenly ill. "Paul, did you ever love me?"

"In the only way I think I'm capable of loving someone. You were dear to me, I cared for you as... I don't know, as I did my mother."

"Hmph."

Like his mother indeed. What, did she look like the housewife, matronly type? No wait, that could be a compliment. Every man loves his mother more than life itself, before the woman he marries. She smiled drunkenly.

Paul brought the coffees in and sat closer to her on a pouffe. "Tell me about Junior," he requested.

"What do you want to know?"

"Remember, I know nothing. Tell me all."

So she did. She told of his reading achievements, his inquisitive mind. Laughed at reminisces of the funny things he said, and did. Told of his maturity, and dexterity. Most of all she talked about the way she felt about him and he about her. How through the emotionless beginning they had grown together and now he was the centre of her world. Her most precious possession. She loved him so much that sometimes she felt it must be impossible for anyone to love that much. She explained how Tony had come into their lives and Junior had taken to him right away. Now there were three of them. She loved Tony, and he loved the both of them. They were a family and would stick together to fight anything that threatened to ruin that. It was nearly two o'clock in the morning when Paul dropped her home. Tony was at the door before the car had even parked up. Jennifer raised a hand to him as she stepped from the car, to tell him she was fine.

"Jennifer," Paul called.

Jennifer leant back inside the car and looked at him questioningly. "Yes?"

He dropped his eyelids for a second, like an embarrassed schoolboy. "Forget the court case... so long as I can see him occasionally... so long as he knows me... I want him to be happy too."

She reached back into the car with her right hand. "Thank you."

He took her hand and kissed it. "He's a lucky man, and I'm a fool."

She watched the car drive off before walking up the pathway and into Tony's arms. He was worried, and no wonder, she had left at seven o'clock yesterday evening. "What happened to you?"

"Everything's okay. We talked."

Tony, still dressed the same as when she left, closed the door behind her. "Until two o'clock in the morning... and where's your car?"

"Tony! You don't trust me?"

"Once bitten..."

She stopped in the hallway and turned to him with a smile on her face. "I had a bit to drink and couldn't drive back that's all. Baby, why have tough steak when I can have succulent chicken? Paul Harvey is not going to be a bother. I made him see that he could only cause disruption by interfering now, he understands that now. This is our time, he had his chance."

"I can't believe he would give in that easy."

"Not exactly," she climbed the wrought iron staircase. "I had to promise him some visiting privileges. I don't want Junior growing up knowing I kept his father from seeing him. So if Paul doesn't see his son it won't be down to me."

Tony followed her up the stairs, his hands on her waist. "I love you, Miss Edwards."

"And I love you," suddenly she turned towards him. "Tony, will you marry me?"

He grinned. "Didn't I ask you that question?"

"Well?" she asked excitedly. Her tired eyes had a mischievously bright light in them.

"Yes. Wherever and whenever you want me to," Tony replied. "You're my lady."

"Make love to me," she breathed before her arms flew around his neck and she kissed him passionately. He held her and kissed back. They walked backwards up the stairs.

"My lady's wish is my command."

Just last week I received a phone call from a very excited publisher. He loved my journals and wanted to publish it as fiction. Would I be interested in doing the rewrite? Would I be interested?! I was too flabbergasted to speak, but after we talked editing and contracts, I accepted and put the phone down. For just a few seconds I sat there letting it sink in and then danced around the living room before calling Tony on his mobile, because I couldn't wait until he got home. People, strangers would be reading about my life. They would like it enough to pay money to read something I had written through some very emotional times.

There was no feeling in the world like it. In fact when I started to tell my friends that I was going to be a published novelist they were more impressed than when I told them I was a barrister.

An author!

I stared at the contract with my name on it. I have this new sense of worth. Like before I only meant something to my family and now I have two careers and a fiancé and a beautiful son.

Paul wrote me a very touching letter. He says that he will not intrude in our lives anymore, all he asks is that I keep him up to date with photographs, letters and a current address so that he can keep track of his son. I agreed, I feel it is the least I could do for a peaceful life.

I'm going to be married, but then you knew that already. But I've actually set a date now, June 24th, it's my mum's birthday. Both my parents will be flying over from Jamaica for the wedding.

This idea of Barbados isn't all that bad, you know. I've been thinking about it and the more I think about it the more I think, why not?

Junior is still young enough to start again. I don't have to be a barrister. With the book contract signed and sealed and a commission to write a sequel, I could write full time. What a beautiful place to write my next novel. I'll feel like Terry McMillan. Plus I'd be so much closer to Mum and Dad. Donna visits from university in the summer. She is being very coy about her sex life, although I get the distinct feeling that she isn't about to become a nun.

I'll miss her if we go, and I'll miss all those friends that I have grown to love, but I can't limit myself. Being a barrister was an ambition that I fulfilled but I don't need anymore. It is in no way as spiritually or emotionally fulfilling or gratifying as my creative ability.

"Mummy, can I have some new trainers?" Junior held up his old ones with holes already in the toes.

"Yes, Junior. Ask Daddy to buy them."

Junior had been calling Tony 'daddy' for about a month now. It had been his choice after hearing Wesley calling the man that he thought had belonged to him, daddy. Junior had asked if he could as well. Tony had accepted it as fate. Junior ran out of the room again. "Daddy..." How many times had I told him about running in the house?

The publisher's agreement was still open on the last page and I turned it over again, reading my name on the front cover. Jennifer Edwards, author of 'Baby

Mother - When a Man Leaves a Woman.' The wedding was six months away and
I now had a book to rewrite as well as organize the wedding and work full-time.
They say things happen in threes, what next?

"Babes," Tony was standing in the doorway in his boxer shorts, "I've just
thought. With your new career we don't have to stay here for anything."

I sighed happily. Number three.

"Oh, we're going to Barbados," Tony picked me up and spun me around the
room, before we fell on the sofa giggling and kissing like newlyweds.

"I'm jealous," there were tears in Karen's eyes. She stared at Jennifer's
traditional white silk and lace gown, the veil thrown back to reveal hair
that had taken Donna an hour and a half to tong, getting each individual
curl to sit perfectly.

"You!" Elaine and a new slimline Beverly said together. Donna caught
the joke and they all burst out laughing. Jennifer beside her groom,
turned around and they all saw the radiance and excitement surround
her like a glow.

"Please ladies, we are trying to take a picture here," the photographer,
a short effeminate man with a tape measure around his neck, bustled over
to them and pushed and pulled at the ladies' peach satin dresses until he
had them in an orderly line outside the church.

"Smile."

The flash went off and Jennifer looked to her left at her new in-laws,
then to her right at her own mother and father who had flown in just a
week ago to be at their eldest daughter's wedding. Her mother had been
eager to talk to the two sisters, lecturing them, especially Donna, on the
evils of the nineties man. "Don't follow your sister," she had said,
marring Jennifer's excitement over the wedding. But as soon as she'd met
Tony, they'd got on immediately and when she saw her grandson for the
first time she had burst into tears. Now she looked happier than the bride
and groom. Jennifer smiled at her before looking back at Tony. He kissed
her gently on the lips as camera flashes went off all around them.

After a long and tiring reception, it was time for the newlyweds to
leave for their honeymoon in Barbados, their new home.

"She's going to throw the bouquet..."

Jennifer stood at the front of the hall watching her friends come
forward. As soon as she saw that everyone was in position she turned her
back to the throng of excited women, raised the bouquet and threw it
back over her head. She turned in time to see Beverly and Donna almost
catch it before it bounced off their fingertips to land in Karen's crossed

arms. She was more surprised than the rest of them. Philip was by her side in a second lifting her in the air. Beverly, Elaine and Donna came to Jennifer's side and as a group they surrounded Karen.

"So what did you say?" Beverly asked.

Karen looked at them all and then turned to look at Philip. "Yes!"

There was a scream from all the women as they jumped up and down excitedly, then they realized that Philip might want to get in there as well and parted. Jennifer clasped her hands in front of her and looked around at her friends, she marvelled at how beautiful they all looked. She was so happy that when Tony circled her into his arms, she jumped for joy nearly knocking him down.

"Think we better be going."

Jennifer and Tony Carnegie took hold of their son's hand and left the church hall, followed by a cheering crowd and a shower of confetti. A limousine waited outside. Before Jennifer climbed in, her hand was grabbed by someone from behind. Jennifer turned around and faced a tearful Elaine. She searched her eyes.

Elaine was nodding. "I'm pregnant."

"Aahh," Jennifer was crying with her, their tears of joy mingling on made-up cheeks. "Why didn't you tell me before?"

"This is your day," she smiled tearfully.

Jennifer hugged her once more. "Congratulations, honey, you deserve it." She let go of her and climbed into the car beside her husband and her baby. She waved to all her friends. Then she saw Donna squeezing through the guests to get to the car, her beaded head-dress already askew.

Jennifer wound down the window. "Did I forget something?"

"Yes," Donna said. "Would you be disappointed if I decided to get pregnant and not get married?"

Jennifer turned around to look at her family in the car beside her. "It's your choice, baby sister. Just promise you'll love the child and not get married or pregnant for the wrong reasons."

Donna smiled. "See, who needs to be single to survive?"

END